THIS CRUMBLING PAGEANT

The Great Plot

THIS CRUMBLING PAGEANT

THE FURY TRIAD
VOLUME ONE

AWARD-WINNING AUTHOR
PATRICIA BURROUGHS

STORY SPRING PUBLISHING
Cincinnati, Ohio

Story Spring Publishing, LLC
P.O. Box 9727
Cincinnati, OH 45209
www.storyspringpublishing.com

Publisher's Note: This is a work of fiction. Names, characters, places, and incidents are a product of the author's imagination. Locales and public names are sometimes used for atmospheric purposes. Any resemblance to actual people, living or dead, or to businesses, companies, events, institutions, or locales is completely coincidental.

Book Layout ©2013 BookDesignTemplates.com
Cover Design: The Killion Group, Inc.

This Crumbling Pageant/Patricia Burroughs. — 1st ed.
ISBN 978-1-940699-03-5

❧ DEDICATION ❧

To my dearly beloved,

My partner in crime,

My high school sweetheart,

My one and only… Sam.

With all my love.

So when the last and dreadful hour
This crumbling pageant shall devour,
The trumpet shall be heard on high,
The dead shall live, the living die,
And music shall untune the sky

John Dryden, 1687

❦ PART ONE ❦

An England Not Quite Our Own

*"In England it is said that
the Furys have the gift of pleasing kings."*

—an adage of the Magi

❧ PROLOGUE ❧

Oxford, 1793

He'd been working on his swagger again, the cocksure walk of the village louts who held power in their brawny shoulders and sometimes coin in their pockets. There was a time when he'd thought the swagger would make him more like them, perhaps even one of them.

It had done him no good, for they'd taunted him still, the bone-thin bastard with a grand name beyond his station, Vespasian Wyltt.

He'd gone back to slinking in the shadows, watching from dark corners, fashioning wands from various tree branches in an effort to find the one that would work for him, would give him the power those lads were too stupid to conjure, even in their dreams.

The sticks had all ended as kindling.

As would the oafs who mocked him, who overpowered him with their numbers, and whose taunts had turned into beatings when the first strands of white showed up in his dirty black hair on the very morn he'd awakened to find his first seed-spilling dream had soiled him.

They would all be kindling to the fire of his ambition, and he would glory in their burning.

But now, upon entering Oxford for the first time, he pulled that swagger back around him, hoping to meld into the tangle of newly arriving students without drawing suspicious glances at his shabby clothes, stolen from an Ordinary family's cottage in Coventry and kept hidden until he was safely back amongst the Magi. Yet those in line with him at the kitchen door to Pendragon College drew away as if he carried the stench of a sty, even though they, too, awaited interviews for servant positions in exchange for tuition.

Watching arrogant young gentlemen select obsequious young scouts made resentment sour in him like curdled milk.

3

This could not be the path to the future his goddess had promised him, deep in the shadows of Wales. These pustulant, primping peacocks could not be the glorious future of the Magi she had foretold. None amongst them could possibly be worthy of his fealty.

None could be the True King.

And then, the hair rose on his neck and on his arms, and awareness tingled uncomfortably like sparks of electricity on a winter's day.

He squinted through the tangled locks of his hair, the better to observe without being observed, and saw a perfumed young gent strolling past, trailing Shadows behind him.

And Vespasian knew, as he knew his own worth, that the promised path was finally opening before him.

He abandoned the queue at Pendragon and followed after, slinking instead of swaggering, watching from the darkness between the buildings, simmering with schemes and dreams.

I know not your name, he thought, *but I hold your destiny in my hands.*

For when she had spoken to him before sinking back into the icy waters of the lake, the goddess had lain their destinies upon him.

❧ CHAPTER ONE ❧

England, 1806

She was pinned like a moth to velvet, pinned against her twin brother's pillow. She couldn't breathe, couldn't move, and yet the tutor had not touched her but held her frozen with his black, black eyes.

"Out of bed and make haste about it," Mr Jones hissed.

His rough hands yanked her from the bed.

She stood wavering, fighting free of the mists that tried to cloud her mind.

"Dress." His voice was harsh and fear pulsed through her. Something was wrong. This was not at all what she had expected.

But she could do this. She *must.* She turned away and pulled her brother's breeches up over his nightshirt and then tugged on a pair of boots he'd outgrown. She hoped—*prayed*—that her disguise wouldn't be discovered before she learned enough to put an end to the presence of the despicable Mr Jones as her brothers' tutor.

He would never hurt Dardanus again.

She tugged a cap over the knot of hair on the back of her head and shrugged on the heavy jacket she'd chosen because she could hide her narrow shoulders in its voluminous depths.

"Hurry, we haven't got all night." He pushed her to the moonlit window.

Gods. The moonlight! She shrank back into the dark, but he shoved her through the open window with a growl.

She leapt onto the heavy limb of the oak tree that spanned the moat below. With a light grasp on higher branches, she scampered across and then fell back against the trunk. Nervously, she watched Mr Jones follow her steps, almost as nimble as she.

She slid down the steep bank with Mr Jones close behind. When they reached the deeper shadows of the sunken garden, she found

Hades, a sturdy black gelding, tied to the gate. Only then did she allow herself to breathe, to realise with a sick clench of her stomach that she'd *done* it. The deception was working.

Tonight, she, Persephone Fury, would discover why her beloved brother had lied to her three times about injuries, had eyes bruised with shadows on the day following every full moon. When she had demanded answers the month before, he'd slid his gaze to his tutor, who stared at her over steepled fingers, his lips curled in a taunting sneer.

She would discover what happened on full moon nights, and finally, her father would have to listen to her and stop dismissing it all as schoolboy antics.

"Put this on your back." Mr Jones thrust a small pack at her. "I'll bespell you to stay stuck."

She snorted her disdain as she saw the magical pillion saddle. As if *she'd* fall from a horse. But she felt a twinge of pity for poor Dardanus, whose seat on horseback was always precarious at best. She remembered the bruises he'd sported the month before and now suspected he'd fallen from behind Mr Jones. But what humiliation, to put him on a magical saddle created for children and women incapable of riding their own mounts!

She smouldered with anger at having to ride the demeaning thing herself but had no choice. Mr Jones dragged her up behind him, and she felt the sharp tug of the binding spell as she settled into the curve of leather. She would be unable to free herself.

The horse moved forward with its steady gait and, once onto the road, was prodded into a fast canter. At least as a boy, she could ride astride. She clutched her cap to her head with one hand, clinging to the edge of the saddle with the other. No wonder Dardanus had been so terror-stricken that morning when she'd coaxed him from bed and he'd claimed to have no memory of the night before.

Never before had she experienced the world at midnight. Strange shapes were etched with silver moonlight. The heavy fragrance of wisteria in the damp night air heralded the bank of tangled vines at the curve in the road. The bleat of new-born lambs and the odour of sheep dung, the rise in the road and sudden gloom of overhanging trees—all were as familiar as her own land, but not at night.

If she weren't so tense in anticipation of being discovered—and of course her trickery would eventually be discovered—she'd have been exhilarated. The rhythm of the horse beneath her was music thrumming through her, and where there was music, she needed no extra magic to hold her steady.

A rabbit darted across the road.

Pride fled. She clutched the saddle and fought for balance as Mr Jones pulled the gelding under control.

Heart pounding, she sucked great gasps of chilly air into her lungs and found herself leaning forward against the tutor's scarecrow back.

"Rutting hell! There's no way that little brat would have stayed astride…" With movements surprisingly powerful for such a shabby excuse for a man, he reined the horse in and swung down from the saddle. He pulled her off so abruptly that she fell onto the road in an ignominious pile.

Hades shied sideways, hooves kicking up a spray of dirt and rock, but before Persephone could respond to the gelding's distress, Mr Jones quieted the beast with a guttural command more effective than any she'd ever witnessed from a groom or even her own father. He seized the reins in one hand and yanked Persephone's cap from her head with the other. He grabbed her chin with hard fingers and angled her face up to the moonlight. *"You!"*

She jerked away. She'd despised him for almost as long as she'd known him, but never had she actually feared him until now, vulnerable and alone as she was in the middle of the road, in the middle of the night, in the middle of nowhere. His features were malevolent contours of light and shadow. She pulled herself to her feet and stood straight with her chin high. "When I tell my papa, you'll never teach in a Magi home again!"

"Indeed." He scoffed, the sound bitter and arrogant in the darkness. "You think I am the one with everything to lose? Must I remind you that at thirteen years of age, you're old enough to create a scandal yourself, caught out with your brothers' tutor in the middle of the night. A scandal that won't just touch you, but your sister as well."

Electra. Persephone's blood ran cold.

"About to be presented at Court. On the brink of her first Season, and by all accounts likely to be the Incomparable. Are you truly willing to bring such disgrace to your family?"

"But… but you're the one who—"

"I won't miss being tutor to spoiled children. Your sister's chances, however, will be ruined."

He dropped the horse's reins and circled her slowly, his boots crunching on loose rocks. When he'd made a complete circuit, he sniffed through his long, arrogant nose. "Should you co-operate and fulfil your brother's role in this night's business, I shall return you to your home safely with not a soul knowing the tale, just as I've always done with your brother. That is, if you think you're up to the task."

She swallowed.

"Well?" His tone was bored, as if her decision meant little to him.

This was exactly what she wanted, to go along with the wretched man, discover his secrets, and finally be able to protect her brother.

She dusted off her breeches and gave a small shrug. "There is nothing Dardanus can do that I cannot."

"You'd best be right." He mounted the horse, then jerked her up behind him.

"Where are we going?"

"London," he replied, as the horse lunged forward with a powerful ground-eating stride.

They flew through the night once more.

❦

Pain throbbed low in her abdomen. Clutching the edge of the pillion and holding herself erect—even with magic—became an act of will and strain, but she was determined to *not touch that man*. She was now grudgingly grateful for that magical cushion of air that protected her from the worst of the jolts and, if she fought hard enough, saved her from the indignity of clutching him for balance as Hades' magical hooves barely touched the surface of the road.

Her mind rang with the things she wanted to call the man. *Beast, blackguard,* and a word that she had never dared utter. She wasn't even quite sure what it meant, but it tasted delicious and powerful on her tongue so she whispered it. *"Bastard!"* She forced her eyes closed against the vision of starry sky and bushes and trees flying past at dizzying speed. She focused instead on staying astride and keeping the pain deep in her belly at bay. His stringy, white-streaked hair, unfashionably long and loose from its ribbon, whipped into her face, stung her eyes, and invaded her mouth.

When they finally slowed to a canter, she opened her eyes to see a mist-choked grove of trees with long, overhanging limbs. Hades stepped amongst them with a sure-footedness that indicated he knew this path well. Mr Jones muttered words she could not hear, and then they burst from the mist into a churchyard crowded with headstones in various states of decay.

The air felt different somehow. Dirty.

With her eyes closed and body tensed, it was her nose that first recognised the place—putrid, disgusting, the sour stench of rot and filth that squelched beneath Hades' hooves—she realised where he had brought her.

Her eyes flew open. Buildings pressed against one another, looming oppressively overhead.

She slammed her fists into Mr Jones's back with all the force she could muster. "Stop!" she demanded. "Stop this instant!"

"Bloody, buggering hell!" He reined Hades in harshly, and they stopped in the middle of the narrow road, the miasma of London hanging in the air around them.

"This…" She gasped. "This isn't *Magi* London!"

"What extraordinary intellect. We are in *Ordinary* London." His soft voice menaced, perfectly distinct even above the harsh, laboured breathing of the gelding. "You will be my son, if anyone should ask. *You will do as I say.*"

Panic set in. She fought the magical bespellment that held her on the pillion. But he grabbed her by the arm and almost yanked it free of its socket. He leaned close to her ear. "You'll not escape, and you'll not cause trouble, is that clear?"

Moving shadows a few feet away resolved into a scrawny, ill-dressed man slamming a filthy girl against the rough wall of a building, one hand tearing at her skirt, pulling it higher as his other hand fondled his own rigid dandilolly. Persephone flushed at the innocent nursery word, for that thing in his hand was nothing like her brother's, though she hadn't actually seen it since they were small.

She tried to look away, but her eyes betrayed her. They wouldn't close, wouldn't shift, wouldn't allow her to stop watching as the young girl spread her fat thighs and the man drove into her with a grunt.

Persephone had seen horses and pigs and dogs and cats and even fowl copulating, but never had she seen anything as horrific and animalistic as these Ordinary folk mating on a public street. She finally jerked her head away.

"And that's what will happen to you if you dare try to escape me, that or worse!"

"Worse?" she choked.

"Girls have been disappearing in Ordinary London, girls like you. *Virgins*—" He hissed into her ear. "—disappearing, never to be seen again. And you will join them if you don't co-operate with me this night."

They trotted through the dark streets until they approached a dirty market square ringed by large buildings, a church at one end.

He leapt from Hades' back, snatched her from the pillion saddle, the release of magic a whisper of sharp, chill breeze. He dropped her to the street with as little care as if she were a sack of grain.

She waited impatiently for him to secure Hades, noting the church's four thick, Greek columns, so similar to those at the Magi Temple of Terpsichore near their home.

She was less approving of the dirty beggar on the church steps, his tattered red coat clearly the mark of a soldier. He had only one leg, and the hand holding out a tin cup was missing three fingers. "Pennies for His Majesty's fallen?" the young man called to her, catching her watching. "Fell fighting Boney on the Peninsula. I has a mum and wee ones at home to feed."

A hand closed over her shoulder and yanked her away. Mr Jones was back, his dark cloak billowing, and he bent low, staring into her eyes with fierce concentration. *"You will do as I say.* And when this night is over, you will forget…"

Something was wrong, terrifyingly wrong.

It was the same feeling she'd had when he'd first awakened her in the night, the same helplessness. She was trapped and unable to breathe, mists swirling within her head.

He was invading her mind with magic!

She fought for air, for life itself, or so it felt, and wrenched herself free.

She gasped in a deep breath, then she looked into his eyes and saw his shock.

"You... *you* can't block me out!"

Emboldened, she fought him with flailing fists.

His hand connected with her mouth, and she tasted blood, but he was the one who drew back with a yelp and a curse. "If you value your life, stupid little Fury, you'll not do that again."

Contrôle de l'esprit? This was why Dardanus never could tell her what had happened to him?

Dardanus hadn't been hiding his shame from her. *He didn't remember it.*

Mind magic.

Mr Jones had attempted to use mind magic upon her and had failed, but he had clearly succeeded with Dardanus. And what about her older brothers? Cosmo and Lysander? Had he used this wicked power on them, as well?

"You're using *contrôle de l'esprit!*" And then, despite herself, she had to ask, "It's real? It really exists?"

"And isn't that sheer perfection, the stupid little Fury embracing French affectations?" He glared down his long nose, his hair tangled from the wind.

"You prefer the term *potentia phasma?*" She felt a thrill of pride.

"Latin? A dead language for a power that reeks of life? Your airs disgust me."

Her cheeks burned. *"Draíocht intinne,* then."

He turned his back to her and began digging in a saddlebag.

It was her turn to sneer. "Or do you not recognise the term espoused by Sir Aengus in *An History of Irish Magic?*"

"If you are quite finished with your pitiful exhibit of knowledge of tomes of dubious scholarship," he snapped, "please tell me, *Miss Persephone,* whether or not you share your family's musical talent?"

"It is no mere talent. It is a *Gift*, bestowed upon our ancestors by Apollo himself, and if you had ever lowered yourself to teach me, you would not ask that question." She rose to her full height, despite the fact that such displays sent her mother into fits of despair. "Yes. I make music."

"Then I pray thee…" He whirled and handed her a battered fiddle and bow. "Prove it."

He grasped her wrist and dragged her into the midst of the stinking crowd of people—*Ordinary* people, for Magi did not stink—and thrust her towards the base of a broken column left over from Roman rule, now less than a yard high and almost as wide. He tossed a cap at the foot of it, leaving it gaping wide towards the night sky.

"Gods be damned—the theatre's patrons are already leaving. *Play!*"

She hesitated, the desire to refuse strong. But then what? Who would rescue her here? Who would come to her aid if he attacked her, or worse, what would she do if he abandoned her?

He had threatened to expose her in such a way that the Magi's Beau Monde would not only recoil from her, but from Electra. Even now, her home was bustling with preparations for the first Fury musicale in decades, when they would use their Gift to remind Society who the Furys were and what they had been and what they would be again— and would secure her sister's place amongst this Season's beauties.

As he watched from between the buildings, she scrambled up the broken column until she balanced on its uneven surface, bracing her weight on her forward foot. It was a most unladylike position, but in trousers it hardly mattered.

Her hands caressed the fiddle's battered and scarred surface until she felt its soul beneath her fingertips, felt it longing to release its voice. It had never been a grand instrument, but it had once known joy. It had once played airs for dancing and now was barely able to hold a tune, she feared, its pegs hardly able to keep its strings taut.

No matter to a Fury. She was quite certain that Dardanus had brought forth sweet music from its depths because, despite the planet-struck nature of his birth, as a Fury, he could do no less.

A small smile quirked the corners of her lips.

But the battered fiddle had never been played by Persephone Fury.

She raised it to her chin and drew her bow across the strings, releasing one long, quivering note into the night.

Deep in her breast, a long, quivering sigh responded.

She met those black eyes across the crowd, and a bolt of fear shot through her.

She closed her eyes, inhaled deeply of filth and all that was Ordinary, tilted her head to listen, and played.

✂ CHAPTER TWO ✄

The music sprang from the girl-brat's bow in a burst of liquid pain that shot straight into his gut.

Fear had flashed her eyelids before she averted her gaze, as well it should, the insolent chit. But then she'd drawn her bow across the strings.

All of Covent Garden stilled under the spell of her haunting, terrifying music.

Theatre patrons stopped in the act of entering carriages; cabbage sellers formerly sleeping in their booths now rose to their feet; nobs and scum alike reacted with confused attention to those first quivering sounds.

She hadn't submitted to him. She'd been immune to his powers. The strongest of Magi couldn't obstruct his ability. How had she?

And now, a mere touch of her bow to the instrument and magic *sang*. Yes, the Furys had a Gift, but this was beyond anything he'd witnessed from any of her brothers.

She was the one?

This scrawny, yammering girl? The knowledge—and the fear that knowledge sparked—clogged his throat with a broken howl of rage.

And the music, the hells-cursed music. She leaned into it, poured herself into it, and held every soul present in the palm of her hand.

Under her touch, *Llwyn Onn*, a song from his childhood, turned itself inside out. A tune made for dancing emerged from her fingertips in a sinister minor key. Her fear and sorrow soared into the air, infecting all present.

Rutting hell, she'd woven a trance. Around him, people wept unabashedly.

People who wept didn't pay.

He dragged a coin from his pocket and with a flip sent it sailing in a high, spinning arc to land perfectly in the cap at her feet.

"*Ysbryd y Myrddin!*" He closed the distance between them. "Cease

15

the bloody dirge and play something else, if you ever want to see your brother again!"

She allowed a single note to draw out long and tense between them. His eyes met hers, and a jolt of power surged from deep within him, and he saw that she felt it, too. Her eyes were wide and dilated and even as that note—exquisite in its pain and beauty—stretched between them, so did this force that was his own peculiar power, yet stronger than any he'd experienced before.

Finally he'd broken through.

He possessed her.

He tasted triumph.

🐦🐦

The world flew into a dizzying spin, and all that held her erect was the power of his piercing eyes as he attempted yet again to control her.

The bow in her hand vibrated. Her arm quivered with the power. The music in her heart wept.

He was winning.

She was drawn into the dizzying, undulating Shadows that pulsed in his eyes. Shadows that whispered Dark and delicious promises. Shadows that called her name in soft whispers. Shadows that tantalised with sweet seduction.

Shadows.

Her heart hammered in her chest. *Shadow magic.* He was using Shadow magic.

The words he'd spat at her, *ysbryd y Myrrdin,* echoed in her ears. He'd called on the ghost of Myrrdin to use against her? She would scorn him for his Earthborn superstitions, if the power he raised didn't fill her with such terror. She tried frantically to summon protection from the Fireborn gods, but she sank more deeply...

"If you ever want to see your brother again."

Dardanus.

He had been her warmth and strength since they'd shared a womb. Just his name brought her strength. For him, she must prevail. "Dardanus," she whispered. "Dardanus!"

In a blinding pain, the spell that bound her ended.

Gasping, she yanked her bow away from the instrument, and the music stopped, leaving her aching and empty where before it had filled her. But one look at the startled face of her enemy—a sinister contrast of dark and light in the flickering lantern's glow—brought a smile of victory to her lips.

She fought for air. She *would* escape him. She would escape him. And lest he mistake her moment of victory for anything else, she flashed him an insolent grin. Oh, she did know how to be insolent, as any in the Fury household would attest.

He wanted the dirge to cease? She shifted her posture, and the opening notes of *Tom Scarlett* floated across the night, a simple melody line, a feather on a puff of air.

Around her, tension melted under the rise and fall of her music. She felt as well as heard the softly released breaths of relief as her toe began tapping against the broken column. Here and there, other feet tapped. Heads nodded and hands clapped as she sent the rhythmic pulse of her magic into the night.

When she began the second verse, a second tune lilted around the melody, circling it as if *two* fiddles played, one taking the straight road and a second a circuitous counterpoint that flirted as lightly and gaily as if terror hadn't danced in her veins only moments before.

A man in dirty homespun made a graceless bow to a young girl, and she curtsied. Their boisterous dance across the cobblestones brought laughter and ribald comments, but as he passed, he tossed an Ordinary coin she didn't recognise at into the cap on the ground. And then another joined it from another hand, and another. More than she could keep up with.

So this was why she played? To make him money? This was his use of Dardanus, as well, to exploit the Fury Gift to line his pockets?

Angry, she attacked the music, and the notes rippled until the sharp night air filled with the sound of three fiddles, now four, each spinning its own web and ensnaring all who heard. Her heart swelled with it.

On this night, she spun magic that could hardly go undetected amongst these Ordinary folk. Thus far, all who listened were too caught under her spell to notice. But the risk, by the gods' blood, the *risk*.

But she could no more stop than she could stop breathing. She sensed Mr Jones's unease and gloried in it. Let him be afraid of getting caught. Wasn't it his greed that had brought them there?

More bystanders followed the lead of the first couple, and soon an uneven line of a country dance formed. Those who didn't join it watched, their expressions rapt.

And still, more coins, a syncopated clink of coins, a part of the music.

And then—

Clank.

A heavy sound, not like the earlier ones.

Gold.

Another piece of gold.

And another.

Two well-dressed gentlemen had been drawn into the crowd by the women on their arms. Were these women an example of Ordinary ladies? The garish shades of the women's gowns, the paint on their faces, the heavy breasts barely contained—she'd never seen such horrid displays. Perhaps these weren't ladies in even an Ordinary sense.

One, her hair a mass of yellow curls that must be a wig of some sort, broke away and drew closer. The woman stared at the violin, then closely at Persephone's face, and then dragged one finger across her downy cheek. "You won't get nowhere on your looks, laddie-me-boy." With a peal of coarse laughter, she cast a coquettish glance over her shoulder at her male companion.

Persephone ducked her head and played as if the woman didn't exist.

The woman raised her skirts too high for decency, exposing plump calves clad in white silk, and her feet in orange slippers began a complicated dance as she flung her head back and laughed giddily.

Until she tripped on what seemed like nothing and landed on her knees with a curse.

Persephone bit back a grin, closed her eyes as if she hadn't caused the fall, and continued to play.

She knew the power she wielded over these Ordinary folk. She revelled in it. And now, she knew how to make it work for her.

The street filled with more people overcome by an almost drunken joy. Mr Jones and his loathsome scowl appeared and disappeared as dancers moved between them. Persephone glanced away, the music buzzing from her fingertips as she worked the crowd to a frenzy, watched it swell and thicken around her.

She paused long enough to let out a shrill whistle.

Before the trance could break, she played again.

☙☙

Her whistle pierced the night air. She was up to something.

He fought his way between dancing fools. He threw an elbow into the hard shoulder of a cabbage-seller and dodged the return punch with ease. He was nearly close enough to grasp the girl when he heard cries and fierce hooves striking stone.

The horse appeared, and the twice-cursed girl had a foot in the stirrup and was leaping onto its back.

He lunged, reached to grab her, to stop her.

She flung the fiddle at him. He grabbed it with his outstretched hand, as she tossed back her head and, with a high, taunting laugh, took off in a crisp canter across Covent Garden's market square, sending people who had so recently danced to her tune diving from her temper.

Idiot girl!

How did she think she could return to the Magi world without him as escort?

He snatched up the cap of coins and took off after her.

She was the power he'd sought since he'd reached his majority, since the prophecy had first been laid upon him, those thirteen long years before.

She'd been under his nose for eight years, and he'd not recognised her, because he'd been looking for one of her brothers to share the weight of Myrddin's legacy.

Chest heaving, lungs screaming for air, he ran, heedless of anything in his path as the voice in his head raged. He'd poured knowledge into their spoiled, lazy minds; he'd suffered through miserable years in their household looking for the sign, the proof he needed that the time of prophecy was truly nigh.

He'd ignored her demands for knowledge, refused to even look at her puling writings, and now the truth rose with the bile in his throat as he collapsed against a crumbling wattle and daub wall, unable to run another step.

He knew this now, when his bridges back to the Fury family were truly burnt.

🕊🕊

She stood in the stirrups to escape the pain of Hades' jolting trot, of hooves striking cobblestones with jarring force. She'd bested him. Savage joy coursed through her veins.

"Take me home, my darling," she crooned. "I don't know the way. You must take me home." Surely loyal Hades could return to the portal that led back to her own world.

The rhythm beneath her became a single pounding word repeated again and again—*bastard, bastard, bastard*—feeding the Darkest corners of her soul.

She'd bested him.

And she'd be making offerings to the gods that the bastard Vespasian Jones would find his way into torment, and soon.

There were few others on the road once they left that horrid marketplace behind. Within minutes, Hades had slowed to a gentle walk, and she had neither the heart nor the energy to urge him faster again. They rode along an immense brick wall to the right, a wall that must encompass acres. Was this the way they'd entered the city? She didn't know; she couldn't remember. She fought down the panic and sank into the saddle. As they passed a pair of gates, she glimpsed a sign in the moonlight and scowled. *Foundlings Hospital.* So this was what the Ordinary folk did with their foundlings? Imprisoned them behind high walls?

What had that magic been, that strange exultation of power unlike any she'd ever experienced? Never had she ached so. Never had she known such exhaustion. A teeth-rattling chill swept down her spine, and she shrank even deeper into Dardanus's coat.

Mr Jones would never dare come within reach of a Fury again, once she exposed him to her father and mother. Finally, she'd be vindicated.

But behind every brave word lurked the memory of black eyes burning with hatred.

Behind every brave vow leered the memory of thin lips twisted in a snarl.

Behind every brave threat lingered the memory of Shadows, and falling, and terror.

Her hands trembled on the reins, and her thighs quivered with fatigue as she caught the scent and sound of water. She allowed Hades to wade into the shallows of the small, flowing river to drink. Tenderly, she stroked his mane and withers, murmuring soft words of praise. Before he could drink too much and risk colic, she pulled his head up. She forced him back onto the road, and they clattered across the bridge.

The splay of black tree foliage against star-spun night stretched overhead in a familiar pattern. He'd brought her to a church with a fog-shrouded cemetery hugging its eastern walls.

Fog. Not on the river, but high on the banks at the church?

Her pulse jumped as she felt the change around her, the quiver of magic in the air. The foggy mist shrouded the portal like a beacon.

"You darling boy, you've done it." She clicked her tongue and urged him forward, growing impatient when—having brought her this far—Hades suddenly shied. The sideways lurch of his body almost unseated her. She was too exhausted for this, too drained to fight with him, but she refused to spend a single moment more in this place of smells and danger. And so she dug her heels sharply into his flanks and urged him forward with her seat.

With a burst of strength, he sprang forward, into the mist—

And her body exploded with pain.

❦❦

The road stretched silver before Robin Fitzwilliam in the light of the full moon. He allowed his mount to cover the ground, trusting her familiarity with these roads. His mind roiled with confusion. On his left hand, the signet ring he'd never dreamed of wearing, never wanted to wear, weighed heavy as stone.

But wear it he did, and all that it symbolised, including the weight of the small estate of Aubrey.

Images spun before him, of his uncle, his cousin, first living and then—*clods of dirt hitting coffins with hollow menace*—dead.

It was with relief that he felt his mare's gait shift beneath him as the beast snorted and quivered, grateful to focus more sharply on the road and the tendrils of mist floating over it.

Mist? The night was clear, the moonlight bright and sharp as a diamond, yet mist clung unexpectedly to this spot.

The mare spooked. He fought to control her as the mist grew heavier, and a weight settled in his gut. He was in the act of turning back when he glimpsed a dark horse grazing in the deepness of an overhanging oak, a figure slumped over its back.

A slight figure.

Why would a child be out alone in the middle of the night?

He forced his horse forward despite her arched neck, aware this might be a trap.

When he'd drawn as near as was practical, he dismounted and secured his irritated mount with a wrap of reins around a low-hanging limb and a practiced tracing of a magical sigil in the air to keep it still.

The black horse seemed less inclined to accept his dominance. Every time Robin took a step forward, the horse took two back. And yet it seemed more nervous than defensive, its movement gentle, or else the youth on its back would be on the ground by now.

"Easy," he murmured, and when he was certain the horse wouldn't panic, he again whisked his hand in the calming sigil and finally chanced the most extreme method of control by running his hand from forelock to muzzle, down its unfortunate Roman profile that arched where his own thoroughbred was elegantly straight. The horse calmed. Robin slid the slender youth's body from the expensive saddle and staggered backwards, not from the weight, for in truth, the boy weighed little, but from the reek of Shadows.

It was a miracle the gelding hadn't tossed the stripling to rid himself of the Darkness on its back.

He eased the boy onto the ground, heaving in great gulps of fresh air as he frantically removed his glove from his right hand. He knelt and touched the slender throat—there it was, beneath his fingertips—a strong, steady pulse. He let out a sigh of relief.

But the boy's body was limp, and his skin was hot and damp with sweat. Robin fumbled with the boy's heavy jacket and grabbed the lapels to yank it open.

Thin fingers closed around his wrists. With a snarl, the boy heaved himself up and delivered a smart punch to Robin's jaw, knocking him back on his heels in shock.

"Don't touch me!" the boy rasped fiercely.

"You're overheated. Let's get that coat off."

Two sharp-knuckled fists smacked into him at the same time, leaving both his cheeks stinging.

"Keep your hands off my coat!" The boy scrambled to his feet and leapt against the horse, attempting to mount.

"Gods damn it," Robin spat, "you're drowning in Shadows, boy, we need to—"

A foot caught him in the chest, and he staggered back, then hurled himself forward, grabbed the boy by the collar, and yanked.

They both fell tumbling into the dirt. "You'd best pray it's the Darkness that has driven you mad, boy, because if it's not, you'll pay for these bruises with some of your own!" He pinned the boy to the ground with one hand braced on a shoulder and continued, "I'm not going to hurt you. Just calm down and let's see if we can relieve you."

The boy relaxed, calming except for his heaving chest as he fought for air.

Robin's mind raced through his options, coming up blank.

"Cat-mint…" the boy muttered. "Tincture of angelica. Blue chalcedony, jet, bronzite, amber—do you have any on you?"

"No," Robin said, confused.

The boy moaned. "Trifolium, then. There's bound to be trifolium…" The boy's head fell back into the dirt.

"Trifolium? I don't know…"

"*Clover,*" the boy ordered, scorn dripping from his voice. "I'm speaking of *clover.*"

Robin paced along the road looking for a clump of clover, unsure whether to laugh or snarl.

"Do you at least know your Greek sigils?" the boy muttered weakly. "The banishing sigil performed with clover…"

Greek, he thought resentfully rubbing his jaw. "I know sigils," he said, amending silently, *if I can remember the Greek ones from the schoolroom.*

If he got the scamp past this spell of poisoning, he was going to thrash him.

And where had he got into such Darkness in the first place?

He found a large clump that looked in the moonlight like it might be clover—*trifolium*, he thought with a sigh. He yanked it up by the roots and sniffed, then paced quickly back to the boy, whose breathing was sounding more and more laboured. Robin was beginning to have real concerns for his safety. "I found your clover."

"Good," the boy sighed. "Scrape the Greek sigil for banning in the dirt and then trace it with the trifolium seven times."

Robin did as instructed, his boot heel making a harsh sound in the night as he prayed silently to Diana, protector of children, that he was doing it correctly, or if not, near enough.

"How long has it been since you were cleansed?"

Impertinent little brat. "My soul is not overburdened."

"You evaded my question, which is answer enough, may the gods deliver me," the boy retorted with equal venom. "Well, I can't tell that it makes a difference, despite what the priests say. If you'd please… promise an offering to Nemesis. I'll honour it myself once I'm home."

Nemesis? The boy wanted vengeance? Something sinister had definitely happened, and Robin was at once alert and protective. At the moment, he just needed to come up with an acceptable prayer. He held his hands over the boy's body and called, "Away, away, from your feet and from all your limbs… erm… Shadows and every muscular pain!" he finished with a wince.

"Did you just use the prayer to rid me of gout?" the boy asked incredulously.

"I said Shadows," Robin muttered.

The boy let out a disgusted sigh. "I'm doomed."

"Listen, lad, I'm no priest."

"No scholar, either," the scamp said weakly.

Frustrated, Robin offered a silent prayer to both goddesses, promising offerings, and finally closed off the sigil.

His energy pulsed within him—*amazing*—skimming throughout his body and then settling into his left hand, the hand that wore—

The amber signet.

Amber.

"Boy," Robin said hesitantly. "If you had amber, what would you do with it?"

❧ CHAPTER THREE ❧

Persephone glared up at the man, seething. "All this time you've been wearing an amber ring and you didn't bother to—"

"Enough," he ordered.

The amber surface of the ring caught a glint of moonlight, beckoning.

She reached. Touched.

And lightning sparked between them, fingertip to ring.

She gasped.

He yanked his hand back, stunned.

For one frozen moment, neither of them moved.

She felt... *bright*.

She looked down and saw no difference, but the feeling was unmistakable, a feeling of bright, molten strength. Like *amber*.

Then it was gone.

She was desperate to feel it again, to feel *more*.

And terrified. The amber should have cleansed her, not done whatever it had done. *First the music, now this.*

She stumbled to her feet and mumbled, "Thank you." Before the man could gather his wits, she leapt to the top of a smooth rock, thrust her foot into the stirrup, and swung her leg over Hades' back. She had to get away before something else happened that she could neither explain nor control.

The man grabbed the bridle. "What in Apollo's name just happened?"

"Release me! I have to be home before dawn."

"Or you'll get the much-deserved thrashing of your life?"

"It's just..." She shifted in discomfort, her hand over her abdomen. "I don't want to vex them today of all days."

He studied her with concern. "You're sure you can make such a ride?"

She tossed her head. "Of course."

"How far are you riding?" the man asked maddeningly.

She didn't know where she was, much less how to get home. But Hades would get her home. Hadn't he got her this far? Yet this man had been kindness itself, despite everything. And Hades clearly trusted him. "My horse needs water."

"I crossed a stream not far back, and I've a flask of watered wine if you think you can tolerate a sip or two…"

Tolerate? As if she were a mere child?

As they rode, she gulped from the flask until he reached across and pulled it from her lips. Finally she sat stiffly, as both horses drank from the gurgling stream.

She felt the man watching her.

"What's your name, lad?" he finally asked.

"Dardanus," she answered without hesitation.

"And your surname?"

"Not for one who doesn't bother to offer his own name."

He laughed. It was warm and comforting and golden, that laugh. A laugh that, at the moment, made her want to weep with exhaustion and fear and pain. She gave her head a shake, trying to clear it.

"Robin—" He broke off abruptly, then said, "Sir Robert Fitzwilliam."

"You have a title!"

"You don't have sisters to marry off, do you? That sounded positively scheming."

"One," Persephone replied, and then quickly, "Well, two, actually, I have a twin sister, but she's hardly ready for marriage."

"Still at seminary, then?"

She froze, forced her voice to be scornful. "No, she doesn't need seminary. She can learn more at home than she could ever learn in a place where all they care about is social graces." That much was true. But so was the shame, the fear that outsiders would learn of her *difference* and refuse to join their bloodlines with a family that could produce such as she. She repeated lamely, "She has no need for seminary, Sir Robert."

"Call me Robin. Nobody has ever called me 'Sir' in my life." Then, as if in explanation, "I wasn't a Sir until yesterday. And now I'm a poor baronet, I fear, not a plum ready to be picked by a miss in the marriage mart. My family is too old and respected to snub but too lowly to respect. If your sister has high aspirations, she'll not be for the likes of me."

"There's no telling how high she might marry. She is astoundingly lovely."

"How fortunate I'm not looking for a wife. My heart won't be shattered on the shoals of her beauty." Robin laughed.

"Not that there's anything wrong with being a baronet. I rather like the simplicity of 'Sir Robin'. Like a knight of the round table."

"A knight out on the midnight road, rescuing damsels—"

She froze. *Damsels?*

"Or rather, lads—in distress."

Heart pounding, Persephone blurted, "I rescued myself, thank you very much!" And now she sounded positively missish! She guided Hades back up towards the road and felt relief as the horse took the lead, evidently knowing the way, and headed west. "Home, boy." She leaned forward and murmured, "Home…"

But in no time, Sir Robin was beside her again.

Blister him!

"What brings you out on such a fine night?" Sir Robin asked, firm. "And how did you end up drowning in Shadow?"

She attempted to mimic Cosmo's air of nonchalance. "Adventuring."

"More adventure than you counted on, I take it."

Persephone snorted. "You might say that."

"I won't let you ride alone, and you must tell your father about your brush with Shadows."

"I'll tell him," she said with a tendril of unease, grateful that he had no suspicion that the Shadows he sensed dwelt within her.

"Would it be presumptuous of me to ask what happened to you?"

Again, she hesitated. Cosmo, she thought fiercely, determined to carry it through. Cosmo. Finally she said in a tone that was near boasting, "I was *abducted.*"

"Zeus!"

"But I escaped—" Now she *was* boasting. "—and left the bas—

blackguard stranded in Ordinary London, and we'll just see if he perpetrates such an offence again on my... on me."

"You—you were taken into the Ordinary world?"

"Hades got me out, bless his withers and fetlocks. However," she said thoughtfully, "I think it must have been the passage from the Ordinary world to this one that caused me injury. That's the last I remember, forcing Hades through because I didn't know the words that the man said, and then pain, and then..." She turned to Sir Robin, wishing she could see his face, his eyes. "You."

"There are portals, of course, but what happened to you could only happen if the portal itself was Shadowed. You say you had to force your horse through?"

"It didn't hurt him, though. It didn't hurt my horse... I think he was trying to protect *me*," she said softly and knew that he was now truly her horse, brave, solid Hades, inelegant as he might be.

Robin shifted in his saddle. "I've heard of such. My mother used to make offerings on this road to Elen of the Ways, 'to smooth passage on roads both seen and unseen'."

"But that's the old gods, the Dark ones," Persephone said dismissively. "It's not as if anybody follows them now." She froze. "Your mother did so?"

He cleared his throat. "So she said."

She had to put more distance between herself and this place of Dark portals and offerings. "I can find my way. My family will be horrid if they've discovered my absence, and you don't want to be caught up in that."

"And that family would be?"

What name to give him? Surely not her own. And yet he was a baronet. He was kind and even rather funny, and it wasn't as if her family wouldn't find out. "How old are you?" she demanded.

"Six and twenty," he said with a startled laugh.

Not too terribly old then. "Fury," she said. "The Furys of Erinyes Manor."

"Not Cosmo Fury's brother?"

Persephone swelled with pride. "You know him?"

"Who doesn't know of that young rake? Well, then, that settles it.

I'll not have you lost, or worse. I wouldn't want to have to answer to Cosmo."

❦

The sun lingered below the horizon, but the sky was already turning shades of rose and lilac and gold as the goddess Eos opened the gates of heaven to show her brother the way home.

She heard Sir Robin's indrawn breath and let a smile curl her lips.

The lane swung to the east then dipped down into the small warded valley that protected her family home.

He reined in and looked out over the vista spread below. "It's beautiful."

What he lacked in eloquence he more than made up for in tone. And who was she to fault him for being awestruck? The land spread below them was green as emeralds, the manor itself a moated jewel of Tudor prosperity, still as grand as it had been the day it had been completed.

"Bardán Fury requested Roslyn Manor from King Henry VIII as a boon," she said proudly. "He was an Irish poet, a musician, a bard, and a soldier. Henry rewarded him for his assistance in routing out the rebel Kildares."

"I learned the history in the schoolroom, of course, but was too young to notice the subtleties. An interesting trait in an Irishman, to be more loyal to an English king than one's own lord?"

"Never doubt a Fury's loyalty." She smirked. "Or our knack for choosing well where our loyalties should lie. Henry seized Roslyn Manor, a stronghold of Catholics, and bestowed it on my ancestor."

Robin lifted his eyebrows. "A member of the Magi who would have been burned for witchcraft, had but Henry been aware."

Persephone glowed with pride. "And having been in Henry's court and noting how quickly the king's fevers flared against his own fellow Christians, Bardán Fury convinced the Magi to withdraw from the Ordinary world. He saw the burning times coming."

"He was a Seer?"

"He was canny."

Sir Robin's smile was wry. "Not many traversed the warp and weave of royal politics so gracefully, and in two different Courts, both

Ordinary and Magi. But afterwards… no Furys have numbered among the Lords, amongst the nobility. For a kingmaker, he had little ambition."

"The Furys need no titles from kings," Persephone retorted. "We have Gifts from the gods."

"Oho!" Sir Robin laughed uproariously.

She chafed at his amusement. She tilted her chin proudly. "Our people were dancing in the temples and pleasing the gods with song at the beginning of time."

"None can trace back that far," he challenged.

"I don't need records to confirm what I know in my soul."

"You're as precocious as you are exasperatingly clever," Robin proclaimed. "Now I understand the old adage about Furys pleasing kings."

"In England 'tis said that the Furys have the gift of pleasing kings." She recited the old verse for him, grinning. "In Ireland, 'tis said, never trust a Fury." But she kept the third line to herself, as Furys always did.

The glow that had begun as the sun slowly cresting the distant hills became alive within her. Never had she felt so free, with no one admonishing her to restrain herself in front of company, to keep her thoughts appropriate and proper.

Was this what her life would have been had she been a boy?

Or was it this man, this Sir Robin Fitzwilliam, who treated her with such dignity and equality, as if she weren't thirteen years old, as if she weren't beneath his notice, or more, as if she were intelligent and *interesting?*

She could hardly breathe with the pain of it. This moment of being accepted was like lightning, brilliant and brief, and already fading, because below them lay her home and her family, and she might never see this man again.

She turned her eyes to him, to drink in what the new sun revealed to remember always, and at that moment, dawn's rays graced his head and his shoulders, and from shadow to light, *he* became the brilliance. His hair was rich auburn, glinting with bronze and red in the ethereal light. His eyes were green as moss, and his skin warm and golden, and his smile, oh dear merciful gods and goddesses, his smile melted her.

His broad shoulders and strong hands and—so much to remember, and yet it was all blurring, because her eyes were filling with tears, and—and—she never cried. She couldn't cry. Only a girl would cry!

She dug her heels into Hades' flanks. He flew down the road, his hooves scarcely touching the ground. She leaned over his neck, fighting back the tears, forcing them down, down deep, deep where she ached and where they would be swallowed up with the rest of her inappropriate behaviours and magics.

They thundered through the gatehouse, across the heavy plank drawbridge that spanned the moat, and beneath the razor-edged portcullis. Finally, they were in the safety of the cobbled courtyard, protected on four sides by Erinyes Manor, with Sir Robin right behind her. But it was all right now, because she was home, and she wouldn't weep, and she wouldn't reveal her masquerade and shame her family and bring scandal to Electra, and she was *home*.

And then she glanced down and saw blood where her legs spread over the saddle.

Her menarche? Of all days, today was to be her menarche?

She bit back a wail of horror. The pains in her abdomen became clear to her. Electra's complaints of aches hadn't been mere maidenly weakness. And now it was her plight, as well!

The first to hear the commotion in the courtyard was, praise the gods, Lysander, who came out of the manor and stood silent and still, his black Fury hair hanging over his brow, his cunning gaze darting from her to Robin and back again, one eyebrow arching in question. And yet, she couldn't speak, couldn't form words.

"I fear I found your scamp of a brother in a bit of a bother." She heard the smile in Sir Robin's voice, though she didn't allow herself to look back at him.

She couldn't tear her gaze away from Lysander, showing poise beyond his seventeen years as he relaxed into his usual slouch.

"My dear *Dardanus,*" he chided. "Whatever are we going to do with you? And look at that horse."

Hades tossed his head and pulled at the reins in an effort to turn back to the stables, fighting as hard as if he weren't drenched in sweat and dirt and pushed to the point of exhaustion. Her heart swelled with guilt that she hadn't taken him there first.

"Get down so one of the stable boys can—"

No, she begged with her eyes.

He strolled closer and his gaze froze on the bloody source of her terror, froze with understanding that would have humiliated her under any other circumstance but now relieved her, because he knew, and he would save her.

"On second thought, take him to the stable yourself. You got him in this state. It's your job to care for him."

But before she could move, Electra arrived at the doorway, her hair a tousle of ebony waves and eyes the darkest grey, her skin porcelain and her dressing gown hastily tied around her slender waist.

Sir Robin Fitzwilliam's gaze fixed on her like she was a vision of a goddess.

As, after all, she was.

Persephone's heart rent in two. He had been hers, *hers,* and for one night it had made no difference that she was only thirteen and he thought her a boy.

For one night, he had been hers.

And now, he wasn't.

Her mother and the downstairs maid appeared behind Electra. Persephone knew she had to leave immediately. Hades shifted restlessly beneath her, then snorted. Her magic was distressing him, threatening to erupt again in public with servants and Sir Robin as witnesses.

With her blood, her magic, flowing from her, she rode back out of the courtyard, through the gatehouse and to the stables, before her shame and her curse were revealed to the world.

➣ CHAPTER FOUR ➢

Persephone huddled in the corner of Hades' stall, aching in a place so deep behind her heart, she'd not known of its existence before. She should be caring for her horse. Instead, she crouched in terror that the stable hands would find her bloody and humiliated in Dardanus's trousers, that someone would call her by her name, that her masquerade would yet be revealed, that—

"Dearest."

She jumped to her feet, even though the movement brought pain to every part of her body, and flung herself into Electra's arms.

"Whatever were you doing?" Electra stroked her hair. "I awakened and found Dardanus in your bed, and then heard the noise in the courtyard, and—"

"Where is Sir Robin?" Persephone asked urgently. "If he sees Dardanus—"

"He's in the drawing room with Mother and Father, and they are nodding and showing appropriate concern and consternation, and you can be sure once he has been sent on his way, they will be demanding answers, so let's get you back inside and cleaned up. We'll go the long way, through old Bardán's hall. No one will see us."

With a clean horse blanket wrapped around her shoulders and hanging almost to her ankles, Persephone allowed herself to be led back to the courtyard, where they slipped unnoticed through the door leading to the old medieval wing, now rarely used. With urgency and stealth, they swept through the cavernous room and up the back stairs, until they finally made it to their bedchamber without being seen.

Upon crossing the threshold, Persephone felt relief course through her. Rose-scented steam—Electra's own salts!—billowed from the copper bathtub under the room's only window, tall and narrow with a stained glass image of the Ordinary folks' Virgin Mother that Persephone viewed as a comforting image of Aphrodite. Unlike her brother's chamber, there were no convenient window escapes to be had here. This had been a chapel for the Catholic family who had built the Manor.

Clover, a maid with apron and mob cap, poured a steady stream of steaming water from her fat kettle, watching the water level climb the linen-lined sides of the tub to near the rim before dismissing the kettle's magic with an efficient flick of her fingers.

"Where's Rue?" Electra asked. "I sent for her."

"None has seen her all morning." The maid blotted the spout with a clean rag so as not to drip water across the jewel-toned Persian rug. She cast a curious glance at Persephone. "I'm not as good with the healings as Rue, but I can assist."

"No," Electra said, distracted. "Find her."

Clover bobbed a curtsey and left.

Persephone's hands were locked over her abdomen as if they could ease the cramping, but they brought her no relief. She turned her face up to the stained glass, whose image glowed with sunrise and spilled a gilt reflection across the floor. As Ordinary as the Virgin goddess might be, she seemed to welcome Persephone with her benevolent smile.

If Persephone were the sort to weep—and she was *not*, she thought fiercely—she would have wept at the sight.

But even though Electra attempted to steer her to the bath and her body longed for the soothing heat on her aching muscles, Persephone pulled away.

"I have to make an offering to—" She broke off. "—Vesta," she finished, for she could admit to Vesta. Her offering to Nemesis would have to remain secret.

"Bathe before you—"

"I vowed to make offerings," Persephone said, fighting to stay erect and not slump to the floor, "and I will do so."

Every movement causing new aches, she lit a candle from the fire and went to the shrine in the corner. With a flourish, she lowered it to the deep bowl of sand on the altar, and in moments it cupped a small fire on which she placed her tiny pot of precious gilt ink to melt.

Electra sighed and knelt beside her as she took a small piece of parchment from the altar, dipped the peacock quill, and felt the flow of prayer spring from her fingertips as she meticulously wrote the Greek characters to express her thanksgiving to Vesta. Upon finishing, she held it before Electra, who murmured the incantation and then pursed her perfect lips and blew across it.

Persephone sprinkled powdered herbs and scented oil across the surface, then gave it a practiced twist with her trembling hands, and it became a tight roll. She laid it across one of the silk ribbons on the altar, and after another incantation, the ribbon coiled and tied itself tightly.

"We call your name, our Queen of Heaven," Electra sang, as, finally, Persephone could close her eyes and allow the music of the cantare to warm her as she added her silent prayer. What god or goddess could not be pleased with such an offering in Electra's pure voice? *"Ceres, Venus, sister of Phoebus, Proserpina or by whatever name, with whatever rite, in whatever appearance it is right to invoke thee, hear our prayer and grace us with your blessing."* Electra's arm circled and supported her as she placed the rolled parchment in the flames.

Together they watched her offering rise as smoke and follow their prayers to the goddess.

"Now," Electra said firmly, "it's into the bath with you, before we're summoned downstairs."

Persephone allowed herself to be stripped of her clothing, covering her mouth in dismay at the sight and smell of the disgusting trousers, surely ruined beyond redemption.

"Not so bad. Your flow hasn't really started yet, it seems," Electra murmured as she eyed them with a measuring glance. "Nothing Clover couldn't handle easily, if we were willing to expose bloody trousers to servants' gossip, which we are not. Into the tub, dearest. And whilst I'm washing you, you are to tell me everything, do you understand? Everything!" Her eyes danced with excitement as Persephone finally sank into the water with a gasp and a sigh.

"I have proof," she said, "proof that will finally convince them that the odious Mr Jones—"

"It's always about the odious Mr Jones! I want to hear all about the beautiful man with hair of flame that you brought home to me."

Hair of flame.

Home to Electra.

How had she not remembered? But... but it had been a stupid prophecy, not even real, just Cosmo playing with a ball of fire and then, his countenance, already handsome at sixteen, turning intense.

I see you, Electra, by all the gods I see you! In the future, marrying a man with hair of flame!

And he'd said more, but the rest of it was beyond preposterous. Ridiculous. They had scoffed and laughed at it, and yet...

Hair of flame.

Persephone sank beneath the water's surface to close out her sister's voice, the world, and the pain in her heart, until she could hold her breath no longer. As she came up to take a gulp of air, Electra lifted one of her thin legs above the surface and began scrubbing her with a soft sponge and her own rose-scented soaps.

Electra caught her surprise and smiled gently. "Today is a day for celebration, sweet. When you go before Mother and Father you'll be a woman, not a child. "

"But I have no—"

"Don't be a goose. Do you really think Mother didn't have your woman's things ready?"

Belatedly, Persephone closed her arms across her almost flat chest, wincing at the tenderness there and relaxing her grip to release the pressure, but still keeping them covered. "How could she tell? It's not as if I'm... well, growing."

"You have the shape of the Furys, long and lean, and I have the shape of the de Lacys, soft and rounded. You'll never be as full as I am, but dear girl, you are definitely showing the beginnings of your womanhood, never you fear. And today, they will have to treat you as such, for which you can count yourself exceedingly lucky." She pressed her lips to Persephone's wet forehead and brushed a sodden hank of hair off her cheek. "Now, tell me what possessed you. You must even tell me about the horrid Mr Jones and the lovely Sir Robin." Her light laughter washed over Persephone, as cleansing and warm as any bath.

"And after you've told me all, *then* we'll decide how much you're to tell Mama and Papa."

🐦🐦

How rude a welcome into womanhood, going from the freedom of her brother's trousers into her first pair of drawers, complete with a bulky wool pad tied between her legs. If that had been the extent of it, she could have borne it with something approaching grace, but of course it was not. Her shift was dropped over her head and then…

"Believe me, today of all days, you will be glad to wear these."

Stays! Ridiculous stays, as if she needed them! By the time Lizzie and Fern were through clucking over her, she was stifling under so many layers she thought she'd die of heat as well as humiliation. But when she stood before the mirror she saw what Electra had promised.

The day before, she'd been a child in a muslin dress with only a shift beneath.

The night before, she'd been a boy in trousers, shirt, and jacket.

On this day, her face and her body were the same, but even before Electra clasped the vestal locket signifying her new status as young lady around her throat, she felt changed. Even in her weariness, the new, heavy undergarments had the odd effect of making her stand taller, straighter and even, she noted, hold her head higher.

She sat stiffly in the chair as Fern, her mother's personal lady's maid, took her hands, clucking at their condition and taking special notice of her swollen knuckles on her right fist.

The fist that had connected with Robin's jaw.

Not that she was going to confess, even to Electra.

Fern took her small packet of unguents for tending fingernails and spread it open on the table. Before long, Persephone's fingertips tingled with the older woman's skilled magic as they were cleaned and smoothed to a gloss by a succession of scented creams and muttered charms, the whites brighter than she'd ever seen them, and the nails as pink as mallow blossoms.

Persephone had only seen these magics applied to her sister's and mother's hands. She looked at them in wonder and wondered how long before her inks stained them and left them smelling of iron sulphate.

But not even magic could save her hair, as straight and fine as ever. Fern's best efforts weren't able to arrange it artfully. She eventually managed to coil it loosely on her head and bespell it not to tumble, and finally, Persephone stared into the mirror and saw a stranger, a girl who was prim and proper, not the bluestocking hoyden Persephone Fury.

Electra squeezed her shoulders and kissed both cheeks. "How do you feel?"

Persephone stared at herself. "I don't know me," was all she could say. But catching the glance the women shared over her head, she forced a smile.

Their peals of laughter were the only response she got.

"Come along," Electra said, taking her hand.

"But they haven't sent for me yet." She stifled a yawn with her hand and longingly eyed the bed that had so recently been vacated by her brother. She wondered what chaos had erupted when he'd been found there, drugged and tricked by her, and what punishment awaited her.

"If we hurry, perhaps it's not too late for Sir Robin to meet my sister," Electra said, eyes dancing with mischief.

"No… I can't… He might recognise—"

Electra shot her a quelling look, and Persephone closed her mouth, aware of Fern's and Lizzie's presence.

With lead in her stomach, she was about to begin the long walk to the drawing room when she remembered. "Go along," she said. "I'll be right with you."

"Darling, they—"

"I have one more thing to do," Persephone said crisply, and Electra sighed, knowing better than to argue.

When she was alone, she closed the door and placed the bolt in place before crossing the room to the old altar. The chapel's original marble altar had been heavy and securely placed against the far stone wall, and early Furys had allowed it to stay. She swept away the brocade cover and revealed the smooth surface of its top and the broken edges of the reliquary. She took an iron file from its notch between the altar and the wall and pried the reliquary's lid off, exposing her dearest treasures.

Tenderly, she stroked the fat stomach of the green marble goddess who had been there from the very first time she opened it. She moved her aside to find the small collection of Roman coins, and specifically, the bronze sestertius with the worn profile of Nemesis on one side and her winged figure on the other. A trader had brought it, claiming to have found it near the Emperor Hadrian's wall to the North. Her father had bought it for her as just another coin for her collection, but Persephone had felt a thrill at possessing such a powerful talisman.

Now, it sent a surge of danger through her, filling her aching limbs with power. She would have her vengeance, and the goddess would help her.

She took the few precious grains of gold and twisted them into a corner of parchment.

All that remained in the reliquary now was a knife of corroded bronze, its edge jagged with deterioration, its handle, however, chased with gold. That corroded edge was a wicked, dangerous thing, more likely to rip and tear at flesh than slice into it with clean malice.

She'd discovered it when she was five years old and even then knew with a thrill that it was dangerous. Now she touched it and felt—

Shadows.

Shadows that called to her.

But they didn't feel malevolent, these Shadows. They felt familiar, and deep, and something within her responded with a slow uncurling.

Heart pounding, she wrapped the dagger in a handkerchief and tucked it deep in the pocket of her morning dress with the coin and the bits of gold dust, then replaced everything until the room looked exactly as it had. Last, she slid the iron file back into its hiding place.

She grimly skirted her way along the walls of the lower corridor, not to the drawing room, but to emerge into the courtyard, which was filled with a bustle of activity. At various spots around the enclosure, tall ladders climbed the walls and male servants perched atop, releasing Chinese spiders to spin their webs into windows, thick-growing vines and corners. Within hours, the interior courtyard would be dripping delicate webs that would then be powdered with silver dust, the better to reflect both moonlight and torchlight as guests arrived. It was an effect often used at Erinyes Manor in past centuries, but on this night, all would see its glory as a prelude to what lay ahead.

Again, she felt a swell of pride.

Her parents had long ignored Society—and some might uncharitably say, their children—preferring to travel through magical lands on the Continent and safely beyond the wars consuming

Ordinary Europe, bored with the narrow world of the London Magi. But now they had a daughter to launch, and after this night, the name Fury would be on everyone's lips, and word of Electra's beauty and voice would grace every breakfast table on the morn.

When she considered how close she'd come to ruining it all, Persephone's head felt light.

Carefully, she found refuge under the low-hanging apple tree in the corner where the family wing and medieval wing joined. She waited stiffly by the bubbling fountain until she was confident that no one had noticed her.

After casting one last glance over her shoulder, she looked at the mossy rock in front of the old fountain and grimaced. She'd soil her dress if she knelt. As Electra kept reminding her, today of all days was a day when she would benefit greatly from her new status as a young lady, lest she wanted to be viewed and punished as a child.

The dizzying thought of standing to address a goddess stole her breath.

This time she had no familiar ritual to guide her, for if anyone made offerings to Nemesis it was certainly not young girls. She took the twist of parchment and opened it, watching the smattering of glittering dust settle on the surface of the water and then disperse into the splashing turbulence. "Accept my offering," she whispered fervently and yet felt its inadequacy. But what god or goddess wouldn't be honoured to accept gold? Her only gold? What more could she want, this goddess of divine retribution, this goddess of vengeance, this remorseless goddess of justice?

And then she knew as surely as she breathed. She had but one thing to give, to tempt the winged goddess to her cause, and perhaps she'd known it all along, because even as the world around her began to grow hazy and indistinct, her right hand found the ancient blade in her pocket, and without hesitation she raised her left hand over the fountain's surface and pierced her palm with the broken tip of the knife.

"*Neimein*," she whispered hoarsely, watching the blood spatter across the water. "*Neimein. Neimein. Neimein…*" It became a chant, and then a hymn spilling from her lips, that single word, over and over until the Darkness inside her unfurled and swept through her with calm, and she knew—she *knew*—her prayer had been heard. Her offering had been accepted.

Neimein.

To give what is due.

To give what is due to the vile Mr Jones.

A fierce joy rose in her.

She finally lifted the coin skyward. And one last time she whispered the words, this time in exultation, *"To give what is due."* She could trust this goddess to wreak the most ferocious vengeance on him. She could not begin to comprehend his purpose, his use of Dardanus, his intent for her before she'd thwarted him. Her head spun with the effort of figuring it out or perhaps, just from exhaustion. But she had no doubt his aim had been sinister.

Would that she felt as certain of her own parents' willingness to bring Mr Jones to justice as she did the goddess Nemesis. Unfortunately, she had no such certainty

She dipped the coin in the water three times and holding, it to the light, saw its surface tinged with blood and glinting with a speck of gold. She kissed it, both sides, and slid it back into her pocket, weak with release but finally satisfied that her obligations were fulfilled.

A shadow fell across her.

She whirled to find, to her dismay, Cosmo, a lock of midnight hair falling across his forehead, his face blanched of colour.

She shoved the knife back into her pocket and crushed the handkerchief in her left hand, her fingers pressing it into her bloody palm in an attempt to stem the flow.

"You stupid little witling!" he snapped, taking her hand and turning it palm up to see the bloody handkerchief. "And whatever is happening to your hair?"

Her hair? She reached her free hand up to find it crackling wildly around her head, no longer a ladylike coil. She looked at him in surprise.

"What mortification are you bringing down upon us now?" He sighed. "What is it this time, goose? What have you done?"

She yanked her hand away from him, gasping at the pain as the movement tugged at her wound and opened it wider. "I did what nobody else in this household will! What you should have done, and now that I know the truth…"

"Whatever are you prattling about?" he asked, dragging his hands through his hair. "Of all days for you to create a stir, you had to choose this one? I've just ridden in from town to let them know that I'm bringing the bloody Duke of Aubyn with me tonight, and what do I find but you doing some sort of—my eyes can scarce believe what they see—*a blood ritual?* Have you finally gone lunatic?"

A Duke? He was bringing the Duke of Aubyn to Electra's musicale? Her heart leapt in her breast. A lowly baronet surely had no chance, hair of flame or not, if a Duke took an interest in Electra, and he surely would.

Hope bubbled up within her, even as she knew herself to be a fool to even think such thoughts. He was twice her age. He thought she was a boy. He would never look at her the way men looked at Electra, but…

"Are you listening to me?" Cosmo demanded, exasperated. "Bratling, what does this mean? This?" He gestured at her hair. "And this?" Again, he grabbed her hand and this time removed the handkerchief and winced. He dropped to his knee, not even caring that he got mud on his fine breeches. He tugged her towards him, and for a moment all she wanted to do was fall into her eldest brother's arms and weep like the child she'd been only the day before.

But she could not. "I have called upon Nemesis," she said, her tone as cool and nonchalant as any he effected. And at the glint of panic in his eyes, she continued. "I have called upon Nemesis to bring justice and vengeance down upon Mr Vespasian Jones."

He dropped her hand. "You're still on about that? Just because he refused to have a female in his classroom?"

"Don't be absurd," she hissed. "I didn't call for vengeance over anything so self-serving. I called for vengeance because he abducted me in the night and carried me off to Ordinary London, thinking I was Dardanus! Because he used his *contrôle de l'esprit* on me, thinking he could enter my mind and clear it of all memories, the way he has done Dardanus at least three times in the past."

"Abducted you?" He stiffened and she knew relief.

But quickly, even before she could be warmed by his concern, came his dismissal.

"Surely not. Surely there is some other explanation—"

"Do you think that I am lying or that I am truly mad?" she demanded, her veins filling with ice. "It must be one or the other. There is no middle ground."

The necklace around her neck, evidence that she was no longer a child, registered. His handsome features softened—for surely he was the most handsome of her brothers, if also so much a rake he was a danger in London drawing rooms, or so she heard gossiped amongst the servants. His grey eyes softened with concern as he affectionately brushed a knuckle down her cheek before squeezing her shoulder. "I think you neither mad nor lying. But this is such a preposterous idea of yours, that Mr Jones would abduct you—"

She flung herself away from him and away from the apple tree, the fountain now bubbling with blood and gold and vows. Fuelled on nothing but anger, she flew across the cobblestones to the door, past the footman.

Her father. She must find her father.

The world spun a half-rotation around her.

She reached wildly—grasping for purchase and finding nothing. Nothing to cling to. Nothing to steady her.

And then the mists were swirling around her once more, all sound muffled, and she felt herself falling.

Falling.

With no one to catch her, no one to save her from the burning black eyes that pierced her very soul.

❧ CHAPTER FIVE ❧

She was so very cold, and yet she felt snug and comforted and baffled in softness as if she were once again a babe in her mother's arms.

The beloved and familiar scent of lilac and lemon balm that was her mother's own blending surrounded her. The tender caress of cool fingertips on her damp brow, accompanied by her mother's voice, pulled her from the dark, cold limbo, back to a present in which her head swam with dizziness. But her gaze eventually rested on her mother's countenance, knit with distress as she knelt closer.

Persephone's head snapped sideways in reflex. Her nose burned, and her eyes stung as her mother withdrew the phial of smelling salts.

"There now. That should bring her 'round and keep her here." She patted Persephone's cheek with no small degree of fondness. "Truly, pigeon, I did not raise my daughters to have vapours."

"Would that you had, Mama," Cosmo said, all charm and indulgence, leaning against the windowsill and tossing a small fireball from one hand to the other. "As it is, we're fortunate she makes such an excellent boy. If she hadn't landed a facer on Fitzwilliam within a moment of discovery, he might not have been so easily duped. I only wish I'd been there to see. Quite the bruise on his jaw."

His deft fingers lifted her right hand, and he carefully examined her swollen knuckles. "Someone fetch Rue. I'll not have my sister battered when we have the best hearth healer in three counties under our roof."

"She's not to be found, the wretched wench," her mother remarked with a snap. "And with all that needs to be done today. But I've sent to the kitchen for Rue's cramp-bark tea, which shall have to suffice."

Persephone attempted to rise on one elbow, but her mother's firm hand on her shoulder held her still. "You are not to move from this bed all day or night or at least half the morrow."

"I'm being punished?" Persephone gasped at the injustice.

"You're being given the benefit of the doubt," her mother returned

47

tartly. "Today you will rest and heal, and tomorrow, once we've recovered from this night's entertainment, your papa and I will be ready to hear your tale and discern what punishment is appropriate. And—lest you think I'm unaware—that wound on your palm and the fact that you were hovering over the water shrine when Cosmo discovered you makes it clear that punishment is inevitable!"

Her mother's stern words set Persephone, for what did they expect her to do if they wouldn't listen? If she had to fling herself at the feet of the entire pantheon to find justice, she would do it.

"La," Electra trilled from the open doorway as she sailed into the room. "You will not punish my sweet, no matter what she has done, for she has redeemed herself by showing up on our doorstep with a beautiful baronet!"

Persephone turned her face away and dug deeper into her pillow. What stuff and nonsense. He wasn't beautiful. He was warm and filled with life and with… with goodness. He listened, even to a thirteen-year-old boy, she thought with a distracted sigh. He listened and he conversed and—and he *rescued*.

And he'd suffered her pummelling without tossing her across the road, as he easily could have done with full justification.

But the more of his virtues she extolled, the more desolate she became. For it was only a matter of time before Electra discovered these same virtues and—Persephone was quite certain—many more.

Fern bustled in behind Electra, carrying a tray with a delicate violet-sprigged teacup and saucer. "I've the tisane, just as you ordered, ma'am."

It smelled dreadful.

"Don't worry, sweet. I dosed it with lavender honey." Electra beamed from her side of the bed chamber as she pulled her exquisite white gown from the wardrobe.

"It's too early to get that out, dear. You'll only soil it," Mama said, followed by, "Drink this while it's hot. It will work faster."

Her arms felt heavy and her hands stiff and numb, but Persephone took the cup and forced the liquid down with a wince. It was difficult to tell whether honey made the bitter dark brew better or merely different.

"I've decided to tea-stain it," Electra announced. "White is not a becoming shade for someone with reddish hair, but a delicate tea-stain would be sublime."

"Don't be absurd! You'll ruin your gown! Electra!" her mama called out frantically, as Electra whisked her way towards the door, her arms full of filmy white fabric. And then, one last desperate attempt at sanity. "You don't even have red hair!"

"But I'll be standing with a man with red hair most of the evening, if I have my way." And with that tart remark, Electra was gone, their Mama fast on her heels.

Cosmo sighed dramatically. "Don't ever grow up, my dear girl. Promise me that. I don't think I could cope with two sisters who are smitten by the mere idea of love."

All she could do was force a smile and finally ask the question that had been driving her for hours.

"Cosmo, where is Dardanus? It was all my idea. Dardanus had no knowledge. Mama understands that, doesn't she? Is he well?"

"As well as any of us on this mad day. Mama has him downstairs, bringing all the instruments into tune."

"Oh." Her eyelids grew heavy, and her sigh felt as if it came from the furthermost reaches of her being. "I don't suppose he can be disturbed, then."

Cosmo leant over close to her, eyes dancing. "For you, poppet? Of course he may."

And within minutes her twin was at her side, peering down at her from beneath a fall of dark hair.

She grabbed his hand and held it tight, like a lifeline, to keep her from drifting.

"What kind of man am I if I let my sister fight my battles?"

"The very best of men." She raised their locked hands. "The best of us all."

Frowning, he dropped her hand and reached to touch the tender spot under her jaw, the spot where a hard thumb had dug when Mr Jones was squeezing her face so fiercely. "He hurt you," he said with a scowl.

"He *tried.*" She smirked up at him, pleasure curling through her. But then, it all came back to her. "Could you really not remember where he took you?" she demanded. "Are his powers truly so strong?" And then, even more hit her, a new knowledge that slapped her with insult. "You *knew*. You knew what he could do!"

He avoided her eyes. "I don't remember, but damn it, you had no right to dose me, and stick me in your own bed, and allow him to—"

She refused to let him divert her. "Perhaps you don't remember where he took you, but you can't have sat in his schoolroom for two years without knowing his powers."

He gave a half-shrug.

"Why didn't you tell me? Don't you realise how dangerous he is?"

That Cosmo and Lysander knew had angered her. That even Dardanus knew hurt. She blinked rapidly and forced down the stirring rage deep within her, the magic uncoiling in an effort to be free.

"Not everyone is like you," he whispered. "I don't like to study. I don't like spending hours poring over ancient tomes and manuscripts."

"And how will you ever go to Oxford if you don't?" she demanded.

"The same way Cosmo and Lysander did." This time, he met her eyes straight on. "The complicated things, the difficult things that he can't be arsed to teach… he plants them in us. He's brilliant beyond comprehension, and he just opens our minds and—" He broke off at the expression she made no attempt to hide.

"You have all allowed that beast into your minds?"

He grabbed both her hands and held her still. "Tomorrow," he promised. "I'll help you tell them tomorrow. When the musicale is over."

"Swear to it."

"Word of a Fury."

They must get past tonight, get past the musicale, allow Electra her triumph.

Again, she reminded herself that there was no good cause to be served by creating more uproar.

And with that, Dardanus leapt upon the bed and crawled across her to take up his spot at the foot, leaning against a bedpost with legs crossed, flute lifted to his mouth to play.

But then…

"Wait!" She sat up, and this time the dizziness was weak, playing around the edges of her vision, even though her limbs were growing heavier and she wondered what had been in that tisane other than cramp bark. His uptilted almond eyes peered over the silver flute at her expectantly. "Your voice!"

His smile was slow and a flush spread across his cheeks. "It changed," he said.

"Of course it did." She laughed, sinking back against the pillows, the pad between her legs feeling strange and bulky, and yet now, finally, right. Even this moment, they shared. "Of course it did."

As his music floated in the air like the golden motes dancing in the shaft of light across the bed between them, she finally allowed herself to sleep.

So heavy was her sleep, so deep and drowning, that only the most disturbing of thoughts could perturb its smooth surface.

Thoughts of a battered fiddle vibrating beneath her fingertips.

Of a dirty couple pressed against a city wall for all to see.

Of the twisted and hated countenance of a man who seemed bent on the destruction of all she loved, if she could but understand how.

And with such thoughts came another, more vivid still.

His room lay waiting in vain for him to return, its secrets hers for the taking.

❧❧

Her head felt light and her steps heavy as she stumbled on the stairs that led to the servants' quarters.

The long corridor wavered before her eyes. She hadn't been in this wing of the manor since her childhood, and yet little had changed.

Vague memory and awareness led her to the last room, the one that had always been set aside for those members of the household who were above the servants and yet not family. The sight of the door, half-open, brought her to alertness.

Three steps took her through the door. Two shuddering breaths braced her. One gentle push of her hand closed the door behind her. And even at first glance, her stomach went from flutters of anticipation to cold frustration.

The room was empty, as cold and barren as a prison cell. Not a book or paper was to be seen on the surface of the small table, only a heavy water jug. No chests or boxes lined the bare walls. The bed bore no skirt, and beneath it, no personal items were stored. The small wardrobe in the corner stood agape and empty.

Whatever had been here was gone.

He had returned and erased any sign of his inhabitancy, all clues of his Dark intent.

The door squeaked open behind her.

Cold fear shot through her.

She whirled, grabbing the water jug and swinging it over her head—

To find Lysander draped in the doorway, leaning against the wall. "How can I rescue my sister from starvation in her state of disgrace if she persists in nosing through the nether reaches of our familial abode?"

She would have fallen over, the weight of the jug overbearing her, had he not lunged forward and caught her with the lithe Fury instincts that had graced Courts and dance floors for centuries.

"Imp." He grinned, one lean arm supporting her as he snatched the jug from her shaking hand. "One would think you expected me to be a demon."

"I did," she said shortly, her heart pounding. "But I see the demon has been here and gone!" She gritted her teeth in frustration.

"Ah, yes, that demon." He helped her to the hard stool and sat her down. "You need food, little one. Can you make it to your chambers on your own feet, or must I carry you?"

She looked around the room one more time. "After last night, how did he dare to come back for anything at all?"

He grew very still, and his lids lowered as he studied her. "Mr Jones was with you last night?"

She thought of the things Mr Jones had threatened to say and her cheeks burned. "Not like *that!*"

He choked a bit, and said abruptly, "Well, of course not like *that*. If I thought there was any possibility of—" He broke off and glared at her. "And what do you know of *that?*"

She rolled her eyes at him. "Do you want me to relay to you what Mama told me? Do you want every detail?"

"Gods, no!"

She nodded with satisfaction. "This room has obviously been cleaned out."

"Perhaps we should presume that he had an accomplice in the household?" At her look of dismay he continued, most soothingly, "But never you fear, I'll find out for you and make sure that whoever it is reveals all."

"Why?" she asked suspiciously, "when you've defended that horrid beast against every claim?"

He gave her a measuring look. "Perhaps because these are new claims," he said. "I repeat. Your own feet, or shall I carry you?"

"I can walk." She got up unsteadily and did not complain or push him away when he assisted her through the busy household, stopping twice to let first a housemaid and then a lackey bustle by.

Upon arriving back in her chamber, she saw the tray on her bed. A loaf of hot, fresh bread torn into large pieces filled the room with yeasty aroma. Several chunks of cheese, a pile of strawberries, and a chipped dish of pickled onions proved that her brother had raided the kitchen, for Cook would never have let such a disreputable spread leave the kitchen. She forced herself to eat in a civilised manner rather than diving into it like one of the hounds. Her stomach twisting with hunger, she took the strongest of the cheeses and bit into it. She sank weakly against her pillows and closed her eyes. "Thank you."

"Who is your favourite brother?" he asked, grinning.

"I have no favourites," she replied crisply. "You are all scoundrels."

"Wretched child."

"I'm *not* a child." She glared at him, then remembered the condition of the trousers he'd seen only hours before and flushed with humiliation.

He merely smiled and popped several small strawberries into his mouth at once, then flopped across the foot of the bed, his long legs hanging over the side. She sighed at the unfairness of it all. Of all her brothers, Lysander was the most like her, as they had the same long limbs that on him were graceful and on her awkward, the same sallow skin that was no detriment to him but, she was assured by her mother, would cause her no end of problems, and the same long nose that on him looked rakish and on her looked unfortunate.

"So," he said, using an ivory toothpick to work loose a seed. "You must tell me what really happened last night. Not the tale you'll spin tomorrow, but the truth of it. What you did. Where you went. And what Mr Jones had to do with it."

She swallowed thickly. She couldn't tell before she'd worked out a plan, before she was certain what to reveal and what to keep to herself.

Not before Nemesis had shown her the way.

But Lysander's devious smile made her catch her breath.

If ever Nemesis were to send her a sign, could it come from anyone better than her sly brother, the one who schemed and plotted?

"Sweet, sweet sister..." He leaned close and tweaked her.

She puffed up, insulted. "Tell me why I should trust you. You've hidden his secrets for him, just as the others have!"

He laughed. Threw his head back and *laughed*. "Of course I have, you silly chit. You think any of us wanted to lose the best tutor in England? You may not like his methods but child, the results are proof of the pudding."

She could have expected no other answer from this brother, after all. But still...

He popped a strawberry into his mouth. "He's gone, isn't he?"

She kept her voice calm even as she toyed with the edge of the sheet. "And what do Mama and Papa say about that?"

"They haven't noticed. Mama is directing every breath anyone takes, Papa is arranging for his casks of Italian wine to be at the ready, and Cosmo is arranging the Moat Room to perfection for his select guests, with a casual display of Electra's sketches of the manor to further exhibit her ladylike talents, should said select guests actually make the trek from London."

"They will. They must! He's bringing a duke!" But Persephone couldn't help wondering how Cosmo could do anything to the Moat Room that could possibly be superior to the Egyptian artefacts and Persian rugs and Chinese porcelains that her parents had brought back from their many journeys and displayed with casual grace in the drawing room.

"Persephone, beloved sister of mine..." Lysander's tone pulled her back to his will. "What happened to our schoolmaster? What mischief did you get up to that finally resulted in forcing him out?"

"It's my mischief, my fault?" It was there, a low-simmering rage, a low-simmering magic, and it was all she could do not to release it in his face.

"Your excitement, your adventure, your fun?" He cocked his brow. "That ended in the removal of one Mr Vespasian Jones?" he purred wickedly.

Fun?

Somehow, his outrageous attitude and reassuring presence turned everything that had passed upside down. She had loved riding in the night, the freedom of being a boy and of being out under the stars. She had seen disgusting and horrifying things, and yet she had surmounted them, had conquered her fear and the villain responsible, had ridden like the wind, had brought home a baronet.

With an arch of his clever and elegant eyebrow, Lysander managed to tease from her the words that had needed release, had desperately needed to share.

If anyone could help her decide what to do about the wretched, horrid Mr Jones, it would be Lysander, once he understood exactly how horrid and wretched the man truly was.

And when she'd told him, and when she found herself suddenly spilling tears upon his hard shoulder as he stroked her hair with soothing murmurs and promises to support her on the morrow… only then did she finally feel at peace and as if this time, this time someone was listening. This time someone believed her. This time, someone would help.

He stuffed his handkerchief in her hand.

But after she blew her nose, his eyes on her were narrowed in concern. She shifted uneasily.

"This vow…" he said slowly. "You have to tell me what vow you made and why you called on such a deity."

She stared at her hands and thought of the small sestertius in her pocket. "My darling sister," he said urgently, and that in itself frightened her. "You have made a powerful vow, you who have powerful and unknown magics. You have to tell someone."

"And if I tell you, you swear you will help me?"

He looked at her with great sorrow, and her fear grew. "I swear on my life I will help you, but I can't swear to help you carry out this vow without knowing what it is."

And in that instant, she felt the relief sweep through her. He would not make any vow easily, but that would make his promise stronger. And of everyone she could tell, this was the one she somehow trusted, this one brother who saw things sharply and from odd angles and acted with great precision.

"I made the vow to Nemesis," she whispered, somehow afraid to stir the goddess's wrath.

He stared at her.

She continued breathlessly, holding out her palm. "And I offered my blood."

He took her hand and touched the edge of her wound gently, wincing. "But... why?"

"I don't know. I didn't plan it. I gave her gold, the only bit of dust I had, but it just—it just felt wrong. It didn't seem enough, somehow."

His piercing eyes fixed on hers. "Where did you make this vow?"

"At the water shrine."

He caught his breath quickly. "In the courtyard?" At her nod, he closed her hand gently and asked one last question. "And what, exactly, was your vow?"

"Neimein." And the word escaping her lips, sounded fierce and strong. *"Neimein,"* she repeated. "To bring her judgement down upon his head. To give the bastard Mr Jones his due."

Something wild flared in her brother's eyes. He breathed deeply, and then he released his breath and his lips curled into the softest and subtlest of smiles. "My dear imp, you have done well."

"I have?" It was as if she hadn't breathed before, that this air that rushed into her brought life itself. "Then, you'll help me?"

"Your vow is my vow, beloved sister."

❧ CHAPTER SIX ❦

"Stand still, miss, or we'll never get it on you!"

Persephone wriggled harder, the white muslin bodice crushing her nose as she struggled to pull the dress over her shoulders. She couldn't breathe.

"She's going to tear it," one worried maid told another.

Suddenly, it was yanked off her in a tangle of arms and hair. She gasped and stared up at her mama in surprise.

"You've outgrown it!" her mother said, glaring as if growing was an intentional act of rebellion. "Fern, surely there's something old of Electra's that will do." She turned back to Persephone. "He said nothing to you about leaving?"

Persephone shook her head uneasily. What was Lysander thinking, disappearing within an hour of the performance? Here she was, being wrestled out of bed and into a dress to take his place, which of course she could do, but what if Sir Robin recognised her?

Fern bustled over with rumpled gown in pale yellow silk. "I can make this do, ma'am."

"Mama…"

"First your sister destroys her gown—*tea-stained,* whatever gave her such an idea?—and then your brother disappears, and now this!"

"Mama…"

"What?" her mother snapped, the ostrich feathers in her turban quivering.

"I need to use the chamber pot," Persephone moaned, for they had dragged her out of bed without a fare-thee-well or a moment of privacy.

"If you must!" Mama gestured in irritation towards the screen.

When she emerged, Fern was smoothing her dress with a sweeping motion of her forefinger, beginning at the top and moving meticulously down, leaving smooth fabric in its wake.

"Not the puce." Her mother dug through Electra's wardrobe.

57

"Perhaps the goldenrod…"

"Don't be silly, Mama," Electra said, entering the room on a wave of light rose scent. "I'm wearing the dress we had made for the occasion."

"That you destroyed!"

"Fern, help me, please?"

Fern abandoned the yellow dress with six inches of crumpled hem untouched. "Of course, Miss Fury."

Three maids surrounded her sister as the dress—the dress that was streaked with uneven colour; no wonder her mother was distraught—was lowered over her head. Finally, they all stepped back, expressions tense.

Electra turned before the cheval mirror, studying herself with a critical eye.

Short ringlets framed her face as the rest of her hair tumbled in glossy black curls down her back. Not only did Electra refuse to kowtow to fashion and cut it, she flaunted its length. The wide scooped bodice displayed the swell of her breasts to perfection, but the streaky skirts…

Persephone caught her breath.

With every movement, the skirts shimmered in the candlelight. What had been streaks were now illusions of light and shadow, moving with each spin as if magic itself danced to her tune.

"See? I told you." Electra turned and smiled. "Where is the gold dust?" she asked. This had been the subject of much debate, to risk appearing gauche by using such for a mere country musicale, yet Electra had insisted.

"Be sparing," her mother warned sternly.

Fern tossed a pinch of gold dust aloft with the command, "Turn!" followed by murmured incantation and a last flick of her forefinger. The gold hung, suspended and glittering, then dispersed into a pale vapour. Electra spun in a slow circle as it settled ever so lightly on her hair, her skin, and the folds of her gown.

So little gold, such subtle effect, and yet the result was the final bit of perfection.

Her grey eyes were large and glowing, her smile confident, and for one breathless moment, every female in the room was caught up in Electra Fury's spell.

Persephone's mother turned. "Child! Finish dressing!" Then her mother, Fern, and Electra sailed from the room, leaving Persephone with a distracted maid, a partially ironed dress, hair that crackled around her head, and a skirt that dragged the floor.

The maid grabbed a jar of pomade from the table and began stroking it through Persephone's hair, which, rather resentfully, it seemed, calmed at her touch.

"That makes it so dull," Persephone said sadly.

"Better dull than wild as a dandelion flying in the wind!"

Persephone stared wistfully at the stained glass window on the wall, its vision of the goddess with the golden hair almost invisible against a night sky.

She didn't know which thought terrified her more.

That Sir Robert Fitzwilliam would recognise her...

Or that he wouldn't.

Holding her dress high to avoid tripping, she was halfway down the corridor to the stairs when her mother reappeared.

"We're waiting, darling! Hurry!" And as if that weren't enough, she cast one parting shot before sailing back in the direction whence she'd come.

"Whatever you do, by all that's holy, do not have an *incident!*"

❦❦

Dardanus awaited her at the foot of the servants' stairs. She noted his new cutaway jacket and perfectly folded neck cloth. Together they would look presentable, which would be sufficient. She didn't delude herself that anyone present would actually be paying attention to any but Electra.

"We're to avoid being seen until it's time," he announced.

"Easily done." She took his hand and pulled him after her. When they emerged into the courtyard, they both caught their breath in amazement.

Knowing that it was spider-web and silver dust lit by the many torchères in the interior courtyard was one thing. Seeing silver-spun lace glimmering in the night, clinging to corners, windows and foliage and encircling the enclosure was quite another.

"Shhh," she warned and then pulled him onto the corner bench, beneath the apple boughs. The comforting splashing of the fountain muted any noises they might make.

"Where is Lysander?" she demanded, not certain why a small knot of panic had taken up residence inside her.

"He didn't come to approve the tuning of the pianoforte, and you know how meticulous he is about that."

"As are you in your tuning," she asserted loyally, and his grateful smile warmed her. "But he can't be gone. Lysander said he'd be here tomorrow," she protested. She clenched her hands in her lap, despite her sore knuckles. "That he'd help me."

"He's taken half of his things! And—" He broke off.

"What?"

"Cosmo was furious, and said it too convenient that Lysander disappeared on the same day as Rue."

The pain in her stomach returned, a new cramping that made her almost double over. "It must have been Rue who cleaned out Mr Jones's room, who took his things and left! She must have followed after him and—" She broke off, confused. "Something is very wrong."

Dardanus closed his hand over hers. "You can't let yourself be upset, not tonight."

"Help me," she begged. She couldn't fail Electra. She took deep breaths and leaned into him.

"Why do you think they have me turning pages for you?"

"What rubbish. I don't even use the music! You should be playing with us." She let her voice fade as she understood. She would fill Lysander's role at the pianoforte, and Dardanus would stand beside her, a calming hand on her shoulder throughout. She let her eyes flutter closed in gratitude and guilt. "You should play. You play like an angel!"

"Don't drool on my jacket," he said, pushing her away. But despite his words, she felt stronger, because he would be there.

Together they watched the continuous arrival of guests. People alighted outside and crossed the drawbridge on foot.

Without exception, each person, pair, or group emerged from beneath the portcullis and stared in wonder.

Persephone squeezed her twin's hand with delight, so proud she might burst with it, as if the glow around them had been taken inside her and left to expand beyond her ability to contain it.

And then she saw him.

Robin Fitzwilliam walked across the cobblestones, his expression alert and fascinated as he seemed not just to take in the artifice of the glistening shimmers of silver, but even to see through to the architecture of webs beneath it all. His coat was dark, his neck cloth a perfect and snowy white, but the heavy wave of hair that fell across his forehead looked more dishevelled than artifice. She sat stiffly until he'd entered the manor, taking all her breath with him.

Dardanus yelped and jerked his hand away from her tight grip.

"Shhh!" she hissed, shrinking back into the darkness. "That was Sir Robin. When he speaks to you—"

"I know, I know. Mama instructed me. After the performance, we're to retreat to the Minstrels' Gallery and not be seen again. If I should come face–to–face with him, I'm to thank him politely for his assistance and then act dim until he lets me leave."

"Act dim? You're to let him think you're dim?" Not only was she offended, she was also struck with dismay. "He'll never believe it. He'll know something is wrong," she huffed. "He spent hours talking to *me!*"

The loud clip-clop of horses' hooves crossing the drawbridge echoed through the courtyard. All heads turned to look, for hadn't they all been forced to abandon their own equipages outside?

Persephone quickly discerned the reason for this aberration.

A footman sprang forward and opened the door with the ducal insignia emblazoned on it.

One long, elegant leg emerged with shining black boot reflecting the torchlight.

Persephone caught a brief but vibrant flash of bronze brocade. Somehow, the Duke of Aubyn managed to glow brighter than the torchères before he was swallowed up by the interior of the manor without a glance at the elaborate decorations.

"Let's go," she said, rising. She brushed a spider from her bodice before it could crawl inside. "We must tell Electra that he's here!"

❦

It was enough to make him despair, Robin thought desperately. One moment she was speaking to him, her eyes alight and dancing, setting his heart alight and dancing as well.

The next moment, her gaze gave the merest flicker through the small group of people gathered by the fireplace and fixed on a movement in the doorway. The flicker became a startled widening of her eyes, accompanied by a catching of breath.

And he knew. As impossible as it might seem that he could know prior to seeing, impossible as it might seem that a country family's entertainment could draw such a personage...

He knew.

He turned with her in response to her brother's hearty laughter and saw—of course—Aubyn.

Or rather, the Duke of. For Cousin Sebastian was in his full personage. Yet his relaxed manner revealed none of the condescension one might expect from a Duke gracing the home of an untitled acquaintance.

And yet by merely entering the small chamber—the medieval moat room, furnished in the height of all that was currently elegant—Sebastian had eliminated all competition for the attentions of the dazzling Miss Fury.

And his attire. Robin could only shake his head in wonder. Cloth of gold had been the fashion this season, but only Sebastian Balmain, Duke of Aubyn, would imagine, much less commission, a brocade of bronze. Its rarity must make it twice as costly. But of course, gold would not frame the duke's colouring in nearly so complementary a manner. Robin considered his own serviceable blue wool that had seemed appropriate for such a gathering but now seemed almost shabby.

And yet, with great surprise he found himself the focus of Miss Fury's attention once more. Her glorious eyes were the deep grey of a lake beneath stormy skies and yet as warm as the sun, and the twinkle in their depths shot through him as she leaned forward, her voice a mere murmur, and asked, "Tell me, sir. Do you know him?"

He smiled. "Intimately. His father was my father's cousin."

"Of course, the hair," she said, acknowledging the ginger colour that had cursed far too many in his family and that both he and Sebastian shared, although Sebastian's was brighter and purer in shade than his own. "He wears his title as casually as an ermine cloak," she remarked behind her ivory fan. "As if it's merely a cloak, and the fact that it is ermine is of no consequence, and yet one cannot escape the fact that the ermine is outside for show and not inside for warmth."

The guffaw that escaped him was neither polite nor quiet, but there she was, her back firmly turned to the Titian-haired god. Instead of doing as any sane young lady would do, Miss Fury aimed every bit of her charm at Robin, a lowly baronet.

He knew a moment's wild instinct to kiss her. "Perhaps," he said, scrambling for polite words, "your opinion is a bit harsh?"

"You know him better than I," she said with a shrug of her smooth, lovely shoulders.

He did his best not to stare at the shadow where her breasts, pulled high by the tight bodice, were pressed together.

"If you vow he is not arrogant…" Her voice gave him focus, and he raised his gaze to her slight smile.

"I vow my cousin is not arrogant," he said, and then added with a smirk, "when compared to other dukes."

"I believe," she said, her eyes narrowed thoughtfully, "that could actually be considered high praise."

"Indeed." As much as it twisted a knife in him to admit it, he was forced to acknowledge the truth. "The Duke is deserving of all praise and distinction and—" He leaned as close as propriety would allow. "—is approaching, so perhaps we should stop discussing him?"

She flashed him such a blinding smile that the weight of a hand on his shoulder took a moment to register. He met his cousin's golden gaze. "Robin," Sebastian said gently, with a glance at the signet ring. "A tragedy, but I know you will fulfil the duties of the baronetcy with grace and valour."

Again Robin was assailed with a flash of memory of caskets and clods of earth, but he shoved them down and nodded his gratitude. "Such duties as there are," he said with a wry smile.

"I think you'll find many honours and duties await you as my kinsman, cousin."

A position at Court for *him?* "I have no political aspirations," he said, startled.

But Sebastian pointedly turned his smiling attentions to Miss Fury.

"Sebastian," Robin said, "may I have the honour of presenting Miss Fury? Miss Fury, His Grace, the Duke of Aubyn."

"Your Grace." She dropped into a curtsey so perfect, it was neither an inch too low nor her lovely head a fraction too bent, nor her obeisance a fraction too long.

Sebastian took her hand, fingers curled under her palm, and brushed his lips against her knuckles. If he held that moment too long for propriety, not a man in the room faulted him.

Nor could Robin fault Miss Fury for the tinge of pink in her cheeks as she watched that crown of dark red waves bend over her hand, tousled to perfection by nature itself, as if titles and money hadn't already weighted the world in Sebastian Balmain's favour.

Robin stifled the urge to run fingers through his own hair in frustration.

"Miss Fury," Sebastian said, "perhaps you can help me lure my cousin to London this Season? I need him at my side in these tense times. Certainly your presence would have better success in wooing him to the public life."

"Surely your cousin can decide for himself what kind of life he aspires to." Miss Fury's smile encompassed them both. "Although I understand your desire for a gentleman of Sir Robin's character at your side."

"A lady and a diplomat," Robin said with a grudging grin. "Careful that His Grace doesn't catch you up in Court intrigues. While I'm sure you would lead everyone a merry chase, your time would be much better spent dancing."

"Speaking of dancing," Sebastian said, "I am told by your brother that you waltz."

Robin froze. What was Sebastian thinking, to drop such an accusation into polite conversation? "I'm sure Cosmo didn't intend that his sister—" he began.

"Mama and Papa learned on the Continent and have taught us all," she said with a pert cock of her head.

Robin felt a desperate need to take her in hand. For all her poise and beauty, her family's lack of experience in the Ton would be her downfall. And what was Sebastian doing, even raising such a scandalous subject? Robin wanted to throttle him, if not call him out.

"Your Grace," Cosmo arrived and said with a smile, "we'll be waltzing at my sister's ball, and then you shall see for yourself."

Gods. The family was going to self-destruct before their musicale even began.

"In fact," Cosmo aimed a negligent flick of his finger at a rosewood music box on a table by the wall, "if it weren't for my mama and her infernal clock ticking away, I would sweep my sister into my arms—" which, as the box released its tinkling music into the room, he promptly did "—and waltz her around the room."

Which he promptly did.

As her brother, there should be nothing improper about Cosmo Fury holding Electra Fury in his arms, with his hand on her waist, their bodies close...

Except, of course, that there was.

Seeing her held just so made it all too easy for any gentleman present to put himself in Cosmo's place. More than one man's eyes grew heavy-lidded with interest, and watched, and *imagined*.

And this was why the waltz was not allowed, and this was why Cosmo Fury should be shot at dawn, for bringing his innocent sister such attention.

Such ruin.

After a single devastating circuit, they parted with his bow and her curtsy—deeper than the one she'd given Sebastian.

Sebastian stepped forward and, again, took her hand. This time he raised her from a pose that dipped far beyond mere courtesy, becoming too much like an offering for his pleasure.

"Miss Fury..." Sebastian stared down into her beautiful stormy grey eyes and said, "You must teach me."

And disaster was averted.

Robin forced his hands together in a series of claps. The smattering of applause and laughter that followed lightened the mood by several degrees.

And if anyone thought Cosmo Fury might take offence that a gentleman, no matter how lofty his title, presumed to make such a proposition to his sister, they had only to look at Fury's confident smile to see his cock-sure pride.

And if anyone thought Miss Fury might be alarmed that a gentleman not her brother presumed to make such a proposition, they had only to look at her triumphant smile to know their error.

A gong sounded from somewhere deeper in the manor. Cosmo reached for his sister's hand. "We are being summoned."

But the Duke did not release it. His eyes never leaving hers, he said, "Allow me to escort you, Miss Fury."

There was no girlish coquetry as she met his gaze straight on. "I would be honoured."

Robin remembered her youngest brother's words. Young Dardanus and his condition had been swept totally from Robin's mind when he'd entered Erinyes Manor and fallen under Miss Electra Fury's spell. But now the boy's words came back to him, as clear as they had been in the crisp morning air:

In England it is said that the Furys have the gift of pleasing kings.

And dukes, as well, it would seem.

His lips twisted in a brief, bitter smile as he followed the entourage from the room.

❧ CHAPTER SEVEN ❧

It appeared to be Robin's destiny on this day to be the focus of one Fury or another; this time, it was Cosmo.

As they walked down the thick Turkish rugs in the corridors, the sheen of the light transfixed him. Mirrors lined the walls, mirrors reflecting more candles than he'd ever seen gathered in one place, and these were simply in the corridor. He slowed to gaze at the reflected light in a gilt-framed mirror the size of a small door.

"Diamond dust."

"I beg your pardon?"

Cosmo leaned closer. "Father claims it fairy dust, but—" He shook his head dismissively. "—diamond dust."

Robin squinted in disbelief. "In the *air?*"

Cosmo threw back his head and laughed. "In the mirrors, a coating with the mercury. Father's father brought them from Vienna. The beeswax for the diamond dust candles, however, came from bees Mama imported from Brazil. Magical bees that are imbued with dust from caves where diamonds grow."

Diamond dust? In mirrors and candles? "Why would your father claim that it's fairy dust? When diamond dust itself is so damnably impressive that—"

"Someone might try to steal Mama's hives? Not that they'd get past the Fury wards, mind you, but with fairy dust? I don't think you'll find many Englishmen who want to take on Irish pookas." Cosmo stopped. "Why do you look at me like that?"

"Just pondering whether it's more impressive to claim you have fairy dust to hide the fact that it's diamond or to claim a source of diamonds to hide the fact that it's fairy, and wondering if both claims are to hide some other source altogether?" Robin said with a grin.

Cosmo slapped him on the back and laughed. "You're too direct for Court, Sir Robin. Some other Fury might have challenged you for your insult. Or..." he said, following Robin's gaze, "for ogling his sister with such open intent."

Robin tore his gaze away from her slender form as she walked beside his cousin enough steps ahead that, please Hera, she didn't hear. "I—I assure you I have no ill intentions," he stammered.

Cosmo laughed again. "Nor have I called you out."

They approached a turn, but rather than take it, Robin stopped and stared in amazement at the tapestry hanging on the wall before him. The colours were rich and liquid, glowing. The figures… He caught his breath. They *moved.* A dragon's wings fluttered. A border of roses trembled on an unseen breeze. Women's hands moved over their needlework. But when he fixed his eyes firmly upon them, all stilled.

"My mother is not musical," Cosmo said, "but she has other gifts."

At Cosmo's urging, they continued into the next wing where the distant, muted sound of a pianoforte drifted down the hallway. Not just music, but music that stirred a yearning that seemed to come from his soul and summoned him to a home he'd yet to see. "My other sister," Cosmo said, his expression soft. "Mama desired that she draw you all in."

And draw them was the precise word, for the delicate tune drew the guests like a beacon. Ahead of him and behind him, guests grew alert with curiosity and tangible yearning as the music grew louder upon their approach.

Entering the Great Hall, he was barely aware of the gilt chairs and delicate settees spaced in semi-circular rows around a collection of instruments.

Playing the pianoforte was a thin young schoolgirl with sallow skin and dull black hair, and beside her, Dardanus. He stood at his sister's side, his hand resting lightly on her shoulder as he followed the music before her.

Sheet music she never glanced at, Robin noted, as she leaned into the music pouring from the glossy black keys beneath her fingertips.

They looked nothing alike, these twins, other than both being tall and too thin. Dardanus had classic, handsome features that at maturity would bear strong resemblance to Cosmo, who now ushered Robin and the Duke to seats on the front row.

Robin lifted the parchment programme, admiring the meticulous presentation that included a most unusual shade of green ink with the subtle scent of fresh outdoors. But he found himself unable to stop watching the younger sister.

On her, the Fury features were drawn a bit too long and thin for beauty, in ways that were unlikely to improve as she matured. He felt a pang of pity for her, forever in the shadow of such a sister. And yet something about her compelled him, refused to release his attention as her hands danced across the keys in a hypnotic rhythm.

Her music flowed into him, through him. So caught up was he in her spell that the song had ended and the gathered assemblage was responding with genteel applause before he realised what he was staring at.

The knuckles on her right hand were swollen.

🙡🙟

Her fingertips tingled with magic, purring to her will. She let them drop into her lap whilst she took a deep breath of pleasure.

It mattered little that her hair was grimy with pomade, that her dress was ill-fitting and ill-hued, that she was called into service under duress. What mattered was that she had played, and these strangers applauded her music. A quick rising from the bench, a quick bob of a curtsey, and a quick smile that burst from within her as warm as honey, and she allowed herself to finally look out at their faces, these people who were not Ordinary, who understood and appreciated her Gift.

And like filings to a magnet, she stared into the mossy green eyes of the man who had haunted her thoughts all day. Before she could look away...

He rubbed his chin and winked.

And his smile melted her.

He knew. He knew she was a girl and that she'd been out at night. He was neither scandalised nor disgusted. He was smiling at her, and winking, and he knew...

And he liked her anyway.

Dardanus yanked on her arm, and she plopped back down onto the bench. "Show off!" he said with a grin.

The door at the back of the hall opened wide. All heads turned.

Framed in the open doorway, her parents stood, tall and proud.

Surely too young and vibrant, many had said, to have such a number of children, one of whom had reached his majority! Her father's hair was as black as the day he'd married. Her mother's softer brown, while too weak to influence a single lock on her children's heads, showed no silver, her face, no lines.

They entered the room with an elegance that might be mistaken for hauteur, had their expressions not been so gracious. Her father's half smirk and occasional nod seemed merely to say, *You have us; we have returned; I hope you are satisfied, for this won't happen again soon,* while her mother's smile managed to be both warm and mysterious. If anyone present had thought the Furys' sudden return to Society was that of prodigals, they now must see the truth.

The Furys were gracing them with their presence.

She felt herself glow as her father welcomed his guests with the same casual poise he used in any of the courts of Europe.

Finally, Cosmo and Electra entered the circle of light to a murmured response of pleasure from the assemblage. They were beautiful together, there was no mistaking that.

Her father spread his arms wide in a gesture both theatrical and self-deprecating. "I am but a humble musician, poet, husband, father… and I am honoured by your presence, by the effort you have put forth to attend our musicale. What we don't have in titles or riches—" He embellished his outrageous statement with an elegant wave, a half-shrug, a comical moue. "—we will attempt to compensate with the beauty of our offering to you, our guests. As you might have noticed, you will find a few selections by Ordinary composers on our programme."

Eyebrows raised and programmes rustled. Persephone stiffened and winced. These guests were probably too stupid to have known the difference.

"There is no such thing as Ordinary music…" His eyes twinkled. "Or Ordinary gold."

The tension melted into laughter. There were none present who would shun a gold or silver coin just because it was Ordinary.

A cap full of coins.

A leering face, too close, a woman who reeked of spirits and filth breathing on her, mocking her.

Coal black eyes, swallowing her whole.

She pinched her forearm hard to bring herself back, to wipe the images away, and grasped for reality. Her father. Her mother. Cosmo. Electra. Dardanus.

Lysander.

No, she couldn't think about him.

But she could think about the music, the pleasure… Sir Robin's wink and smile.

Her father's voice broke her reverie as he introduced each of his children. When her name was called with that of Dardanus, she rose for another quick curtsey. Dardanus placed his hand on her shoulder again, but she said to him, "I'm well. You must play."

He darted a look towards their mother on the front row.

"We're to present a family musicale." Again, she ignored the sharp twinge that marked the missing Lysander. *"Play."*

His smile as he crossed to the violoncello was all the answer she desired.

Persephone moved from the pianoforte to the old, unfashionable harpsichord, for Electra preferred it for the Bach.

With a sharp sling of his head, Cosmo lifted his violin to his shoulder.

And finally, Electra raised her violin, graceful as a swan, slender fingers arched on bow and neck. With a glitter of eye and the slightest of nods, she signalled and they all began.

The selection had caused much argument, but Electra had won. Rather than making Electra the focus, the first song would be their group together—absent Lysander. Once more, she forced the thoughts of him down, deep down.

The music flowed from her fingertips in such an outpouring that she could have closed her eyes and simply let it take its course, had she not wanted to watch the beauty that was her brother and sister, leaning into the music with sensuous abandon—Cosmo, whose black hair hung into his eyes as his arms whipped the music into a frenzy, and Electra, whose entire body swayed with it, glory pouring from her with each note.

These were the Furys and their music, the Gift that they had carried from when the gods walked the earth. The Ton did not deserve the gifts laid out before them in such an outpouring of wealth.

But her father said, not even the Furys themselves deserved such gifts, and thus they were compelled to share them, and in the sharing, reap the rewards of such creation, for in the creating, they were as the gods.

And so the evening went, until one last performance remained, a duet of airs her father had chosen from his vast knowledge of the alchemical art of combining heart and harmony to incite or soothe or woo…?

Now, when the assemblage was sated and it seemed that to add one more song would push them past the precarious balance between pleasure and tedium, there would be two more songs, performed together.

Persephone sat at the harp, poised, willing her hands to still their trembling as exhaustion and exhilaration took their toll. At the slightest of nods from her father in his seat on the front row, she sent a melancholy trill of music cascading into the air. A sidelong glance revealed goose-bumps on a woman's bare shoulder, and another covering her mouth quickly to disguise a choked gasp.

Electra parted her lips, and her true instrument was revealed. *"I saw my lady weep…"* The sorrow rounded her voice, quivered in the air, and her voice alone would have broken hearts. But with the harp unleashing its subtle but painful passion, not a soul could help but tremble. And as the poet extolled the beauty of his lady's sorrow, the air vibrated with a voice pure and rich and throbbing, with Electra's very own pain, until another note—a single note more—would break open a beauty and a pain beyond endurance.

And it was ended, met by stunned silence.

Before any recovered to applaud, Persephone's fingers stroked a gentle glissando. Her voice bright with delight, Electra moved forward from pain to promise, *"To see, to hear, to touch, to kiss, to die…"* If only her lover would but come again that she might cease to mourn.

Was there a man so numb that he didn't long to leap to the challenge of meeting her joy with joy, to assuage any pain he might have caused? Not on this night, not in this room, not with this elegant Miss Fury whom none had seen before and now none would forget.

In the second stanza, Persephone found herself overcome with a choking awareness. This was where Lysander's voice should enter. No one present would imagine anything amiss, but the Furys knew. Persephone's fingers froze, as despite the lilting tune, all sorrow and pain broke within her.

Lysander, oh, Lysander.

For she could keep at bay no longer the guilty knowledge that there could be only one reason he was gone.

"Your vow is my vow, beloved sister."

She remembered his rigid reaction to her revelations, his probing for detail after detail. He'd believed her and understood her and now would avenge her.

But he had not even eighteen years to draw on. Vespasian Jones was not only mature in strength and diabolical in nature, but who would better know Lysander's weaknesses than his old tutor?

If anyone noticed the harp's silence, Persephone prayed there was not a glance to spare for the sister who blinked back tears, clutching its frame to keep from collapsing.

But *she* heard the missing voice, which was meant to anchor Electra's soaring soprano. She heard it and quaked with longing, and she knew that Electra felt it, too, that beneath her light soprano lingered profound loss.

And then Electra was no longer alone.

Dardanus stepped forward to take his brother's place.

In a newly-minted voice that occasionally cracked when it should not, he added the counterpoint to her melody.

Electra seized his hand as their voices joined in a vocal dance, an allemande, circling each other to pause and touch in breathless wonder, sharing a single, pure note, and then twirling away in different directions. Sometimes one would hold true while the other wove in and out of the melody, and sometimes it was the other, but together their voices danced until the room quivered with the radiance of diamond dust, of subtly scented candles, of the gifts of the gods funnelled through nothing but Fury magic.

Not a soul present would ever forget this night.

🐦🐦

Somewhere outside Persephone's blurred vision, people applauded, even cried out their praise. Somehow, she knew that the success was complete, that they had done it, had launched Electra into the heights where she belonged. At some level, she was even aware that the Duke of Aubyn was the first at Electra's side, with Sir Robin watching, his heart in his eyes.

But she knew she must leave. She must leave before it broke loose, this spasm of Shadow threatening her from within, now that she'd exhausted the strength to control it.

Heads turned towards her. She had drawn attention.

Do not have an incident!

Eyes were on her.

Watching her.

Staring at her.

Clenching her fists in her borrowed skirts, she fought the trembling that threatened to overwhelm her. She forced her chin higher and prayed to the gods that she could escape the room before the staring eyes saw what was struggling to break free from deep within her:

Her shame, her secret, her strange and terrible magic.

She made it to the door—through the door—into the corridor.

Dardanus grabbed her arm, and this time it was *his* eyes she felt on her, his murmured, comforting words pouring into her ear.

With him at her side she found strength; she walked faster, faster, until she was running for safety, for a place where, if she shattered, nobody would see. But what place? Where? She heaved in dry sobs of air that tasted of candlelight and perfumes and powders and—

"Here!"

He jerked her arm, and she fell after him as he tugged her into the dark conservatory. Torches sprang to light upon their entrance.

It smelled of damp and earth and green, blessed green, and she fell to her knees and grabbed the ground and took in great heaving gulps of earth-scent as the plants around her crooned their magic into her ears.

A tearing, a roaring that came from within her split her open as she tossed back her head in a silent howl of pain. It escaped—the Shadows escaped. She stared through fear-glazed eyes at the glass panes overhead and saw herself reflected, so small and so far away like some wild thing, with dark hair flying, and eyes slanted with pain, and mouth open to the night, and… One last twist inside…

And the reflections were gone.

The glass was gone.

A series of strange, loud cracks turned to gentle spatterings of sound all around her.

Soft, cool dustings of crystalline snow shimmered in the air.

What have I done?

It was beautiful, reflecting lamplight and candlelight. The air danced with magic, and could such magic truly be Shadows? Could anything so shimmering and bright be Dark?

Music swelled in her, music like she'd never heard, vibrating through her veins.

Somewhere far away she was aware of something very wet between her legs, and she remembered Electra's warning that her blood hadn't reached its full flow yet, and part of her worried, was she bleeding, was she soiling Electra's dress?

But part of her was floating in the air, somewhere apart from it all, somewhere high above, looking down at the strange girl in the yellow dress who now had people around her and arms lifting her, a newly familiar voice near her ear saying, "Quick, where can I…" and fading away as she closed her eyes and leaned her face against the strong, warm body that held her so safely.

She floated, she danced, she sang in her head as the world spun around her.

And then she saw the beautiful goddess with the silvery hair smiling benevolently down at her, even though it was night and there was no light to illuminate her.

Now she was on her bed, and there was Dardanus, sweet beautiful Dardanus, looking so frightened.

"It's all right," she whispered. "Did you see it? Wasn't it beautiful?"

"It was beautiful," the voice said.

She turned her head slowly to find its source.

"You..." she breathed, looking into his mossy green eyes, at his russet hair, and his kind—his oh, so kind smile. "It wasn't Shadows," she said. "It can't be Shadows."

"Of course not," he agreed, tucking the bedcovers under her chin. "I've never seen anything so beautiful in my life."

And he wasn't speaking of Electra.

He also wasn't speaking of her.

But he was speaking of something of her making, something terrible, something beautiful. She blinked, confused, and the terror began to creep back in. "What did I do?"

"The glass in the conservatory," Dardanus said slowly. "I think you... I think you broke it all."

"Oh!" she gasped.

But then a strong, warm hand closed over hers, and she found herself drawn once again into those eyes of moss, and she felt safe.

"You changed the glass back to sand," Sir Robin said in awe. "You *changed* it."

She felt her lips trembling but refused to cry like a child in front of him. "I don't know how to stop it."

"Your hair..." Dardanus gasped. "Your hair!"

She tried to touch it, but her arms were heavy, so heavy.

Dardanus stroked it and then, after hesitating, held a long strand so that she could see.

Silver.

She choked in fear.

He lifted a larger clump, black laced with silvery threads.

"What does it mean?" she asked, frantic.

Dardanus shook his head mutely, and she turned to Sir Robin, looking desperately for an answer.

"What is happening to me?" she pleaded.

His face creased in concern, he could only shake his head. But then, again, he smiled. "I don't know, but it is beautiful, too."

Beautiful.

"Shall I fetch your mother?" he asked gently.

When she couldn't answer, Dardanus answered for her. "Please."

He climbed on top of the bed and pulled her close, and she closed her eyes and let her heartbeat join with his in soothing unison, felt their souls mingle as they had from the moment their lives began.

What had happened wasn't Shadows, couldn't be Shadows, because it was beautiful, and Robin had said so.

But deep in her heart lived the hard cold knot of icy fear that had been with her since she was able to understand the things people whispered, the things that the Furys hid from the world.

That Dardanus Fury, the last child, had no magic at all.

Because Persephone, his Dark, wicked sister had stolen it in the womb.

That she was a child of the Dark.

Of Shadows.

❧ PART TWO ❧

England, 1811

❧ CHAPTER EIGHT ❧

England, 1811

Persephone had not intended to eavesdrop.

She had taken refuge in the priest hole where nobody would know to look. The manor was filled with women tugging and pulling on her, the days pressing in upon her until she couldn't breathe. The dark soothed her, the heavy, musty smell a tolerable exchange for an hour's sanctuary.

And so she sat, her back pressed against the cold, damp wall, half-dozing as she kept worrisome expectations and thoughts at bay... thoughts of muslins and silks, of endless shopping trips to acquire the proper wardrobe for the sister of a duchess and myriad orders from all directions to stand straight, speak gently and...

For Aphrodite's sake, they must keep the charms strong to mask the silver threads in her hair.

The priest hole under the Oratory at the end of her bedchamber was small and cramped. She could not imagine the terror that would compel someone to hide there, stretched flat beneath the floor, waiting for the trap door to wrench open and light to spill in.

The priest hole behind the kitchen wall was a long space with a bench for sitting. It was often warm and scented with yeasty baking and savoury roasting, a comfort of darkness and scent and solitude.

But on this day, she'd slipped into the dark space that had been added behind a false wall in her father's study because it was in the male domain, quiet and cool, and not a soul would ever think to seek her here. At first, she shrank back instinctively from her papa's and Cosmo's voices, strained harder to block them out, and not to hear beyond the occasional alarming words such as 'rebels' and 'filth' and 'treason'. Somehow, old King Pellinore managed to linger on with rumours of desperate illness suddenly replaced by joyous news of near-miraculous recoveries. But he couldn't live forever, and all of Magi society, both common and aristocratic, fretted over what lay ahead—a peaceful transition into a new Royal house or full-scale rebellion and bloodshed?

She pressed the heels of her hands against her eyes to relieve the pressure. She had enough concerns without adding politics. What good did it do to worry about the business of men when even the business of women was more than she could bear to contemplate?

A chill shuddered through her.

And then came the word—the name—that pulled her out of her isolation and had her pressed against the secret door, straining to hear more.

Lysander.

"Where did you hear this?" came Cosmo's voice, sharp and hard-edged with astonishment.

"Aubyn, though for obvious reasons, your mother and sisters can't know."

"Gods, no. Of course not."

What? She wanted to demand. *Can't know about what?* There was word of Lysander, after all this time, almost five years, and they weren't going to tell her? They would let even his own mother continue to dwell in fear of his death?

"Why wouldn't Aubyn have told *me?*"

Of course he'd wonder that, wonder why his position in the duke's circle hadn't won him such a confidence, as if that gave him more right to know than Lysander's own father. She almost snarled. She wanted to hear more about Lysander, not petty Court politics!

"There's more, and worse," her father said. "There's a child. A son."

"For the gods' sake, what was that idiot thinking? How did he let himself get trapped that way? If any woman knows how to avoid increasing, it would be she!"

"It happened under this roof when he was young enough to be tricked."

"What?" A heavy sound, as if Cosmo dropped into a chair.

"The child was born mere months after they ran away. It's—it's a boy. A strong son." Her father sounded weary and worried, and his revelation was met with stunned silence.

All Persephone could do was force her breathing to stay soft and barely audible as her head reeled at the thought of Lysander at her age—seventeen—a father. He'd run away because of this?

It had nothing to do with her at all?

She bit her knuckle until she tasted blood, fighting tears.

"We owe Aubyn much," her father finally continued. "If this came to light, the scandal would destroy your mama and sisters."

"You're certain?" Cosmo said. "He's certain?"

"You know him better than I," her father said sharply. "He would scarcely have delivered such news if it were mere rumour. You know what this means. You have to marry, have heirs. We can't let the only living heir be—for the sake of the gods, be half-Earthborn."

"Don't say he married her!" Cosmo's shock rang through the room, and she flinched at the sound.

"If they weren't married, it wouldn't signify! If he'd come to me, I could have bought her off, which was probably what she wanted all the time. At worst—set him up, set her up with a place. He wouldn't be the first man with a mistress in household, even if—gods! He was hardly a man at all, or he wouldn't have made such a cock-up of it! It's hardly a scandal for a young man to bed a maidservant, or even to have his share of by-blows—but to marry her?"

Persephone sank back onto the bench, aghast.

"It had to be deliberate," her father bit out, his voice low, for it would be a disaster were the servants to overhear. "A hearth healer getting with child could be nothing else. And she was older than he by several years. She trapped him, and he was fool enough to—" A moment's silence, followed by "Enter!"

Head reeling, Persephone clutched herself as a servant delivered a message, and her father and brother made leaving noises.

She was alone in the dark, with the musty smell of age and dirt pressing on her from all sides.

She had thought the tuggings and pullings of women were relentless.

Tears streaked her face as she took in the knowledge of men. Tears of anger and disgust, tears of loss and pain.

And finally, to her own shame, tears of relief.

Her beloved brother hadn't left to avenge her.

It was not her fault.

🦅🦅

Robin lingered beneath the stand of chestnut trees, holding his horse still, stunned at what he saw.

Persephone hurled rage from her fingertips—bolts of shimmering air that hit the water in the gurgling stream with explosive impact, carving smooth-walled holes that shivered momentarily before filling with the gush of returning water. Again and again, her body too thin, too rigid, she expelled her pent-up emotion in releases of magic flung free and then absorbed by the flowing water.

He had known since the beginning that this girl was a seething mass of barely controlled magic. More intellect, more power, more life than one small body should be forced to contain.

But never had he seen her like this, with the skirt of her morning dress swelling around her, her hair flying in a wind that didn't exist. And what hair. Fine and straight, lifeless and dull in the dappled sunlight, seeming to swallow up light rather than reflect it. He knew, as few did, about the charms that kept the strange silvering hidden, stealing her lustre, and giving her one fewer opportunity to allure, she who already lived in her sister's shadow.

His horse snorted and crackled in the undergrowth, restless and wanting water.

She froze in place, then whirled on him. "How dare you!"

"I—" What? He had no words to excuse his spying.

She raised a quivering hand, and it was his turn to freeze, staring at her forefinger, aimed at him.

She wouldn't.

Surely she wouldn't.

He met her gaze without flinching, unable to force his dry mouth to swallow, much less speak.

"Tell me," she said, pacing slowly toward him, her finger aimed straight at his throat, the air crackling between them. "How many by-blows do *you* have, Sir Robert Fitzwilliam?"

By-blows? She was asking him about… about *by-blows?*

"Good gods, girl!" he sputtered, aghast. "That has to be the most bloody inappropriate thing you have ever said to me, and considering what you've dared say, that's a remarkable feat!"

She stepped closer, vibrating with tension. "You did not answer."

"I—I most certainly have none, though why you should even think to ask such a—" He broke off and tried again. "Why you should even know that—" His mouth was moving but words did not emerge. "Whom have you been talking to?" he finally demanded. "I'll call them out for putting such knowledge in your head."

"Oh, never you fear, Sir Robin," she sneered. "Nobody has spoken to me. I have to skulk around like the lowliest of spies to accidentally trip across the way men—" This time it was she who broke out in blushes.

"So this—" He gestured from her to the brook. "This is not because of London, your Season?"

She blinked her confusion, seemed to see her pointed forefinger for the first time and gasped, pulling her hand against her middle and covering it with its opposite member. "I didn't—I wouldn't—" She shook her head, her distress evident in her wide eyes. "I wouldn't hurt you!"

"I know," he said softly, his heart still pounding. "I know."

"It's just that…" She dragged her fingers through her hair and spun away from him. "I can't tell you."

Now that he could breathe again, he gave his head a shake. "Perhaps that's best." But he knew it wasn't. He knew by the wild tension still radiating from her. "However," he said cautiously, "there may be some aspect of what troubles you that you could speak of."

She clutched her arms tightly around her waist, still facing away from him, but her voice was falsely steady. "I've decided. There will be no waltzing at my ball."

His laugh broke free despite himself. He would grow grey himself, attempting to keep up with her on this day. "As if your sister would allow a ball without waltzing!"

"It's my ball!"

There were more responses to that than he cared to enumerate. She was a Fury; of course there would be waltzing at her presentation ball.

Her sister's balls were known for waltzing. And most important, Persephone Fury danced like a dandelion wisp, so lightly that she seemed to drift and twirl on the breeze. She only looked lovelier when she played her music, and the ball was intended to display her at her best.

She must waltz.

Except... When had this happened? Was he the only one to see how fragile she was? If she was in this much distress in her own home, how would she survive London? He forced an even tone. "Have you considered waiting a year?"

"Oh, no. We couldn't do that. Papa is expected in Arabia and, after that, the Orient. He has already postponed his trip for my debut. Once he and Mama set out on their journey, we may not see them again for three years. And besides, what does that have to do with waltzing?"

He drew in a deep breath. The point was, what did waltzing have to do with *anything*?

"You don't have to be so bloody careful," she snapped. "Just say what it is you have to say!"

"Good gods, language, Persephone! Language!"

She snorted. "You said it first."

"That doesn't signify, and I shouldn't have."

"Ask!"

"As you wish," he said, exasperated. "You're bouncing from barely controlled magic—"

"It was controlled," she snarled.

"—to by-blows, to things you can't tell me, to waltzing. Tell me what you're willing to answer, but permit me this one thing, my dear Persephone, make it simple enough that my poor intellect can follow you!"

"Poor intellect, indeed," she scoffed. "Your intellect is adequate. You're simply lazy."

He folded his arms and glared.

"Well?" She spun and faced him, arching an eyebrow perfectly, a technique she had clearly picked up from one of her brothers. "Are you telling me that you didn't bring me figures that you should be able to work out yourself?"

Damn it all, he had. He sighed and reached between his waistcoat and his linen shirt, where he'd tucked the small, flat ledger.

She crowed softly and snatched it from his hand but then, with a deliberate snap of her wrist, flung one last bolt of magic at the water. Not only the water, but also the small boulder beneath the surface exploded as well, and they both ducked from the falling debris of water and gravel, Persephone laughing, Robin cursing.

"Sir Robin," she said severely. "Language!"

Soon she was perched on a large rock, dangling her feet in the water like a hoyden, brow furrowed as she went down the column of figures and did a mental tally.

"You're a pigeon for the plucking." She sighed. "I swear by Hera, you don't even try, do you? Anyone could see that your tailor is taking advantage of you, and there's no way your horses could consume as much oats as the stable claims and—"

"Why don't you want to waltz?"

She almost dropped the ledger in the water, and would have, if he hadn't rescued it himself.

"It's an inappropriate dance," she said, her voice strained. "Men I don't even know, putting their hands on me." She shuddered. "I thought it would just be my brothers, but—" She broke off.

He wanted to tell her she was being silly, but was she silly not to want to share such an intimate dance with partners she barely knew? He wanted to tell her that she could sit out the waltzes, but at her own ball? She would appear the worst sort of wallflower. And of course, he knew which brother was missing, which waltz would be left open for strangers.

"There are only three waltzes at your sister's balls," he said briskly, coming to the obvious solution. "The first will be your father's. The second will be Cosmo's. And that leaves the third—and last before supper—well, Miss Fury, would you do me the honour of saving your third waltz for me?"

She stared up at him, and then covered a choked sound with her fingers and ducked her head, hiding her eyes from him.

She didn't want to?

"You would dance with me?" she asked softly.

"If you'll have me," he answered, watching her clutch the skirts of her morning dress in her fists and wrinkle them beyond redemption. "People still speak of your sister waltzing with Cosmo. Those who were there that night—"

"—say they will take the vision with them to their grave," she finished for him. "But my dance with Cosmo will only emphasise how inferior I am to my sister. However," she said firmly, speaking over his protest, "I will dance with you." She tossed her head, adding, "Though I'm sure I'll live to regret it, because you are certain to step on my toes."

"Hellion," he said.

Her smirk widened to a grin that warmed him from the inside out. And then, just as quickly, faded.

"Persephone," he said, "you have to tell me. What is wrong?"

"The third waltz would have been Lysander's."

He couldn't stop himself. He reached for her hand. It was cold in his, and trembling. He had no words of comfort, only whatever she derived from having his large, warm hand close over hers.

Even though it was patently inappropriate, he realised with a surge of dismay.

He was about to remove it when she spoke, her voice so low and hoarse, he leaned closer to hear.

"He's alive."

It took a moment for her words to sink in. "Your brother?"

She nodded, staring into her own lap, denying him her expression.

"But that's... that's good news."

"Robin, you have kept my secrets for close to five years—things only my family knows—and now, you must promise me to keep this one."

"I swear it, of course."

She took a shuddering breath. "He's married and has a child."

Again, news that should be good, that should send the household into a frenzy of preparation to welcome back their son from the seeming dead.

"You didn't know him, of course. He was cunning and wicked and wonderful, which is why none of this makes sense." She appeared to be listening to the brook, her head cocked thoughtfully, before she finally went on. "We had a maidservant, a very powerful hearth healer."

"I remember hearing of her, the maid who ran off with your family's schoolmaster on the day I met a rapscallion wastrel of a lad on the road from London."

This at least pulled a small laugh out of her. "That very day. But she didn't run off with *Mr Jones.*" How bitterly her tone rang when she spoke that name. "She and Lysander ran off together, and they married, and they have a son, and my father thinks she should have been bought off and that Lysander was a fool, because that's what young men do, get by-blows off the maids it seems, but Lysander was nobody's fool, and it makes no sense—"

He broke off her wild torrent of words with a finger to her lips.

The face she raised to him was heart-breaking, her eyes liquid with unshed tears. "They say he can never come back to us now."

He had no words, and yet he must find some. And finally, inadequately, "Never is a very long time."

"Do you have any by-blows?" she whispered. "Do all men? Do you think... do you think my father does?"

By all the gods in the pantheon, this was not a conversation she should be having with him, and yet he had never felt so honoured with her trust. "I have none. Not all men do. In fact, I dare say most don't..." He hesitated, but in for a penny... "And I find it very unlikely that your father or brother does. Clearly, Lysander has a strong code of behaviour, and clearly, he got that from somewhere, and clearly, that would be the family in which he was brought up."

Hope leapt in her eyes, even as she began to argue. "But I heard my father. He said that Lysander was a young idiot and that he—"

"Your father is a man in pain. Allow him that."

"Oh!" She buried her face in her hands, and her shoulders quaked with her sobs, and now that his hand no longer held hers, he felt a ridiculous urge to stroke her hair and soothe her.

Which would be highly inappropriate.

"You make... you make it all sound so different."

"I'm a man," he said ruefully. "I see it differently." He handed her a handkerchief.

"I still think it's horrid." She stopped to blow daintily. "And that men are horrid, and—"

And you don't want strange men touching you, and is that any wonder?

"And that you are going to step on my gown or my toe and send me sprawling." She gave another impertinent sniff. "But I'm glad you are my friend, despite it all."

"And my figures?"

She sighed. "I will set them to rights for you, although, Robin Fitzwilliam, you are truly too lazy for words and should be ashamed."

This time, he did reach for her hair and gave it a rough rumple. "Only because it gives me excuses to visit the impertinent Miss Fury of Erinyes Manor," he replied.

This time, she wasn't quick enough to hide her blush. He caught a glimpse before she ducked away again and felt inordinately pleased.

🦋🦋

The blood sang in her veins.

She gave Hades his head and allowed him to break loose beneath her, leaving Robin to catch up if he could. She needed time to recover, to restore her balance, to revel.

Robin had asked her to waltz.

She should feel embarrassed to manoeuvre him in such a way, for she had known that raising the issue would result in him rescuing her. She laughed aloud at her audacity and his predictability. Yet the gentle twist in her chest at the thought of waltzing with him justified any manipulation.

Stupid man.

Dardanus would have taken that dance. It was his first ball, too, and he was no more looking forward to it than she had been, before…

Before Robin asked her to waltz with him, in his arms, the last waltz before supper, which meant she'd enter the dining room on his arm and be his partner for the midnight hour. She wanted to crow to the sky and, instead, rode like the wind.

When she could speak without laughing her delight and her triumph, she pulled up and awaited him. "That horse is not fit for stew meat," she said with an arrogant toss of her head.

"There was no need for you to wait for me, Miss Fury," he announced in mock-serious tones. "I'm sure I would not get lost finding my way back."

"One can't be too careful." She joined him, riding side-by-side, at a more sedate pace. "I suppose while I am forced to share nuncheon with the *women*, you'll be off with the gentlemen discussing *politics*."

"It seems likely. At the very least, I'll be delivering missives from Aubyn."

"Missives? Goodness, we must be an important family if the duke is sending his most trusted aide to deliver secret missives."

"Impertinent," he shot back. "I'm nowhere near his most trusted aide, your brother comes closer to that, and I'd hardly categorise these as secret missives. They are, after all, to his wife and her father and one would presume regarding matters of a personal nature."

She sighed. She'd known that he hadn't really come from London only to bring her his accounts, but it had been nice when he'd pretended such was true. "I'm sure he is sending love letters to Electra, because the two of them are still so disgustingly in love, and it's equally apparent to me that whatever he might send my father must be political." The words were out of her mouth before she thought about them and realised her cruelty. Even now, with almost five years past, there was no doubt in her mind that Robin still bore a *tendre* for her sister.

Just as there was no doubt in her mind that he saw her as a child, still, despite the fact that the entire household was in a tizzy, preparing her for the marriage mart.

"What have you seen and heard of your father's politics?"

"Rebels and treason and danger, and we should not be part of it! We have a Gift, and it's not to be soldiers and politicians. I'll be happy when he and Mama are in Arabia and there are at least two people in my family whose lives I don't fear for!" She gave him a sharp look, waiting for him to attempt to soothe her.

But the expression on his face was grave, and after a long moment of no sound other than squeaking leather and hooves on earth, he broke their gaze and stared ahead. "Follow me."

He pulled ahead and veered sharply off the path. They wove

through the forest so surely that it made jest of her taunt that he could get lost anywhere, for Robin might be a baronet with a position at Court, but he was first and always a country gentleman who was raised on the land.

If only his cousin hadn't found him a position and he still lived as a country gentleman... Together they could build a home as magical as Erinyes Manor. Not that she had any idea how one would do such a thing, for her mother's attempts to teach her housewifery had failed dismally.

Eventually they wound their way down the side of the hill to join the path from the south, and then, just another furlong, and Robin had led her to the hilltop view they had shared on that magical dawn when she'd first brought him home.

This time there were no mists floating from the river. This time the land sparkled bright and green, cradling the aged, red brick manor surrounded by ancient oaks that reached across the trim moat and sometimes touched it with a benevolence that seemed to come from the earth itself.

She never wanted to leave this place. Its magic had created her; its beauty fed her; its strength held her safe at night. They all said it was normal for young girls to be nervous about the future; she mustn't fret over such things!

She felt his eyes on her and forced her chin up, for whatever else she was, she was proud. "Someday," she said, "you must show me your home."

"It's nothing like this, I fear."

"But you could make it so." *We could make it so.*

"Do you remember what you told me? That Bardán Fury was a poet and a bard and a musician but he also created this. That he recognised danger when he saw it and not only pulled his family back to keep his people safe, but also kept our Magi world safe. This is what is in your Fury blood—not just the Gift of music, but the Gift of what music does. Your father and Cosmo have the Gift of reaching into people's souls and pulling out the best in them, inspiring them to do that which is hard but necessary. Bardán Fury persuaded a magical people to pull away from the world before the burning times. *Before.*

And even though the first fire had yet to be lit, he convinced them that they needed to shield themselves from the Ordinary world, and to find their own king. They believed him, because of his Gift. When the times need it and the gods show the way, Furys lead. And when the times change, Furys do the even more remarkable thing."

She stared up at him, breathless at his passion.

"They retreat to their magical home and their Gift and leave political power behind."

"And soon I will no longer be one."

"You will always be a Fury, and any man who stands beside you will know just what a gift that is."

"Am I weak to be afraid of what is coming?"

"You are wise to be afraid."

"The duke was wrong to force you to London."

"Perhaps, if we're lucky, we'll both be able to leave it behind."

Yes. Oh, yes. If they were lucky, and if there were any way on Earth she could make it happen, they would.

❦ CHAPTER NINE ❧

The air was clotted with the smells of warring perfumes. Electra had taken to wearing an expensive French blend the duke lavished upon her. Her mama wore her preferred lilac and lemon balm. Persephone had no idea what the milliner and seamstress wore, only that the mix was making her ill. She waved her fingertips beneath her nose to perform a simple air-clearing, despite the fact that it could be taken as insult.

Better that than to lose her eggs and toast on the dressmaker's pretty carpets.

She didn't miss the longing glances Mrs Beauchamp cast in Electra's direction. The woman clearly would much rather be dressing a beautiful and wealthy duchess than the plain younger sister. Not that Persephone blamed her. She herself wished Electra were the one standing in the centre of the small room, framed by mirrors that threw back every flaw in multiples. If she could just suffer through this last fitting, perhaps there would be time to finally get Electra alone, to tell her what she'd been longing to tell her since arriving in London.

Tell her about Lysander, and the child, Lysander's child. Despite the shame, she needed to share the burden with the one person in position to do something about it.

She shivered in the sleeveless, linen chemise that hung loose from narrow shoulder straps to mid-calf. Mrs Beauchamp circled her with a sharp eye, occasionally sending one of several shop girls off with directions for a bolt of fabric, a roll of lace, a card of buttons.

"I believe you will be surprised and pleased with your gown," the older woman said, beckoning to an assistant who came forward with prettily embroidered stays. "Raise your arms, dear."

Persephone held them outstretched as the lovely torture device was held up to her torso by one girl and another stood behind, ready to do the laces. Persephone stared at herself in the mirror, confused. Her breasts were suddenly full where before they'd been, well, inadequate.

Ignoring the dressmaker, she dropped her arms to tug the bodice away from her body and turn it inside out.

"There is a layer of small ruffles sewn between the lining and the exterior fabric to provide fullness," Mrs Beauchamp said crisply. "I find it a very pretty effect for young ladies with less generous attributes, and just think how lucky you are to have such a narrow body without tight cinching."

She took Persephone's hands and held them out again. One girl quickly adjusted the stays, while a plump girl with mousey curls smoothed the ruffled bodice back over her breasts. Only this time, Persephone felt something odd pressed against her skin.

Paper. A note?

The plump girl stared straight into her eyes and held them, not breaking contact until Mrs Beauchamp sent her to fetch a box from against the wall.

"But what if people can tell? I'll look like a fool!" Persephone's cheeks warmed with embarrassment even as she wondered what had just happened. She snatched her hands free and reached for her bodice, only to find the plump girl's eyes drilling into hers again from the floor, where she was lifting white silk from the box. Persephone, dropped her hands to her sides.

"None will guess," Mrs Beauchamp said.

A silk petticoat settled over Persephone's head. Like the chemise, it hung loose from narrow straps, and clung to the shape provided by the stays beneath.

She graced Persephone with a practiced, almost-warm smile. A gesture toward a curtain, and it swept aside to reveal the pale blue evening dress in all its pastel loveliness.

Persephone couldn't help it. She caught her breath at the sight.

"My darling," her mother said, "you will be beautiful."

And with that word, her spirits deflated. The dress was beautiful, but once it was lifted over her head and smoothed into place, one glimpse in the mirror revealed the painful truth.

The colour should have been perfect with her black hair, but instead, her skin looked even more sallow. Her hair hung straight down her back rather than in fashionable curls to frame her face. And her mouth looked more drawn, wider still.

"It's very pretty," she forced through stiff lips

Mrs Beauchamp approached her with a long coil of blue satin. "We aren't finished yet." With a snap of her fingers, the woman sent the coil writhing into the air. Alarmed, Persephone almost ducked, but Electra's glare held her stiff.

The satin wound and wrapped and finally knotted atop her head, hiding her dull hair beneath the most fashionable of turbans. A few wisps of baby hair escaped in a soft, thin fringe across her forehead. Persephone saw the silver glints and prayed the shop women did not. Even so, with her hair off her slender neck, she found herself feeling almost… presentable.

Her heart fluttered in her breast. What would Robin think? Would he finally look at her and see, not the girl he'd known for years, but a young lady who might… She couldn't continue the thought, for fear someone could read her hopes and know her for a fool. She closed her eyes and inhaled deeply.

"That's correct, Miss Fury. Hold your breath and keep your eyes closed."

They were barely shut before something soft caressed every inch of exposed skin. She caught her breath in surprise and something clogged her throat; she came up coughing to see Mrs Beauchamp with a wide-mouthed bowl of powder and a large puff. "Next time, hold your breath?" she said with a sigh. "And now, look."

Persephone spun to look in the mirror and gasped. Her skin was like porcelain. She reached to stroke her cheek.

"Don't touch!"

She jerked her hand back in alarm.

Again, the shop girls descended, this time with bottles and cold mists.

"Close your eyes." An order snapped with the expectation of obedience.

Long moments passed before she felt a gentle tap on her shoulder. Mrs Beauchamp took the ivory fan that had supplied the tap and placed it in her hands. The sticks were pierced in a delicate filigree. When she held the fan, she realised that the blue dress also had narrow ivory lace at the neck, sleeves, and hem, with an ivory silk ribbon tie under the bodice.

Mrs Beauchamp pinned a perfect ivory silk rose on the turban, and stepped back.

At the sound of a delicate sniff, Persephone turned to find her mother weeping and dabbing her eyes, while Electra beamed. "My dear Mrs Beauchamp, you have surpassed yourself."

The woman gave a light nod, her smile smug.

For the first time, Persephone felt hope.

"Your Vigil Gown has been prepared for you," Mrs Beauchamp concluded. "It has been sealed in its travelling bag, but if you want to try it on..." Her expression showed that she clearly found such an event unnecessary.

"I'm certain everything is prepared as required," Persephone's mother said, to Persephone's relief.

When the final selections were complete and arrangements made for Mrs Beauchamp to send one of her dressers to complete Persephone's toilette the night of the ball, Persephone surprised them all by insisting on wearing the stays home. She couldn't risk removing them and letting anyone see what she had next to her skin. Whatever was hidden there, she did not want to examine it in front of others.

Her mother patted her cheek and winked affectionately. "Of course you want to wear your new pretty."

Persephone asked, "Is there a retiring room?" She blushed madly.

"Of course, my dear. Clary, will you show Miss Fury..."

The plump girl looked up quickly and stepped forward, her expression carefully guarded, but Persephone was certain she was alarmed at the prospect of being at Persephone's mercy outside her mistress's earshot. "Yes, mum," she said, staring rigidly at Persephone's feet.

"Let me go with you, darling," Electra said, dashing hopes of any such tête-à-tête. "Mama, we'll be back quickly, I promise."

In a flurry of movement and swirling skirts, not to mention a new onslaught of overpowering scent, everyone made way for the duchess and her sister.

As they moved quickly down a dark hallway, Persephone hissed, "I need to talk to you. When can we be alone without being overheard?"

Electra led her into a prettily decorated room that evidently had a toilet chair behind the screen in the corner, for the heavy violet scent was not strong enough to mask the room's purpose.

"Yes, of course, perhaps tonight before supper I can find a few minutes."

Persephone sighed and moved behind the screen where she did a convincing amount of skirt-adjusting to make it appear that she was taking care of her needs. She reached into the bodice of her chemise and found the small, folded note the shop girl had put there, a torn, dirty corner of paper with a familiar bold scrawl. Only the strongest of will kept her from gasping aloud.

Imp —

Did you think I would forget our waltz?

I will be in touch with you soon. Say nothing to anyone, but know that I'll be near.

L

She pressed his elaborately scrolled L to her lips and fought for air, wildly blinking back tears. His hand, so elegant and achieved with such practice, relegated to a scrap of dirty paper.

Lysander, what have you done? She considered how very little pocket money she had, determined to get more and keep it with her at all times. If she saw him—*when* she saw him—she would press it upon him, no matter what his prideful nature might claim.

"I'm considering wearing a deep rose to compliment your blue," Electra's voice trilled from the other side of the screen.

Persephone pressed one more kiss on the note and then tucked it back beside her heart.

She emerged and stood blindly at the washbasin, where she splashed her hands with violet-scented water. A dark purple vial was beside it, evidently the source of the heavy scent.

"Are you all right, darling?" Electra stroked Persephone's hair back, her face knit with concern. "We can talk here, if we must."

Money. Electra would have money.

But he hadn't reached out to Electra.

Did you think I'd forget our waltz?

"No—no, it's just nerves." Persephone lifted the vial without thinking. "I was wishing I had a dress this colour," she lied and immediately realised it wasn't a lie at all. What a beautiful, rich shade it was, the colour of the stained glass violet blossoms that ringed the goddess window in the room she'd shared with her sister for most of her life. Her fingers closed around it convulsively.

"Don't be a goose. Only old dowagers and widows wear aubergine." Electra laughed and pressed a kiss on her cheek. "Come. Let's go get an ice before we return to Aubyn House."

As they made their way to the front of the shop, Persephone darted glances in all directions, looking for the plump girl who had delivered the message. It wouldn't be difficult to find out where the Duchess of Aubyn shopped and even where she'd been taking her sister with the same goal in mind. Clever Lysander, to get a message to her this way. Could she return a message?

Before they reached the door, Persephone stopped and asked a woman arranging silk ribbons for display, "Excuse me, but could you tell me the name of the girl who assisted me, with light brown curls?"

The woman looked up, alarmed. "Did she offend you? I must summon Mrs Beauchamp!"

"No! She was…" Persephone reached wildly and could find no logical reason to want to speak to her. "She was kindness itself," Persephone finished lamely.

"Darling, of course she was," Electra said quickly. "As well she should be." She smiled at the shop woman, still frozen in indecision, then back at Persephone. "Come along, I do believe you're overcome!"

❦❦

The following afternoon, Persephone drew back into the dark corner of the carriage, making room for Dardanus.

"They said she is no longer employed there." He tossed her a small package wrapped in scented paper. "Your gloves."

She sighed in frustration, or at least she hoped it was frustration she felt inside, this jittery sense that felt ominously like her powers demanding release. "How will we find her?" she asked.

"In London?" He glanced out the window and shrugged. "We won't. Though I wish you'd tell me why you want to talk to a shop girl." He gazed out the window, entranced with the passing street life.

Persephone stared at his profile, the reason she'd sent him in to ask. Dardanus turned heads wherever he went. If ever a male could get information from a shop girl by simply smiling, it would be Dardanus. Unlike Cosmo, whose dashing smirk might be considered arrogant if not delivered with such charm, Dardanus had a softness about his expression that could almost be mistaken for shyness, if one discounted the confidence in the set of his shoulders. To everyone's surprise, he was the tallest of the brothers, taller than most men in the Magi Beau Monde, it seemed, and his youthful awkwardness was endearing. But it was all for naught on this day.

A short ride found them back at the imposing townhouse, and within minutes they were seated in a small family drawing room, Dardanus with lemonade and Persephone with the small pot of 'tea' she despised. She spooned honey in and then squeezed a wedge of orange into it, attempting to mask the taste. She carefully schooled her face not to show her dread as she raised the cup to her lips, but Dardanus's lips drew taut. She never fooled her twin.

He said nothing. There was nothing to say.

She drank deeply and quickly to have it done, and when she drew in a deep breath, he pressed his lemonade into her hand.

She was too grateful to turn it down. The tart lemon cut through the putrid flavour of the tisane, and she couldn't prevent the shudder. She handed him back a half-empty glass. "Thank you," she whispered.

And still, he said nothing, though his eyes stayed on hers.

"And what scheming am I interrupting?" asked a voice from the doorway.

She leapt to her feet without thinking, the tea forgotten. "Robin!"

His curious gaze shot between her and Dardanus.

"None," Dardanus replied, shifting into an easy slouch.

Robin's eyes rested on the cup, and she realised belatedly that the residue revealed that this was no mere tea. "It's nothing," she said with a careless shrug. "My London medication. We mustn't have me emitting sparks, must we?"

He stiffened. "You're drinking something to suppress your magic?"

"Really, Robin," she chided. "Can you think of any other way to bring me safely into such a place? Let me ring for some tea—"

"No," he said quickly. "I'm sorry, but I'm here to see His Grace."

"Of course," she said, hoping her smile didn't waver and reveal her disappointment that he had not come to see her. She'd been here almost two days.

"Perhaps later? Or another time," he amended. With a shallow bow and a last glance at her cup, he was gone.

She sat down, feeling more than a little foolish.

The numbness was creeping back into her fingers. "I think I shall have a rest," she said and would have left quickly to hide her unsettled state had not Cosmo entered at just that moment.

"Poppet," he said. "Just the brilliant mind I'm seeking." He offered his hand. "Could I press you into service for the afternoon?" Before she could ask for elucidation, he included Dardanus in his invitation. "Feel free to join us, if an afternoon in Aubyn's library appeals."

She shot to her feet again. Aubyn's library? She'd been wanting time in there since they'd arrived but had been warned against appearing too odd, and a young lady perusing volumes in the duke's library was odd, indeed.

"I'll beg off, if you don't mind," Dardanus said.

"I thought as much." Cosmo tucked her hand into the crook of his arm. "We'll take the back stairs, why don't we?"

Of course they would, so as to be seen by as few people as possible.

Upon entering the luxurious library, she could wait no longer. "What is it?" she demanded. "What do you need me to do?"

With a wave of his hand, he closed the doors, and Persephone heard the bolt slide home. "Can I trust you not to discuss this with anyone? Not even Dardanus, I fear?"

She considered Lysander's message, still pressed against her skin for safekeeping. What a secretive bunch her older brothers were. "Of course."

"You know that the king's health is precarious."

"As it has been half my life," she agreed, her curiosity now thoroughly aroused.

"And you know that since he has no heir, there have been fears about unrest," he said delicately, "should he die without naming one."

"They are saying it will be the duke, for the queen and king love him so," she said, feeling a thrill of amazement.

"Hush. Don't speak so," he ordered, with a glance at the door.

But if predictions were true and the newspapers correct, her sister—her very own Electra—would likely be queen.

The tisane suddenly got the better of her, and she sank into a chair.

Cosmo went to a bookshelf on the far side of the long room. He withdrew several ancient-appearing volumes and brought them to her, not using magic to carry them, she noted. "There have been rumours from the less fortunate classes, what they are calling the return—" His lips, usually so generous with good cheer, twisted. "—the return of a 'True King', a belief that springs from some ancient Welsh prophecy."

She frowned. "I've never heard of such a thing."

"Nor has anyone else. In fact, we have reason to believe it's a Banbury tale fabricated to stir up rebellion amongst the ignorant." He placed the books with their cracked and crumbling covers on the table beside her. "But on the chance that such a prophecy might exist in some form, would you mind spending your free time reading these?"

Her fingers had already closed over the top volume. "The *Prophetiae Merlini?* Surely you jest! Nothing but romantic claptrap."

His laugh was reassuring. "I do not jest, but neither do we take it seriously. At least, not in the strictest sense. However, it never hurts to be aware of what might be twisted to nefarious ends, and who better to ask than my own sister? I know I can trust you, and there's no man or woman who can handle the translation with such facility."

She felt her face flush and knew that she could not hide the pleasure she felt at having her intellect recognised. "Well, it's not as if I have more compelling things to do."

"Perhaps you'd rather read them in your own suite of rooms?"

"Indeed," she said wryly. "I wouldn't want to be caught in the library." But the indignity of being ushered out bore no sting, as her mind already raced ahead as she caressed this ancient volume of—she shook her head in amusement—the *Prophecies of Merlin.*

❦

Robin paced Sebastian's study restlessly, practically gnashing his teeth with rage. He whirled at Sebastian's entrance and did not attempt to hide his displeasure.

"Robin," Sebastian said, "whatever is wrong?"

"They're drugging her!" Robin spat. "For your benefit! For I can't imagine anyone who would be more averse to scandal at this moment than the Duke of Aubyn!"

"Brandy?" Sebastian asked, pouring two glasses without waiting, and then pressing one into his hand. "Be seated."

Robin sank resentfully into the offered chair. "She shouldn't be in London at all. She certainly shouldn't be offered up on the marriage mart. Do they propose she keep herself drugged for the rest of her life in order to hide her odd powers from a husband?" He tossed the brandy back in a manner to which he was totally unaccustomed and barely managed to avoid choking.

"You're very protective of my wife's sister."

Robin looked away. "I'm appalled that her own family isn't."

The silence grew taut between them.

"They are concerned," Sebastian finally said. "She is an odd thing, to be sure. However, she must be presented now, to Queen Ygraine."

Rather than to her own sister, should she become queen. Politically, it was an intelligent choice. But this wasn't about politics. This was about a girl's life, a girl's future.

"As for her potions, that's none of my concern. She's evidently prone to mishap, so…" He shrugged, ready to dismiss the subject.

Robin was not. "Then present her to the queen and take her home. She doesn't have to be offered for marriage!"

"Robin." Sebastian's voice was musing, almost idle, and yet Robin sensed him to be anything but. "There is to be an announcement tonight. Elevations in rank. The creation of new titles."

Robin sat straighter. Was this it? What they'd all waited for? "Are congratulations in order?"

Sebastian stroked a finger down a rolled scroll and circled the glowing Royal Seal that held it closed. He touched it with his signet ring, and it opened. He offered it to Robin, his expression intense, watchful.

The parchment was heavy and crisp in Robin's hand. *"By Royal Prerogative and unanimous Parliamentary Proclamation,"* Robin read aloud,

"Sebastian Balmain, Duke of Aubyn, is named on this tenth day of April the Duke Regent of Glastonbury... Glastonbury!" The very word resonated with history and magic.

Sebastian's clear blue eyes met his, and in them was quiet triumph. "The Duke Regent."

Regent.

The palace was finally acknowledging the need for a regent to perform King Pellinore's duties, as the king had clearly been unable to for a very long time. By royal prerogative... meaning, the king's action, not needing approval, yet with a Parliamentary Proclamation supporting it. But the queen had been the power behind the throne; this was also common knowledge. "Queen Ygraine supports this?" he asked, hesitantly.

"She chose me."

Robin grabbed his cousin's hand. "Sebastian... I don't know what to say!" Years melted away between them. "I will be honoured to call you 'Your Majesty'."

"No," Sebastian said in sharp warning. "The regency is not the throne."

"But the intent is clear. You are to be the next king."

"It is not the throne," Sebastian repeated.

Always cautious. He would make a good king. "As if the public would stand for anyone but you," Robin said. "When is the installation?"

"It's not necessary. This was a legal matter, settled by letters patent. To turn it into a time of pomp during the king's illness would be unseemly."

Robin allowed the scroll to roll up in his hands and placed it carefully on the desk between them. A simple legal matter handled with dignity and solemnity, as if the course of a nation hadn't just been altered and secured.

"There is honour enough in its bestowing. I need no pomp to adorn it. And besides, my mind is on more important issues. For one, I'm thinking that the new Earl of Monmouth could not have a better political position—" He broke off to sip from his brandy. "—than to be married to my wife's sister."

Robin heard her voice again, usually so crisp and bright, now soft with fear. *Men I don't even know putting their hands on me.*

And she'd been fearing a mere waltz.

All good humour drained from him. Robin wanted to reach across and rip out the throat of the duke who would be king. "Are you mad?" Robin demanded incredulously. "And her parents agree that she should be offered as political boon?" Disgust rose in his throat.

"All agree that there could be no better arrangement for her, no better way to keep her safe and to keep her odd vulnerabilities protected than to be wed to the Earl of Monmouth."

"Who is this Earl of Monmouth? No such title exists!" Robin snapped.

"Haven't I mentioned it?" The gleam in his eyes brightened. "I'm speaking of you."

Robin froze, his heart thudding in his chest.

"Surely this isn't such a dreadful thing. Worse marriages have been made for worse reason. You're fond of the girl, and anyone can see she's smitten with you."

"She's seventeen years old, and I'm thirty-one!"

"As if that signifies."

"She's been like a sister to me. You're insane. All of you." He felt a sickening twist in his stomach. "You brought her here and put her through all this to press me into offering for her hand?"

"No," the duke said softly, regret colouring his tone. "We brought her here to present to the queen, to have her vigil and her presentation ball, and to marry. We only *hoped* it would be to you."

Robin lurched to his feet and left the room before he could betray his rage.

❧ CHAPTER TEN ❧

Two days had passed since Robin had seen her tisane and had been unable to hide his disgust.

Two days without a word from him.

She had attempted to bury herself in old books about old legend. The idea that the ignorant could believe that the True King—Arthur—could actually return dismayed her. But then, hadn't the royal family taken the name Pendragon upon ascending the magical throne in the sixteenth century? The conceit of the Pendragon name had been Bardán Fury's idea. But none had ever believed there was a true connection. None would give even a moment's thought to such legend being true in this time of reason.

Perhaps having a House of Pendragon for three centuries had influenced the ignorant to believe ludicrous prophecies but, whether reading the Latin in which they had been first recorded or French discussions of same, there were no such prophecies of Merlin that gave substance to the whispered rumours.

She turned at the swish of silks and smiled tremulously at her mother.

"It's a great honour to hold Vigil at the basilica," her mother reminded her.

"Of course it is," Persephone said crisply, hoping to reassure her mother in ways that she herself longed to be reassured. Electra's first Vigil had been at the rustic shrine near Erinyes Manor, but at the time of her marriage, Aubyn's lofty position made her worthy of a basilica Vigil, and now as a duchess's sister, Persephone was granted the same. If—when—Aubyn became king, he would have to keep seven full-moon vigils in that holy place before coronation.

"You will do us all proud," her mother responded. "And now, your bath awaits."

With her cleansing, surrounded by those women who would be offering her to the queen on the morrow, the ritual would begin.

107

Persephone allowed herself to be drawn away from the window.

He would surely come. He would surely want to be one of the male attendants who accompanied her to the basilica.

Surely.

❧❧

She sat alone in the dark and oppressive carriage. As they rolled solemnly down the magical streets of London, she was certain that young girls watched from bedroom windows, dreaming that someday they might be the ones in such a carriage, with such attendants, on such a night.

She touched the Vestal locket at her throat and gazed through the velvet-curtained window. On one side, her father was proud and handsome astride his prancing black stallion, brought to London for just this event, with the Duke Regent taking the lesser position behind him. Such lack of pretension was only part of what endeared Aubyn— now Glastonbury—to the common people.

On her left rode Cosmo, followed by Dardanus.

At her heart, Lysander's note felt like second skin.

Robin had not come.

All too soon, she stood inside the doors, her head high, her back straight, wrapping herself in the pride of the Furys even as her father's hands lifted the hooded cloak from her shoulders.

She turned to place a kiss on each of his cheeks and then dropped to her knees for his blessing.

She did not allow herself even a glimpse of the others, for to see them standing there on this most important night was to remind her of those who were absent.

Her father took her icy hands in his warm ones and raised her to her feet. She projected a serenity that would rival her mother's, for this was what the occasion demanded.

She would step forward into this night of decision with serenity and confidence. She would erase the doubt from his eyes. She would pretend that the hesitancy she saw reflected in his beloved grey eyes was that of a father watching his youngest daughter step into adulthood, not fear that he was doing the wrong thing by allowing it.

She took one step forward and heard the doors close behind her like softly echoing thunder.

The night stretched before her.

Her decision hung over her.

Her future loomed ahead of her.

She dropped to the floor and prostrated herself, arms spread wide on cold stones, eyes squeezed shut against her tears, waiting for the toll of bells at midnight and whatever lay ahead at this, her dedication to her goddess.

❦❦

Robin's rage had reduced to a slow simmer. For two days, he had remained in his rooms, ignoring the summons from Court. *Let Sebastian rot*. Ignored, too, was the quick, questioning note from the duchess. *Let Electra rot with him.*

Persephone had never *asked* him to be an attendant at her Vigil.

There was no reason for him to feel this gnawing guilt.

But they had all expected it. Without question, as if he were already such a part of her life that to be her attendant was natural.

It seemed the act of discovering her and returning her home so many years before had sealed his place as her protector, and none had seemed to question that fact.

He had *wanted* to be there. He held her in the greatest affection.

Except, they had misconstrued his affection in ways beyond his imaginings. They thought he would see in her a wife? They thought the attentions he paid to her, the minor indulgences, the long conversations about ideas and subjects he never thought to raise himself—they thought this smacked of ardour?

Surely her brothers and her father didn't look at him as anything but a family friend.

If they had thought otherwise, they should have called him out for it, for she was only a child!

And if they thought otherwise, now that she was truly becoming a woman, did they have reason to call him out if he did not ask for her hand?

Did he deserve to be called out for breaking her heart?

He wasn't blind. He'd seen her infatuation. But Zeus, that's all it had been, an infatuation that would evaporate like the mists as soon as she found herself in London, surrounded by men of suitable age and ambition.

Faces flashed behind his closed eyes, faces of unmarried, ambitious men who would snatch up the duchess's sister in a heartbeat.

Men I don't even know putting their hands on me.

He bit back a snarl.

But of all the questions rolling through his alcohol-infused mind in the dark of this long night, one rang out the loudest and with the harshest impact.

How had this strange girl with her odd mix of power and fragility become such an anchor to him that the mere thought of her being thrust into the arms of someone undeserving could eat him from the inside out?

When every shred of decency demanded that he remove himself from London and from her orbit until expectations such as those Sebastian voiced were void, why didn't he leave?

ᚱᚱ

With her eyes closed, despite the cold seeping into her, she could almost imagine herself at home again. The sound of the Naming fountain, bubbling down by the apse, gentled her much as the fountain in the courtyard at Erinyes Manor would. Surrounded by stone walls, with bright moonlight streaming through stained glass and spilling across the floor, she could almost smell the colours of the glass, smell the magic that made them.

The midnight pealing of bells in the tower overhead sent vibrations straight through her body from the floor, yet she lay there still, clinging to hard, cold stone, dreading the quiet when they ceased.

Midnight.

When she must make the choice that would shape her destiny.

There was no easy decision for her this night, and no amount of prayerful deliberation had moved her closer to one. Hadn't she once chosen a goddess, begged a goddess for help, given a goddess her blood, only to be ignored?

The scar on her palm throbbed in memory.

There was no shrine to Nemesis at the ever-so-civilised Basilica of Apollo. Had there been, she would not have given the goddess a second chance to reject her.

She finally forced her stiff limbs to curl and rolled to her side, staring at the far wall lined with curved, recessed shrines. Votives of all colours ringed the floor beneath the fresco of the Shrine to Aphrodite that showed the goddess rising from the white foam froth of sea, streaked with the red blood of Uranus.

She rose and walked as quietly as a spirit to the shrine and fought to focus her heart, her spirit, on the beautiful goddess. Many girls chose Aphrodite to guide them and came back throughout their lives to soothe their hearts, to ask for children, and to beg for the return of their beauty when their husbands strayed. Each candle glowing in the darkness represented such a request.

This would not be the goddess to guide her through her trials. They would never be so simple.

She drifted down the niched wall, clenching her fists spasmodically in an attempt to keep her magic at bay. Slowly, she walked past familiar gods and goddesses, all surrounded by burning requests for patronage. She longed for a sign of hope, a calling for her heart to recognise, and yet none offered peace, or strength, or wisdom.

She stopped and looked across the nave to the wall far opposite, its two stories of arched windows dark. On earlier visits, for Electra's wedding and state occasions, she'd hardly been able to pull her eyes away from the jewel-toned images and patterns.

But on this night, it was the shrine to Minerva that suddenly caught her eyes and heart.

Wisdom.

Could there be a better goddess for her?

She almost flew across the basilica, her bare feet skimming over cold stones, and she dropped breathlessly to her knees.

Why hadn't she thought of Minerva? She fought to still her breathing, to calm herself as befitted a supplicant. She fought for the words of entreaty. Her mind searched wildly for the proper offering.

But she found no words. She found no offering.

For though she desperately needed wisdom, and Minerva's Gift of music was in her blood, she felt no healing here. Minerva didn't still her trembling hands.

Once again, Persephone stood, the jittery feeling in her chest growing. She'd had her tisane pressed upon her before she'd left the townhouse, and had swallowed it all—every drop—in total obedience and desperation, because this was not the place to lose control of her magic. Yet here she was, pacing, apprehension and pressure building.

Hera.

She was almost certain that Electra had chosen Hera to bless her future. Hera, the Queen of the Gods, the goddess of sky, and women, and marriage. Electra could pose for an image of Hera, her beauty was so pure and ethereal, her grace so profound. One simply didn't say which goddess one had chosen, but Persephone felt deep in her heart that Hera had guided Electra forward into a future so bright, it hurt mortal eyes to gaze directly on it.

She found herself in front of Hera's image, and wondered, if she flung herself on Hera's mercy, would the goddess take pity on her, the lesser sister? Would Hera have room in her heart for one such as she?

Again, she stilled herself and waited in silence for a sign of acceptance that did not come.

🦋🦋

The goddess's scent came to him in his sleep.

Elen. Elen of the Ways.

He'd waited half a lifetime to see her again, had sought her, had dreamed of her, and finally she had come. Her presence filled his mouth and soaked into his skin, leaving him moaning, reaching with arms too heavy to lift. It surrounded him like the bottom of the lake from which she sprang.

The scent of earth... Of death... Of power.

🦋🦋

Music called her, drew her near, echoing delicately in the quiet of the night, like a harp... only not. Or a lute... and yet, not a lute.

She turned to find its source, listening, craving...

Music as delicate as the gently bubbling fountain.

She found herself walking, searching, until the fountain was in front of her, the place where someday Electra would hold a baby as it was Named. Persephone reached into the water, letting it flow over her hands like music.

The music was everywhere, as light as the air it floated on. Music pulsing deep in her soul, like air and blood and prayer. Like cold water, streaming down her arms, soaking her thin Vigil gown, sending shivers throughout her body.

She turned slowly, spinning, arms outstretched, reaching as if to draw the music into her, into the ache that opened like a wound and begged filling.

She knew not to whom she made her offering, but she knew what she must do. She pulled the thin, silver flute out of her sleeve and raised it to her lips. She offered her breath, her soul, her heart, her joy, her pain. The flute's sweet sound poured forth and joined in the music of the night, and Persephone fell into its embrace.

And then—the voice. The woman's soft trilling voice, like the coos of doves before dawn, sweet and bewitching in its purity. *Persephone...* Like a slow-drawn breath. Like laughter. Like song.

"Yes!" she cried out, clutching the flute in fingers that still trembled with song. "I'm here!"

Why do you seek to bestow your loyalty on these unworthies, you whom I chose before your birth, you who are my child, my joy?

And her soul took flight. Claimed, wanted, desired. She fell to the floor, not in the prostrate stretching of ritual nor in the kneeling of supplication, but in the boneless wilting of relief that her goddess was here, and had found her, and claimed her and—

Falling.

She was falling.

In a dizzying spin, down, down, down.

Into Shadows.

❦

Behind his closed eyelids he saw her now, her white hair floating like moonbeams around her head, her white skin almost transparent, her eyes silver, and all of her more corporeal than any woman he'd ever beheld in his waking hours.

He flung a hand out, desperate, grasping. "Choose me," he groaned. "Choose me again!"

🦋🦋

They were sucking her under, these dizzying, undulating Shadows that pulsed, that whispered Dark and delicious promises, that seduced. She'd been here before in these Shadows, had felt these promises before on the wretched streets of Ordinary London.

"Noooo!" she cried out, swaying on her knees, her nose filling with the smell of earth and decay, her hands tearing at her hair. "Nooo, I'm not yours! Not—"

She fell to all fours, the music swelling in her ears in heavenly torture, and scrambled across the cold stone floor. "No, I don't choose you!" she cried out to her unseen tormenter, the unknown goddess who called to her from the Shadows.

She scrambled blindly, looking for sanctuary… for…

Above her, over her head, Hera, the Queen of Heaven.

"I choose… I choose Hera!"

🦋🦋

Boy, Elen said, her voice more lyrical than any paltry memory his dreams had ever produced, *did you think I wasn't watching? Did you think I wouldn't see your betrayal?*

Weighed down with the heaviness of sleep, he couldn't speak, couldn't make his mouth work.

He'd spent half a lifetime, sold a piece of his soul for her words, and now he needed more. His scream started deep in his throat and fought to erupt, but was stoppered as surely as if her cold hands choked him.

And perhaps, after all, they did.

🦋🦋

"Please," she begged of the goddess on the wall, choking on her sobs. "I promise you anything! Let me marry and be normal. Let me be safe! Please, let me have Robin!"

But as the words erupted from her in a wash of pain, so did the magic from her fingertips, and before her eyes the fresco melted— golden hair streaming in gilt rivulets down creamy skin; azure eyes dripping until only smears were left behind, limbs and robes dissolving and flowing until the wall was bare, while paints pooled on the floor, flowing ever closer to the votive flames.

"No!" Persephone moaned. "No…"

My poor child… the liquid voice whispered into her ear, a cold caress of air and music, *our moonpath will lead you to me, in the now and in the now to come.*

Persephone screamed.

❦

A scream shattered the night, leaving behind the scent of stale air, the sound of heavy snoring in the next room, and the absence of all that he craved.

He sat up, head pounding, and opened his eyes and saw before him, not the image of the Lady of his obsession—

But the image of the girl, the wretched, despised girl.

And then he sat, gasping for air and seeing nothing but blackness.

❦

Silence. The voice and music were gone. The cold air was gone.

She opened her eyes not to darkness, but to a hazy glow.

The image of Hera gazed down from the wall again, with her vague smile that promised nothing, her eyes that saw blindly, her image that was nothing but paint and plaster.

Voices—muffled, frantic voices—came to her as if from a great distance. Familiar voices. She strained, listening for that one voice, that one needed voice. And she did not hear him.

But all was well. Everything would be well. She had chosen Hera. She had chosen Robin. She could be what she was supposed to be, could do what she must, if only Robin would be hers, and he would be, she knew he would be.

She turned her face away from the flat fresco.

Because she had chosen Hera, not the goddess who tempted her from the Shadows. Robin would not fear her. He would never be disgusted by her. She would be worthy of him and would spend her life being so.

It was dawn, the night was over, and the air was scented with roses. She inhaled deeply and sat up and saw her dress, her body covered with a jewel-toned pattern cast down from the stained glass dome over her head. Beside her, the Naming fountain kept up its unceasing flow of sparkling water, and around her like a thick layer of snow were rose petals of every hue, and centred in the middle of a low mound of petals lay her silver flute.

Her goddess had accepted her.

The voices grew nearer, and then they stopped.

The men stood a short distance away, a frozen tableau, until Dardanus broke free and dashed forward to grasp her hands and yank her to her feet and into his arms. "I felt something wrong—your distress... but they wouldn't let me enter."

"I had to do it alone. You know that. But it's over, and it's... it's wonderful, isn't it?" Sinking against him, she clutched her flute to her heart beside her absent brother's note and allowed herself to be led away, out of the silent basilica and into the dawn of the first day of her life as a young lady.

They watched her warily, though she couldn't imagine why.

"The flowers..." the duke finally asked. "Did someone send them for you? Were they a presentation gift?" He exchanged a quick glance with Cosmo, and she knew in an instant why he asked, who he thought might have sent them, and felt the twist of pain. But it didn't matter that they were not from Robin, not now.

"Why are we standing here?" she asked without answering, looking from the group of men to the carriage with its open door. Cosmo stepped forward and reached for her, but she twirled away from him and began dancing down the steps that seemed to stretch forever.

She had chosen Hera. She had chosen what her family and her society expected of her, and what she *wanted*. What she *needed*. She was not of the Shadows.

"I have to prepare to meet the queen."

She was a Fury.

She would prevail.

❧ CHAPTER ELEVEN ❧

The ride to the palace was as different from the ride to the basilica as it could possibly be. Instead of dark and silence, Persephone was surrounded by gay chatter as her mother and Electra recounted their own presentations to this very same queen.

The sun shone golden on the verdant grass of Ordinary Hyde Park as carriages ranging from opulent to serviceable wound their way down Serpentine Road through unseeing Ordinaries, protected by the powerful cloaking spells that had hidden the Magi in this special place for centuries. The concentration of magic required for such a thing was fearsome, and she felt it tingling around her like a familiar scent or sound.

"She was dazzling when she was young, they say," Persephone's mother sighed. "By the time I made my debut, the blush was gone, but she was still lovely."

Persephone stared through the curtains at children running with kites, totally oblivious to the magical conveyances passing them. This was a different view of the Ordinary world than she had seen before.

Seeing the direction of her gaze, Electra waved her fan. "The Ordinary world is a dangerous place, and if we didn't have to pass this way to get to our own palace…"

Persephone suppressed her memories with a shudder. "I know."

Soon they were veering off the public road and following a much narrower one that wound past the Serpentine and into a copse of trees, where the very air began to feel heavier, then passing through a shimmering veil that felt oddly familiar and left her gasping.

"Breathe deeply," Electra leaned across the carriage to take her hand. "Odd, most people hardly notice when we pass between the worlds. You're sensitive to so many things."

Persephone took several deep breaths, remembering meeting Robin at such a place. "Is there a trick to passing through?"

"A spell. The driver casts it when the veil comes in sight." Electra laughed. "Don't tell me you're going to want to learn to cast your own."

"What happens if it's not cast?" Persephone asked, suspecting she already knew the answer.

"I've heard it can be quite horrid," her mama said. "One might lose consciousness, lose one's wits or—so they claim—one's life. A body can't properly shift between worlds without proper magical protections."

"And Ordinaries?"

"Can't make the change at all. We're here, darling. Don't crumple your gown." She twitched the fabric into place for the transfer through the narrow doors of the carriage. Queen Ygraine demanded the fashions of her youth, thus Persephone was swallowed up by voluminous skirts belling from her thin waist.

With a footman taking each hand, she stepped out of the carriage and saw the pink-stoned palace rising ahead, reflected perfectly in the mirror-calm of the Long Water.

Persephone followed the others up the wide steps and into the airy entry of the palace, where the line of young ladies and their chaperones wound its way down a wide corridor and out of sight.

Oh, goodness. She'd no idea there would be so many here today.

The poor queen.

Electra stepped forward, and upon seeing her, a footman immediately cleared the way for the duchess and her family. Persephone's cheeks burned as she passed those who had been waiting longer, but she was hard-pressed to mind the special treatment.

Finally, a thin, reedy voice announced her. "Miss Persephone Fury, daughter of Mr and Mrs Apollo Fury, presented to Your Majesty by Her Grace, the Duchess of Aubyn."

And it was Persephone's time to walk up the wine-red carpet toward the small woman who sat dwarfed by her ornate throne.

The poor queen, indeed. Her face was creased with wrinkles, her figure frail. Persephone dipped into the lowest curtsey possible, her nose almost touching the floor to demonstrate how deeply honoured she was by the queen's attention.

"Rise, girl," the old woman said in a quavering voice. "Look at me."

Startled, Persephone did just so. It had never occurred to her to do otherwise.

"So you're the other Fury girl," the queen said with interest. "You have odd eyes."

"Yes, Your Majesty." Whatever appropriate response could there be to that?

"Your hair isn't your best feature, either."

"No, ma'am."

"You'll make a good match anyway. You should be grateful to your sister."

"I am, ma'am." Slowly, the old woman held out her right hand, wrinkled and heavy with jewels.

Persephone reached uncertainly toward the queen, prepared at any minute to snatch back with abject apologies. *Whatever you do, don't touch her!* she'd been told.

The queen's skin was like paper, dry and cool. Her eyes were watery and yet their shade was a piercing blue. Frozen, Persephone allowed herself to be studied.

Finally, her hand was released. "You'll do," the old woman said dismissively.

"Do?" Persephone blinked rapidly. "For what, ma'am?"

The old woman leaned closer and whispered hoarsely, "For life, Miss Fury. For life." And then she smiled, and the sun broke through the clouds.

"Thank you," Persephone breathed, dropping into a deep curtsey again. "And bless you, ma'am."

The queen looked beyond her to the next girl. Persephone backed away the required twelve paces before she could finally turn. She found her mother with a handkerchief pressed to her lips and Electra triumphant.

"Whatever did she say to you?" asked her mama as they ushered her back toward the carriage.

"That I have odd eyes." Persephone met Electra's gaze. They burst into giggles, as if they still shared a room and dreams, and there were no secrets between them.

Even as the torn corner of paper pressed against her breast and absorbed each beat of her heart.

Did you think I would forget our waltz?

And the promise.

… know that I'll be near.

Tonight.

❧❧

Persephone stared at herself in the mirror.

The pale blue dress, the turban giving the illusion of fashionable hair beneath it with a short fringe of dull black framing her features, the ivory fan, the pearl choker at her throat—all combined to make her look almost pretty.

She didn't look so very different from other young ladies. She wouldn't be an embarrassment to Electra.

No, she looked like a young lady of the Beau Monde, and if it had taken two tisanes to still her enough to maintain such an illusion until dawn, that had been a small price to pay.

She'd only to give the dresser the nod, now that her mother and Electra were downstairs greeting guests. Her father, her brothers, and the Duke Regent were outside her door, waiting to perform their last duty as attendants on this blessed day.

The door swung open. She looked up, startled, and felt a rush of fond delight. Cosmo lounged in the doorway, examining her from head to toe, and she caught the scent of violets and lemon blossoms. After much discussion, Cosmo had convinced her mama and Electra to use roses and lilacs on some other auspicious date. Thus Persephone's desires had been indulged. The ground and first floors were festooned with delicate bouquets of deep purple and creamy white with bright yellow centres dusted with glittering sugars. The scents wafting up the stairs soothed her with memories of childhood hours spent in the conservatory with nothing but her flute or violin to keep her company.

She owed him so much for siding with her, despite her unfashionable choice.

"Good gods," he drawled. "So this is what they did to you?"

She blinked up at him, not believing her ears.

"I told them at all costs to avoid yellow, but I never dreamed they'd stick you in infant shades."

She swallowed thickly. She looked nice; she knew she did.

"You're fortunate to have me as your brother, poppet." He sauntered into the room, waving the door shut behind him, locking it with a flex of his fist. "I thought they'd never leave."

"What are you doing?" she demanded, fighting tears, all warm feelings gone in a flash. She curled her fingertips into her palms in an effort to calm herself. "You're a wretch, Cosmo Fury, a wretch!"

He cocked a brow at the dresser, and the foolish woman's cheeks flushed bright pink as she produced a large box that had been hitherto half-buried under tissue on the bed.

"I asked, what are you doing?" Persephone demanded, her chest swelling, her fingertips tingling despite her best efforts.

He winced. "Oh good gods, and they even put a padded corset on you?"

She crossed her arms across her breasts, her humiliation complete. She wouldn't go downstairs, would never go downstairs, would leave London and never return.

"My sweet poppet, you'll thank me." He gave the turban a brisk tug. It tumbled down in folds of silk and strands of dull black hair.

"Minnie," he said. "I'll wait behind the screen whilst you attend my sister. And get that insipid powder off her. She looks like a dowager hiding wrinkles rather than a pretty young lady." He gave Persephone one last, quick apologetic glance and tweaked her chin. "Trust me."

The maids were goggle-eyed with shock but never dreamed of disobeying. Amidst a flurry of brushing down and stripping away, she could do nothing but watch her sallow skin emerge again, her petticoat revealed as the blue dress was whisked away, and the stays that she had never felt comfortable in disappear while she pressed a hand to her breast, feeling the soft crackle of paper between the thin silk chemise and her skin.

"Here," his voice called from behind the screen. Something flew over the scrolled edge and she reached without thinking to catch a circlet of pearls. "For your hair," he said.

Finally she turned to see the dresser—Minnie? And however did Cosmo know her name?—holding a different dress.

Persephone gasped in horror.

❦

Robin wandered through the ground floor drawing room, relieved that the announcement of his arrival had been swallowed up by the low cacophony of genteel discourse surrounding him. The ball was yet another of Electra's successes, an out-and-out crush that should thrill any young lady.

He caught snippets of conversation that ranged from small political intrigues to talks of impending rebellion from the Earthborn, and beneath it all the urgent awareness that a new Court was on the horizon, if not soon, inevitably, with positions to be earned by those who found ways to prove their loyalty now instead of waiting.

He could hardly blame Sebastian for using this night to further his own plans. There could be no society function these days that was focussed only on pleasure. Fortunately, most members of the Beau Monde were finding as much pleasure in political manoeuvring as they ever had in social machinations, so the night would be declared another brilliant success.

Some might even deign to notice the wraith of a girl purportedly at the evening's centre.

As if he were much better. He knew not whether his motives were generous or selfish, whether his presence would bring her comfort or more pain, whether she knew her family's plans to manipulate her into a 'safe' marriage.

He simply knew that he was here.

He paced restlessly, his eyes lighting on the odd choice of flowers. Electra preferred profusions of elegant cream-coloured roses, sometimes with edges and hearts tinged pink or yellow, always chosen to be the most complimentary to her evening's attire. He found himself wondering what colour the duchess would be wearing tonight, only to have her appear at his elbow as if summoned.

"My dear Sir Robin," she said, "how delightful."

She wore green.

"Indeed, an honour to be invited," he returned with a bow.

A shade of grey-green that should have been drab, but on her was elegance itself.

"As if there were ever a doubt," she scoffed with a gentle laugh.

"She's been in high fidgets for days. I'd hoped you would drop by. You always do have a calming effect on her."

"Not that I can tell," he said acerbically, recalling a quivering finger pointed at his heart.

"I must find Mama. Come and join us. I'm certain she would welcome your presence," she said breezily, and he found himself following in her wake as her slim, green form glided through the crowded room. Her hair had been cut into a dark crown of Greek curls that any goddess would envy, and the way she could briefly give each individual the impression of a personal exchange without slowing her progress left him in awe.

They stepped onto the first floor landing outside the ballroom as a sudden stir caught his attention. He stepped onto the first floor landing to realise that from below him, people were gathered, looking up. Guests who had been milling near the ballroom entrance were now turned, also looking up expectantly. He followed their gazes up the stairs.

Dardanus and Cosmo Fury descended, Dardanus's expression one of ill-masked concern that caused Robin's heart to leap.

Cosmo, however, exuded confidence, his eyes glittering.

And why did that leave Robin uneasy?

Sebastian descended next, as regal as if he already bore the crown. The slight tension around his eyes was all that betrayed that he, too, might have concerns. It was a detail few would detect. The tight grip on Robin's elbow made it clear that Electra noted it as well.

When the three reached the foot of the stairs, they turned as one and awaited the announcement of her name.

And finally, the slow, graceful descent of Apollo Fury and his daughter.

A soft gasp echoed through the assemblage.

Beside him, Electra muttered in a whisper that he doubted any heard but he, "Bloody hell..."

And he... he could do nothing but stare up as Persephone came into view...

Wearing a dress of purple so dark, it was almost black.

Her hair was a sleek fall of ebony, usually so flat in colour, now shimmering, with a silver laurel wreath its only adornment.

Her skin wasn't the fashionable milky white of her sister, but in this light, against such a dress, it had a honeyed cast that glowed with life. The wide neck of the gown was low on her shoulders, exposing the delicacy of the joining of sinew and bone, the hollow at the base of her throat. Her mouth was wide and tinged with rose.

But it was her eyes, large and liquid, that dominated her face with their dark intensity.

Her presence was magnetic. There was no way any eye could have been on any other woman in the room.

She appeared to have stepped from a medieval portrait at Erinyes Manor, despite the fact that her dress was of the most recent fashion, with snow-white gloves that covered her from fingertip to above where sleeve met wrist—an effect obviously created by a modiste of the first stare. Down to the finest detail, it could not be faulted in any way.

Except for its hue that no young lady of fashion would ever choose.

A hue that made her glow.

The blood-draining grip at his elbow, the carefully composed expression on Electra's face as she looked—simply looked—at Cosmo, and his return smirk told Robin everything.

This presentation was Cosmo Fury's doing.

And the Duchess of Aubyn was rigid with rage.

Persephone drew closer. Robin looked into her eyes, and his breath caught at the intensity of her apprehension.

Oh yes, her chin was high, her shoulders straight, her posture impeccable. Few would know that she reeked of tension, only those who knew her well.

And yes, he knew her so well.

And it hit him.

Persephone didn't know. Electra had yet to recognise. The first shock had not worn off.

None of them, with the exception of Cosmo, and it was apparent, his father, had quite yet realised.

Persephone Fury was stunning.

❦

Persephone's eyes locked onto Robin's, her Robin, who stared at her with an expression she couldn't read. Impossible. He was always an open book to her.

One more step and she stood on solid floor, surrounded by people she knew, who shielded her from those she did not.

From those who stared and gasped, for yes, she had heard the gasp that met her unfashionable appearance.

Electra's carefully composed smile masked outrage. Mama's placid smile was tempered by eyes narrowed in suspicion.

In that moment she went from wanting to obliterate Cosmo for what he'd done to wanting to protect him. So she produced as wide a smile as she could manage and accepted the duke's token kiss on each cheek before turning to the others.

The orchestra began the long, soft introduction to the first waltz, allowing guests time to gather.

She clutched her papa's arm with such anxiety that she wondered if he'd have marks where her fingers had been. But he patted her hand reassuringly and guided her toward the dance floor.

A tall young man with golden brown hair stepped into their path. He gave a low bow and looked beyond them for assistance. Persephone watched the duke's pleased expression as he recognised and gave a short nod. "Mr Fury, Miss Fury, I present Lord Greylund."

Lord Greylund took her hand and brushed his lips across her gloved knuckles, the essence of propriety, but the eyes he turned to hers were a strangely familiar blue that left her off balance.

"Mr Fury," he said, without sparing her father a glance. "Miss Fury," he said, studying her face thoughtfully. And then, as if making a sudden decision, he flashed a smile and asked, "Might I have the honour of this dance?"

In less than a moment, Persephone sensed that the duke was very pleased indeed, and to her shock, her father was offering her left arm.

She firmly pulled her arm back. Despite the fact that the lord was so much taller than she, she managed to look down her regrettably long nose and reply crisply, "This dance has already been promised, my Lord." She gave him as cool a smile as was in her arsenal, and after years of watching her sister, her arsenal was heavily armed. "Perhaps later. Perhaps the minuet?" She immediately regretted that offer, for there were dances that left far less opportunity for conversation than the minuet. But there was no way she would waltz with this arrogant man whom she did not know.

When she and her papa were in the centre of the ballroom, she'd grown quite stiff with anger. He'd almost allowed that man to dance with her. His dance!

"Pray don't scowl at me so prettily, my dear. While I see the grace behind it, I fear these London nobs might not."

She forced a smile. "You were going to let him take our dance."

He only laughed at her distress. "How was I to guess that you'd rather dance this most romantic of dances in your old papa's arms?"

"Old," she scoffed. As many female eyes followed his movements as followed Cosmo's.

"However, I'm delighted that your near brush with the disaster of waltzing with a young, eligible gentleman has brought back your fire."

She would have met his mockery with true fire, but the music started, and they began the slow, graceful circling that had been much anticipated. A Fury waltz. Comparisons were being drawn and she would suffer.

"Stop thinking, my love," he whispered. "Close your eyes."

It was easier with eyes closed. Even though she felt the eyes upon her, she felt the music more. Almost imperceptibly, the tempo increased and the music swelled, and she could imagine her father's flashing smile as he spun her faster, until she was laughing up at him, eyes wide open, giddy as a little girl that this was her father, that this music was theirs, that together they spun magic. She lost awareness of anything but the music, of anything but her father, of anything but the circling, dipping, and spinning that would have left lesser mortals dizzy but for them was sheer joy.

And when the dance ended with a hushed silence and they stood again in the centre of the ball room floor, she no longer cared that she was wearing a dowager's dress and that she wasn't beautiful. She was a Fury, and that alone lifted her above any who dared judge her. Her father spun her out to the side and bowed as she curtseyed, and she felt the tension in the room release as people dared breathe again.

The ensuing conversation and laughter was almost frenetic with gaiety. The Furys had infected their guests with their energy, and the floor filled with couples. This time, when her father handed her off to a stout cousin of Aubyn's, she accepted his hand with a poise that belied her churning stomach.

She wondered where Robin was.

Lord Greylund arrived precisely at the start of the minuet, as nonchalantly as if he'd merely shown up by chance. He flashed a smile and took her gloved hand to lead her onto the floor. As they took their places in the square, she asked succinctly, "Who are you that you think all you have to do is stand before me and I will forsake my first dance partner?"

His eyes widened in surprise and then he gave her a slight smile. "Very well. I am Lord Greylund of Lyngthorpe, and my given name is Gawain, although only my great-aunt calls me that."

The set started, and they performed the honours to their audience, and then to each other. Then, facing one another, joined their inside hands in the centre and began the graceful half-circle turn. "Who is your great-aunt?" she asked, her eyes narrowed in suspicion. Only the House of Pendragon took knightly names, but there were no living members of the royal house other than the king and queen, so clearly he'd been allowed the name as an honour only.

"The queen."

The dance separated them briefly enough for her to cloak her reaction. He was the queen's relation. No wonder Aubyn had been so pleased. That didn't mean she had to be.

When the dance brought them together again, she gave her head a slight toss. "And this is why you found yourself unwilling to acknowledge the most simple expectations of etiquette?"

"I'm afraid it's worse than that." His smile was wry but confident.

She refused to prompt him for more as they made the reverse half-circle. She chose instead to gaze away from him and across the gathering, longing to see Robin.

"My great-aunt sent me. It seems she is intrigued by you, Miss Fury."

She snapped her gaze back to him. "Indeed."

"I came early and made your acquaintance by presenting myself discourteously, even at the risk of offending you, because I have another engagement this evening."

She smiled in a manner that she presumed, on Electra, would be considered pretty. "You succeeded at both."

Again, the dance separated them, and in the nick of time. What madness had got into her?

Following the steps of the dance, she once again faced him. She hoped her flushed cheeks could be attributed to exertion and not the confusion she was feeling. "You've fulfilled your duty," she said. "And it is no longer early. Surely your other engagement—"

"Is forgotten."

"I must remember how lightly you make and break commitments."

"You have a sharp tongue."

"You have an air of conceit."

"Because I am conceited. And thus, I suppose this means that you are sharp."

Their eyes locked, and she found herself staring into those familiar blue eyes she'd seen just hours before, the same the old queen had pierced her with.

"That," she said crisply, "should have been evident when we first met. I believe you must also be slow."

And he laughed. His laughter was so genuine, it caught the attention of all around them, although in truth she had felt people watching from the moment he approached. A turn resulted in her facing Aubyn amongst his guests. His expression was pleasant as he inclined his head to listen to a short, stout man whose every urgent movement bespoke of more political discourse, but the duke's eyes met hers with approval.

And then, she was facing Lord Greylund again, and finally, the dance ended.

They presented honours out, and then to one another. She rose from her curtsey. "I hope you enjoy your engagement, my Lord. I'm sure your companions would still welcome someone with such excellent connections as yours."

And she spun away to weave a path through the crowd, her heart pounding.

What had started as annoyance had ended in something that—she couldn't deny it, having watched Electra for all these years—was very close to flirtation. With her mouth dry and head beginning to ache, she was quite sure she didn't like it.

She immediately felt guilty. She had insulted someone whose attentions could only be considered advantageous to her sister and the duke. It was poor repayment indeed for their many indulgences and generosities. She steeled herself to do better, when all she wanted to do was find a corner and hide.

She wondered yet again where Robin was. Would he really abandon her so completely? Her throat thickened with tears.

Behind a hanging brocade drapery, the balcony offered dark refuge.

❧ CHAPTER TWELVE ❧

One moment, she was there, shimmering with a glow that went beyond diamond dust candles and hinted at a more troubling source, and the next moment she was gone.

Robin scanned the large ballroom twice. Uneasiness gnawing at him, he sought the nearest open door, unencumbered by people seeking his acquaintance. Despite his place in Sebastian's orbit, he was not viewed as worthy of toadying, for which he was eternally grateful. Sebastian could keep his world of people wanting to give convenient favours in return for later, far less convenient reciprocation.

He left the bright ballroom for the dark balcony, its air heavy with the scent of roses slumbering beneath the moon.

He paused as his eyes adjusted, and then saw her at the far end of the balcony, clutching the stone railing as if clinging to a bobbing plank on a roiling sea. Her head snapped toward him, her eyes black hollows in her face.

"Where have you been?" she demanded. "For two days, I've needed you, and you weren't here!"

Guilt sliced through him. He grabbed her hand.

She snatched it away. "What are you doing?"

"You need to dispel your magic—"

"I have it perfectly under control!"

That he doubted, though he didn't doubt she was dosed to the gills with calming potions.

"Come with me." She whirled away in a billow of gossamer overskirts, leaving him to follow her into the shadowy corner of the balcony and a discreet door.

Even though he opened it for her, he said, "If we're seen, this will be disastrous. You can't just leave a ball with a man."

"Oh, piffle," she called over her shoulder, diving into a dark corridor.

He followed. What else could he do?

131

They turned onto a slightly wider corridor clearly meant for servants. A liveried footman stepped from a doorway with a tray, but spying them, quickly whipped around and went the other direction. "Poor fellow will have to detour through another wing because of this, you know," he muttered. From her sharp look, she didn't have the grace to care.

Soon they were entering the library, where two braces of candles were lit at opposite ends of the vast room, their light almost swallowed by the darkness between.

"None will look for us here." She smoothed her skirts and hair with satisfaction, then turned on him, eyes snapping. "You didn't answer me. Where have you been?"

"I had business."

"What business? You didn't go home to your estate. But, of course, Aubyn sent you somewhere."

He didn't disabuse her of the notion, instead, watching as energy crackled off her. And she claimed she had her magic under control?

"Persephone... let me help you."

"That's why I brought you here!" She glared at him, then paced to a tall mahogany stand where a heavy atlas was open to a map of England and Wales, with Scotland truncated to the North. She retrieved a small pile of books from the under-shelf.

"Cosmo set me to a task, and I—" She broke off and cast him a strained look. "I discovered something, and I don't know what to do."

"What kind of task?" He stood behind her and looked over her shoulder as she opened the top book across the atlas.

"You've heard of this... this ridiculous prophecy?"

Bloody hell. Cosmo hadn't pulled her into that, did he?

She angled her head back to look at his face. "I hope you don't think you are hiding anything from me, Robin. It's clear as candlelight that you're trying."

"I know there is rumour," he said carefully. "A rumour of a prophecy stirring the common people to rebellion."

"I don't think he truly expected me to discover anything. He hasn't asked me about it again, so I suspect he meant to distract me, nothing more." She lifted a slender, leather-bound book. "You know this?"

"*Prophetiae Merlini?*" Robin read. "*The Prophecies of Merlin?* Any Magi schoolboy has studied them, but not necessarily in the Latin. Most use translations."

"And you?"

"Translations." He braced himself for her scorn, but she just nodded and turned the page carefully.

"They're ridiculous, really. Geoffrey of Monmouth translated them in 1135, yet claimed they contained prophecies that had already come true, like the sinking of the white ship in 1120. As if he couldn't have put them in himself to give them more veracity. People took them seriously. People like being fooled."

She spun away from the table and faced him. "And that's what is so maddening about this so-called prophecy of a True King—whatever that means—returning when the 'old king' dies without heirs. Any charlatan could look at the present situation—King Pellinore and Queen Ygraine being without children since Prince Arthur's death— and rouse the rabble with a new, false prophecy designed to fit, claiming it to be lost from the old ones."

"Perhaps 'any charlatan' saw Geoffrey's success," Robin agreed, "and did just that? Is that what you think?"

"Well, you certainly don't believe a mad Welshman who lived centuries ago predicted this, do you?"

He opened his mouth to respond, and then recognised the urgency in her tone, the tension in her body, the way her fingertips were now curled into her palms and braced against the book stand. "But... you do."

"No! Well... not exactly." She twisted her fingers until he thought she might snap them.

He placed a hand on her shoulder in a wholly improper way, as he'd seen Dardanus do to calm her. Her thin shoulder stiffened under his hand, and his first instinct was to withdraw it.

But he did not.

"Explain," he said, his voice even.

She stood very still. Finally, she turned her face to the glass cabinet against the wall. "We'll need to... to go over there."

He dropped his hand, and she took a slow, shuddering breath.

When she finally began moving to the cabinet, he realised that he, too, needed a breath. A deep one.

She dropped low to bring the small cabinet lock to her eye level.

Though the key first seemed stuck, she clearly knew its idiosyncrasies, for after a deft twist of her slender wrist, the glass door swung open with a soft squeak. "Like Lord Mudleigh's stays," she muttered, "creaking throughout our dance. If that's not enough to throw one off one's rhythm."

He choked back a laugh as she withdrew an old, wooden-backed book with the greatest caution and reverence.

"This is a 12th Century copy of the *Prophetiae*." She cupped it in her hands and leaned over it, as if inhaling ancient history. "Lock the doors," she said suddenly. "Now."

Without question, he flicked his palm toward both doors and felt the resonance of locks slipping into place.

She rose gracefully and carried the old book to the table where a brace of candles cast better light. She lay the book face down and opened the back cover. Then, taking a letter opener from the silver cup beside the candle brace, she slipped its sharpened tip under the shredding silk lining of the cover and with a murmured spell, eased out a folded sheet of vellum that crackled with age. Another murmured spell—leave it to Persephone Fury to know the magic to protect ancient books—and it opened to reveal faded script, ornate and distorted enough to make it difficult to read.

"I don't know who wrote this. I don't claim it was Geoffrey himself, but…" She pointed to the Latin words written so closely it was difficult to tell where one ended and the next began. *"Caput draconis."*

"Head of a dragon," he said, relieved that his schoolboy Latin didn't fail him.

"Pendragon."

"Whom Geoffrey of Monmouth wrote about. Uther Pendragon, King Arthur's father…?"

"This is not about Uther Pendragon or Arthur himself."

"Then what?" he asked, caught up in her disquiet. "What does it say?"

"I will ask of my beloved brother,
Who sees the days unseen,
When will the true king come?

When the old king dies with no heirs
In the time of unseen messengers,
Will come the true king,
will come the head of the dragon."

Robin's heart skipped a beat. The rebel prophecy existed. But how could they know? Who else could know of this? *No,* he thought desperately, *no.* "This could have been three centuries ago, when the first king in our House of Pendragon was crowned."

"Henry VIII had heirs. Our House of Pendragon has none."

He looked back at the faded writings in her hand, his mouth dry. "So you're saying…"

"That this might be interpreted as a prophecy of Merlin that fits the rumour."

"Might be?"

"I will not go so far as to claim that it is."

"Because…"

"Because I don't want to start a war."

And that is when he saw the trembling of her fingers, heard the quaver in her voice, and recognised the burden she'd carried for two days.

Alone.

Because he'd wilfully refused to visit her for reasons that no longer made sense.

He eased the vellum from her fingers and placed it carefully on the table, then turned her to face him. "I am so sorry," he said, his heart in his throat. Her eyes—those intense, alarming and yet beautiful eyes—swam in tears.

I don't want to start a war.

He wanted to believe that it was her words and the terror they revealed that moved him to touch her.

He wanted to believe that it was guilt and sympathy and the strange brotherly concern he'd always borne for her that moved him to reach out.

But none of that explained nor excused the slow movement of his hand as he brushed that fall of oddly shimmering hair back from her throat. Inexplicably, he dragged a fingertip along her jaw and up her cheek, the entire time lost in her eyes, wide and thick-lashed, staring at him in disbelief. Neither of them breathed.

Neither guilt, nor sympathy, nor brotherly concern explained the surge of his spirit as his lips found hers.

Neither guilt, nor sympathy, nor brotherly concern explained how he felt when her lips parted in a gasp, and he pulled back, prepared for her horror. Instead, she stared at his lips, and then, returning to his kiss, pressed her delicate body against his until he felt as if they shared a pulse, a heartbeat, the very air they breathed, so great was his need to hold and protect this girl, this woman, this fragile creature in his arms.

So very right.

Something swelled within him, something that felt safe and secure and anchored, that sent roots deep into the loamy earth to find bedrock and claim it.

Nothing else mattered. Not age, nor thoughts of her sister, nor the fact that Aubyn would be all too pleased, and this union would be all too convenient at a time when convenience for Glastonbury carried with it risk, nay, danger.

What mattered was that in a blinding flash, as her hand covered his and she turned her lips into his palm, recognition jolted through him. This girl, this woman, was connected to him in a way that went beyond reason, and he had never felt so whole.

❦❦

Something alive and tingling welled up in her as she turned her face into his palm, found his amber ring beneath her lips and kissed it. She rested her face in the palm of his hand until she felt she would weep with the overwhelming feeling of connection, of belonging, of desire.

Desire for what? She could not name or define it. She only knew her body was alive with purpose. She turned her face to his and found his dark green eyes staring at her in wonder. "Perfect," she sighed. And then, because she could no more hold the words back than she could stop breathing, "My first kiss—" She nuzzled his hand again. "—is in a library." And she collapsed in laughter against his chest.

He stroked his fingers through her hair, his amazement clear. "Your hair… it's gleaming."

"That's from Cosmo! An obscene extravagance!" She blushed with embarrassment that something so normal for other girls required such an extreme measure for her. She studied the floor. "He had it dusted with diamond dust."

"Circe!"

"It was wrapped in a turban and looked ever so fashionable, and in fact, I looked as fashionable as the other girls. I looked like them," she said earnestly, "and I was so happy that I could. I never suspected I could look so Tonnish, that I could fit in so well and not be the odd one. And then he pulled my hair down, and no one in London wears their hair like this, and you know how dull the mask to hide the silver makes it, and—and he put me in this dress—"

She was babbling. She knew it and couldn't stop, but she did stop short of mentioning that she didn't fill out the top, once Cosmo had made her remove the padded stays, and she had nearly lost Lysander's note in the process.

Still, she rushed on, her frustration boiling over, "This dress makes me look like an aubergine, and I could slay him for it!"

Robin stared down at her, clearly shocked by her outburst. "You can't believe that!"

"This colour—when I showed it to Electra she said it looked like an old woman's colour, an old dowager, and yet Cosmo put it on me and—"

"Persephone Fury, you do not look like a vegetable or a dowager. You are stunning, and if you were anyone else—if you were your *sister*—I would know you were simply fishing for compliments."

She flamed with embarrassment. "Don't be absurd."

"Have you not been surrounded by men all evening? Does that mean nothing to you?"

"I've been surrounded by those who see me as a political prize. I'm not blind, and I'm not stupid," she snapped.

"The young Lord Amberley is so smitten with you he has scarcely left your side. Many a young lady shot daggers at you for that conquest."

"Who?" She blinked, trying to remember who he could possibly mean.

"Tall, brown hair, gold waistcoat?" he provided helpfully, his eyes dancing.

"Oh," she said, with a dismissive wave. "That puppy—"

"He's five-and-twenty if he's a day."

"I know what men who are five-and-twenty are like, for the gods' sakes. I have brothers! And please," she said miserably, "don't flirt with me. It's not necessary and… and if you must know, it makes me feel like you think I'm a fool to believe such flummery. I'm not beautiful and—"

"You aren't beautiful," he agreed placidly.

She stared at the floor in horror. Oh, this was worse than the flummery.

"I said you were stunning, and you are."

He forced her to look up at him.

"It's not your hair nor is it your body, nor your eyes nor your mouth nor the sum of all those things. It's you, something radiant and vital and alive that glows from within you. Tonight, everyone is seeing you as I do. You walk by, and they can't tear their eyes from you, not because you're beautiful—that would be easy to admire and then ignore. It's because you capture their gaze, and they don't know why, nor can they define what it is that draws them."

"Robin Fitzwilliam," she said waspishly, "you talk too much."

"As you will," he said.

Sweet Hera, she wished he'd kiss her again. Oh, how she longed for it. She looked up at him from beneath her lashes, hoping…

Muted music found its way into the room, disturbing the hushed silence, and Robin jerked into movement. "We have to return. They'll be looking for you, and if they—gods, this is a disaster."

"You go back the way we came," she said, suddenly shy, of all things. Shy, with Robin! She slid the old parchment back into its hiding place and replaced the wooden-backed book in its glass cabinet, keeping her face averted, because, what if it wasn't perfect for him? What if she was the silly girl who believed a kiss meant something, when to a man of one-and-thirty years...

She rose quickly. "Go on," she snapped, scowling, suddenly annoyed with herself and with him and with the night. "I'll take the front stairs and go to the retiring room first, and then downstairs, and—"

"You will waltz with Cosmo and share a country dance with one of your many admirers—"

"I have no admirers! And—*we* can't dance?" Her heart skipped a beat.

"We will have our waltz." His smile was warm and golden.

And she melted at those two beautiful words. *Our waltz.*

He quieted her with a finger on her lips. "Shhh," he whispered into her ear, and then, another kiss, this kiss was so different, so short and sweet, and that promised everything.

"Hurry," he said sternly, as if she hadn't been the one telling him to hurry just a moment earlier.

She couldn't find it in her to argue or point out his unreasonable nature, because the blood in her veins was singing, and Robin had kissed her.

He pressed his lips against her gloved hand.

She gave him a watery smile and pressed her lips against his hand, making him laugh.

And then they were in the corridor, going in opposite directions, and her head was filled with memory and sensation, her lips still tasting his, her hand still tingling where she'd held his.

"Excuse me, miss." The liveried footman who had dodged them before barely snatched his tray out of danger again as she ran smack into him.

To her astonishment, this time he didn't duck away to give her room to pass. "I beg your pardon," she said stiffly and raised her eyes to his and saw—

"Lysander!"

His black hair was pulled back in a neat queue but his long nose was unmistakable. "Did you think I'd forget?" he asked, arching one perfect brow.

"But you're—why are you wearing a servant's—" she stammered and then grabbed him and kissed his cheeks, tears spilling down her own. "You did it. You… you came! We have to find Mama, and Electra and—"

"We can't," he said, pulling her into the nearby alcove and checking the corridor.

She tried to pull herself back under control. Already off-centre, now she was reeling. "We have to tell Mama, we truly do. I don't care what you've done, she needs to know and—Why are you dressed like a footman?"

His wide lips curved into a gentle smile. "I've missed you most of all, my little imp."

"And I, you."

"Where is Mama?" he asked, his voice so familiar and so beautiful to her ears.

"Downstairs, I'm sure. We can—"

He darted a hasty look in that direction. "Not the front stairs. Not together. You certainly can't be seen dragging a footman around. We'll go down the back stairs," he said firmly, already leading her in that direction. Following behind him, she saw that his long queue of hair did not end at his collar but was obviously inside his footman's jacket. She wondered how long it could possibly be and was disturbed by the sight of it, a style of hair that was so—so *common*.

But she couldn't think of him that way, despite the things she'd heard her father say, not when he was *here*, with her, at her ball. And her mother—oh, her mother would weep with joy when she saw him.

"When we get downstairs, I'll send someone to fetch Mama," she said, hurrying to match his long stride.

Their feet clattered on the narrow stairs, faster and faster, until, heart spinning, she felt almost as if they truly were dancing, going so quickly it was a wonder they didn't trip, and the laughter bubbled up in her again, and this night was perfect.

Reaching the bottom of the stairs, when she would go left toward the kitchens to call a servant, he pulled her to the right and out the door into the crisp night air still filled with the startling scent of roses.

A hood closed over her head.

Sharp, stinging stench filled her nostrils, and she collapsed into blackness.

❧ CHAPTER THIRTEEN ❦

Robin watched the doorway for the flash of dark purple that would announce Persephone's presence in this room of misses who were pallid beside her.

But the movement that caught his eye was not purple and was not in the doorway. He turned to find that Dardanus had peeled himself away from the pretty young misses who had claimed his attentions for most of the evening and was approaching, his face pale and brow creased in concern.

"Yes?" Robin asked and felt a prickle of unease on the back of his neck.

"Something's wrong," Dardanus said, his voice hoarse, his panic evident beneath his attempt at a calm facade. "I feel it—I feel her. Something is wrong with Persephone."

Robin didn't pause to question.

"Tell your father," he ordered. "And the Duke. But, whatever you do, don't let word go beyond them."

Dardanus nodded grimly.

Robin followed the path she would have taken from the library and found no sign of her.

Minutes later, he was at the foot of the stairs again, where he found Electra awaiting him.

"Where was she when you last saw her?" she demanded. "Did you say something to distress her? Perhaps she's hiding. She does that sometimes, you know. She disappears…"

"She isn't hiding, and she wasn't—" He broke off, gripped by the expression of tremulous joy he'd seen on Persephone's face. "She wasn't distressed."

Electra visibly stilled herself, replacing her frightened expression with one of cool, placid beauty. "I'm sending my most dependable maids—"

Loyal maids, not prone to gossip.

"—from room to room. If she's hiding, they will find her. If anyone asks, Mama and I will say she was overcome and had to rest. Papa and Sebastian are waiting for you outside, along with Cosmo and Dardanus." Her steady gaze met his. "Find her, Robin. You must find her."

She returned to the din of music and laughter, as unruffled as if she weren't a hostess with a missing guest of honour, a sister with a missing piece of her heart.

She would make a magnificent queen.

It mattered not. It mattered not that Electra was born to be a duchess, a queen, and not to be the wife of a lowly baronet.

All that mattered was that something was horribly wrong, because Persephone had not returned to the ballroom for their waltz.

❦❦

If she stayed deep in the black hollow of sleep, she could forget the piercing pain in her head. If she didn't move, maybe the world wouldn't roll about behind her eyelids, bringing bile up into her throat. If she could only sleep and be still…

But her tormentors wouldn't let her sleep. Strong arms hoisted her up, and a jolt of agony shot through her. She should be fighting these arms, she should be strong. She should rage, and strike out, and fling her magic.

But her magic was far away, somewhere beyond her reach, and that terrified her.

Now the arms nestled her and held her close against a hard chest with a heartbeat that soothed and protected her. Sweet music caressed her, as Lysander's beloved voice crooned softly into her ear.

If she could sleep… if she could sink deep enough into the blackness, maybe the pain would go away.

❦❦

Tremors shook her. Her blood was ice, and her skin was fire, and it hurt to move. Shards of pain sliced into her. Stop—why couldn't they be still?

"Calm her!" Lysander's voice ordered, echoing hollowly in her head. "Help her!"

Cool fingertips stroked against the heat of her eyelids, and another voice, a woman's voice, murmured magic. She should know this voice, she did know it, but thinking of that only brought tears to her eyes.

She wanted her mama.

And Robin... She had forgotten Robin. He would find her. He would save her. Robin would take her to a place where it was her mama's voice and hands that soothed her, where her magic was able to float free.

Why did she feel so young? So afraid?

But then, the fingertips withdrew, and perhaps the pain withdrew a little, as well.

She drifted once again into the blackness.

❦

"... won't wake up..."

Voices like angry midges buzzed about her.

"... wasn't supposed to affect her this way..."

Broken pieces of words that made no sense.

" ... again... I don't care that you've already... have to try again!"

Someone was carrying her, running, jostling her... *Stop*, she wanted to cry, but couldn't.

Lysander's voice called to the night for help. How odd, to the night, not Nyx the goddess of night, but to the night itself and—

Pain shot through her, and the voices were no more.

❦

A voice as old and cracked as ancient stone spoke somewhere near her, and the familiar voice, the beloved voice, Lysander's voice responded.

A rough touch to her eyelid opened her eye, and light blinded her.

A sharp slap stung her cheek. It should have hurt, but instead, it was merely an annoyance. It would take more than that to dwarf the throb in her head, the ache in her body.

A cold cloth covered her face, and a chill rippled through her.

"What have they been giving you, girl?" the cracked, old voice demanded.

Water like ice splashed across her face and dripped down her throat and shoulders. She gasped, her eyes opening wide to see a wrinkled, gap-toothed crone staring coldly down at her. "What did you drink?" the old woman asked harshly. "What did they give you?"

"Help us, Imp." Lysander's face, wreathed with concern, hovered over her.

Her Lysander, her beloved Lysander.

She reached for her magic, but it wasn't there.

Instead, drawing on sheer physical strength that a moment before she thought gone, she drew back her hand and struck him a blow across his beloved face.

"Do not speak to me." She turned her face away from her tormentors, closed her eyes, and sank into the deep blackness where they could not reach her.

☙☙

Pain. New pain. A new nightmare, a fresh evil, an assault she couldn't fight because she couldn't reach her magic.

She smelled Darkness. Tasted it. Felt Darkness pulsing around her and pummelling her.

Pain... Fear... Shadows. She knew these Shadows.

She knew *him*.

Her eyes flew open. Black eyes burned into her, pinned her like a moth to velvet, frozen and unable to do more than breathe.

She felt herself yanked painfully from her refuge and into the frigid night air, and still, he sneered down at her, his tone dismissive as he spoke to someone she couldn't see. "I've got her."

He pulled away. She could breathe again and inhaled the scent of green, and freshness, and—

Wood fire, and savoury stew, and—

Dark and Shadows, filling her nose, her mouth, her veins.

Never had she smelled so much Darkness and Shadows.

Bile rose in her throat.

She flung herself forward, slamming the vile Mr Jones sideways with a wave of her hand—of magic! her magic!—and dove for open ground, where she knelt and vomited in gut-wrenching, body-heaving spasms.

"Cover your filth with dirt," the old crone's voice ordered harshly from nearby, and weak as she was, Persephone took shuddering breaths and swept loose dirt over her vomit with her bare hands, humiliated. All around her, people sat in the darkness, watching her warily. She felt an intense need to hide her shame, and her hands went faster, until all that was left was the bitter taste in her mouth and the stench in her nostrils.

Lysander must be there somewhere. Her betrayer. Rue. She sat back suddenly. The child. She found herself momentarily distracted, seeking a small face in the flickering glow of the fire. But then, she felt her enemy and turned to find him advancing on her, lean and menacing, somehow worse than he had been in her nightmares, his voice a silken snarl. "You do not use your magic against me, girl."

"Don't touch me," she said, not recognising the raspy croak of her own voice. Then she called out sharply, "Lysander Fury, you slithering worm, present yourself!"

From behind Mr Jones, Lysander rose slowly, his movements elegant and lithe, until he was fully standing, his arms spread and head cocked slightly in a wry shrug. "Forgive me, imp. It was the only way I knew to get you. We had no idea you'd—"

"Silence!" The snarl cracked through the night like a whip, and the beast pinned her with his glare. "You aren't the one to demand answers!"

Her eyes and nose and throat burned, and she was so weak she could hardly stay upright, but she forced herself to stand and face him across the fire. "How dare you! I was abducted from my family, from my own ball—"

"Oh, you were abducted from your ball," he said in a whine that even she had to recognise mimicked hers uncannily. He waved his hand at her and turned away. "Be seated, before you fall," he said contemptuously.

Her heart pounded in her chest. She knew not where she might be and was surrounded by people who, from their expressions, held her in no manner of high esteem. She trembled so violently, she thought if she didn't sit she would collapse.

But she would collapse into the fire before she would obey that man.

"No." Let the snivelling fools who followed this bastard see her for who and what she was, not someone to scorn but someone to fear.

He would not win.

She would die first.

She reached deep, heart racing, and found rage.

She didn't care that Shadows clung to it, that it reeked of Darkness. Her scarred palm throbbed with it. She embraced it, erupted with it, felt herself shatter from within as she shrieked, "Bastard!"

In one blinding moment she felt all her strange magics coalesce into one brilliant surge of power. It shot through her like cold steel and gave her strength.

They stared at her, all of them, mouths agape, scrambling backwards on the ground. Even her hair snapped with it, wildly writhing around her head, as power uncoiled from her core and flowed to her extremities.

She hurled it from her fingertips at the bastard Vespasian Jones.

His eyes flew wide with shock, and then he whipped a wand from his sleeve—*a wand!*

Then her own Dark power slammed back into her and through her.

"No!" she heard Lysander shout.

This time, when the world went black, there was no safety or hiding.

There was only void.

❧ CHAPTER FOURTEEN ❧

Robin's eyelids burned as if scraped by sand, and his face was coarse with the rasp of unshaven whiskers. His clothes were rumpled, his neckcloth loose and wrinkled beyond redemption. A long night had passed, but no one had slept.

He stood in the library yet again, a fifth time or even a sixth—he hardly knew any longer—looking for a sign, any sign that would lead him to her. The others were combing the lower floors, the stables, all the doorways she might have been taken through, probing for signs of magic, but all they detected was the strong residue of the routine servant magic, as it was they who expended the most to keep everything running smoothly in the background while the Quality enjoyed their ball. The faint magic of guests was only barely detectable, as they, after all, had not had cause to use any at a ball so exquisitely planned.

Persephone's passage from the townhouse had been magically masked from them.

"Fitzwilliam." Cosmo's voice was weary yet urgent.

Robin turned to find Cosmo framed in the darkened doorway.

"Nothing?"

Robin shook his head.

"Do you think we're wrong?"

Robin shook his head again, this time more slowly. "If word got out, she'd be ruined. Forever ruined, no matter that it's not her fault. No matter what happens to her—" He fought down his panic. "—or doesn't happen, people will always assume…"

"Yes. So everyone says. So I know. And yet…" Cosmo looked lost, uncertain. Then, collecting himself, he gestured sharply. "Come downstairs to the study. Aubyn can't sound an alert, but our family aren't without our resources."

What a bitter truth.

All the resources and power at the call of the new Duke Regent,

149

and yet they must remain untapped. His sister-in-law's absence was being blamed on physical collapse, a sudden malady during her own ball. No official search could be mounted without the truth escaping.

The ball had proved to be more political than social when, after a few 'tuts' and 'tsks' at Miss Fury's unfortunate absence, the business of politics resumed as the main course, with dancing and dining only the side dishes.

Persephone had gone absent from her own ball, and other than her family, no one cared.

He stepped into the wide corridor, still brightly lit by sconces along the walls, to find Dardanus. He stared into a distance that Robin could not see, but something about his posture sent a warning.

"What is it?" Robin demanded "What do you know?" *And how?* he wanted to add.

The younger man's eyes were closed. He raised a hand to gesture quiet, so Robin complied, despite his frustration. The hand finally lowered. He looked at Robin and said, "I don't know… but it worries me."

"I'll be downstairs. Are you coming?"

The young man shrugged, and his cheeks flushed with colour. "For what purpose? I'm the one who would be the least help."

And the most hindrance, for without magic, he would be someone to protect, not someone who could fight.

Robin wasn't sure how to respond. He gave a brisk nod and headed down the stairs.

❧❧

Robin entered the study to find Apollo Fury and the Duke, both standing tensely by the fire.

"I've sent to Erinyes Manor for men and horses," Apollo said without preamble.

Robin spoke slowly, carefully, in an attempt not to offend. "London is such a vast place. I'm not sure what those unfamiliar with its territory could do."

"I know that," Apollo snapped impatiently. "We will divide them into four groups, and each group take a section of the city. If she's here, we will be able to sense her magic. *If* she's still here."

And alive.

"Each group will have one of us leading it. Our knowledge of London will suffice. I need my own men in case there's a fight, not to do the actual tracking. They would die for her," he said.

"As would we all," Robin said fiercely, then turned, suddenly aware of Sebastian, standing silently, staring into the flames. Sebastian couldn't join them without calling attention to their quest. "You have no idea why someone would take her?" Robin asked him.

Sebastian met his eyes and his voice, usually so confident, was strained. "To hold hostage, to force me to… What? Until they make their demands known, I can't be sure."

"You think it's the rebels," Robin said, his stomach heavy with dread.

"Who else?" Sebastian responded. "But we won't stand by waiting like eunuchs. When the sun rises—" He pushed away from the mantle and faced the other men. "—we hunt."

As a plan, it seemed woefully inadequate, but Robin had none better. Each tick of the ormolu clock on the mantle grew louder and more ominous.

Persephone gone. Held hostage.

Roots ripped from the earth. An anchor tore free. He was drifting, empty, and the thought of her missing staggered him, left him breathless and frozen.

Then it hit him. What did it matter if she was ruined? He wanted her. What did he care of scandals and whispers? Why need she care about the opinions of Society, his fierce Persephone, who was better than any of them? He snapped his head up and felt his fingers roll into fists. "Are we all insane? To Tartaros and the damned with the Beau Monde and their rumours. To Tartaros with all of them! Your men should be combing the city, even as we speak!"

"You will not ruin my sister in that way," a low feminine voice snarled. They all whipped towards the door and Electra, her hair long and loose around her shoulders, her dressing gown fastened high on her neck. The intimacy of the garment made him flush, and he looked quickly away, but not before glimpsing her mother behind her and Dardanus bringing up the rear. They entered the study, which now felt stifling with heat and too many bodies.

But looking away did not save him from Electra's wrath. She flew across the room. She was shockingly different from the cool, sedate duchess who had continued her duties as hostess without a wobble until the last guest was gone. No, this Electra was a Fury, indeed. Her eyes snapped, and he realised that he'd supplied her with the one thing she'd needed all night.

A target.

"So easy for you to say, Robin Fitzwilliam, that my sister's reputation is not a precious thing to be protected!" She was almost spitting fire, she was so enraged, and at first all he could do was stare, slack-jawed in wonder that she could be so blind.

"Do you not realise the danger—" he began and then realised his error, and yes, the impropriety of what he was about to say. But he didn't care. He whipped around to face Apollo. "Sir, I have no words strong enough to express my horror that she is out there, and we aren't doing enough—not nearly enough—to find her. There is absolutely no need for restraint. Whatever happens, I aim to make her my wife, and the opinions of Society mean nothing to me. I implore you, use Sebastian's men. Use every means at your disposal. We must find her!"

"No!" Electra cried. "I'll not have my sister's future decided in the middle of a panic—"

"I don't believe my ears," Robin said, aghast. "You value a potential political match over her very life?"

Electra's hand sliced through the air and she slapped him. "Swine," she growled. Cosmo grabbed her from behind and pulled her away, but that didn't stop her from continuing with a cry of rage. "I won't have her life decided when she is not here to voice her own desire, because I don't care how noble your intentions or how true your heart, Robin Fitzwilliam—If you are not a woman, you have no idea how the stench of scandal can follow a woman throughout her entire life!"

"Darling," Sebastian said, and she went into his arms and buried her face against his shoulder. But she didn't weep, oh no. Her rage was still palpable in the room. Sebastian raised his eyes to Robin's and spoke softly but with the weight of authority, "The decision is neither yours nor my wife's to make, and I'd ask you to respect those who bear the burden of making such a choice, Robin."

Robin quivered with rage. He whirled, searching for and finding Dardanus. "You sensed she was in trouble. You knew it immediately. What do you feel now? Is she in pain? Is she—is she injured? Can you tell?"

His eyes hollow with distress, the youngest Fury gave his head a single negative shake. "Nothing. I haven't felt anything." He looked away, his cheeks flushing with shame. How painful it must be for him, the youngest and the weakest, to know she was in danger and he could do nothing to help her. Less than nothing, without magic.

There was a scratch at the door, and all turned as Sebastian granted entry to a footman. "The men from Erinyes Manor have entered the city. They should be here within the hour."

"We will not betray her plight," Mrs Fury said, her voice cool, her eyes resting on Robin in close examination. She turned to her husband and found comfort in his arms. "Not yet."

That was clearly the last word.

"I'll have pigeons readied," Sebastian said. "And as many of my men as can leave without arousing questions." He pressed his lips against Electra's temple, and she gripped him even more tightly. "I'll take the first round. My duties at Court are not pressing this morning."

What of the one Fury who remained silent? Cosmo leaned against the mantle, braced on his forearm, his head hanging, as he stared into the fire, seemingly letting the conversation wash over him unheard.

But when Robin would have entreated Cosmo to take his side, the younger man grew rigid, flung out his hand, long, sinuous fingers splayed wide. Reflections of flame danced over his skin and in the depths of his eyes. He opened his mouth to speak, and none dared breathe for fear of breaking his spell.

Robin's eyes darted from face to face in the room, but only Sebastian revealed a confusion that matched his own.

"My sister—" Cosmo spoke in a voice ethereal in its beauty. "—is safe in the arms of her goddess."

"Praise Hera," Electra breathed, making a circle on her forehead with the heel of one hand.

"She is safe in the arms of a brother."

A brother...?

"Lysander?" their mother gasped, turning her face to Apollo. "It has to be Lysander. But... that means he lives!"

Apollo's gaze darted to that of Sebastian, even as he held his wife close.

"My sister is safe...." Cosmo gasped again and fell to his knees, his head buried in his hands, his body trembling. As the women dropped beside him on either side, cosseting and pressing their concerns, Apollo did not wait for his host's suggestion or permission but walked straight to the brandy and poured a generous amount into a tumbler. If his hands shook despite his efforts to still them, Robin would be the last to comment or scorn.

What had they just witnessed?

Apollo pressed the tumbler into Cosmo's hand, and the younger man stared at it, confused. "What... what happened?" he asked, and then before any could answer, "After all this time? It happened again?"

His mother turned her tear-stained face to him and said, "Thrice-said, thrice true. She is safe. And your brother—Lysander—he lives!"

"Cosmo, a Seer?" Sebastian asked, clearly stunned. "And this prophecy can be trusted?"

Robin stared at the Furys, his doubts too large to dismiss.

Electra rose from the floor, her eyes filled with wonder and relief. "We didn't believe it before. How could we? The first time—oh, my darling, the first time this happened," Electra said, offering her hands to her husband, "he claimed that I would marry a man with hair of flame, and it seemed so ridiculous that we could do nothing but laugh... Darling, he said that I would marry a man with hair of flame and that I would be Queen."

Sebastian stared from brother to sister, and his thoughts were clear to those who knew him well, as Robin most certainly did. His carefully veiled scepticism melted into shock and then slow comprehension, as the full import of what they'd witnessed sank in. As he pulled his wife—his heartbreakingly beautiful wife—into his embrace, his face reflected the final realisation that if there had ever been hope that he would be King, it was now full-blown.

Robin turned his back on the scene before him, his mind racing.

They believed this, and perhaps they had reason, but...

He met Dardanus's intense grey gaze.

No one paid attention to the twin.

But the twin paid attention to everything.

Robin closed the distance between them. Before the younger man could even open his mouth to speak, Robin jerked his head towards the corridor.

❦❦

"What are you withholding?" Robin demanded when they were alone.

The look Dardanus gave him was resentful and measuring, catching Robin quite off balance, for what had he ever done to the lad to merit such distrust?

"You sense something else," Robin pushed.

"Nothing. I sense nothing."

"Then—"

"If you don't know, you won't be responsible."

"Gods damn it, just tell me!" The answer came to him in a flash. "Whatever it is, I'll keep your confidence. I'm not going to tell anyone."

"You'll try to stop me."

Stop him? Good gods, what was the idiot considering? Of course he would stop him. He must. Whatever it was, it had to be dangerous, or he wouldn't be withholding knowledge of it, and no responsible person would allow the most defenceless Fury to attempt something dangerous.

Still, the intense grey eyes measured him and found him wanting.

Something is wrong with Persephone, he'd said, and she had been gone.

Robin met the younger man's gaze steadily. "I'll help you."

Relief flooded Dardanus's countenance, brief but visible. But then, the caution again. "Why should you?"

"Because she's your sister. She's not your possession, or your reputation, or your pawn. You only have one reason to find her, and with my magic and your instinct, that's the reason you will."

Boy warred within man and man within boy, as Dardanus struggled against tears. The man won. He said, "I don't know where she is, but I know Lysander has her. I know he wouldn't hurt her. And I know she needs me…" He studied Robin carefully, seeming to see more than what could possibly be visible in the dim light of the hallway, then corrected himself. "Needs us."

Robin was besieged by questions, but knew better than to push. In that respect, it was clear the twins were not far distant in their temperaments. "Do you have a plan?"

"Not yet."

"I do. Come."

❧❦

She awakened to dim light and shadows seen through cautiously opened eyes. She kept her breathing steady and took stock. Her shoulder throbbed with pain, but her body tingled with magic in a way it hadn't since she'd entered London. Fresh, vital, alive.

And aching. Not just her shoulder and her body, but oh gods, her heart.

Where was Robin? What was he doing and thinking? He knew she wouldn't leave him, not after he'd kissed her.

Her eyes closed against burning tears as she ached with the memory.

Oh, Robin.

Outside, birds sang and she heard the low murmur of voices and the sounds of movement. But inside this rustic cottage she heard nothing but—

Breathing.

Her heart stopped.

She was not alone.

Whoever was with her was as still and watchful as she. Her fingers longed to flex in defence, but she kept them still. Was it someone she could overcome? With her magic tingling in her veins and her rage at what had been perpetrated upon her, she knew she could. She could overcome anyone who dared stand in her way. Even Lysander.

Especially Lysander.

She allowed her eyes to open completely and, after a moment, saw beyond the feeble light from the small window and into the gloom of the dark corner. Another blink, and shape emerged. Long legs stretched forward. Elbows were planted on the arms of a chair. Long, pale fingers steepled and glittering black eyes stared over them at her. A predator, watching. Waiting.

She shot up, the pain in her right shoulder tearing through her. "How dare you!"

His wand flicked out, aimed at her heart, though beyond the movement of that one agile hand, the rest of his body remained as still and dangerously relaxed as before. "Quite easily," he purred.

Her purple gown, once a source of horror and then of wondrous pride, now was ripped open with a bandage and too much skin showing beneath it. She covered herself with both hands, enraged. "What sort of blackguard watches a young lady sleep?" she demanded, her heart pounding. "And... and..." She found herself unable to voice her shock and alarm at being faced with a wand again, much less the sort of man who would possess one.

A shudder of revulsion rippled through her.

"I've not been watching you sleep. I've been watching you awaken." The wand twitched. "Consider carefully any move you make, because if I even suspect that you are about to attack me again, you will be chastened. Again."

Chastened? Was that what he called it?

His voice was silky and menacing in the gloom. "Unless you'd like a wound in your left shoulder to match that on your right?"

She drew back in fear, despite herself.

"Ah, so we have an understanding."

Her mind raced as she sought a way out of this place, a way to deal with a wand—a wand!—a way to...

"By now you must have noticed that you have regained your full magical capabilities."

It clearly would do no good to deny it.

"And you must be wondering how I think it possible to control you and your—" He paused as if considering his words carefully. "—quite unexpected powers, since clearly your family could not do so without resorting to crude and desperate potions." He waited politely for a response.

She denied him the pleasure of her admission, though yes, such thoughts were flitting wildly through her mind.

"It's Miss Fury, now, isn't it? The young lady of the household," he said with a sneer. "Miss Fury, first you must understand that whatever ill thoughts you have towards me, I would never have authorised diminishing your powers for the convenience of conforming to Society's expectations. It is just such the thing I abhor about you and your world."

Oh, so easy for him to sneer and condemn, he who had no idea of the unexpectedness and strength of her outbursts. As if finding a way to control them was only about convenience!

"I'll admit, they do raise issues that must be addressed. When your brother persuaded me to bring you here, I did not expect this kind of complication."

Lysander. Her blood boiled at the thought of him, at the realisation that he wasn't only a conspirator in her abduction, but the cause of it!

"Here is where we stand." He shifted forward, his eyes gaining in intensity, his face more clearly defined in the shaft of weak light, sharp contours of wickedness, more filled with evil and malevolence than her memories had supplied. For the man in her memories was a horrid old schoolmaster, powerless and ragtag, nothing but skin and bones, whom she had hated simply because he denied her knowledge, denied her respect, and, as she'd always believed, had malignant intentions for her family.

This man was not powerless, and while his clothing wasn't fine, there was nothing shabby about it. Where before his hair had hung in limp grey-streaked hanks, now it streamed long and heavy down his shoulders and back in a gleam that was silver with strands of black, giving it strange, fluid movement when he shifted. His frame was still long and whip-thin, but this man—this man reeked of power. And now, his intentions were clearly more malevolent than she'd ever dreamed.

Now, they were aimed fully and distinctly at her.

"Your people know nothing about your magic," he said. "They hide it and make excuses for it because they are fools."

"And what do you know of it?" she retorted, part in scorn that he should speak of her family in such a way, and part in fear. Yet, she felt a traitorous flicker of hope that he held knowledge that they did not. Knowledge she could never trust.

He rose to his feet and towered over her where she lay on her pallet on the dirt floor. "I could tell you what I know, but I fear it would overset your feminine sensibilities."

She watched the wand he dangled so casually from his fingertips.

"I think it best to have Night give you at least the rudiments."

"Night?"

"Our healer."

The calls to 'night' for help—not to the night, but to a woman.

A movement at the window drew her eyes, and dismayed, she saw the old crone approaching.

"Treat her with the dignity her position commands," he snapped. "It is she who healed your shoulder and who has nursed you back from the excessive and dangerous dose of potion that almost killed you upon your arrival. She is bringing you broth—"

"I won't drink anything you present me!"

"As I suspected you to be a fool, I suspected you'd react predictably. So let me lay out my expectations for you, Miss Fury. You will cooperate fully with your healing. You will eat and drink what is offered you. You will treat Night with the deference to which she is due."

"And if I don't?"

"In case threat of physical harm isn't enough to influence your cooperation," he said almost cordially, "perhaps the knowledge that in plain sight outside this window, your brother Lysander is bound and gagged. He awaits whatever punishment I choose to give for his most unwise attempt to interfere with you when I regrettably—" His lips twisted in a smile that showed no regret at all. "—was required to control you with the use of my wand."

He twirled it through his slender, nimble fingers and then back into his palm again.

"And why should I care what you do to that unfaithful, scheming, unloving excuse for a brother?" she cried. "It's his fault I'm here and in this condition!"

"Ah, yes, so unloving that he flung himself between you and the curse I cast and is now the worse for it."

"How badly?" She felt a pang of fear despite her resentment.

"He has his wife to care for him and did not catch as much of it as you did." He shrugged. "I'm sure his bonds are uncomfortable, but nothing beyond endurance."

"Then he's already been punished enough!"

"If you honestly believe that your 'unfaithful, scheming, unloving excuse for a brother' has been punished enough—" The lips curled into a sinister smile. "—are you willing to give your word that you will refrain from using any means—magical or physical—in an attempt to escape or harm or betray in any way any person who is in this camp for the next sennight?"

To not attempt to escape or harm anyone—especially Vespasian Jones—for an entire seven nights? Her first instinct was to spit in his face.

But her condition was weak, her shoulder injured, and she knew not where she was. Seven nights to listen, to learn, to grow stronger and then... "Will you give the same word, that you will not use any means—magical or physical—to harm or compel or betray me in any way, for the next sennight?"

"More easily than you. For you see, none of those things were ever in my plan." He smirked and slid his wand up his sleeve. "Shall we make a magical bond?"

He held out his hand, and it was all she could do not to flinch away. But it was the best plan she could make under such circumstances, and thus she clasped it, determined to show no fear.

She gasped as the jolt of magic passed through her body.

She saw by the slight widening of his eyes and flare of his nostrils that he, too, had been caught off guard, and it was he who broke their clasp and stared from his hand to hers, eyes narrowed.

And then, he stared at the tangled mess of her hair. "How long," he asked slowly, "has your hair been turning?"

She clutched a hank in her hand as if to protect it. She glared at him without responding, but now found her own eyes taking in his hair, glistening even in the dim light, and then, quickly, his face.

He was not as old as she'd imagined. His hair had always made her think so, and the fact that he was an adult when she was a child. But the lines at his eyes and the creases in his cheeks were no worse than her father's, a man who admittedly looked young for his age. She jerked her gaze away and stared blindly at the floor.

Finally, with the slightest and most insulting of bows, he left her alone to fret that perhaps her agreement had been made too hastily.

❦

Even with his promise of food and care, none was quickly forthcoming. She barely noticed, when so many other thoughts circled her mind in wild confusion. She paced restlessly, despite her weakness, with an occasional stumble and grab at the wall to steady herself.

She needed a mirror.

There was certainly nothing like that in this rude hut. But she'd seen his hair, his eyes, and for the first time realised they were like her own.

And he claimed to know about her magic.

She paced until her legs could no longer support her, and finally, she half-sat, half-fell onto the crude pallet and sank into an exhausted sleep.

↬ CHAPTER FIFTEEN ↫

"She talks to the gods."

"You mean, she prays?" Robin had never thought of Persephone as a religious girl.

"No, well, yes, that, too. But that's not what I mean. All of her life, she prayed with such urgency…" Dardanus stared straight ahead down the hedgerow-lined road, avoiding Robin's eyes. "It's as if she expects an answer."

"I suppose that's not a totally unusual thing in a child."

"She went to her vigil expecting a goddess to claim her."

"Claim her?"

He saw Dardanus glance at him from the corner of his eye as they rode down the centre of the dusty lane. Finally, the lad spoke. "Send her a sign. Speak to her."

Robin didn't know whether to laugh or sigh. Of course she did. "She told you this?"

"Afterwards, she asked Electra which goddess chose her and was disturbed to discover that none did."

The reality of what he was telling gradually sunk in. "But she thinks she was chosen?"

"She says a goddess spoke to her and claimed her, and she—she rejected it."

Robin stopped his horse, unable to simply ride forward in broad daylight on an empty road whilst having such a conversation.

Dardanus did the same, straightening his shoulders and meeting Robin's eyes, finally disturbed enough to reveal the secrets he had held back. "She heard a voice. She believes a goddess claimed her. She was afraid, and she rejected it and chose another goddess."

"Do you think this voice—" Robin forced the words out. "—is madness?"

"When we went in at dawn, she was surrounded with roses. She says they were a gift of the goddess."

163

"And your father—"

"Doesn't realise! He and Aubyn assumed they were gifts from an admirer who was seeking to curry favour with the duke through her. But she told me that they appeared after the goddess spoke to her, chose her, blessed her."

"If this is true…" Robin's mind sped from one thought to the next, unable to find sanity on which to light. "Truly she is blessed."

Dardanus's grey eyes grew darker. "Except that the goddess my sister chose in the deepness of her pain and anger was Nemesis. She believes Nemesis has accepted her and will attempt to use her to avenge old wrongs. And now she is old enough to understand that Nemesis might view such things far differently than the thirteen-year-old girl who called upon her."

"Zeus," Robin muttered, attempting to gather his thoughts. He urged his mare forward, brought her under control when she attempted to kick Hades, who he ponied beside him, ready for Persephone when they found her. Hades was unexpectedly calm, praise the gods, for two irritable horses would be torment to control.

They were on a familiar stretch of road, one he'd ridden many times. It dipped low near a stream, often the last area to hold mist. A prickle of awareness danced over his skin; Hades twitched his ears and snorted uneasily.

It was the same mist-shrouded stretch of road where he had first met a slight girl in her brother's clothes.

Though it was morning and the buttery yellow sunshine spilled across the road, he felt a tug of memory, followed by a wash of concern. "Do you feel her now?"

Dardanus shook his head. "Nothing."

"Perhaps she's not frightened now, or…"

"Farther away," Dardanus supplied. "Too far."

Never had he felt so impotent, so desperate. She *needed* him, this strange girl that he would have for his wife, if the gods were merciful.

He thought of her praying, expecting answers. He'd been to the basilica once, the local shrines on rare occasions. He didn't know the rituals or the protocols. He didn't know how to seek—how to *presume* to seek a boon from the gods.

He just knew need… Urgent and sharp need.

His breath coming in short bursts, as if he couldn't catch enough air to sustain him, he sought words, prayers, and found none, until finally, a single word hissed through his mind.

Please.

And again, *please.*

He found the strength to continue. *Whoever you are, take me to her. If not out of mercy, then from justice. Because she does not deserve this. She does not.*

At first, there was nothing, and he felt almost as big a fool as if he'd spoken aloud. He caught Dardanus staring at him strangely and wondered what his expression had betrayed, despite his attempt to guard his thoughts. But then it didn't matter, because deep amongst the trees, tendrils of mist began to curl where he had never before seen them, drawing him forward with an elusive scent he thought he recognised.

Beside him, Hades sprang forward, ripping the reins from his gloved hand, and all he could do was watch helplessly, breathlessly, as the gelding plunged into the mist and disappeared.

Without thinking, Robin leapt from his horse and snagged a fistful of clover from the bank. He tossed a clump to Dardanus, who caught it, confused. Robin remounted and turned off the road, into the forest. The mist swallowed him in sparkling brilliance, and a voice like liquid laughed and said, *Welcome, my child. I've been waiting.*

Then the woman's voice was gone, and he found himself on another road, this one with the overpowering odour of droppings fallen from the manure wagon making its way down the road in the distance.

Dardanus appeared beside him, breathless and astonished. Across the road, Hades pranced, tossing his head with pride, his greying coat showing more silver than it ever had before. He was going to be a trial to recapture.

And indeed he was. It took a full five minutes of coaxing and soothing before the gelding finally calmed and began munching at the tall grass by the road. Robin allowed it, stroking his mane so that he could finally ask his desperate question. "Did you hear the voice? Did she speak to you?"

Dardanus's expression was almost frantic. "I heard nothing, and what's more, I don't know what just happened!"

Robin stilled the panic in his own breast. This was good. This had to be good. "We just passed through a Way," he said. "We're in the Ordinary world."

Dardanus paled. "Persephone's here?"

"Do you feel her?"

Dardanus shook his head again. "No."

Robin forced his breath to slow. "Do you sense anything? Even a direction?"

Again, Dardanus shook his head.

Well, then. They were spit out on a road, and judging from the shadows, facing west. There was nothing for it but to keep going in that direction.

He would try not to worry about strange voices and the wisdom of binding oneself by obligation to strange goddesses.

🦅🦅

Someone was tugging her hair, muttering with disgust.

Who dared comb her hair with such disdain and so little care for snags and tangles?

She shifted on the hard bed, found herself face-to-face with blue eyes narrowed in concentration as a young woman worked relentlessly at her hair.

Persephone probed cautiously and found her magic still present, still strong. She sat up. The girl drew back, startled and clearly afraid.

"What are you doing?" Persephone demanded, massaging her tender scalp. "I can comb my own hair." Her stomach gurgled loudly. She ignored her hunger and focussed instead on the small earthenware bowl in the girl's hands and its glittering contents. "And what is that, pray tell?"

"He told me to do it," the girl said frantically, cupping her hand over the bowl protectively. Clearly unable to restrain herself, she added, "What kind of people are you, putting the dust of diamonds in your hair to make it shine!"

Persephone reached and felt her fine hair, no longer weighted and glossed with its artificial gleam.

"Vespasian says this proves how wasteful you Fireborn are," the girl said resentfully. "You mask your hair with dullness and then use riches to bring back the shine!"

"It's unheard of for a girl my age to have ugly grey in her hair," Persephone said.

The girl rose quickly to her feet, the bowl clutched tightly to her. "I'm to tell Night that you're awake."

Persephone realised quickly that this girl was her best opportunity to gather knowledge. She clearly didn't guard her tongue. "Why isn't Rue your healer? She was the best hearth healer for several counties."

"Rue is Night's granddaughter. Night is our Crone."

And with that explanation that explained nothing, the girl left. Persephone, aching with hunger and filled with foreboding, awaited the return of the bitter old woman.

She didn't have to wait long. When Night entered, Persephone forced herself to her feet, bracing one hand against the rough wall, determined to meet the old woman eye-to-eye. She would not be loomed over again. She raised her chin. "He said you would tell me about my magic."

"Eat." The old woman put a chipped bowl on the rough table, with bread and no utensil, and Persephone only barely managed to control her gasp.

Night had no forefingers.

Only scars remained.

Persephone focussed on the floor, fighting down nausea and panic. Only outlaws who had used magic for the vilest purposes suffered such a punishment. Without forefingers, the old woman's ability to focus her magic was greatly diminished, possibly destroyed, a punishment that was worse than death for most Magi. In truth, most ended their lives upon hearing their sentence rather than suffer the injury and live without magic.

What offence had a healer committed to receive this violent and irreversible retribution?

The bastard!

Her promise had seemed so benign on the surface. She'd known she would regret it. But a healer who had lost her magic for misusing it was hardly the person to be trusted with one's food. She glanced up and saw the woman's rheumy eyes narrowed in disgust. She knew what was in Persephone's mind, it was clear. A slow, vindictive smile exposed the gaps in her teeth. "Maybe I'll just take that back," she gloated, reaching for the bowl.

Persephone grabbed the bowl. If they wanted her dead, she'd already be dead. If this was a test, she didn't intend to fail it so quickly. She lifted the bowl and sniffed. She detected nothing more than the familiar scent of mutton broth and herbs. How many times had she been given just such a broth when suffering from a childhood illness? It was unsettling to be offered the same comfort by enemies that she'd received as a beloved child. Clearly the crone was the source of Rue's receipt. Bracing herself and all too aware that her stomach might rebel, she sipped it.

She tasted nothing rank or unpleasant. She sipped more, and her stomach clenched not in an effort to expel but in welcome to sustenance. She forced herself to drink slowly and placed the bowl back on the table after only a few swallows.

"Please," she said carefully, "would you tell me about my brother's child?"

Night whipped around and jabbed a misshapen claw at her. "You keep your Fury hands off my blood!"

"He has Fury blood, as well," Persephone snapped back. And then, softly, "I don't even know his name."

The old woman propped her disfigured fists on the table between them and leaned forward menacingly, wisps of white hair flying around her head. "He says I have to tell you about your magic. But I will tell you nothing else!"

Persephone shot to her feet. "Then tell me!"

"You were born with it, with more than you can handle, but then it got worse, oh I know, it got worse." The old woman leered. "On the day you got your woman's blood, it reared up inside you, and you've never been the same. Look at your hair, look at your hair and see it! It's crone magic, magic that shows in the white in your hair. You and your kind—you hide it out of vanity?" The old woman spat in the dirt at her feet. "That's what your magic is, and you never deserved it, and never less than now, may the goddess preserve us all!"

With that, the old woman limped from the cottage, and the door slammed shut behind her.

The sound of a key scraping and turning in the lock was the only sound that broke the silence.

Persephone clutched a fist full of hair in each hand and tugged until her scalp stung, tears burning her eyes, a scream threatening to erupt from her lips. Only the fiercest pride stopped it from doing so.

She was turning into a crone.

This wasn't magic.

This was a curse.

❦❦

Vespasian stood high above the camp, looking down at the fires glowing in the dusk. The wind whipped his cloak around him, tempting him to flight as if he were a hawk surveying prey.

Oh, to bloody well fly away and leave them all behind, to take his wand and turn the insolent chit who now slept in his cottage into a pile of smouldering ash.

It was one of many evils he could perpetrate, any one of which tempted him with an itch in his fingertips as they caressed the smooth wand he held so lovingly in his right hand. The wand that terrified her, as well it should.

It should curdle the blood in her veins.

He had been called a hawk in those hell-cursed days at Oxford. Being a hawk did not bother him. Being told he had a Roman nose had driven him to duel, because he was young and all too volatile about things that didn't matter. As much as he despised being named for and bearing the profile of a revered Fireborn honoured by those ancient invaders, it was not worth duelling over.

He forced those memories from his mind. On this night, he had problems that rendered his days at Oxford benign in contrast, even though his days at Oxford had been anything but benign.

It was there that the evil had been born, and with the evil, his power revealed.

No.

He could not let himself get distracted, not when he needed all his wits in the coming hours. Not when he had to handle her, to teach her beyond question that he was her superior in every way. Not when he had to bend her to his will, break her, and remould her.

He shoved away from the boulder and stared down at the cottage where she slept the day away.

He could snarl without being heard, could curse and swear, up here above them all. But he didn't. He held it in, as always. Swallowed it down. Tasted the rage simmering in his stomach and nurtured it, fanned its heat, relished its power.

The wind shifted, and he smelled hares roasting on spits. Every third night, they had meat, by his orders. Every night, a measure of rum or wine. Every day, full buckets and skins of water fresh from the stream above them. The crone watched over the cooking, but it was his orders that rationed food yet kept them strong.

Below him, they moved about in the gathering dark, all except Lysander, who sat under the twisted oak just as if he were still bound. In another man, Vespasian would have suspected bitterness and pique. But he knew Lysander itched to go to his sister and comfort her, to convince her that he'd meant her no harm. Time enough, and Vespasian would allow it. It was part of his plan, after all. And if he could trust anyone, it was Lysander Fury. The fact that Lys actually loved his sister would help him win her over.

Vespasian's anticipated the conquest that lay ahead of him.

He would finally put her in her place, where she'd begged to be. Only now, there would be begging of an entirely different sort.

❦❦

A throbbing rhythm vibrated through her body with every beat of the unseen drum.

She opened her eyes to darkness and saw the faint, flickering light dance across the dirt floor. It pulsed with the music, golden and vibrant, beckoning.

The air was scented with the tang of burning wood and meat sizzling on spits. Her mouth flooded with moisture as she crawled from her pallet to the wall and inched carefully along until she could peer from the corner of the small window.

Three fires formed a triangle in the centre of the encampment.

Around the campfires was the source of the strange music: instruments she knew from books but had never hoped to see or to touch.

Her eyes widened at the sight of a woman cradling a Greek lyre. It was clearly ancient, and yet as the woman's fingers flew across its strings, plucking and strumming with wild, rhythmic abandon, the music that filled the air was as young and fierce as a babe's first cry.

A lithe young man with flowing white hair played a fiddle unlike any she'd seen before, its shape strangely square and the bow that crossed it oddly curved, and yet she knew it from drawings—a crwth, an archaic Welsh instrument. Yet despite its awkward shape, it released a stream of molten melody into the night.

She knew that hair, knew it from her childhood, remembered the tiger riding on the back of her family's coach, the beautiful young boy with white hair and pale blue eyes who sported the satin uniform with such pride. She had not been able to run the fields with him as she had some of the other children of Erinyes Manor, for even though he was nearly her age, he already had a demanding job, and thus she had watched him from afar.

He had disappeared without a trace, and Persephone's mother had been distraught. But his own father had been strangely silent. Persephone had worried about the boy at night, wondering if he was safe, if he was having adventures, if he was captured by pirates, if he was dead.

She'd wondered what kind of world he'd found outside Erinyes Manor and had even prayed to Hera for his protection, this boy she didn't even know.

Could there be another head of hair like his, so pale a blond, with lashes and eyebrows to match? Of course there could, and yet…

Rue and Mr Jones were here in this group of traitors, and deep in her belly, she knew that this had to be her family's tiger, grown up.

Others played as well, swaying with the beat of the ever-driving pulse of the drum, the primitive cadence his fingers pounded across tautly stretched skins, a beat that drew her until she found him. Lysander's dark head was bent, and his black hair blew around him in the night breeze. His shoulders hunched oddly, his body curved and formed a hollow.

She caught her breath in a soft gasp when she saw the child in his lap, a laughing boy with hair as black as any Fury's, but where a Fury's hair would be sleek, this child's hair was a wild halo of tangled curls.

Her heart tugged with memory at the sight. How many times had she cradled against her father's strong chest as he played one instrument or another, never pushing her away or complaining at how awkward she made his movements. No, instead he'd crooned into her ear, "Feel it, my darling, feel it in your blood. It's your Gift from the gods, and you must take it in and then release it back to the heavens."

But never had Apollo Fury's music held such heathen magic, and the thought terrified her as she saw her brother swept up by it, along with his innocent child. The child threw his head back and laughed with a wildness that called to her as if he were her own blood.

He has Fury blood, as well, she'd said, and now she felt the fierce need to protect. She couldn't tell if he was sturdy or slight, his manner Fireborn or Earthborn, lost in the dark and in the folds of a child's dress as he was, but it didn't matter.

As she watched, Lysander arched his neck and threw his head back in a luxurious cat-like stretch without once losing the driving beat. Her eyes adjusted yet again to an even deeper darkness. She saw the woman standing behind him, curled around him, her fingers trailing through his hair and stroking beneath it to the bare skin of his neck.

Rue.

She had never seen Rue's hair in loose waves down past her shoulders rather than pulled tight under a servant's mobcap. Persephone stared, hypnotised, as the woman's body writhed gently to the music, her focus clearly on her husband and his part in it.

She had seen Electra's gentle touches when she and Sebastian shared public but tender moments. The subtle brush of fingertips across the back of his hand and his quickened glances in return. The tightening of her hand around his forearm as they walked, and the closeness of their bodies. Seeing such things had made her flush and need to look away, embarrassed to have witnessed what seemed to be private expressions of affection.

These public caresses should be obscene to any gently raised young lady. Instead, they made her ache more deeply for the loss of her

Robin, her love.

She fell away from the window and crouched in the corner of the hut so none could creep up on her and catch her spying. She wrapped her arms around her knees and buried her face in them, feeling the music build in her until it raised the hair on the back of her neck, feeding her magic.

With no food to fill her and no voices to soothe her, she was left the victim of the magic that swirled around her in ways she'd never experienced.

She hid alone in the dark, forgotten, it seemed, and lost, trembling with need she couldn't define, aching with magic churning to break free.

She almost—almost—missed the darkening of the light-pattern on the floor as someone walked slowly past the window.

But she didn't miss it, and thus, her chin was raised in challenge and her nerves hardened with resolve when the bastard Vespasian Jones towered over her.

❧ CHAPTER SIXTEEN ❧

The girl's need radiated from her, and Vespasian knew that if he had a shred of decency, he might feel pity. But he wanted her this way, desperate for what only he could give her. In one hand, he held a bowl of food he knew she could smell like hell's own temptation. In the other, he held a soft bag that dangled heavily halfway down his leather-clad thigh, the contents of which would send her reeling.

"Up," he ordered. "At the table."

She stared at him from her corner. She was barely able to contain herself. Her eyes darted to the window, not to escape, but to the pull of magic in the air.

He lowered to his knees without strain, grabbed her arm, and pulled her up smoothly. "At the table," he repeated. She fell into the chair but refused to meet his eyes.

He lowered the plate for her to see, to smell. Bread. Roasted rabbit. Boiled onions and herbs. All things that filled the night with redolent scent.

"You don't have to eat." He allowed his voice to go silken as he bent closer to her ear, gauging the amount of silver in her hair now that the magical glamours had faded. He marvelled that there was still more black than silver. When the change was complete, the powers she would have…

She turned away, but he saw her jaw clench with hunger.

"You may eat, or not. It's your choice and yours alone," he said.

Despite her weakness, she met him with defiance. "I require my tisane."

"Your people may think your power is something to suppress through sedation," he snapped, "but it is not. You must nurture it and learn to control it."

"Shadow magic?" she spat. "Something to nurture?"

So she knew the nature of her power? Well, that would make things easier in the long run. He only needed to demonstrate how urgently

175

she needed him to help her. "You don't trust me. But in this circumstance—" He trailed a leisurely hand through the air, indicating the small hut's interior. "—you have no choice but to cooperate. Now, will you eat or no? Pray, make your choice now, for if you refuse to eat, I have another task for you."

"Task?" she asked sharply, her voice as clear and crisp as the night air. "I will perform no tasks for you."

"Again, it's your choice," he said. He leaned against the wall in the deepest shadows with a private smile she would not see. He reached into his cloth bag and stroked the long neck, the throat… and when it was clear that she would refuse to eat just to spite him, he pulled it out so that the flickering light from the window caught it just so.

He heard her soft intake of air, the faint moan that was almost a whimper, her need was now so strong. "Your task—" He slowly turned the battered fiddle in one hand so that it made one fluid revolution. "—is to join your brother. You know you want to."

He watched with interest as she fought it. Her hand clenched in her lap, her body visibly stiffened with distress. "I have no brother in this place."

"Pity," he sighed, feeling little pity at all as she played into his hands. He placed it on the table just beyond her easy reach. "It would have done you so much good."

"How?" she grated. "How would it be to my benefit to play for you?"

"Your task was to play for yourself, stupid girl," he replied evenly. "You are the one who needs the music. Tonight, it's the only release you have. If you have a fraction of the intelligence you claim, you'll seize this as the lifeline it is."

He pushed off from the wall and whirled to the door and into the night and sat under the low, twisting branches of the ancient oak to watch.

🐦🐦

She stared blindly at the plate, waiting until she was certain he was truly gone and would not return. Then she tore at the rabbit, pulling flesh from bones, biting into the crackling skin and sucking it into her mouth, weeping as rosemary and salt flooded her tongue and oily meat slid down her throat, only half-chewed. Each bite whetted her hunger to a sharper edge, until onion and potato and bread were gone and her fingers dripped with grease, and through it all, she couldn't tear her eyes away from the fiddle.

She recognised it, of course... She had dreamed of it, of that nightmare night in Ordinary London.

And now that it was here in front of her, instead of hatred for its role in her nightmare, she craved its heft in her hands, its scratched and battered surface beneath her fingertips.

She craved the music it would play and the balm it would pour into her soul.

And she despised this man all the more for knowing her need, for knowing how to assuage it, and for using it against her.

That was the agony of it all. She didn't know what he wanted from her. Why had Lysander brought her here?

Until she knew the answers, no matter how desperate her need, she could not give in.

Tears stung her eyes, and she twisted her fingers and then bit down on them, hard, to stop from taking the fiddle. She staggered from the chair and turned her back on the instrument's enticement, desperate for the oblivion of sleep.

But she could no more close her eyes against the sight of the instrument than she could cease to breathe.

Instead, she fell into the corner again, with the security of walls at her back, and stared at it, felt every scratch and scrape on its surface as if on her own heart.

Once it had sung with joy, released its music like prayers into the air, but now the music was trapped within it.

She ground her teeth in frustration.

She could feel him listening, and if she played even a single note, he would win.

Worse still, she knew that if she played a single note, she would not be able to stop.

She couldn't be alone like this. She needed her mother, or her father, or Dardanus. She needed her potion.

She needed.

And instead, he tempted her with Shadows.

The music outside her window grew wilder, pulsing within her. The Shadows built within her, and she wept at her weakness. What made this music, this place, so powerful? What evil did it possess?

And why did she long to embrace it?

She trembled in her corner.

Finally, she rolled away from it and faced the dark, willing it to swallow her, to rescue her from temptation and need.

❧❧

Furys. They were the prophesied key to destiny, if they weren't his downfall first.

The music circled and spun, a vortex with Lys at its centre. His fingers on the tabour shaped the rhythms of the night as surely as his presence in the circle now formed the pulse of the encampment.

A presence and pulse that was controlled, of course, by Vespasian Jones.

Even now, when the musicians and dancers slowed in anticipation of a night's hard sleep, Vespasian caught the younger man's eye. All it took was a nod, and the rhythm increased. Behind Lys, Rue trailed her fingertips down his shoulder and nuzzled his neck, but Lys merely smirked and cocked his head, and the magic spun again into the night.

Lysander Fury had entered their ranks on the sharp-edged cusp of adulthood but with a confidence and cunning far beyond his years. His arrival had been stunning and unexpected—a young Fireborn aristocrat with every reason to be their enemy.

He'd joined in the most menial of labours, working side-by-side with them, stripped to pale skin, though his blue blood soon disappeared under sun-bronzed skin.

Vespasian had entertained no misconceptions. It was no egalitarian spirit that moved Lys to toil like a peasant, but a calculated effort to overcome the suspicion that greeted him.

He'd been exactly what they'd needed at that moment in time.

He electrified them with both suspicions and possibility.

The new king? The True King?

A spy? A wastrel bent upon seducing their daughters?

Was he here to save them or destroy them?

They'd turned to Vespasian for a verdict, but Vespasian treated his former Fury pupil no differently than any other member of their community. Lys was there because he chose to be. He had passed through the ancient wards on the outskirts of their lands. His intent was not sinister. He had even woven layers of Fury magic to strengthen them.

And if they had wanted to believe that the young Fireborn man was there to fulfil prophecy, Vespasian hadn't bothered disabusing them of that thought. Why should he? It might even be true, one way or another, though certainly not in the most direct manner they hoped.

Lysander Fury was no True King. But hope, after all, fuelled rebellions. If he never proclaimed Lysander their king, he couldn't later be blamed for their misplaced expectations.

And then, within weeks, Lys put all suspicions to rest. He'd won their hearts when he stood as husband to their Rue, even as her stomach swelled larger. At night, the camp heard him sing to her, his clear tenor soft and tender, as if she'd never been his family's servant and was not four years his senior.

And with the birth of the son, Night had lifted the squalling infant, still streaked with his birth blood, up to the goddess, her gnarled old hands steady and her voice strong with conviction. "Bless him, our mother, and bless his blended blood."

Blended blood.

More prophecy fulfilled. And the sudden idea had filled the camp with wonder and despair. Wonder, that the new king might be theirs, their very blood. Despair, that their wait and their fight could last years before this child was ready to take his place at their head and deliver them their future.

Again, Vespasian knew their hopes to be unfounded, and again, he allowed them to hope.

And now, four years later, the child squirmed from his father's arms and danced around the fire with Fury music in his blood and Earthborn spirit in his soul. Never had a child been loved so well by so many.

Vespasian drew to his feet. Memories plagued him this night, not least the memory of what had driven Lysander Fury truly to appear in their midst. And that memory drew him around the edges of the sprawled gathering, skirting his way through the dark, circling until he reached the hut where Persephone Fury still resisted the call of her desperation. Vespasian had felt her need from across the camp, and as he drew nearer, it throbbed in the air.

To resist this meant she was stronger than he'd ever suspected.

But she'd been too silent for too long, and now the need was his— the need to see her, to once again see the insolent girl who had been thrust upon him by prophecy and whom he would, at all costs, control.

He slipped into the hut and found the fiddle, still untouched. The food bowl was empty, save for bones. The girl was sound asleep.

He crossed the floor and stood over her, staring down at hair streaked with silver, at a thin blanket twisted around her restless body, at an upper lip beaded with perspiration as she trembled and slept.

He drew in a deep breath.

Impossible.

And yet... sleep she did.

She had denied the call, even as it moved within her.

Even with no drug in her veins to soothe her, she had prevailed.

He scowled, his rage coiling within him. Not bothering to be silent, he snatched the fiddle and swept from the hut, and catching Lysander's eye once again, put a stop to the music with only a look.

As the instruments faded to silence and they began settling into the night for whatever bodily needs were strongest—sleep, bladder, or loins—he settled back against the oak and watched the hut through slitted eyes.

He would get no sleep this night.

🦅🦅

It was all Vespasian could do to sit there, to watch the hut, to wait for her to break. She had to break. For break she must, if he was to remould her.

He sat and stared and fought the power within him, the power that coiled and demanded something unnameable. He shoved it down, refused to let it surface.

As he sat, staring across the cold embers of the fires, shivering in the cold of the night with sweat shimmering on his body, the entire thatched roof of the hut erupted in flame.

One moment there had been nothing. The next, fierce flames shot into the sky, an inferno.

And knowledge surged within him, equally fierce, equally hot, that everything was going up in flames. Everything, in the form of a wretched girl.

Then he was on his feet. He was running, flying across the campsite, stepping on coals—not cold, but burning, burning into his soles, into his soul—only to hear the shouts, the cries of horror, as the entire campsite came alive with fear of their great enemy.

Fire.

And just as he reached the doorway and blew it open with a fling of power that threatened to bring the entire structure down, Lysander sprang ahead of him and dived into the flames.

"Persephone!"

Rue's screamed, "No! Noooooo!"

From behind him, chaos.

Before him, a hell-image worthy of the Ordinaries.

He whirled, barked orders, his heart in his throat, his rage rising in his veins. He sprang forward into the hut, for the entire future was in this nightmare of smoke and flame.

Another fling of magic, and a swathe of smoke swept aside to show Lys with the girl, limp in his arms. The walls buckled and snapped with a loud shriek.

"Out!" he shouted. "Now!"

He stood in the conflagration with embers, flames, and sparks whirling around him, holding it all together through will and terror until Lysander had staggered out into the clear night.

But when Vespasian tried to dive after him, the world collapsed in flames around him.

❧ CHAPTER SEVENTEEN ❦

Smoke and cinder choked her. She coughed until she felt as if her throat was bleeding and her chest ripping in her body.

Fire. She had lost control and caused fire.

Two gulps of cold air were all she allowed herself before staggering to her feet.

Two gulps, not enough to clear her lungs, barely enough to clear her mind.

Around her, children cried, men and women shouted, and she saw the angry and frightened looks they shot her way as they went about the frantic business of dealing with the disaster she had wrought.

Half the cone-shaped roof had fallen, and she knew the other half would follow, but...

He was still inside. She wanted him to die, and yet, she felt an unreasoning fear that he might.

Men descended on the cottage, hoisting, prying, as buckets of water flew through the air, hoisted from one set of strong arms to the next, sailing between.

She took a step forward, but whether it was to help or to get a more intimate glimpse of his death, she could not say. She just knew she was compelled to return to the fire with a vicious need that drove reason from her mind.

Strong arms grabbed her. She felt hands grip her upper arms. She flung a wild fist out and felt the jarring impact all the way up her arm as her knuckles connected with Lysander's cheek.

He released her and fell back. She craned forward as Vespasian's body was pulled out, his shoulder gashed and burned where a beam had fallen across it.

Before anyone else could touch her—assuming they would even want to—she stumbled away into the dark forest, leaving the crackling flames and shouts behind her. She collapsed against a tree to vomit until there was nothing in her but pain, fear, and rage.

Her mind whirled with questions. How had she made fire? Was Lysander unharmed? What use did he have for her, that her enemy would risk himself to pull her out? And, most particular, why in the name of all the gods and goddesses had she felt compelled to dive back into those flames?

She sank to the ground, her back against a tree, weak and trembling.

She could walk away and they would not stop her. She could escape.

❦❦

She heard someone approach and saw that it was Lysander. Numb, she allowed him to take her arm, to lead her back to the encampment. Where there had been a cottage, now were partial walls, still smouldering.

Silhouetted against the flames, she saw him sitting, the centre of her nightmare. The crone leaned over him, pouring a steaming unguent over his shoulder, chanting. Persephone stared at the working of magic unlike any she'd ever seen, as the bastard gritted his snarling teeth and hissed, while his blackened, angry flesh was cleansed.

Her own shoulder ached in response. She wondered what it looked like beneath its bandage, whether her wound had been one of fire or one of slicing, and if this was the same magic the old woman had used on her. Was this Shadow magic? Was it even now in her body, in her blood?

And as she stared, transfixed, glittering black eyes found hers.

She froze, unable to breathe, and then, with a curl of her lip, turned away.

"She will stay with me," Lysander said, his tone defiant. "My sister stays with me."

"Lys." Rue stepped forward, her eyes slanted with suspicion. "Not with us, Lys."

Persephone stared from one to the other and blurted, "You let her call you Lice, like a common vermin?" To be called like an Earthborn Commoner was bad enough, but lice?

Rue sneered.

Lysander burst into laughter. "Come along, Imp."

She didn't budge. "Aren't you afraid of me?" she demanded. For *she* was afraid, her insides quivering with fear of what she might do next time she slept without anyone to watch her, without her potion.

"Do you trust me?" he asked gently. "Do you trust me not to hurt those I love?"

Her eyes filled with tears. "I want to," she whispered.

He drew something bright and shining from up his sleeve. Her silver flute, the one she'd played for the goddess, the one that had been in her own sleeve at the ball. "Play for me, Imp. Play for me, and all will be well."

The surge of magic from within her was gentle but strong. The need still called to her, despite the fire, despite the fact that she'd already let the Shadows escape to do their worst.

But Lysander, the brother who had betrayed her, took her gently by the hand and led her away from the chaos, into the dim interior of yet another hut. Rue slipped in behind them and slithered onto a pallet covered with soft rabbit skins sewn together, and then Persephone saw the child, already sleeping.

Rue curled around her son, wrapped her arms around him, her eyes catching a glint of firelight from outside and shining in the darkness as she glared.

The flute in Persephone's hand felt cold and hard, yet it thrummed with promise.

"Play," Lysander whispered. "You remember how."

She closed her eyes in pain and memory. Of course she remembered—dark nights with low, sweet lullabies, sometimes played and sometimes sung, sometimes by her parents and sometimes by her sister or brothers, lullabies that wove love and protection.

She had begged her mother for more siblings, feeling so cheated that she and Dardanus had never been the older ones, the ones who got to cast sleep spells.

She had released fire. She could have destroyed them all.

Lysander sank to the ground and pulled her into his lap, holding her as he'd held his child. He crooned gently into her ear. "I'm holding you, Imp. I won't let harm come to you."

Her eyes burned, and her heart ached.

His arms wrapped around her, and again, he whispered, "Play."

Yes, he had brought her here, and for that she could not forgive him, but he would not hurt her and would not let her hurt his family. If he told her to play, she would.

Aware that a sleeping child lay in the dark, one who was the first of a new generation of Fury magic, she lifted the flute to her lips and released bright strands of magic into the air. It eased the ache in her heart, and the pressure in her chest melted into sweet nothingness. Soon, all too soon, she felt herself drifting to sleep.

There was someone who loved her watching over her. Finally, she felt safe.

❧❧

They had wanted to empty a hut for him. They had wanted to find him a place that befit his position. But he couldn't bear the idea of walls. He'd endured the agony of cleansing, of burned flesh sloughing away and unguents that healed without soothing, and finally, of bandages, all the time refusing any other offers of comfort.

He insisted on straw piled beneath the oak. His vision was glazed with pain, but he had to watch over his people, to protect them from whatever ill intent the girl next chose to release upon them.

Night snarled angrily at him and forced a steaming mug into his hands, promising vile putrefaction should he refuse it. He knew within minutes that she'd laced it with herbs to force sleep upon him. He wanted to strike out at her, at anyone.

At the girl.

But Tern, small and wiry yet ever alert, took a position behind a fallen tree trunk. Bramble sank into a crouch near a newly built fire, providing another set of watchful eyes.

He finally allowed his own eyes to close, until the music began. He started with awareness. He was too weak and drugged to fight it, curse them all. If they'd all been soothed and warmed by the gentle songs Lys had sent into the night during Rue's times of distress, nothing had prepared him for the delicate tune that now floated in the air, silken and lovely and dangerous. Sleep, it sang in sinuous notes. *Sleep.*

Around him, movement slowed. Panic attempted to find purchase in his mind, to waken him.

Fury power, Fury gifts. He had needed one, and now he had two, but at what price?

Sleep swallowed him, despite his best efforts to fight it.

❦

He knew by her stiff spine and her raised chin when she emerged from the cottage that she sought him, and that she meant trouble. Her features drew into a fierce scowl as she strode across the open ground. She did not look at him or acknowledge his presence in any way, but he knew.

Her progress through the village did not go without notice. How could one not notice the wild tangle of hair, the grime smeared across her oh-so-arrogant features, the mud that smeared her dark purple gown? And yet, her bearing was that of a queen, as if she either knew not her appearance, or cared not. She moved through them without glancing in any direction, her gaze fixed ahead of her as if no twig, stone, or small child would dare present itself to trip her.

A confrontation lay ahead.

"Bram." The exertion of the single word sent a shot of pain through his body. "Get me up."

"Don't be a fool," Bram muttered from his place on the felled tree trunk that blocked the area from the rest of the village. His eyes narrowed as he followed the direction of Vespasian's gaze and saw her. "I'll cut her off," he said, unfolding his lanky limbs and rising.

"Get. Me. Up." Vespasian forced the words through gritted teeth. Bram looked unhappy but looked to Tern, and they got him to his feet, straw clinging to him from his rough bed. When he was standing, jaw clenched in pain, black spots flashing before his eyes as his body threatened to betray him, he hissed, "Leave us alone."

"You're mad," Bram muttered, releasing his arm.

Vespasian fell back, would have fallen over, but the ancient tree's trunk braced him, and he drew from its strength, leaning against it in a determined show of languid ease. "Leave."

Despite their obvious frustration and reluctance, the men faded into the trees.

She was only a few feet away from him when she stopped and met his eyes.

Her voice as prim as if she were at a bloody tea, she said, "I believe

I told you that I needed my potion."

She laid her outburst at his feet? She sought to make it his fault? He almost sprang for her throat, he was so astounded and enraged.

"When I don't have it at night, I lose control."

As if she'd merely pissed in the straw rather than burned up his home and risked taking the entire village with it.

"Which," she said, raising her chin higher, "is why I'm here. You claim you can tell me how to control my—" She swallowed, and her gaze flickered away as she seemed to look for the right words, then snapped back to him. "—my unusual sort of power."

"Your Shadow magic," he said precisely, enjoying the way she flinched. It took every ounce of his strength to stay erect, but he refused to let her see his weakness.

"I insist we begin immediately." Her stare was hard and cold.

She knew.

She knew that he was injured. She knew that he was weak. She was counting on that.

"You insist?" He sneered. "You are captive here, victim to powers you cannot control, and you think you can insist?"

"You refuse to give me potions. And yet you have more to lose than I do if I choose not to learn. You can't force me to play."

She twitched her filmy, filthy skirts into place as if preparing to leave. "I see you're unable to comply. Perhaps after I burn down another hut, or…" She glanced around the area. "There are a lot of trees. Large trees. It would be tragic if they fell."

She had felled trees?

He allowed himself one slow blink to clear his vision, a slow inhalation that—hopefully—betrayed none of the pain that laced through him, a slow clench of his right fist to stop it from trembling.

"So. At last you are using the wit and intelligence for which you would like to be known. You admit you know nothing, can do nothing without me, and thus, you are willing to submit to my will."

Her cheeks flushed red, and she closed her hands in white-knuckled rage. "I admit no such thing!"

He arched one sceptical brow.

"I admit that you have knowledge that I seek."

"You will submit to my will," he said, his voice low and silken as he watched her gnaw her lower lip in frustration. She was an open book, ready to be examined, page by insolent page. And still, she didn't answer. "Miss Fury, this is not a lesson you will learn from a book, or that you will learn by thinking. This requires you to open yourself to my tutelage, to open yourself as your brothers did before you—"

"You will not invade my mind!"

Which raised the question he had pondered for almost five years. Had he been unable because she had the power to block him, or was there some other reason his mind magic had failed? And which answer was more devastating? He thrust such thoughts aside and fixed his deathly glare on her. "It's not an invasion if you allow me in. And if you don't allow me in, I cannot teach you."

She whirled from him then, frustration rolling off her like thunder off a mountain.

As she walked away, his strength faded.

He had won a brief respite, time to heal, to regain his strength. He felt his legs crumpling, and he sank to the ground, his head back against the rough trunk of the tree, watching her retreat. Relief and grim satisfaction eased through him.

Until she stopped, pivoted back to face him, her face pale and eyes haunted, but her air as haughty as ever. "I will try."

She would try? Try to cooperate and give him access to her mind?

Long years of practice made it second nature to hide his triumph.

"But," she added, her voice thin, "we start now. Today. This minute."

And at this, he allowed himself a smirk and tilted his head in the most mocking of bows. "But of course. I am totally at your bidding." She took a determined step towards him, but he raised a hand.

He flicked a finger.

Bram presented himself, not bothering to temper the black look he aimed at the girl.

"Fetch Lys," Vespasian ordered. "Tell him to bring the book."

Her scowl returned. "You said the answers I seek aren't in a book."

"You seek my tutelage. If you are to benefit from my knowledge, I am also to benefit from yours."

As Bram loped off to find his quarry, Vespasian let his triumph colour the tones his smoke-rasped voice produced.

"I think, Miss Fury, it is time you discovered why you are here."

She stiffened but said nothing.

"First, however…"

She let out a sharp huff of air, her annoyance evident in every breath. "First?" she finally repeated, unable to restrain herself. "What now? How many requirements are you going to pile upon me before you do what you offered to do before I even asked?"

"At this time? Merely one." He curled his lip in disgust. "Bathe."

Her loud gasp drew attention from all within sight. Her fist clenched, and he watched it idly, wondering if she'd dare try harm him, and how many would stop her, and in how many ways, both physical and magic.

Cheeks flaming, she said, "That is a highly improper suggestion!"

"Still yourself, girl. I'm not offering to participate in the act. Your stench offends me. You will bathe, and you will return to me within the hour, ready to begin your first lesson."

An hour was hardly generous, considering the state she was in, but any more would give the appearance that he needed the time himself. Even an hour would grant him reprieve to regain some of his strength.

She could hide nothing from him. The tendons in her skinny neck were rigid with tension, and her hair seemed at the point of writhing yet again. Amazing, that hair. Despite the filth that coated it, silky strands of silver shimmered, perhaps her magic attempting to break through.

More questions to tuck away, more avenues to explore.

"Rest yourself," he finally snapped. "Don't you want to be clean? Or do Fireborn ladies prefer stench to submission, even though submission is only a matter of sinking into a bath of steaming water with an abundance of soap in the offing?"

The mention of hot water and soap brought a soft exhalation of longing from her lips, though her eyes were still wary.

He needed her gone. Now. Before he collapsed—or worse. "No one will see you who hasn't already seen your scrawny body," he snapped, unable to enjoy the sight of her folding her arms across her breasts in horror. "For the gods' sakes, give in and be done with it. Clary!" His barked call rang across the open green, and he saw the girl emerge from the seamstress' hut. "Take Miss Fury to the women's hut, and be quick about it. I haven't all day."

He wiped the beads of perspiration from his upper lip and waited for his man to return.

❦

"Miss!"

Persephone found herself being watched from a safe distance by the girl with mousey curls who had slipped her the message in Mrs Beauchamp's fitting room. Why was she surprised to meet the girl here? But now, the girl acted like Persephone might catch her on fire with a mere blink. Persephone glared at her. "You have something to say?" she asked.

Clary nervously tugged at a lock of her frizzy hair. "I'm to take you to bathe."

"I don't have time for that," she snapped. "I want my brother."

"Mr Jones told me to take you to bathe." Clary's voice broke with fear, but she remained firm.

Persephone crackled with rage, and in that moment would not have been at all surprised to ignite the girl, nor did she feel much inclined to restrain herself if igniting were to be imminent. Though it was the man she would want to ignite.

"He was in that burning cottage far longer than I was, and he has the nerve to question my scent?"

The girl took a few steps backwards but said with a none-too-subtle wrinkle of her nose, followed by an offended sniff, "Mr Jones is very particular. He was cleaned last night when his wounds were tended. Now, if you'll just follow me." She turned away without waiting to see if Persephone followed.

Her face was gritty, her hands grimy, and she couldn't imagine what the rest of her was like. Belatedly, she remembered the gleaming fall of hair that framed the man's clean-shaven features. Worse, she could even smell herself. "Wait," she demanded, and the girl paused.

Persephone cast a sidelong glance towards the oak tree where the former tutor now lay, his eyes closed, surrounded by men who were clearly caught in the spell of his powers. He probably had the entire village under his Dark thrall. This insistence that she bathe was not just insulting, it was also clearly a ploy to keep her away from him and exert his power over her.

Well, she could clean up faster than he could heal, and what's more, she'd feel more herself once it was done. If he thought treating her like a mere schoolgirl was gaining him any advantage, he would find himself mistaken.

"What about my dress?"

Clary shrugged. "My sister Clover can clean that for you, right quick."

Persephone allowed herself to be led through the village to a small hut. Children scattered at her approach. She noted with surprise the ring of ancient earthworks surrounding the village, wooded and eroding, but clearly once a line of defence. All the cottages were round and whitewashed, with conical roofs of thatch. They had clearly claimed an ancient hill fort and rebuilt it. The thought puzzled her, but she had no time to ponder, for they were at the door, where Clary gestured her inside.

Inside, a deep hipbath sat, already filled with steaming water, with a pot of creamy soap on a small table beside it. "Whose is this?" she asked, dipping a finger in and lifting it to her nose, relieved to smell the most delicately fresh hint of lavender.

"It's the women's. The men's is on the other side of the village."

She looked at the girl, startled. "You all bathe in this hut?"

"You didn't think we washed in the river, did you?"

For the first time, she noted that these rebels were remarkably tidy, as was the village itself, despite their crude living conditions. She pondered that, as she removed her dress and placed it in Clary's waiting arms.

After the removal of her chemise, Persephone examined the dirty bandage on her shoulder. Gritting her teeth, she removed the bandage and exposed a garish scar of pink, puckered skin.

"That sealed up nice and proper," Clary said matter-of-factly. "You're lucky Night agreed to heal you. It was nasty, but no more than you deserved, attacking Mr Jones that way."

"I'd been taken from my home." Persephone lowered her lashes in an attempt for sympathy. "I was dreadfully afraid, and he's so very powerful and frightening." The words almost choked her, but they must have worked.

"Aye, he's powerful, he is." Clary seemed very proud of that.

"And he's brought people here from all over. I hear by their accents. From Scotland, from the West Country, but most sound Welsh, like he is." When Clary didn't answer, she continued. "But that would make sense, as we are in Wales."

"You may think you're going to fish information from me, but knowing you're in Wales is hardly going to help you, is it?" Clary's smirk galled her.

"Might I have privacy?" Persephone asked, her tone chilly. But beneath it, she felt the satisfaction that her conjecture was correct. Knowing she was in Wales might not help her in this moment, but every bit of knowledge she tucked away was more valuable than gold.

Clary flashed her a dirty look. "I'll be taking this to Clover and then will be back in a trice. Don't even think of trying to get away." And then she was gone, with Persephone standing nude, wondering that such a warning was even deemed necessary. As if she'd wander without her clothes.

Finally, she sank into the tub with a relief akin to bliss, determined to enjoy what little time alone she had. It wouldn't take much to convince herself she was in her own hipbath, with these salts that were so close to those used at Erinyes Manor the scent made her ache. Eventually she took a cloth and worked soap into it, then scrubbed until her skin was raw, save the tender, fresh scar.

Clary finally returned to find Persephone staring at her fingers in dismay. Even after soaking followed by such cleansing, her nail beds were still lined with grime.

With an obsequious air, Clary handed her a small, sharp stick. "Unless you want me to do it?" the girl asked with a falsely-sweet tone and malicious glint in her eyes. Obviously she'd enjoy applying a sharp stick to Persephone's tender flesh.

Persephone fixed her with a cold stare.

The girl dropped the stick into the water and quickly hung the newly cleaned dress on a hook and then turned her attentions back to the chemise and stockings. With a soft murmur of spell-words, she swept her hand across their surfaces. Wafts of smoke and ash rose and hovered filmily in the air before dispersing. By the time she finished, the garments gleamed white. Even the pale blue ribbons at the high waist of the petticoat were fresh and pretty again.

Persephone sluiced water over her shoulders to rinse. The cooling rivulets danced down her skin and rolled off her nipples, causing them to pucker into tight nubs. Embarrassed, she folded her arms.

"I don't know where we'll find you more dresses," the girl said. "Any that are long enough to cover your legs decent-like, will swallow you up top." She lifted her own plump breasts as if calculating their size. "My dress would be both too short and too full."

Cow, Persephone thought bitterly. "I don't need any other dresses. I am quite satisfied with my own."

"But for how long?" the girl asked.

Persephone stood, dripping, waiting for the sheet of soft fabric to dry with. Her clothes looked almost as fresh as when she'd donned them for the ball.

For how long, indeed? A sennight, that was her bond. Beyond that, not a moment.

The hut's interior shimmered as her eyes filled with tears. Robin… where was he? What was he thinking? Doing?

Fierce knowledge surged within her.

He would find her.

Clary's narrow-eyed scrutiny as she passed her the sheet caused her to lower her eyes, lest her tears be seen and her weakness be reported. She rubbed her head angrily, not caring that her hair would come out tangled and matted. There was nobody here she cared to impress. She had only one need in this place and that was to draw as much knowledge from the bastard Vespasian Jones as she could. Knowledge of her powers, of this location, and of Jones's Dark goals.

She would return to London, and when she did, she would take a gift beyond measure.

The means of avoiding war.

CHAPTER EIGHTEEN

This time he didn't rise when he saw her coming.

The way he slouched against the tree trunk, one long, leather-clad leg stretched out and the other cocked, his knee pointing skyward, was both insolent and insulting.

And yet it pleased her, because she knew this meant he was too weak to stand to intimidate her, and she knew she had him at as much of a disadvantage as she could hope for. The fact that it was all her doing—the fire, his injury— no longer horrified her, since no one else had come to harm.

She walked towards him, aware that the sunlight dappling through the trees touched threads of gold woven into the fine aubergine, and her black kid shoes were more handsome and expensive than any in this village, and her hair lifted on the breeze, wild and untethered.

She knew everything about her appearance galled him. She galled him just as he galled her, simply by existing. That, too, gave her strength.

She walked up to him, so close that she loomed over him the way he had loomed over her.

She did not think he truly felt threatened, but her act was clear and deliberate. She knew he would recognise it.

"Thank you for your kind attention to my comforts," she said sweetly. "I feel very refreshed and most eager for my lessons."

He flicked his hand at the fallen log.

She backed away from him with a gracious nod and lowered herself as gracefully as she could, imagining how Electra might handle the awkward task of sitting on a log. She folded her hands demurely in her lap. "Before you begin," she said, taking control, "I have questions."

"Truly, I am amazed." But his sarcasm was wasted on her, for she refused to rise to his bait.

She met his black gaze and asked the one question that had haunted her since the old woman's pronouncement. "How do I slow that which is happening to me?"

That seemed to catch him off guard. Beneath the heavy fall of black-and-silver-streaked hair, one ebony eyebrow arched high.

She rushed on, "Or stop it. How do I stop this—this magic—from happening to me?"

His glare grew fierce. "You're brimming with magic the likes of which most people will never taste, and you want to stop it?"

"I didn't want it, even before I learned what it was. If you can teach me to control it, you should be able to tell me how to rid myself of it. I hardly imagine that you are happy I possess it. You should be happy to rid me of it."

His voice was ice. "Be careful what you say, for the gods and goddesses are listening."

"Is it they who cursed me? Am I supposed to be pleased that I will wrinkle and my teeth will fall out, and that it has already begun with my hair?" She grabbed a fistful of her hair and gave it a vicious yank. "As if the lot of women isn't already enough of a burden, now I'm to lose my youth and my... my—" Her fear closed off her throat. Would she sacrifice her ability to bear children, to be a wife, to live her life at Robin's side, Robin who had kissed her and—at long last—had seen her as a woman? Would she now have to tell him this foul truth?

"You are a disgusting, spoiled creature."

She clenched her hands more tightly. "How long do I have before I am fully changed?"

"Changed?"

"The old woman—"

"Night."

"Night," she amended, "said my hair and—" She refused to mention her menses. "—and other aspects of my powers are crone magic." He merely continued to stare up at her from beneath his knit brows. Her mouth was suddenly dry. "I want to know how long before I turn into a crone."

"You insolent little—" He broke off with a twist of his features as he raised himself higher against the tree trunk. His white shirt gaped open at the throat in a way that not even a worker of the lands around Erinyes Manor would allow around a lady, and she saw heavy bandages—far heavier than hers had been—beneath it. "You should be so graced by Ceridwen! Though any tribe so cursed to have you as its Crone would be despised by the gods, indeed! And think you to refuse this Gift, to fling it back at the goddess who so graced you?"

His disgust and anger rolled over her, but her heart lifted. "I don't have to be a Crone? I may not be?"

He lifted a strand of his own hair and sneered. "And you think I am turning into a Crone?"

So their hair being the same was not mere coincidence. "A man can have crone magic?"

"It seems I am mistaken," he said dismissively. "There are things you still need to learn from your books. Suffice it to say that you will keep your teeth and your complexion for many years."

"We do not have books on the Studies of Shadows in our library."

"Which is why your education is so woefully inadequate. You have relied on a deficient library—"

"It is not deficient! It's one of the finest in England! And the only opportunity I had for more knowledge was denied me, as you might recall."

"If there are no books on your magic in your much-vaunted library, it's because one of your foolish ancestors tried to cleanse his family tree of Shadows, despite the clear fact that Bardán Fury was a purveyor of the deepest Shadows."

She leaped to her feet, energy crackling from her fingertips and hair and—even her toes. She felt it in her toes! "Liar!"

"Lys, control your sister before I have to take matters in hand," he drawled, insolent and, had she not known better, bored.

She whipped her head around to find Lysander approaching, a leather-wrapped bundle in his hand. "Calm yourself, Imp. You're giving him too much."

"I give him nothing!"

"Other than the ability to send you reeling every time he wants to unbalance you?" He winked at her, and now she wanted to turn her rage onto him.

But as he handed the bundle to the man on the ground, she felt something clench in her belly. Those long, elegant fingers untied the leather lacing and unfolded the wrapping. By the time the book was revealed, longing awoke deep within her, and she found it difficult to breathe.

The cover was delicately carved wood, with patterns of twining vines and a leek in relief at the centre, with leaves splaying out in a fountain on top. Her fingertips were about to graze it when she realised what she was doing.

She was on her knees beside him, reaching to touch the book in his lap. She yanked her hand back and stared at him, too close for safety, and his black eyes bore into hers.

In her haste to rise she almost fell backwards into the dirt, but he seized her forearm. "Sit."

"No—" she began. He yanked, and she collapsed, sprawling.

"I said, sit. That is, if you want to hold it." His voice was low and seductive. Once again, he held something in his hands she longed for, only this time it wasn't magical need that welled up in her, it was sheer desire.

She adjusted her legs until they were curled gracefully to the side. Her slim skirts were not made for sprawling on the ground. Her mouth dry, she held out her hands and then pulled back and hurriedly tugged the gloves down her elbows and forearms and off her hands.

Again, she held out her hands—her bare fingers—and let out a soft gasp when he placed the book in them.

How ancient it must be. Older than the Latin volume she'd been asked to translate.

The wood was cool against her palms, worn smooth either by expert craftsmanship at the time of its making or by the hands that had touched it through the passage of time. Her fingertips charged with sensation as she traced the pattern across the front, traced its labyrinthine coils and knots and felt her breath grow slow and deep.

Finally, she lifted the hinged cover open and found the aged parchment inside.

The title inked in black and red and gold, centred on the page, was almost lost in scrollwork: *Ir Proffwydoliaethau ohono fe Myrddin.*

Awareness shot through her. For the second time in days, she was being handed a copy of the *Prophetiae*, but this time, the words weren't in Latin.

This volume was older, its pages thin and even more yellowed with age, the ink brown rather than black.

The words, Welsh.

Not Welsh as any would know it in this time, but an older dialect, as old as written words.

She turned to the first page. The letters swam before her eyes—some clear and others confusing and dizzying. Such an illogical language, spoken with aspirations that were rude to her ear. It was a language she'd never had reason to learn and thus had largely ignored, beyond the lyrics they'd sung together in various Welsh tunes.

And yet, the language hummed beneath her fingertips, beckoned to her, a challenge with power far beyond the mere Latin Cosmo had put before her.

The Prophecies of Myrddin.

Foolish, ridiculous, with the power to spill blood, rip apart families, and destroy their magical world.

She wanted to close the book and give it back with a contemptuous sniff.

No, she did not want that. Good sense told her to put it down, screamed at her to give it back.

But her curiosity, her intellect, urged her to turn another page, to look at these words that, if her eyes could be believed, predated the foolish Geoffrey of Monmouth by centuries. These words were, perhaps, his source. Words she didn't comprehend, but might, given enough time. Wasn't that one of her strengths, languages? Had she ever been presented a language she could not crack open like a nut?

She had not. Thus, as the Welsh text flowed from her lips as she read, her mind supplied the translation: *Woe to the Red Dragon, for his banishment hastens on.*

"This has already happened," she said. "The English King—"

"Celt," Vespasian Jones supplied roughly.

"—was the Red Dragon, the *Ddraig Goch*," she spoke over him. How beautiful to taste the words as they were originally intended, not rude at all as they brushed across her tongue. "The White Dragon was the Saxon invader. If these prophecies were truly written prior to the invasion—" She ran her finger down the edge of the parchment, pondering its age. "—then perhaps they were true prophecies, but they might just as easily have been written afterwards."

"They are true," Vespasian Jones spoke again, his voice rigid with offence.

"And how can you know such a thing?" she demanded.

The two men shared a quick, secretive glance, and she could only shake her head in irritation and turn another page, sucked into the words, even the ones that spilled into her mind without clear meaning.

Leaf after leaf, she turned, awash with this language she'd never heard, adrift on its gentle sea of strange sounds that made music from the inside out. She no longer attempted to understand but instead allowed the sounds themselves to sing to her.

Beside her, both men remained silent, tense, attentive.

And she allowed a soft smile to curve her lips, for she knew why they had brought her, to spill this book's secrets to them, just as Cosmo and the Duke had wanted her to do.

Foolish men, looking for new reasons to stage a war.

Looking to her to give them reasons.

And here she was, a mere girl unable to make the slightest decision about her own life, with the weight of the future in her hands. And he thought she would be too stupid to understand.

She let the music hum through her and knew it for what it was—power.

She didn't want to close the book, but suddenly it seemed the necessary thing, and so she trusted that instinct and did so. "Fairy tales," she said with a regretful smile. "But oh, such beautiful fairy tales."

"You understood it?" Lysander asked quickly.

She gave him a most serene smile. "Not all, but enough. I've seen this before, of course. It's all been translated before. It's all nonsense, and like all prophecy, only obvious after the fact."

"When have you read this before," her adversary asked smoothly, "that you are so sure it is, as you say, nonsense and a fairy tale?"

"Who knows?" she said with a shrug. "Despite your scorn, our library has many books."

"But it does not have this one."

"You surely don't claim to know my family's entire—"

"I know which books have been omitted, which lessons your brothers only learned because they had me to teach them."

She bit back an angry retort. The blackguard's gaze went from her to Lysander, watching them both almost idly, as he also gazed beyond them and into the village green.

"I knew," she said. "I knew that if you poured your knowledge into their heads, you also poured poison. And even so, the Fury blood was too strong for you. You only managed to find one son whose mind proved fertile ground for your noxious seed."

The look Lysander turned on her was filled with frustration. "Truly, you try my patience."

"I try *your* patience!"

Mr Jones stared intensely up at her, his chin resting on his joined knuckles, his eyes deep in shadows and yet gleaming with something she could only define, with great apprehension, as the knowledge she so desperately craved.

"Had you kept reading," he said, "you would have seen that the translations your Royalist compatriots gave you—"

She looked up, startled.

"—were incomplete. There is material here you could not have seen in any language. Pray, continue your examination."

Her pulse quickened, but she kept her eyes pinned on him without flinching. "First you will answer more of my questions."

His lips thinned with displeasure. "This is not a game, Miss Fury."

"Indeed it is not."

"Return the book."

Persephone tried to take satisfaction from the fact that her tormentor's voice cracked and his parchment-pale skin was beaded with perspiration. But all she felt at the moment of parting was a deep sense of loss when she released the ancient book back into his hands.

"What questions?" he snapped.

"Why me? Why was I given such a burden?"

His jaw clenched and an even whiter line appeared around his lips. With a movement as graceful as it was violent, he swept an acorn off the ground and sent it flying at her.

She deflected it with a flick of magic from her fingertips and then deflected another, and another, and then a handful all at once— "Stop!" she cried. "What do you think you're doing?"

"Testing you," he hissed, and then with evident pain and great effort, he hauled himself to his feet and barked, "Coal!"

When a dark, slender man approached, Vespasian said, "The stones. Now!"

"Vesp—" Lysander began.

But Vespasian cut him off with a snarl. "Bring her!"

🦋

An unholy energy crackled from his body as he strode ahead of her down the path, between lush, moss-covered boulders and gracefully twisting trees, with an occasional stagger the only indication of his weakened state. Behind her, Lysander's hand touched the small of her back.

Finally they broke from the cool dark shadows of the ancient woods and into an area open to the sky, a vast area of bracken and broom, gorse and heather.

And a stone circle in the near distance. At its far end stood a cromlech with a magnificent table-top stone balanced precariously on three others. Yet it couldn't be precarious. It had clearly stood this way for centuries beyond memory, back to the time before the new gods brought light and wisdom to these island kingdoms.

The path to the circle was clear and straight and beaten down, trodden for centuries by those who clung to the Shadows. Before her, Jones still walked as if drawn by the beacon of the stones, and she found herself staggered by the sheer force of will that must fuel him on this trek.

Only when she found herself standing beside him in the centre of the tall stones and turned to see the man, Coal, with a quiver of arrows on his back and a bow in his hands did the full panic begin to set in. "What are you doing? No!" She tried to move but found her feet stiff and unyielding, as if rooted into the earth.

"Your lesson continues, Miss Fury," Vespasian said, his voice roughened with fatigue and anger. He lifted a hand and let it drop, and with a soft twang, an arrow was flying towards her, faster than she could see, think, react—

She repelled it with a slash of her hand and gasped at the sense of magic that sprang from her.

Again, he signalled.

Again, an arrow flew.

Again, she deflected.

And then three in fast succession. She felt tears welling in her eyes, a sob in her throat, and still she deflected until the final arrow sliced the air, aimed at her heart, but burst into flames at her gesture and fell into the grass.

When it was clear no more were coming, she whirled on him and screamed, "How dare you!" She raised her hand to hurl magic, not at the archer, but at the man beside her, his eyes dark hollows in pasty skin.

He grasped her wrist and held it. "How dare you call this a burden!"

And then his grip loosened as he swayed, and he collapsed in the grass, and she saw the blood oozing from beneath the bandage. Men were running towards them.

Her feet were free and she could walk again.

Only she could not leave.

She could only stand there and stare at the burning arrow in the grass. "That makes it no less a burden," she whispered.

"Nor does it make it less a Gift," her brother said, taking her elbow to pull her away. "To think of the things we could have done to better prepare you for this day. Wait until Dardanus knows we could have used you for target practice instead of apples on rocks. We could have even used cherries on your head!"

"I-I could have been killed just now!"

"Why do you think he stood beside you? He would not have let you die." He gave her arm the kind of tight, domineering squeeze only a brother would attempt and snapped, "Stay."

His tone was overbearing enough to raise her hackles under ordinary circumstances, but at this moment she merely stood numbly and watched the circle of men surround Vespasian on the ground, Lysander taking the most prominent role as he leaned close in an exchange of tense words.

His brow smoothed in a way that seemed deliberate rather than a true response to the situation at hand, and he rose. "You'll live, you stubborn fool, despite your actions on this morn." Ignoring the older man's pained scowl and shallow breathing, he signalled the other men. "Take him to Night. Perhaps now he will listen to her when she tells him to stay abed."

Then he pulled Persephone under his arm and gave her a gentler squeeze, one born of affection rather than threat. "Next time, perhaps you should let him feed you the knowledge straight into your brain, my dear sister?"

He was saved from her bitter response when she was distracted by the sight of a woman running—not Night with her healing, or even Rue, but a woman she hadn't noticed before, blonde hair flying behind her and a strange bronze circlet around her throat. She shot a frightened, angry look at Persephone and only stopped her flight to the stricken man's side because another man grabbed her and held her back.

But from that moment her eyes, wide and worried, never left the still form of Vespasian Jones.

"Come with me," Lysander said into Persephone's ear. "They will care for him."

"What if he dies?" The words bubbled out of her as he led her farther across the flat hilltop to a spot where the earth fell away in steep, rugged cliffs, and a green valley spread below them. She stared, unseeing, at the vista he showed her. "Does the power he holds over you end if he dies? Because I want him dead, Lysander. I want him dead."

"No, my sister dear, you don't want him dead. Because if he dies, I take his place."

❧ CHAPTER NINETEEN ❧

Persephone tried to spin away from her wretched brother, but he tightened his grip on her upper arm.

"We need to talk away from their ears." Lysander led her to the far side of the circle, to the cromlech that overlooked the grassy plain slope that disappeared beneath gentle mists.

She felt the tingle and knew that the Ordinary world lay beyond those mists. But the cromlech itself—the massive table-top of stone with a small fire burning in the centre of the ground beneath it—gave her a strange kind of chill. She walked closer, but found herself unwilling to walk beneath.

"It won't fall," Lysander said with a chuckle. "It's been this way for centuries."

"Why is there a fire?"

"Ah, and that is unknowable. As long as there has been a cromlech, there has been a fire. Or so legend says."

She gave him a sceptical look. "That your Earthborn rebels feed with fuel on a daily basis?"

"Nay, sister. It burns on its own."

She backed quickly away and instead, attempted to go to the edge of the mists, to explore beyond. They called to her as strongly as the cromlech repelled her.

"Be seated," Lysander said as he hitched his own hip against one of several boulders beneath the canopy of aged woods.

But she couldn't stop, not until she saw for herself. She ignored him and cut away from the well-worn path, through the bracken, towards the mists.

"Beware the adders," he said casually. "This is the time of spring when they dance."

She froze, her mind circling wildly between scoffing at an older brother's attempt to control his younger sister through childish fears and the very real fear that he spoke the truth.

205

His low chuckle released her from indecision. She forced herself forward until another step would take her into the mists, where she felt the Fury wards he had woven into the warp of ancient wards before them. She glanced over her shoulder and glared at him, and he finally rose gracefully and brushed the seat of his leather breeches before following her.

"Hold my hand," he said. "You'll be fine with me."

They stepped into and through the mist, and suddenly, the world grew brighter, warmer, wider, more terrifying.

Behind them was the cromlech. Before them the earth sloped away into a flat plain bounded by mountains on three sides and water to the west.

She inhaled deeply and realised the vague scent that had tantalised her all day was salt. Salt air.

She'd never seen the sea before.

"This is how I came," he said softly, pointing to the east. "Vespasian had told me about the village, but to pass through the wards without being escorted was… unprecedented. I crossed the valley and kept my eyes on these stones. I climbed until I reached them and the mist reached out to me."

"You journeyed through the Ordinary world?"

He winced. "For days."

"But Papa would have taken care of everything. He would have—" She broke off, remembering her father's words and how disturbed she'd been by them. She couldn't form the words that would dismiss his wife, no matter how base-born she might be, and his child. "If you come back now, they will welcome you."

"Hush, Imp," he said softly, his expression incredibly sad as he peered to the east, towards home. "I can't go back. Maybe someday, but not now."

"You've no understanding of how much we miss you, of how much you are loved, and what we would do to have you back." Her need to convince him was so strong, she felt lost in it, floundering. If only…

"Your son belongs at Erinyes Manor," she said softly. "He is a Fury. It's his home, his heritage. You belong there. Not here, chasing after a madman who could get you killed for treason, but with your family. Please, Lysander, please—choose your family. Choose us. All of us who love you and are ready to love your wife and child."

She didn't realise she wept until he used his sleeve to wipe her cheeks dry. He pulled her close and held her as she calmed. Only then did he finally speak. "Imp, I already made my choice." He turned his back on the view. "I'm here."

She pulled away. "What has he done to you? What did he tell you, promise you? What lies and poison?"

"You're so sure it's poison?"

"Did he steal you away in the night, too? Did he take you off to Ordinary London to... to—" She broke off. She still didn't know why. "Why did he use us in such a way?"

Lysander's laugh was easy and smooth. "For the coins, girl. For the money. Remember what Papa says, there is no such thing as Ordinary music or Ordinary gold. If you want to understand why, come back to the village, and this time, read what he gives you. Read it."

"If you already know what it says, why did you need me?" she asked bitterly. "Why did you bring me here?"

"We know enough for me to know what is right, but not all."

"And how could you know enough—or know anything—if I am your only hope for reading it, and your need for me is so urgent that you must snatch me away from London and my Season?"

"Vespasian knows he is right because the goddess told him."

Her heart raced. "Which goddess?"

"Elen of the Ways, our goddess and yours."

The Ways across the worlds and between them...

"My goddess spoke to me in the Basilica of Apollo. She is not a goddess of Shadows and of commoners!"

But if she was so sure, why had she fled from that goddess? Why had she flung herself at the mercy of Hera and refused the voice that called her, refused to claim it as hers?

His grin was slow and triumphant, and his eyes were lit with wildfire. "You think that Elen couldn't enter the basilica of the usurpers? The goddess who was here before them and never left, even when our people abandoned her? My dear little fool, and you tell me she actually spoke to you?" He shook his head in disbelief. "You've been wandering lost when the light was shining down and showing you every step of the way! You prayed the perfect prayer but to the wrong goddess—you prayed *Neimein* to Nemesis!" He said it as if not quite believing it himself. "That prayer, your plea that Vespasian Jones would get his due, was answered. It was you who sent him what he was due, what he needed." He paused and then said, "It was you who sent *me* to him."

"You're mad! I sent you nowhere! You promised to help me and instead you left and... and they thought it was because of Rue, but it wasn't, was it? It was to follow him!"

"They?" he asked sharply. "Who knows about Rue?"

"Father! And Cosmo! And... and the duke, of course. It is he who knew first, that you married and that you have a son."

His eyes glittered with an emotion she couldn't name as he took in a deep breath and then released it. "How long have they known?"

"I don't know. Not long."

"And what else did they say, pray tell?" His words were clipped and cool. "What did Cosmo say?"

She wasn't sure how to answer, what would be fair for him to know and what would only be cruel. She stared at the ground, her cheeks burning. "They would welcome you back. All of you."

He stared into the distance, and then, suddenly, as if the subject of family had never arisen, said, "Vespasian was given a prophecy and a power and a responsibility beyond what any single man could fulfil. The goddess Elen brought me to him to help him find and bring forth the True King. You wanted him to have his due. My darling sister, be careful when you bargain with gods and goddesses, for they do listen, love. They listen."

This time, when she tore away from him, he didn't attempt to stop her. This time, when she headed across the flat plain, she was running. And because she was running, she almost stepped on them.

Adders.

Coiled together, their upper bodies raised as they danced their deadly dance where her foot was about to tread. She shrieked, flung herself backwards, and fell into Lysander's arms.

Her heart pounding, she couldn't tear her eyes away from the serpents with their black and silver patterned bodies twining, coiling, and then—with a quick flip—rolling together towards her.

Lysander pulled her out of the way, steadying her. "I warned you, Imp," he murmured.

She scanned the entire area, looking for more, fearing more.

"It's what the males do," he said, "the way of the world, two males fighting for the right to take the strongest female."

"Strongest?" she scoffed, proud that her voice was almost steady, even if her pulse was not.

"The smart ones do, yes. They seek the strongest, the most clever."

"Then it's fortunate for me that I'm strong and clever rather than beautiful. My dance card will always be full."

He released her then. "The adders won't bother you if you don't go stepping on them. Just watch the path. They like the gorse and the bracken, and this is the time of year when…"

"They dance," she finished for him.

"Yes."

She walked towards the forest, but she couldn't cross the wide open bracken quickly enough. Once reaching the trees, she glanced back to see Lysander still standing there, watching the battle between serpents play out before him as if it held answers to some unspoken question. She shook her head in disbelief. This brother of hers, who sought out Dark company with the sort of men who sought power from the Shadows, and who found a pair of snakes battling for supremacy fascinating rather than alarming… Did he have a desire for death? She shuddered as a sudden chill rippled through her. She plunged into the cool darkness beneath the canopy of twisting oaks.

I already made my choice. I'm here.

Her hands trembling, she found a split in the path that took her away from the village and drew her deeper into the woods with a winding path and a tangible sense of safety, almost a beckoning. She went faster, seeking refuge from those who sneered and glared at her, whose dislike for her ran bone deep, who resented her and everything about her.

She had to get away from the brother whose madness caused him to blame her for his own Dark deeds. She had not sent him to the bastard, whatever he might claim! And no goddess had done so, either.

She had much to ponder and needed relief from pushing and prodding.

When she broke into a deep green glade, she could have wept with relief. Instead, she stood and stared in wonder. Never had she seen such a place, a place out of myth, with moss-covered rocks and boulders beneath low-hanging branches of trees, with a gurgling brook twisting its way through its centre, waters tumbling from one rocky pool to the next, sometimes frothy with foam and in other spots glittering like the facets of emeralds where sunlight filtered through the trees.

It was a place of peace. She could do naught but sink to her knees in a large patch of grass and seek relief from her distress, as a gentle breeze rustled the leaves overhead and kissed her cheek with the softest of benedictions. The velvety moss looked soft enough to sleep upon, but not the hard, smooth rocks and boulders beneath. She laid her head upon her outstretched arm, the grass beneath her seemed soft and cool. She found herself drifting to sleep and was grateful for the release from the world.

She dreamed of a liquid voice whispering in her ear

Persephone, my child…

❦❧

Blinking away darkness, he realised that they were attempting to take him into a hut. "No," he snarled, "Not here. Under the tree."

"Night said—"

"I don't care what that old woman said. Do as I…" He lost the words in the pain.

"You forget yourself," Night spat.

"I forget nothing," he thought he might have said, if she could only understand his mumbling.

"You forget your place."

He clenched his teeth, swallowed, and listened to her giving orders. "I have to watch—"

"Fool. You let the girl see you weak. That cannot happen again."

"Take me under the tree. I shall be strong enough by the time—"

A rustling in the room, a familiar scent. He struggled to sit up.

"I'm here," the gentle voice said.

"No!" he growled. "Get her out!"

"Enough!"

Pain exploded in his shoulder, bringing the release from consciousness that his weakness had merely dangled as temptation.

❦

When Persephone awoke, she was not alone. She jerked upright, staring at the familiar-appearing man who sat cross-legged a respectful distance away, his expression attentive but not menacing. "Why are you staring at me?" she demanded.

He shifted to touch his forehead, as if doffing a nonexistent cap, and she saw the quiver beside him, the arrows, the bow, and realised he was the archer who earlier had been firing arrows at her person.

She stood quickly, her feet braced, prepared to protect herself.

"No, girl, I'm not goin' to hurt you." His accent was rough, but his tone was calm.

She remained standing.

"I never shot at a girl before," he said thoughtfully, staring up at her from his spot on the ground. "I just wanted to tell you that. I don't make a habit of it. No need in you bein' upset over it all. Vespasian can be severe-like, to be sure, if you not be used to his ways."

"You say you won't hurt me? What if he tells you to shoot at me again?"

"I'd shoot, plain as you stand there."

"Then how can you—"

"He wants you too bad to hurt you. If he says shoot at you, it's because he has a plan, and that plan doesn't include hurting you. That's all I want you to know." He rose slowly, the quiver still on the ground. "But if you'd like, I'll show you how to shoot."

He was lean, his skin dark as a nut from his outdoor life, his hair brown and tousled, his eyes narrow and his mouth wide. But when he flashed a smile, his teeth looked white against his skin, and he had a certain amiability that allowed her to relax, just a little bit.

"Why would I need to learn how to shoot?" she asked.

"I didn't say you be needin' to. I just said, if you'd like."

"What would I shoot at?" she asked, suspicious of his intent.

"There'll be no shooting at me, if that be your thinking." He scowled at her, and she saw the twinkle in his eyes.

Without warning, a bit of laughter bubbled up, and she covered her mouth but couldn't stop it.

His mouth cocked up on one side.

They both laughed.

She couldn't remember the last time she'd laughed so. It seemed like her world had been consumed by tension and unease. But here she was laughing with a dark Welshman who had been shooting arrows at her heart a short time prior.

"We have to leave here. There's no shooting arrows in this place."

"Where are we?" she asked, gesturing at the glade. Would he reveal knowledge that would help her escape?

"*Y cysegredig on,*" he said with a shrug and a tone of surprise, as if she should have known.

The sacred grove. She should have known, indeed. "How far does it reach?"

"As far as needs be."

"If I keep walking, how long will it take me to cross it?" she asked, not willing to let the subject drop.

"As long as it be supposed to." This time, he smirked.

"I think I'd like to learn to shoot," she said, smoothing her skirts. She allowed him to lead her back out the way she'd come, casting one last glance around her. She'd be back. And next time, alone.

She could hear voices from the village when he stopped and pointed to a broken stump in the distance, as tall as a man and as wide around as a whisky barrel, with a number of arrows clinging to it at odd angles. "*Y targed.*"

The target.

"Aim it over there."

She chose not to tell him that she'd been using a bow since she was ten years old. It didn't take him long to figure it out, however, when her arrows found their mark on the tree trunk more often than not.

"And if I thought I was going to get to put my arms around a pretty girl to teach her to shoot, I was mistaken, is that it?" Coal asked, teasing gently.

She stared at him, at a loss for words. Her first instinct was to hand him back his bow, his arrow, and withdraw quickly, politely, and put as much distance between them as she could.

He was mistaken, or worse, was sly, because she wasn't pretty and the fact that he thought he could use such words and not have her laugh in his face distressed her, because she was not some simpering female who would succumb to clumsy flattery.

And he was Earthborn. He was her enemy. He had fired arrows at her! And would do so again, by his own admission, if so instructed.

And he was not Robin. Only the strongest resolve kept her eyes dry at that thought, but it repeated itself, *You aren't Robin,* like a wild tattoo that echoed her racing pulse.

And yet a thrill rippled through her, a feeling of power.

And she found herself smiling coyly, averting her eyes. Calculating. Thinking of her sister.

"You flatter me, kind sir," she said, reaching for the words of flirtation that Electra would use, if the man had been her equal and not totally ill-suited. She glanced up from beneath her lashes. "Of course I would delight in your tutelage."

A wide smile split his face. "Take off your shoes."

❦❦

Dim light should have brought comfort. Instead, it felt heavy on his chest, weighing him down, making it even more difficult to breathe. Pain, agonising pain… Shards of pain pierced him, the weight on his chest threatening every breath.

He opened his eyes to find Lysander sprawled on the earthen floor, hands braced around his knees. "Coal…?" Lys asked pointedly.

"He knows what to do."

"And that would be…?"

"Ground her to the earth," Vespasian snarled. "Push her until she's spent her magic." And then, on a low purr, "Let her own power seduce her."

He closed his eyes. It wasn't as if all could be accomplished by the archer, but he could take the edge off for a short time.

"I could have done the same," Lysander said, his manner stiff.

Vespasian longed for the strength to hurl magic at him, to hex him, or worse. Would the insolent Fury dare question him, were Vespasian not flat with injury done by his even more insolent sister? "Leave!"

"The ritual is tonight," Lysander said nonchalantly.

"No."

"Night has spoken. Preparations have begun."

"Where is Lark?" he asked, his anger simmering despite the weakness, despite the pain.

"In Night's cottage, preparing for her sacrifice."

If he had an ounce of strength, he would stop them. If he had an ounce of fortitude, of integrity... He could not laugh, but the back of his throat ached with a bitter attempt.

"My sister is proving to be difficult."

He snarled, baring his teeth. "Your sister is the root of all our evils."

"I must tell her more," he said, his voice urgent. "I must show her, if she's to understand, if she's to help us."

"You claimed she would be pliable."

"Time has passed. I misjudged."

"You forgot she was an insufferable brat."

"I need to tell her more."

"No."

"You realise—" The Fireborn examined his nails. "—you aren't in any position to stop me."

"You realise," Vespasian forced through gritted teeth, "that once you have your way, that will change."

"Not my way. Night's. And—" The younger man narrowed his eyes. "—Lark's."

Vespasian turned his face to the wall. "Leave."

From the rustling behind him, it was clear that this time Lysander left.

☙☙

At first she'd been annoyed when he'd corrected her stance, her grip on the bow, the tension on the bowstring.

Arms around her.

Arms that were not Robin's.

Her feet found intense connection to cool earth, despite the distraction of a crackling dead leaf biting into her tender sole.

Around them flew a whirl, the merest shimmer, of Shadow.

She fought down panic and instead smiled up from beneath her lashes and said, "Is this better?"

"Elbow higher," Coal said, touching it gently to adjust.

She shifted, feeling her muscle tighten, seeing her aim grow steady.

But as he raised her elbow and she tilted her head to get a better eye on the target, she began to feel something similar to the feeling when she was first learning music, to feel it in her bones, in her fingertips, pulsing in the bow.

And her aim grew surer.

Her shoulders ached, especially the injured one. But it was a strange ache, a satisfying ache, an ache like she hadn't felt since her drills in the sedate lady-graces begun. It had been years since she'd held an archer's bow, since her mother had put an end to such pastimes.

You're stronger than I expected, he'd said. She hadn't been able to restrain herself from giving a very unladylike sniff. Years of practice on bowed instruments had built deceptive strength.

She felt alive, loosing arrows, watching as they hit the tree trunk time after time.

She felt like a girl again, a girl who didn't have to act like a girl, who could just do as she wished, without a thought to appearance. A girl who could run across the countryside with her brothers chasing after her, or who could climb after them out onto the old oak and cross the moat and dance in the moonlight.

Who here would care? And if they did, why should their opinion mean anything to her?

Joy coursed through her, joy and, again, that shimmer of Shadow.

She shivered in the warmth of the sunlight and nocked another arrow into place.

She released it and watched it zing straight into the heart of the target, the dead centre.

"Now, try this," he said, again, reaching around her, too close to be seemly, too close to be a man who was not Robin, and yet she allowed it and met his gleaming eyes with a smile because he had called her a pretty girl, and in this moment, she almost felt pretty. Not beautiful, of course. No plain girl with Electra for a sister could ever make that error. But this man had never seen Electra.

The way he looked at her made her believe that he truly thought her pretty.

And so she smiled and felt the cool earth against her feet and the warm sun on the back of her neck and the strength in her arms and the shimmer of magic and this time, when the arrow sprang it split the first one in half.

She crowed with laughter, with triumph, with exhilaration and delight.

Her laughter found an echo. Male laughter rang out across the clearing, laughter that cooled her delight, laughter she recognised without looking up from the quiver where she reached to pull another arrow free. With a movement like liquid, she had the arrow nocked and aimed before the laughter could break off, before Coal could stop her.

"What do you find so amusing, brother?"

"That he thinks he's teaching you, when I taught you everything you know years ago." He did not seem at all disturbed by the fact that she had the arrow aimed at his right eye.

Coal, however, grew tense, his gaze flickering between them uneasily.

"Everything you know," she returned evenly, "but clearly not enough, since he has taught me more in an hour than you taught me in your life."

"You've made your point. You could fell me with one twitch of your finger. But you won't, so put it down."

"Why should I put it down?"

"Why should you kill me?"

"Because you chose to betray me and all who love you. Because you stole me away from my family. Because—"

A loud squeal pierced the air, shrill and joyous, and with it, an explosion of dry leaves, a child arrived in the clearing.

"Papa!" he cried, raising his arms. Lysander scooped him up, laughing, then hoisted him onto his shoulders where the boy grabbed two fists full of hair and continued laughing.

"Not all my family." Lysander smiled indulgently, his hands on the boys' bare legs, sticking out of the child's dress he wore.

"Your point is made." Belatedly, she lowered the bow, her game ended. She had wanted to see those cock-sure eyes flinch, that poise falter. Such was not to be. Not this time.

"My son, Otter." Before she could voice her dismay over such a name for a Fury, he continued, "Otter, this is your Aunt Imp of whom I've spoken so often."

Aunt Imp? She wanted to protest, but she found herself lost in the child's dark eyes—a green so dark they were almost brown—and curly hair, the nose so like his Uncle Cosmo and the lips so like his Aunt Electra and—

Robin's curls and her hue, Robin's green eyes and her fair skin. He could be her own. She could have a child such as this. He terrified her.

She wanted to hold him.

His mother's blood, heritage, and influence should set him apart, make him clearly not a Fury.

It did not.

He calmed long enough to study her, his head cocked. "Aunt Persephone?" he asked, each syllable as clearly articulated as if Apollo Fury had raised him.

"Indeed," she said primly, handing the bow and arrow to Coal so that she could cross the clearing to offer him her hand. "I am your Aunt Persephone." And with that, she aimed a glare at Lysander, who mouthed, Imp, and grinned. "What an interesting name you have. Is it your only name?"

"Unless I get a True name," he replied, then grabbed onto Lysander's hair with a squeal of giggles as Lysander's quick jostle threatened to unseat him. He turned his large eyes back on her and asked, "Will you play for me?"

"What would you have me play?" She drank in his air, his confidence, and most of all, the easy affection he seemed to have for her, she who was for all intents a stranger.

"I play the flute," he said. "Would you play with me?"

With a fluttering of her heart, she answered, "I would be delighted when we return to the village. But for now—" She slipped her own silver flute from her sleeve and offered it up to him, where he sat balanced on his father's shoulders. "—you must play for me."

Eyes dancing, he examined the bright instrument carefully and then raised it to his lips. Clear and pure as birdsong, the childish air lifted to the sky. *Llwyn Onn*. Lilting and lovely. Her breath caught in her throat. Eyes filling with tears, she met Lysander's gaze and said softly, "You have no right to keep him from Papa, from us all."

"More than a right," he responded, his voice grave. "A duty."

"To whom?" she demanded.

Before he could answer the song ended, and Otter asked shyly, "Did you like it?"

"It was beautiful," she responded sincerely.

"It's Mr Jones's favourite."

That name, that hated name, spoken so lovingly by his childish lips.

He leaned precariously from his father's shoulders to return the flute and almost toppled. Lysander steadied him with a graceful stretch of his arm. But as he reached, his sleeve slid up his arm—

Exposing the tip of a wand.

The blood froze in her veins. Her fingers stiff and numb, she accepted the flute. "Ah yes, Mr Jones," she said, her words like chips of ice.

She pinned Lysander with a look, and the firming of his jaw as he adjusted his sleeve was more confirmation than she'd ever wished to see. What a sinister duty it must be.

"We shall play together later," she finally said, forcing a stiff smile and keeping her voice light for the child's sake. She gave a curt nod to her brother and the archer. She had to put distance between them to deal with the pain of loss, that this beautiful child whose music rang with such magic was already lost to her.

Coal snatched up his quiver to join her, but before she could dismiss him, Lysander stopped him with a look. "Mine, now."

"But Vespasian told me—"

"'Tis my job, now," he said. "Thank you."

His job? To stay with her, watch her? She watched Coal slip into the trees without using the path and suddenly understood his presence.

Any pleasure she'd had for the time she'd spent with bow and arrow in hand dissolved with those few words.

'Tis my job now.

Vespasian had sent him. Of course he had. She was a job, a burden, a duty.

She slipped her feet back into her kid slippers, lifted her skirts above the forest floor, and walked regally, following the sound of voices, of children laughing, of women singing in the distance.

She ignored the brother who followed her, his son chattering about the birds, the trees, the girl in the village who pulled his hair. She ignored the brother who called this village home, chosen above the family of his birth.

But as she walked, she memorised every rock, every tree, every twist and turn in the path. She would be leaving, the sooner the better.

CHAPTER TWENTY

Nearing the village, she slowed her pace. She would not enter such a place where everyone had been set to spy on her.

Well enough, she thought. She could spy on them.

She found shelter in the shade of an ash tree, continuing her alert perusal of everything within her sight. Vespasian Jones wasn't to be seen anywhere, but she was hardly surprised.

He'd been bleeding. Barely conscious. Alarming, if she'd cared, but she only cared that he still lived.

Activity in the village seemed normal, with laundresses working in the open over bubbling, soap-smelling cauldrons at the far end of the common, their strong arms bare to the sun and their voices raised in a song with a lyrical tune and bawdy words.

Several stone-walled enclosures held a few cows and horses, and chickens, dogs and cats roamed free. A few men stood round a mare tethered within one of the enclosures, examining her swollen belly, and a smithy hammered away at a set of glowing-hot horseshoes nearby.

The mood that hung over the village appeared as calm and agreeable as ever she saw at Erinyes Manor, with distinct threads of magic enhancing each activity.

And yet the tension was palpable. It overhung every movement, and despite their diligent attention to work that could not be ignored, tense glances were being cast at a cottage on the other side of the open green.

The Crone passed by inside the window, her gait slow and laboured. Persephone's stomach knotted as the blond woman who had flown to Jones's side when he was stricken came to the door with a heavy bucket and sat it outside, then returned to the dark interior. Finally, Rue hurried across the green clearly intent on assisting with the healing, her hair flying, her apron filled with dried herbs that Persephone had seen many a time in Fern's herb closet—nettles, yellow dock, and comfrey. She paused at the bucket and glanced down at it, her expression grim, then disappeared within.

One of the men who had guarded her earlier now took the bucket and, with a grimace, carried it near the edge of the wood where she sat frozen. He didn't enter, didn't see her, just poured the bucket's contents into the soil.

Persephone stifled the intake of breath that threatened at the sight of the bloody water.

When the man turned away, she forced her dry throat to swallow.

She would not think about the graphic evidence of Jones's injury. Instead, she would take advantage of his weakness and the distraction it provided. She would make her escape. And she would take with her the knowledge that would end this rebellion before it even started.

Her heart hammering, she imagined her favourite quill sliding across the surface of her mother's finest vellum, saw the straight lines and small circles and sharp angles take form in a far more effective manner than if she'd actually had a quill, ink and paper at hand.

It hadn't been difficult to detect that this village was built on the remains of an ancient hill fort, though forest had encroached upon it, cutting off its vistas. But the rocky summit overlooking the village provided the lookout needed against enemies, and there was no mistaking the layout, including the distinctive round huts that made a partial circle of one end of the village… she counted twenty-three of them, including the remains of the one she'd destroyed. They all had stone bases of varying heights, but rougher stone and fresh wattle-and-daub revealed where ancient foundations ended and new structures began. Their cone-shaped roofs completed the image, and if the rebels hadn't been dressed in modern clothing, she might have believed herself transported to an earlier age.

When she'd done her best to note every distinctive aspect of the village and the three trails leading into it—one from the summit overhead, one from the stone circle, and one that disappeared into the forest and appeared to lead to the sea in the West—she closed her eyes wearily.

She was so dreadfully weary.

"Aunt Imp!"

Her eyes flew open. She'd actually slept, to her chagrin.

The sun was lower in the sky; the laundresses and their cauldrons were gone; the pregnant mare stood alone, munching on a tuft of gorse.

And Otter stood in front of her, bent over double to stare at her face, giggling. "You had a nap!"

She rubbed her eyes and tried to straighten up, but he plopped down in her lap. The unexpected force and weight knocked the breath out of her.

"Otter!" Lysander called, and then he, too, stood there, towering over the two of them. "Come along. You can stay with—"

"Aunt Persephone," Otter announced. "I'm staying here until you come back."

Speechless, Persephone didn't know what to say. She stared at the tousled head in her lap, astounded that he curled against her, staring up at his father with pure obstinacy.

"Where are you going?" she asked numbly, wondering if the child expected to stay with her for minutes, hours or days, and with very mixed feelings about any answer given.

"To check on Vespasian. Come along."

She cautiously eased an arm around the small boy. "Of course you may stay," she said. If Lysander would prefer that the boy go with him, that was enough reason to keep him.

Lysander gave a stern warning and then loped across the green to the small cottage which, by now, must be getting quite crowded. Persephone felt her nephew nestle even more snugly against her. She sat there, afraid to move.

But no sooner was Lysander gone, than Otter jumped to his feet with a scampish grin. "I know what we can do!"

She'd known too many Fury males to trust that grin and those words.

But she had never known four-year-old boys, and thus, when he flung himself from her arms and took off running down the path from which she had emerged earlier, she was caught unawares. She flung herself after him with a desperate hope that she could catch him before he got into trouble.

His squeal of laughter was now familiar to her as she followed it through the woods. The path itself was also familiar, as it became evident he was headed back to the same clearing where she had practiced her archery.

When feminine voices greeted his, she hung back, unwilling to make herself known.

Otter had no such reluctance. "Will you let my Aunt Persephone play with you?" he asked sweetly, and she stiffened in dismay as she recognised the laundresses in their damp gowns and rolled-up sleeves, now equipped with quivers and bows.

One of them, a buxom girl with curling ginger hair, cast a look over her shoulder and their eyes met. The girl's expression hardened into a sly smirk and she tossed her head without speaking, then notched an arrow into her bow and let it fly—

And split one of Persephone's in half.

Laughter rang through the trees, and one after another, she saw her arrows split as these girls missed not a single shot and picked off her arrows one by one. Their muscles rippled beneath sun-browned skin and their movements had the grace of young, wild animals.

Girls. Women. More skilled than any man she'd ever seen.

And she thought she'd done so well and had preened under Coal's tutelage.

Otter grabbed her hand and pulled her forward. "Come! You can play with Vixen and Lily and Phlox! They'll let you. Sometimes they even let me!"

To resist would be to look weak. She allowed him to pull her into their midst. She lifted her chin, aware of their sullen reception. "This probably isn't a good time," she began.

"Another day," the ginger-haired girl said, ruffling Otter's hair. She tossed a laugh over her shoulder as she sauntered away. "We've had our fun, little one. We have work to do. But if you clean up the mess, I'll give you a sweet."

He was delighted with the prospect and took her quiver, which was almost longer than he was. He dragged it toward the target stump, undaunted.

"Yes," said another, carefully avoiding Persephone's eyes as she studiously rearranged the arrows in her own quiver. "We don't leave our debris in the goddess's forest."

As Persephone had? But it was Lysander who had interrupted her practice, and neither he nor Coal had mentioned the arrows.

Their animosity was evident in their thinly masked sneers as they took their leave.

Persephone stood stiffly until they were gone, cheeks burning. They had work. The meaning was clear. She was the spoiled usurper and had caused injury to the bastard they called their leader. She was despised.

Some part of her wanted to flaunt the fact that she read many languages, that it was her skill the men needed so desperately that they stole her from her sister's home. That she had more value than they did, not less.

But the scattering of splintered arrows that Otter was gleefully collecting left her feeling more inadequate than she had felt before.

Women and girls. And this was what they could do.

"Otter," she said softly, and when he turned his green eyes to her expectantly, she drew a breath and asked, *"Mon animal de frère vous a-t-il enseigné le français?"*

"Oui," he said, returning to his chore. "He does, even though Mr Jones doesn't like Papa to teach me that language. Why do you call my Papa a beast?"

"Because he is my brother," she said shortly. "Because he is a beast." And then, belatedly realising to whom she spoke, she added, "He is a beast of a brother, and someday you may have a younger brother or sister and you will be a beast, as well. But he is a very good Papa. You are blessed, sweet one."

She helped him retrieve the last of the arrows, a bittersweet pang twisting in her heart at the renewed thought that this child could be a child of hers and Robin's. And that if she were more ruthless, she would steal him and save him from this place and these people.

❦

A damp cloth covered his eyes. Any movement brought him agony, but he heard the movements outside, mothers calling for their children, supper being called, sounds of the nightly pause between work and play.

And finally, finally, the distinct scraping of boot against earth, the particular rhythm of the approaching footsteps and rallied himself to speak. "Lys."

"You sent for me?"

Finally, he could deliver the order that would allow him to relent. Finally.

"Drug your sister. Do not let her witness anything tonight."

"You told her you would not."

"I told her I would not dampen her power. This is to protect our secrets."

"Rue will take care of it. I don't want her anywhere near this place tonight."

"Good," he sighed and gave himself over to the pain.

❧❧

She sat in the deepening dusk, and this time when Otter climbed into her lap he felt… right. His soft, sleepy body snuggling into hers brought her comfort and pain. She could not allow an attachment to form, or else to leave him would tear at her heart.

And leave she must.

Her heart already had enough aches without compounding them, and thus, she'd made her decision. Upon waking in the morn she would demand a table, quills, materials to begin the translation.

And… the book. Already, she regretted allowing her fears to get the best of her. How could it have hurt to read it? To translate myth and fable for these deluded souls. Upon reaching her home, she would have information for Aubyn to stop this war before it began.

"Aunt Imp…" Otter's voice was sleepy, his face pressed against her purple-clad breasts.

"Yes, darling?" she asked, trailing her fingers through his hair.

"Why are Fireborn and Earthborn different?"

Persephone stopped and stared at him, at his lovely eyes, wide in question.

"My papa says they are just words, but my mum says they are different as night and morn."

"That's all your father told you? That they are only words?"

He nodded solemnly.

She felt annoyance grow. How like Lysander, to brush history and fact aside just because they were inconvenient.

"Well," she said, settling herself more comfortably, "It all started eighteen centuries ago with the Roman conquest of Britain..." His brow furrowed, and she took a breath and tried again. "The people who lived here in Britain were ignorant. Uneducated, I mean. Do you understand that?" At his nod, she continued. "They were Celts and they drew their power from the earth."

"Like we do!"

She winced. "They worshipped lowly gods. And then the Romans came, and brought the greater gods of Olympus, and the Fireborn religion they gave us." She circled her wrist on her forehead, and watched with a pleased glow as he copied her. "Many of those who lived here recognised the truth, and welcomed the new gods, but not all..." She groped for a way to make it clear. "For almost a thousand years the magical people fought amongst themselves, until the year 1066, when the true gods won. The true gods sent us forward with their powers, and those that had been here before finally had to acknowledge their defeat. Those who still worshipped the earth ran to the furthest reaches of the isles or fled to Ireland, and now all educated people—and most who are not—worship at the basilica of Zeus in Glastonbury, or the Basilica of Apollo in London, or at any of the shrines around the countryside to the true gods."

"We don't," he said, unperturbed.

"Exactly," she sighed.

His beautiful mouth stretched into a yawn. "My True name will be Arthur."

"True name?" she asked, bewildered.

"Yes, if I am the True King, my name will be Arthur, not Otter."

She clutched him to her, horror sweeping over her.

He was the one they thought to be their leader, their king? This innocent child was at the centre of their rebellion? "Who said that you are the True King?" she gasped.

"Papa says I am not. But the others, they say I must be..." Another yawn, and his head fell heavily against her again. "I think maybe I don't want to be Arthur, even if he wears a crown and carries a sword."

She rocked with him in her arms, her head spinning.

She had to stop this war.

🦋

And she was thus, rocking the sleeping child in her arms, when the blond woman stopped and stared and pointed, and then shrieked. "Take him away from her! She has his death upon her! Take him away!"

Before she could react, Rue swept forward and snatched her child.

"You can't believe that!" Persephone was surrounded by faces filled with fear and with loathing, and it was clear that they did believe, they believed it very well. "I'm not bringing death. It's your evil Mr Jones!"

Lysander pushed them all aside and pulled her to her feet and into the protection of his arms.

"Who is she? Why would she say such things?"

"Lark is our Seer," he said calmly, waving them all away and guiding her toward his hut.

"You don't believe her! Surely you don't believe I would bring harm to him!"

"Of course I don't, but this is not the night for me to challenge her."

"You're afraid of her?" she demanded, aghast.

"I respect her. And tonight of all nights… is not the night."

"I want to go home, Lysander. I want to go home."

"And I will take you home. Did you think I would bring you here without a plan? When you have translated the prophecy, I will return you to Erinyes Manor, and none will think a thing but that you spent a few days with your brother's family." He pressed a kiss to her forehead. "But now, I'll have Rue bring your supper. You need rest, Imp. Tomorrow, all will be well."

She tried to take comfort in his words, but instead felt emptiness where a child had lain in her arms.

🦋

The air was heavy with choking clouds of burning herbs. Lys would insist on infecting them with his Fireborn ways.

Night chanted in an ancient tongue not so terribly distant from Vespasian's native Welsh, close enough that he could follow her words as she called on Elen to grant them power, then croaked out praises to the herbs wafting their way into the heavens—mugwort to protect them from Dark forces, webgrade to protect them from septic toxins, lavender to protect them from ill effects.

A chill trembled through him.

He wanted to shout out his distress, to stop them.

He could not.

At Night's command, Lys had prepared to gag him, had threatened to spell his hands and feet to the ground.

And of course, none was necessary.

How could he require a coward's preparation, when on the other side of the green, Lark was meeting this night with utter calm.

How could he refuse what his Crone commanded?

And so he squeezed his eyes shut against the smoke and turned his mind to the one delight that soothed him: nurturing his hatred for the girl who made this necessary, whose existence was so vital he risked everything to save her from her own undeserved powers.

Whose continued obduracy, whose unmerited gift, required every fibre of strength he would ordinarily have at his disposal—and more.

Rage and hatred were so much easier to nurture than the ever-present guilt that clung to every moment of every day.

And then, through his pain, through his low-seething bitterness, he heard the women's voices in soft counterpoint to the harsh, guttural sounds from Night's throat.

They brought his deepest shame, and when this deed was done his contempt for himself would be amplified beyond endurance.

They came.

❦❦

As night fell, Shadows grew. She felt them deep in her bones.

The Shadows in this place were stronger than she'd ever felt before. They terrified her and sucked at her, plying her with tantalising hints of what might be if she allowed herself to succumb.

But this was something new, something different.

Magic was rising, the magic that knew her name and her soul, that drew her deeper towards depths she dared not explore.

Her fingertips tingled.

She squeezed her hands into tight balls and rolled onto her side on her pallet in Lysander's hut.

Otter's sweet breathing… that's what she would listen to.

Not the voices floating like webs of silk on the wind.

Not the shimmers of magic that seemed to rise from the earth at their beckoning.

Not the wet, muddy spot beside her where she had poured the tisane Rue had given her, lips pressed tight with distrust.

They thought her a fool, to drink from that cup?

And so she lay in the darkness, rocking in her distress, fighting the pull, fearing what they sought to hide from her, battling the fierce need to discover its secrets.

But how to feel the magic without succumbing? How to fight it and still learn? When she realized the low keening throb of sound came from her own throat, she broke it off and held her breath.

Who had heard? Who would come? She bit her knuckles until she tasted blood. And still, the magic rose.

❧❦

Lark stood in the doorway of Night's hut, her ephemeral gown transparent against the light of the bonfire behind her. Her hair hung loose, as it hadn't since she'd been the young girl he'd—

Not rescued. No matter how she saw it in her pitiful gratitude. He would never consider it a rescue.

Not when it was he who had selected her to begin with.

His pulse brought pain with every beat.

Think of the other girl. Cling to the rage.

Night raised her gnarled hands high and called out a ritual warning.

Three times, she called it.

Three times Lark refused to heed it.

At Night's bidding, she crossed the threshold.

If his descent to the bed of dried herbs and straw had been reluctant and angry, hers was filled with grace. She lay beside him, just beyond his reach.

Stay there, he wanted to snarl. Stay out of my sight. But he did not say it. He gritted his teeth against what he knew was coming.

Outside, a psalm rose pure and clear into the night as only Lysander

Fury could send it.

Inside, the heat and smoke built, and finally, even though he knew it heralded the beginning of the horror, he welcomed the approach of the water from the sacred grove's holy well, the ancient song that filled the night.

He welcomed it and the relief from his pain it would bring.

For without pain, with strength, he could better nurture his hatred.

He could better keep his guilt at bay.

⁂

No one came. Perhaps no one heard.

But then, her beloved brother's voice, the voice she heard in her dreams, rose with the magic, and she could not deny her heart and soul.

She stumbled to the open doorway of the hut. He sat on a log by a low fire, the strange harp in his lap, his eyes closed as his song called her, until to deny it would be to deny herself the air itself.

She spared no thought to the others. She gave no more than a glance at the men who carried buckets of water, at the women who trailed behind them, scattering fresh herbs on the ground.

She stumbled forward, the earth cold and welcoming beneath the bare soles of her feet. She found herself at her brother's side, her face wet with tears.

Without missing a beat or a note, he drew her to him. They sat close, souls bound by magic and blood, and though she did not recognize the song he sang, she lifted her flute to her lips, and her harmony wrapped round his melody until there seemed more than one voice, more than one instrument, until the music they made was far beyond the skill of two mortals. Such was their Gift, that together, even magic was too weak a word to describe them.

⁂

At the first note of the flute, the earth held its breath.

At the second note of the flute, the smoke was gone.

At the third note of the flute, the magic within the hut rippled.

He witnessed it all and recognised its source in the girl.

It made him hate her all the more.

❧❧

The air melted around her, like liquid it caressed her, like a balm to her soul and a solace to her heart. She existed for the music to pass through her. Such glory she had never known, so that even when the voice, the hated liquid voice whispered in her ear, *Well done, little one, know that you please me...* she could not stop. She did not want to stop, despite the Shadows that wrapped round her in the night.

❧❧

He knew what came next. He knew it, because it was *his* power.

His, and more than his.

It rose within him, rose like fire, like life. Lark lay beside him, as still and calm as death. If her gift to him was life, his was the taking of life. If her gift was strength, his was the stealing of strength. If her gift was adoration, his was the abuse of same.

And thus, when the dagger of bronze, traced with runes of silver and gold, was held high, it sang to him through the sound of the flute.

It called him. And when it descended and sliced with its precise razor's edge and Lark's scream split the night...

His spirit leapt in his breast and drank in the sound of rebirth.

Then finally, so near his ear he felt the cold, sweet whisper curl into him, the voice he'd longed for, waited for half a lifetime to hear...

Well done, little one... know that you please me.

And it spoke not to him, but to the girl.

❧❧

A scream split the night.

The music within her died, but the magic spun tighter, faster, stronger.

She was filled with horror, but she could not escape the enchantment. She did not want to escape it. Shadows embraced her.

A woman's scream.

Awareness penetrated the fog of melody as a scream tore at the fabric of the night itself, splitting the air and leaving ragged edges of pain. And as surely as she knew she breathed that same, pain-wrought air, she knew that she had fed the magic that caused that scream. She had joined in it, fully knowing that she played in Shadows.

A woman's scream.

She trembled. Her breath came in short, broken gasps. What had she done? What in the goddess's name had she done?

She turned her horrified gaze to Lysander, sitting beside her, his fingers still rippling across the strings of the harp, his pure voice lifted, sweat beading on his forehead as he worked the magic, strengthened it, more burden on his shoulders now that she had broken off.

Around her, tense eyes focussed on the hut where the bastard lay injured and the beautiful blond woman had gone arrayed in gossamer.

A tense hush held sway, as Lysander ended his music and all held their breath in fear and expectation, staring at the now-silent hut.

Whatever had happened there was part of her doing.

In an instant, she was running across the green, her bare feet finding traction and comfort in the soft, cool soil, in the bite of pebbles, in the tickle of grass—all sending life surging through her, life… life… life.

The air vibrated with life.

Despite the scream.

Because of the scream.

Behind her, voices were raised and heavy footsteps chased after her. But her anger was swift, her need urgent, her magic strong, and she dived through the door and into the hut and the horror that awaited her there.

❧ CHAPTER TWENTY-ONE ❧

It had been so long ago, yet it still haunted him with both the seduction of dreams and the horror of nightmares. So many years since he'd last felt this tension of surging strength and magical energy.

But this was different, terrifyingly and seductively different.

He thought he'd known power before, but he'd only known the whispered promise, the tantalising tease.

For now, on this night, the light within him was transcendent.

From the moment the flute's song took flight, any power he had felt in the past had dimmed in comparison as new sensation rose in him. This was what had been promised; this was promise fulfilled.

He wanted to hate her and did. If any knew how to hate it was he, who had honed hatred to a skill.

But hatred was too pure a description for this complex reaction brewing within him, feeding on magic she was spinning even as it fed on his rage.

That he should even need her was a canker on his soul.

Possessing her was sheer triumph.

And thus, he lay on the straw with magic spiralling through and around him, magic fed by Lark's sacrifice but fuelled and strengthened by the wretched girl's Gift.

He felt her approach in the ripple of the air and the prickling on his skin.

And with that approach, he sensed something new and alarming.

He drew on his newfound strength and rolled to a cat-like crouch, withdrawing into the shadows to wait, even as the women continued their urgent business, unaware of the approaching Fury.

When she appeared in the doorway, her dark gown shimmering with the residue of the magic she had wrought and her hair flying and coiling with her powers, his own powers leapt in response.

Wasn't this what they had been created for, to perform this magical dance, to fulfil a prophecy almost lost to the mists of time?

To take life and raise it to new heights?

But again, the rage that it was she.

And yes, her rage that it was he.

What twist of fate left him with his soul bound to such a creature as this, with her arrogance and her absurd youth and inexperience?

And yet, wasn't it that arrogance and inexperience that ultimately would be to his benefit?

His heart pounding in his chest, his fists clenched and pulsing with strength, he watched her.

He needed to learn her instincts.

He needed to learn her.

With such knowledge he could control her.

With control came conquest.

He didn't stop his smile from forming as he watched her survey her accomplishments with horror.

❦❦

Blood.

Skin.

A writhing body, bare from the waist down.

The sickening stench of burning flesh.

The beautiful woman, her abdomen slick with sweat, biting on a leather tether as Rue tenderly stroked her hair, and with an odd-shaped phial collected her tears.

The old Crone bent over her body. Her wand sizzled against tender skin as a precise, bloody wound burned and turned black.

The air smelled of blood, of burning flesh, of burning herbs, of—how did she know this, and how could it be?—life.

Vile and terrifying.

But life.

She swayed in the doorway and fought not to vomit, fought for the presence of mind to know how to stop this horror, how to help this screaming woman, how to atone for whatever heinous sin she had committed when she willingly played with Shadows.

The Crone raised her wand again—

The woman cried out in a deep, strangled rasp—

Persephone dived forward and snatched the wand from the old

hag's maimed hand. Snatched it and felt it pulse against her palm, as if even the wand itself protested her interference.

But—the torture would end.

"Stop her!" the Crone commanded.

A form took shape, rising from the dark. Strands of silver, catching the light. Eyes of flat onyx meeting hers. A strong, bare chest, pale like the underbelly of a fish. A purple, oozing scar on his shoulder.

His arm reaching—lightning fast—for a wand.

His weakness was gone. He pulsed with power.

She could do nothing to protect herself without risking everyone present, for what did she know about this stick in her hand other than the fact that it pulsed with menace?

She sprang from the hut and saw the circle of people, all ready to stop her. She raised the wand like a sabre. She was a girl with no knowledge of wands, yet the wand in her hand was enough to freeze them in fear.

She would not be stopped. She would not be caught.

She felt it again—the pulse of wood against her palm. Fear shot through her, and temptation, and power.

She snapped the wand in two. Flung the pieces. Heard a shriek from within the hut.

"Persephone!"

Lysander's voice sliced through the night, but she spared him no glance, and she ran—ran—

"Let her go," the hated voice sneered.

She plunged into the black wood, running blind. She couldn't stop, couldn't slow. The earth beneath her feet rose steadily. She was going up to the lookout over the village, to the mountain top—and once there, what escape then?

Her heart beating a wild tattoo in her chest, she pushed thought from her mind, she who craved knowledge, because knowledge would paralyse her. She could only focus on each step, not where they led her, as long as they led her away from the nightmare scene she had stumbled into and away from him.

Him.

He had let her go. He knew she was trapped.

What had happened to the injured man who had collapsed and then been hidden away all day, who should be beyond the ability to give her chase?

What had she done? What Shadowed ritual had she been part of that resulted in the woman writhing on the floor and the man radiating Dark power?

❦❦

So, he thought with satisfaction, she was all impulse and youth, without cunning or consideration. Raw reaction and energy and unheard-of power.

He flicked a glance at Night and tossed her his own wand. She snorted in disgust and caught it in a hand that was agile and deft, despite its mutilation. She jerked her chin toward the open doorway. "Stop her!"

She had felt the power, too. But of course she would.

"As you wish," he said. He paused long enough to stroke damp hair from Lark's face, to meet her blue eyes, relaxing into lassitude as the pain receded. "I have never deserved you," he said, "and never less than now."

Her soft smile was her only reply, and then her eyes slipped shut.

"The girl," Night repeated impatiently.

Leaving Lark to Night and Rue's healing, he snatched up his cloak. He stepped from the cottage and into the clear, cold night.

The women had played their part. Now it was his burden to carry. He couldn't fail. Not now. Not after Lark's sacrifice.

Tern stood at the foot of the lookout path, ready.

Vespasian waved him off, anticipation rising within him.

"She is mine," he said.

No one responded, not even her brother. No one had ever doubted it.

He slipped into the darkness, intent on tracking his prey.

❦❦

Slowly, the wood took shape around her, moonlight casting glimmers of light to paint patches of gorse and outcroppings of boulders with silver. The path before her switched back against itself, winding its way higher.

Nobody was following her.

She stopped, gulped in huge breaths of air, held herself still to listen. She stood frozen, waiting for any sound to betray the presence of another and heard nothing.

Only her own heart, her own gasps, her own terror pounding in her veins.

Why had she chosen a path to a place with no option except to turn and retrace her steps to where he lay in wait?

She took a step off the path and found the earth tingle beneath her feet in comfort, as if it welcomed her.

She eased her way through the brush, flinching at the noise of her passing.

And then, as if blessed by the air itself, the wind stirred around her, the leaves high in the trees begin to sway and rustle loudly as if a storm was on its way. She could move faster without fear.

Deeper, she pressed into the dark of the forest. With each step she took, her eyes revealed more to her, and she found her way narrow but clear.

She would escape, and she would find Robin, and her father, and those men who defended all that was right and good. She would give them the knowledge they needed to bring these people back into the light and to visit ruin on the monster Vespasian Jones.

To bring this youngest of Furys back to the family where he belonged.

The family that would not use him as a pawn, but would welcome him as a beloved child of music and magic and light.

And then she felt him.

Tendrils of Shadow, lighter than smoke, softer than a baby's breath, coiled around her and caressed her.

He was near.

Her heart thudded in fear, and yet... the Shadows filled her with want. With desire.

She closed her eyes and rocked, fighting the lure

A twig broke. A branch rustled. She stiffened, remained still, but she did not flee.

He was near.

And coming closer.

The Shadows spiralled at his approach, around her, within her.

She turned slowly and stared into the deep blackness where she sensed him, battling the urge to step closer. She caught a movement where moonlight did not venture.

"Do you know how many hours I pondered how to tempt you?" His voice was velvet, Dark and seductive and promising the forbidden. "I thought to offer you power… but I might as well offer candles to the sun. You have more power than you can command, and you're not tempted to use power over another."

Light against white hair, white skin, stark in the midnight hour, and not where he was supposed to be. When had he moved? She pivoted slowly to faced him once again.

"I thought to offer you knowledge, for isn't that what you always craved? I showed you the book and you trembled with desire. Knowledge… knowledge would draw you to me. I saw that, and had I been stronger, had I not been injured, it would have been enough, I think."

When had he moved to the other side of her, and how, without her knowing?

"Finally, I offered you what you are desperate for, what you need more than anything. Control. And you leapt at the chance, didn't you? But you delude yourself. You don't want to control it. You want to destroy it. Such a dilemma. How do I control you long enough to teach you control? How do I initiate you into the power so that you forget such thoughts, so that you reach for more?"

She realised she had taken a step closer to him, two steps, three… hungry for his next words. She froze, tried to remain still.

He spoke again. This time, his words came from behind her.

"The irony is, I didn't need to do anything. The power, the craving for knowledge, they devour you. The real temptation was already part of you… the Shadows."

The word pierced her.

"I could stand here and not say a word, and you would come to me. You can't resist it, can you? Our ritual drew you to us. All I needed to do was use the Shadows, and you would come."

She heard her breath, short and broken. She shivered with the cold as the wind whipped dead leaves around her feet. Her teeth chattered. She tasted snow in the air, April snow, not unheard-of, but rare. She concentrated on that—snow—and pushed the magic down.

When that didn't work, she thought of Otter and fought to see his face in her mind's eye, that face that hinted of a child of her own.

And when that didn't work, she called out to all that was warm and true and safe.

Robin. Robin. Something deep in her soul stirred, and she choked back a sob. She wanted and needed Robin. But deep within her, something wanted and needed what the bastard Vespasian Jones offered even more.

A cloak, heavy and warm, settled over her shoulders. She wanted to fling it away but clutched at the warmth instead.

A hand closed over her elbow and gently led her back in the direction whence she had come. She wanted to fight it, but she wanted to follow it even more.

Before they stepped onto the wide path, she stopped. Her mouth dry, her voice cracking, she asked, "What is the truth about Otter?"

He paused, clearly considering his answer carefully. "There is more than one truth. There is the truth that you will dismiss. There is the truth that you will believe. And there is the truth I can't share with you yet, possibly ever, because frankly, Miss Fury, I need you, but I don't trust you."

"How can I earn your trust?" she asked, because wasn't this the truth she would need to take back to London?

"You can't. Had this Gift been bestowed on any of your brothers, I would have trusted them."

"Cosmo belongs to the king!"

"Had this Gift been his, I would have trusted him," he repeated, his voice turned to steel. "Had this Gift been given to your beautiful sister, I would have trusted her."

She jerked away from him, stung. What was it about her that he despised?

"Had the Gift been freely bestowed to you, I would trust you," he continued. "But it was not. And that's what I didn't understand until today. It was never supposed to be yours. I would wager my soul on that."

Truth hit her without any need for explanation. Hadn't she heard this all her life, that she had stolen her brother's magic, that she had held his life hostage until she'd received all the magic her mother had to bestow to her two children, and finally, during the dark of the sun she had emerged, a squalling brat already bringing terror to those who saw her? And then, her brother, smaller and weaker, had slipped out behind her, just as the sun emerged from behind the moon, eclipse conquered by the light.

This was the story that angered her parents, but that the servants at Erinyes Manor told when they thought none could hear. But *she* had heard, for she was the girl who hid in the shadows and listened.

"Dardanus," she whispered.

"You want to refuse it? And now you seek to break the vow you made to me by escaping? Yet I should trust you?"

"You impugn my honour by suggesting such a thing. Do you think me so stupid that I would run up this path to escape, with no way down lest I leap from the summit, spread wings, and fly? Which is it you suspect me of, you blackguard? A lack of honour or a lack of intelligence?"

"Which would disturb you the most?" he countered.

"I have four more nights in this place whilst I am honour-bound to cooperate with you, and you are honour-bound to treat me with respect. I would remind you of your vow, as well! And I would have you know that I will not stay here a moment longer than necessary, so whatever work you have for me to do, present it to me quickly, while you have the opportunity."

"You speak with too much arrogance for a captive," he said, his tone dismissive.

But she refused to let him turn away and end this conversation without returning to her most urgent concern. "What about Otter?" she repeated. "How many ways have you doomed that innocent child?"

"That is an easy and simple truth. He is not the True King they wait for."

She snorted. "True King!"

"Prophecy is clear."

"Then let me see it!"

"That, Miss Fury, is why you are here."

This time when he used slight pressure to turn her down the path, she allowed it.

As they descended, she heard music and did not know whether to laugh or to weep. Her footsteps quickened at the sound of her brother's harp, and she blinked back tears of anguish and of joy.

☙☙

Where there had been darkness and the Dark, shadows and Shadows, there was now light.

Bonfires flared high, laughter rang through the crisp, clean air. Children ran the periphery of the green, sometimes taking a tumble and then leaping back up to rejoin the chase.

She stopped, frozen, as she saw relief and joy unleashed.

If she had thought the music was compelling on her first night, this night it was jubilant. A celebration, but of what, she could not be certain.

Lysander still played, but now Rue sat at his feet, leaning against his knees with her eyes closed, her face lined with weariness, but a satisfied smile on her face. Otter danced around them, twirling and spinning and laughing, and the years fell away, and she danced with him in memory and imagination. As a child, music had swelled in her until she would burst if she didn't twirl like dandelion fluff on the wind.

So many nights when they'd performed the wardings of Erinyes Manor, after all their people gathered to watch and sometimes add their magic to the procedure, she and the other children had been just like these, running wild in the night. Then she was back, standing at the edge of the village, trapped between dark and light, her chest swelling with the desire to be that girl again. To be the girl who was different but not yet frightening, to be the daughter of the Manor, not the Other, the enemy.

Cold rippled through her, and she realized she still wore the cloak. A quick spin and she saw he was no longer behind her but was ducking back into the hut where terrifying magic had changed her forever.

She flung his cloak from her shoulders with an urgent need to rid herself of anything that was his.

If only she could rid herself of his magic so easily.

She plotted a path to Lysander's cottage that would weave behind and between the rebel villagers without garnering unwanted attention. But before she could take two steps, a hand closed over her elbow, firm and sure, and she caught her breath to protest and found Lysander, his eyes somehow sad despite his smile. "My sister," he said gently. "One of my deepest regrets is that I did not get to dance with you at your ball."

Her breath caught in her throat. Her ball, could it truly have been only three nights before? Three nights and two worlds away. She had no words for him, for she certainly couldn't forgive him for anything that involved that night. She averted her eyes and pulled her arm away from him.

But this was Lysander Fury, and he did not accept her rejection so easily. He stepped in front of her and made a deep bow with such flourish, he might have been a Cavalier from a different age.

Her brother was nothing if not calculatedly dashing when he saw an advantage in it.

"May I have the honour of this dance, milady?"

The music had fallen silent. They were being watched.

She stiffened under the scrutiny. As he rose, he took her hand gently in his and pulled her into his arms. "They've never seen a waltz," he whispered. "Surely you won't deny them one of the great joys of life."

"A Fury waltz," she finished with a sigh that was half laughter, half despair.

She realised he was waiting for a word or a sign before he continued. In that moment, with the moon shining overhead and the wind whipping through the trees and all around them frozen in uncertainty, she felt every bit a Fury.

"Are any here able to play such an air for us?" she asked, her chin high in challenge.

He called out to the musicians around the fires and suddenly a lilting *Llwyn Onn* began. She felt a moment's anger. Knowing it was the favourite of their brutal leader was enough to pull her out of her brother's arms and yet…

It had just the right lilting rhythm. She felt her eyes filling with moisture—not tears, oh no, not tears, she would not cry, she would not, for this was not her ball and her family wasn't here.

Only Lysander, her beloved betrayer.

She wanted to simply melt into the music, to return to her home, that place of grace and beauty that had borne them both. So she nodded, and with the slightest of pressures on her back and hand, he swept her into the dance. He spun her in fluid circles and people scattered, until a wide path opened before them. Suddenly, Lysander tossed his head back and laughed, and what could she do but laugh with him?

This was not the graceful dance she'd shared with her father, but a wild and flying waltz that took all the grace of the Furys and fuelled it with his new, wild fire, and she could do nothing but fly with him, fly through the night as the stars spun above them and the music swirled around them, and they waltzed as none had waltzed before, dipping and twirling faster, and faster, and if any but they had attempted such, they would have tripped and fallen. But not Persephone Fury and her wicked brother, never they, for they spun like quicksilver and drove the music faster, and yet faster.

Until with ebony hair flying, dark eyes flashing, magic soaring, they waltzed until their breath was gone and all that remained was joy.

❦❦

He heard the shift in music but ignored it and continued his concerned assessment of Lark's still figure, until he was reassured that she slept, only slept.

Night sat on a stool nearby, watching, a fresh poultice ready for the wound and a weak draught of opium to help Lark sleep, should she awaken in pain.

He stood. Something about the music disturbed him, and he knew not why. Its cadence was subtly wrong.

He yanked the window covering aside to look out and see Lys and his contemptible sister waltzing.

Buggering hell, what next?

He slipped quietly outside to stand under the thatched overhang and watch his lieutenant flaunt his Fireborn origins.

And flaunt, they did. The girl with the dark dress and pale skin and hair flying like midnight and moonbeams around her face and the man with his contagious laughter, spinning with feet never touching the earth, as though they flew on Fury magic.

He gritted his teeth and watched his people stare in awe, as if they suddenly found themselves unworthy, for as never before they remembered that not just the girl, but Lys himself was of the Quality.

Vespasian knew a desire to fly into the midst of it all and tear the two apart, to stop them and punish them both—yes, even Lys, especially Lys—for bringing this unrest. These people deserved more than to be made to feel lesser by the man they'd taken in like a lost son.

And he would have—he would have acted and let all else be damned, had not he caught a flash of red as Rue stood, her eyes narrowed, and spoke to Turtle who nodded his balding head. With a subtle shift of rhythm on the drum in his lap, he brought the music to an end.

And the blasted pair didn't even notice that their performance had been stopped, not by their own design, but by deliberate action. Lys made a deep bow, and she responded with a curtsy, and eyes flashing. They fell back in exhausted laughter, oblivious to all around them.

But Rue was not oblivious.

She caught Vespasian's eye and at his unspoken agreement, stepped into the firelight.

ॠॡ

Persephone hadn't caught her breath when Lysander swung her out to the side again, her hand lifted high in his. He announced to their awestruck audience, "My friends, my family, at last I may formally present to you my sister, Miss Persephone Fury."

It took a startled moment for her to realise he waited with a smirk and a challenge for her to curtsey. Without hesitation, she swept her foot as wide as her skirts would allow and dropped low. She did her best to grace the dirt with a whisper-touch of her nose. She rose again, having accepted his dare with smug confidence.

But he wasn't finished. With a flourish of his free hand he

continued, "And now, my dear sister, you are finally, and officially... in the marriage mart."

She froze for a split second, long enough for Tern's familiar Welsh voice to call out, "I'll take 'er off yer 'ands, Lys, just say th' word!"

Sudden wrath warred with humiliation until she caught the expression in his eyes, the new challenge, the reality that this was not an idle jest he played, but a test.

At which point she steeled herself, flung her hair behind her shoulders and forced out, as bold as she could muster, "It will take more than a shouted offer from a coxcomb in the darkness to win my hand, sir."

Lysander broke the stunned silence with a shout of laughter.

Tern's figure took form as he stepped closer to the light, his teeth flashing white in the fire's glow. "That's a challenge I'll meet," he said with a grin.

"Alas, tonight, it is not," Lysander said smoothly, to her great relief, and she would have let it drop and mentally prepared the tongue-lashing she would aim at him later had she not seen the dark scowl on Vespasian Jones' face. In that moment, knowing that something about their actions displeased him, could she do aught but press for more? "And would it be such a bad thing if I danced with him?" she asked her brother in a low, curious voice.

"There are many worse things you might do than earn the respect and acceptance of Tern Trevarthan, as he gives neither easily, and where he goes, others may follow."

She had no desire to earn the respect and certainly not the acceptance of the people around her. She only wanted to flout the disapproval of the bastard.

She spun toward the archer, her chin high, announcing, "I would turn you down with much regret, if my brother's words held any sway over me. But, as they do not..."

The world became a blur of shouting and energy as she felt herself swept into the figures of a rough country dance she'd danced many times in the Furys' elegant ballroom, but never with such fierce abandon. Women held their skirts high, exposing lengths of shin and ankle no lady would dare, and more than one man snatched a kiss as he met a lass in the centre of the square before the steps split them up again.

To Tern's credit, he never took such a liberty, and she found herself slipping into the mood, almost able to join in the merriment, did she not still catch glimpses of resentment from the other women and of hesitancy from the other men who partnered her briefly.

It was not her imagination that as the rhythm intensified and the passions rose, such flashes of limb and such brazen kisses were often accompanied by taunting leers tossed in her direction, lest she think that her presence in their dance indicated any welcome on their behalf.

And worse—these were not decently gloved hands that grabbed at hers. They were bare, rough hands, broad and strong from work. Had there been even a brush of fingertips she would not have been able to stand it; she would have broken away. But it seemed these rebels did retain a shred of decency, and clasped hands were carefully palm to palm with those most magical and sensitive tips of the fingers left clear.

It was music. It was dance.

How her Fury spirit had longed to escape back into the wild night, ever since that first terrifying yet exhilarating trip to Ordinary London. And yes, she'd slipped out into the ancient oak on many occasions and breathed in the dark air, but this was different, this place where night came alive around the blaze of bonfires, where Shadows rose instead of fell, and where her brother thrived and laughed and loved and found happiness that did not include the family of his blood.

Spinning faster, breathing harder, she found herself more confused than ever. But if she accomplished nothing else, her presence in the dance provoked the man who stood and watched with black eyes and mood. And that, in the final analysis, was enough to bring her a thrill of triumph.

The song ended, and without pausing, she spun away from the shouts and ribald laughter and fell against a large boulder at the edge of the green, fighting to catch her breath.

"Will you dance with me, Auntie Persephone?"

"My sweet nephew…" She dropped to the ground, her back pressed against the rock, and stared wearily into his large, pleading eyes. "I would be honoured."

"Otter!" Rue's voice sliced through the night like a blade. "Come to bed this instant."

Persephone saw the look in the older woman's eyes, the distrust that had always been there, and now, a sharper fear brought by the foolish Seer's words.

"Tomorrow," she promised, when Otter looked as if he might protest, or worse, cry. "I promise."

She would fulfil that promise, if she had to wrangle a deal with Vespasian Jones to do so, for she felt such a deal would be fully within her power. She had what he wanted, and she intended to give it to him—give him anything, if only it meant she'd get to leave this place. But that didn't mean she wouldn't get more from him than he anticipated or would ever know, until it was too late.

With that, she lifted her skirts just high enough to clear them of dust and twigs and whirled away from the frantic music and dancing, and away from the man who loathed her, and whom she held in equal loathing.

❧ CHAPTER TWENTY-TWO ❦

Her dreams that night were disturbed by a rustling of leaves, by moans.

Unease trickled over her skin and through her to parts forbidden, rousing her from her restless sleep. She pushed the blankets from her overheated body. Glancing over to where Lysander slept with his wife and child, she rose and escaped through the door into the freedom of the night.

Beneath the heavy sky, her toes digging into the ground, she felt a thrum of connection to the earth and knew without a doubt that it was not escape she was seeking—she was being drawn to something.

She cast a quick look around. A guard sat at the far end of the village. He raised his head and turned to look straight at her. She stood stiffly, watching the silhouette of his long, bushy hair. She waited for him to call out, after a long perusal, he looked away. He must assume she was going to relieve herself. Her heartbeat thumped a ragged rhythm.

She heard the moan again. This wasn't something she heard outside of herself. Whatever was happening, she felt it *within*.

She lifted her face to air so cold, it felt as if it could shatter on her skin, but somewhere nearby there were rustling and moans, and it made her itch and heated her skin and filled her mouth with moisture and tickled her belly in strange ways.

She found the mouth of the path she'd traversed earlier in the day and stopped, lifted her face to the night, and though she could no more name a scent or sound than she could create them, they were there, beckoning her.

Chafing her arms against the cold, she hurried forward, ignoring the cutoff that led to the archer's practice field, drawn instead toward the narrow path to that place of moss and twisting oaks and green refuge, the sacred grove.

The moans were clearer now and made her tremble down to her

core in a way that the icy air did not, for this was a heated trembling, a melting trembling, as she watched the shadows move.

And then a glimpse of ghostly pale that slowly became long hair, white in the darkness—her family's old tiger.

The slow movement of his head resolved into the movement of kisses, trailing down a girl's tender jawline. She moaned and arched her neck, and he followed it down to the dip at the base of her throat... Her insides growing hot with confusion, Persephone realised they were naked.

In this cold, in this place that they thought holy, they were naked, rutting like animals.

Except... this was not rutting. This was something other... a sacrament.

The strong line of his back took form, the round curve of his buttocks, the long lean thighs, straddling the girl as she moved beneath him.

Persephone couldn't breathe. Her mouth went dry even as she felt other parts of her throb, and she didn't understand it. She stood frozen, unable to move, unable to stop watching through still leaves that barely fluttered with her breathing.

She clenched her legs together, as she felt the tingling grow, and fought to stand still when part of her wanted to move with them. Her eyes widened as he drew away from the girl and, after short, wet sucklings at her full breasts, dropped low on her body until his head dived between her thighs.

Persephone gasped. His face—his mouth—was down there. And only their own noises and gasps kept them from hearing her. The girl arched off the ground and grabbed a fistful of his hair and... By the gods and goddesses, she'd seen dogs sniffing and licking each other's parts, but not people, surely people didn't do such things.

The girl threw her head back. What started as a low whimper grew to a keening, hoarse and frantic, and coursed through Persephone like sound become sensation. She felt it from her tingling scalp through tense muscles all the way down to her feet, clenching and unclenching in the frigid, wet decay on the forest floor.

She tried to make sense of it, and even caught a glimpse of his cock, stiff and white in the night. She put her hands to her lips, swallowing the sounds that threatened to come from her own mouth.

They were beautiful.

Persephone wanted to scorn her own romantic notions, but they moved together like silk, and they almost glowed in the dim light.

Like dancing, floating stars drifting down in benediction, snow began to fall.

He rose over her, and in an act that left Persephone quaking, he plunged between the girl's open thighs and she cried out with a laughing gasp, like something holy.

Holy.

Somehow, deep inside, Persephone knew they did not feel the cold because they had been blessed, and these fragments of icy lace dusting the April night were proof.

She stood shivering, pressed against the rough bark of an oak, and tears stung her eyes. She felt the pain of loss, that she was not in that grove, under that sky, warmed by a goddess and graced with snow.

She had to look away, could not watch more. She dug her fingers into the bark until pain blurred her vision and then, heaving in a deep breath, forced herself to turn.

Only force of will wrenched from the hatred she bore for him stopped her from screaming when she saw the bastard Vespasian Jones leaning against a rowan tree, arms folded, his lips twisted in a sneer that even darkness could not hide.

She forced herself to swallow, tried to slow her thundering heart.

He cast a long, lingering glance over her shoulder and she covered burning cheeks with icy hands, determined to walk past him. Only at the very last moment did he ease out of her way and allow her room to pass. She no longer cared if they heard her. She took off down the path, twigs tearing at her hair, a small branch whipping across her face.

She took the path back to the village, back to Lysander's hut to lie in the dark and shiver and try to clear her mind of all that she'd seen. But a rough hand closed over her mouth, another over her shoulder, and she was yanked back.

"Come with me," he growled.

The snow barely pierced the heavy canopy of new spring leaves, but now that she was aware of the cold, she felt it from her bare feet to her fingertips that tingled not with magic but with numbness. She clenched her fists as he dragged her, and her stomach suddenly clutched in fear.

How long had he been there?

How long had he been watching?

What if he thought that she would want to do those things?

What if he intended to make her?

She wrenched free, and even if the hand she flung at him and the fingers she pointed at him were trembling like aspen, she dug down to find the strength to defend herself.

And again, he sneered. "I don't even need to pierce your mind to read you."

She gasped for air, but did not relax her stance.

"Don't delude yourself," he said, his disdain evident in the set of his shoulders and the angle of his head as he glared down at her from his superior height. "Your arousal at the sight of what was supposed to be a private matter is puerile and disgusting."

He couldn't have shocked her any more if he'd slapped her. Worse, this time his barbs hit home. She should never have gone to the sacred grove, and once there, she should never have stayed. Her cheeks burned with mortification.

"I would return to my bed," she said, fighting for dignity and finding none.

"Answer my questions. Why did you come to the grove on such a night?" Before she could think of an answer, he asked the more pointed question. "How did you know to?"

This was part of her curse that he called a Gift. This awareness of what was happening. The need to follow the beckoning until it was too late, when she was caught in the spell and unable to move.

She didn't want to tell him. And yet, he had said he would teach her. He had said he knew of her Shadows and could teach her to control them.

She raised her chin and said through chattering teeth, "It woke me. They woke me."

He cocked his head. "You felt them? You knew what was happening?"

"Not what—I didn't recognise the—" She refused to use the word 'sensations'. "I didn't know what it was, but something awakened me, and once I felt it—" She cringed at the word 'felt' and prayed he didn't understand her meaning. "I had to go. I was drawn. I had to follow."

The snow was coming down harder, and now it even dusted the ground beneath the trees.

"Why?" she asked, determined to at least learn from this horrible night. "Why would I feel it and—and why would they do such a thing in your holy place?"

"As if holy places have never been used for such things? Surely your education has not been that inadequate." His derision was tangible in the air between them.

She snorted her frustration. Of course the Ancients had used their temples for such activities and had even incorporated carnal acts as a form of worship, but not civilised people, not the Magi of London in these modern times!

He took pity on her. "They're using the grove for a private ritual. Had you not sensed them, none would have known. If ever there was a night when they wouldn't be stumbled upon, it should have been this one." He raised one languid hand, its fingers long and starkly white in the darkness, as if to catch the snow.

"But they're too young!" she protested. "I know that boy!"

"You are not in the protected realm of Erinyes Manor and pampered Fireborn aristocracy, Miss Fury," he said, his voice rich with barbed irony. "In this world, the world where the Quality never venture, girls already have children at your age. They have taken a man to be husband. They aren't polished to a fine sheen and dusted with magic and paraded before the worst of Society's dandies in search of a wealthy husband. They aren't cosseted and spoiled and—"

"Your point is made!" she snapped. "And now, if you will allow me passage, I must return to my bed. It will soon be dawn." She turned sideways to edge past him, and if he didn't make her passage easier, he also did not stop her.

When she'd put several desperate yards between them, she suddenly stopped and spun and called back, "I will be ready tomorrow to do your translations, and once they are done, I would have my lessons. I am weary of this place and am ready to finish our bargain so that I can return home."

Without waiting for his answer, she hurried back to her bed in the straw.

❦❦

Until she disappeared, swallowed up by the night and all it foretold, he could not breathe.

He wanted to rail against her for her impertinence, for daring to set her own terms.

He wanted to rail against the fates that had cast this demon child into his path.

He wanted to rail at anyone or anything other than the deity responsible, for even he did not dare question the very goddess he so yearned to please, to see again, to hear again. Tonight he had heard the goddess speak to the girl with words of tenderness and praise, not to him.

He whipped his cloak around himself and trod the path he knew like his own heart, which would take him back to the stones where he had collapsed only a day before.

He stepped out of the forest and onto open snow-covered ground, unnaturally bright in the darkness. He stood, feet braced wide.

At the moment of healing, at the very moment when the small glow of life that had been released from Lark's belly found its way into him, his soul had leapt.

At that moment, when the magic spun fast and brilliant and beyond their ability to control, he'd felt another's pulse beat with his own. He'd tasted another's joy as if it were his own. He'd heard the goddess call another, *"my child"*, as she had once called him, and he had known that something horrible had happened. Against all expectation and foretelling, the girl's magic had joined with his, and tantalising promise had been fulfilled. There could be no doubt that she was the one he required. And like all gifts from the gods, he now knew what an unforgivable price must be paid.

❧ CHAPTER TWENTY-THREE ❧

The hedgerows towered above them as they rode, heavy white clusters of hawthorn blossoms filling the air with the scent of death. Robin wondered that the Ordinary folk lined their ways with faery trees and bad omens, but perhaps they did not know. He only knew that he, not usually a superstitious man, would feel better when they'd left this narrow road with its darkly aromatic sentinels behind.

"Hades senses water," Dardanus said, and indeed, the gelding already wanted to prance ahead of his mare, but the young man controlled him much more efficiently than Robin would have ever dreamed when they first began this journey. Hades was always the first to scent anything new, which made the gelding a valuable companion in this world that was not their own.

As the road turned, they saw the narrow opening in the hedge and the well-trodden path through it. Just wide enough for a mounted man to pass through without thorns scraping him or his horse, it was not wide enough for two horses side by side. But there was no doubt that this was the direction Hades chose, with his nostrils flaring and his prancing growing more difficult to control. Thus Robin rode through, but Dardanus dismounted and led both his beasts.

They were startled to find three young girls gathered around a high stone wall that had water burbling out of it and into a pool beneath. The girls looked up, clearly afraid. One gasped in a breath, as if to scream.

Dardanus stepped forward, his boyish smile shy and winning. "Please, don't be afraid. Our horses are thirsty, and we've a long way to go before nightfall."

As easily as he had calmed the horses, his voice and manner calmed the young maids. They neither ran nor shouted an alert. They still huddled nervously, though they kept interested eyes on this handsome young male.

Robin hung back, the better to mask his other-ness. It had not been

257

difficult to decide that Dardanus, with his decided lack of magical aura, would best serve their purpose by speaking to the Ordinaries when they could not avoid it. And when it came to young females, his grace and shy charm would have carried the day, even amongst Magi.

"This is a holy well," one of the girls said, "but we often allow our cattle to drink further downstream." She pointed a bit further away where a second pool formed without the benefit of masonry or lush foliage.

Dardanus doffed his hat again and smiled, then shot Robin a look. With a sigh, Robin took the horses downstream, with an ear cocked to hear the conversation he left behind. Damned whelp, more interested in flirtations than in finding his sister, or so it seemed.

As their horses drank from the lower pool, Robin angled his body to study what he recognised as deliberate ornamentation and plantings of herbs. He wondered if they carried some sort of religious meaning in the Ordinary world, so careful were the choices. The overhanging apple tree—sacred to Venus and Pomona, goddess of all fruit trees—shaded the water, whose depths were dark with algae and moss. The water's edge was dense with fern, and at one end, clearly planted by design, stood the graceful, drooping sword-like foliage of irises, with a single, late bloom of pure white glowing in the shadows, reflected in the rippling surface of the pool.

"I hope there was nothing about my appearance to inspire such terror," Dardanus said gently, again using that smile. Robin had yet to determine whether it was sincere or calculated. The young man was a Fury, after all, and they did seem aware of their gods-given charms.

And yet, there was something innocent about the youngest Fury, and even now it seemed the maids couldn't reassure him quickly enough, so concerned were they that they might have hurt his sensibilities.

"Please, sir, don't think we thought you a brigand," one said.

"It's just that—" another began hurriedly.

"It's just that—well, you know, the disappearances," the third rushed on and then covered her mouth and glanced at the others, and it was clear that their alarm was still present, not totally, though they did not seem to focus on Robin and Dardanus any longer.

"Disappearances?" Robin repeated, his brow creased with concern.

"Girls," the first one said. "And... and they never come back."

Robin felt an icy edge of concern.

Dardanus stretched out his hand, beseeching. "Please," he said, "we seek my sister. Have you seen a lady you do not know, who looks something like me? She is my twin, you see..."

But the maids drew closer together and stood stiffly, as if even hearing of the missing sister bore its own danger.

"I've seen no such lady," the darkest one said. "I hope you find her."

"We will pray for her," the youngest said, her voice earnest. "We will pray to St Agnes."

"Thank you," Dardanus said, swallowing his disappointment.

"If you have a lock of her hair...?" the dark-haired girl spoke suddenly, "An offering to the saint from your heart for your sister's well-being?"

It was then that Robin saw, caught amongst the foliage at the edge of the frothing pool, a small lock of hair tied with limp ribbon.

"You've lost someone," Dardanus said softly. "Tell us about her, and we will watch for her."

And the girls spilled over with words of a plump girl with blue eyes and sweet demeanour who had disappeared from her father's field as she sowed spring wheat. Robin stared at the limp, dark hair and felt a heavy awareness that she would not be seen again. He saw it in Dardanus's eyes, as well, in the tender way he listened, even as he grew tense with need to move on.

Dardanus caught Robin's eye and raised his chin in a manner so much resembling that of his sister that Robin had to blink away his pain. He gave the girls a slight bow and returned his hat to his head. "You must return home before it gets dark."

The girls gathered their baskets, and it was only then that Robin noticed they'd left offerings of herbs and a fat tallow candle in a niche in the rock overhang.

Prayers of protection, no doubt, but such would not save their friend from whatever perils preyed on young Ordinary females.

He was disturbed by his knowledge, but he did not question it.

He gathered the horses and led them back to the road, leaving Dardanus to follow.

Clearly they needed to find out more about these disappearances, the kinds of things that young maids could not tell them.

He reminded himself that there had been no such disappearances amongst the Magi and felt comforted. He tried not to think about the fact that if his instincts had been right, if the goddess was leading him, Persephone was not amongst the Magi, and the peril might include her, too.

🦋

As simply as that, the nature of their journey had changed.

It had begun as blind desperation and a mad gallop across the countryside on what seemed like a whim. He'd known, it seemed, as soon as they'd struck out to find her, that somehow he needed to go back to where it had begun—to the place that this strange girl-child had first claimed a piece of him.

It had been a moment of blind faith when he threw himself on the mercy of her goddess and had flung himself and his companion recklessly into the Ordinary world, where they set out wandering with nothing but the deep-seated conviction that he would be guided.

It finally became an act of blind obedience as they found that the path to a holy well, at the behest of Persephone's horse, was not an end to itself, but a beginning.

Robin wondered which goddess would give them such a guide, even wondered if he was mad to make such an assumption, but then, Hades was not just any horse, and the compulsion to give him his head was too strong to doubt. Since that night long ago, when their dangerous leap through an unopened portal between the worlds had left Persephone injured and unconscious, the bond Hades shared with his mistress and the magical blood in his veins made him a formidable partner. With quivering nostrils lifted to the wind, he led them from one holy well to the next.

The first holy well had been near London, but farther and farther west they went, the horse's manner seeming more driven, more certain with each furlong they travelled.

And thus, with a strange certainty that they were somehow right,

Robin and Dardanus continued to put their faith in the beast.

There had been wells with stone benches or well-tended gardens, with pilgrims come to pray and dip their ailing limbs or bodies. Wells with colourful ribbons fluttering from the overhanging oaks or ashes or lindens, where young maids had tied their prayers for husbands.

There were crutches, wedged in rocks or brambles or laid lovingly beside the flowing waters, proof of the lame who could now walk. Even without knowing the saints they prayed to, it was easy to divine what gifts the saints bestowed.

There were candles, flowers and offerings, and sometimes, written notes on twists of paper stuck in crevices.

And then there were the other wells, no longer marked or visited, yet just as holy, even more magical, but somehow abandoned by the Ordinaries and lost in time.

But not to Hades, who would snort and stamp and sometimes drink, sometimes not, but then would lift his head to the air once more.

When they came across Ordinaries, it was always Dardanus who spoke to them, who coaxed their problems out of them, who learned their petty or tragic reasons for visiting the wells. Robin hung back, his aura of magic too threatening to expose to the curious. But he heard, again and again, the stories.

How often they were of young girls, missing.

And always, floating in the water, locks of hair.

~ CHAPTER TWENTY-FOUR ~

"Aunt Imp!"

The full-throated chuckles that pierced through the fog of her sleep were possibly the only sounds she might have heard on such a morning without flinging a curse at the person who dared awaken her.

But Otter's laughter was enough to make her smile through her bleariness. "What is my name?" she admonished with a yawn.

"Aunt Persephone." As always, the clarity of his vowels and consonants warmed her. Oh, if only her father could see this boy and hear him speak and play and sing.

"What do you want, sweet one?" she asked.

"Mr Jones sent me to—"

She sat bolt upright. She'd claimed that she would be waiting shortly after dawn, and now the man had the satisfaction of sending for her to be fetched from the bed like a laggard.

She flew from the bed, donning her slippers before stepping outside into the early morning.

She decided to make Jones wait longer. She washed her hands and face in the bucket of water left by the door for that purpose and cast a thoughtful look toward the bathing hut, where several women were gathered, gossiping as they awaited their turns within. How many water girls did they have? If more than two people in the Fury household chose to bathe within an hour, the poor water girl had to rest and restore her magic before filling the tub again. The Furys sometimes doubled up on bathing water if they all needed to cleanse themselves in short order. But here, not only did these peasants keep clean, but there seemed to be no shortage of water to service them.

Again, she was surprised by the strength of magic in this place.

As for her own bath, whom should she ask about it? She refused to speak to Rue, would prefer not to ask the Crone, and would rather smell Ordinary than make such a request from Jones. Lysander was nowhere to be seen, nor was Clary, and even had she thought Otter able to help her, he'd disappeared into the woods with a shouting mob of other boys.

She crossed to the table of flat oatcakes, bacon and weak ale and milk. Only when she'd broken her fast did she finally turn her attention to the man, or more specifically, to his book.

She finally approached him where he stood giving orders to various men for their day's work. Not once did his black eyes flicker in her direction, although the gazes of the other men certainly did. She feigned unconcern. If he aimed to make a point, she aimed to ignore it.

Jones gestured at a small, fair man whose garb was grimed from travel. "You've brought word from Penwith?"

As he took the missive the man offered, she thought quickly back to the maps in the Fury library. West Penwith... Cornwall? There were rebels in Cornwall, in England? How many were there, and how widely were they spread?

She felt a tremor of discomfort and found herself under scrutiny. One man in particular studied her through narrowed eyes. His face was as wrinkled as a dried fruit and his hair sparse and white, straggling down his back, save two thin braids that framed his face. His back was stooped, and she wondered what kind of job he might be able to perform in such a society where most apparently earned their keep by physical or magical brawn.

She averted her eyes, finally determining it best to give him the same treatment she did Mr Jones, for he stared at her with too much intensity.

"Do you have a problem, Miss Fury?" Jones finally asked, snapping his head toward her.

She stared at him, startled, and then realised she'd been shifting her weight, and her feet and toes had been curling within her slippers as they longed for the earth beneath them. "My toes were going to sleep," she responded blithely and then began twisting a strand of her hair, holding it up to the light. "I believe I've acquired more silver since I've been here," she remarked as casually as she could manage, despite the fact that such knowledge struck her with horror. When she returned to London, Fern was going to have even more difficulty masking it.

"It's not seemly," he sneered with a curled lip, "to flaunt your powers. In future, keep such observations to yourself."

"I was not flaunting my powers."

"Oh, then it's vanity you exhibit?"

Vanity! As if she would want to have this malady! She bit her lip in exasperation. She glanced warily at the old man, who still studied her from beneath bristly grey eyebrows.

If her hair was truly an outward manifestation of her inner powers, she ought to use them to return her hair to its natural shade.

"If you would but give me to the book and the tools I need for writing, I can begin," she said serenely.

He didn't answer, but instead gave the slightest jerk of his chin to the old man. "Grebe will provide you with all you need. I'm too busy to oversee your progress."

Oversee!

"He will bring each leaf to me for my perusal as you complete it."

Grebe nodded and took her arm as if to steer her away.

"No you will not," she said sharply to him, yanking her arm free. "I will determine when it is ready."

"Miss Fury!" Jones's voice cracked like a whip, echoing off the mountain behind her. "You overreach yourself!"

He paced toward her like a cat, and she swallowed, refusing to show her fear.

"You do not speak to anyone here as if they are your servants."

"I did not speak to him as if he were a servant," she said stiffly.

"Indeed, you did not, for you treat your servants with courtesy."

His words struck her like a cold slap because they were true.

But her servants weren't plotting treason.

She dared not say these words. She turned her head to the man with the odd grey braids and bowed slightly, avoiding his eyes. "My most humble apology," she said, and oddly, she meant it. "I'm ashamed to have acted like a person of poor breeding."

The old man stared at her through rheumy eyes that seemed to absorb more of her than she wanted to give. She recognised too late the authority in his visage and the respect shown him by the others present.

Jones's voice turned to ice. "I've changed my plan. You will come with me."

She could do nothing but follow him mutely, aware of all the eyes that watched them.

❦❦

She entered the hut with its two finely crafted cases of books, three small tables, each with two chairs, and an open-front cabinet holding various writing instruments, tallow candles and lamps.

Strong light poured in through the open door. A quick perusal of the bookcases revealed them to be meticulously ordered by subject—much history and geography, along with accounts of Boudicca, the writings of Caesar, herbals and Celtic lore. In her first glance, she saw titles in French, Latin, Greek, Welsh and Gaelic.

This was clearly the study of an educated man.

She wondered what need he could have for the several tables placed about the room.

One of them had been prepared for her use, the one that got most light this time of day. It basked in the glow from the open doorway, with a lamp ready, should the sun shift.

Arranged neatly were several goose quills, a penknife, a pot of ink, a stack of blank pages, and a small book bound simply with a leather cover, sewn with silk thread. Opening it, she saw it appeared to be a meticulous recreation of the ancient text she'd held so briefly the day before. She turned quickly to Jones, watching from the open doorway. "I require the original," she announced.

"This should suffice. I won't risk the other with you again."

"Risk? As if I'd ever harm a thing of such beauty!"

"Perhaps," he said silkily, "I refer to the risk of having it out at all. Perhaps you take my comments all too much to heart."

"Perhaps," she returned, "but I doubt it."

He gave an elegant half shrug and then entered, making the hut seem suddenly too small, too close, too confining.

She stood straighter. "Who made this copy?"

"I did."

It was beautifully done, in a script that was tight and controlled.

"I can't verify that the translation will be all that it should be if I'm dependent upon—"

"You want to touch it."

Of course she did.

She held her hands still instead of allowing them to clench reflexively as they longed to do. She met his gaze without blinking. She calmed her breathing. "If accuracy is not important to you, I shall begin."

Ignoring his presence, she walked to his bookcase and pulled out a small volume of Welsh poetry.

He glared at her down his sharp, long nose.

She did not give him the benefit of explanation but instead spent several minutes reading the language, letting its rhythms sound in her ear, its vocabulary fill her mind. Finally, carrying it with her, she turned and took her seat at the table and began, despite the crawling feeling on the back of her neck where she felt his eyes on her.

Any knowledge valuable to him was of equal value to the duke, to the king. As well, the deluded babblings he relayed to his people— possibly believing them himself, though she found that unlikely— needed to be understood by those who would destroy him.

Her pulse increased as she thought of her father, her brothers, of Robin. Were they thinking of her, as well? Were they even now trying to find her?

She held little hope that they could.

But if she returned to them with the means to avoid a bloody war by stopping the traitor who would start it, then anything that happened to her here would be worth the sacrifice.

She stilled her racing mind, lost in her task, letting the oddly syncopated words absorb her.

By the time she had completed three pages, which consisted of a repetition of Geoffrey of Monmouth's work, her right hand was cramped and aching. She had not anticipated working under Jones's scrutiny. But there was much she needed to learn about this place and these people, and who better to learn it from than he?

If she could give him an opportunity to boast without raising his suspicions...

"I note," she said evenly, placing her quill in its stand and rubbing her throbbing fingers, "that everyone here is well-fed and well-dressed.

You must pride yourself on the care and organisation of your people."

"That is hardly my doing."

"Is it not?" She met his eyes with careful consideration. "Then whose is it?"

"Whilst it is true that the organisation is mine, the Earthborn take pride in their skills and talents."

"Ah…" she said thoughtfully, thinking of the leather breeches the men all wore, perhaps not fine like gentlemen, but well-tailored and serviceable, such that any Fireborn farmer or tradesman would be proud to wear to shrine or basilica, much less while doing their workday activities. Skill and talents… yes, it made a certain amount of sense. She kept her face blank as she probed further. "This location is remarkably powerful. The magic is tangible in the air, in the soil…" She didn't finish her thought, for the slow smirk on his face startled her.

"The *place* is powerful?" he asked, idly toying with an unused quill. "How observant you are." His tone implied anything but.

If not the place, then… "Are you saying it is the people themselves who are powerful? Surely you don't claim their magic is superior to that of the Fireborn."

"You are surrounded by truth that you are too blind to see." He smirked. "And you consider yourself bright."

She turned back to her translations, seething.

But within minutes she'd found it… a new verse. A verse that had not been in the Latin translation. She wrote quickly, the quill scratching in the silence, his body looming over her shoulder, until she completed it.

> *He will be known by the word of y Deraon,*
> *Borne on the shoulders of the madman,*
> *Created of prophecy and blended blood.*

"I don't know this word," she said, pointing. "*Deraon?* What does it mean?"

His only response was a twisted smile.

"You knew this already," she accused.

"Continue," was all he said.

She bent to her work, losing herself in her task. After many hours, she turned the final page. The emotion that had fuelled her all morning drained away.

The beautiful book that hummed and called to her with the promise of tantalising secrets had none. It was little different from the Latin volume presented to her by Cosmo, its prophecies as simultaneously precise and yet vague, as direct and yet open to a confusion of interpretation as any other prophecies. The single extra verse made even less sense than those that had gone before, and it clearly was not the knowledge he sought.

Her cramping fingers slowed the quill as she completed the last words of the translation. The book held no pointed promises of a returning king to fuel a rebellion. It was clear by Jones's lazy sprawl in a chair on the far side of the room that he had expected no different.

And yet, outside these walls, a community of rebels bustled with an assurance borne of false promises spoken by a lying prophet.

The question still remained. Why had she been brought here? Would they take her translations, change them, turn them into lies? Why not take the existing translations and do the same? Why did they need her?

What had persuaded Lysander to turn his back on his loved ones and turn to this demon in a man's guise?

This time, when a shadow fell across the table she did not raise her eyes. She continued to stroke the cover of the volume in her hand. It held thoughts and words and ideas written by a madman long dead, and now perpetuated by a man whose only goal was evil.

She did raise her gaze at that and found the black eyes, flat and impenetrable, staring down at her. Was he driven by madness, as well?

Such she could not believe. His intellect and perception were rapier-sharp. He wore a hard shell of ambition, not madness. She decided she did not like playing his games and thus held the book out to him, finding it much easier to release than the ancient book he'd shown her. "I found nothing," she said sharply. "Nothing on which to build your war. But that should hardly matter to you. It hasn't mattered yet."

It was then that she noticed what he held between his fingers.

A tattered piece of parchment with a deep crease where it had been folded.

Was it an illusion of her traitorous mind that made her breath catch and her eyes see a shimmer of light surrounding his outstretched hand? Dust motes danced; surely it was merely a slant of sunlight that illuminated the scrap of parchment. Yet the shimmer teased her, and her trembling hands reached for it…

She snatched them back, but not without the humiliation of seeing his lips twist in a satisfied smile.

She clenched her fists in her lap, her anger turned inward.

"Thank you, Miss Fury. If you'll grant me a moment's perusal…" Without releasing his hold on the fragile parchment, he took the stack of pages she'd translated and flipped through them, his eyes darting smoothly, his expression cool. It took mere moments for him to scan, absorb and dismiss her morning's work. He dropped the pages back onto the table. "Your work is… adequate."

"And how would you know?" she snapped.

"Because you caught the error on the second leaf, you navigated the tricky portion of the second prophecy and gave me both options, but, alas, you missed the subtlety of the seventeenth verse."

She jerked to attention. "I missed nothing."

His wide, bony shoulders shrugged within his fine wool jacket. "Adequate." He lifted the parchment, and had she been less distrustful, she might have interpreted his movement as an offer, a presentation. She found herself unable to tear her eyes away from his hand.

"Your brother might be correct. You might be able to help us."

"Help you," she repeated, her tone flat with disgust.

"Ah yes, I'm afraid that to give you what you crave, I must require that you give us what we desire." He placed the creased, shabby leaf of parchment gently before her. "A translation of the last and secret prophecy of Myrddin."

"Or so you claim." But deep in her soul, something leapt and responded to this last temptation as to none before.

Her eyes roved the faded script, and her head swam with words and permutations of words. The air shimmered and danced, and she could not deny herself the delight of stroking one fingertip down the dry surface, and could not suppress the husky gasp that this mere feather touch provoked.

She could not restrain herself—her eyes rose and met his and saw them dilated with a desire that equalled her own, as his hand—sculpted so elegantly of clearly defined vein and bone and sinew—reached slowly...

One long finger touched the page with as much trepidation and desire as she had shown. She stared at the ancient page, at the two forefingers touching it, at the soft luminescence of power.

In this moment, the fact that her soul seemed perfectly content to lie alongside the evil heart and soul of Vespasian Jones was immaterial.

Shadows called.

Shadows responded.

And she would not turn away from them, even if she could.

❧ CHAPTER TWENTY-FIVE ❧

What was happening?

The parchment that he had held dear, almost worshipped, had turned luminescent. The faded ink no longer lay flat and brown against the surface, but shimmered in a dull, wet red, like blood.

And her fingertip hovered closer, closer, as if to stroke, to smear—

And an instant—a very instant—before she touched it, he felt the sizzle in his own fingertip, smelt the singe of paper, smoke stung his eyes—

"Apples," the girl said softly. "Do you smell them?"

The parchment glowed. The ink beckoned with its message.

An army will be moving to and fro,
Blood will rule the land,
He will be met with rejoicing
and will bring the time of golden peace to all.

The books on the bookshelf were smoking; the thatched roof was singeing over his head; his world was burning down around him.

He grabbed her chair and hauled it away from the table. She landed on the hard-packed dirt with a cry of outrage, but he only had eyes for the parchment.

Which was a parchment again, nothing more. No glow, no wet, blood ink. No secret ready to be revealed in shimmering words of war and welcome.

He snatched it up and tucked it safely away in the pouch that he wore against his heart.

The books merely smoked, and the thatch overhead already showed a few blackened patches but no spark of red. He'd stopped her in time.

He whirled around and grabbed her by the arm, jerking her to her feet.

Her eyes flared with fear and fury. "But there's more! We haven't read it all! You can't hide it from me..."

"Haven't you burned enough?" he snapped in reply, pulling her

273

towards the door.

He dragged her from the hut and into the dying sunlight. "My staff," he ordered calmly, even though his mind raged in terror.

If his people knew, they would lose all faith.

If they knew he'd lied.

A flurry of activity resulted in his light woollen mantle settling over his shoulders. He fastened the brass frog with a single hand, never releasing the girl.

He'd lied.

The cloak presented for her use was a dark red, reminiscent of the ink that haunted his mind's eye. He recognised it as Night's and would have questioned the offering of the old woman's best and warmest covering if not for the urgency that drove him.

"We will not be back tonight," he snapped, ignoring the exchanged glances, the knitted brows, some scandalised, some knowing and speculative. "Lys," he barked. "You will be in charge until—"

"Excuse me," Lys said, his voice soft and eyes hard, "but I do believe I misunderstand your intent. You do not plan to remove my sister from my protection, and you do not plan to take an action that will ruin her by fact or by implication. Of this," he said, his voice cold as the razor edge of a blade, "I am certain."

"You brought her here," Vespasian replied with equal chill. "You said you could control her and persuade her to cooperate with us. Any agreement I made as to her treatment was made before she arrived with her utter disdain for my people and her determination to destroy us all. Any agreement I made prior to her attempts on my life was null when she showed herself to be an ungovernable, selfish baggage, and you will either stand back and allow us leave or I'll be forced to—"

"Forced to what?" Lysander asked, stepping in front of him, his eyes glittering with danger.

Vespasian met his gaze, allowing his lips the most subtle of twists as he raised a single finger.

And that was all it took.

Bram, Tern, and Coal had Lysander pinned within seconds, with others at hand to assist should he fight.

"No!" Rue cried out, her fear and anger palpable in the rapidly cooling air.

"Convince your husband that his inability to control his sister abrogated any authority he had over her," Vespasian said easily, "and there will peace amongst us. If not…"

Another flick of his finger, and this time Lysander Fury was being dragged away, despite his struggles.

"Lysander!" The girl spoke calmly, as if a battle for her reputation and her person was not being fought over her head. "Listen to me, my brother!"

He stilled briefly, and in that moment she cast a longing look at the spot over Vespasian's heart where she'd last seen the pouch disappear. Her gaze touched him like fire. She wanted the parchment, and she wanted its secrets with a desire that consumed the blood in her veins and the air in her lungs. He knew this because he'd felt it, too, ever since he'd received the prophecy nearly eighteen years before.

Slowly, her posture grew confident and her eyes cleared, and then, with a hint of a lazy smile, she turned to her brother.

"I shall be safe," she said with an arrogant toss of her head. "He can't harm me." There was no doubting the sly look she slanted in Vespasian's direction. "His goddess will not allow it."

Vespasian caught his breath in a hiss.

She removed her arm from his grip with the grace of a queen.

"Beloved brother, do not think I haven't noted that he broke his vow with you."

Brother and sister exchanged a secretive look that burned Vespasian to his core. He yanked her to his side and turned to the boy who held his staff at a diagonal across his thin body, its weight supported by the ground. Vespasian took a step toward the boy to retrieve it, his hand outstretched.

His palm tingled. A… beckoning. He squeezed his hand shut then flung it open again, allowed the sensation to grow, a phantom weight in his grasp a moment before the staff flew from the startled boy's grip.

Instinct brought his hand up to catch it. He took an inadvertent step back to absorb its momentum. His hand stung at the blow, but more, his entire body rang with it, not just with the staggering recoil of the heavy piece of carved wood, but with the power he'd just exhibited.

He knew before he even looked that the faces around him would be gaping.

With presence of mind, he tossed his hair back out of his face and down his back and spun smoothly to face them as if this had all been in his plan. This time it was his chin that rose as he aimed the fullness of his antipathy at the girl.

Her thin face had gone even paler, her eyes larger, and for the first time, he felt the true taste of triumph. He watched her absorb how outmatched she was. He thrust the staff at her. "Carry it."

He watched critically as she staggered under its weight but then straightened, holding it horizontally. Ever insolent, she demanded, "Do I look like a pack animal?"

"You'll need it where we're going." He swept his people with one last, hard glare.

From their expressions, he knew that not a soul amongst his people believed her wholly safe in his care.

But he also knew that none would lift a finger to protect her.

It was clear that she saw this as well. She braced the staff on the ground and watched him warily.

Taking a bag of supplies held out to him by one of his men, he dismissed them all with a nod before he proceeded up the path, his long stride not allowing the girl any kind of graceful exit at all, as she scurried to stay with him.

They'd been one mere instant away from disaster, from her bringing yet another hut down on their heads, and they could never know the truth.

He'd lied to them all.

He could not control her, either.

❦❦

She had no concept of how long or far they'd walked. All she knew was the throb of her arms, shoulders and back under the weight of the staff. She could no longer alternate sides to relieve her muscles, for the ache was a low, constant companion, no matter which side of her body bore the brunt of the burden. The path climbed higher.

He kept a steady pace in front of her. She used the staff for support, even if it was only for the briefest of moments before she dragged herself forward to keep up with him. She blinked back the perspiration that burned her eyes; the day had gotten unexpectedly warm after such a cold night.

Her toe struck a stone and she went sprawling. She landed across the path and avoided striking her head on a rock by sheer reflex. She lay gasping, every part of her body crying out for rest. Her knees stung and her injured shoulder ached.

Her captor huffed and turned as if to assist her, but she hauled herself to her feet and panted, her tone acid, "Your hypocrisy astounds me."

He recoiled. "Hypocrisy?"

"Why yes, Mr Jones," she said, turning her voice to sweetness. "I find it so intriguing that someone who scorns everything I am finds me so indispensible. I find it particularly intriguing that you have a Fireborn name. How you must loathe yourself. I'm amazed you haven't cast it aside and chosen something more fitting, like Crow!"

But to her frustration he met her contempt with an amused smirk. None of her darts had struck home.

"Miss Fury, whatever makes you think I have not cast aside my name?"

She blinked, confused. "Vespasian—the name of a Roman emperor—isn't your real name? Your hypocrisy grows!"

"And your ignorance surpasses it."

He would not have taken on such a name, of course he wouldn't. She met his cold gaze, considering. "Jones is not your name."

"Brava."

"Which raises the question, why do you hide it?"

"I save it." He snapped his cloak tight around himself and, with a raised palm, took the staff from her loose grip. It flew through the air toward him and arrived with a slap into his hand. "We are about to emerge from the forest. I would advise you to watch your step more carefully, for not only will there be more stones and a path less defined, but there are adders about, should you decide to stray."

She couldn't hide her shudder. Dark was falling, and they were walking through rough terrain, inhabited by serpents?

"Keep up." He moved forward, the staff held easily in his left hand, only occasionally brushing the ground as he walked.

Finally relieved of its weight and torment, she immediately wanted it back. It would have at least provided a weapon against adders.

❧❧

When they broke out of the heavy forest and into the open, she could only stare. It was the magic hour, that time when the sun's low-slanting rays painted the world with a warm glow. The footpath skirted the edge of the low mountain, above a patchwork of fields and wide expanses of brush and gorse, rolling away to a shimmering body of water. The sun on the horizon turned the sky all the colours of persimmons and deep plums. Never had she seen such a sunset. Surely the Hesperides had rarely spun such magic across the sky. The earth was washed in golden magenta as the sun prepared for its descent into the sea.

"Come," he snapped. She scurried forward, her attention torn between the treacherous ground ahead and the map of the world spread below.

For a moment, she stopped and glanced back in the direction of the village. She'd seen diagrams of such hill forts, could supply the hidden details from memory of the village itself. Quickly, she scurried forward, clutching the dark red cloak tightly around her, watching the ground for stones or—worse—movement, and darting quick, attentive glances at the rest of the land.

Another small village was barely visible at the edge of the sea. She had no idea how distant it was. She had no experience judging such things, but the narrow footpath that appeared and disappeared with the rise of the land seemed likely to lead there. Belatedly, she realised he was drawing away from her, clearly willing to trust her fear of being alone in the dark to keep her close.

And, rot his soul, he was right. She again picked up her speed, hating herself for her fear, but fearing all the same.

❧❧

The air held the fresh tang of spring, of new growth crushed under foot and the soft undercurrent of salt from the sea.

He heard the girl dragging behind him and was pleased at her physical distress. The shadows were growing long and they hadn't much further to go. Not that he would give her any such reassurances. He quickened his pace as they reached a small ridge of low rocks that appeared to drop away but actually hid the curved path he sought.

He whisked past the broken rock and wove along the overgrown path to find the old shepherd's hut awaiting him.

Its thatched roof had collapsed. Its dry-stacked stone walls stood open to the darkening sky.

"Bloody hell!" he muttered. He had heard no word that the hut had fallen into such disrepair.

He cast an angry look back at the limping girl who became a silhouette as she moved between him and the sun. Standing with her back to him, she shielded her eyes, gazing out over the last lavender twilight as if her bed were waiting along with servants to do her bidding, once the dark was upon them. "Miss Fury, if you desire food, you will come now while we can still see to prepare it."

She turned in a swirl of cloak, her gait had lost all arrogance as she made her way to him. "What I desire," she said, "is the knowledge you promised to give me. What I desire is for you to live up to your word, as I have done my best to do."

Very prettily said, if not for the loud gurgle from her belly. He could practically see the blush flame her cheeks as one hand clutched her middle. "Then if you don't desire food," he said, reaching into the bag hanging from his shoulder and pulling out a dried apple, "there will be that much more for me." He bit into it and tore off a strip of sweet, leathery flesh. He did nothing to hide his pleasure at the taste.

Eventually, he deigned to notice her hand, held palm up as she glared at him, for yes, even in this dim light he could not miss her scowl. He looked at the apple in his hand, half-eaten, and with a shrug, tossed it to her.

She gasped her outrage, but she caught it. After a long minute's seethe, she bit into it, and he turned to rummage through the hastily packed rations. Dried venison, poached from the Ordinary lands to the South the prior autumn, crusts of bread, some cheese, and a skin of wine made up the rest. He ripped off a portion of bread and pressed it into her free hand. "Eat fast. Night draws nigh."

He left her standing as he paced the circumference of the hut. The thatch had been swept out of the interior and off to the side, and he cautiously gave it a wide berth, not wanting to risk the very adder bites he'd taken such pleasure in describing to her. Satisfied, he studied the doorway, what he could see of the interior in the waning light, and again, cast a glance over his shoulder to see the girl finishing her meal.

"Come," he commanded, and she did. He handed her his wineskin to drink from and watched her take three swallows before he snatched it back. "There will be more later, but now, you have a task." He thrust the staff at her, then indicated the hut with a jerk of his chin.

"Go inside and flush out the snakes."

❧ CHAPTER TWENTY-SIX ❧

She stared from the staff in her hands back to the dark figure looming over her. "What?" she asked weakly, not even attempting to hide her dismay.

"The wind will pick up tonight, and I don't want to be in the open. We may not have a roof in this godsforsaken hovel, but at least it has walls. Do as I say, while I eat."

Whatever defence she'd thought the staff would give her, it offered her no protection or comfort if she was entering a darkened place that might be nested with adders. It had to be a cruel trick. "You wouldn't sleep there if it had adders. You know I can't remove them. You're surely—"

"—growing impatient, Miss Fury! Take the staff and enter the hut and rid it of any adders that might be sheltering there!"

She took a hesitant step toward the hut, her hands trembling so violently that she almost dropped the staff.

"Are you so weak you cannot support the weight of a stick?" he asked, his voice velvet and coming from too close behind her ear.

A shiver rolled through her. "Not—not weak." But she bit back the words *terrified* and *horrified* and *please, please don't make me, I'll do anything!* In an instant, that sinister idea snagged her panic-stricken mind. Was that his plan? To terrify her so that she would do and promise anything?

And what would *anything* mean?

She kneaded the staff convulsively. She raised it from horizontal to diagonal, and lifting it high enough not to drag the ground, put one foot in front of the other until she finally stood at the doorway, now black against the dimly glowing walls of dry-stacked stone that reflected the last rays of the setting sun.

She hated him with a hate so pure and cold it burned her from the inside out. If she'd had an adder to hand, she would have held it up and let it strike him until his face flowed with blood and poison. Her

281

hatred was so bitter she tasted it, smelled it, and before she knew it, she was inside the hut.

For one wild, horrifying moment, she saw the ground writhing. Terror froze her in place. She took in a broken sob, only to realise that the ground did not writhe with snakes. It swam with her tears.

Now the sobs broke free, sobs of relief, no matter how temporary. Her rage returned with a vengeance. She held the staff tightly, calculating how far he was from her, how strong a swing she could manage, with what momentum it would strike his skull, and the thought that she might kill her enemy on this night, at this moment, filled her with such passion that—

The staff began to thrum in her hands, and the air to vibrate around her. Beneath her feet, the earth warmed, discernible even through the soles of her slippers.

And the interior of the hut began to glow, not with the gold of the sun but the silver of the moon.

She looked overhead and saw that the full moon shone down, lighting her surroundings. Nothing. Bare dirt. No nests of sleeping creatures or debris from either man or nature. Again, she sobbed, dropping to the ground, but she did not release the staff. She refused to release the staff. And when the hated man made a move to take it from her, she snatched it away. "You will sleep outside," she said. "You will not ruin me. And if you try, I will kill you." She clutched the staff against her body like a babe or a lover, but whether she thought to protect it or thought it would protect her, she could not say.

❦

He felt both triumph and satisfaction. He'd accomplished what he'd intended. Her level of exhaustion was such that she could hardly do more than cower.

She had no comprehension that the staff in her hands was simply a large wand, a focus for her power, a manner of controlling it. He would have laughed, had he not been hungry, thirsty, and oh so rutting, bloody tired of being nursemaid to this spoiled young brat. Always complaining, patently unworthy and without appreciation of the great honour bestowed upon her.

And now she clung to the piece of wood as if it had power or authority in and of itself. As if it could help her.

He allowed her a moment of victory… and then brought it to an abrupt end with a snap of his wrist, a flattening of his outstretched palm, and—he disguised his relief with a sneer—the sight of the staff flying through the air to hit his hand. He'd have bruises on his palm if he didn't learn to bring it more slowly.

He held the staff aloft as if examining it for damage in the moonlight and then, with a casual movement, dropped it to the ground between them. "I must assure you yet again that despite your airs and delusions, or perhaps because of them, I have no interest in you beyond the benefit of your translation abilities.

She sat up quickly, reaching, as if she thought him about to hand her the parchment at that very moment.

"Which will wait until daylight," he snapped, "when you can actually see to do the job." He slipped his right hand under the edge of his frock coat and rubbed the pouch through his soft linen shirt. He did so partially to reassure himself that it was still there, as had been his habit for many long years, but also to feel her hunger as she watched him.

"You are a liar and a deceiver," she snapped. "I've done all you've required of me, and still you refuse to honour your part of our bargain and *teach* me!"

"Idiot girl, I've been teaching you since you first arrived in our village on that hell-cursed night, and you've been too stupid to see it. If I'd acceded to your demands at Erinyes Manor, I would have ended up killing you out of sheer frustration at your slow wit and inability to comprehend what is in front of your very eyes!"

Her offended gasp pleased him to the aching soles of his feet.

"Wrap yourself in the cloak. It is finer than you deserve. Any attempts you make to cross this staff and escape this miserable excuse for a hut will not be met with good humour."

"Miserable?" Her words were laced with disdain. "You see this sky with all the stars in the heavens, given to us by the gods, and dare call it miserable? It is no wonder that they despised you and cursed you as Earthborn!"

He was left speechless, so unexpected was her defence of the squalor in which they found themselves. He turned his gaze heavenward. The sky was as soft and deep as dark velvet, the moon a fat pearl, the stars chips of diamond…

"How am I to sleep with you looming over me?" she demanded.

"Perhaps you should roll over and face the other direction," he said silkily, leaning against the uncomfortable stone wall, folding his arms. He gave his cloak an impatient twitch. He'd been about to sink to the ground, but now to do so would appear to capitulate to her demands.

He watched as she gave him her back, but he felt little satisfaction. For all his threat, he wasn't sure how to keep her on her side of the enclosure and away from the door and freedom, though the gods only knew what she'd do with her freedom if she stole it.

Unless… he eyed his pack on the floor and considered its contents.

Perhaps he would get some sleep on this night, after all.

❦❦

She awakened from uneasy dreams with an urgent need to relieve herself. She squeezed her thighs together, her mortification growing. The night was still heavy with darkness. Dawn was hours away. She rolled her head slightly to see the sleeping form of Mr Jones and heard his steady breathing. Was she supposed to waken him and beg permission to relieve her bladder? Worse, what if he insisted upon following her, lest she try to escape?

No. Absolutely not. She would not beg, nor give him opportunity to dog her footsteps like the cur he was. Cringing at each soft rustling sound, she pulled herself to her feet and took a moment to stare down at his lanky form, not curled into sleep but stretched out, his legs almost as much a barrier as the staff still on the ground between them. His hair fanned long and gleaming around his head, down his shoulders and back, its silver catching light.

Almost trembling with nervousness, she braced one hand against the stone wall, stepped over the staff, and froze—waiting for noise or hex or any other magical trigger to betray her.

But none came. She leapt lightly over his feet. A few more steps and she was outside the hut's walls, the night suddenly bigger and more brilliantly spangled with stars then any she'd ever seen.

If she could crouch in the area on the far side of that clump of heather, perhaps she wouldn't have the humiliation of waking him and bringing him down upon her like the wrath of Zeus.

She rushed forward and was almost there when she felt a sharp tug on her ankle, and looked down to see a thin, silken twine, fine and shining in the moonlight, stretched taut between her ankle and the hut. He'd tethered her like an animal!

She was thrown off balance and fell into a lurching tumble as she fell face first into the heather. It scraped her face and shoulders and snagged in her hair. She hit the ground, the impact knocking the air from her so that she knew nothing but a desperate need to breathe.

And then a rough slither crossed her hand. In a wave of primitive fear, she saw a serpent's body rise from the ground, moonlight glinting on its flat, deadly eyes.

❧❧

The jerk on his wrist was sharp and painful. He sat upright, his wand in his hand, to see bare ground where the girl was supposed to be.

The bloody little brat was trying to escape.

He heard the scramble, the crash and movement in the brush outside and his heart twisted in ill-suppressed pleasure. She honestly thought she could give him the slip?

And then she screamed.

He sprang through the doorway, to find her thrashing, her skirts hiked high, exposing her bare legs. Even by moonlight he could see the tangle of twine in the heather, limiting her freedom. And then he saw the adder.

It struck.

And struck again.

And would have struck a third time, had he not sent a sizzling blast at it from his wand. It burst into flames and flew through the air, landing in the heather, a twisted coil of burning flesh.

She stared at him, clutching her bare leg, whimpering, rocking. "Don't!" she said, as he started forward. "Stay away!"

"Damnation, you've been bitten."

"Stay away!" The strong scent of urine soured the night, and he knew her vanity, that she would shun his assistance to hide her soiled state. "Stupid, stupid girl. Do you think I care if you pissed yourself? Let me see your—"

This time all that emerged from her lips was a snarl, and he caught the flash of her teeth as she bared them at him like a wild animal. Her magic pulsed in direct attack

He deflected it with ease. This time, he didn't ask. He grabbed her leg and found the puncture wounds, four tiny holes visible only because of the blood streaming from them.

"Unhand me!"

It was one thing to see them and know them for what they were, but without Night and her herbs and spells, he felt the first stirrings of unease. "Don't move," he ordered.

He left her to dig through his pack, hurling its contents onto the ground until he found the small packet of salt. Returning to her side he paid no heed to her missishness. He spat on the wounds and then rubbed in the salt, gripping her calf so tight the only reason there wouldn't be bruises visible was because soon her leg would be swollen and black with the adder's venom. "Do you need to vomit yet?" he snapped.

She didn't answer.

He turned to see her face, even paler than he thought possible in the glow of moonlight. "Do you?" he demanded.

She shook her head. "I'm fine. It doesn't even hurt very much. I think I was just upset, seeing it happen."

"Stupid girl, falling into a viper nest," he muttered again. "In an hour you will be begging me to kill you, to put an end to your torment."

She stiffened, and her tone was insufferably snide, considering she was the one whose wild flight into the night had resulted in catastrophe. "I don't know what you think you're accomplishing with this. If I had an agate—"

"An agate will not be strong enough for this bite." He dropped her leg without ceremony or care. "Don't move. I don't care why you think you need to—don't move!"

"But—" He heard her deep intake of air, but her voice, when she spoke again, was small. "What if there is another one?"

"If there is a snake within a league of this place, I would be astonished. They all fled from your screeching and floundering. The only reason you were bitten to begin with is because you were clumsy enough to fall on top of one!" He crossed to the heather and the still-smouldering serpent. He yanked his blade from his boot and with fierce economy sliced the charred remains of the head and let it drop into his open palm. He then muttered a spell and cut the twine that still bound them.

"I hardly think that will work," she offered oh so unhelpfully from her spot cringing on the ground. "It's going to be entirely different composition from a dried adder head—"

"Do you have a dried adder head?"

"Of course not."

"Neither do I! Now if you prefer I not make the attempt... if you prefer I allow you to suffer, it would bring me great delight to accede to your wishes."

Her voice was small, suddenly very young. "Is the water near?"

"There is a holy well further down the mountain side. It won't take me ten minutes to get there."

"People don't die of adder bites. Not usually. Hardly ever!"

"What feeds adder venom?" he spat. "Have you managed to stumble across that bit of information in your efforts to educate yourself?"

"Of course! Magic! Which is why Ordinaries rarely die, and if they do, it is theorised that perhaps they had magical blood somewhere in their ancestry, the remnants of which..."

"Continue," he said coldly.

"If adder venom feeds on magic, and if an individual has strong magic... do you think that makes the bite worse?"

"What a clever girl you are. Finally you understand your plight, or had you forgotten your *burden* already?"

"I could walk with you. I feel almost normal. I'm sure it was just the sight of the—the snake—biting me—" She fell silent, but her silence was fraught with emotion.

"Bloody hell, take my wand, and if anything moves, incinerate it, if destroying innocent beasts will make you feel safer."

He held it out, growing impatient when she didn't snatch it immediately. "Choose your fear, Miss Fury. Fear of the wand or fear of the night. Which terrifies the little girl most?"

She took the wand as daintily as if it were a cup of tea. "Thank you," she said primly. She held it betwixt her fingertips as if afraid it would bite her next.

He snorted his disdain and wheeled away to retrace their steps back down to the cut-off that led to the holy spring, a gurgle of mineral-strong water pouring from the earth into an odoriferous pool below.

Pulse pounding, he flew down the path as quickly as he could without falling headlong himself. Clenching his jaw tight, he fought the slight rise of nausea in his own throat, enraged that he might share even a twinge of sympathetic feeling for the wretched girl.

❧❦

He'd left her.

He had left her alone, in the dark, on the ground, with adders, with a wand—a wand she didn't want, didn't know how to use, and shouldn't he—didn't he know it was his fault? She wouldn't have fallen, wouldn't have been bitten, wouldn't have pain gnawing at her, climbing her leg, burning into her until she could only fall back into the dirt and moan...

His fault, and he'd left her. She wanted to curl into a tight ball, to hide from the moon, from the air, from the snakes... but... but she couldn't. She couldn't move, lest the pain devour her. She couldn't even raise the wand to her defence. Her fingers, numb and cold, barely held it. Moving them, raising her arm... it was all just too difficult... She rolled her head to stare up at the sky, at the diamonds swimming in the night sea, bobbing, shimmering, moving, until she thought she would retch.

Do you need to vomit yet?

He had known. He had known what was coming. He had known, and yet he had left her. Her heart pounded in her chest, but not steadily, not the heartbeat she sometimes felt when she ran across the fields or crouched low over Hades' back as they thundered down the road...

Images floated before her eyes.

The night road.

Hades' back.

Wild freedom.

The bastard Vespasian Jones.

Robin.

Her heart felt oddly—frighteningly—off-tempo. She wanted her papa. He would clap his hands and wave his baton and keep the rhythm steady. He would not allow her heart to lose tempo. He would not let it hurt. *Make it stop make it stop make it stop.*

She hiccoughed once, twice, barely managed to roll her head sideways before she lost what little supper she'd eaten, clots and bits of it clogging her nose, coating her tongue and mouth with its putrid remains, and all she could do was lie there, her mouth filling with dirt, and weep…

Robin.

He was supposed to find her. Save her. She knew that, somehow deep inside, deep as her soul, deep as her very magic. He should have come. Her Robin…

She was going to die alone. She, who had always been loved. Had always been, even before her birth, loved.

"Dardanus…" His name was a rasp in the cold air, but a balm to her soul. Dardanus… He should be holding her, crooning her to her death with music that needed no magic to bless her.

Her precious brother.

Who would protect him when she was gone?

Mr Jones had left her to die alone.

She should be glad. She didn't want to die in his arms. He would never offer, he who treated her leg like a nerveless piece of meat, when his every touch and movement sent agony knifing through her. She hated him with a passion that went beyond anything she'd ever imagined. She despised him, would dance on his grave, dance with wild glory and sing songs of jubilation.

She wanted him to die.

He had tethered her like an animal and had brought her to her own death, and left her there to die alone, surrounded by night with a blind moon staring down upon her.

Surrounded by adders.

❧❦

He smelled the pool long before he reached it, but after a moment's debate, he decided he must climb to the source of the water and collect it flowing rather than still. Not quite as confident as he'd professed that the commotion they'd made would scare away any annoyances, he hurled magic at the area and waited for a telltale rustling or scurrying. When the silence had stretched long enough, he scrambled up the craggy hillside and perched against a smooth rock, within easy reach of the spring.

He used his teeth to open the wineskin and drank deeply, before pouring the rest into the pool below, an offering to Elen or any other deity that might bless or interfere. He then rid himself of his ghoulish trophy by dumping the charred head into the pouch, carefully avoiding its gaping fangs. Finally, he stretched out and leaned over the ledge to fill the pouch with water.

Leaning caused the world to spin. He vomited up the wine. Eyes stinging, nose burning, head pounding, he concentrated on holding the pouch and numbly wondered if his fouling of the pool negated the offering of wine.

And then he thought little, except of the need to return to the ungrateful little bitch, the bane of his existence, and… and wonder why he was so sodding sick, almost as if he were the one bitten, not she.

Preposterous.

He staggered as he climbed back up the path, staggered with weakness, even felt a knife-sharp pain in his calf, followed by a throb that kept rhythm with a pulse not his own. His wrist burned where the silken twine wrapped it.

He reached the fork in the footpath and stopped abruptly, confused, before he remembered to keep climbing, that was the direction, up… climbing… Bloody, bloody hell.

Blood. Oozing from four holes in pure, white flesh. Four points of pulsing pain, radiating up *his* calf. *His* wrist. *Burning.*

The dizzying revelation of what this meant washed over him.

Adder venom fed on magic. Magical twine had connected her to him at the moment the adder struck and provided a path for the venom to follow. And now, the venom was feeding off his magic as well as hers, and if he didn't get back to her, if he didn't find a way to save her…

They would both die.

He staggered into the clear area with the roofless hut gaping its open maw at the sky above and saw her on the ground.

Not moving.

The wand loose in the dirt.

Her hand limp.

He smelled the vomit and excrement she'd released in her trauma.

Another wave of nausea rose in his throat, shuddered through his body, until he collapsed and heaved, splashing his leather breeches and cape and the hand that braced him in the dirt and kept him from falling face first.

When he was spent, with the world spiralling around him, he dragged himself the rest of the way and poured the water with its essence of charred—not dried—adder over her leg.

His legs buckled. His head struck the ground beside her like a fist striking a wall. He knew nothing but spinning and pain as he squeezed his eyes shut and fought for air.

And then, he knew nothing at all.

❧ CHAPTER TWENTY-SEVEN ❧

Something skimmed her cheek, warm and moist, leaving cool dampness behind.

Leaving comfort… sweet comfort.

Arms cradled her.

Her blood, slow, sluggish and Dark, pulsed through her veins. It felt thick and heavy with venom she could taste and smell, though she could not name the scent or flavour beyond the Dark, deadly knowledge that it was poison.

A voice—a liquid voice of equal parts music, laughter and sorrow—crooned to her. If her brother couldn't croon her way to the other life, this voice, this beautiful voice, was not unwelcome…

Her eyelids were heavy, as were her arms, her fingers, her limbs. She couldn't move, and she was suddenly overcome with sorrow, that in these, her last moments, she couldn't feel the last pulse of magic, couldn't create even a last spark of light before her life drained from her.

Shhhh… the voice said. The arms tightened, and she nestled more deeply.

Again, the warm, moist touch flickered over her cheek, her throat, her eyelids, her lips.

And a cool breeze, light with a fresh, sharp scent of apple. And elder… She tasted tears. She felt them sliding from the corners of her eyes, burning her throat.

She couldn't move. She couldn't speak. She couldn't see. She couldn't tell them goodbye, tell them that she loved them, all of them, all of them…

So many to leave behind. They were slipping through her fingers, and she couldn't stop them, couldn't hold them close, couldn't…

Calm, my sweet. Be calm. You are safe.

Of course I'm safe, she thought mournfully. *I've nothing left.*

How you do carry on, the voice laughed. *I come to bring you comfort and you*

293

think you are dying.

I feel it in me. Death. My heart, it labours so…

That is not your heart you feel, not your death.

Who are you? she thought, at the very moment she realised this was the goddess who had chosen her. The goddess who wanted her. The goddess who held her, now that she was too weak to refuse. The goddess who trailed comfort across her forehead.

Not me. That is Cysur, my hound. Again, laughter tumbled around her like falling blossom.

A hound? A hound's tongue licking her face? If she had had the strength, she would have pushed it away.

The licking stopped, as if the hound heard, and she tried to relish the power of having made it do so, but instead, she only felt bereft.

You are so alike, in the most unfortunate of ways. Each of you refusing the comforts I send, turning away from the roads I create for you, blind to the light I shine before you.

Am I dying?

You are healing.

I can't move.

Shhhhhh. The arms held her, and the voice crooned, and now, now she felt it… like liquid flowing through her, a gentle tingle of life.

Why do you hold me? she asked.

Because you were in pain, and I wanted to spare you.

Why did you choose me for the gift? Why did it have to be me?

That power was not from me.

You said you chose me at my birth!

This time, the voice did not sound as light. This time, it grew grave. *I would not have had you receive such a burden, my child. It was never my will.*

A chill rippled over Persephone's skin that had nothing to do with the cool, fresh, green breeze. It was a chill of fear and of the knowledge she had always carried, that this magic of hers was wrong. Dark. Wrong. Terrifying.

When you received the power, my child, I knew you would need me. I chose you then.

But, I don't want—

It can't be changed. Your path was chosen for you. You must be strong. He needs you, your Robin. Your world needs you. They need you and your gift.

With that, strength stirred within her, within her heart, her soul. She took a shuddering breath.

I am always here for you. Do not forget that.

"But—I did not choose you!" Her voice was a rasp but it was hers, it came from her throat, and she relished the sound and feel of it. "Does that count for naught? Am I not allowed to choose?"

You will have many choices, my child. The first awaits you now.

Persephone felt the ground growing firm beneath her, even as the cradling arms faded away. She flung her hand out; it struck a stone. She struggled to sit up and saw her legs splayed disgracefully, and Mr Jones sprawled beside her, a wineskin in one hand and a gaping, charred serpent's head, its fangs bared, beside it in the small patch of mud.

She scrambled to her feet, the nightmare back upon her, the snake, the pain, the horror. Only, she was standing. She had no pain. She looked down again, and her leg bore no scar, nor was she even soiled with her own waste.

Without thought or plan, she fell to her knees and blessed the goddess she hadn't chosen, blessed her for her healing, her voice rising rough and crude and unlovely, and yet pure with intent.

Persephone stared at the former tutor's body, at his face, twisted in a rictus of pain. His breathing was harsh, and he showed no awareness of her, or of anything.

In fact, he appeared... he appeared to be dying.

"It's your fault," she ground out. "Everything—it's all your fault!" She had wished him dead and wished it still. Now, as she stared down at him, hatred welled within her for all the evil he had brought upon her family and the evil he would bring to her people, to all the Magi, Fireborn and Earthborn. The rending of families. The violence. The deaths.

And she realized—at this moment she could change the future. She could stop this war before it started.

She could kill the bastard Vespasian Jones.

Power surged; her fingers tingled; her chest swelled, and she knew his life was thin and fragile and so easily, oh, so easily snapped.

She raised her hand, pointed her finger, felt the magic crackling through her.

She gasped. "No!" Her fingers trembled, and she found she couldn't aim them. Then she saw the wand on the ground—the wand he had left for her to slay serpents.

The largest and most vile serpent of them all lay at her feet, covered in dust and in his own vomit, as pasty white and pallid as if death had already claimed him.

She snatched the wand from the dirt.

But he had come back. He had come back to save her.

The wand was a malevolent weight in the palm of her hand, frightening in its ability to concentrate magic and focus it into such a power for death and destruction that no decent Magi would even consider touching one.

It sang to her.

He had come back to save her, not because he had even a shred of honour, but because he had Dark intentions for her and her magic. He wanted to keep her alive to use her. His motivations were impure, his intentions vile.

She owed him no debt because he had attempted to save her. The adder bite was his offence against her.

The wand warmed in her palm. She aimed it. She sought the pulse...

The wand fell from her grasp. Her body trembled, and she fought to keep her feet beneath her. She would have run like the wind in terror and relief, had there not been one last beckoning. A need both logical and elemental drew her close to him. It was so strong, she would even step closer to his stinking body, to the hands that had done her violence. She would draw near enough to touch him.

She snatched the leather cord from around his neck, taking the pouch that held the prophecy, and she pulled away from him, not letting herself care whether he lived or died. Whatever became of him, it would be none of her doing.

With the grey sky turning pink on the eastern horizon, she remembered the path that had brought her there, the play of patchwork over the land, the spread of sea to the west, and she turned and ran.

❧ CHAPTER TWENTY-EIGHT ❧

My dear Duchess,
Please reassure your Mama that her darling son is eating well, is in good health, and is avoiding trouble despite his unfortunate choice of travelling companion. I will leave it to your discretion whether or not to relay that he is proving to be as charming to the rustics as to the Ton and consistently leaves awe-struck females in his wake without ever seeming quite aware.

It feels we have been absent longer than three nights, but if this is so for us, what must these minutes, hours and days have been to— Please forgive me. I should not have gone down such a melancholy road. I would cast this aside and start again, but I am rationing paper. I am not certain how many more correspondences I will need to send before we find her.

And find her we will. I do not want to raise your hopes too high and implore you not to pass this along to your Mama, but… I feel oddly like we will find her, and soon. The feeling grows with each day.

And if I have to spend another April day inhaling the stench of blooming hawthorn I think I may give up riding until May, once this is over.

Yours ~
Sir Robert Fitzwilliam

⚜

C ~
What is it about you Furys that draws females to you like bees to nectar? You are not that sweet, I swear to it, and yet females seem blind to this fact. Although, I must admit, if there is a sweet Fury, it is your youngest brother. It would certainly be neither of your sisters. Everywhere we go, it is he who coaxes information from young maids and old women, never appearing to do so. It is he who wins their confidence. It makes me wonder what delicacies and delights would have come my way if I'd had a quarter of his Fury charms when I was still eager for same.
R

⚜

Sebastian,

Having endured the strain of writing to those family members for whom my news might be more distressing than reassuring, I am finally putting onto paper what I did not tell them.

There is time enough, later, when we know for sure.

I'm torn between hope and terror.

Dardanus awakened in the night in a sweat of fear. He claims it all mere dream, yet trembles with agitation. The images that filled his sleeping mind were of his sister—my dear Persephone—in agony, crying out to him. He heard her voice, again and again.

Sebastian, she begged him to sing her to her death, to hold her in her last moments on earth…

And yet—even now, I am too confused to make sense of it. I had my own strange dreams, from which I awoke with the certainty that we must go to St David's. The certainty that she lives. That she will be there. I cannot explain my certainty for you would—do, I fear—think me mad. But we are near that place and will head directly there.

We awoke to find her gelding gone.

I send this pigeon to you, separate, with the desire that these words not be shared for any reason. Perhaps because I don't want to cause unnecessary dismay to those who love her. Perhaps because I don't want to raise hopes that should not be raised. Perhaps because I am afraid of my own madness and only trust you to understand and not judge.

If we find her, I will send another pigeon immediately and give you our route home so that you can meet us with full retinue, for protection and for—please and praise the gods—celebration.

I sign, as ever, yours,
Robin

❧ CHAPTER TWENTY-NINE ❧

Once again, she breathed in the blessed air of the magic hour. Before, the sun had been sinking into the black sea, leaving the sky alight with jewelled colours. She'd been captive.

Now, the sun was rising.

Now, the winged goddess Eos painted the eastern sky the colours of the roses she loved, pinks and golds with deepest reds closest to the sharp-ridged silhouette of the mountains on the horizon. And in painting the sky, Eos cast her warm glow over all she touched, bringing Persephone to her knees again in thanksgiving at the place where the narrow path joined a road.

No sooner had she knelt than the loud crunch of wheels and the heavy clop of hooves broke the silence. A wagon was approaching with a single figure in a dark cloak driving it. As it drew near, her heart sprang to her throat. She clutched her cape around her and jumped to her feet, prepared to flee.

For the driver of the wagon, when her face came into view, was a crone.

But something stopped her from running. The placid, gentle expression on the old woman's face calmed her, along with the recognition that this woman was harmless, wasn't a Crone with allegiances to those who were her enemies, but an Ordinary woman taking her crops to market.

The wagon stopped, and the woman's face broke into a gentle smile, and Persephone felt a hard knot of fear break open and relief flow.

"Ye must be daft, alone on the road like this, with young girls disappeared and ne'er heard from again. Are ye needin' a ride into town?"

Persephone nodded, fighting tears.

"Ye look tired. If ye want to climb into the back ye can sleep. We won't be there before the sun is full up."

Persephone scrambled onto the back of the wagon, finding a soft nest of hay amidst the piles of onions, turnips, and greens. It was only when they were once again moving forward and the rhythm of the wagon threatened to lull her to sleep that she felt the absence of that heavy, sluggish heartbeat. Her own heart lurched with the knowledge. Had she really managed to leave him behind? Had distance broken their contact?

Or was the bastard Vespasian Jones dead?

She lurched upright, startling the old woman. With her hand covering the place where the ancient parchment in its protective pouch pressed against her breast, she finally thought to ask, "What village? Where are we going?" And then, though she felt foolish and sounded weak, even to her own ears, she added in a small voice, "Where are we?"

The old woman reached back and patted her head, and she felt as if she'd been blessed by that smelly hand, that simple touch.

"To the cathedral market," the old woman said in her cracked, old voice. "St David's."

Wales.

❦

"Wake up, merch," the old voice scolded. "Ye can't sleep the sun through, under that fine red cloak o' yours."

But it wasn't the summoning or even the glow of sunlight that pulled Persephone up from the depths of the deep sleep that accompanied the first safety she'd felt in days. It was the word 'merch,' a puzzle her mind snatched and examined. "I'm not your daughter," she said, confused, as she raised from her bed of straw and realised the wagon no longer jogged along rutted road but now stood still.

"But ye're a girl." The old woman climbed stiffly down from the wagon. "Come along, if you want your blessing. It looks to me that you be needing one."

Persephone scrambled out, brushing straw from her cloak, her wrinkled gown, her hair. She had no need for Ordinary blessings, and she certainly had no desire to spend time stopped on the cart track while the old woman performed gods knew what kind of ritual. But the appearance of cooperation seemed more expedient than refusing what was kindly meant. And then another word that puzzled her sprang to her mind, a word from the parchment she now wore against her skin. "Do you happen to know the word *y Deraon?* I read it, but I don't know its meaning."

For all her age and decrepit appearance, the woman's movement across rough ground was swift; she clearly knew this terrain and made this pilgrimage often. But she stopped and scowled at the ground as she stepped over a large rock. "No words a girl like you should be speaking. It's a she-devil, a whore."

Which made absolutely no sense in context of the prophecy.

Persephone caught up with her as she halted by a pool of brackish water, surrounded by smooth stones and the remains of a low wall.

"This is the place where St Non gave life to St David," the old woman said gently, clutching Persephone's forearm as she eased herself to her knees. "'Tis sacred ground and holy water, and many's the miracle that has been worked on this spot." Then, not satisfied, she tugged on Persephone's skirt. "Kneel, girl."

"I do not pray to your god," Persephone said in a tight voice, remembering the tales of Magi death at his followers' hands.

"Nor did I say nothin' about praying."

Persephone dropped to her knees in the thick grass.

"I dipped each of my *babanod* in this well and never lost one to death, and that is powerful protection. Now dip your hands and your arms and your face, girl, and ask St Non to protect you."

Persephone hesitated, fear of offending her own goddess the overriding thought.

"Do it, lass." The old woman's voice brooked no dissent.

Reluctantly, Persephone leaned over the green, sludgy water and splashed it over her hands and arms and finally—gritting her teeth—onto her face, the smell of it overpowering. She thought of the voice in her head, of the arms that had held her, and felt their absence in this rugged spot with the sea crashing below and the wide sky spread above.

But something spoke to her. Something drew her.

She shivered and her eyes stung with tears. "Save me," she whispered and felt an empty chasm inside, desperate for filling.

A familiar sound came to her, on the edge of hearing. No—not a sound, a rhythm, a pounding that echoed in the recesses of her memory. The striking of hooves—ones she knew as well as her own footsteps.

Impossible.

And yet—it was more than memory, now. She heard the gallop of hooves on earth, even felt the earth itself move with it and—

"*Y diawl!*" the old woman cried.

But this was no devil. Chunks of earth and pebble flying from beneath his hooves, eyes wild and nostrils flared—it couldn't be, and yet it was. Lathered and dirty, it was her Hades, her magnificent Hades, flying toward her.

Persephone leapt to her feet and scrambled down the embankment towards the road, and only through sheer strength of will did she remain standing when the horse skidded to a stop before her, breathing hard.

"Where did you come from?" She sobbed into his neck, her loyal and faithful Hades, and knew what this meant, what this had to mean.

They were near.

Her father and brothers? Someone sought her, had come close, and sent Hades, her beautiful Hades…

"When a great, wild beast such as that'un chooses a young thing like you," the old woman said fearfully, keeping the low, broken wall between them, "it must mean something fierce. And look at ye, both of ye, Lor' I didn't see it till now but ye has the hair o' wisdom, merch."

Persephone reached for her head, suddenly realising what the woman saw—her hair, with its silver crone threads, stark and dreadful in the sunlight.

"Not that it means a thing in a horse, mind ye, but the two o' ye standin' there together…" The old woman gripped her skirts with white-knuckled fists.

"Hair of wisdom?" Persephone repeated numbly, her heart pounding as she stroked Hades' long, arched nose and he nuzzled her neck with equal intensity of affection.

"Aye, when it comes in one so young, it means wisdom beyond yer years."

"And this is my wise, beautiful Hades," Persephone crooned, "who found me."

"Hades! What a devilish name for a beast. Ye should rinse your mouth with water from the holy well, that ye should," the old woman said, huffing with indignation as she made her way back to her wagon.

Persephone thought guiltily of Hades and led him to the well, regretting there was no sweeter water for his drink, but he plunged his nose in and drank as if it were nectar of the gods.

"Will ye be ridin' him into town, then?"

Persephone frowned. "I'll not go into town, now," she said, her heart taking wing as the reality sank in. "If he's here, my brothers must be near. I should stay here until they find me." Again, she sought comfort in the sweaty horse smell of his neck, until the old woman cackled.

"Just climb on him and let him take ye to 'em. If he's smart enough to find ye, he's smart enough to take ye back."

"But there's no saddle!"

The old woman spat in the dirt and then smirked at her with eyes squinting into the sun. "And that's the problem with the Quality. With girls too weak and genteel to spread your legs over the back of a horse and—"

Persephone drew up to her full height. "I'm not weak."

"Then climb on that rock and throw your leg over the beast's back." She gestured at a broken boulder near the edge of the road. "Grab two fists full o' that fine mane o' his, squeeze him hard with your knees, and hold on. Make yerself be one with 'im, like he was a man." At that, she cackled again.

Persephone was torn between outrage that the old woman would speak so to her and the desire to fling all of her misgivings to the wind and do as the woman commanded, to put her safety and faith in her horse and pray she didn't fall off,.

She raised her skirts high so that she could step precariously up the broken edges of the boulder until she was high enough. Hades eased gently close to her, only the arrogant toss of his head indicating his restrained spirit.

She swallowed, took a deep breath, and tugged her skirts even higher, her bare legs goose-pimpling in the brisk, early morning breeze. Unable to see a more ladylike way to do it, she finally did just as the old woman had advised and flung her leg over his back. His coarse hair felt warm and bristly against her legs and inner thighs, and when he shifted his weight, she squeaked and grabbed for his mane. He was raw energy beneath her, not safely contained by saddle and reins, but a living, breathing beast and she nothing but a young woman a fraction of his weight.

And then he turned his head back and snuffled at her leg, a gentle, reassuring touch, just as he often did, and her world shifted back into place. This was her Hades, and he would take her to her family.

She could barely speak, and so she nodded at the old woman and finally forced a hoarse "Thank you. For everything!"

And then, leaning over his neck and grabbing his mane she whispered, "Take me home," and rejoiced when, with a smooth surge of strength, Hades started forward.

"Home," she murmured, "home… home…" and she marvelled at his heart and faithfulness, and yes, the shimmer of magical connection between them.

❦❦

His hooves barely seemed to touch the ground as he flew down the road, and had she not known better, she would have thought they'd shifted back into the Magi world, where a magical horse such as he could have had her in London in a few short hours, rather than days. But this world was Ordinary still, and her heart ached at the thought of London, of her family. Of Robin. It ached even more at the thought of Lysander and stout, stalwart Otter, the family she had left behind her in her flight.

But deep inside, where she was reluctant to look, was a different ache. A cold, empty place where a pulse belonged, where tendrils of Shadow groped and reached for something to cling to. She hoped— she prayed—it meant he was dead, the bastard Vespasian Jones. Suddenly, her skin began to tingle, and warmth filled the chill hollow within her. She knew then without question where Hades was taking her, whose arms would hold her, who sought her and had found her. His hooves thundered, and they rose over a hilltop, the road stretching before them,

And galloping toward her, his horse as lathered as hers...

Dardanus, whose sweet voice had not sung her into death, but who had come to find her and take her back to her life.

In moments, they were together, the horses standing still, flanks heaving, as brother and sister clung to one another, and his strong chest absorbed her sobs and her laughter, and her hair absorbed his tears and his joy.

"How?" she finally gasped. "Oh my gods, how did you find—"

"Where have you been?" he demanded. And then, growing very still, he met her eyes, his own filled with hope. "Lysander?" he asked softly. "Is he near?"

Her heart broke. She found no words to soften her blow. "He's lost to us. He's lost."

She watched his jaw clench, his knobby Adam's apple work as he swallowed, and she longed to pull him into her arms and comfort him, but what comfort could there be? For all his lack of magic, it didn't surprise her that Dardanus had sensed Lysander's part in her disappearance. Dardanus was not without his own perceptions. "You're alone?" she asked, as much to distract him as to resolve the confusion that such could be.

He glanced over his shoulder, and beyond him, she saw sunlight touching a head of rich auburn hair with fire and gold and bronze. On a distant hill, frozen, as if horse and rider were cut from stone, was her Robin.

She straightened with an indrawn breath. "We must go to him!"

"No, you can't. He can't," he said, his voice rich with a strength and maturity she'd never heard before.

"Are you mad?"

He gave his head a hard shake. "It's not acceptable. You can't be with him on the road to London. It would be a scandal. He rides ahead."

And even as he spoke, Robin raised a hand in greeting and farewell, and after one more moment of frozen stillness, he whipped his horse around and galloped away from her.

"A scandal? Robin? Who has been our friend, true and strong, since

I was but a girl?" she demanded.

"It would not be an appropriate because he is no longer your friend."

His voice was firm, and finally, she met her brother's eyes, and saw something warm there, something secret he withheld from her. "What is it, you dreadful scoundrel?" she demanded.

"He has made his intentions known. He is your suitor."

Her world stood still.

"Dear sister, he would marry you."

"And he's riding away?" She broke off, unable to voice her thoughts, that his arms should be around her, his lips pressed against hers. Just the thought was so heady, for a moment she thought it might be this moment, this place, with Hades as still as stone, that she would fall from his back and into the dirt, so limp was she with wonder and relief and joy.

Her tangle of hair, her filthy clothes!

"We're off to London, m'love," Dardanus said with a grin and doff of an imaginary hat. "It's many miles before the misty passage between the worlds. We must begin now."

"Erinyes Manor," she corrected him, suddenly certain of where her need led her. "I want to go home."

"They'll kill me if I don't bring you to London. Persephone, a pigeon found us this morning, and you have been summoned to the palace. The Queen wants to see you!" She had to clench her jaw and swallow hard in the face of disappointment. London was not home. Instead... the Queen, the balls, and...

Marriage to Robin.

"To London," she agreed softly, and leaned over Hades' neck to stroke him, not meeting her brother's eyes.

"I would not deny you anything on this day, if I had a choice."

"London," she repeated. And the sun burst within her. Her world awaited her. Her life. Her future.

❧ CHAPTER THIRTY ❧

*A*nd now, what to do with you, boy…
Ice ripped through his veins, turning his moan to a bleat of pain. He was cold to the core, deathly cold, so cold that he waited for the rattling chills to break his bones, to shatter his frozen flesh.

If there had been a way to grab death, he would have seized it in his teeth.

When he thought he could bear no more, the numbness began.

Creeping, blessed numbness, embracing him with absence of pain, with absence of… everything.

After a life such as his, absence was both blessing and reward. Even his heart, with its sluggish, traitorous attempts to beat, ceased to feel cold and jagged in his chest, and slowly, the comfort of numbness, of absence, seeped into his innermost being.

Death, blessed death.

❧❧

Oh, nay, I cannot let you die, boy. You know better than that. Your service hasn't ended. My need for your special talents hasn't been fulfilled.

The hand on his forehead seared his skin with a pain so sharp it was made of both heat and cold, fire and ice, but not ungentle for all that.

Breathe…

The lips that covered his, the air that pulsed down his frozen throat and into his lungs scalded him with a screaming return to life. He knew her voice, her scent, her touch.

Elen, blessed Elen.

He'd waited half a lifetime for her to grace him with her presence again, had yearned and raged and begged for it, but she'd turned her back on him. And now the raging and begging and yearning faded, and he could only form one stupid thought.

It's you.

And who else?

You despise me because I betrayed you.
Indeed, and betrayed your power, and betrayed my trust.
Then... why save me?

In his breast began the fluttering of hope, warm and ripe. She hadn't abandoned him. After all these years, she still was here, and in his distress she saved him. For the first time since his betrayal, he felt the grace of her concern, her benevolence and dared hope...

Don't be a fool. Do you think I'd save you if I didn't need you? Do you think after your treachery I would possibly offer you forgiveness if I did not have use for you?

A new pain of salvation offered and snatched away, of hope shattered, bloomed in agony in his chest, pulling a humiliating groan from his lips, and moisture to his raw, burning eyes.

Listen and listen well, boy. You cannot do my will if she doesn't trust you. You cannot do my will if she knows you hate her. You cannot do my will and you cannot please me.

What had been ripe with sweetness was now oozing and rotten, poisoning him from the inside out.

He fought to open his eyes, to see her once again, as he had so many years before. To see her silver eyes, her body made of mists and magic. To see her placid smile, and instead saw only haze and blur and light and dark.

This was all for the girl.

A poison of rage and despair welled up in him.

Don't be a fool. It's not about the girl. It's about my use for the girl. If she is worthy she will not betray me. If she is worthy, she will not fail me. But she cannot act alone, and thus, you are reprieved. That is the reason I spare you.

And his true shame was that, despite her scorn, despite the fact that he was a mere pawn in her plan, when all of his frustration and anger boiled away it left him only with a yearning so deep it cut through his flesh and into his heart.

If only he could see her...

I do not leave you without comfort, her voice, liquid and gentle at last, whispered into him. *I do not leave you alone.*

But leave him she did. A new absence hollowed him. An absence of the divine, leaving him alone in the blackness again, all the more aware, all the more stricken, because despite her scorn, she had saved him, embraced him, breathed grace into him, and yet, not enough, never enough to quench his desperate need.

She was gone. He would have howled his anguish, had he possessed the strength. Instead, the emptiness claimed him again, and the world went black.

❦❦

A stench of rot and offal assaulted him in short bursts of hot air, punctuated by sharp howls, too near his ear, piercing as a blade. Something was snuffling against his neck, followed by snarling and growling. He knew a desire to laugh like a madman, that after everything else, he'd been found by a wolf.

He braced himself for an attack he had no strength to fend off.

The brief, clear whistle of a flute, three sharp bursts of clear sound, floated through the air. He knew that signal. Twice more it sounded, and then, silence, until, in the distance, the signal was repeated.

"We've got ye, Vesp, although the goddess only knows where this baying hound came from that called us to ye," a calm voice said. When he tried to rise in response to the voice, it continued, "Lie down, man. We've got ye."

Coal. It was Coal. He felt himself lifted on magic, felt it flow and pulse around him, with the occasional sound of a snarl or growl and once, a manly oath breaking through his haze.

❦❦

The world flew by her in a blur, colours brighter, scents sharper, every one of her senses alive with triumph. She was vaguely aware that Hades matched his stride to that of Dardanus and his own horse, for her valiant beast had bested her brother's on many occasions. She leaned forward on his neck, inhaling the tang of horse and sweat, and letting her tears flow. Even now, Hades knew what she needed. Her magical bond with her horse had been strong since their escape from Ordinary London those many years before, and never had the connection been so welcome, so urgently necessary.

Once again he bore her weight in an escape, and once again she trusted herself to him.

Until, sharp as a blade, pain pierced through her.

She gasped, felt her entire body wrench sideways, and beneath her, a fierce movement of horse in response, and instead of falling, she was safely clutching the strong horse's neck.

But the pain pulsed through her like a sharply-focused rage, like a second heartbeat, strengthening and growing.

And then, it was gone.

But in that lightning-struck moment of awareness, a terrible knowledge seized her.

He lived.

☙ CHAPTER THIRTY-ONE ❧

London

At first he thought it was only his imagination, the sound of hooves on cobbles, muffled by fog and by magic, but a silver bridle caught moonlight and flashed.

The horse almost glowed.

Suddenly the courtyard was filled with horses and shouting, and in the middle of it, tall and straight as she had no right to be after such a journey—Persephone, her remarkable cloak billowing down her body in sensuous folds. Its blood red had been a beacon in the distance as he rode ahead, always there to reassure him every time he glanced over his shoulder. But now it rippled and flowed as if moonbeams themselves were woven into it.

A groom ran forward to take her horse, and only the strictest control stopped Robin from being there to catch her in his arms as she dismounted. But Apollo Fury was off his own steed, arms outstretched for his daughter before Robin could make it halfway through the churning of restless, snorting horses and confused euphoria.

The daughter of the house was returned, from all outward signs unscathed. He refused to think of the harm that might not show.

She was safe. Truly safe. The front door of Aubyn House opened, and Electra and Mrs Fury stood for a tense moment and then, all dignity cast aside, ran down the brick steps. The butler stood as formally as if there were not midnight chaos before him.

Then the seas parted, the noise faded into nothing, and it was Persephone, his Persephone, flying from her father's arms across the cobblestones and into his.

The entire universe shifted into place, stars and comets and moon.

He had air to breathe again, blood to pulse in his veins, a heart to beat.

She became aware of their observers long before he was willing to let go, for she carefully pushed him away and stood before him, her hands in fists as if she did not dare relax them. Her voice clear and crisp, she said, "Thank you, Sir Robin, for your part in finding me."

He bowed.

She curtsied.

She was swept away by her family, their urgency to speak to her, to bombard her with questions and receive—please the gods—reassurances, undampened by the relief of having her home.

He made to follow and was stopped by the butler, who stepped into the doorway to block him. "I'm sorry, sir, but family only."

He stared in disbelief.

Dardanus dashed back across the entry toward him, his clothes dirty and dishevelled but his air easy and confident. "Come, Robin, we owe you everything," he said, and the butler reluctantly stepped aside.

Robin passed him quickly, aware that—expressionless though the servant might be—he would never have made such a move to block a guest, much less the duke's relation, had he not been ordered to do so, leaving Robin to wonder upon whose orders he had been blocked to begin with.

⸛🙰

Something was different. Something was wrong.

Persephone's mama drew her into soft arms smelling of lilac and lemon balm. She was home, as close to home as she'd ever be outside the walls of Erinyes Manor.

"Imp," Cosmo began, "were you—"

"Don't call me that! Never call me that again!"

"Leave," her mother told him. "Leave us. I'm taking her upstairs to—"

"But, Mama, we have to know—"

"Don't you see she is stretched to her very limits? I will ask the questions—the important questions."

Suddenly she knew what was different, just as she felt the coil of tension tighten within her. She saw it in their eyes, the love and the fear and the delicacy with which they greeted her, and she knew it by the surprising absence of servants.

They were afraid of what defilement she might confess.

Her mother took her hand and after pressing yet another quick kiss to her forehead began pulling her across the entrance hall toward the stairs, away from her father, the duke, Robin.

But even as she allowed herself to be drawn forward, Persephone suddenly knew what she must do. She stopped, and when her mother turned to give her hand another gentle tug, her eyes filled with joy, and yet, the fear, always the fear, Persephone stiffened her backbone, drew herself taller, and refused to move. Gently, she disengaged her hand from her mother's. She attempted to reassure her with a smile that didn't quite work and then turned her aching body to face the men of her family, clutching her red cloak around her to cover the ragged purple gown. "Where can we be private?" she asked her papa.

"There's time for that after you clean up," her mother said. "You need food and rest and—"

"Not yet. First, there is knowledge I must share." She met her father's eyes straight on. "With my family. My father."

Let the duke take offence. Let Electra bristle. Anger trembled within her, anger that no one had listened to her when she'd attempted to tell them their tutor was evil, when now he was raising arms against them and had stolen her brother. His list of transgressions grew, and these were the people who had scoffed. Her father. Her brothers. Her sister and mother.

The duke glanced between them. "I will excuse myself," he said, with a polite bow. "I understand your need for your closest family, but I hope you know that I would protect any secret you shared with me."

"Daughter, you have no idea how much assistance he has given us, how concerned he has been. To insult him in this way, to imply that he is not in our family—"

"It is your choice, Father. But know that I may have things to say that you might wish he didn't hear." At her mother's gasp, she recognised her error. "Please, Mama," she said, grabbing her mother's arm and pressing her cheek to her mother's, "not that. I am unharmed in that way. My virtue is intact." She pressed down the curl of resentment that such a confession need be made. "These aren't the kinds of things that need to be said. There are other things. Family things." She broke free from her mother's embrace and stared at the floor.

The air grew tense.

Electra shifted impatiently, made as if to speak, but at a glance from her husband, did not.

"We have no secrets from the duke," her father finally said. "Although, it might be best if Sir Robin—"

"I have no secrets from Robin." Persephone glared at them all, daring them to contradict her. Again, their fear and unease was palpable.

Before she could process the knowledge of their fear, new knowledge took its place. There was no uncontrolled magic surging through her. It stayed under her tight command, deep in her body.

The duke broke the tense silence. "Perhaps we should take this to my study."

He offered his arm to Persephone rather than to his own wife. After a split-second of surprise, she placed her hand on his sleeve and allowed him to escort her, finding herself grateful for his strength and concern.

She was aching from the journey and weary to her bones, and she had worse to face before she finally allowed herself to be truly "home."

☙❧

The house was strangely quiet and empty. She had never experienced it without servants hovering at the ready and doubted that the duke had, either. When they entered the study, it was his hand that brought the candles to full flame. He approached the fireplace and would have brought it to life as well, had not Cosmo entered at that moment.

"Please. Allow me," he said and took Persephone's hand and pulled her close to him before the hearth. "Shall we?"

The warmth in his eyes and the half-smile quirking the corner of his lips took her back in time, and she blinked back the moisture in her eyes and forced a small smile of her own.

"At the count of three," Cosmo stated. "One... two..."

As he spoke "three", she took a deep breath and blew into the fireplace with all her might, pretending not to see his finger flick as he brought the fire into a roar of flame. "That, my friends, is all the proof you need that my sister is a fire-breathing dragon."

How quickly he brought ease into the room with relieved laughter, reminded them of their childhood, when as an older brother he'd played such games with her, turning her difference into a matter of insignificance.

How quickly she would change it.

She braced herself, drew deep for strength and—yes—anger, for without it, she wasn't sure she could speak the things that must be spoken and show them the things that must be shown.

Her mother and sister were seated, having turned the only available chairs to face her by the fire. She stepped away from Cosmo, putting distance between herself and them all. With a twist of her wrist, she allowed the cloak to fall away and settle to the floor around her in sumptuous folds and allowed them to see her, truly see her. Then she bared her shoulder. Dardanus gasped, and Persephone saw his horror and his rage at the sight of the purple gown, ripped and hanging to expose her jagged red wound.

"Who—my gods—who did that to you?" Her mother sprang to her feet.

"I'll kill him with my bare hands," Cosmo said.

"No," Electra snarled. "I shall."

But it was Robin's eyes she sought, Robin's reaction. Her scar was brutal and unlovely, and she expected his wince, the dismayed twist of his features. What she had not expected was that before she could breathe, he would cross the room and pull her tightly to him and hold her close, so close, his strength coursing into her like liquid soothing a parched tongue.

She leaned into him, allowing his embrace even as she was too numb to return it. She turned her face up to his, searching, fearing, and found only compassion.

"It's nothing," he breathed for her ears only. "It's nothing."

She knew what his reassurance meant and gloried in it, even as she knew he was wrong. "No, it is not nothing." She pushed him gently away, praying he saw the gratitude in her eyes. But it wasn't his reassurance she sought. It was vengeance. A vengeance that began in this moment as she turned to the rest of them and said, her voice crisp,

"It is more than you can imagine, my dear Robin. Far, far more."

"Who?" her father demanded. "Who dared, and why? Why would anyone take you and harm you in such a way?"

"Who took me? My brother, Lysander took me, as you already knew. Why? Because he has joined the rebels—"

Electra flinched.

Her mother stared resolutely into her eyes, though her cheeks paled and a slight tremor whispered across her lips. Her mother appeared to have aged years in the few days Persephone had been gone.

"Like Cosmo before him, he wanted my special talents to translate an ancient prophecy."

The men in the room exchanged quick glances, but her mother, oh, her mother.

"How does he fare?" her mother asked softly. "Is he well?"

"He's Lysander, Mama. Of course he fares well. He's cunning and laughing and full of himself, just as you might imagine and… might hope and pray for." Despite her determination, she could not help but soften in that moment. "And he has a son. A beautiful boy, as bright as the noonday sky and with the music of the Furys in his veins."

"Despite the taint of the Earthborn blood?" Electra asked quickly.

"Yes, oh yes, despite all that." She caught her father's eyes and saw the gleam of moisture therein. "Someday you will see, and you will be so proud… We must get him back," she said earnestly. "We must get them both…." She thought of Lysander and Otter, but she also thought of Rue, her arms around her son, her tender care for her husband, and forced herself to say, "We must get them all. Before the rebels ruin him completely. Before they fill his head so completely with lies of prophecies that he believes the things the Earthborn peasants do."

"Which is?" the duke asked crisply.

"That the child might be their True King."

Her mother's hand went to her heart. Electra stiffened, her eyes quickly darting to the duke. The Fury men exchanged worried glances.

Only the duke stood calm. "*Might* be?"

"That's the idiocy of it all," Persephone said. "It's all so ridiculous, so foolish! They are so gullible—" She broke off, realising she had yet to play the trump in her hand.

She dipped gracefully to the floor to take up the red cloak and then rose, tucking it around her shoulders. "You ask who did this to me? Who fills them with lies? Who seeks to raise arms against us and has stolen my brother and his son, and who leads those poor people down the path to their destruction? Have you truly no idea?"

She could tell by the confused expressions on their faces that they had none.

"Why, it is none other than your old schoolmaster, Cosmo, who pleased you so by using mind magic to pour knowledge into your head. Only what else must he have poured to turn Lysander against us all? And now he uses it to turn the hearts and souls of those people to war, with a false prophecy and a promise for a future in which we are all naught but gravel under his heel as he grinds us to nothing!"

"It can't be," her father said, and now it was his turn to pale, only he paled with guilt, just as she'd anticipated. His open remorse tempered her longing to proclaim how right she had been and how wrong they had been to dismiss her. In reality, her father was a strong, wise man who had made an error of judgement, and she had been nothing but a jealous girl. Why *should* they have heeded her?

"Mr Jones," Cosmo said. "I can't believe it. He was not a man whom others would follow."

"Lysander followed him."

They had no response to that.

"There is a part of the prophecy that your Latin translation did not have. Only the gods know how he could have come across it, but he had—" She found herself making a correction, though she could not fathom why she chose not to reveal it was in her possession. "—*has* the prophecy, and it is writ in Welsh so old, it is almost unrecognisable as a language."

"You saw it?" the duke asked, suddenly alert. "You could read it?"

"Could it be the original prophecy from Myrrdin's own hand?" Cosmo demanded.

"I saw it." *I have it.* "It had a word, *y Deraon*, that made no sense, about a wild, evil woman. And then I knew, he thinks the wild, evil woman of the prophecy—the *y Deraon*—means *Fury*."

"The Roman Furys of our religion in a Celtic prophecy? He's mad," Cosmo scoffed.

"Unless," the duke said slowly, "it means a different kind of Fury."

And they all knew exactly what kind of Fury he meant.

"Which is just as preposterous," Persephone pushed on, grimly determined to force them to see. "But it doesn't have to make sense to sensible people. It is just enough to give the desperate false hope. Bardán Fury put the House of Pendragon on the throne. And Mr Jones became part of our household because we are the Furys. Because he knew that Furys would be there to aid the next king. Because he's conniving and—and—if it brings the last breath I take on this earth, I will see the end of the bastard Vespasian Jones!"

A sharp crack broke the frigid air.

"Language!" her Mama said.

Electra cried out and sprang to her feet, rushing across the room to her husband, who held a broken crystal goblet tight in a fist that dripped blood.

"Sebastian," she gasped. "Let me call for—"

"Call for no one," he said, turning his fierce gaze from Persephone to Cosmo. "Vespasian? Your tutor's forename was Vespasian?"

They all looked at him without answering.

He jerked his head away and stared blindly into the dancing fire. "There could not be so many with that name and certainly not so many ambitious, corrupt men with that name. Is he near my age?"

"Older," Cosmo said, though as soon as the word was out of his mouth, he seemed uncertain.

"A little younger," her mother supplied. "Despite his grey hair, his face was unlined."

Persephone felt the eyes of every person in the room avoiding her, but more important, she thought of the girl Clary, who called her silver hair 'magic', and the old Ordinary woman who called it 'wisdom'.

She remembered the sinister man with hair like hers, who had done his best to break her and had left her alone with the Dark and the adders. Hatred welled within her once more.

She studied the duke's face, so strong and handsome, barely lined despite the fact that he was two and forty years. Vespasian Jones's face was not aged, but his hair was streaked with silver. "You are possibly of similar age," she finally said.

"At Oxford," the duke said slowly, "I had a servant, a young Welshman some few years my junior whose only opportunity to study was to take on a servant's position. He stayed in the background, performed his duties with sullen adequacy, and was clearly resentful of his betters. But he was ambitious. So ambitious. Finally, he revealed himself to me, revealed power unlike any I'd seen, and yes, I was tempted." He turned his face away briefly and swallowed, then forced himself to continue. "He showed himself as more evil than any I've ever known, and he would have been expelled for his atrocities, had he not disappeared without a trace." He raised haunted eyes. "His name was Vespasian Wyllt."

"Wyllt?" Electra stared at her husband in dismay.

Myrrdin Wyllt, the madman of Wales, the seer under whose prophecy they now were burdened. The very thought made Persephone dizzy. "Could he be a descendant?"

"Indeed, he has powers, but I will not speak of them before ladies."

"Oh, Sebastian," Electra chided.

"*I will not.*" He was rigid with anger, his jaw clenched, and the pallor of his face was so profound, it appeared that the blood had fled his skin in fear. No one dared question him. For the first time, Persephone saw the kingly authority that dwelt in him and made men look to him in this time of uncertainty.

Yet she needed to know what evil they faced, *she* faced, for deep inside she knew that she would face Vespasian Jones again and would know the taste of battle and—might it please the goddess—victory.

She would find out what powers he possessed that the duke chose not to share, if not from Cosmo, from Robin. One of them would tell her. She would be sure of it.

"Darling," Electra murmured, "your hand."

As if seeing the dripping blood for the first time, the duke opened his palm to her tender ministrations, and soon both Electra and her mother were tending him as Persephone stood by, impatiently staring into the fire.

"What must we do?" her father asked. "Whatever it is, I am with you. As long as…"

"We will spare your son."

"And his son," Persephone interjected. "You must spare Otter."

"Otter!" Her mother stiffened. "That is no name for a Fireborn child, much less the only heir to our name!"

Electra drew up. "I believe as the eldest son, it is Cosmo's duty to supply you with heirs, and that is a duty I certainly intend to assist, even if I have to find him a bride and drag him to the altar."

"That will hardly be necessary," Cosmo drawled, his jaw tight.

"It makes no difference," Persephone said. "Don't you understand? He is a beautiful child, a Fury, not just an heir, but a bright and talented little boy… and…" She loved him. Already, she loved him.

"Of course he will be spared," the duke soothed. "He is a child. We are not in the business of harming children or of using them to our own ends."

"Give me your word," Persephone said, crossing toward him, an urgent fear growing within her. "Your word that my brother and his child and—and his wife—will not be harmed."

With a look almost tender, the duke raised his uninjured hand to her cheek. "You are my sister, as surely as if you were my blood. I give you my word that those whom you love will be unharmed."

"You won't wreak vengeance on those who are deluded by the lies? Those who are innocent, who fell under the spell and power of an evil-tongued devil?"

"If there is battle, I can make no guarantees," he said carefully, but meeting her gaze, he nodded. "I will give such orders, that sufficient force will be used, but not excessive force without necessity."

"The bastard Vespasian Jo— *Wyllt*—will die?"

"Of all you ask, this is by far the easiest to swear. He will die. If I could, I would deliver his head to you on a silver platter."

She felt the surge of satisfaction grow within her. "Then I will help you."

He arched one fine brow in query. "Indeed? Then how can we do anything but succeed? But… in what way can you help?"

"I observed much," she said. "I can tell you their weaknesses. His weakness. And…" She thought of those moments before sunset with the world a patchwork of undulating hills stretched out before her to the east, and the sea to the west. She thought of the stones where she'd been attacked with arrows and had seen the Ordinary terrain stretch out before her as far as the eye could see, as clear as any map. "I can tell you where they are and how to get there."

Even so, with such a vow and goal embedded deeply in her soul, she did not tell them of the parchment she kept placed by her heart and that she might possess the words of Myrrdin Wyllt, just as they'd come from his hand.

Words that had turned to blood when she and Vespasian Jones laid their hands upon it together.

She did not tell them that whatever evil power he possessed, she possessed it also.

❧ CHAPTER THIRTY-TWO ❦

She dragged herself up the stairs towards her room—a bed! But instead, her mother led her into the dressing room, where a tub of steaming rose-scented water awaited her, yet still there were no servants. Her mother and sister bustled about with armloads of towels and sheets.

She shrugged out of her cloak and laid it carefully across a chair. She refused to think of its provenance and instead thought that never had she had one so soft and fine and so resistant to weather.

Her sister's quick fingers made short business of the tiny buttons down her back, but before her gown could fall free, Persephone clasped it to her body. "I need the necessary," she said, hurrying to the commode placed behind a decorative screen. Once there and seated, she allowed the bodice of the gown to fall forward and pulled the cord and packet of parchment over her head. Her business complete, she lifted herself from the painted wooden toilet, her thighs and legs and back aching, and stepped free of her gown and underthings. She then tucked the packet securely in the aubergine folds and stepped from behind the screen in all her nakedness, the gown clutched to her.

"We'll burn that thing," her mother said.

"No. I must keep it."

"But—why?" Electra demanded.

She allowed tears to fill her eyes. "I don't know. I just know that I must keep it."

"Of course, dearest," her sister crooned, pulling her close and stroking her hair. "Whatever you desire, it will be yours."

Persephone sank into the hot bath, but the tears had become real. They poured from her, and she felt as if finally, finally, she would be cleansed from the inside and out and be whole again.

With water that smelled of her sister's favourite scent and with her mother's strong hands rubbing the lathered sponge tenderly on her neck, her throat, her shoulders, and delicately across her scar, she felt

323

safety flow into her, and with it, peace.

⚜⚜

In the morning light, what little peace she'd found disappeared.

A gasp broke through the mists of slumber, not because of its volume, for it was unnaturally quiet, but because of the depth of its dismay.

She blinked her eyes open to find Fern, her mother's maid, standing by the chair by the window, where sunlight lit the red cloak. The maid bent to examine it more closely, then rubbed it against her cheek as if it were a beloved and not a garment. When she saw Persephone staring at her, she showed not a glimmer of embarrassment or impropriety. "Where did this come from?"

"From an old woman who was amongst the rebels."

Fern lowered the cloak and stared at her from haunted eyes. "Her name, child. I must know her name."

"Night. They called her Night."

The older woman sank to the floor in a dead faint.

⚜⚜

A maidservant had come at Persephone's quick tug of the bell pull, and upon her command, had fetched her mother. If Persephone had expected Fern to be bustled away to the servant's quarters, she was mistaken. Her mother took one glance at her shaken maid and sent for tea.

When the pot of tea and three cups arrived, the maidservant was dismissed.

Fern sat in the chair now, a cup of tea in her trembling hands. Persephone's mama took the other chair, leaving her to return shakily to her bed.

"Mama, what is wrong?" Persephone asked. Her own tea steamed sweetly, the first she'd had in days. But now, she found herself unable to drink it until her mother responded.

"That cloak. Who made it?"

"Night," Fern said, her voice soft and raspy. "She said the old woman's name was Night."

"Nightingale." Her mother gave her a sharp glance. "Drink. Drink and eat. Then you must tell me everything you know of her, and then… I must tell your father. How many of our people from Erinyes Manor were there, pray tell?"

"I saw three that I recognised for certain. Four, if you count the bastard—"

"Daughter! I will hear no more of that from your lips!"

She closed her mouth and took a deep breath. "If you count our *tutor*. Lysander, Rue—"

She caught the anguished expression on Fern's face.

"And the tiger, the one with white hair."

"Truly? He was only a child. However did he end up with them?"

"Mama, who is Night? Why are you so distraught?"

Her mama stroked the soft red fabric that lay across her lap. "How were her hands?"

"She had been punished," Persephone whispered. "Her forefingers were gone."

Her mother's deep sigh told her that this was what she'd expected to hear.

But Fern—Fern stifled a sob with a handkerchief.

"She still worked magics, though." With the cold clenching her chest Persephone said, "She, too, used a wand."

Again, her mother nodded wearily.

"Who is she, Mama? Is she from Erinyes Manor, as well?"

"Once she was my most trusted servant and had been since I was a young girl."

Persephone darted a quick look at Fern, who showed no surprise or hurt at such words and only kept her eyes downcast.

Her mother placed a gentle hand on Fern's shoulder. "She is Fern's mother and Rue's grandmother."

Persephone sank back into her pillows, trying to rearrange these relationships in her mind.

"Nightingale was our hearth healer, but she was much more. She taught me the ways of dying the tapestry wools and silks in colours that lived, the ways of stitching and weaving, of working earth magic into the tapestry so that it moved with magic as it told our stories, and that is how we recognised her hand behind this—this cloak of yours." For a moment, her mother's eyes softened. "It was she who was at my side when my children were born, who brought each of you living and screaming into life when so many died."

"Then why was she punished?"

Her mother's eyes hardened. "It was she who delivered you and Dardanus. She declared that Dardanus was born into the light and that you were born in the dark of an eclipse that none could see, but which astrologers confirmed." Her mother looked away. "It was she who claimed you would bring destruction to us all.

"She claimed that you had stolen his magic in those moments before birth and thus must die.

"As a consequence, she suffered punishment and exile under the king's justice, when I would have had her dead."

Poor Fern flinched, but her mama continued, her lips twisted with bitterness. "They didn't listen to me, and they did not put her to death, and now she lives to wreak her vengeance."

"She uses—" Persephone broke off, uncertain. She felt dark waters swirling around her, and didn't know how much to share, and when to share it, and with whom.

Robin. Robin above all others would know. Robin would help her.

"She uses…?" Her mother prompted suspiciously.

"Shadow magic." Persephone bit her lower lip.

"I knew it, but she used it in such small ways it seemed odd, rustic, not dangerous," her mother said bitterly. She cast her eyes at a tapestry on the wall, a tapestry of maidens dancing and musicians playing, in which nothing moved, no colours glowed, and it was clear what she was thinking—that her own tapestries with their rippling movement and hues, her own artistry so enhanced by—by Shadows?—had lured her to temptation.

Persephone stared at the cloak, glowing like wet blood on the floor where it had fallen. "Is it dangerous?" she asked sadly, for she had grown possessive of it.

"Not the threads or the weavings," her mother said as Fern retrieved the fine wool garment and folded it neatly, her hands lingering and stroking perhaps more than strictly necessary. But who could blame her, with a garment so fine? Who could blame her, when her own mother had created it?

"If that had been the extent of it, there would be no harm and much beauty. If that had been all…"

"She has Dark powers," Persephone said. "She is evil."

"Both she and Rue have betrayed us with their powers. But not Fern. Not my Fern." Her mother trailed tender fingers down Fern's cheek. "You, my dear friend, are faithful and loyal."

Fern sniffed and placed the folded cloak back on the chair. "I know my place, ma'am, and it is with you. I was born on Fury soil and will die there, may it please the goddess, despite the shame my kin have brought me."

"Their shame does not touch you. Would that your character could grace them." But then her mother turned to Persephone. "My darling, you need your rest."

Sitting on the edge of the bed, she stroked the hair from Persephone's face. A slight frown crinkled her brows as she rubbed a strand of silver between her strong, slender fingers. "We must do something about your hair before you go out again. But drink this. You'll feel better."

She pressed it to Persephone's lips, and the onslaught of scent and taste overwhelmed her.

The tisane they gave her to control her powers.

Her mother was still afraid of her.

Her eyes filling with tears, she drank it and sank deep into the covers. She closed her eyes, needing silence. Needing solitude. Needing to think.

But just before her mother slipped from the room, Persephone said, "I would see Robin after nuncheon. Please, send him a message."

"I'm not sure," her mother said, "that this is wise."

"Please."

Something in her voice must have touched her mother's heart, for she quickly returned to the bed and pressed a kiss upon her forehead. "I will, my darling. I will. Now, sleep."

But when her mother was gone, Persephone knew that she would not be drinking the tisane again. She knew that she would not be cloaking her hair under dull, heavy glamours again. And she knew that there were things about her time with the hated rebels—her own Shadows, her shame—that she would not share.

You stupid girl, I've been teaching you since you first arrived in our village on that first hell-cursed night, and you've been too stupid to see it.

Had he? Was this the source of her confidence? If so, it was to his own bad end, and that she vowed fervently into her pillow before finally drifting off to sleep.

❧ CHAPTER THIRTY-THREE ❧

Persephone was sitting in the library with books spread around her when Electra found her, drew her close, and pressed a damp cheek to hers.

"I was so afraid, even though we knew it was Lysander. You can tell me if you tell no other. Were you…" Electra drew back and her eyes were probing and fearful. "Were you violated?"

"I was treated like a servant and worse. I was blasted with magic and injured and despised and cursed." Persephone allowed a small smile to spread across her face. "In other words, nothing worse than what you and my brothers have done to me on many occasions."

"Minx!" Electra squeezed her close again and then settled back into the chair beside her. "He's truly well?"

"He seems so happy." Persephone shook her head. "Sleeping on straw." With his arms around Rue, with Otter sometimes snuggled between them, sometimes curled under his father's arm. "He *is* happy," she corrected. "But if we accept Rue as his wife, he would be happy *here*, I know it."

"Impossible."

"If they lived at Erinyes Manor, wouldn't they be a bit of a scandal, a tittering behind hands, but then forgotten? They wouldn't want to be in Society, I'm certain."

"When did you become so familiar with the ways of London Society? Is there a book on these shelves that teaches such politics?"

"I've listened to enough gossip to learn."

Electra became more solemn. "Then perhaps you will be more understanding of what I have to say to you."

Persephone sighed heavily.

"It's about Sir Robin. About his intentions for you. He has made it clear that he would offer for your hand, but Papa insists he wait until you are eighteen."

"That's not so terribly long," Persephone said, her heart lifting.

"Only September."

"Long enough for you to look around," Electra said firmly.

"Do you think there is a finer man than Sir Robert Fitzwilliam?" Persephone demanded. "He has been my friend, my protector, my—"

"Calf love." Electra closed her hand gently over Persephone's, her gaze intense. "Do you not understand what my marriage has won for you? You have *choices*. Do you understand how rare that is?"

"Robin is already loyal to the duke. You want me to make an alliance that suits your political needs."

"You think I would put political aspirations above your happiness? Don't you understand? Your ability to marry well rested on my ability to marry well!"

"You're saying you married the duke because of me?"

Electra blushed furiously. "No. But—but it was vital that I marry well. I was blessed to win Sebastian's favour. Persephone, you must allow yourself to see beyond your girlhood *tendre*. You have never held anyone but Robin in your heart. I ask you to keep your heart open for… possibilities."

"Excellent advice." At the firm voice from the doorway, both sisters jerked their heads around.

"Robin!" Persephone pulled free from her sister's grasp to fly across the room.

He held her at arm's length, his eyes warm but firm. "Your sister is correct. You must honour your father's wishes, as must I." But his eyes drifted to her lips, warming her. "Now, what work is ahead of us that you must see me in the library, surrounded by books?"

"I need your help. I'm searching for a history of Wales. At least, we can begin there."

He nodded. "I am your servant."

Electra snorted. "For this, I must play your chaperone? To watch the two of you bury your noses in books?"

"You could read," Persephone said helpfully.

The only response was another snort, this time not so gentle.

❦

Once more, Persephone was accompanied by her mother and her sister to an audience with the queen.

No long line of young ladies with their chaperones snaked its way through the palace's corridors. No clouds of perfumed scents wafted, and no subdued giggles and nervous laughter punctuated the quiet.

Instead, liveried servants moved silently, carrying trays with messages. Important men stood in quiet clusters far enough apart for a semblance of privacy.

She stood straight and unfashionably tall, her chin raised. She knew not why she was here, but a summons from the queen could not be a bad thing. The high colour in her mother's cheeks and the proud tilt of Electra's head supported her in her confidence. Whatever confusion and speculation the invitation might have caused at Aubyn House, in this public place the Fury women presented an aura of rank, privilege, and the expectation that of course their youngest daughter had been summoned to tea with the queen. Why would she not? She was the sister of a duchess, and she was a Fury.

The gallery they entered was high-ceilinged and long, with a vast wall of Pendragon portraits stretching its length.

Persephone had slowed to look at a thin man with a thick ruff around his neck, regretting the need to rush to keep up with the others. Suddenly, the sound of a great many approaching footsteps startled her out of her musing, and she realised she was being overtaken from behind.

She turned. Silhouetted in the doorway behind her was a massive litter being floated forward by the magical efforts of ten strong men wearing the livery of the king's guard. Belatedly, she saw the heavy crown atop the wizened old head and dropped into her deepest curtsey, her head swimming under the assault of details of what she'd glimpsed in that half-second of startled awareness. A face like dirty wax, not white but grey. Eyes clouded over with age. A neck so thin it seemed impossible to imagine it holding up his head, much less the weight of a crown of such ornate design. Gilt brocade robes draped over what must be a frail body.

And the scent of decay.

If she hadn't known better, if she hadn't seen the trembling of his hands as they clutched his sceptre, she would think him a corpse. Her head swam and her stomach roiled as she stared at the blood-coloured carpet before her nose.

The feet passed her, and still she remained down, clammy with cold sweat, with the assault on her senses.

The footsteps faded but the sensations remained, and she thought she might swoon. Would anyone believe it was the honour of seeing the king and not the horror that caused it?

Then the stench that clogged her throat was replaced by the cold, sharp tang of outdoors, and for the briefest moment, she was on a Welsh mountain and felt relief.

Frightful thought!

Whatever could have brought such to her mind?

A cold, gloved hand gripped hers, and she was raised to her feet. She staggered slightly as her legs betrayed her, but the hand steadied her, and finally she was breathing again. The scent of fresh air was the fragrance of outdoors that clung to Lord Greylund.

His blond hair was wind-tousled, his cheeks red with cold, his eyes dancing with life as he smiled down at her. "Miss Fury, the queen told me she expected you today."

"My Lord." She dipped a small curtsey.

"I'm late to my duties with the king, held up when my horse threw a shoe, if you must know, but now I consider myself fortunate to have been so delayed."

"Would that the horse feels the same," she replied tartly without thinking and then shot a startled look at him, expecting a tightening of his features at her careless words.

For a moment, his features betrayed nothing, and then he gave a startled bark of laughter. "Your point is barbed and has found its target. For your concern, I am sure my steed will thank you."

With a practiced snap of her wrist, she retrieved her fan from where it dangled from a loop on her wrist. She had it open and fluttering to cool and hide her flushed cheeks from his eyes. "I beg your pardon. I spoke without thinking. It's the burden of having too many brothers, my Lord. One sometimes is too quick to speak one's mind in a way most unbecoming to a lady."

"Your oldest brother is one of my favourite gentlemen at Court, and if you should feel so comfortable with me as with him, I will consider myself fortunate."

She allowed herself the slightest eye roll and a half-smirk. "I think I should avoid Court if there are this many silver-tongued charmers roaming the corridors."

Again, he laughed. "May I escort you to the queen's sitting room before I continue on to my duties?"

"I fear not, as it would make you even later. I'm too early to the queen's appointment, you see," she said regretfully. "My sister was going to show me this gallery, thus we came early. And now, I must catch up with her and my mother."

"There is no duty that demands my immediate attention, and my queen will be most satisfied if I show you some of the delights of the palace."

She cast her eye down the length of the portrait-lined Long Gallery to the remarkable fireplace and surround centred on the wall. "May we spend the time I have remaining here? I've heard of the Fury marble all my life, but this is the first time I've seen it."

"The honour is mine." He took her hand politely—his fingertips had now warmed, and even through the supple leather of his gloves and the silk of hers, the warmth was a comfort. They walked slowly down the gallery, their footsteps first muffled by thick carpet, then gentle clicks against polished wood floor, then muffled again as they reached the next carpet.

When they reached the fireplace, all other thoughts fell away.

The Fury marble, the warm, dark green of a forest glade touched by sunlight. The gift of Bardán Fury to King Constantine, it was a miracle of art and magic and skulduggery, an emblem of his support and a reminder for the ages that it was Bardán Fury who had made this king a king. Carved into its surface high on the wall was the handsome countenance of the king in all his splendour, but the mantle itself was supported by the exquisite nude carvings of an unnamed god and goddess, physically and symbolically supporting the king and his progeny.

All knew that the god, his tightly curling crown of hair and classically perfect body with strong shoulders and long-fingered hands carrying the weight above, was patterned after Bardán Fury himself, his eyes cast at the floor in all modesty.

She stepped forward and laid her hand against his shoulder and gasped at the contact. It was warm, despite the fact that the fireplace itself was cold and empty. Persephone's eyes closed, and she felt the marble beneath her palm throb in recognition. She reached deep for some inkling of that first Fury, some bit of magic to soothe her, to resonate, and felt nothing more, after that first quick pulse. Finally, regretfully, she let go and found Lord Greylund's eyes upon her, curious.

"The marble was stolen from its quarry under the dark of the moon, and the Irish Magi still hold a grudge," she whispered, awestruck, trying to carry on as if she hadn't just touched ancient magic.

"In Ireland it is said that Furys—"

"Are not to be trusted, yes, I know," she cut him off, then forced a faint smile, her eye then lighting on the goddess supporting the right side of the marble monument. She approached her and frowned. This woman's body was slight compared to that of the Fury god, but she supported the weight above with equal strength. Her arms were like those of one of the laundresses in the Earthborn village, tight with muscle.

But this was no Earthborn goddess. She wore a laurel wreath in her hair, which tumbled in tight curls down her neck. "Who was she?" she asked, surprised at her own ignorance. For all the tales that she'd heard of the marble, she'd never heard reference to this figure other than an unnamed goddess, but surely she had been modelled after someone.

"Ah, the mystery. Time has forgotten her, it would seem, though speculation is that perhaps she was a favoured mistress. The king had an eye for a comely lady, as did the queen, it is said."

Persephone blinked. "The queen?"

Lord Greylund cleared his throat. "A question for the duchess. Perhaps it would be best if you didn't reveal the source of your curiosity."

She arched a brow but released him from his embarrassment. She brushed the back of her hand against the marble to find the tingle of recognition again. She didn't understand the need but felt a deep desire to stay there longer. She angled her head upward to a life-sized painting beside the fireplace.

It took several long moments before she recognised the king. The style of his clothing was that of a generation earlier, and the beautiful young woman beside him, whom she surprisingly identified as the young Queen Ygraine, was wearing the excessively wide skirts she still preferred.

Beside them stood their young prince, his crown too heavy upon his head, though he was tall and strong and seemed more than willing to shoulder its weight and responsibility. The royal prince had died so young, so tragically, changing the course of history, leaving the king without an heir and the Magi people a prophecy ripe to be fulfilled or abused.

The taste of decay in the back of her throat rose once again. "I'm afraid if we linger longer, I'll be late," she said, suddenly needing to put distance between herself and this place.

He escorted her down the remainder of the Long Gallery, past a parade of Pendragons, each looking more regal and alive than the frightening cadaver of a King she had seen, the last of their blood.

She forced herself to venture a question. "The King appears… unwell." Lest her comment appear critical she added, "I always remember him in my prayers, but his illness never seemed so real to me when it was only reports. I will renew my prayers most fervently."

"I'm certain that your sweet prayers can only be welcomed in the pantheon. As for his illness, it always appears the most frightening before his treatments, and then he regains his strength, praise to Zeus and Hera."

"Truly?" She could not keep her astonishment from him, under the circumstances. "You've seen him this way before?"

"He will improve markedly."

"Praise to Zeus and Hera, indeed. But, these treatments… they must be miracles."

"Indeed they are, though I have no intimate knowledge of them. And here is where we turn." He guided her to the right and into a different wing. She felt an easing around her heart and throat.

"The king's chambers are that way," he said, indicating the corridor which they'd left behind. "The queen's are ahead of us."

She tried not to wonder what she'd sensed in the king and its effect on her, and why leaving his path and domain behind brought her such relief. There were magics afoot here that she didn't understand and knew enough not to even want to.

☙◈❧

The queen's sitting room was a vast, cavernous space with arrangements of delicately carved chairs spaced around the fireplace in the centre of the long wall, and at either end of the room. Four ladies-in-waiting were seated in a semicircle across a low tea table from the queen, their dresses artfully arranged. Their quiet talk stopped on the arrival of Lord Greylund and Persephone, and their heads turned as one to identify the newcomers.

From the surprise on their carefully painted features, they had not been forewarned of the queen's guest, Persephone surmised, for she found it difficult to imagine that the queen's nephew could engender such a reaction.

As he bowed, Persephone dropped into a deep curtsey.

"What brings you into my presence when you should be attending the king?" the scratchy voice asked, as Persephone once again found herself with her nose almost skimming the carpet.

"My dearest aunt, I have had the profound delight of escorting Miss Fury into your presence."

Lord Greylund rounded the tea table with a twinkle in his eye and a roguish smile for the queen, who revealed clear affection as she allowed him to kiss her cheek. "Well done," she said, patting his cheek in return. "Leave us and go about the king's business."

He backed away from her with a half-bow and then sketched a quick nod to Persephone before removing himself from the royal presence and leaving her alone to meet whatever fate the queen had in store for her. In the meantime, she felt the eyes of the ladies-in-waiting resting upon her with thinly disguised disdain.

"Heliotrope, my ladies would like to play Tarrochi. Fetch the cards and remove their refreshment for their convenience."

Servants whisked away the tea things, and the ladies rose as one, making their curtseys to the queen and darting sharp looks at

Persephone. A fresh tea service arrived, this one with only two cups, and by the time the queen indicated her desire for Persephone to be seated, only one chair remained.

"We would have privacy."

The servant blandly performed a brief but intricate bit of spellwork, her fingers forming a pattern Persephone strained to observe. But it ended almost as quickly as it began. The air around them fell still, and the murmurs of the ladies silenced. As the servant bowed and returned to her place by the wall, Persephone's mind raced. A privacy spell such as this would be incredibly useful, if it weren't dependent upon the magic of the palace to work.

A cup of tea already awaited her as she took her place across the gilt table from the queen. Persephone felt a clutch of uneasiness as she lifted the tea to her lips and hesitated.

"Go ahead, sniff it." The old queen glared imperiously at her. "I will not take offence… this time. But in future, you must learn to hide your distrust with more success and in my presence, know that it is unwarranted."

"I beg your pardon most humbly," Persephone said, horrified that she'd committed such a blunder.

"I said, sniff!"

Persephone sniffed and detected nothing unusual. Sitting primly, cheeks burning, she waited until the queen finally gave her own cup a single stir with a tiny golden spoon and then raised it to her lips and took a most delicate sip.

Persephone followed suit.

The queen seemed to enjoy her brew, but her glare did not disappear. "What is that you're wearing?" she demanded.

Persephone glanced from her silver bracelet to her afternoon gown of mint green, sprigged with pale yellow blossoms.

"I'd been led to expect that you would appear in something astoundingly inappropriate. I quite looked forward to it."

Persephone replaced the teacup and saucer on the table and fumbled for a response. "If you're referring to my ball, Your Majesty, I'll admit my gown was… an unusual colour."

"*Imperial purple.*"

"Yes."

"I heard tales."

"Was it that dreadful?" Persephone asked, frustration renewed. Three lifetimes had passed since that night, when her most important issue seemed to be the choice of a gown. With everything that had transpired since, she should be immune to such issues now. But in a gown which both her mother and sister had insisted was perfect for a young lady's formal afternoon visit at the palace, all the insecurities seemed poised to come crashing back down upon her if she were so silly as to let them.

"You quite captivated Gawain," the old woman said petulantly, "and I wanted to see it for myself."

Persephone felt a brow arch and was hard pressed to force it back down. "You wanted me to arrive in inappropriate attire, Ma'am?" she asked in disbelief.

"Perhaps it would be more accurate to say that I wanted to see the attire that some found inappropriate, others captivating, but none were able to claim was scandalous. That is quite a feat, and I admit that having clear memory of your Presentation, it was not a feat I would have attributed to the young lady I'd met, nor, I might add, the young lady I have now in my presence." Again, the eyes narrowed in an imperious glare.

"I'm very sorry to disappoint you," Persephone said.

"If I invite you again, will you do better the next time?"

"I'm sure I must. I couldn't refuse a queen, nor would I desire to."

"Very well."

Persephone realised she was being dismissed. She rose to her feet and was about to make her curtsey when the old woman stopped her with a raised hand. "Is it true that you are a bluestocking?"

"Yes, Ma'am." There was no sense denying the accusation.

The eyes gleamed with speculation. "I've never understood the desire myself, but if you truly like sticking your nose in dusty old tomes…"

"I do," Persephone said.

The queen raised her hands—still elegant and graceful, despite spots of age and knuckles that must pain her when the weather turned damp—and tugged a ring off the smallest finger on her right hand. She offered it, dangling from her fingertips. "Here. Take this."

Persephone accepted it with a startled gasp. It was a lovely trinket, a narrow gold band with a pearl nestled in a bit of golden scrollery.

"Show it at any of the royal libraries in the palace, and you will be allowed entry."

This time, Persephone's gasp was deep and from her heart. "Your Majesty!"

"Yes, yes, I know. Come to visit me next week at the same time, and afterwards, you may explore the caverns to your heart's content. It's not as if anyone else does, other than ministers looking for obscure precedents and loopholes to suit their own needs."

For a moment, it felt as if the parchment that was pressed against her breast, hidden from all, warmed in anticipation.

With the ring on her finger and gratitude on her lips, Persephone kissed the hand that was offered her and then curtseyed and barely remembered not to turn her back on the queen as she made her exit.

Sometimes it felt as if ants were beneath her skin, stinging her from the inside out, as she suffered under the impotence of being female and excluded from the plots and plans that went on behind closed doors.

But... The royal libraries. The queen had no idea what a gift she offered. But Persephone did. Oh yes, she did indeed.

CHAPTER THIRTY-FOUR

"What do you mean, she disapproved of your gown?" Electra demanded, her eyes flashing with disbelief.

"She expected me to show up inappropriately attired and was quite peevish when I didn't," Persephone said blithely. "She'd heard rumours, you see, and I disappointed her."

"Well, I never!" her mother said, sinking against the carriage seat in dismay. "In fact, I quite disbelieve you. Queen Ygraine is known for her elegance and grace, and I find it quite unlikely that she'd—"

"I suspect she's bored." Persephone stared thoughtfully at the passing view. "I'm sure I would be."

"I don't believe my ears!" Electra retorted.

"Then why else would she invite me back next week with instructions not to disappoint her again?"

"Again?" Both women responded in unison.

Electra recovered first. "She continues to do you such an honour. It must mean something significant. I must tell the duke."

Persephone sighed. "In the meantime, I'd better consult Cosmo about my wardrobe." She stood on the threshold of knowledge beyond her dreams, and Electra would not stop her.

"You'll do no such thing."

Persephone slid her a glare. "Indeed, I shall, for I am the one who stands at risk of offending the queen, and that is the end of it."

To her astonishment and satisfaction, it was.

Cosmo arrived at Aubyn House in a most ebullient humour, his eyes dancing. "So!" he announced, as if that single word said everything.

"Indeed," Persephone responded in kind.

His smile spread. "My baby sister has captured the curiosity of the queen, and Electra's nose is quite out of joint, for I am the one who gets the credit. I do believe this Season is going to be a delight."

"I don't trust you, you know," she said stubbornly, "but I'm at your

341

mercy."

He pressed his cool lips to her forehead, then held her at arm's length. "They insist upon draping you in colours that make you look insipid, which you are not."

"I think they wish that I were."

For once, her brother's eyes grew intense and urgent. "Never. You will never be, and it is important that you accept that."

"I was never the one who needed convincing."

His smirk returned. "You needed persuading to wear aubergine."

"Ah, well. That was only good sense," she sniffed.

"You don't need good sense. You need flair," Cosmo said.

The smart ones seek the strongest, the most clever, Lysander had said. She mustn't—couldn't—think about him. Not now. She had her own game to play, and if it meant she must pretend to be a doll to be dressed and paraded rather than a warrior, perhaps she should consider herself lucky. Or try.

Cosmo whisked her into the drawing room where a new dressmaker and new assistants awaited them. In minutes, they'd fallen under his spell and were offering sample after sample for his perusal, quite ignoring Persephone and her mother.

Electra had chosen to shun the proceedings.

Persephone stood in her muslin shift as, one after the other, an array of fabrics were draped around her.

"Too orange," he pronounced of one shade of red. "Something more garnet... yes, that one. Perfect." Followed by deep topaz—"It doesn't make her look sallow at all, Mama."—and emerald—"Lords will duel for the honour of her waltzes."—and sapphire—"The Queen has a coronet with stones this shade and will demand to know whence came your gown."

The modiste left, bristling with excitement over the size of the order and the honour of sewing for the household of the new Duke Regent. Cosmo had set course for her Season with Persephone gowned in tones that would never allow her to fade into the woodwork, no matter how much she might want to. Her morning dresses and afternoon gowns were simple but of colours just as rich. Her evening dresses would be trimmed with thread of gold and bronze and silver, and the laurel wreath she wore in Fury tradition would display discreet but perfect gems to match.

Electra's entrance was timed perfectly. "You realise that everything you have planned for her goes against anything proper for a young girl's first season, not to mention against all that is fashionable. It's as if you were preparing her to be on the stage!"

"Thus, my career as consultant to young ladies in matters of fashion will be short-lived," he said. "But my sister shall be proclaimed an Original, and she shall have her choice of husbands."

"Indeed?" Persephone snapped. "Then I choose Robin, and we can save ourselves all this bother."

Three sets of eyes glared at her.

"It's not fair!" she cried. "It's not fair that Electra should get a prophecy and a marriage of political advantage and a man she loves! What about me, Cosmo? Where is the prophecy that gives me *my* heart's desire? Isn't Robin the duke's cousin? Isn't that honour enough? Why must I be the pawn in a game of knights and bishops and kings?" The words poured out of her on a wave of anger and pain, and to her dismay, she choked on her sobs as everything overwhelmed her.

She tore herself away from them and fled to find a place to lick her wounds and cry in private, without platitudes and demands, without pity.

She ended in the library, of course, with the weight of war on her shoulders.

❦

Upon her return from the exhilarating nightmare night with Mr Jones in Ordinary London, she had spent many sleepless hours assaulted by memory of the world flying by in a flurry of scents— wisteria and sheep dung and the rough, nasty tang of a musty cloak.

No.

Not him.

Never him.

She had learned to force her thoughts past the terror and into the magic—the world surrounding her with softness, with a slow plodding ride home, Hades carrying her as gently and as comfortably as a ride on a down-filled mattress, with conversation winding into the night, because Sir Robert Fitzwilliam had thought her male and thus worthy.

How she'd loved riding in wee hours, flying down the road into nothingness, an experience no girl should have. Such exciting memories would drive away the others—the memories that had awakened her in terror and sweat from uneasy dreams of a man pressing a whore against the wall of a building, of his... cock... in his hand, of a silken, menacing voice telling her, *That's what will happen to you if you dare try to escape me.*

For a year, longer, such images had brought her awake, sitting straight up, gasping for air and fighting tears and in Electra's arms as her sister soothed her and urged her to spill the content of her dreams.

But she never had. She had wanted to save Electra from such images, such knowledge. She had wanted no one to know her shame, that in the dark of the night these images taunted her with an awareness of things she should not know, did not want to know, and mostly, did not want others to know she knew. Such knowledge made her feel dirty, and if she felt dirty, wouldn't they see it?

She had spent those hours replacing tawdry memories with the others, the ones that made her feel strong and free as she never had before and never had again, until the wild escape from the man who had once again become the source of nightmares.

But she *had* escaped him. Again, she had triumphed.

Her return to London at her brother's side was as much a triumph as a flight, for she had bested Vespasian Jones again and had left him as good as dead. If he'd survived after all, she refused to bear the shame for that.

But now that she was tucked into another soft bed, and once again surrounded by warmth and safety, she found there were new images haunting her dreams. She had finally, successfully banished the old nightmares.

But the new ones... She flushed with new shame to think that such dreams held such power over her.

She insisted on sleeping behind drawn curtains around her bed, closed off from prying eyes, in fear that someone would spy her in her sleep, whilst her mind was filled with images of the tiger with his long, flowing, moonlight-drenched hair, his face nestled between the unknown girl's open thighs.

Again and again, her memories assaulted her—and sometimes, it was worse. Sometimes it was a head of dark auburn hair touched with sunlit fire and the thighs were her own. To her horror and embarrassment, it was Robin, and she fought between the glory of it and the shame that her mind fed her such images that she awoke to the sound of her own whimpers. The gods forbid she should ever awaken with Electra hovering and demanding to know what kind of dreams haunted her now. Gods forbid Electra should see her and *know*.

But then came the night when nightmare turned to pure horror, when she awakened on a strangled scream, because the head between her thighs brought her to a place she'd never been. And when the head had lifted, the eyes were black with menace and the hair long and coarse and shot through with silver.

And her scream split the night.

❦

Outside her room, footsteps came running.

Inside, behind the dark velvet curtains, she shuddered with aftershocks and confusion, fighting for control. Her bed curtains were yanked open and a spill of yellow candlelight fell across her face.

"Imp?"

She rolled away, curled into a foetal ball.

Cosmo reached for her, touched her shoulder.

She recoiled. She scrambled away from him for fear that any touch or sight would reveal her shame.

Cast in sharp contrast, light and shadow, her brother's face contorted. "What did he do to you? What did that blackguard do to you?"

"You saw my wound," she snapped. "You know what he did."

"That's not what I meant."

She whirled on him then, that he—he of all people—should dare ask. "He slithered into the bosom of our family to steal, and he succeeded. He stole my brother, and thus, his child! If you could see him, Cosmo, if you could see that beautiful boy—"

Cosmo flinched in the dim, flickering light. "We have failed you so miserably," he finally said, his voice strangely hoarse in the darkness. "We will not fail you this time, my sweet sister. We shall not fail."

She dug deep for strength to feed her voice, for air to fill her lungs. "That's guilt if ever I heard it. Since when am I your sweet sister?"

"Since you showed yourself to be more valiant a warrior than any of your brothers, my sweet," he said, his voice forced but with a smile, a sign that he, too, fought for normalcy. He clearly could not let it rest without one more urgent query. "If he hurt you in any other way—"

"Do you call me a liar?" she whispered harshly, "after all I have told you? Do you truly think I would hide—"

"If you were intelligent—and you are quicker witted than any of your brothers, as well, my sweet," he said, and she longed to be Imp again, because she did not feel like his sweet, or anyone's sweet, "you would know which revelations would destroy your chances on the marriage mart, should they ever come to the ears of Society. If you felt it necessary to keep such violation silent in order to protect your reputation and your future, I would have you know that I would keep your confidence even as I avenge you to the full extent of my ability, and, my dear sister... my ability for vengeance is strong indeed."

"Then use it on the man who would destroy our world as easily as he did our family with his evil, for surely, *dear brother,* that is cause enough."

She drew in a silent, shuddering breath and held it until he nodded, and she prayed to the goddess that he believed her.

When he was gone and she was again alone in the darkness, her heart beating a dull, numb rhythm even as the blood in her veins seemed to rush with fear, she stifled one last sob at the thought that some untrustworthy part of her put the bastard Vespasian Jones exactly where her brother suspected and feared that indeed, people could see into her and see her dreams.

❧ CHAPTER THIRTY-FIVE ❧

The Lord Librarian of the Royal Libraries did not approve.

It was clear from the way he raised his lorgnette to his eye and peered down his sharp nose at her, from the way he hovered, and from the way his cheek twitched whenever she displayed the pearl ring for him, as if he hoped that the queen would withdraw her permission.

It was worth suffering his disdain and his supervision to enter that hall with its four galleries of bookcases stretching to the painted ceiling where Aphrodite and Ares frolicked with nary a book or scroll between them. Each gallery had a narrow, iron-railed balcony that circled the vast room. Small seating bays at each level held long tables where branches of candles awaited the trigger of magic to spill their light across the tomes and books that no one bothered to read.

Until Miss Persephone Fury, she thought, tilting her chin and passing the Master with a polite nod.

This was her fourth week in pursuit of knowledge, and if the Master refused to reveal his organisational scheme to assist her, he also had no power to refuse her entrance. Her very soul reached out for comfort as she entered and was embraced by the scent of beeswax rubbed into every wooden surface, of old leather and parchment—the very atmosphere of words and ideas. As her stomach curdled with the watching and waiting for the duke to finally move against Vespasian, she spent her hours searching for her own answers.

The knowledge she desperately needed might be here. She dared not speak of it aloud, but she needed to understand the Shadows that held her in thrall. No one must know she was bound to Vespasian Jones with such a Dark connection, but she had to learn why it held her and how to break it. She wanted to believe that it would vanish with the vile rebel leader's death, but she feared that it would not.

She couldn't eat. Her family watched her, their attentions unnoticeable to any but those who knew the things of which she was capable. Dardanus lingered often, his hand resting against the nape of

347

her neck or on her bare forearm. Even Robin's eyes watched her warily, tenderly, as they met over tea or in the Library at Aubyn House, never left alone to their own devices anymore.

She had spent the first three weeks under the Lord Librarian's suspicious eye, traversing the periphery of the lower level bookcases, working her way through Latin canticles and French poetics and Middle English tales, finding nothing in Welsh, modern or old. She sensed nothing that had been touched by Shadow, nor did she find any volume that spoke of the old Earth magics. She dared not ask and reveal the subject of her enquiry.

At various spots around the room, half-ladders braced against the cases to allow closer look at the top shelves of this bottom tier, and she had climbed them, despite her skirts. In the east corner of the north-facing hall, a beautifully wrought spiral staircase twisted its way up to all four levels. It was time to climb to the highest tier, higher than any cottage roof at Erinyes Manor. She had taken two steps up the spiral staircase, her grip tight on the rails, when a familiar voice greeted her from the doorway.

"Miss Fury."

She stepped back down to the thickly carpeted floor and turned to smile at Lord Greylund. "My lord." Her curtsy was shallow, but the air came more easily into her lungs. For all the problems his attentions raised, he brought something into the room with him that she rarely felt anymore.

He didn't know to be afraid of her.

He ignored the Lord Librarian, crossing to take her hand and lift her gloved knuckles near to his lips for the most perfunctory and proper of greetings. Then he scanned the distance up the staircase, and his face broke into a grin. "By Jupiter, it has been years since I played here! Are you going up?"

A loud slam sounded as a book landed on a table. A quick glance showed the Lord Librarian's rigid posture and fierce glare.

"Play?" she repeated.

"How could we resist? My sisters and I spent many hours leaping from these shelves."

This time she could not hide her dismay.

"Surely our esteemed Lord Librarian has explained its workings to you?"

"Not a word," she murmured resentfully.

Again, he grinned. "Then," he murmured just as low, "we shall annoy him, much as my sisters and I always did." In a more normal tone he added, "Climb up, go ahead, no, don't stop, keep going."

She'd gotten so high her knees were above his head when he stopped her. "Turn around."

She hadn't scrambled in and out of her bedroom window throughout her childhood without feeling nimble as a goat. She turned and faced him. The laughter in his eyes and the clear assault on the Lord Librarian's affronted sensibilities drew her into his game.

When he shouted, "Leap!" she did, expecting his hands to catch her from the air.

Instead, he stepped back, and she floated slowly to the floor, her skirts billowing around her.

She landed gently—toes first and then the balls of her feet, and finally her heels—staring at him in shock.

"This old palace has more magic woven into it than any of us will ever know. It only makes sense that anything so valuable as a book would not be allowed to plummet to the floor if someone lost his grip. Fortunately the magic supports bodies, as well." He pointed to the highest tier of bookcases. "Leaping from there is like flying!"

Her stomach turned over. There was no magic strong enough for flight, but floating seemed almost as wonderful. But she was not a child who could leap from the rafters with skirts billowing around her, exposing her nether regions to any below. She felt the heat of a flush climb to her cheeks at the very thought of it.

"You were going up?" he asked politely.

The Lord Librarian was now quite rigid with suppressed frustration.

"Perhaps you need a guide, since my aunt's librarian has had responsibilities too onerous to teach you the secrets of the Royal Library."

This time, it was the Lord Librarian whose cheeks flamed red.

Persephone felt a twinge of sympathy on his behalf. He loved books, as surely he must, and had been forced to suffer the presence of children treating this beautiful domain like a bear garden. Now he must fear his lack of cooperation would be reported to the Queen herself.

"The Lord Librarian has important work," she said firmly. "But if you'll guide me, I'd be ever so grateful."

She began the climb with Lord Greylund behind her, finally reaching the top tier of books. She stepped onto the balcony. As her foot touched the floor, candles sprang to light on the tables.

"What kinds of books are you seeking?" He touched a cracked red leather spine and frowned as it flaked. "It appears some care is needed on this level."

She didn't want him watching her choices so attentively. "I have a thousand questions," she said, deciding to be the young miss from the country, overwhelmed by choices. "I've seen so many spells or charms used here that I've never seen before. The silencing around the Queen to give her privacy, for example. Are such things recorded or only passed from one servant to the next? This floating spell would have made my childhood an utter delight. And the old gods, the false gods," she babbled lightly. "I've found carvings and shrines around Erinyes Manor that date back before the Normans or Romans brought the true faith to these isles and have always wondered what tales they told."

His smile was wry. "No leaping games for you, I see."

"No," she said primly, giving him a stern look. "I am of the most unusual opinion that a library should be for books and reading and study."

He sighed theatrically. "I know nothing about the spells and charms. Such things are always done by others of a lower class, are they not? But these false gods you speak of, such are Shadows." He cocked his head. "Are you not afraid of them?"

"Why would I fear that which is false?"

"Then, if you're looking for the Forbidden books, you are in the wrong library."

She let out a sharp gust of frustration. Four weeks, and all in the wrong place! She glanced up at him from beneath her lashes and waited.

This time it was *his* sharp gust of air as he shook his head and then laughed. "They warned me you were a bluestocking, but I never dreamed I'd be courting you in libraries. Very well, then. Come along. But—you have to leap."

She stood frozen in place. It was the first he'd openly spoken of it—*courting*. She wanted no courting from him.

He glanced back at the staircase and angled his head in query. She gave a sharp nod. In a trice, he'd dragged a pair of chairs to the rail. The seats were scuffed, most likely from the heels and shoes of mischievous children.

He offered his hand to her, and she allowed him to assist her onto a chair, as if she hadn't spent her childhood scrambling across rocky outcroppings and up ancient trees.

"Don't look," he said. "Just close your eyes and—"

She refused to be missish, to simper and need his coaxing.

She released his hand and leapt.

Clutching her skirts to her legs, she fought the urge to squeal as the air rushed up her legs and nether regions, over her neck and chin and face, for this was no gentle floating, this was *falling*. Not a plummet, praise the goddess, but much faster than she'd anticipated, and it took her breath away. With the hard polished plank floor only a few breaths away, the air thickened around her and slowed her to a graceful float. Relief exploded from her in a burst of giddiness she hadn't felt since she was a child.

She was floating. Quite near flying. The knowledge amazed her, and the sensations filled her with wonder. Her toes touched down, and before she'd quite caught her balance, she spun to face Lord Greylund as he joined her. She flashed him a triumphant smile, and his full-throated laughter joined hers.

Long after the giddiness passed, her hammering pulse and leaping spirit still rejoiced. She was finally, finally going to find the forbidden knowledge she so desperately needed.

❦❦

They had reached the Fury marble, and as always, she slowed to stroke it as she passed. She paused before the would-be god, Bardán.

"He was a wise scoundrel, they say."

"That describes every Fury male I know," she said with a smile.

"Not the females?" he asked, his blond brows arching.

"To profess wisdom would be vain, and to admit to scandalous traits would be unseemly."

The blond lord placed an accusatory finger between Bardán's eyes. "I've often wondered what prompted him to place himself here. Was it his fervent desire to be known as one who served and welcomed the yoke of a king where there had been none before? For magical people who had always been able to skirt the restrictions of an Ordinary king, a king with their own powers was not necessarily a welcome change. Or did he put himself here to accept responsibility, come what may? For it was his silver tongue that convinced them of the need to withdraw from the Ordinary world before the Christians stopped burning each other and turned on us. Or—" He turned to face her and placed the same finger gently between her eyes for the briefest of moments, a gesture not quite tender or intimate, but a breach of etiquette all the same. "—was he leaving behind a legacy, a reminder that would serve every Fury who came after him, a reminder that the Furys are a force to be reckoned with?"

"Our family has avoided politics for centuries," she demurred.

"But clearly is prepared to step in when a new King is needed."

She thought of the prophecy and lowered her eyes, lest they betray her unease.

"Being a Fury certainly didn't hurt your sister, even though she was a commoner, when it came time to wed the future king, and one can't help but wonder if the duke was securing the family as well as a bride."

When she trusted her voice not to betray her anger, she spoke with a light, razor-sharp laugh. "One would think you had never seen the duke and duchess together, had never seen the deep and abiding affection they have for one another, Lord Greylund, to assume that he must marry her for her brothers. I can assure you, the Furys need no such ties to be faithful and loyal to the rightful king."

"Forgive me, Miss Fury, but such marriages are not lightly made, and her family connection strengthened her position. It was certainly part of the equation." He met her gaze straight on, and there was no artifice there, nor was there true apology. "The first thing that brought you to my aunt's attention was your family name. The next thing was that your mother bore so many healthy sons and yet still retains her own vigour and loveliness, meaning strong breeding blood."

Though it remained unspoken, it was clear that they both understood the significance of the single prince whose life had ended so tragically and so young.

"There is also, of course, the fact that you will one day be sister to a queen. All of these are reasons why my aunt took notice of you and pushed me in your direction, because she is nothing if not ambitious for me and an experienced and crafty politician."

Persephone was startled that he, a subtle creature of Court politics, would be so brutally blunt.

"But those facts do not change that she also is charmed by you, Miss Fury. She respects your intellect and wit and thinks you would be a wife who would challenge and, dare I admit, improve me, not to mention improve my prospects. Imagine being told that a young woman with no title will improve my prospects, with my family lineage. It's quite unheard of, and yet she is right. And that is before we even consider that you are unexpectedly lovely, that by refusing your waltzes to any but your family, you leave the rest of us staring in envy."

"Stop!" She whirled away from him and began walking quickly toward the long wall of windows to stare blindly out at the rain. "Don't, please don't. It's not necessary." She caught herself twisting her fingers together in frustration and stilled her hands with some difficulty.

"What isn't necessary?" he asked, perplexed.

"To wax poetic about my charms, such as they are. To do what gentlemen do when they are courting. It's not necessary." Her cheeks burned with heat at the ridiculous words he spoke with such ease.

"I was making you understand that there are many reasons why a titled gentleman chooses a wife. That your sister brought the support of your family with her into marriage was a reasonable and intelligent consideration on the duke's part. It does not negate the fact that within weeks he was so smitten with her the entire Court was amazed. The duke has not been a warm man, and yet, with her…"

As he was waiting for a response, she gave a sharp nod, accepting what he said was true. "If we're finished with the lesson in the politics of marital alliances, could we please go to the Forbidden—"

"Not quite yet. My point, dear Miss Fury, is this. Just because my aunt pushed me in your direction and quite openly is campaigning for our alliance does not mean that I don't have equal if not stronger reason to pursue your hand. Never have duty and political ambition been so sweetly combined with desire."

She stared blindly at the pane of glass before her, at the water streaming down in rivulets.

"I've gone beyond the boundaries of what is proper. I must redeem myself by fulfilling my promise. If you will allow me, I will take you to our promised destination. However…"

She finally raised her eyes to his.

"You must follow my lead. I would not have us seen there, and if any question us…"

"Of course," she answered quickly. "Of course."

He offered his forearm, and she placed her hand lightly atop it. He led her away from the public halls and deeper into the palace, speaking blithely of this vase and that portrait, of the history and art of the palace, for all intents a guide doing his duty to the queen's guest. It was only when they entered a narrower, darker hall and she felt the four-square panelling closing in on her that she thrilled with the knowledge that they must be close, in this oldest wing of the royal domicile.

"Your ancestor spent much time in these corridors and chambers," he remarked casually, opening a door to show her an interior that was musty from disuse. "The queen has never cared for this oldest section."

"This feels like home to me," she breathed. "It's very like Erinyes Manor."

He eyed her thoughtfully with unveiled speculation and then closed the door and led her deeper down the corridor until they stood before an arched Norman doorway.

"Do you… feel anything?" he asked, his voice low, his curiosity palpable in the air between them.

At first she was puzzled and was about to speak her confusion, but stopped, startled. She did feel something. She felt it in her bones. A connection. A thrill. A recognition. But what was it, and how would he have known to wonder?

Faint, but so certain it was almost a taste on the back of her tongue, she sensed it and knew its source, and yet she could hardly believe it.

"Has my father been here?" she asked weakly, knowing the answer even before it was voiced.

"It is highly unlikely."

"Then he didn't set these wards."

"No, I'm sure not."

She felt his eyes fixed on her in fierce concentration but brushed the awareness aside impatiently. She closed her eyes and inhaled. She opened her eyes to see a gossamer webwork of subtle lights shimmering before her. She caught her breath in wonder.

"What do you see?" he asked, his voice hoarse.

"Silence!" As if it were she who was his queen.

He did not speak again.

She reached forward, almost to touch—and then, gathered deep within herself, she found knowledge. "Bardán Fury set this ward," she whispered. Her ancestor, whose skill at crafting wards and hiding things had won him royal approbation from four monarchs—three Ordinary and finally, the Magi king he had lifted to the throne.

She was touching *him*, touching the past, and that knowledge flowed through her with a power that robbed her of air.

She flicked her fingers. The gossamer warding vanished, and she—not her father nor her brothers—had done it.

She heard Lord Greylund's soft gasp. "A door," he breathed softly.

"Of course. You could not see it?"

"Not until you… released the wards, I suppose?" She felt Lord Greylund's eyes upon her, and they glowed with recognition, with understanding, with *pride*. Whatever else he claimed, there was another reason he was willing to consider her, a commoner, as his bride.

"The queen knows we're here, doesn't she?" she asked. "This was her plan all along."

He stood straighter.

"Who else can open this door?"

"Until now… no one."

Without thought or plan, she flashed her fingers through the air and felt the surge, felt the spinning from her fingertips, and once more, the gossamer web shimmered.

"I don't believe I'll be doing more until I speak to Her Majesty," she said calmly, and she turned and walked away, leaving him to follow, even as that piece of ancient parchment pulsed in recognition against her breast. Even as every fibre in her being fought desperately to turn, to drop the wards and fly into the room. For she knew as surely as she breathed, it held the answers she craved. Let them scheme and plot behind closed doors. She held the key to the door that mattered. She knew she did.

And it seemed, perhaps, the queen knew she did, as well.

❧ CHAPTER THIRTY-SIX ❧

She took three deliberate wrong turns, forcing Lord Greylund to correct her path before they finally returned to the public hall so that he would think her incapable of retracing her steps, which she fully intended to do when there was no one at her side.

Pulse pounding, she realised he was steering her toward the queen's chambers again.

"But she didn't want to see me today," she said tentatively.

"Perhaps her wishes have changed."

A footman opened the door and Lord Greylund escorted Persephone through. The ladies-in-waiting greeted their entrance with arched eyebrows. The queen, however, did not raise her eyes from the small volume of love poems in her long, knobby-jointed fingers.

Lord Greylund did not slow his pace, and thus Persephone found herself before a monarch who had specifically requested her absence for the day.

The queen continued to stare at the page before her.

Lord Greylund swept into an elegant and deep bow, sending Persephone belatedly into the requisite court curtsey. Together, they remained in obsequious poses until Persephone's limbs and knees trembled, and she thought she would shame herself, though she was uncertain which shame would be worse—collapsing sideways or standing to relieve the strain.

"Rise," the queen said, her disdain clear.

Lord Greylund dropped all pretence and leaned forward to kiss her cheek. "Will you forgive me?"

"You?" she asked. "Always." Her eyes slid to Persephone. "I suppose I must forgive any you drag into your disrespectful ways, as well."

Persephone dropped another quick curtsey, this one neither as deep nor as long. "I beg your forgiveness, Your Majesty."

"It is freely given." She closed the book gently and laid it on the small table beside her. Her eyes met Greylund's again, and this time it seemed they spoke a language unheard by others. "Have you had a pleasant morning?"

"The libraries have proven to be as pleasant as ever, Your Majesty."

Had Persephone not been alert to the slightest change, she might not have detected the almost imperceptible reaction which accompanied the queen's almost bored, "Libraries?"

"Miss Fury does not approve of my use of the Royal Library," he admitted with a charming half-shrug. "Nor was she willing to enter another without royal permission."

The queen studied Persephone closely. "You still wear my gift to you."

Persephone raised her hand, and the pearl caught a warm ray of sunlight, its glow such that it made her wonder if it bore some sort of magic on its own. "I never remove it."

"Then perhaps you suspect my permissions are flighty?"

"No, Ma'am!"

"Then I do not understand, nor do I appreciate, this interruption."

What little strength and determination remained from her quick decision outside the old Norman arch drained from her, leaving her quaking. "I beg your forgiveness. I never intended—"

"I will accept your desire to respect me," she said with a slow, thoughtful nod. "Perhaps on another day—" The queen broke off, and the mood in the room shifted as all eyes turned to the doorway where a footman wearing the king's livery stood stiffly.

"Enter," she said.

"Your Majesty, His Majesty requests the presence of Lord Greylund." The man's voice was rich with tension.

The Queen nodded. "You are both dismissed," she said, and Persephone found herself backing away once more until Lord Greylund's touch at her elbow indicated permission to turn and leave.

In the corridor, he bade her a warm farewell. "Another time, Miss Fury. I look forward to our next meeting." He glanced at the footman. "If you will accompany Miss Fury to the Long Gallery—"

"I know the way, my Lord," she said quickly and held her breath as he smiled politely. His features grew more solemn as his thoughts clearly flew ahead to the scene that awaited him in the king's chambers.

Persephone turned and walked away from him, her mind racing. Had they managed their way to the old library without incident because it was in a section of the palace that was little used or because the queen had cleared their way?

She was about to discover which.

❦❦

No one paid her any mind.

It was as if she didn't exist. Servants passing spared her no glance, and once into the oldest wing, there was nobody else within hearing. Stillness hung like a shroud over a sleeping spirit, long silent, yet still expectant. That feeling of expectancy shimmered through her, and the knowing deep in her bones returned.

She was comfortable here. She belonged here. This place wanted her. It was a ridiculous notion, but she was unable to dismiss it.

She arrived at the arched door, released the wards as if she'd been doing so all of her life, and entered.

Billows of dust sent her into a choking spasm until tears streamed from her eyes. Oh, to know the cleansing spells her servants used! Instead, she finally managed to still herself long enough to scan the room and see, beneath the dust, a room that was largely empty. Her spirit plummeted. She had expected a vast collection to be behind such wards, but instead…

She allowed herself a few shallow, calming breaths.

Surely an empty room hadn't been declared forbidden and dangerous and been warded so effectively for three centuries.

With a leap of her heart, she spotted a small casket-shaped mound on a long table. She moved slowly forward, careful not to stir up another cloud of dust, bemoaning the hem of her skirts and the layer of pale grey that already clung to her clothes. But such thoughts fled as she tugged her gloves from her hands and stroked her bare fingers down the table's edge and felt carving. She held her breath and carefully used a gentle magic to lift the dust.

Runes, the kind of runes she'd seen on broken pieces of old stone around the periphery of Erinyes Manor.

She longed for a quill and parchment to record them and instead tried to hold them in her mind, this ancient language she had yet to learn. Then, the first experiment relatively successful, she inhaled again and used the same gentle magic to blow dust away from the carved box. The cloud was dense but contained and moving away from her, so she finally released her held breath and examined the casket, a thicker layer of dust still clinging to it, but at least not soft and ready to fill her lungs at the first movement.

She rolled a layer of dust away with her palm. It curled before dropping, soft and dense, to the table top.

The ensuing cloud of dust sent her coughing again, and had her heart not been stirring with excitement, she would have been in terror of her appearance. But the parchment at her breast had gone beyond pulsing and now was hot against her skin, hot with tension and promise and urgency.

A heavy iron latch on the front of the casket hung open. Someone had been here before her! But it opened easily, and inside lay four long rolled parchments, tied with leather, and a thick tome, its cover of ornately-tooled leather stretched over a thin wood base.

Her hands trembled as she sought the wisdom to know which to open first.

The scrolls were older, and she was less likely to know their language. She had no knowledge of their state, of whether they would crumble if touched, and she had not the knowledge to restore their flexibility. If only the Lord Librarian were less prickly, she could get that knowledge from him.

Well, what good was it being a Fury, if she couldn't find a way around his prickly demeanour?

That settled, she reached for the book and lifted it, almost staggering under its magic. Lush and beautiful, it flowed through her like honey, and her entire body spasmed in response. "Goddess save me," she cried, as her knees buckled, and she fell to the frigid floor, cradling the volume to her breast where the parchment warmed her from the inside out.

Answers.

They called her name.

She opened the volume and turned page after sumptuously

illustrated page, the colours glowing like molten jewels in the dim light, not just because of their rich hues, but with the same magic that made her cloak glow like garnets and her mother's tapestries shimmer with movement. These were the same Shadows the crone Night used. Instead of shrinking back in dismay, she wanted to cradle them against her.

She needed to read—to read closely—and yet, she turned page after page, allowing each new scrolled and detailed image press into her until she thought she would swoon with the ecstasy of it. Somewhere, her mind kept count. Some rational part of her mind counted each leaf she turned until she reached the last one and felt a lurch of loss.

She turned back to the beginning, this time to read, but felt something new, a heavy presence, a *waiting*. She looked over her shoulder at the arched door and knew without opening it that someone was outside. Lord Greylund? The queen?

The knowledge made her uneasy. They couldn't enter, but did they know she was inside? How much time had passed? Had her mother noticed her absence, yet? Was someone seeking her?

Fear and need warred within her as she fought the impulse to gorge on the knowledge that was within her grasp. But she couldn't go further on this day. Her absence would be difficult enough to explain, and her filth even worse. She must return home as quickly as possible, before a message could be sent to the palace looking for her, alerting the queen that she had never left.

She closed the volume and placed it in the casket, which she shut with the heaviest reluctance. But then she did what Bardán Fury had not. She warded the casket itself. It might not stop another Fury from opening it, but it would stop all others. She pressed her cheek against the arched door, listening, probing, and felt nothing but the same emptiness she'd felt when first entering this wing. Whoever had lurked outside seemed to be gone.

She opened it slowly, escaped into the empty hallway, and with one last tremor of relief, re-set the wards on the door behind her, Bardán Fury's ancient magic welling within her again.

A new certainty overcame her. If this wing was original, wouldn't it have its own door to the outside? Perhaps long disused, but still…

She walked deeper into the ancient corridors, and as if her feet had trod this path before turned right instead of left, and came to a window, tall and narrow but easy enough for her to squeeze through.

Again, the warding fell before her hand, and the window opened. She found herself a short drop away from the ground at the rear of the palace.

Within moments she was outside, leaving the window closed and warded and walking quickly through one of the palace's many gardens, headed toward the perimeter of the Magi's park. She had traversed Ordinary London before without disaster striking. It seemed the only option now.

When she broke through the veil into the smells and noises of the Ordinary, her body vibrated with new promise. She would return to the Forbidden Library and she would find a way to free herself from Shadows so dangerous, her ancestor had locked them away.

❦❦

Persephone found Aubyn House blessedly empty of family. She entered at the back and dashed up the servants' stairs without notice, then shed her clothes and scrubbed her hands and face as best she could in cold water before ringing for a mid-afternoon bath. If the servants wondered at such an afternoon activity, they did not question, nor did they comment on the state of her dust-grimed dress. Being the sister of the duchess had its benefits, and her mother need never know.

The family usually gathered in the duchess's sitting room before dinner, unless the men were kept away on royal business. Strange, to think of her family conducting royal business. These new activities were unsettling, betokening as they did a war that she prayed could be avoided.

Persephone sat wearily at the window, contemplating the dusk as Dardanus sat at the pianoforte and played a tune quite calculated to calm her.

How urgently they all worked to keep her calm.

She stood up abruptly, crossed the room to the pianoforte, and took a seat beside Dardanus. She leaned her cheek against his shoulder, closed her eyes, and found peace.

❦

Too much time had passed and still the men did not come.

Her mother kept to her needlework, but Persephone noticed that the threads sliding through her mother's gifted fingers were not the rich, beautiful tones for which her work was known. Persephone knew that it wasn't artistic choice that drew her mother away from the colours she loved but the cloak hanging in Persephone's wardrobe.

Persephone had refused to allow them to remove it, and her mother assented, much to her surprise. She'd watched her mother stroke the fabric one last time before closing the wardrobe door. There was a great sense of loss in that touch.

Now, with a sharp pang of sorrow, she understood why. Her mother had given up the magic that had shaped her creations and set them apart.

Dardanus took her hand and placed it on the keyboard above his. His fingers shifted into a teasing, dancing melody, and with a twitch, she threw herself into the game. He challenged and she echoed. She sent the melody scampering into a new key, and he followed. Back and forth they battled in the game they'd shared as long as they'd known music. She sometimes believed they'd hummed their game in their mother's womb, their melodies tangling and twining in harmonies as yet unheard.

Electra and their mother rose abruptly. For once, it was they who felt it first, the return of the men, the urgency that crackled even before they entered the room.

The music drained from her as she, too, rose, with Dardanus standing beside her.

Something was wrong.

Her father entered the drawing room, his face tight, and without a word he crossed to her mother and took her into his embrace.

The duke entered behind him, and Electra didn't wait. She flew into his arms.

Cosmo sauntered in behind them both, his air elegant, the tension beneath it anything but, as he walked to the fire.

And finally, Robin.

Oh, how she longed to fly to his side, but she could not, with

Dardanus standing beside her, cold with the fear that entered the room with this contingent from Court. But Robin, true Robin, ignored all the restraints that had been put upon him, and she found herself caught in his one-armed embrace even as his free hand rested on her twin's shoulder.

"What is it?" she asked. "What has happened?"

"Nothing yet," Cosmo responded briskly, the only one alone. He gathered heat in his hands, a flare of fire that crackled with power. Suddenly, the reason why she could enter the old wing of the palace, enter the Forbidden Library and even escape without detection was clear to her. The footman's summons to Lord Greylund in the queen's chamber, surely not a thing done lightly, was explained.

The plans were set and the attack against the rebels was imminent. That which had seemed to take forever in the plotting had now come to fruition. Had blood been spilled? Had they killed the bastard?

And Lysander, her maddening brother Lysander, did he still live?

These were the questions she wanted to spill from her lips and yet could not. To ask was to have answers. Answers held terror.

"We ride tomorrow," Cosmo announced, as it seemed clear none else would.

That word—that horrible word—*we.*

Her mother jerked back and stared into her husband's eyes. "No," she said.

"We," he repeated. "You didn't think we could send others out to do what we would not?"

Persephone's father was strong and vital, and she had never once considered him anything but young. His hair lacked the silver of her own, and his body was taut with energy. But he was not a fighter. Was any Fury? They pulled music from the very air, but fighting—blood— attacks—

She touched her scarred shoulder and flinched at the knowledge that she knew more of these things than they did, that she was the only one who had suffered an attack.

She did not want this for them. It was the very magic they feared and hated—the Dark that coiled deep within her, that had demanded release and sprung forward to attack, the kind of magic with which they were not cursed.

She began to tremble, pressed against Robin's chest. Robin was true and decent and strong, but what did he know of battle?

She reached blindly—found Dardanus's hand—grabbed it and clung. Only he would be spared.

But touching him, she felt his bitter regret like a knife. His inability to join them was the taste of blood on her tongue, the burning of shame.

They rode on the morrow.

Cosmo broke the tension with a burst of laughter, tossing his flame so high that it almost kissed the high ceiling with its scorching tongues before falling back into his hands. "We ride tomorrow," he repeated, his eyes meeting Persephone's with hard promise belied by his tone.

"Not all of us," the duke responded briskly. "Not all can be spared." He crossed the room toward the pianoforte, and Persephone felt her brother tense as his shame increased. But when she tried to send him comfort through their touch, he shook his hand free and stood, straight and strong.

Thus he was already on his feet when the duke reached their side and clasped his hand on Dardanus's shoulder and met his eye with grave confidence. "I'll need you with me tomorrow. I've come to rely on Furys, it seems."

Dardanus's cheeks flushed with colour, and Persephone's heart swelled with love for her sister's husband.

This man destined to be their king.

❧ CHAPTER THIRTY-SEVEN ❦

She dug her toes into the sweet earth beneath the heavily laden rose arbour. Like a parched root, she sought the calm and strength she craved.

I've been teaching you since you first arrived—

—you've been too stupid to see it.

The voice hissed and sneered, and she would have shut it out if she could. Instead, she had forced herself to examine his claim. Yes, somehow using assault and taunts, and yes, shaming her with his sheer disdain, he had forced her to control her magical impulses. She reminded herself viciously that he did so to serve his own purpose and felt unreasonable satisfaction that when it came to teaching the supposed tutor was a miserable failure. If he couldn't force knowledge in through mental assault, he used physical force.

But that was no longer her problem. It was his. For if he'd driven her to control, then he'd also shown her ways to fight back.

She had no staff to weigh her down, no bow to hold and stretch, no arrow to let fly. So as the tension built, she sought relief in the soil and wished she dared dig her fingers into it and cup it to her face to inhale its loamy odour.

She waited.

This time, she waited for the light in the duke's study to be doused, for Robin to leave through this garden, by this path.

She ached with the cold. Surely a servant had failed his duty and left the candles burning into the night, and all were gone and already warm in their beds.

The door opened. It was Robin's form that emerged.

"Robin…" she breathed.

She felt more than saw the sharp movement of his head. He moved forward quickly, his steps crunching on the gravel path until he was beside her beneath the arbour and its low-hanging canes of blossoms.

"How did you know?" he asked, his voice low as he pulled her into his arms.

Her spirit leapt at his words, at this connection of what seemed like more than hearts, but even souls. "How could I not know?" She pressed her cheek against him and clung, inhaling and finding the strength she needed. She vowed even more ferociously that she would find a way to free herself of the evil that called to her, she *would*.

Again she was reminded of all she had to lose, of things she had yet to taste, and a new urgency drove her. "You need me," she said, a flat statement between them.

"Beyond comprehension," he agreed, burying his face in her hair.

"Then I shall go with you and—"

Suddenly, the night was cold, and he was not holding her. "You will do no such thing!" The concern in his tone was evident, verging on fear.

She pulled him close again. "You know that you cannot stop me, that I know the way."

"I'll tell Electra—"

"You will not!" This time it was she who opened distance between them, with a sharp shove that caught him off guard. "You will not," she said again, her voice lower and more controlled. "Those of my blood and my bone are going where I have been, where I could lead you, and—"

"Do you think any of us could function knowing that only one of us need fail for that viper to take you? Do you really think your presence would not weaken us, no matter how strong you are?"

Frustration boiled deep within her. "You call me strong at the same time as you say I can only weaken you."

His groan of frustration was too loud. She slapped her hand over his mouth and then pulled him close and used her lips instead. If he dared push her away again—

He did not.

His groan softened, deepened, and she savoured it, revelled in his arms closing around her, the intensity, the connection rejoined, and this time it wasn't comfort she found there.

It was fire that left them both gasping as they broke apart for air.

"Persephone..."

"Don't."

"We mustn't—"

"But we must. You feel it, too, and you know it. We must."

"We aren't animals without choices, and if you think I intend to take you in the dirt under your sister's chamber windows—"

Her pulse skidded, and she fought for air. His open acknowledgement of the desire that hung between them was a triumph, music in her blood, heated and demanding.

She would not allow him to refuse what she had to give, for she realised—fully understood—what before she had only dimly sensed. "My virgin's blood," she whispered, astonished.

He froze.

"There is a power in a virgin's piercing, in her blood, and it will protect you."

"You're mad!"

"It will bring you back to me."

"If such were true, there would be no safety or refuge for virgins when war called to men, because they would all be securing their safety between a virgin's thighs—willing or not!"

"We're not talking about them. We're talking about me! About my—my peculiarities."

"You think your virgin's blood, can stave death away?" he asked incredulously.

"I know that you have a need of me, as I know there are stars above us and worms below. I know if you don't return to me, my life will be nothing! I know that we are bound in ways that are good and worthy and even—even holy—" She broke off, unable to complete her thoughts because they were the secrets and the terror and the shame she could share with no one.

She was bound to Robin Fitzwilliam in ways that were good and worthy and holy, just as she was bound to the bastard Vespasian Jones in ways that were not.

Without Robin, she was lost.

"Hold me." Desperation drove her beyond the limits of her pride.

He gave in. He pulled her to him with a low moan, and she felt him against her, that part of him so hard and long that she would have gasped had he not covered her lips with his own.

She knew triumph.

A low throbbing pulse leapt between her thighs, and if breathing meant not kissing her Robin, not feeling that pulse, she would never breathe again.

"Persephone!"

She felt Robin freeze. They broke apart, and she stifled her frustration by covering her mouth with a trembling hand.

Dardanus. His voice called softly across the garden as he drew nearer.

"I told you that when you need to come out here at night you should—" He broke off, finding them together. "—call me to go with you," he finished, on a sigh.

"Well, I did not need you to come with me," she said, her voice edged with frustration.

"Evidently," he responded, his own voice placid. "But you need to come inside now."

"Are you my keeper?" she snapped, astonished at his temerity.

Robin took her hand and placed it in that of Dardanus. "Until my return," he said softly. "Keep her safe." Despite her brother's presence, he kissed her once more, then he whisked away into the darkness, his boots crunching against the gravel.

"I'm sorry, but Cosmo sent me."

"He knew?"

"I don't think so, but he wanted to see you before... well, before tomorrow."

She whisked ahead of her brother, unwilling to give him any taste of forgiveness.

❦❦

Cosmo, as always these days and especially these nights, stood staring into the fire.

She entered her bedroom and dropped into a chair, where she began wiping her feet free of soil on the piece of folded linen she kept for that purpose.

She wondered if it had become a contest of wills, the wait to see who would speak first.

But Cosmo showed no sign of being aware of any such contest when he finally turned towards her and fixed her with his stare. "You have asked, repeatedly, how we could allow him to invade our minds."

He dropped to the floor before her and sprawled, facing the fire from a new direction. He looked ridiculous in his evening wear, stretched out like a child. He looked like her dear Cosmo. She reached forward and brushed his hair off his forehead, pulling his attention back to her.

"Sometimes, he drank."

She felt sudden dread that he was about to finally reveal things she was not sure she was ready to hear.

"At such times... I don't know whether that is when he dropped his armour, or whether—gods help me for not seeing it—it was when he set his trap. I was the oldest and exposed to him the longest, so if any should have succumbed it should have been me..."

"What?" she rasped. "What?"

"One afternoon there was such a storm—rain pelting down in sheets, lightning flashing, and even though I must have been... fifteen? Sixteen? Old enough not to be afraid of storms, anyway, the schoolroom felt like a small fortress of safety in a world gone wild. Mr Jones smelt of brandy, and it did cross my mind to wonder whether it was Father's brandy he'd dipped into, but it didn't cross my mind to care. He held something in his hand, something he worried and turned in his fingers, staring at it as though he'd seen it so many times, staring was now pure habit. I thought he probably knew every contour."

"What was it?" she asked.

"A coin. A denarius. Not one of ours, not of Magi mint, but an old one from the Roman times."

"Was it hexed? Did it have power?"

"It held memory, and perhaps that is the greatest hex. It held memory."

"Cosmo, stop circling and land on the story. You are not here to entertain but to—"

"Inform, yes, I know. I'm sorry. It's difficult remembering, now that I look back with more awareness. He was always such a shabby thing, unkempt, all prickly angles. You didn't want to get crosswise with him. But on those occasions, he revealed himself, it seemed. That day, he turned the coin over and over until he could hold his hand still and it danced on his fingertips, spun and twirled and caught sparks in the firelight. I wanted that coin. I, who had coins to spare, lusted after the one that danced on his fingertips. And then he told us the story, with that voice of his—"

That voice. Yes, she knew that voice.

"Raspy with drink, smokier, somehow." Cosmo lifted his own brandy to his lips and sipped, his eyes trained on the fire as if the scene he described was playing out before him in the flames. Knowing Cosmo and his powers, perhaps it was.

She gave up on prodding him and found herself sinking back against her chair, caught up in his spell.

"He said his mother couldn't read. Lysander and I exchanged a look that, had he seen it, he would have had us pinned against the wall while he took stripes from our backs because if there was anything he would not have tolerated, it would have been our stunned—and condescending, I am sure—pity."

"Stripes? He beat you?" She clenched her skirts in her hands until they were numb.

"He cuffed us from time to time, but no more than we deserved, I'm sure. You truly had no business in his schoolroom. It would not have gone well."

Because she was the one who never minced words, who made demands, who was, if anything, as prickly as their tutor.

"He said his mother couldn't read, but that she had *aspirations*, if you will. She held him in her arms, a babe newly born, and watched a man in the village pull out a denarius to pay a debt, only he dropped it in the dirt, and instead of picking it up, dug into his pouch for another one. Mr Jones's mother snatched it out of the dirt and handed it back to the gentleman, hoping for a reward of some sort, even though the man could have easily picked it up himself. Did he realise how pathetic he made her sound? Or was he too foxed to notice? Scrounging in the dirt for a coin, hoping for a reward..."

Cosmo shook his head.

"She handed the coin back to the gentleman, showing him the face on it and said, 'I never seen one o' these afore, sir. Who is that there on the thing?' And the gentleman said, 'The emperor Vespasian,' and she said, 'There'll be no lowly names for my babe, then. I'll name him that. Vespasian. Aim him high, I will.' And the gentleman gave her the denarius and told her to spend it on her babe, then, to buy books for him… and instead, she saved it and gave it to him before he left for Oxford and said, 'This is who you are, this is the father I chose for you, and this is what you will be.'"

Persephone swallowed thickly, her head swimming with reactions from empathy to horror. "He would be emperor… or king."

"We felt something for him, there's no denying it. He was scruffy and unkempt, but he spoke of a life we'd never have to live, and I suppose, sometimes, made us feel guilty for it."

"Planting the seeds."

"And in Lysander, he found fertile ground."

She blinked back tears. "But you'll stop him."

"For you, for all of us."

After that, there seemed little to say. They shared the time before the fire, each with their own thoughts, and when she awoke the next morning, it was to find herself in bed with a soft, harmless ball of his conjured fire glowing on the pillow beside her, as if in farewell.

❦

Breakfast swam before her bleary eyes. They were gone. The thought of tea curdled her stomach, and the smell of eggs brought bitterness to the back of her throat.

With a gentle scraping of his chair, the duke drew away from the table. "I shall be leaving for the palace once I retrieve some papers from my study. Dardanus?"

Her brother leapt to his feet, so eager to help, so relieved that someone believed him capable of doing so.

"Persephone?"

She looked up sharply at that, as did her mother and sister.

"I think you might find time passes in a more palatable fashion in the Royal Library, would it not?"

"She has a fitting—" her mother began.

"Which can wait," Electra interrupted, giving Persephone's hand an encouraging squeeze.

"I'll postpone it until after lunch," her mother said, her expression softening.

Persephone scampered up the stairs to fetch her things, the prospect of exploring the Forbidden Library again tantalising her.

❦❦

The scent of smoke reached them in their carriage before they pulled into view of the palace.

They all three stiffened, and when the duke yanked the velvet curtains aside to reveal the view of the palace, they all breathed with relief. Whatever the source of the smoke, it must not be the palace itself that burned. Perhaps someone was burning refuse somewhere behind?

But Persephone's heart clenched in a tight squeeze as the stench grew stronger. It smelled of Shadows. Sweet and evil, Dark and deadly.

She grabbed the duke's arm in a grip made vice-like by her fear.

He turned his face to examine hers intently. "What do you sense?"

She couldn't tell him. She shook her head helplessly. "Just... wrongness." She lowered her eyes to shield them.

The carriage pulled under the Royal entrance to the palace that the duke, being the named heir to the throne, was privileged to use.

A footman opened the carriage door. The duke did not wait for Persephone to precede him, but leapt out. "What is burning?" he demanded.

A courtier stepped forward. "It's nothing, Your Grace. A small fire, but it did not spread."

Persephone stepped from the carriage. When Dardanus joined her and made to speak, she silenced him with sharp glance.

"Where?" the duke asked, his voice still hard with concern.

"In the old wing, a small room that is not in use."

Persephone grabbed Dardanus's arm and kept walking, now blind to anything around her.

"A hidden room, Your Grace, with an arched doorway, one that just appeared yesterday."

"But it's open now?" the duke asked, confused.

"Yes, Your Grace. We don't know how, just that the door was

open and fire within."

"And it didn't spread?"

"No, Your Grace. By the time we found it, it was burning itself out. Rather uncanny."

Her answers.

Gone.

≈ CHAPTER THIRTY-EIGHT ≈

They left her in the Royal Library with the Lord Librarian and a leaden heart.

She pulled a slim volume off the nearest shelf and sat down, the book unopened on a table before her as she stared blindly through her tears. How many men were travelling to the north and west? How long would it take them?

How long before they returned?

At best, she thought, six days. At worst... some would never return.

She choked back a sob and almost shrieked when the Lord Librarian stepped into her line of sight, startling her. She grabbed her handkerchief and dabbed at her eyes as he cleared his throat. "Miss Fury."

She inclined her head and met his gaze, brazening it out, daring him to note her reddened eyes.

"Her Majesty has summoned you." He indicated a liveried servant waiting a few paces away.

She stood. "Thank you."

"Would you like me to keep your book out until you return?"

She blinked in confusion. Since when did this man offer her any assistance? "No, but thank you." She straightened herself and tried to dispel her sense of worry, lest anyone wonder what occasioned such distraction. The force had been sent out on this morn under cover of darkness and secrecy. None should know of the threat that smouldered in Wales. None should know to be concerned.

She took a deep breath and followed the queen's servant out of the hall, his quick, astonished glance at the walls of books making her wonder whether he'd ever been in this place before.

❦❦

Once again she found herself behind a wall of silence, with ladies in waiting shooting irritable looks in her direction as they joined in

377

desultory conversation and plied their needles.

"Do you find it odd that you opened a door that had been hidden for centuries, and now your discovery is nothing but ash?" the queen demanded, her tone as cutting as a razor through silk.

"I find it a tragedy, Your Majesty, such a tragedy that I had not even considered the timing. I had not considered that I might be deemed culpable," she babbled, panic-stricken.

"Do you perhaps know a charm to cause fire to wait hours to erupt?" The queen's eyebrows almost disappeared in her mock surprise.

"No ma'am, of course not."

"Then how could you be culpable?" The royal exasperation was unleashed.

Persephone swallowed thickly. "No ma'am, I wasn't and couldn't have been, thank you, Your Majesty."

"I saw your map."

"You did, ma'am?" The change of topic tossed her off balance.

"Yes, the map of the village of traitors. Meticulous. Detailed. Impressive."

So the queen knew of the threat, the plans? She flushed with shame. Her abduction?

"Did you think such an action as that from this morning could take place without the knowledge of the king?" the old woman asked snappishly.

"I… I hadn't considered, Your Majesty." But once again, she made herself find fascination in her tea. The king she had seen had been incapable of knowledge. After two swallows, she finally found her balance. "He's very fortunate to have you at his side to trust, and you are fortunate to be so trusted…" she said, her tone almost wistful.

"Miss Fury, if one is to be at Court, one must learn to curb one's tongue and not let it go rambling every time one has a thought. Particularly when that thought is to ponder the relationship of your king and queen. Particularly when your queen is the recipient of said ponderings!"

This time her eyes opened wide in horror, and she met the queen's angry gaze and quailed. "I beg your pardon, Your Majesty! I did not mean—I never thought to—"

"Oh hush, girl, and drink your tea. You notice too much and comment too freely. The time will come when your presence at Court will be far more frequent, I would presume, and these are lessons you need to learn."

"Yes, ma'am," she repeated numbly. "I will do better," she finally said, and then remained silent, needing to be elsewhere, anywhere but in this place where she'd been so close to ridding herself of her curse and now smelt the stench of burnt dreams on the air.

"We did not summon you be a mealy-mouthed miss," the old woman eventually complained. "We summoned you to see what you might be wearing and whether you have covered up your horrifying hair."

"No, ma'am," Persephone responded, bracing herself for a command she refused to obey.

"Are you so determined to be an Oddity? Do you think to ruin your chances at marriage? The gowns can be thought of as Original, but the hair," the queen said querulously. "We are sure gentlemen do not like the hair."

"I am not determined to be an Oddity." Persephone chose her words carefully, fighting for presence of mind in the midst of inner chaos. "I do believe a gentleman who desires me for his wife should know what he's getting, and if this displeases him, look elsewhere."

"Pah!"

Persephone clenched the teacup more tightly and braced herself.

"Any who choose you are choosing to marry close to the crown as can be got. They will be choosing position and access to the king. You could have warts, spots, and an extra nose, and you would still be a prize."

Persephone felt the blood drain from her face as she placed the teacup on the table between them. "Of course," she said softly, her throat clogging with tears. Those she loved were at this very moment tearing across the country towards a confrontation that terrified her, the Forbidden Library was burned, raising issues she hadn't had time to consider, and now, she was sitting before the queen, making missteps at every step, humiliating herself, and bringing shame to her family.

"I said," the queen's voice raised to a sharper edge, "that we did not summon you to be mealy-mouthed! Do not weep in our presence! We do not desire to watch you weep!"

"I beg your pardon most humbly," Persephone said, her own voice rising to her dismay, "but I am not in a state of mind to be pleasant company, no matter how much I might desire it!"

The queen glared at her. "Miss Fury, what would it take to put you in the proper state of mind to be pleasant company?"

Persephone's eyes darted wildly in all directions, looking for something, anything calming on which to focus. She belatedly felt the tremor of magic deep within her, the subtle but growing threat. Her gaze snagged on the tight-faced Heliotrope standing at a distance, outside the ring of silence that she herself had woven.

Persephone met the queen's gaze without flinching. "I desire to learn the silencing spell, if it please Your Majesty." She dropped her eyes and held her breath.

"You wish to learn a servant's spell?" the old monarch demanded, shock and disapproval ringing in her tones so loudly, it was a wonder that all in the room didn't react, despite the spell.

"I like learning," Persephone said. "It will be a useful skill in a house of brothers."

"You will not be in a house of brothers much longer."

Persephone nodded, swallowing her disappointment.

"It could be a dangerous bit of magic for a wife to use, a bit of magic that could hide her indiscretions if she chose to entertain gentlemen, for example."

"I would never—" Persephone began in horror.

"Until you know who your husband is, you do not know what you might do. Until you spend long nights remembering what might have been, you do not know." The old queen sniffed with satisfaction. "Do not tell me what you wouldn't do."

But she'd gone too far. Persephone did not weigh her words, and she did not pause to consider that the old woman was possibly even speaking of her own indiscretions, for such would be treason. She only knew that such an accusation could not be born. "Your Majesty, you have seen many things and you are wise, but you *do not know me*. When

I vow, it is my honour and the word of a Fury that is at stake. I will not betray that vow, and I will not betray my husband."

The old woman's eyes grew soft, as did her voice. "I fear what life will do to you, Miss Fury." She took a thoughtful sip of her own tea. "But I believe watching you learn the servant's skill of silencing charms will be diverting." She summoned the servant with a slight, curt nod, and the sounds of the room returned. "Dismiss everyone and then return. I have a task for you."

As the servant turned to do so, the old queen's eyes glittered with anticipation. "I knew you would entertain me, girl."

The tension in Persephone's stomach loosened, and as she prepared herself for new magic, her spirit lightened, despite it all.

❦❦

It wasn't until later, much later, that she realised the time spent with a disapproving Heliotrope had done more than entertain a bored monarch. It also ate up her time at the palace, so that when she emerged from the queen's quarters, a servant awaited her with a message that the duke had called a carriage for her.

She passed the corridor that would have led her deeper into the palace, into its oldest and most secret depths, and instead walked towards the sunlit entrance hall, away from any opportunity to see for herself that all that remained of her answers was ash. Impossible now to follow the faint stench of burning shadows to its source and to mourn.

❦❦

Five days and nights they had been gone, and by any calculation, even if the size of their party slowed their travel, they must be at the rebel village soon. Whatever would happen in that place, whatever blood would be spilled, would be happening soon. That knowledge gripped her with a certainty that threatened to turn her bowels to water.

She found herself wanting to hide more and more often these days. She longed for the priest holes at Erinyes Manor, for the security of seclusion. She no longer trembled with suppressed magic. She found that playing the pianoforte, pouring herself into its passions, relieved her.

Your task was to play for you, stupid girl. You are the one who needs the music. Tonight, it's the only release you have, Jones had told her. She wouldn't burn Aubyn House down over their heads.

She took long walks through the Magi trails of Hyde Park, servants trailing after at a distance, and on one occasion she destroyed a large rock there, just to feel the delicious release as it went to powder.

At night sometimes, when sleep didn't come, she sought the garden, where she could step off the gravel path and dig her bare toes into the moist earth.

She did not need to hide for any magical reason, but her heart needed seclusion. Responsibility weighed heavily upon her shoulders. She remembered the people of the village, and even though she'd found no friends there, she thought of them in their rustic lives and imagined the forces of the king riding down upon them and—

She longed for a priest hole.

Or perhaps, that odd Ordinary practice of confession the Catholics had done in their chapel at Erinyes Manor. Was there someone who could absolve her? Would her goddess absolve her, if she asked? Did she deserve to be absolved?

She shot to her feet. The basilica. She must go and pray, for her father and brothers, for Robin, for all who were on their way west, for the innocents who were caught up in the rebels' malevolent schemes.

She hadn't been since her vigil. Suddenly, the memory of the discomforts of that night seemed less important, and the beauty and peace the basilica offered seemed a refuge from the world.

☞☜

She was not surprised to have to make the trip alone in the carriage, for neither her mother nor her sister were prone to public worship, preferring the small remembrances performed at their own personal shrines.

Persephone entered the basilica and took a moment to allow her eyes to adjust to the dim light of the narthex before stepping into the nave. It stretched before her, its stone floor beginning to show wear after three centuries of use, the stained glass in the various shrines lining the nave spilling jewels of light across the floor. The faint scent of incense still clung to the air from the early morning rites.

She passed the shrine dedicated to Ares and stopped. Candles burned low, their flames sputtering in the thin films of wax that remained. Offerings were piled before his altar. All evidence pointed to a ritual performed to this god on behalf of those headed to Wales.

To *Ares*. The god of war, and so they, the men, chose him to bless their endeavour, but at what cost? Ares, who cared little for strategy but loved fighting. Ares, who raped and relished massacres.

She wanted to sweep the alcove clean with a blast of magic. How dared they? Her fingers curled into fists at her side. She forced herself to find the chapel of Athena, to drop to her knees and beg for her blessings, her guidance, and her protection. Hadn't she the power to disarm her brother, Ares? Hadn't she done so when he threatened to add his own mischief to a battle she cared about? She was the clever warrior, the one who used cunning and magic rather than brute force. She would care about protecting the helpless as well as guiding the worthy.

Why couldn't they have chosen Athena? Why hadn't they? Because in their manly endeavours, they had no respect for a female deity? Because they feared Vespasian Jones so much, there was no room in their retaliations for cunning and protection of the weak?

Tears coursed down her cheeks as she thought of all those who stood to suffer, and instead of absolution, she found new fears.

When her tears were spent, when she'd laid her own offerings on the altar, she reached into her sleeve and pulled out the flute. She cradled it in her hands, then lifted it high to catch a ray of cobalt light shining through the goddess's robe in the window. "I have not a flute of beechwood but pray thee that my offering of silver music is pleasing to your ears," she whispered, then raised it to her lips.

The first note floated like clear, sweet nectar to the ears. She did not attempt to play a recognisable tune but instead let the notes trip and tumble from her lips, sometimes flowing like velvet, sometimes a staccato spray of unexpected joy laid upon the air. It was in the playing, not the praying, that she found her peace. She found her absolution.

If she closed her eyes and the goddess she saw, the goddess she yearned to hear, was not the one pictured in the window, she refused to admit such a thing. Athena, she knew and trusted. Elen, the old goddess, she knew not and trusted not.

Finally, the last note had been played and her coins lain on the altar. She stood wearily, her knees bruised from the hard, cold floor, and turned to face the immense front doors of the basilica. A soft murmur caught her ear. It was a familiar voice, and yet so soft that she could not place it. There was little doubt that prayers were being spoken, rhythmic and urgent. To interrupt the petitioner would be at the very least, rude. And yet, that voice…

She walked quietly down the nave until she approached the apse, and only then did she spy the duke kneeling at the high altar of Apollo, his head bowed, his hair of flame glowing in the noonday spill of light through the halo of the sun that circled Apollo's head. He had no retinue. No group of men prayed with him or were nearby waiting. He was alone.

With a tug at her heart, she thought, *alone and lonely.*

What a burden he bore on this day, and here he sought his own absolution? Guidance? Blessings on those who had been sent forth?

Without further thought, she dropped to her aching knees again and joined him, praying to the god of the sun to shine down on the venture and, she couldn't help but think a mite rebelliously, curtail Ares if necessary.

❧ CHAPTER THIRTY-NINE ❧

"What an unexpected delight to find you here."
She whipped her head up as guiltily as if she'd been caught doing something untoward, shocked that the duke's prayers had ended without her notice. Only upon her completing her own and starting to rise had he made his presence known with an offer of his hand to assist. She sketched the faintest curtsey to her sister's husband. "Your Grace," she murmured.

He kissed the back of her hand. "Persephone." Without releasing it, he said gently, "You pray for your father and your brothers."

"And Robin, and Otter, and…" She studied the floor as avoided his gaze. "Any who might fall without deserving such a fate."

"You are a remarkable young lady." He released her hand. "Did you perhaps need a ride to Aubyn House?"

"The carriage is waiting for me," she said.

"Come with me." He led her to a low bench at the back of the nave and motioned for her to sit. "I had hoped to speak to you."

She took the seat he indicated, holding herself very still. She had wondered when he would seek her out and was torn between insult if he did not think her observations merited deeper conversation and distress at what he might ask her.

"We must speak of Vespasian Wyllt."

She gave a jerky nod.

"If it would make you more comfortable, I could ask Electra or Cosmo… your mother, perhaps? To join us?"

"No!" The word was too abrupt, but she did not want any others to share witness.

"Has he taken a wo—" The duke drew in a careful breath and sat back in his chair. "A wife?"

"I don't know. I don't—I saw no indication that he had." What a thought!

"But you're certain that there was no Ordinary woman there.

385

Someone who would be… beholden to him."

She thought of the woman writhing in blood on the cottage floor and barely restrained a shudder.

"What is it? What are you remembering?" he urged gently. "I know this might be difficult, but it is vital."

"There was a woman, and there seemed to be a connection between them, but she wasn't Ordinary."

"What is her name?"

"Lark."

He frowned, clearly disappointed. But then, again alert, he asked, "And her appearance?"

Persephone gave a half-shrug. "She has light hair, curls." But then, because it *was* vital, she forced herself to add, "The colour of wheat at harvest."

"Ah…" He steepled his fingers under his chin, his eyes glittering. "Did she perchance… sing?"

"Like an angel," she replied.

"So, Lark might be an Earthborn name given to her after she joined them, replacing her Ordinary name."

"Your Grace, I would know if she were Ordinary."

He nodded. "Of course. Perhaps I'm simply wanting rather than accepting, and that, my dear, is a dangerous mistake to make."

The hardness that entered his gaze belied his words. He most certainly believed he'd discovered something important. "The connection between them?" he pushed. "Was it… intense?"

She turned her head away from him, closed her eyes, fighting off the images. Worse, she did not want to recall her own participation. She probed for a way to respond with truth, if not the whole truth. "She was eager to please him. Almost desperately eager. He did not find it difficult to use her desperation to his own ends."

The duke drew back and arched his brows.

Belatedly, new images flashed across her mind. She forced the blush down, not wanting to betray knowledge that would be unbecoming a young lady. "He's a wicked creature who is capable of taking advantage of any weakness, of imposing his will on those unable to refuse him."

"What bothers you, my sister? Something is distressing you,

something beyond those things of which we speak."

"I worry that I will bring destruction on innocents whose only sin was falling under his mind magic and getting caught up in his web without any ability to protect themselves. Is it fair?" she asked softly. "Is it fair for them to suffer?"

"That is the injustice of the world," he said, his face turned to stare into the heart of the basilica. "It's the heaviest of burdens, knowing that your decisions determine whether people live or die."

"Not heavy for him."

"No. But heavy for our king, and heavy for... for those who must act on his behalf."

"The king seems so very ill."

The duke nodded gravely. "But he has amazed us with his ability to rejuvenate, and I pray that he continues to do so for many years."

"When I saw him..."

"After his healings, he comes back to us with his spirit and his wisdom, even if each time, a little more of his physical strength is gone forever. His presence brings such joy and comfort to us all. We are blessed to have such a king."

"May the gods continue to grant him long life and happiness," she said automatically, tracing an eternal circle on her forehead with her wrist.

He smiled softly. "Indeed."

He took her hand in his, and alarm jolted through her. Her bare hand, stripped of its glove in order to play the flute, and he was touching her hand, too close to her fingertips. Was it impropriety if he was married to her sister, and his intent so clearly to reassure, and he didn't even notice that he was holding her ungloved hand? Her stomach settled, and her pulse slowed, and she allowed her hand to soften and relax in his as he spoke, his voice tense with concern.

"I must ask you something more, and I beg your pardon for this, but..." He cleared his throat uncomfortably.

She'd never witnessed him thus. The duke, the future king, uncertain and ill-at-ease! "Yes, Your Grace?"

"When you returned, we all had such fears and concerns for your physical safety. Concerns that you might have been subjected to unthinkable—" He broke off.

"But I wasn't," she said, cheeks burning with embarrassment, and also with that slow-burning rage that it always came back to this, to her maidenhood. "As I reassured you all, I am now as I was before I left."

His eyes locked onto hers, probing and urgent. "That is not what I meant. I meant—did he hurt you in any other way? Did he perform a ritual and include you and— Do you have any unexplained marks or injuries on your—" His gaze flickered down to her abdomen and back up.

She felt a wash of Shadow sweep over her as she pulled her hand free. *He knew.* "I... witnessed something. But he did not do it to me." Oh, no. Not to her. *With* her. She covered her cheeks and squeezed her eyes shut, lest he see them and read the truth.

"I must ask you these things, Persephone. I must. Please forgive me, but... whom did he use?"

"Lark," she breathed. "He used Lark."

"Then she is still virgin?" He was no longer looking at her, to see her horror that he would discuss such things with her. He was lost in his own thoughts, his brow knit in concentration. Finally, he murmured as if only for his own ears, "He... he is farming her."

Trembling, Persephone began tugging her glove onto her right hand, covering it, attempting to erase the memory of Shadow that lingered, summoned by his questions, his *knowledge.* He had said he knew Vespasian Jones to be evil, but she had never dreamed he knew so much. Would know to suspect so much about her. So much, and yet, blessedly, not all.

She had both hands gloved and was reaching to tug her shawl more securely around her shoulders, to rise, to leave, when he stopped her with a gentle word.

"Peace..."

She raised her eyes to his and found no censure, nothing but gentle concern.

"Be at peace, beloved sister of my wife. You have been afraid and guilty, and I've seen you struggle with it, even to come here to pray to the wisest of deities for your purpose. I have seen, and I know what you seek."

"How could you?" she sighed miserably.

"Because I have struggled, too. But now I know as I couldn't be sure before. We are doing what needs to be done. There is no reason for your sweet guilt, my dear, for you seek to protect those you love, and there is no action more justified than that. We protect the helpless, the weak, even the strong and mighty, and when that monster is gone, whatever the price, our world will be safe again."

Like Sisyphus with his boulder, Atlas with his world, she'd felt bowed beneath an impossible weight. But now, in the soft glow of these holy walls, she felt it lifted from her and carried by another, and she felt absolution and hope and... something growing deep within her... renewed power, and more, a renewed need to act, to join the battle, to add her magic.

As if sensing her desire, he leaned forward with even more intensity. "Your family believes that you have unusual powers, Persephone. If you do, is it possible that... that your power... could help us?"

She felt the blood drain from her face, but there was only one answer. "Of course, Your Grace."

"Ah," he said, "the priests await my leaving so that they can continue their prayers." He nodded at the bishop across the depth of the basilica. A line of dark-robed men filed into the quire. Voices raised, they sang prayers to the gods, their song wafting like smoke into the high arched ceiling, and beyond.

"Your Grace." The bishop joined them. "Miss Fury," he added with the barest glance in her direction, his dismissal of Persephone clear.

"My Lord," she responded with a curtsey. "If you'll excuse me," she said, the Shadows within her seeming to flare at his presence, "I will return home to weave prayers of my own, however inadequate they might be."

The duke kissed her gloved knuckles as she curtseyed.

The magic within her demanded release, and if such a thing were possible, she would send it west to protect those she loved.

☙❧

Robin's eyes felt filled with grit, and his beard as grizzled as the old shepherd who managed his flock at his familial manor. He ached from riding. His heart bled with images of all that he had seen, one melting into the next…

Apollo Fury, eyes closed, head cocked, lips curved into a smug smile. "Ah yes, excellent…" Assessing the wards that protected the rebels in their hill fort, hid them and their path from view, and finding a source of pride, because he recognised them and knew that his ne'er-do-well son had cast them with Fury skill.

Apollo Fury, with his arm raised and a whispered chant, brought those same wards down.

The shock in the wide eyes of the first man they saw—with light brown hair and big ears and sunburned skin—as he saw the King's horsemen riding down upon him, and reached for a bow and arrow of all things—

The gash across his face and throat as a hex sliced him.

The blood gushing in spurts as he crumpled to the ground.

Blood splashed across Robin's trouser leg as he rode by, a voice in his head screaming to stop, to give aid, that man was bleeding, was dying…

He'd been reaching for a bow and arrow.

A bow and arrow, against magic? Did he really deserve death?

Robin had killed game; he'd witnessed slaughter with blood and entrails spilling and had seen hides cast aside for tanning. The smells had coated his mouth and nose and permeated his skin.

Nothing prepared him for the sight of human blood spilled, for human terror, for feeling the need to protect those whom he was sent to attack when they thundered into the village. Fowl scattered, children cried, women grabbed them and ran.

And then the scream, the scream that split his soul and sent him careening to the left, to follow its sound, to do something—anything—to stop it, for that scream was torn from the depths of a soul.…

And the child, oh the child, in a pool of blood, the woman holding it and screaming her rage and her pain and her grief—

His eyes met hers for one ragged moment.

He knew himself dead, if she'd had her way.

Dead for being one of the invaders.

Liberators, he wanted to explain. Here to release her, to release them all, to save them from the Dark bonds that held them wrapped in magical lies and deceptions.

It made no difference why they were there.

She rose to her feet, her limp child clutched against her with one arm as she flung her hand forward, and he sensed it—sensed it all—knew what was happening before it could happen and wheeled his horse sideways into the flank of the one beside him, before his companion could cast the spell to stop her—*gods, don't kill her*—and in so doing, knocked them both clear of the pulse of death she sent from her fingertips, screaming past with echoes of her savage cry.

But he stopped her death, as well.

"Go!" he shouted to her, opening himself to a second attack if she should try again. "Go! I can't protect you again!"

Somehow he pierced her pain, and against all odds, her eyes locked to his for a sharp-edged moment. She whirled away with her bloody burden and took off running, leaving him to numbly absorb the verbal abuse of the soldier whose killing hex he had sent astray.

It had all been chaos, and the idea that this was a camp of rebels that could somehow threaten the authority of the Crown brought bile to his throat.

Ludicrous. Insane. They were meant to only get the leader. His fingers itched with the longing to bring that villain down.

Where was he?

Then—as if summoned—the villain was there.

Standing atop a cottage roof at the highest point in the village, legs braced wide, his mouth twisted in a snarl as he roared his rage.

Shadows, Dark and pulsing, streamed from his fingertips as he stood there, daring them to take him down, and all granted him that desire, as Robin felt and saw all his fellow riders reining, turning, firing magic at the towering Earthborn rebel who taunted them with his position.

No spell, no hex touched him. He neither flinched nor staggered.

Instead, he stood, a raging savage, his hair long and wild, streaming around him, black as night and streaked with silver—shouting a word, a strange, foreign word—*'Encilio!'*—that was repeated by any

Earthborn within sight or hearing, repeated in an urgent command, as they all turned and ran.

Like cowards.

Leaving their leader alone, standing there, a taunting figure above them all, untouchable. His power was horrifying to behold. Had any of the Fireborn such apparent invulnerability? The man reeked of Shadow and malevolence, and like a dagger to his own heart, Robin thought of Persephone in this demon's control, of the scar she bore on her flesh that this man had put there.

A howl of anger built within him, and suddenly, he was charging forward, riding for the cottage as if to charge its wattle walls.

He felt the eyes—black with evil—turn on him. He felt himself the focus and tossed back his head and raised his hand to do that which he had thought himself incapable—

To hurl death.

With a prayer to Ares on his tongue, he released the spell and felt the wrenching pain all the way up his arm to his shoulder as the power exploded from him, a power and pain he'd never experienced before.

The world slowed and air lit up like white fire. Pain screamed through him as his eyes locked with his target. Something pulsed between them, and he knew in that moment how vulnerable he'd left himself, that his very life was as brittle as the thin shell of an egg.

He felt the tremor as the man of Shadows slid his gaze away, dismissed him as insignificant, and whirled away in a billow of dark cloak and wind-whipped energy, leapt, and disappeared from view behind the cottage.

It was over, the skirmish that had begun as horrifying carnage and then, upon the command of their enemy, their true enemy, had ended in confusion and a village empty save the king's men riding in circles, looking for an enemy who was no longer there.

Men took off for the forest on the far side of the village, regrouped.

Robin sat frozen, staring at the rooftop, assaulted by memory of night-black hair streaked with silver, of pulses of the Shadow that lingered around his Persephone, even though she was safe with her family. He hadn't understood before what that Shadow might be and now was fearful that he did—a link between her and an evil he'd never dreamed could exist.

But it made no difference.

He burned with a restless and aching desperation that drove him forward on the road to London, to his anchor, his roots into the earth, and the odd and fragile girl who seemed to own a piece of him.

❦

By the time she reached Aubyn House, urgency rose in her like a storm-driven tide. She was tugging her gloves from her hands before the door closed behind her and had her pelisse unbuttoned and off before the footman was standing there to take it.

"The duchess?" she asked, unable to form a more coherent thought.

"In her sitting room, miss."

Hair in her face, in her mouth, tangling in her eyelashes, she burst into Electra's upstairs sitting room to find her entertaining Lady Dupree. Both looked up from their tea, Electra startled, Lady Dupree scandalised by her abrupt entrance.

"Darling, is something amiss?" Electra asked, rising. She glanced back at her companion, who clearly was not meant to know of the situation in Wales.

Persephone gave her head a helpless shake. "No, nothing is amiss. My apologies for bursting in so rudely." With a look of longing at the small pianoforte, she bobbed a curtsey to them both and withdrew.

Upon entering her own chambers, she fell against the closed door, gasping for air.

She might be female, they might have left her behind, but she wasn't helpless. She slid the flute from her sleeve and stared at it. Didn't these instruments focus her magic into a thing of power? Whether a violin, or a pianoforte, or even a drum, didn't they wrap magic tighter until it was a fine but powerful weave that ensnared all who listened in its web? She who could bring tears or joy to her listeners could certainly bring triumph and protection to those who deserved it.

She felt a desperate laugh bubble up, felt the incipient onset of hysteria. It was ridiculous, nay, insane to think she could do anything that would have effect on those two hundred miles away. She cradled the flute in her hands, blew her breath across it, and watched the metal fog briefly and then clear.

She had pressed it to her lips when the door behind her opened, sending her stumbling.

"I rid us of that tedious woman; now tell me what is happening."

"I must play magic to protect them." Persephone wondered if she sounded as mad as she felt.

"Then we both shall," her sister—her beautiful, beautiful sister—said, without hesitation. "I will join you."

Somehow, it did not astonish her that Dardanus was climbing the stairs when they went back into the hallway. He crossed the distance between them and took her hands in his. "I felt you," he said. "Felt your need of me."

She pressed her lips against the back of his hand. "You are the brother of my flesh and my spirit; how could you not? I feel something, as well. Something is happening in Wales, and I refuse to be helpless, I—"

"Nothing can be wrong now that we are all here together," Electra said. "Now, enough talk. We must play."

Electra led them into the room she had just abandoned and took her seat at the pianoforte, Dardanus at the violoncello.

Persephone almost joined them with the flute yet found herself hesitating. She went to the painted cabinet with figures from the far off Orient and opened it and wrapped her hand around the throat of the old Stainer violin with its carved lion head, its strings already vibrating against her palm as she lifted it. Her other hand closed around the bow, and so intense was her need to play and its need to be played that it seemed to leap in her grip.

She turned into the room where her mother now sat with clenched hands in her lap, with its slanting rays of sun falling across the floor and her sister's rose silk skirts swelling around her on her bench.

Persephone closed her eyes and summoned the night.

The night of terror and discovery when, humiliated, she had played for money in the nasty heart of Ordinary London. The night when she had, for the first time, outwitted and outplayed the bastard Vespasian Jones.

She inhaled deeply and could almost taste the stench of Ordinary.

She cocked her head, nestled the gleaming instrument under her chin, and reached back to the memory of dancing and laughing and overwhelming power. She played, and the spirit rose within her. She was only barely aware that Electra and Dardanus joined her in counterpoint. She played with her body, her heart, her soul.

And her magic was released with its Shadows, and its glory, to soar.

❧❦

She was the first to feel the heaviness in the air, the shift from music to discord. Suddenly, her arms throbbed with weariness, ached with it, and she dropped them so heavily the violin almost struck the floor. Only years of training and instinct tightened her grasp in time to save disaster. She focused her attention on the doorway, felt every muscle and tendon in her body tense as it opened.

The duke stood there, his face drained of colour, his stature erect, with eyes for none but Persephone.

Electra's fingers stuttered on the keys, and the violoncello ceased its luxurious tones abruptly.

"Sebastian?" Electra's voice was tremulous. "You've had word?"

Still, his eyes locked onto Persephone's, as he said, "A pigeon. I came immediately."

Her mother let out a low moan, covering her mouth with her hand.

"No," he said abruptly, visually putting himself together. "It's not—not what you fear. We lost only one man, and he was not of your acquaintance or blood. Other than that, we took only minor injuries."

Persephone found herself unable to speak, could only stare at him, waiting for that which he did not want to share.

Finally, he approached her, holding out his hands. "Sister of my heart," he said, his voice low and rich with pain. "I have failed you."

"He lives," Persephone said.

"Vespasian Wyllt escaped with his life…"

Rage boiled up in her. "And the innocents? Did they survive?"

"There were deaths, and injuries, but then—" He spread his hands wide in confusion. "—they disappeared. Not even our most skilled spell-casters recognised the magics that hid them. They were simply… gone."

She had heard it said that when one's rage spills over even the eyes saw red. In that moment, she knew it to be true. She clenched her fists, and it was a wonder that the bow and the violin's throat didn't snap.

She longed to smash them, to take that violin and smash it over something—anything—to watch it explode into splinters as—

"Sebastian!"

Her sister's voice pulled her back, drew her back from her boiling rage, and to her shock, the duke—the future King of all the Magi in England, Wales and Scotland—had knelt before her, his face turned up to hers and twisted in agony.

"My sister…" he whispered. "I have failed you."

Cold crept into her veins. As quickly as they had roared with fire, they now froze with ice. "No," she said.

"I made a vow, and I have failed you. I told you that we would not harm him, but… your brother's child—"

"No!" she cried, and took a step backward.

But he grabbed her hand and held it tightly in his, the bare hand that had been playing joyous magic only moments before and now was cold with Shadow.

"One of the peasants—an ignorant, wicked woman—thought to stop us with magic, thought to raise up their—their king—" He broke off.

Her mother wept openly; she heard her sobs, even as her own were hard, jagged things caught in her chest, unable to find release, and she could do naught but stare into his face.

"It was too late to stay the sword, and he—the child—was killed."

The world spun slowly, so slowly… every surface around her glowed, shimmered, wore a halo, as she stared numbly down at the head of flame bowed before her, at the hand that clasped hers, the lips that pressed themselves against her hand in desperate supplication.

At the tear flowing from her sister's eye as she dropped beside her husband, as slowly and delicately as a handkerchief caught by a breeze, settling beside him in a crumple of silken skirts, beautiful even in her pain, the tear like a diamond, so slowly it slid down her cheek, so brightly did it glitter in the light of candles.

Candles—everywhere—glowing with diamond dust, scented with

the dew of roses, lighting the room with beauty when within Persephone's heart stretched and curled Shadow black as sin and red as blood.

Until all she could do was open her mouth in a silent howl of anguish as the world circled slowly around her and she heard the echo of Lark's prophecy that she would bring her precious nephew's death.

The black Shadows swallowed her from the inside out, swallowed her whole.

❧ CHAPTER FORTY ❧

Sometimes… sometimes she could feel Electra nestled against her, holding her through what seemed to be an endless agony. She heard her sister pleading to her to come back to them, to wake up.

She sank farther away, into the Darkness of grief and guilt.

Sometimes it was her mother who held her, who spoke to her of things she did not want to hear—of forgiveness, and lack of blame, and things happening beyond our control and the will of the gods being at war with our own, and she fled, she fled these words of torment, words that were meant to comfort and instead pierced her to the quick.

Sometimes it was Dardanus, her beloved twin's voice that sang to her, wrapped her in soft wool and nestled her in comfort, and still… she drifted further away, seeking to become lost in an underworld of her own making.

The blackness was a refuge, a Dark comfort filled with shadows and Shadows and for once, instead of frightening her, it was frighteningly seductive. Please, she heard herself cry or moan into the smothering velvet of Dark, *please…*

Nothing more. She knew not what she begged for, only that she begged from the depths of her Dark soul for something and that it meant going deeper into the chasm, running from the people who loved her. All she wanted was to kill the one responsible for it all.

His eyes, black as coal and burning with hatred, stared at her from her nightmares, and she was pinned like a moth, but this time he had reason to hate her.

She had reason to hate herself. She had set the hounds of Hades loose, and that black coal, those smoking embers were in her, burning her from the inside out, an everlasting punishment, and she was willing to suffer it, and more, if it meant bringing that sweet child back.

She clutched the Dark need for vengeance to her breast and nursed it, even as it threatened to burn her soul beyond recognition.

Whatever it took, she would do.

Someday.

But for now… for now… she drifted in the churning, nauseating, oily black waters that chilled her to the bone and kept those who would love her—who did not understand the depth of her wickedness or the threat of what she carried inside her—at bay.

❦

"Sir Robin!"

The last person he'd expected to greet him was her mother. Of the entire family, he had the least connection to her, the least understanding of how she might view his suit for her daughter's hand.

He bowed over her hand, excruciatingly aware of his dishevelled state.

She trapped him with her fine blue eyes, narrowed in appraisal.

"I hoped to see Persephone."

"She is indisposed and not receiving." A slight arch of one brow indicated without question that she thought perhaps he should be in the same state and not in her daughter's drawing room. The drawn nature of her appearance, however, indicated much more, and reminded him…

He reached into his inner pocket and retrieved a small scroll, tightly wound and sealed. He offered it to her with another slight bow. "From your husband, madam."

She snatched it from him with no pretence at civility, turned away from him, and carried it to a window where she could read it with her back to him. Straight as an iron rod, she stood, only her head bent as she absorbed the contents of the missive. She continued to stand there long after the time it would take to read, and finally he saw the slight tremble of her hands, her shoulders.

He groped for a handkerchief, then remembered that everything he possessed, everything on his person, was begrimed from days of travel and of— He cut off that thought, unwilling to return his thoughts to Wales, except, of course, he must, for it was Wales that made her weep.

"He won't find him," she said, her voice broken. "Lysander won't allow himself to be found, especially not now…"

"He knows. He must try."

She nodded her head, still facing away from him and finally reached for her own handkerchief.

"Mrs Fury, if you could please tell me of Persephone. Is it…" Shadows swirling, devouring… "Is it her old malaise?"

"She hasn't awakened since she learned of the child's death."

The child, a broken thing in his mother's arms, their flesh and blood. He could offer no comfort, for there was none in that death.

She turned to him, and her lovely face showed signs of age he'd never seen there before. "I will take you to see her. I will remain with you."

"Thank you. Of course… thank you." What more was there to say beyond that?

She led him up the stairs and down a hallway he'd never seen, having never been a guest of Aubyn House. Its interior was vaster than he'd suspected, but all that meant to him was that it was taking longer to find his Persephone than he thought he could bear.

She opened the door to a darkened room with candles burning dimly by a four-post bed and a body so still it appeared lifeless.

He closed the distance without thought or care that he was being improper. He stood and stared at skin so white it threatened the linens around it for pallor. Her hair lay long and tangled from her thrashing. One hand clenched into a tight fist outside the covers, the only sign of life other than the slight rise and fall of her chest.

"Persephone…" he breathed.

She did not move.

He sank to the bed and took her hand in his, stroked the tender skin, willing her fingers to relax… helpless. Helpless. He meant the words to apply to her, lost in her misery, and yet didn't they describe him? Helpless in the midst of chaos and blood and fear, helpless to stop it, helpless to do what she'd bid him to do? Did he even deserve her?

"Please come back to us," he said, his voice cracking. "We need you so." Not caring that her mother was present, he pleaded, "I need you so."

❦

The urgency quaked through her with enough power to find that tiny core that was rage as well as Fury.

No, she wanted to say, *no. Not me.*

And then the words of the goddess, *Your Robin needs you.* Words of liquid seduction, to entice her and draw her back.

But they couldn't need her. She was a creature of Shadows, and any who needed her would fall.

The world spun wildly around her until vomit rose from her gullet, and perhaps she would die of it, drown in it.

Light of every colour exploded before her, and it should have been Cosmo who brought such light, but it wasn't.

"Robin." Her voice was unrecognisable to her own ears, but his hand tightened on hers, his head snapping up to find her staring at him, and she saw the joy on his face, the horrible joy. He didn't know—he didn't understand what she was.

He laughed, gods damn him. He laughed, broken and sounding too close to tears, and then there were tears streaking down his face. How dare he sit on her very bed and call her back only to weep?

"You do not need me," she snapped, or tried to, but her voice would not cooperate and came out more like a whining thing. "You can't need me. You don't—don't understand. It's you—you who are good and strong. You whom we need!"

He caught her hand and turned his face into it, pressing his lips against her palm.

She whispered, "I need you," and this time it was her voice that broke on a sob.

He gathered her into the strength and goodness that she craved, that would chase away the Shadows and save her. He smelled of horse and rank male sweat and things she did not recognise and did not want to recognise, but he smelt also of Robin, until finally she clung to him, tears choking her, and knew that as long as Robin lived, there was hope and reason for her to live as well.

Slowly, with the scent of lilac and lemon balm, came the awareness that they were not alone and that she held a man in her tight embrace, even as she languished in her night-rail. She choked, this time on embarrassment and dismay, and pulled herself free. "Mama?" she said, finding her mother's still form standing in silhouette against the west-facing window.

"Sir Robin," her mother said firmly, "I thank you delivering my husband's message, and for... being a friend to our family, but now I must ask you to leave us in our grief."

Had her mother's voice not reeked with despair, she might have protested this chilly dismissal.

Once more, Robin pressed his lips to the back of her knuckles— her bare knuckles, and this time a tremor swept through her. He bade the most formal of adieus and, with one last, long glance in her direction, bowed and left the room.

The clatter of arrival came up the stairs and through the door in the brief moments it was open, and then when it closed, she asked, "Is that Papa downstairs?"

Her mother shook her head. "He is still in Wales, searching for Lysander."

"Mama," Persephone said softly, "please hold me."

She did and spoke the words that she had not spoken in all the time since Persephone's return. "Tell me of him. Tell me of the child..."

And thus, Persephone was speaking of sweet flute music and tousled curls and beautiful eyes when the door opened once again, and it was Cosmo who stood framed in the doorway, rigid with pain.

"Come," she said, offering her hand. "Come, let me tell you of your nephew."

But after one long frozen moment, he forced a smile and shook his head. "Maybe... maybe someday."

He left them to their sorrow, and finally, their comfort, as she gave her mother a grandchild she would never see and found comfort in her mother's arms.

❦

Robin stood by his horse and contemplated leaving him there for Sebastian's grooms and stable to tend. The weary beast had earned its right to oats and a good brushing and sleep. As had he. He was about to ask to borrow a mount when Cosmo entered the stall, whatever hold he had on elegance a slim grip indeed.

"I am the bearer of unfortunate tidings," he said, his handsome features twisted into true regret.

Robin felt a fissure in his own ability to remain calm. "Which are?"

"The duke requires our presence."

Alarm filtered through his exhaustion. He hadn't gone with the others to report, had believed he had nothing to share that they couldn't tell, and—and he had needed to see Persephone. For Sebastian to command his presence could mean disaster. Had he heard that Robin had blocked Reginald of Surrey from killing the young mother? Surely he would understand.

I'm afraid, Sebastian had said, his eyes hollowed by lack of sleep, his face lined with exhaustion. *I'm afraid of war, of what it will mean to us. I'm afraid of what I will have to do to save us from it.*

"Robin?" Cosmo's hand gripped his shoulder, and his voice was laced with concern. "Are you ill? Should I tell him that you can't—?"

"No," Robin said brusquely. "I'm well. Tired, but well. However weary I am, my problems are nothing compared to those of my cousin."

"They are going to execute the captive. He wants us there."

Execute.

Robin stopped breathing. His eyes locked with Cosmo's, and he read the same shock there, the same distress. Neither of them had lived a life to prepare them for this. No one of their acquaintance had. They'd all been only peripherally aware of the troubles in the Ordinary world, of wars and spies and betrayals, of punishments, of... execution.

He nodded. "Of course."

If Sebastian must order it, he must stand by him and be grateful that their kingdom had such as Sebastian Aubyn, Duke Regent of Glastonbury, an honourable man strong enough to make the hard decisions when necessary.

They had one last chance at avoiding civil war, and they must take whatever steps they could to do so.

🐦🐦

Cosmo led him to an unfamiliar part of the palace. Deep down narrow hallways they found the oldest part of the structure, two joined wings clearly original to the building in the sixteenth century. Finally, they came to a door that opened into an area of the palace grounds he'd never seen—a small courtyard with a free-standing building on the other side, octagonal, with a roof that rose to a high point, topped by a cupola from whose windows came smoke, redolent with herbs and sweet-smelling wood.

"The original kitchens." Cosmo's features were tight. "We wait."

"I'm here," Sebastian's voice broke in. "Waiting for you both." He stepped from the shadow of an arch, his dress crisp and in the most recent style of fashion. He waved away their bows. "It took many long hours to come to this moment," he said. "If the king were… were stronger, perhaps more able to make a decision that goes against our tradition and recorded judicial practices…" His voice drifted away into distraction.

"What is it, Sebastian," Robin asked quietly. "What distresses you so?"

"The problem with having a peaceful succession for three centuries, for having a kingdom that has remained untouched by external strife and wars, is that we've never had to revise certain laws that, once established, were never used." He inclined his head to Cosmo. "In fact, I have found letters from your esteemed progenitor that, had they been heeded, would have left us without this practice today. But it seems that once he withdrew from palace politics, his voice was less powerful in argument. Those who had the king's ear daily insisted we retain some of the Ordinary practices, in case rebellion and treason were ever in the offing."

"As they are now," Cosmo remarked.

"Indeed," Sebastian responded softly, "as they are now."

"What is it?" Robin demanded. "What is it that burdens you so? And—where is it to happen, the hanging?"

There was no scaffold built, no gathered witnesses.

"The hanging will be done inside." He indicated the old kitchen. "I would prefer no witnesses, for surely the knowledge alone is enough deterrent, without resorting to the carnival atmosphere the Ordinaries have revelled in through the centuries. An execution should be solemn, not a cause for celebration. But—" He broke off again. Rarely had Robin ever witnessed his cousin so distracted. "It's to be somewhat more than a hanging. It seems our documented practice, should a rebellion ever occur, was intended to be hanging, drawing, and quartering."

"Gods!" Cosmo gasped.

Robin could not speak at all.

It was clear that Sebastian's rueful smile was forced. "If I stand unwilling to do this on my own, it's not a good recommendation for a future king, is it?"

"We will stand with you," Robin announced firmly.

"You are my brother, my regent, and some day—may the Gods let that day be distant and King Pellinore's life be long—my monarch," Cosmo said solemnly, his wrist circling his forehead. "I serve you in any way you need."

The duke slapped a heavy hand on each man's shoulder. "You are my foundation," he said. Together, they crossed the short distance to the kitchen.

Inside, everything became clearer.

The scaffold stood near the centre of the vast, wattle-and-daub walled room. Already standing in place, a man, battered, bruised, and cut, with dull, stringy hair hanging into his rebellious eyes. Even bound and standing in the place of his death, he showed not an ounce of fear.

Before him burned the sweet-smelling fire that had greeted them when they first approached. Two priests flung herbs onto the coals, sending billows of smoke high into the air where they wafted into the cupola and out across the palace grounds.

Robin wondered what people assumed about the sweet scents, what pleasant source they attributed them to, and then stopped himself from thinking further, thinking ahead to the foul, new scents that would fill the air. He wanted to raise his grimy handkerchief to his nose, to use whatever vile smells it already held to block what would come.

But beside him, Sebastian stood resolute. Could Robin do any less? He straightened his aching shoulders and drew in a deep breath.

The priests chanted low prayers as they circled the flaming embers. Finally, they stepped away and stood on either side of the scaffold, arms raised in entreaty to the heavens.

"State your purpose." Sebastian's voice rang sharp and clear, bouncing back from the high, sharply steepled ceiling in command.

The executioner stepped forward, and with heavily accented words announced, "Upon the charge of treason against the Crown of King Pellinore, Coal Buckthorn stands accused and condemned. His punishment is death."

"Do you offer information to aid us in exchange for your life?" Sebastian asked.

His answer was a glob of spit flying through the air to land impotently at the duke's feet.

"Do you offer any prayers?" Sebastian asked, unmoved.

"Not to your foreign gods!"

"This is your last chance; what say you, Coal Buckthorn?"

"I say that ye'll never wear the crown o' this kingdom, not as long as those breathe who fight for the True King!"

Sebastian leaned forward with new intensity. "Who is this True King you die for?"

The man stared stonily ahead, refusing to answer.

"Then perhaps," Sebastian snapped, his control clearly stretched past his ability to control it, "the conditions of your execution are justified. Perhaps when word gets back to the other traitors just what punishment awaits them, they will reconsider the treacherous lies they believe."

"We have the prophecy of Myrddin of Wales to guide us, the strength of Vespasian of Wales to lead us, and the glory of our sweet goddess, Elen of the Ways to protect us. We shall prevail!" the man shouted, his eyes wild, his body beginning to tremble with frenzy. "And we will—"

Sebastian gave a sharp movement with his hand, and the floor dropped beneath the traitor.

With a harsh, guttural sound that was quickly cut off by the hangman's noose, he swung and jerked at the end of the rope.

Which should have been enough. Which, please the gods, *was* enough to any civilised creatures. Enough by any terms, by any standards, except those of the time in which the Pendragon dynasty had been founded.

The executioner yanked the rope and brought the man back high, swinging him forward to land hard on his knees on the front of the scaffold, still breathing, still choking, still alive.

With one vicious sweep of his arm, he brought his razor-sharp, hooked blade across the man's torso. It snagged, the hook deep, but the executioner threw all his strength behind it and jerked, ripping open the peasant's leather shirt, his skin, and his muscle walls.

In a gush of blood and liquid too vile to name, guts poured out of him, tumbling like long, glossy ropes, churning and twisting and tangling as they spilled through the air and landed on the hot coals, leaving the man screaming in horror as he burned without dying.

"This is your last chance," Sebastian spoke, his voice cracking. "Do you have anything to say to ease your way into the hereafter? Any confession?"

It was a useless question, for even had the man the will, he had not the ability. Nothing would come from his mouth but agonised groans as the stench of his burning bowels assaulted them all. They hissed and writhed on the burning coals, and before Robin's horrified eyes, they began to blister and crackle and—

Cosmo Fury fell to his knees, his entire body shaking with tremors.

Sebastian dropped beside him, held him, and Robin took his other side, relieved to have something—anything—to pull him away from the atrocity before them. Cosmo's skin was cold and clammy under his touch, and his eyes rolled back in his head.

"We have to get him out of here," Robin said, attempting to stand and lift his friend with him.

But Cosmo went rigid in his grip, terrifying Robin, and his grey eyes fixed on the fire before him, its writhing contents, its billowing black smoke. "*We are the people of the sacred grove...*" he said, but it was not Cosmo—it was a wretched voice, a voice Robin had never heard, wrenched from hell itself. "*You cannot find us, nor touch us, nor harm us, for we are the people of the sacred grove, and our power is that of the Earthborn, and the glory of the coming of the True King to all the peoples...*" And then, a cry of pain worse than any preceding it. "*Vixen, my Vixen! My Kit!*" And, when it seemed there would be—could be—no more... "*My loves...*"

Cosmo collapsed in a heap on the floor, and at that moment, the traitor's screams stopped, leaving only the crackling, hissing fire to fill the silence with its wicked sounds and stench.

❧❦

"You must tell no one what we witnessed this day."

They had each been taken to separate chambers in the abandoned wing, had burned their stench-ridden clothes and bathed, and if the servants had questions about the nature of this venture, they wisely let no curiosity show. Cosmo was, even now, naked on a low bed in an adjoining room, under heavy covers, his features haggard with exhaustion. He had yet to awaken from his trance. Robin and Sebastian had retreated to the larger chamber.

"What *did* we witness?" Robin asked, numbness spreading through his body. He needed sleep. He needed... "I'm still not certain I believe it." He accepted a goblet of wine but feared that even one sip would send him sprawling, so deep was his own weariness.

"It went beyond prophecy," Sebastian said, his hair gleaming and eyes glittering with the reflection of the fire he was staring into. What did he see? The gruesome fire they had witnessed? New plots? New plans? Robin could not bring himself to step near the fireplace, even though he shivered in the growing gloom of night in a wing of the castle that had gone unheated for centuries. "Though if we ever had any doubt, it is by now crystal clear that our Cosmo truly has the gift of pyromancy and in ways he's never explored, it would seem."

"But if it wasn't prophecy—"

"They were the traitor's thoughts—his last rational thoughts, a spilling of his mind and his soul at the moment of death, when he was beyond thinking and praying and speaking. Had I known, had I any idea—I could have questioned him."

Robin snapped his head towards his cousin.

"Surely you don't mean that."

"To prolong a traitor's death while we extract information from him that he didn't want to give? Is that so wrong when we're saving the lives of our people?" Sebastian met his gaze steadily, and again, Robin was grateful beyond words that these were not his decisions to make.

"You don't want my answers," Robin finally said. "But then, I am not responsible for an entire kingdom."

Sebastian finally turned to him then, and on his face, Robin read despair.

"It doesn't matter," Sebastian said. "Not at all. It's over. Praise Juno and Zeus and all the pantheon of heaven, it's over now." He braced himself against the fireplace. "If you would stay and care for Cosmo and alert me when he wakens, I need to go home. I need Electra. I'm sure you understand."

Robin let out a long breath.

Oh, yes. He understood the need of a Fury woman to soothe him and bring him back to a belief that the world was not truly such an awful place. And if he envied his cousin, he could not begrudge him.

"Go with the gods," he said, as Sebastian left him alone in the empty place with questions and no answers.

❧ CHAPTER FORTY-ONE ❧

Persephone came to the stable for comfort. The smells of straw and hay, of horse dung and sweat, came closest to taking her home to Erinyes Manor behind her closed eyes. Here with her cheek pressed against Hades' strong shoulder, she could almost be in the place she loved above all others.

Several stalls away, she heard the soft humming of a stable boy, a tune not from town but from country, and wondered if he had come to London with her family.

A shadow fell across her, and she raised her lashes to see Robin standing there, clean and buffed and ready for the palace, and yet here, in her stable with her. She allowed herself a small smile, but it did not reflect the ache that was in her heart.

"This is all the welcome I get?" he asked, and that same ache was in his voice, his eyes.

"If I fly into your arms," she said softly, "I will get horse hair on your fine clothes. But even that, I would do, if…" She turned her face back into Hades and inhaled, fighting the tears that threatened to fill her eyes.

"If…"

"If… I didn't fear that I'd be scolded like a child and told that it isn't proper, that we mustn't—"

Then she was in his arms, pulled roughly from her refuge, his face buried in her hair. "Foolish girl," he sighed.

"Am I?" she asked mournfully. She took his face and pulled it to hers, where lips could find lips, and then there was no mourning, only desperate seeking and blessed finding, as the world ceased to exist for the length of their kiss and a few breaths beyond.

"No, I'm the foolish one," he breathed into her ear. "I'm the one."

He pulled away and looked at her, truly looked at her. "You haven't been sleeping."

"Nor have you," she replied, the hollows beneath his eyes testament to that truth.

"This is a burden I have taken on willingly. It's not one for your shoulders."

"Yet it landed on my shoulders, did it not?"

His quick, chagrined glance at the place where her scar was hidden beneath her dark green dress brought a frustrated huff of air from her lips. "That's not what I meant."

"But it happened, and it happened because you were not believed, and you were not protected, and now this has all exploded beyond what I ever imagined in my wildest nightmares."

Suddenly, the hollows, the lines, the rigid lines of his body took on new, more sinister meaning.

"What do you mean? What is happening?" she asked.

"If you don't already know—"

She grabbed his lapels and jerked. "Don't you dare, Robin Fitzwilliam, don't you dare try to hold this back from me. If anybody—anybody—deserves to know—" A low growl formed in her throat, and she allowed it—nay, she forced it out. *"It is I."*

"If you tell your sister—anyone—that I've told you. Hells, she might not even know."

She jerked at him again, and he put his hands on either side of her face, his palms hot and dry against her skin, soothing despite her desire to stay angry.

"I'll tell you. It... it should reassure you. Sebastian is taking your warnings very seriously and agrees that Vespasian Wyllt must be captured and put to death, and it must happen now, without hesitation and without fail."

The words tumbling from his lips seized her with fear and a tightening of her throat that made it difficult to speak. "When this was attempted the first time, it did not work, and it ended in disaster. Yet he sends you again?"

"It was not viewed..." He averted his eyes. "It was not viewed as disaster. We lost only one man, and that through a fluke. We weren't out-battled. We were out-witted, and Sebastian swears that cannot happen again. Not with..."

She fought down her anger at the previous skirmish being

considered anything but a disaster, having ended with the death of an innocent child, but his last words... "Not with?"

"We've been blessed by the gods with a strong royal dynasty and no borders to defend. What wars the Ordinaries have fought don't touch us. But now... now we need experience that we don't have. An army that we don't have."

"What is he doing? What is the duke doing?"

"Under the guidance of our king—"

"Pah!"

"Persephone, he has to at least maintain the appearance that the king is fully functioning or risk offending the queen. She—"

"I know," she snapped. "I know all about the queen."

"He has brought troops from the Continent, troops and individuals with the expertise we need to—"

"He's turning foreign soldiers with no love for our land or our people loose to attack innocents who have done nothing but fall under the spell of—" She couldn't finish it, so distraught was she.

"Not turned loose on anyone, not that. But Vespasian Wyllt will not escape again, and he will be brought to hand. He will be executed for treason." At that Robin turned away again, and his throat worked.

"He trusts foreign soldiers to take more care with his people than his own men did?"

Robin shook his head. "I would think if anyone would see the need to act quickly and decisively, it would be you."

She spun away from him, digging her fingers into her scalp, and sent Hades stomping nervously. She willed her hands to soothe and sang a low crooning tune until he calmed, only the occasional snort and stamp of a hoof showing his earlier upset. But she was not calmed. Her concerns were not stilled.

But Robin drew her from the stall and pulled her close. "You understand how carefully Sebastian has to walk. How much thought and prayer he puts into every decision."

She remembered his time on his knees in prayer and then, on his knees, begging her forgiveness. She trusted the duke. She trusted him implicitly, and this was his decision. These were his people, too, and soon... soon, his kingdom. Robin took one finger and tipped her chin until it was just right, and he kissed her. He tasted of tea and sugar and…

Tasted.

His tongue found hers. Heat shot through her, and she was melting. She curled her hand around his head, pulling him closer, tighter, until nothing in the world existed, nothing but this man and this moment, and if they thought they were going to force her to marry any other, they were so very wrong.

A gentle cough broke through her haze, and she found her face turned against Robin's waistcoat as she stared at Cosmo, standing in the stable doorway. "Do we have no stable hands?" he demanded, a portion of his old joy finally emerging after days of malaise. "If this is the only way you can get your horse curried—"

"Sorry, milord," a shrill voice rang from a nearby stall. A young stable boy emerged, covered in hay, rubbing the sleep from one eye. "I was—I was polishin' th—a saddle."

Robin, now standing at a respectable distance, cleared his throat.

Persephone folded her arms and scowled at the dirt beneath her riding boots.

"The duke sent me to fetch you, to find out what caused you to disappear into the stable and not return." Cosmo raised his glance to Robin. "I don't think I shall tell him."

She looked between them, these two men she adored. They both bore the weight of what they'd seen in Wales and what had been lost there. Cosmo, in particular, had never been able to be present whenever Otter's death was mentioned. She crossed to him and pulled him close to place a kiss upon his cheek and smooth his hair—that one lock that always would fall across his brow. "You're a beast," she said.

"And you a brat." He returned her kiss with one of his own in the middle of her forehead. "Fitzwilliam, are you coming or must I send the duke to roust you out?"

She did not get a kiss from Robin as he gave her a regretful smile and followed. She stood silently, watching them enter the townhouse before she whirled on the stable boy.

"How long were you in there, and just exactly what did you hear, you little weasel?" she demanded.

"No, milady!" he gasped, and to her dismay, he was trembling. "I was asleep and dint hear nothing!" He backed away from her, his hands twisting on the rope he clutched, his eyes looking everywhere but at her.

"I'm not a lady, just a miss, as you well know," she said automatically, but his behaviour was unsettling. "What is your name?"

"Oh, no, miss. Please don't tell the duke. Please, I beg o'ye!"

"Surely you don't think His Grace would—"

At that, the boy swallowed a sob, turned, and fled.

Without hesitation, Persephone flew after him and, before he could escape the stables, lunged. She grabbed the back of his shirt, and fortunately it was good, coarse fabric, for it held without ripping as she yanked him to a halt. When she finally had him turned to face her, she was surprised. Small though he might be, but this was no young child. This was a boy old enough to be ashamed of his tears, and yet he sobbed openly.

"What is it, boy?" she asked. "What has you struck with terror?"

He shook his head, refusing to answer.

"I won't be telling the duke anything. You've done nothing to fear his punishment." Even as she spoke the words, it occurred to her that she did not know. Perhaps he'd done something heinous and had good reason to fear the duke's attentions.

"Neither had the child!" the boy blurted, and then catching himself, let out an anguished moan as he dropped to his knees. "Please, forget I said. Forget my words!"

The child. There could only be one child…

Persephone dropped to her knees and grabbed him by the shoulders. "You were in Wales?"

"I was, with my uncle," he said.

His sobs turned to deep, racking hiccoughs that made her fear he was going to lose his meal.

"It was a horror, so much blood, and so—"

"But it was an accident," she said.

He grew still… as still as well water, undisturbed by wind or current, cold with winter chill.

"What do you know?" she demanded, her voice low. "What did you see?"

"You're the duke's family. You'll—"

"The child was my blood," she growled. *What did you see?*"

"Before we left, when my uncle was alone with his horse…" His voice was a mere whisper, and he stared at the dirt between their knees, as if remembering something from long ago, not mere weeks. "The duke told him that there was a great threat to our way of life, our kingdom, and that my uncle was the only man he trusted to handle it."

No. She refused to believe this. This could not have happened…

"He said that these rebels were going to rise up, and that they believed they had a king of their own, a mere child, and that as long as he lived—"

"Noooo." Now she was the one who trembled.

"I don't lie," he said, his voice still low, a dull tone as he spoke things he clearly had no desire to speak, but had no will to refuse her demands. "He wanted the child dead and said that if my uncle took care of it, there would be a title and a manor for him once the duke is king."

Lies. These had to be lies! Her fingers dug into his shoulders as she felt the rage boil up within her. "Who is this uncle who filled your head with such excrement?"

He raised his eyes to hers, and they filled with tears. "Reginald of Surrey, miss. He was Reginald of Surrey."

The only death suffered by the king's men.

No.

"Miss, he didn't have to fill my head with—with whatever you said. I was there, asleep in the stable, only I wasn't, y'see. I heard it all, when he was told."

She forced the words through stiff lips. "How did he die?"

"A knife in the back, miss. They said it was flung by one o' the Earthborn, but none saw it happen."

This couldn't be true. Not the duke who had prayed, who had begged her forgiveness. It could not be true.

"A woman—a woman raised the child and called him the True King and said he would—"

"No, miss. She was his mum, and she had him in her arms and was running. She was fleeing."

"Oh, gods…" Now, it was she who wept, who sobbed, releasing the boy so she could clutch at her own middle and rock back and forth in her grief. The dagger was in her, in her heart, the pain of this knowledge that she wanted to deny, needed to deny. It had to be lies….

They believed they had a king of their own, a mere child, but that as long as he lived…

She had told them that. She had told them, but she had told them it was foolishness, that even Vespasian Jones, as vile as he was, thought it foolishness.

She had told them everything.

She had drawn the map—oh, how impressed even the queen had been with her map, and she so puffed up with pride that she had noticed so much and could record it with such detail.

The entrance through the old burial stones, standing tall on the horizon and visible for miles.

The path that led to the village.

Which cottage Lysander lived in with his family.

She had drawn it to save them, to save those she loved.

And, finally, it was she who lost her food into the dirt, in great retching spasms, as the boy sat beside her, numb.

❧❧

She had to see him, had to speak to him, had to find Robin…

Without Cosmo.

Without—oh gods, without the duke.

"What is your name?" she asked the boy.

"You'll not tell—"

"Tell no one what you've told me," she said. "No one, under any circumstances. No one shall ever learn of you from me."

"Bertrand," he said then. "My name is Bertrand."

"Ready the duke's and my brother's mounts," she commanded, as if the ground beneath her feet was solid and not so much shifting sand. As if her world still made sense and wasn't as fragile as a soap bubble, and built on air. "Do your work, keep your head down, and speak to no one other than what your tasks require. I… I shall return later. I promise, within the boundaries of my ability, I will protect you."

His mournful glance let her know without a doubt that he had concerns about what a young woman's abilities could possibly be, but that was a matter best settled later.

Before the clock in the drawing room had ticked away five minutes, she had returned to Bertrand with a note. "Give this to Sir Robin."

"The duke's cousin," he said.

"Yes, and let no one see you give it to him. Tell him to read it without being seen."

There was nothing left to do but go to the back corner of the garden, beyond the rose arbour, past the kitchen garden, beside the wall of espaliered pear and apple trees. It was the only spot on the grounds that could not be seen from any window in the townhouse. Once there, her heart fluttering like a moth trapped behind glass, she sat on the low bench and raised her eyes to the overcast sky. "Sweet goddess, please, if you ever loved me, guide me!" For she, Persephone Fury, who always had words to speak and prayers to pray, was helpless to do anything but fling herself on the mercy of the gods.

She heard him coming, recognised his steps by weight and rhythm. By the time Robin rounded the bend in the path, she was standing. He raised the note, smiling and more than a bit confused. "Before I can even leave, you're summoning me back?" His expression quickly changed. "You've been weeping!"

She nodded and stared up at him. Still, words failed her. How could there ever be words to tell him this horrible thing?

He pulled her close to him, stroked her hair. But being held could not make the frightening knowledge go away.

As if sensing her withdrawal, he peered down at her. "What causes such fear in you?"

Of all the things she could have answered, one seemed most important. "I'm afraid you won't believe me."

"Don't be ridiculous," he said, teasing the corner of her mouth with his forefinger in an attempt to make her smile. "Did I not just tell you that my biggest regret is that no one believed you when you tried to warn them?"

"My parents should have named me Cassandra," she said with an attempt that she was sure ended up being little more than a twist of a smile. "Cursed to speak the truth and not be believed."

"I think you need to try me," he said.

She closed her eyes, took a slow breath, fought to believe... to believe that he wouldn't dismiss her as others always had. She had no choice. If he didn't trust and believe her, who would?

"You're trembling."

"I'm trusting you with... with everything," she breathed.

"May the gods make me worthy of such trust."

"Indeed." She held his eyes with hers, watching their depths for any sign of scepticism. "If I were to tell you..." She swallowed and tried again. "If I were to tell you that Otter's death was not an accident, that he was killed because his mere existence was a threat to the Crown..."

"Who told you such a thing?" he demanded.

Tears stung her eyes. "I can't tell you, but you know me, Robin Fitzwilliam, you know me, and you know I would not make up wild tales, nor would I be taken in by them. I am not my brothers. I am not my father. I am not easily swayed by tales spun by liars."

"Of course. I never thought you were. But whoever told you this— Persephone," he said, his voice a hoarse whisper that gave her reason to hope he believed her after all. "Do you not understand? They speak treason. They imply that the king—that... that Sebastian—ordered a child's murder."

She met his gaze without flinching. "Believe me... or not."

"I believe that someone told you this, convinced you this. I believe—"

"That I couldn't possibly be speaking the truth." She felt it like a physical blow. She'd known her words to be unbelievable, and yet, had hoped, had prayed—that he would feel the truth she had.

Without the evidence.

Of course. She felt herself deflate. Without the boy's story, without the boy's fear so palpable she could taste it in the air, bitter with the taste of blood and iron—without those things, would she even believe such a thing?

"I must know who told you this lie," he said urgently. "Don't you see? He must have connections to the Earthborn rebels. If he has been close enough to speak to you—for the love of all the gods, Persephone, he was close enough to harm you!"

Her mouth was dry as dust. If she'd ever considered betraying Bertrand's trust, now it was impossible, for to do so was to have him seized, questioned, and possibly worse, much worse. "I will not tell you."

"Then I'll tell your brother. I'll tell the duke, if that's what it takes to keep you safe."

"If I were going to be harmed, it would have already happened, would it not?" she snapped. "I'm sure you're right. I'm sure it's someone wanting to start rumours, and I will make sure not to open myself up to such a connection again."

She pulled away from him, wanting nothing now but to put distance between them. "Go on," she said. "You have royal business to attend."

"Don't do this. Don't be this way."

"What way? Tired? Exhausted? Worried about my father? About Lysander? About the fact that the bastard Vespasian Jones is still breathing while my beloved nephew is not? How can I be any other way? But of course, these are the reasons I'm vulnerable to wild tales of treason, are they not?"

He stroked her cheek, his brow knit with concern. "You must tell me. Persephone, you simply must. This is dangerous. This man who told you these things—"

She jerked away from him, rigid with her refusal to speak.

"Will you stay here today and not leave? Stay safe for me, I beg of you, and I will return tonight and—"

"I'll stay," she said because until she had a plan, there was no other option, and because she did not want to hear whatever promises he planned to use to sweeten his plea, for they would only tear her heart further.

"Stay safe," he repeated urgently, and then kissed her. It was bittersweet, that kiss, neither long enough nor warm enough. Merely desperate and needy, and she returned it in kind.

He left her, his last glance over his shoulder filled with concern and regret. She turned away and stared at a stunted green pear tree splayed against the wall like a moth to a velvet backing and felt she shared the sap that rushed through its limbs, struggling to find a way free to reach for the sun.

CHAPTER FORTY-TWO

Robin entered the Duke Regent's study in the palace, mind racing, one fist clenched at his side, the other flexing nervously. If only he could have stayed longer. If only he could take her from this place where all her problems were amplified and exploited, where her very presence seemed to set off sparks of reaction that were beyond his comprehension and her ability to endure without losing all reason.

"Good gods, Robin, whatever has you so tense?" Sebastian asked from behind his desk, peering over his spectacles. He gestured towards a side table with various cut glass decanters throwing sparks of amber, gold, and garnet wherever the sunlight struck them. "A drink, perhaps?"

"No," Robin said, forcing his hands to relax. "You sent for me?"

"Indeed." The duke stared up at him a moment and finally removed his spectacles and inclined his head. "Forgive me. Please. Sit down."

Robin did so. "I'm at your service," Robin said, forcing a casual smile.

"For which I am ever grateful. What bothers you, cousin? What has you so distracted?" He sighed heavily. "I've pulled you into State affairs, and now my concerns are weighing you down," Sebastian continued. "I am selfish enough to keep you here. Do you realise how few people I can trust? Fewer than I can count on one hand, and of them all, you the only one who did not attach himself to me after my royal connections formed."

After he had become the prince's closest friend and a regular resident of the palace as playmate and companion. And then the tragedy, when he had become the nearest thing to a son that the king and queen had left. And then, he'd become duke upon the death of his father. The litany of events flew through Robin's mind in an instant, and he thought how lonely Sebastian must have been after the prince's death, never knowing who truly sought friendship and who sought position and power.

Robin felt all the more guilty for not caring, for wanting to shove it all to the side, take Persephone Fury and whisk her away—not back to Erinyes Manor, but to his own Roe Hill, to protect her and make her his.

Sebastian leaned closer, suddenly urgent. "What is it, Robin? Whatever it is, you must let me make it right."

Robin let out a snort of laughter. Was there anything Sebastian couldn't do in his own mind? Yet wasn't that as heavy a burden as any, to look at each problem and feel that the 'making it right' was within one's power, and the inability to do so was one's weakness? But if any could help him, it would be Sebastian. "It's Persephone. I fear for her."

"We have her protected—"

"I fear for her—her mind. Her rational mind."

Sebastian stiffened. "You all fret so much about her 'events'. Has there been another? Need I warn Electra to take precautions?"

"No." Robin started. He had to reach back to remember the last time she'd lost control.

"What is it, then? Surely a mind as sharp as hers—"

"She's as sharp-witted as ever. But the loss of her brother's child—Sebastian, it has shaken her to the foundation. She's... she's falling apart."

Sebastian's interest quickened, evidenced by a sharp look, which he quickly hid behind his spectacles again. "She did have a very rough time of it for a few days, but once Cosmo returned, she seemed to get stronger."

Robin fought the urge to correct him. *Once I returned. And why do you continue to skirt that issue?*

"Give her time, Robin. Her father will also return soon, and her grief will fade. She hardly knew the child, after all. She'd only shared a few days with him, at most."

"I shared your thoughts, more or less," Robin said, unsettled by Sebastian's ability to dismiss her condition so easily. But Persephone had been under his roof such a short period of time, he did not truly know her, neither her depths nor her abilities, nor the strength of her compassion and her heart.

"You shared my thoughts, but no longer? What has happened?"

Sebastian flipped a sheet of parchment on his desk, the movement crisp, his eyes never leaving Robin's.

Robin cleared his throat uneasily. "I'm sure everything is as you say, and she's merely having a difficult time this morning. I'm clearly distracting you from important matters. You said you needed me to meet with the Minister of the Treasury to discuss improvements to the Basilica of Apollo—"

"Stop." Sebastian whipped off his spectacles and placed him before him. "You're speaking of Electra's sister, and nothing that concerns her could be unimportant. The Ministers can wait. *Tell me.*"

What to tell? How much, how little… or any at all? He truly had no choice. Sebastian needed to know. "There are evidently… rumours that the child's death was not an accident. That somehow—it was expedient, and was ordered by—" Robin met Sebastian's gaze without blinking "—the king."

Sebastian paled. "That's—to even speak such words—it's treason. To suspect our king of slaying children?" He rose abruptly. "Who is saying such things? Who fed such lies to her?"

"She wouldn't say."

"Whom has she seen recently? Who could have told her such lies? Who is making such accusations against the Crown? Against me? Robin, it is I who am being accused."

"I'll find out. I'm sure she'll—"

Sebastian cut him off. "I'm sorry. I shouldn't have let my anger out in such a way. You've done right to bring this to me. The poor girl. The poor, poor girl. I must find a way to help her."

"I am the way."

Sebastian stiffened, and then, slowly, his shoulders drooped. "And that quickly, I'm to lose my oldest and most trusted confidant?" Before Robin could respond, he shook his head. "No, no, perhaps I can convince Electra that her sister need not marry a Viscount."

Greylund, of course. Robin inhaled and let it out slowly.

"Give me a bit of time, Robin. But for today…" Sebastian handed him a note-sized sheet of vellum. "Write to her. Tell her to come here and meet you in the Library this afternoon. She likes the Library. Best not to mention me, but together we will gently discern who has filled her with such ideas. Together we will help her. The blackguard responsible will be stopped."

As Robin scrawled the note, thinking of how she would chide him for his penmanship, he felt a twinge of unease. Would she consider it a betrayal? He added an addendum, urging her to bring Dardanus. Her brother's presence would steady and reassure her.

The duke reached for a pull and in moments, a servant appeared. "Have this delivered to Aubyn House immediately," he said, then turned back to Robin.

"By the time she comes, the king will no longer require my presence, and you will have concluded your meeting. We will meet her together." Again, his hand rested on Robin's shoulder, and again, it brought comfort.

❦❦

Heart pounding, she made her way up the stairs to her bedroom, desperate to kneel at her shrine, to hold the talismans that would bring her closer to her gods. But it had been easier to slip through the old corridors of the palace unnoticed than to do the same at Aubyn House. Her mother spotted her and beckoned, and all she could do was follow her into the family dining room for a light nuncheon.

"Mama," she began, "I truly have no appetite—"

"You need sustenance." Her mother brooked no argument.

Persephone sank into her chair at the end of the table, with her mother and sister her only companions. She watched them eat cold chicken and fruit and tried to follow suit, but every bite threatened to come back up. She sipped from her wine and knew she was drinking too much when her efforts to maintain normal composure began slipping and tears rose in her eyes.

Despite the fact that she finally dabbed at them with her napkin, her normally eagle-eyed mother didn't notice.

Electra, radiant in her daffodil yellow morning dress, practically glowed. Their mother's cheeks were flushed as she patted Electra's hand, and it slowly occurred to Persephone that the two of them held a secret, and unlike her own, it was something that brought them joy.

How would their worlds shatter, how many ways, how many painful ways, when the truth about the duke—oh, my gods, Electra loved him, she *loved* him! Persephone floundered, uncertain which was worse, that no one would believe her, or that her sister's world would shatter in more ways than could be counted.

"Mama?" she asked, her voice too tremulous for her liking.

"Yes, dear?" Her mother turned a distracted glance her way.

"If I might be excused... I'm not feeling well."

"Poor sweet," Electra said, "I hope it's not something you ate. I'm the one who should be unwell, if anyone should be."

"What's wrong?" Persephone asked, suddenly terrified, despite the fact that there could be no reason the duke would rid himself of the wife he clearly adored... could there?

"Electra, it's hardly proper to discuss this in front of her."

"She's to be married soon," Electra replied. "She's not a little girl any longer."

"Married? Soon? Whatever are you talking about?" She clutched the damp napkin more tightly as her world spun out of control.

"Exactly my question," her mama said. "There have been no offers and any discussion of marriage is ridiculously premature. And as for the other—"

"Sister," Electra said, her eyes shining, "I'm increasing."

Persephone drew in a harsh breath.

"We decided it is time for a baby," Electra finished softly, her hands cupping her abdomen.

The subtle sadness that had clung to her family in recent days had vanished. With news of Electra's condition, all thoughts of the child they'd never known had faded. He was forgotten because he'd never been real to them. What would they say if they knew? Would they share her horror, her agony, or would they trust the duke to know what was best? Would they accept it as uncomfortable, even tragic, but necessary to maintain the monarchy?

Before she could find words to speak, Electra had snatched up the small golden bell by her plate and given it a delicate shake. "Darling, you really are ill, aren't you?" she asked, rising from her chair and moving to Persephone's side.

"You shouldn't," her mother said. "Let me."

As a servant arrived, Electra gave orders to have tea taken to

Persephone's bedside, and with her Mama assisting, Persephone allowed them to guide her to her room, wanting nothing more than to be alone there.

"Your Grace," a servant said, "a message came to Miss Fury from the palace."

Persephone whirled to see what the servant bore on his tray. She snatched it up before her mother or sister could and tore it open.

"Is it from the queen?" Electra asked, her hope clear.

"No. It's from Robin. He's asked me to come." She folded it tightly, keeping the rest of its contents to herself. He wanted to see her. Could he possibly believe her?

"You'll have to send back a message saying you're indisposed."

"No, Mama. I'm not—I'm not indisposed. I'm better now, truly," she gasped, pulling away from them. Heart pounding, she felt hope begin to flower within her.

She snatched her bonnet from her dressing table and tying it under her chin, took off for the stable. She would not take Dardanus. She would not wait. She had her own business at the palace.

"Your gloves," her mother called.

She darted back and grabbed the top pair from her drawer, not caring that they were ivory kid and the lace on her gown snow white. Not caring about anything, other than that Robin wanted to see her.

❧❧

This time there were no false starts or turns-by-error for stealth, and within short minutes she was slipping around a corner into the narrow, dark corridor that led to the forbidden knowledge, the Forbidden Library, the one that was nothing but a gaping door and ash, if that.

But she hadn't seen it for herself, the destruction. Hadn't checked to see if anything remained, some scrap of ancient incantation, some whiff of knowledge...

Just as she was about to pick up her pace and scurry on, the approach of footsteps, many footsteps, sent her scurrying instead into the deep shadows of a niche where at one time a statue must have stood. Now, she stepped onto the low ledge and pulled close against the wall, thanking Cosmo and the queen and any deity willing to accept her thanks that she was wearing a dark gown that faded into the recess of the alcove.

The footsteps grew closer, and with them, an unsettling feeling of jubilation in the air, of relief, as men would sometimes emit like a heavy scent of sweat when swelled with accomplishment after a hardy hour's work or play.

Perhaps it was that sense of accomplishment, relief, and jubilation that saved her, for as they passed, not a one spared a glance in her direction. Not a one noticed her. Not a single attendant.

Not the Viscount Greylund.

Not the duke.

Not the king, borne on a litter by proud liveried servants, a goblet in his weak hand, a soft smile on his lips, no scent of decay or death clinging to him.

Then they were gone. She stood frozen, unable to believe that this man—frail, yes, and old, certainly, but very much alive—was the same she'd seen so recently, a mere skin and skeleton and stench. If they had wrought such a change, they must use very powerful magic indeed.

As the footsteps finally faded, she emerged carefully, finding the corridor empty in both directions. She edged forward to the turn that would take her to what remained of the Forbidden Library, down the same dark corridor she'd traversed before.

And yet it felt different. Empty. Instead of ancient magics, she felt only the hollow places where they used to be. She arrived at the arched door and felt no wards. Sensed nothing forbidden. She pushed, and the door opened to an empty room. She entered and circled it, feeling a loss deep in her bones. If only something had remained. Anything…

A gust of air whirled, and a small corner of parchment spun at her feet. She snatched it up, heart leaping—only to find that it was just the singed corner of a page, not ancient, just… the page of a book.

She held it in her fingertips, so much hope bound in this one scrap of paper, ridiculous hope as if even a scrap of ancient paper might have brought her knowledge.

She tucked it into her pocket, all the same. As she was closing the door behind her, intent upon returning to wait for Robin, she felt something. Felt it so deeply, she staggered, caught herself with one gloved hand braced against the rough stone wall. *Tendrils. Oily tendrils of Shadow.* Pulling at her like the tug of rope on an anchor, moving her despite her rising fear.

She swallowed thickly. For a wild moment she expected to see Vespasian Wyllt looming over her, for only in his company had she ever felt such power.

But these Shadows were so very different.

She stood at the window through which she'd fled before, into the courtyard, the old outbuildings, the gardens that eventually let her slip through the wards and into the Ordinary world.

She should turn back.

She should go to Robin.

And yet… even as she was repelled, she couldn't resist. She opened the window and stepped through into what should have been fresh air, and was instead—

Death. Shadows. Stench. Horror. *Ordinary.* An assault from all directions, an assault of all the senses. The octagonal building was the source. She wanted to flee.

She wanted to *see.*

She edged around the walled courtyard, past the cascade of thick ivy grown wild and the low bubbling fountain where she scooped a handful of water and let it trickle through her fingers as she passed with a quick prayer to the goddess.

There was no doubt to which goddess she prayed. The goddess she hadn't wanted, but had claimed her anyway.

She felt more danger, more need of that goddess than ever before. The air grew heavier and the stench so strong she knew she'd never be able to wear this gown again, and how to ever explain—

Then she was at the building, and the first window, with its heavy wooden shutters closing it from outside curiosity.

The wards were strong, but she felt her mouth twist with triumph. She knew them, and they knew her. She brought down Bardán Fury's wards and dragged her fingertips down the rusty hinges, willing her magic into them and daring them to make a sound.

A slight pull, and one shutter began its slow swing open. There was no movement within. No one there. But gods, the smell, the heavy air.

She clung to the wide stone windowsill. When both shutters were open, she saw what horror awaited her.

Seven bodies, naked and bloody and crumpled like broken dolls.

Girls. Mere girls. On the cusp of womanhood, their breasts tight swells of promise that would never be fulfilled, with a few threads of hair at their pudenda.

Ordinary girls, as evidenced by the stench of their sweat and filth and—low on their abdomens, gaping wounds where they had been sliced open.

Where Lark's wound had been small, precise and cauterised to heal, these girls had been opened viciously, their life force ripped from them, and then...

Blindly, she managed to get the shutters closed and warded. She collapsed into the soil, heaving in great gulps of air, fighting to keep the vomit down. She had to leave. She had to leave before anyone knew she'd been here, especially *here*.

Checking to make sure she had her gloves, her reticule, and even the scrap of burned paper from the Forbidden Library, she slipped into the garden, keeping to the path shielded by tall hedge, putting one foot in front of the other, until she was free of the weighted, Shadowed air, and back in the fresh.

And then she ran.

Ran past lilacs long past their bloom and calendula overflowing with flower. Past topiaries and knot gardens.

She knew what she fled.

She knew who was keeping the king alive, he who had looked at her abdomen and *had known*.

His knowledge—his knowledge of evil—brought her world crashing down upon her.

But who would believe her?

Who would believe that Sebastian, Duke Regent of Glastonbury, husband of her sister, father of their unborn child—the future king of magical England—

Wielded evil. Nurtured it. *Embraced it.*

She knew the answer to that and knew an even deeper fear.

She wrapped her magic around her like a cloak as she fled through the streets of Ordinary London and wondered what Robin would think when she didn't return to the library.

She had so little time, so very little time.

She plotted the most surreptitious path into Aubyn House, the least travelled staircase at this time of day, mentally cataloguing those precious things she must take with her.

The boy. Bertrand. She could not leave him.

There was only one horse she could take without arousing immediate suspicion, one horse that none would seek, for he wasn't a fine thoroughbred to attract the jealous eye.

She longed for parchment, for quill, for ink, for orderly lists and time to plan, but she had none of those things.

She could rely only on her mind, and her will, and—

Please, please, please—

Her goddess.

For there was only one person who would believe her and was powerful enough to have even a hope of stopping the duke from ascending the throne. And he would kill her on sight, if she dared return.

🦋

Robin took off at a gallop. The uneasiness he'd carried with him ever since he'd left Aubyn House earlier, abandoning Persephone to her wild fears and accusations bubbled to the surface.

The butler met him at the door, and before Robin could ask, intoned, "In the family drawing room, sir."

Robin dashed up the stairs.

Upon entering the room, it took but a scant glance to see who was missing. "Where is she?"

"Gone," Dardanus said, his jaw clenched and eyes haunted. "Gone."

Mrs Fury crossed to him and took his hands in hers, pleading, "Did she say anything to you? Anything that would explain… why she might disappear?"

"You think she left on her own?" he asked, flabbergasted. Yet he knew what might have caused this.

"Yes, Robin. Do you know anything?"

Sebastian's voice was rich with concern and with innocence. Robin didn't meet his gaze, didn't have to, to understand. There would be no talk of her suspicions here, not amongst her family.

"She has been distressed," Robin said. "But she has said nothing to—" He broke off, confused. "What makes you think she left of her own will? Did she leave a note?"

"No note, and I think—I think we were just hoping," her mother said. "If she left on her own, she could come back. If she were taken again…"

"Was there sign of an abduction?" What weren't they telling him?

Sebastian stroked Electra's hair, soothing her. "We will find her."

An aide appeared in the doorway. "Your Grace," he said with a bow. "We know who the boy is."

"Enter."

The aide approached, his stance stiff and proper. "It was a boy, Bertrand. His uncle was in the party that rode to Wales. Reginald of Surrey."

Sebastian grew very still. "The man who so valiantly lost his life in defence of King and Crown."

The aide bowed his head in agreement.

"Had he other family?"

"No, Your Grace. He was alone."

"The poor boy." Sebastian raised his head and circled his wrist over his forehead. "That poor, lost boy. Had I only known—"

"You would have taken care of him, my love," Electra said. "You would not have left him alone in his distress."

Robin sought his attention, attempted to send him a silent message, a request.

Sebastian understood. "If you will excuse me, I must take Robin to my study for a private conversation."

Robin felt all eyes on him as they left.

The fire flared to life as they entered the study.

"The boy," Robin demanded. "He seems unlikely to be an Earthborn spy spreading tales, unlikely to be involved in anything that could lead to her abduction."

"But his grief could make him vulnerable to a pretty girl's distress, if she showed him kindness," Sebastian said gently. "If she believes the madness that was spoken to her."

Robin paced restlessly, desperately, unable to hold still, needing to be gone, to find her. "She's gone mad with grief. Her mind, her brilliant mind—" He raised his eyes to meet the concern, sympathy, and grief in his cousin's gaze.

Sebastian crossed to him and shoved a measure of brandy into his hand, which he accepted as a drowning man grasps a lifeline. He tossed it back, savoured the burn that for brief moments wiped everything out of his mind but the explosion of flavour and fumes and fire.

"I am under the impression," Sebastian said carefully, "that her mind has always had a precarious balance."

Robin's hand clenched on the glass, but he found it difficult to dispute such an assertion. "If she were my wife, I would take her away from all of this. She was strong and happy at Erinyes Manor. I could give her safety. Stability. Room to be what she is without hiding it behind tisanes and the monumental effort to be what she is not." Again, he raised his eyes to his cousin's. But this time he was filled with determination. "Promise me that, Sebastian. Promise me you and Electra will stop these machinations. You'll stop trying to make a political match. You'll let me take her away to the life she and I both desire."

"You would leave me when I need you most?"

Robin swallowed, deflating. "Once the throne is secured and the rebellion eliminated, I will leave you, as I always intended. Keep your lofty titles to bestow on those who will use them. I never even expected to be a baronet, and this is more than enough title for me."

Sebastian's hand was warm on his shoulder. "Even knowing you as well as I do, I was surprised you did not find the baronetcy an unexpected boon. Most men would have leapt at the lands, such as they are, and the position." He glanced at the battered ring on Robin's left hand. "If I weren't in such need of those I can trust, I would release you from my side immediately."

"I know you would, and thus, I have hope for my future."

"I think you'll find your next duty one that assuages your heart."

Robin went alert with expectation. What could possibly do such a thing?

"A ship sails at week's end, filled with foreign soldiers under my command."

"A ship?" Robin had never considered such a thing.

"Large numbers can be moved more easily this way, without detection. It is a French ship, one that possesses powers to hide in the mists and go unnoticed on the horizon by Ordinary eyes. If Persephone ran away in her madness, it was to join the rebels. If she was taken, it was by the rebels."

"And the rebels are on the Welsh coast."

"Indeed. And I am taking you with me, with a single duty." His eyes pinned Robin, and in those depths Robin saw the command of the throne, past and present and future, and swelled with the need to fulfil whatever duty was put before him.

"I have the wherewithal to locate her, wherever she is. You will be the one to rescue her and bring her back, for you above all others have her love and trust, and whatever Dark power is influencing her, you alone can overcome it." Overpowered by the instinct to serve the crown and to love this man who saw so much and had such wisdom, Robin dropped to one knee, brimming with relief and purpose. "My honour is to serve you, Your Grace."

At last, at last, action.

❧ CHAPTER FORTY-THREE ❦

Vespasian had been there at dawn, the wretched dog a short distance away, giving him meagre hope. The dog would know if its mistress was coming, would it not? He had watched the thick mist coat the surface of the lake, unable to discern whether it was still as glass or rippled with the slight movement of air. She had appeared through mist before, as was fitting, since travel between worlds always involved mists of one sort or another. It had been midday that first time, and even then there had been mist.

They had argued with him—Night had commanded him to stay in the village, not to go on a fool's errand.

He had disobeyed and taken men with him. He felt it in his soul, this need to see his goddess again, to hear her words and this time not in condemnation as he had heard the night of the adder, but with instruction.

What were they to do now? What was he to do with this gift that had become curse when he'd flaunted it for dreams of glory? What was he to do now that Aubyn had found him? What was he to do without the cursed girl, or worse, *with* her?

He cursed himself for being a whining child. He knew what he must do, and he knew with a surge of pride that he'd done it. He had prepared his people for what lay ahead and prepared them well.

But none had been prepared for the one thing they had failed to anticipate. None had believed that those wards could be breached.

Lys had never dreamed his own father would be amongst the forces that attacked them, or his own brother. Furys weren't fighting people. That had been the assumption they'd accepted without ever considering any other reality. Fools, stupid bloody fools. With Lysander Fury the fiercest fighter amongst them, they'd never dreamed the others would fight as well?

He sat on the slope above the lake, counting his errors, staring blindly, now that its surface was clear and the mists gone, and another midday approached. He'd prayed she'd condescend to appear again, but she had not.

He wasn't surprised—just tormented by the burn of loss, of need, of rage. He'd been young and he'd been stupid, and he'd been the sum of his mother's foolish dreams and his own arrogance, and he'd betrayed Elen's trust. But was there no forgiveness in her? None for the aching and weary man who still did her bidding, even after she'd withdrawn her grace from his shoulders?

He'd feared she wouldn't come, and yet he'd allowed himself to hope. Now his disobedience was for naught. This was the last thing his people needed—another reason for unease, another reason to doubt him.

He bit back a snarl and leapt to his feet, careening down the slope with sure-footed speed that would have sent a lesser man sprawling, and when he reached the shore of the lake, he seized a stone and hurled it, not to skip gracefully across the water, but to land with a loud splash where she had appeared before. If she was there beneath the water, mocking him by withholding her presence—if she was there... *May it strike you and show you my anger.*

The low, bitter laughter he heard was his own, as he dropped to a crouch and watched the ripples spread across the surface, so similar to those he'd seen before when he was barely a man, and yet so clearly different. Ripples made by man, not goddess. Ripples made by something sinking, not rising.

Still he stared, unwilling to give up that last remnant of hope.

Stared, seeing a slow bubbling in the centre of the ripples, bubbles popping across the surface. Heart pounding, he fell forward on his knees. "My lady," he breathed. "My goddess."

First, the crown of her head appeared, long silken tresses of glowing white streaming down her shoulders. Her head tilted as she gazed at him, her features milk against moonlight against glass, white and ethereal.

She rose, and he choked on a gasp as water streamed down her body—only it wasn't her body—not the slender, beautiful goddess of his youth. This was a full, round creature, her belly swollen and her arms heavy, and this was not his goddess—not Elen—

"Vespasian!"

The shout came from behind him, and before his eyes, the vision vanished, leaving a surface as still as glass, despite the chilly breeze that swept across.

Rage boiled up in him, sheer and deadly, as he whirled to attack the blackguard who had made her disappear.

Tern and Kale, grim-faced with their own anger, held Persephone Fury between them.

"We found the little bitch trying to—"

"You did not find me. I found you," she said, but her voice was weak, and she would not meet any gaze and instead pulled the cloak—Night's red cloak—tightly about her body and stared at the ground.

It was all he could do not to close the distance between them and take her slender neck in his grip and—

She met his gaze then, and he was stunned to see how hollow her eyes were, how empty.

"Please—I have to warn you," she begged. "They're coming again—they know where you are—"

"Take her away from me," he said, giving them all his back.

"No, please, you have to believe me—"

"If you want to live past the noon, you will let them remove you from my sight." His voice was harsh with threat, and if she had any sense of self-preservation, she would heed his words.

"Do what you will, but do it after you hear me!"

He snapped back around, feeling the power crackling through him. One offence after another rolled past him, but if the disappearance of that strange—wrong—goddess had been first in his mind, now seeing the men's expressions, her previous and far more grievous offence swept over him. "Hear what? Lies? They sent you here to deceive us? Do you have more of our children you want to kill, or will it be your brother this time? How many ways do you desire to destroy us, *Miss Fury?*" His last words hissed, and if he'd had the venom to go with his bite, he would have sunk his teeth into her himself, and this time let her writhe to her death.

If he expected her to be stung, he did not expect the devastation he saw play across her thin, agonised features.

"Release her."

They did, and she collapsed into the mud, her face smearing through it before she gathered her balance and drew up on her elbows. "The duke has brought foreign soldiers," she gasped. "And he knows you hide in your sacred grove!"

He stared down at her, willing his face to be cold, to reveal nothing. "I have no reason to believe one who sent a child to his death." She sobbed, she *dared* to sob! He drew back his boot and released his anger into a kick—watched mud splash across her and snarled, "You have no right to mourn that child! Do you know what the murderer said as he threw the hex that killed him? He said, 'This? This nit would grow to nothing but a louse, and you think him a king?' and then he killed him, and our Rue held him in her arms as his blood poured, and *you* dare to grieve?"

She had no answer. She collapsed into the mud, sobbing, a disgrace, and he stared at her in frustration.

This was the hell-bent bratling who had left him to die? Who fought him tooth and nail at every turn? "Stand," he ordered, only to see her remain a crumpled heap.

"*Stand!*" he roared and grabbed her by the upper arm and yanked her upright. "This is what you become among their lot? A puling, whimpering infant? You disgust me!"

That, more than anything, seemed to rouse her. She tried to pull free, rubbing her face and only smearing the mud across it more thoroughly. "I can stand," she finally said.

He released her and, allowing his lip to curl, reached for a handkerchief and began meticulously wiping his hands clean of her grime.

"Vespasian," Tern said, his voice rough. "You know what must happen, what Night will demand."

One knuckle proved difficult, and so he applied himself to leaving its creases as pale as the skin around them, his mind racing with calculations. Finally, he folded the handkerchief so that no soiled portion was evident and placed it back in his pocket. "Of course I know." He raised his face to Tern, to the girl. "Death."

She did not flinch but only stared resolutely past them all, out towards the water.

She had known. She had known that if she came back into their grasp, the question would never be life or death, but how painful and lingering a death she would experience.

He spat his disgust at the dirt and whipped away from her.

"There's the boy that came with her."

"Boy?" Not another Fury, surely not the inadequate brother.

"He knew too much." She dug her fingers into her hair, revealing more distress over this unknown boy than she had her own safety. "I couldn't leave him there. The duke—he would have killed him, if he discovered what Bertrand knew."

"Bring him."

The boy was not over tall but sturdy, well-fed, and dressed in the clothes of a Fireborn servant, his hair neatly shorn as befitted that station. He didn't meet anyone's eyes. In less than a moment, Vespasian had the boy's chin in a tight grip, his head tilted back, and—

"No!" The girl flew at him, her face twisted with fear and rage as she recognised his intent. One quick slash of his arm, and she fell back, gasping, though he hadn't touched her.

He found the boy's brown eyes and trapped them easily with his own, as if the boy had never been warned—stupid girl—the images he most wanted to hide were uppermost in his mind.

Bouncing images—disjointed—

The village?

Bloody hell, this boy had been in the village?

King's men.

His rage started low in his throat and erupted in a roar. He had not seen, because he had not been in the village. But this boy had seen—

Otter Fury split open by a hex that ripped flesh into jagged edged death, spraying blood across the dirt, the wattle and daub wall of the cottage—

Rue's face.

Her arms.

Her body.

Clutching the child, her mouth open in a silent scream.

He released the boy's chin.

The boy fell back, staggering, dark smudges on his flesh where Vespasian had pressed too tightly, where there would be bruises, where blood that still beat in his veins would rush to fill, while Otter's body lay in a grave, cold and bloodless.

Then the girl—the arrogant Miss Persephone Fury—flung herself in front of the boy, *this* boy, and was babbling, shrieking—

Vespasian grabbed her by the hair and yanked her to him and snarled, "Silence!"

"—but you can't, you can't kill him, he didn't do it—he couldn't have stopped it, and—"

"Miss Fury," he hissed, *"we do not kill children."* He watched his words find their target.

She turned ashen.

He whipped back to the boy. "And you? If you are truly innocent, we'll find a place for you." A new thought rolled through his mind, and he pinned the girl with a look. "What is your age?"

"What is the d—day?" Her teeth chattered in her head, from fear or shock, he did not know nor did he care.

He released her hair and drew back. The irony, that she should not even know the day which was so important to him, the day that had brought him to this place. "It is the fifth day of September."

She nodded, clearly struggling to regain purchase on her thoughts and emotions. "Then—then I am eighteen today."

"Today?" he asked sharply.

"At noon. I was born at noon." Her voice drifted and her face clouded over. "And Dardanus twelve minutes after."

On his eighteenth birthday, at the exact moment he was receiving the prophecy—both gift and curse—with a task that would change his life forever, Persephone Fury, the Power that had been prophesied, was taking her first squalling breath.

The Power that would lift the True King to his throne. The Power he would wait eighteen years to finally receive, and yet, there still was no True King. The throne would be vacant, and then would be filled, and there was no bloody True King. He felt the eyes on him, from them all, his men, the girl, and the boy she protected.

"Alas," he said, turning his voice to silk and watching her grow wary. "Had you only come to us a day sooner, your youth might have saved you."

He didn't spare her a glance to see how she received that information.

"Tie them both up," he said. "We're returning to the grove."

❦❦

She put one foot in front of the other, despite the sharp pains that shot up her legs, thighs, and back, from long days on horseback. She refused to ask to stop to rest. Her cheeks stung with shame, that she had grovelled, that she had begged, and then—with wrath. He dared kick mud in her face, handle her like an animal? And finally, with guilt. For deep down, she knew she deserved no better.

But she had more to tell him, much more he needed to know, which she would save for the time it was most likely to save her.

The path climbed higher, out of the wood and into the open where it crossed the mountain top, and she felt horribly exposed, despite the fact that it was too soon for the duke's new dragoons to have come west. Vespasian Wyllt wouldn't lead them across an open mountain top if they were in danger of assault. It went beyond irony that she found herself relying on the same blackguard to keep her safe who was even now planning her death.

She refused to think about that. She would go mad if she thought about that.

In front of her, Bertrand stumbled, even less accustomed to days of horseback and then long treks than she. No one helped him, though, and bound as he was, he had trouble regaining his footing.

The men trained all their attention on her. Their hatred radiated off them in tangible waves. Where before they had tolerated her presence, now, they despised every breath she took. If Vespasian Wyllt was planning her death, they were relishing the prospect of it.

She could not think about that now. She could not allow herself to think about that now.

❦❦

She recognised the twist in the wooded path, the limb she ducked, the broken boulder she stepped over.

She recognised the approach to the village, and a tightness started in her belly and climbed, making it difficult to breathe, to swallow, as though rocks were in her throat, clogging it.

They entered the village, not slowing their pace, Vespasian Wyllt so close behind her she felt the heat of his rage.

She saw Lysander's cottage and splatters of mud on one white wall.

No, not mud.

Splatters of blood.

She could not breathe or swallow for the pain that lodged within her, and yet—she did both. Just as they all did. Walking past and to the path on the other side that led to the sacred grove, the grove that had welcomed her when she'd first found it.

She began to tremble, not with fatigue but with fear. What awaited her in that grove? What justice, so well-earned? Would a sacred place allow itself to be defiled by her presence?

Blindly, she walked, seeing nothing but the splatters of brown on the white wall, her ears filled with the echoes of silent screams.

❧❦

Anticipation of this moment had weighted her feet, making her journey west as harrowing as it was necessary. And now, the moment was here.

Lysander.

This man was hardly recognisable as her brother, his hard face etched with rage, his body seeming to waste away to nothing but raw sinew and bone, held together by agony.

Lysander.

He showed no surprise at her arrival, just a long stare that cut through her. The words she'd thought to speak turned to ashes in her mouth.

Bertrand stopped ahead of her as he stared at the emerald velvet moss coating boulders and climbing tree trunks, turning the grove into a magical place of worship that rivalled—nay, surpassed—the Basilica of Apollo in all its glory. A tremor of anxiety rippled through her. The leaves overhead sheltered the Earthborn rebels, but she heard them shiver with a rustle of hissing malignancy at her entrance.

Faces stared at her with venom. The hatred rose from them like mists from the ground. Bertrand must wonder what fate she had led him to.

These people had kept their distance before. Now, even though they didn't move, they were a body of threat closing in on her.

She forced her eyes straight ahead and kept walking, and she had a sudden need to feel earth beneath her feet, between her toes, that strength, that comfort, that release.

Then the moment she hadn't allowed herself to think of at all.

Oh, merciful gods and vengeful goddesses, she had not allowed herself to think of it, and now it was upon her and she could not have been prepared for it, in no way could she have been prepared...

For Rue.

Her eyes blazed with madness, fingers curled into feral claws, breath coming in sharp pants as she crouched on a moss-covered rock, twitching with each move Persephone made. Rue, who had never liked her, now had reason to hate, to destroy, and for one mad moment Persephone felt the need to drop to her knees, to bare the back of her neck for swift and final retribution.

Instead, she blinked back tears and walked deeper into the heart of the grove, closer to its power until there was no further to walk, for they had arrived at the massive, ancient oak with its heavy, twisting limbs shimmering with moss and magic.

At its gnarled, knuckled roots, sat the Crone, Night, as surely enthroned by a seat of bark and moss as Queen Ygraine had ever been in her finely wrought gilt.

Without thought, without plan, without consideration, Persephone fell into a curtsey so deep, her breath stirred the crackle of leaves.

Vespasian Wyllt sneered, "*We* do not kneel. *We* do not grovel. To *anyone.*"

She rose quickly, remembering how she had grovelled in the mud at his feet. She turned away from him, quickly, and to the Crone. "It was respect."

"I do not want your kind of respect," Night said.

There were layers there, layers of meaning. Persephone could only bow her head in shame.

"You," the old woman said to Vespasian, glaring, "I will deal with later."

"Had I not disobeyed, we would not have found this *woman* prowling our border," he said, the emphasis on woman a taunt.

"Silence!"

Persephone felt him withdraw from behind her, felt the cool air where before there had been solid body. "I am here to warn you," she said quietly, "and to assist you, if you trust me, and I beg of you to trust me in this, for there is a great evil coming."

At which words, the world broke into roars around her and over her head. Roars of outrage, of frenzied, lathered lust for vengeance. Roars of men and women all determined to make her pay for what she had seen as duty, as an attempt to save them.

Their words broke over her, a babble from which she could distinguish nothing, for she stared into the old woman's pale, rheumy eyes and felt true despair. This was the woman who had wanted her killed at birth.

But whether they liked it or not, they must listen to her. They must.

One voice cut through the others, the voice that had cursed her or prophesied, Persephone knew not which, that Otter's death would be on her hands, the golden voice, the soft, sweet voice of a lark.

"The time is ripe for prophecy to be fulfilled. In the fulfilling, the sky will rain blood and sorrow. If it is not fulfilled, there will be peace and devastation."

All fell silent in frozen expectation as Lark stepped from behind the Crone, one slender finger outstretched in accusation. *"There are as many ways as there are mistakes to be made. And she—she will make all of them!"*

"Not with my people," Night said, her voice harsh with age and with anger as she rose to her feet and added her gnarled finger, pointing in accusation and curse. "No more mistakes with my people!" She sank back into the twisted base of the huge, ancient oak. She raised her head and spoke a single word. "Grebe."

The people fell back as the small aged man Persephone had seen once before walked forward, his movements much more agile than his wrinkled face and almost bald pate would have led her to expect. The long, thin plaits hung from his temples, reaching down almost to the low-slung belt he wore low on his bony hips. His steps were sure-footed, even though he kept his gaze trained on hers, steady, unreadable.

When he reached Night's side, he seemed to grow in stature, his bent frame more erect.

"Speak to us, oh Judge, what is the law?" the old woman asked, her tone indicating this question was more rote and tradition than sincere query. Her eyes glittered with anticipation as they swept down Persephone's form and back up to her face.

"The offence is against people and person," he said. "The most severe penalty for these is banishment from our people, from our worship, to curse the guilty to wander the face of the earth an outlaw without kin or goddess." His eyes drilled into hers, merciless. "When the betrayer is not of our kin or goddess, the punishment is death."

A ripple of satisfaction swept over the gathering.

"The offence against the person takes precedence over the offence against the people when it is death of a kinsman, and thus it is the kinsmen of the dead who choose the form of death."

She could not restrain her gasp. The choice of the kinsmen—of—of Lysander? Her brother, her beloved brother, now to choose her form of death? She could not see this as a mercy but only as an agony of the worst proportions as she met his stony gaze. A scramble of movement barely caught her eye, but then Rue was at his side, and if Night's eyes had glittered with anticipation, Rue's sent chills through her.

One man stepped in front of them and laid his bow and arrow at their feet.

Another man offered a knife.

One of the women she recognised as a laundress placed a phial into the cradle of the bow—a poison? Persephone wondered if it was fast-acting or one that would bring many hours or even days of excruciating death. The narrow-eyed sneer the woman flashed in her direction seemed to answer that question more than adequately. No easy death from that party.

Swaying on her feet, Persephone suddenly needed strength, comfort, and within moments had quietly eased her feet from her slippers to feel sharp pangs of twig and dead leaf piercing the soles of her feet, just as the cold earth nourished her. *Please*, she begged her goddess. *Please*. Without understanding why, she found herself searching for the face of the man least likely to offer her any comfort or salvation and wondered why he, with his position of authority, was not in the midst of the anticipation. Instead, to her surprise, Vespasian Wyllt stood where the path first entered the grove, as if guarding. Guarding it against her flight? If Rue's expression had chilled her, his turned her straight to ice.

She jerked her head forward. Were these offerings piling up before Lysander and Rue tradition, part of the rite being enacted, or were they more specific and more personally aimed at her? Did it make a difference, when the rage against her was so palpable she could cut it with her knife? She shifted her heavy sack over her shoulder, her few possessions that seemed so important when she hurriedly put them into the heavy box and sealed it with her own magic now meant nothing.

Against her breast, the pulse of the parchment vibrated, just as it had since she'd first been thrust back into close proximity with the bastard Vespasian Wyllt.

She would have begged, she would have grovelled, she would have debased herself in any way possible to receive Lysander's forgiveness. She would fling herself into the storms of Hades for all eternity to bring back his fierce, sweet son.

But she could not bring back a soul from the dead, and to ask Lysander's forgiveness was to ask him to be stronger than the gods, who would themselves smite her, had she treated their sons so.

But she could give his people her knowledge and her possessions to use as they would, and in her wake she would leave them the potential to win this desperate fight.

The sky would rain blood. Hadn't it already? But what was peace if it brought devastation? It became clear to her, that she was treating Lark's words as true prophecy, for they rang true in her heart and mind. She looked at the woman, her hair shimmering gold even in the shadow of the oaks. How could she be Ordinary and yet be in this magical place? So many questions to ask, and they would remain unasked.

She shifted her body then, turning to face Lysander and Rue. She didn't cast herself at their mercy. She awaited their decision, as Rue stared at the instruments of death at her feet, her expression hungry and fierce. Through it all, Lysander remained as cold and still as Nemesis herself, judging and ready to give her what she deserved.

He turned away from her, giving her his back, and instead, presented himself to Night. "You know what she has been taught. I took her from everything she knew, brought her here as an abductor, not a brother, and used her as a weapon, not as a sister. She has suffered throughout her entire life with powers she could not control and no one helped her. She was injured and reviled here and given no reason to trust or believe. I cannot accept her death as the proper punishment—"

Rue's scream split through the air, and she flew at her husband, claws outstretched, streaking blood down his cheeks. He grabbed her, wrestled with her, and then held her against him as she fought to free herself, but his eyes did not leave those of the Crone, who spat at the ground and then turned her attention to the struggling woman, who stilled under the old woman's scrutiny.

"Daughter of my daughter, it was your son who died. Tell me the sentence."

Rue trembled, and her eyes danced between those of her husband and her grandmother and finally, at the pile of offerings.

Persephone froze.

Rue crossed the earth to the pile with an unearthly grace, reached into it, and withdrew a blade with three jagged notches on its sharp edge. Her face transformed into a strange beauty that was nothing like when she danced for Lysander in the campfire's light, when she cradled her son—she took the phial and twisted the stopper out of its neck and dripped it down the blade of the knife.

Long, glistening strings of viscous yellow coated and clung, before finally dripping to the earth—

They sizzled into putrid smoke.

Rue's smile was deadly as she whispered, "I have decided."

❧ CHAPTER FORTY-FOUR ❧

And just like that, it all unravelled beyond saving.

He clenched his fists to stop from hurling bloody Lysander Fury across the grove and into a pile of boulders to land as broken bits. He'd counted on the man to use his glib tongue to save the bloody chit, and instead—

Instead, Lysander's eyes met his over Rue's head, and whatever was in them, he had no time to read—

Only to react—

As Rue lunged forward, the knife in her grip—

Vespasian held up his hand and willed—that's all there had been time for, his *willing*—and before he could form the word or thought, he had summoned the blade and its hilt was in his hand.

Rue whirled, looking for the knife, snarling in confusion and rage.

Lysander let out a deep sigh of relief.

Vespasian waded into the chaos, snapping orders. "Control your wife, Fury!"

Night shot to her feet. "You have no authority to disrupt!"

"No authority? I have spent half my life waiting for this moment, and now the time of prophecy has come, you think I'm going to allow all hope for our future to die under a poisoned blade?" He glared at everyone around him. "You can't kill her, not unless you are willing to lose everything!"

"I've already lost everything," Rue shrieked, fighting against Lysander's hold on her.

"Then kill her after she's put the True King on his throne!" Vespasian replied. He slid the poisoned knife carefully into the pouch at his belt and secured it. "But not now, and not today."

"Boy!" Grebe's voice, usually so gentle, cracked thunder. "You are not the law!"

Wrath boiled up within him like molten earth and rock. They could not truly mean to allow this to happen. To fling the *law* in his face? To

451

snap at him like a child, he who had given them all that he had and more? His fists trembled, and the power to force them to his will surged within him. For one wild moment, he was tempted, because if he didn't, there was only one way to save the arrogant Fury brat, and the thought of that brought his rage to an even more savage pitch.

What about *her* power? She could have stopped Rue, could have destroyed them all herself, had she so chosen, and in fact, he was astonished that she had not—that fear had not erupted from her, and if it had not, that could only mean that she, like him, was controlling it.

Brava, Miss Fury, he thought savagely. *Brava, for finally learning when it's too bloody late.*

He grabbed her hand and yanked her to him, and then raised his free hand in subtle threat. "You will not kill her. You will not hurt her. She has brought us warning, and we should even now be preparing for attack."

"There's plenty o' time after we—" one voice snarled.

"You can't protect her all the time." Rue's hands were empty, but her threat was not.

"Oh, there is a way," he said, "and you will not be able to touch her."

He saw recognition hit Grebe and Night at the same time, saw them both tense with understanding, Grebe in outrage, Night in calculation.

"There is only one way you could do such a thing," Grebe said harshly, "but it would be an outrage to all we hold holy."

"She is a woman." He watched Night's eyes for recognition. "Today."

Night stood more rigidly. "Today?"

"Yes, mother Crone, on this day, she was born. On the day when the goddess appeared to me with her prophecy. At the very moment."

"It was supposed to be the boy," Night said, her anger still crackling. "It was supposed to be the boy, but this—this thing— insisted on being born first, on being so difficult, her brother could not be born at the right time, and now you want her to continue to exist to thwart us!"

"Not want. *Command.* I am leading us into battle, and this will be my decision." He placed his hands on the girl's—nay, the woman's—shoulders and turned her. She stared up at him warily, stiffening at his touch even as she allowed his proximity to protect her. "Whatever self-sacrificial choice you have made, the choice is no longer yours. You will live under my protection, and—"

"Nooooooooooo!" Rue screamed, finally understanding.

Vespasian raised a hand and blocked her, never dropping his eyes from those of the black-haired wraith before him. Still, she did not speak.

"You cannot," Grebe repeated. "She's not one of ours and doesn't live by our laws—"

"Miss Fury, are you faithful to the Fireborn dynasty that dares to call itself Pendragon?"

"No." She shuddered and clutched her bag more closely to her chest.

"Do you desire to give up your Fireborn loyalties, family, and friends, in order to bring the True King to the throne, may the goddess show him to us in her good time?"

She swallowed and blinked back tears. "Yes."

"Do you swear this with your body and your heart and your soul?" he demanded, his voice rising over the gasps and mutterings of the gathering as they all realised his goal.

She stared up at him now, and her voice was an open expression of grief. "Yes," she whispered. "Yes."

"Tell me again that I cannot—"

Grebe was trembling with rage and affront.

But it was Night who spoke.

"Vespasian Wyllt, if you do this thing—"

"What thing?" Persephone demanded, turning to him in entreaty. "What are you all speaking of?"

Staring into her face, he knew the deepest most venomous rage of his life and felt it spilling over until he tasted it, metallic and bitter, on the back of his tongue. He had no choice. He had no bloody choice. He curled his lip into a snarl and lowered his lids and forced the words out. "If you are my True Wife—"

"*Outrage!*" Grebe shouted.

"—none can touch you. You will be bound to my will—"

She drew in a sharp breath, her own outrage visible.

"—and none can touch you," he repeated, and this time it was Rue's anger that rose above the clamour of all around them, even as Lysander wrestled her away.

He saw the girl's knuckles go white, her jaw rigid and her eyes squeezed shut. He wanted her to refuse. He couldn't allow her to say no.

Again, Grebe spoke. This time, his words quieted everyone. "There can be no binding, none at all, and certainly no True Bond begun between two such as you," he said, his tone serene. "The magic will not happen."

"What kind of bond? What kind of magic? Tell me!" She, whose life was being spared, was making demands? His own control came dangerously near slipping. "You were put on the marriage mart to find a wealthy husband," he grated.

"Not necessarily—"

"A suitable husband," he corrected, "meaning wealth and social position—"

"It's not—not like that." But her cheeks flamed in her pale, narrow face.

"The idea of marriage is not foreign to you—"

"Yes."

That stopped him.

"Yes," she repeated, her voice strangled with tears, her head bowed so that her hair hid her face. "If that is the only way, then do it."

"So you want to live after all," he sneered.

At that, her head snapped up. "I will atone for my mistakes, and I will see that the Duke of Glastonbury never takes the throne, no matter the cost, and if that means I must—" She broke off, and it was clear the horror of what she was agreeing to overcame her.

The horror. She looked at him with horror, and he raised his eyes to the sky, wanting to send every Fury that ever breathed into the most distant caverns of the underworld to freeze into ice. "Must... what?" he asked finally, forcing her to say it.

"Must marry."

"Marry?"

"You."

"It will not work!" Grebe said and kept speaking.

But his voice, all the voices of outrage, were as nothing, for one other voice rose over them, liquid and silver and cold with rage.

"No, no, my child, you will not join yourself with him!"

She flinched back away from him. He knew they had both heard the voice of the goddess, even as he knew by the cacophony around them that no others had.

Vespasian felt the rejection down to the very bone, that still his goddess despised him. After everything.

Dust. It was all turning to dust.

Then she reached for his hand, grabbed it with more strength that he had suspected she could possibly possess and said, "Yes, whatever it takes, *yes.* "

"You will regret this many times," he snapped.

She raised her chin a notch and glared at him through unshed tears. "As will you."

Threat made, threat returned.

"When?" she asked. "Is there a rite?"

It would be so easy, too easy—too fast. "We stand on sacred ground."

"It can't work," Grebe shouted. "It's an outrage. She doesn't even know what it means!"

"Will you join your path with mine?" Vespasian asked, "With—" and honesty and fear made him add "—or without the protection of the goddess?"

Oh, stupid girl, stupid, stupid girl.

For her answer was "Yes."

Their hands warmed, palm to palm, and he stared down in shock and triumph at the soft flash of light.

It had worked.

How? It had been a wild gamble, and it had worked, and yet—how could they have the commitment to mark the beginning of such a bond?

He raised his eyes to find Lysander Fury's attention fixed rabidly on their hands, to see the relief that crossed the younger man's features as he clutched the sobbing Rue against his chest. How neatly he had been played by the cunning bastard, who—knowing his own inability to protect his sister—had spectacularly failed so that another, more permanent protection had been put into place.

Vespasian reached for her bag and, despite her attempt to hold onto it, flung it over his shoulder and took off, dragging her behind him.

"Is that it?" she asked, running to keep pace. "That's all?"

Oh, surely she could not be so innocent.

"No, that is not all. We're leaving sacred ground to complete the rite, for there is nothing sacred that will happen between us, of that you can be certain."

She asked no more questions.

With a clench of his gut, more rage, more frustration, that his burden had become so heavy, he surged faster down the path, leaving her to trip and stumble but never fall, for he had her hand and she could not fall and slow him. They broke out of the wood, and the wide western sky was before them, bruised with dark hues left behind by the setting sun. He chose the path that took them down into the Ordinary wood, a place where there was threat and risk.

A place that would not be defiled by their actions.

❦❧

Robin had dropped his mug of ale, shoved away from the table without apology or excuse. Scrambled up the narrow stairs to the deck and into the blast of howling wind and churning sea—

She needed him.

His blood roiled with the knowledge, burning in his veins.

He'd known it, known she needed him, and he needed her from the first moments of their meeting on a moonlit night so long ago.

He'd known it when she disappeared, known deep to the bone that he had to find her.

But this was new, this was desperate, this was a gnawing, eating him from within.

Now, at this moment.

She needed him, and he was on a ship in the Channel, his

helplessness a howl of rage and fear and desperation growing within him like a tidal surge.

He had been graced with a seaman's stomach. This is what the sailors told him as they scrambled across the deck, securing things against the high waves. While most were below decks, hiding and retching, Robin stood at the rail, staring out at the coastline they circled, high, sharp cliffs and rolling green terrain. His hands clenched the rail with white knuckles. His legs were braced wide for balance, but his stomach managed to remain stoic as long as he could fill his lungs with the bite of sharp salty air.

She needed him.

And he was on a ship in the Channel, a howl growing within him, a howl of rage and fear and desperation.

She needed him.

And he was helpless to save her.

❧❧

Vespasian finally stopped to catch his breath when they were at the small clearing where he felt the most protected, for it was shielded by thorny bracken and by dense foliage.

Only then did he finally turn and look at her, and brace himself for what was to come. If there were tears… if she dared cry… But she did not. She took her pack from him and placed it carefully in the crook of a twisted log, then removed her cloak and draped it over the pack. He watched in stunned silence as she began working the buttons at the nape of her neck, and when she could no longer reach them, she whispered a command and the rest fell open to expose her white chemise.

She could not be this calm. She could not be this placid. She could not be so very uncaring.

She was not. Her face, when her hair swung back, was strained and white. But still she kept moving until, clad only in the thin white shift, she had backed herself up against a tree and stared at him with those large black eyes and waited.

Waited. For what?

"Isn't this the way it's done?" she asked crisply. "Isn't this the way the Ordinary women do it when it is a transaction of business?"

It flashed before him, that night when this—this child, for she had been a child then—had ridden before him on the horse and he had forced her to see, had threatened her with what she saw.

Now she taunted him with it, because yes, wasn't that exactly what they were doing? He took a step towards her but could not go farther, disgust welling up within him. "No," he snarled, "that is not the way."

"How would you have me?" Her chin rose higher. "On all fours? Like a dog?"

"Damn you! Do you think I want this? Do you think I would ever choose this?" He snatched her cloak up, not even bothering to use magic, and with a wave of his arm, watched it spread and drift to land on the ground.

A marriage bed.

She walked regally to it and eased herself down, raising the drape of her chemise until it was bunched at her thighs and then lying back to stare up at him and finally say, "I am ready."

As if she could ever be ready for what lay ahead of them.

He knew a moment's mad hope that perhaps they would fail after all—but his body betrayed him.

As much as he despised everything she stood for, everything she had done to bring them to this place and this moment, the sight of her long white legs splayed on the blood red cloak... of her quim, shadowed with dark curls but open to him, brought him to life.

He did not want to do this. *He did not want to do this.* He fumbled with his breeches, ripped them open, and when the length and heft of him sprang free, purple with blood, she turned her head to the side.

"Do it," she said. "Just do it."

He gnashed his teeth with fury—even that did not chill his blood.

He tried to form words, but there were no words.

She rose up on her elbows and, her eyes cold as steel, hissed, "I have waited all day for my death, do you think I cannot take this? Just do what you must!"

He lowered himself between her legs, his heart pounding, his mind *raging.*

He did not want this. He had never wanted this. He would do it—would consummate and draw her blood, but that was all, nothing more—

He lowered himself between her spread thighs and felt a wave of humiliation. Was she stronger than he? But for all her bravado she was innocent, she didn't know—

"Now!"

With a gasp, he found himself between her legs, pushing through her virgin flesh and into the depths of her.

CHAPTER FORTY-FIVE

The pain was sharp. Fast. Almost before she could cry out, it was over—almost but not quite, for she did cry out, and then felt her skin flaming. With embarrassment for allowing any sound to escape, with the aftermath of pain, with the indignity of it all.

He held himself raised over her, his body weighing her down but his face—

She stared up at him, into his black, black eyes, and this was the face of her nightmares, only he was not leering and there was no pleasure.

Where were the Shadows? The connection that sang to her and tempted her; if ever she was to feel it, wouldn't it be now?

She couldn't breathe, she couldn't breathe, she couldn't breathe—

Suddenly he was rolling away from her, and it was done. She could breathe again. She stared up at the dense cover of leaves—ash leaves, they were in an ash grove, and her head was filled with the memory of a night long ago, a night when she'd played *Llwyn Onn* until people wept.

This was not supposed to be. It was meant to be Robin and not a rushed, urgent act but a loving one, but that could never be, now. Her eyes and throat were dry as if her grief were too deep for tears, or perhaps, she had finally at long last run out of them.

Chill shimmered over her skin, and she realised she still lay there, her legs and lower body exposed, and it seemed like too much effort to cover herself, to move.

"That was quick," she finally said, testing her voice and pleased that it functioned in an almost normal fashion.

"Surely—"

She turned her head at the sound of that strained, gravelled voice, which wasn't working nearly as normally as hers.

"Surely you aren't complaining, Miss Fury!"

He was curled away from her, his back and shoulders so

overwhelming in close proximity, rigid and curled over himself.

"No, of course not. Just..." She reached for a word and couldn't find one. "Confused. When I observed it, it seemed to last longer. Perhaps when one is in the midst of it, it seems—" But no, she'd witnessed rapid thrusting, urgent and somehow dirty, up against the side of the building. What had happened between them had been one thrust, one sharp, painful thrust, and then no more.

She studied his back, its movements with his short, fast breaths, and frowned. "Is it—is it supposed to hurt you, as well?" It wasn't that she felt pity, exactly, but perhaps breaking through her barrier was painful on a man's nether parts.

"Miss Fury," he snarled, "if you do not cease speaking—"

"I'm not. I'm not Miss Fury, am I?" Panic clutched her. Were they married at all? What had she just done?

She sat up abruptly—saw the blood on her thighs—and reached over and slapped him on his arse, not intentionally, but in a wild flail of instinct and desperation. "A phial, we need—oh gods, I never dreamed this—I don't have a phial!"

It wasn't her duty to have one. Robin would have had one. He would never have taken her to their marriage bed without one, and now her virgin's blood was on her thighs with no way to collect it. Virgin's blood that was not Robin Fitzwilliam's. That was—was this man's. But no matter. It was powerful, and they needed its power.

He turned his upper body and his glare towards her. She got a glimpse of him, still jutting and stiff, and wondered how long it would stay that way and thought it no surprise at all that he was in pain and tried to imagine Robin that way and—stopped herself. She squeezed her eyes shut against tears that would not come, shut her mind against images that were not hers to imagine, against a future that was no longer hers. Against the foolish dreams of a foolish girl. Against her heart.

She thought instead of the box in her pack, of its contents, and could think of nothing that would suffice. "Have you nothing to collect my blood?" she asked forlornly.

"Don't be stupid," he growled. "Your blood is worthless."

Ah. There they were, the tears she thought she'd exhausted. She blinked desperately, swallowed. She would not let him see how his barb struck home. Damn him and curse him if this meant so little to him! Not knowing what else to do, she sat up, clenching herself closed between her thighs as if holding back piss and looked wildly around the clearing for something—anything—and saw a short distance away, an acorn cap. She strained her hand towards it, and the tips of her fingers touched, then closed over it.

Relieved, she sat up to examine her thighs more closely. This was magic she'd never learned, for it was man's magic. Such boundaries had never been a thing to stop her, but this was work she had never spared a thought to need.

She gritted her teeth against tears. As little as it might hold, this small cap of virgin's blood should not be wasted, even if her—she choked at the thought—her *husband* thought it worthless.

She held the dry, brown cap against her thigh and watched, relieved, as the damp streaks of blood filled it.

Well, then. Not filled at all. For all that it looked like a lot of blood, it hadn't been so very much.

"For Arawn's sake, do your vows mean nothing?"

He was sitting up beside her, and a quick, embarrassed, surreptitious glance revealed that he was no longer erect. She ducked her head to let her hair hide her cheeks, which now flamed more hotly than before. "Just because you find it worthless doesn't mean I must. There is power in a virgin's blood, and—"

"Miss—" He broke off, and she met his gaze and saw his cheeks were flushed, as were her own.

"Am I still a miss?" she asked, worried.

"You are not."

Before she could examine the sense of relief she felt, he was tugging his trousers up, and she thought of the blood on his—and stopped that thought, as well.

He stood, towering over her, giving her his back while he adjusted his clothes.

Belatedly, she finally tugged her chemise down and closed her thighs. If tears were harder to come by, the blood in her veins certainly had no trouble flushing her skin. She rose to her knees, holding the acorn cap gingerly.

"What would you prefer to be called?" he asked, his voice as stiff as his stature.

There was only one answer, as odd as it felt on her tongue to give him the freedom. "Persephone, of course." She rose to her feet. "Although, I am sure it will be as difficult for you to cease calling me 'idiot girl' and worse, as it will be for me to stop thinking of you as the bastard Vespasian Wyllt."

He froze.

Even before he turned his face to her, she felt his ire.

"It's not as if you've given me reason to feel any different!" she said.

His eyes were burning. "I do not know who my father is, nor do I want to. If calling me a bastard brings you pleasure, feel free. You will hardly be the first."

The blood that flamed her cheeks was hot with shame. If she had known, would she have called him so? Oh yes, she would have called him so with even more venom, revelling in her power. But not now. "I'm sorry."

"Why? I hardly care."

But he did. He clearly did. She felt chagrin. "I shall not do so again."

After a long moment, he waved a dismissive hand at the cap of blood. "I told you, it's worthless, and still you do this?"

"I never dreamed I would have a husband who did not want my bride gift, but even if you have no respect for it, I will not let it be wasted." She raised her chin and glared at him.

And—oddly—he winced and sighed. "Did you not promise to forsake Fireborn ways? Or was that a matter of saying what must be said to save your skin?"

"You mean, the Earthborn don't—"

"The Earthborn do not put a value on virgin's blood, no." He snatched her gown up from the log.

It looked absurd in his surprisingly elegant, long-fingered hands. He held it out to her, an offering of sorts, she supposed.

She clutched the cap more closely to her body. "It can't be—against my vows—to keep it?"

"Miss—" He gave a long-suffering sigh. "Persephone. The value put on a virgin's blood is the value defined by men who view women as property. Proof that a bride has never been possessed, never known another man, nothing more."

"You say that as if it were a bad thing. As if—as if the Earthborn have no value in virtue, in chastity?"

He gave a toss of his head. "The Earthborn value respect and fidelity. They do not seek to possess, to own, to control. A virgin's blood is simply that—a few drops of blood with no more or less power than any other." He stared significantly at the cap in her hand. "It is up to you to decide which you will honour, Fireborn or Earthborn."

Until you know who your husband is, you do not know what you might do. Until you spend long nights remembering what might have been, you do not know. Do not tell me what you wouldn't do.

That place in her that was hollow and cold grew larger as she finally, painfully, watched the bit of blood—the blood that Robin would have collected with love and reverence—drip into the soil.

❦❦

He waited impatiently for her to dress, wondered if he should offer to help with her buttons, but she magicked them herself. He felt a sense of relief. Spoiled and pampered she might be, but she was not without her areas of self-sufficiency. He was about to lead the way out of the clearing, his mind already on what awaited them upon their return, when he realised she was not behind him. Was, in fact, on her knees.

Praying.

He felt his lip curl. To which deity? Which of her Greek deities received her pleas?

He'd a mind to shake her shoulder, bring her to her feet, but couldn't. He sank onto a rock and buried his head in his hands. So bloody weary. A long time passed, and when to linger longer would be dangerous, he raised his head to speak and found her already standing before him, her face haunted in the moonlight.

"What is it?" he snapped.

"She won't speak to me."

She had been praying to Elen? He'd hardly expected the girl's loyalties to shift so readily. Nor did he actually trust that they had. But as for not speaking... his gut twisted with sharp-edged bitterness. "It is her way when you betray her, when you disobey her. To stop speaking."

The stricken expression on her face, the way she clutched her heart, satisfied him that he had found his mark.

"But if she doesn't speak—how will I know what she wants me to do?"

"That is, indeed, the dilemma." He jerked his head, impatient now. "Come."

But.

He stopped, turned to study her once more. What was he missing? He sensed something within her, an unease as yet unexplained. She waited for him to precede her, confusion evident. She hadn't told him everything. Something sent her back to him in terror. Not just grief. Not just guilt. Terror. He did not believe the terror she felt was for the well-being of his people.

He folded his arms and leaned into the cradle formed where the thick trunk of an ash tree sent forth a heavy branch, still fully-leafed for a few more weeks before winter set in. "What have you not told me?"

She made no pretence of misunderstanding. She wrapped her arms around herself inside the cloak, as if fending off a chill, avoiding his gaze.

He waited silently, allowing the silence to work for him.

"When I was in the village... what you did to the woman, to Lark..."

Again, he did not speak, though unease tightened within him.

"You took something from her, and it restored your strength."

He forced a nod, forced himself not to react.

"The duke said you were evil, that you did evil, that he knew you when you were both young and—"

"He speaks the truth."

"Oh." She took a step backward, though he doubted if she was even aware of it.

Again, he sensed the flare of terror and wondered that he should sense such a thing, yet knew that he did.

"He asked me about it, asked me if you had an Ordinary woman with you, and I said no, but—but it seemed as if he knew what I had seen, what had happened, and even—he wanted to know if her name was Mary."

"Not anymore."

"But—but how could she be Ordinary and live amongst the Magi? Even the Earthborn would be so high above her—"

Even the Earthborn. Even the lowly Earthborn. Had the source of her fear not been his most urgent need, he would not have let that pass. "She is our Seer. We respect her."

"He said you—you must *farm* her."

He went rigid. Farm her? What sick, vile creature did Aubyn think him?

"What did he mean?" She chafed her arms uneasily.

"He suggested that I used her to restore my strength regularly. When in fact, I had never done so before. Never had I sunk so low, until you came amongst us." He did not attempt to keep the vicious tone from his voice, nor did he feel any pang of empathy when she winced, and his patience snapped. "What has you so terrified you do not sleep at night, you ride night and day to get to us, to warn us? What convinced you that we were worthy of saving and your people deserved betrayal?"

"Not my people. Never the *people*. Just as I did not believe your people deserving of what would happen to them. The people are pawns, all of us, in a game I don't understand. But he—the duke—" She raised bleak eyes to his, and the terror rose so sharply between them, it was scent and taste and texture and he knew it all. "He's using the same... the same power?"

"He does not have the power," he said.

"The same ritual?" she asked. "He's doing the same thing, only worse, so much worse. They—they died."

"Who?"

"Girls. Ordinary girls. Seven of them."

Like a punch into his ribs, he felt the blow, lost his breath. "Seven?"

"All dead. Their middles split open." She swayed on her feet.

He grabbed her, pulled her onto the log to sit, and found himself sitting beside her, knowing that sheer force of will kept his hands from trembling as hers trembled. "For what? For what purpose did he need so much power?"

"He's keeping the king alive. I'd heard of healings, but... I recognised the feel and scent of it, and it pulled me, it tried to pull me in, just as you did, only this was different, so different, and it felt like filth and dirt, and I thought it was because the girls were Ordinary, but if—if Lark is—"

"It wasn't the girls that were filth. It was him. He got the knowledge, and it seems, the knowledge was enough, if he found some other source of power."

"The duke told me—once he knew I had seen the ritual, and that I knew about it—he told me that he could use my power to fight—to fight you. But when I saw what he'd done—those girls—" She twisted her fingers together in her lap, a frenzy of nerves revealed despite her attempts to hide her emotion. "He ordered Otter killed! He planned it, even though I told him—I told him that Otter could not be the True King, and he promised me, and then, he ordered him killed! And—and he is killing girls, and even if they were Ordinary, they were girls, young girls—"

"Girls approaching their first menses," he said flatly. "Girls filled with ripe eggs, with new life, the newest and freshest life. The first time we experimented, it was with such a girl, and it was clumsy, but we... we did it. We took that bit of life from her and used it, and it restored life to a dying cat." He rubbed the scar on the pad of his thumb, felt the ghost of an ache where a wild claw had ripped it open as the cat made its escape. "We sent the girl back with no memory of what had happened, with a coin in her pocket and a scar on her belly, and... it seemed harmless enough. The next time, the scar was smaller. I took away that girl's memories and sent her back with a coin and told myself she was none the worse for it and had more money than she had ever known."

"And... Lark?" she asked softly. "Mary?"

"When I found her, I did not know that Glastonbury was changing our experiment. He did not want a single egg. He wanted them all.

When I saw how he took my—my Gift—and was willing to use it to destroy—when I saw how cavalierly he shrugged off my concerns and the fact that she could not survive such an action—when he mocked me and held me and my power in disdain and told me that I should count myself fortunate that he paid me for my service as his servant and still allowed me to be treated almost as one of them—" He broke off, wanted to hold something back, and yet, now, at this moment, could not. "He was right. I had used this Gift to buy his respect and a position amongst his peers, for even then there was speculation that he was King Pellinore's choice to succeed him to the throne." He rubbed his hands together. "I had demeaned myself and my Power seeking glory and position, and in that moment, I did not reject him because he was doing wrong. I rejected him because I would never be allowed to be his equal, would never be elevated, would only be used and then discarded. I refused to leave the innocent young Ordinary girl that I had brought him to her fate. So I took her and escaped, and they tried to find me but could not, for I knew Ordinary London and they did not.

"She saw me as her saviour. From that day forward, I have known I was not—not in any way that counted."

"Except that you did save her."

"She had no family and was already being watched by the whoremongers. There was nothing I could do but take her to Pentreafal. She found a place there, and as it turns out, she had her own gift."

"She would do anything for you," she said softly. "You broke her heart when you—when we—"

"I never asked for her heart, nor did I deserve it, nor did I want it."

Eventually he realised her silence was as eloquent as his own. "And you? Have you broken a heart on this day?"

He thought she would not answer, but then, so softly he strained to hear, she said, "Two hearts."

He had no doubt she spoke of her own as well as another and could spare no pity for a girl's first affections. There would be much more ahead of her that would take a harder toll.

But he could reassure her in one small, painful way. "You will not be asked to spend your power or your gift on our behalf."

She looked up at him, astonishment writ plain across her features.

"For whatever reasons you might have for running and for whatever guilt that drove you to warn us of impending attack, we will not trust you. You will not be part of our plans, nor will you know of them. Your power will not be used. I will not rely on it only to have you unable or unwilling to use it against those you formerly considered your equals, whom you now still clearly consider our betters. I do not trust you."

She jerked to her feet and reached for her pack, but he grabbed it first. Whatever possessed her to bring such a heavy burden on her flight from London? Whatever could be inside?

"I will carry it myself."

"You are weak. Until you have eaten and recovered, I consider it my duty to take your burden."

Her face shuttered against him, she stood stiffly, and finally, he started down the path, leaving her to follow him. He turned his thoughts back to Night and Grebe and to the rejection that awaited them upon their return.

He had given his people good reason to reject him. It was his own fault. Why did it sting so? Wasn't that the habit of his life?

His bitter laughter was so low, it barely sounded above the rustling of leaves as they broke through the thorny bracken and back up the path to the misty wards between the worlds.

❧ CHAPTER FORTY-SIX ❧

They had gone only a few steps into the open when harsh male voices carried through the night toward them. Persephone froze, but Vespasian drew her back up the path, with its tugging limbs and crackling leaves. Each step left her more breathless with panic. When they were in a dark crook in the path with only the dimmest spattering of moonlight, he pulled her into the bracken, leaving the path open. They were still visible, all too visible, and she had no idea what he planned. The voices grew louder.

One voice, harsher, more guttural than the others, spoke. She strained, attempting to understand what was very bad French. She could barely understand the words—"track her like a hare"— "this way"—and another voice, also French but with a different accent, laughing scornfully, saying, "Easy as tracking a lame doe."

Beside her, Vespasian started to move, but she silenced him with a sharp squeeze of his arm. Someone was following them, tracking them, tracking *her* so easily that they were following in her exact footsteps.

"I've found her again." This accent was… Spanish? One of them was German and one was a Spaniard, but they were speaking in a common language—French—and doing it badly.

These men were coming straight towards them, even with silence as the only guide.

Again, Vespasian moved beside her, but this time she caught a glimpse of pale moonlight on his hand and on what he held—two wands.

He pressed one into her palm. Hadn't he said he didn't trust her? Yet he was handing her this most deadly of weapons, and she didn't even know what to do with it. She tightened her grip on it, and as the sounds came closer, she thought of the wards she had brought down at the palace and that she had raised again.

Bardán Fury's wards.

With one last warning squeeze of Vespasian's arm, she raised her hand and felt for the memory of movement, of gestures. With nothing present to remind her, no echoes to follow, and unable to speak the words aloud, she simply reached... moved... felt a sharp pull within her... felt *something* happen.

Suddenly, the men were so close she could smell the smoke of a camp-fire on their clothes, the memory of spicy foods.

When Vespasian flexed his arm to attack—the two of them against three men who were without a doubt foreign soldiers of fortune sent by the duke to find her—she again squeezed his arm desperately, praying he would not move.

They stood in place as the men approached, close enough to touch—

The men kept going.

Vespasian turned to stare at her, but she merely shook her head.

The men's voices rose in confusion and frustration.

"Gone."

"Can't be! She was here!"

How had they managed to come so close that only the Fury wards had stopped them?

Her heart pounded like the hare they compared her to.

One of them, taller than the others, his hair fair in the darkness, peered closely into the bracken all around them. "She is here," he said, and she recognised his accent—the German.

The shortest of them spun in place. "She was here, and now she is not? Impossible."

"Which means," said the German, his French getting more heavily accented as his scrutiny grew more intense, "she is here, whether we can see her or not."

He whipped out his wand and spun—unluckily—straight towards her. His eyes were not focused, but his wand was dead on target. "We were told to bring her back alive, but not before I have my way with her. Not before I—"

She didn't know whether his attack could broach the boundary she'd erected, but taking no chance—

She dropped the wards.

Power streaked from the tip of her wand and hit the man in the middle of his forehead. It burst open and blood poured from it; his eyes widened, his mouth fell open, and he dropped to the ground.

Two more streaks, and the other men joined him.

And she could only stare, as the wand fell from her limp hand.

"Did I...?" She couldn't finish the thought.

"You killed him. I killed the others."

He snatched up her wand, then the wands of the other men, and then again yanked her forward, running this time, and she followed.

Would the wards have protected them? Could they have been safe without—without—

Again, she could not finish the thought.

She ran through the too-bright moonlight, praying that they would reach the sacred grove quickly.

Once there, when she was almost doubled over, gasping, Vespasian whirled on her, wild with rage. "What was that?" he gasped. "What were they saying?"

"They were... looking for me." She heaved in deep gulps of air, and fell back against a tree trunk. "They knew how to follow me—they knew I was there—right there—but they couldn't—my wards stopped them from knowing where, but—"

"Wards? Your father taught you wards, as well?"

"No, no—he didn't, but—"

"But *what?*"

"They were too close before I put up the wards. So they knew I—I disappeared—at that spot. But if I hadn't dropped them to—to—" She swallowed the lump in her throat. "The wards might have—might have protected us. We might not have had to—to—" She could not finish.

"*Might?* Perhaps you are willing to risk everything on a *'might'*, but I am not!"

He dragged his fingers through his coarse, dark, moonlight-streaked hair, and the magic seemed to ripple off him in angry waves. "How did they follow you? How did they know you were there? Not me, but you? Are you certain?"

"I don't know," she cried. "I don't know! They said they were tracking me, like—like an animal!"

She dropped to the ground, wrapped her arms around her knees, and shivered in the cold. It seemed she couldn't breathe for a very long time. So Dark, so cold... So alone.

He was rigid in the darkness, and she sensed his tension, but not impatience. For once, he was not prodding, pushing, pulling at her. If he did, she thought she might shatter.

"Are you able to continue?" His words were emotionless.

She reached into her gown, her hand going to her breast, and her pulse leapt and Shadows swelled within her, for she was pulling out the pouch containing the prophecy. She tugged it over her head, grunting when it caught in her hair. Finally she held it out to him, her eyes filling but her voice strong. "It was not mine to take."

The tension between them stretched to the breaking point. "Were you wearing this when we consummated the vows?"

"Yes." She avoided his eyes. "But it didn't call to us when we were... doing what we did. I don't understand."

It should have driven her wild. Both of them.

"Evidently, whatever power it uses to join us," he said, his voice even, "was not meant for copulation."

She looked up and felt the old shame anew. "It was meant for my brother."

Finally, he took it out of her hand and she wondered what kind of control he could have to not snatch it immediately, when she already wanted to snatch it back. "Why are you giving this to me now?"

"Obviously," she said with a sniff, "it doesn't work without us both. So it's not as if you won't be needing me still." She raised her eyes to his this time and repeated the important truth. "But it was not mine to take."

☙☙

The aroma of food reached her even before the flickering firelight of the encampment. Food, and how long had it been since she'd eaten anything substantial? How many long hours had passed since she'd eaten at all? Over a day.

They finally broke from the narrow path and into the grove. It felt strange at night, though the memory of one other night and the things she'd witnessed caused her skin to heat and the soreness between her thighs to acquire a new and different throb. She wanted to duck her face, to hide behind her hair again, but she thrust her chin forward instead. Staring straight ahead, she followed Vespasian towards the fire and the large kettle that clearly was the origin of the scents that made her stomach clench in an agony of hunger.

Vespasian raised a hand, and several men and women rose from their places around the encampment, coming forward with trenchers in one hand and mugs in the other. "We must prepare," he said harshly, and as he turned to the kettle, Persephone watched as a lithe figure sprang forward, an empty trencher in her hand, and pressed it into his. Golden hair shimmering, eyes wide and searching his face, Lark's pain was evident.

As was her ill will when she finally allowed herself to look past him and meet Persephone's gaze. Her eyes flickered down Persephone's body, took in her mussed hair.

Persephone realised in a startled moment what the other woman saw. What they all saw. She felt their stares like things crawling on her skin and stumbled, catching herself before she fell, but, they knew. They all knew. They knew where she had been and what had transpired.

Just as she had seen the tiger and his girl and still remembered every movement, sigh, and nuance of that, these people were seeing her, imagining her, imagining her humiliation at the hands of Vespasian Wyllt.

She wanted to turn and run, but such was not the act of a Fury.

She thought of the women of the *Beau Monde*, the women of Erinyes Manor, women who seemed to walk with a... a *knowing*. Women whose movements men watched with a hungry look in their eyes. She forced her body to slow, her movements to take on a more sinuous glide. They would not see her shame.

She reached the kettle, but Vespasian had already moved on, caught up in urgent plans.

She stood alone. No trencher was offered, nor was any evident. The steaming, simmering stew so redolent of leek and potato and the barest trace of chicken taunted her, bubbling before her, with no way to eat it. Their intent was clear.

She could ask.

But she'd seen those eyes staring at her, felt their sullen rage, and—oh gods, how she hungered—could not give them the opportunity to watch her further humiliation, to intensify it by their deliberate refusal to offer her the hollowed out bit of bread she needed before she could eat.

But she could not stop her hand from clutching her stomach as she turned away. Nor could she prevent the gurgle of hunger, and prayed none heard. Without food or drink, she turned and walked away, determined to find a place where she felt protected and safe.

When she finally found a boulder with a craggy notch in its side, she sank to the ground and pressed her back against it. Only then did she allow her body its release, and only then did the shaking take over, trembling that rocked through her. She closed her eyes, and even though the first sight that danced there was a faceless blond man with a jagged, bloody hole in his forehead, she still did not let herself cry.

"Miss…"

At first the voice seemed a part of her haunted memory, but when it repeated, "Miss!" she opened her eyes to see the boy, Bertrand, a crust of soggy bread in his hand and a mug half full of ale.

"I can't let them see me help you," he said, his voice gruff. "Take it quick."

She snatched it from him, too desperate to do else. But he couldn't let them see, couldn't stay? "Were you told not to feed me?"

"Nay, but if they think I am on your side—well, they seem grudging to accept me, already," he said. "They don't like you by half, and if they think—"

"I see," she said wearily. She tilted the mug to her lips and drained it, then handed it back to him. "Thank you. But—just go."

He needed no further encouragement.

If she thought she couldn't be any hungrier, she discovered that a few swallows of ale and bites of broth-soaked bread did nothing but ignite her hunger to a new pitch.

The fires burned low, and around her, people began settling for the night. She did not want her new husband by her side. If ever there was a reason to stay huddled up by a cold slab of rock, then that would be it. Yet she burned within to see the beautiful Lark watch his every movement. Seeing again how the other woman had waited with a trencher in her hand for him, looking at him with adoring eyes, Persephone wondered if he truly never responded in kind.

She wished with all her heart that the Ordinary woman had been the one to lie beneath him, and that she were somewhere else, somewhere warm, somewhere in a civilised bed with the warm-hearted Robin Fitzwilliam.

She felt a sharp stab of pain that such could indeed have been her joyous consummation, if Robin had only believed her. He above all others should have.

If he had believed her.

Pain was subsumed by anger. Robin Fitzwilliam had failed her. It made no difference that her tale had been so wild even she would not have believed it without the evidence of Bernard's terror and his stammering words. On this night, in this place, she found it easy to hate Robin for not being what he was supposed to be, what she knew deep in her soul he *should* be.

It had been her right and her calling to be at his side, but the life they were meant to have was lost because Robin Fitzwilliam was less than he should be.

She was alone.

Yet the task was still hers, even without him. Especially without him. She stared across the clearing at the man who now had claim to her loyalty.

He would never be deceived by the duke, nor would he underestimate him.

Which meant nothing. Vespasian Wyllt had a small group of poorly equipped commoners who had already demonstrated their inability to fight the king's men. The duke had riches, power, and the foreign soldiers who even now must be drawing closer to them.

Soft sighs broke the crisp night air. She looked for its source. With a start of embarrassment, she recognised the curve of a back, the slow thrust, even cloaked by a blanket.

Had they no shame, these Earthborn? Rutting like animals where anyone could see?

A quick frightened scan revealed family groups sleeping together, sometimes with children cradled between them, but here and there, others who coupled quietly in the night. New sounds were suddenly evident, a soft moan, a quiet gasp. She covered her ears and squeezed her eyes shut. With hunger gnawing, memory haunting, and now this—would she never find refuge? How would she ever sleep?

What if he came for her? What if he thought this his right, to mate again? She tested the old wards and felt the shimmer that told her they were there. She remembered the old Queen and the silence spell. Moments later the cocoon of emptiness was complete, and with it the knowledge that none could see her, and she couldn't hear them, and Vespasian Wyllt would not come to her this night.

She sank back against the sharp, chilled surface stone, knowing that none could sneak up from behind her, pulled her cloak more tightly around herself, and slept.

❦❦

The hell-cursed, gods-be-damned girl was gone?

He flung the remains of his morning meal into the fire, while a twisting, burning thing coiled in his gut. As if there weren't already enough coming down upon his head, she'd run? Was she mad?

If ever he'd suspected her capable of more betrayal, he couldn't imagine such a thing after—

He clenched his jaw and shoved that memory away, but it would not remain gone. He couldn't think the words "bound" or "wife" without choking. The image of what they had done—what he had done—brought him even more rage. The girl taunting with her acid mouth, and then grimly accepting as if—as if—

As if it had been forced upon her, which it bloody well had been—on them both—and now she dared disappear when he did not have time for such distraction.

The search had been diligent, with expressions and mutterings of satisfaction all around him—"knew no good would come of it"—and suspicion—"probably leading them to us even as we slept, the little bitch"—and all he could do was fume and continue to draw the battle plan in the dirt and pretend he wasn't a mass of gnawed flesh inside, leaving it to others to deal with.

Had the spoiled chit vanished because no one was catering to her whims?

"The dog is acting strange," Tern said.

"Why the rutting hell should I care?"

"Like it's guardin' somethin'."

His mind raced. Guarding? There was no reason for the cursed beast to guard anything, and certainly not *her*. He dropped his stick into the dirt. "Where?"

He followed Tern to the pile of boulders that marked the western edge of the grove, a single large oak with roots that tangled amidst them in search of earth.

The dog crouched low before them, its dirty grey ruff bristled, its lip exposing fangs in a snarl.

"What is it, you mangy cur?" Vespasian snapped, as if the dog would answer.

It raised up into a half-crouch, gave two low snarls and then edged sideways.

Vespasian smelled the tang of expensive perfume that had clung to her skin. She was near. He spun around and found nothing of her, nothing but scent. "Bloody hell."

He slid his wand free from his sleeve and held it thoughtfully. If she had warded herself away from them, just as she'd done the night before, he would never find her. She said she didn't know if the ward would protect her from attack. Perhaps it was time to find out.

He scanned the area, waving everyone back. He closed his eyes, inhaled deeply.

He hurled a small stone at the dog, striking its flanks. The dog yelped, then snarled again, but edged further away. "Someone feed the damned beast."

He paced closer. The scent was easy to discern, now that he was attuned to it. He circled the boulders until he came to a notch, deep in shadows, and knew—from every sense in his body—that she had to be there.

He raised his wand and stopped. "Go on with you," he said, waving them all back, sending them off with a glare. When even the dog had crept away, following the new boy who had pulled a crust of bread from his pocket and dangled it cautiously, Vespasian turned back to the rock and studied it.

She was here. Watching the uproar she caused. Revelling in it.

With a snap of his wrist, he sent a stinging hex straight at the darkest of the shadows.

One moment… two moments… three moments passed. He raised his wand again.

The shimmer of magic was tangible in the air, even if he couldn't actually see it, and suddenly she was in front of him, her hair wild and face swollen with sleep, one slender arm swinging toward him—

The stinging spell caught him in his gut and sent him flying. He landed in the dirt a few yards away, gasping.

Her hand was raised to strike again.

He barely dodged the next stinger, rolling sideways, sending a blast of force that swept her feet from under her. "How long," he gasped, pinning her arms to the ground and flattening her legs with his weight, "were you going to watch us search before you had enough of your game? This, from the bluestocking Fury who prides herself on her great intellect—to distract me at the moment we must be ready for an attack?"

She stilled herself beneath him, and he saw how shadowed her eyes were, how drawn her face, and saw a form of recognition cross her features. "I was asleep."

"You slept through half the encampment searching for you? Through that miserable cur of a dog barking?"

"I used a silencing charm so I wouldn't hear—" She turned her face away from him, avoided his eyes. The pallor of her face stained pink. "So I could sleep."

"And you learned such a charm where?"

"From the queen's lady." She shifted her arms, strained. "Release me, for Circe's sake! Or are you that afraid I will attack you and get the best of you in front of your people?"

He rose to his knees, rubbing his stomach where he still stung from her attack and knew he would be bruised, and saw her rub her thigh in similar manner. *Rutting hell.*

"I'll have—" not Night, certainly not Rue… "—Clary tend your bruise."

"No! I can take care of myself."

"Don't be absurd. I did not note any knowledge of healing magics when you were here before."

"I can learn."

Now she was rubbing her shoulder, too. The shoulder he had blown open. He curled his lip. If she thought to inspire guilt in him, or pity, she had much to learn. "Whatever you wish." He rose to his feet and did not offer her his hand, leaving her to clamber up on her own. But when he saw her clutch her stomach, he had had quite enough. "If you think to make me feel pity for you, or guilt, you will be disappointed. I was merely testing your warding to discern whether it would block a hex, and as you see, it would not. If you refuse healing—"

She dropped her hands from her stomach. "You've quite made your point." She began walking away from him, away from the encampment.

"Where in bloody Hades do you think you are going?"

"To relieve myself," she said crisply. "If I might have privacy!"

He waved her on, disgusted at not discerning the nature of her discomfort without being told. He leaned against the boulder, waiting. He would not leave until she was back and with him. He would not return without her obediently at his side.

When she finally returned, she seemed even paler than before, strung tightly as if held together by fine wire, one snap away from collapse. "Are you ill?"

She gave her head a shake and walked ahead of him, not waiting for his demand or an invitation.

When they reached the heart of the grove, he found himself watching her, even as he hurled orders right and left for the placement of various bins of arrows, the final assigning of position for their defence. Thus, when he saw the boy she'd brought with her steal to her side, careful of being seen, the hair on his arms and neck rose. What secrets were whispered?

Rage stirred, rage that she had tricked him, carrying out what kind of plot?

Then he saw the scrap of meat, the tiny chunk of cheese the boy pressed into her hand and saw the gratitude on her face, the tremble of her fingers, the relief with which she turned away, and the speed with which those scraps of food found their way into her mouth.

He left the small huddle of people around him gaping as he spun away and made his way to Night seated in the oak, surrounded by her women.

"What were the arrangements for supper last night?"

"The cauldron was for all, but each woman prepared bread for her own family."

He glanced at Lark. She smiled softly. "I knew you had no one so made extra for you."

"What of those who had no women to prepare for them?"

"Our people were all fed."

"I understand." And he did. He whirled away, the burning in this gut growing hotter, like acid bubbling away.

He found the boy and curtly demanded his assistance. He led the way to their stores, the baskets of apples and the round cheeses, the nuts, and the casks of ale.

He detected a certain secrecy in the boy's manner. "What is it you hide from me this time?" Vespasian gripped the boy's chin, lifted it, and the boy blinked rapidly. Vespasian dipped into his mind with a rapier's sharp delicacy. Images flashed by of the boy currying a horse, sleeping in straw, fast images, desperate images and then—

Persephone Fury in the arms of a man, like a lowly housemaid playing slap-and-tickle in the stables.

"Who is he?" he asked, releasing the boy to the pain the intrusion most likely left behind.

The boy's cheeks were ruddy with shame. "Sir Robin."

"Who is he?"

"The duke's cousin. He wanted to marry her."

And clearly, he thought, examining the way she had moulded herself against the man's body like a sinuous mink, she had similar feelings for him.

He snatched up an apple for himself and tossed it thoughtfully. So she'd left a lover behind. *Such a shame, truly,* he thought, languidly taking a bite and pondering the advantages this brought him and that it wasn't truly a shame at all.

He resolutely placed the haunted expression of her eyes out of his mind. There would be no room for sympathy in the days ahead.

❧ CHAPTER FORTY-SEVEN ❧

She sat in her niche of rock, using shadows rather than wards to hide her. They weren't as effective, but they did the job well enough. Of course, other than to send suspicious glances in her direction, no one approached her anyway.

Thus, when the sound of scuffling rocks grew louder, she was surprised. Bertrand eased closer, his cap in his hands. Without speaking, he thrust it at her. Two apples, a wedge of cheese, and a few nuts were piled in precariously. "For you."

She seized them and dumped them into her skirts. "Thank you," she said fervently, biting into the apple and relishing its sharp juices, even as her empty stomach cramped in response. "But you mustn't do this again. If you get caught taking so much—"

"*He* told me to."

She didn't need to ask who *he* was. "Thank you," was all she could manage, so desperate was her hunger.

Bertrand doffed his cap and dug awkwardly in the dirt with his toe. "He knows about Sir Robin," he finally said, his tone miserable.

"Knows what?"

"About you and him in the stable."

She stopped chewing and wasn't sure she'd be able to swallow.

"Ye ain't really married, are you? I mean, if you wanted, you could still—"

"I'm married."

"But there were no priest, and their gods aren't real," he protested, clearly disturbed. "That man, he's a bad'n, ain't he?"

Everything she'd endured, each sacrifice she'd made, washed over her. She rose to her feet and placed the food—oh gods, the food—on the rock and gave a sharp gesture with her chin for him to follow her.

She cut through the midst of the activity, ignoring those who slid sinister looks in her direction, and shoved Bertrand towards the path. They had gone half a furlong before he asked, "Where are we going?"

485

"I'm taking you to the standing stones," she said, her voice as brittle as her mood. "And when we get there, I will point you to the mists, and will help you through them."

"What?" he asked, alarmed. "What mists?"

"The mists that ward out the Ordinaries, and if we are very lucky, the duke's men. If the fact that *that bad'n* is saving your life isn't enough to win your loyalty, go find the duke's men and see how well you fare."

"No!" He stopped, frozen on the path. "I didn't mean—that's not what I meant!"

"Then watch your tongue and show some gratitude to those who have taken you in, to *that man*, or you will have far more to fear than your connection with me!"

He clutched his cap in his hands convulsively. "Beggin' yer pardon, miss. I didn't mean—"

"I am not a miss. Now go on, leave me be. Find some way to make yourself useful, or I'll toss you to the mercy of the duke's men anyway!"

She left him behind, her need to put distance between them stronger than any desire to make sure he followed the narrow path successfully. How dare he question her choices?

How dare he ask the very questions she was trying so desperately to suppress? Once opened, that box of doubts refused to be stifled again. Her words to him had rung with truth. She had made her choice, and she would not regret it, no matter what. The queen's portentous remarks be damned.

But such a decision made left her to worry about how much Vespasian knew about Robin and what it all meant to her.

The memory of strong cheese set her mouth to watering, and she thought of nothing but food.

Only to arrive at the rock outcropping and find it bare.

A squirrel chattered at her from a low-hanging branch, and she thought of all the various creatures that might have made off with her food and stifled a sob.

The long-fingered hand holding out a rustic earthenware mug of ale should have surprised her. She should be alarmed that he had caught her unaware. She remembered not trusting anything he might offer her.

Now, she took it as politely—not desperately, no, she refused to let desperation show—as if it were tea and he the queen. "My most gracious thanks," she murmured before drinking deeply and gratefully.

"Did you have enough food?" he asked, his voice sharp. "Did the boy bring you enough?"

She swallowed thickly. "He brought me enough," she finally said, carefully averting her face from his intense scrutiny.

He finally let out a snort of derision.

She glanced back in time to see him toss the wedge of cheese at her, time enough to snatch it from the air and—damn his scrutiny—pop even the crumbs into her mouth and close her eyes in ecstasy at its salty flavour.

"If you don't want me to consider you a stupid girl, perhaps you should cease doing stupid things." His hand appeared, holding two apples.

She dropped to the ground and then took all the food he offered and immediately thought better of it, since instead of leaving, he towered over her.

When he eased to the ground some distance away, tension climbed her neck. She bit into the apple and chewed methodically, determined not to let it show.

"Hold up your hand," he ordered.

She stared suspiciously and finally raised her hand, fingers outstretched.

With a quick twist of his fingers, he sent something small twirling in a high arc, something delicate and silver—

It landed perfectly on the tip of her ring finger and slid into place.

She dropped the apple into her lap, snatched the ring and pulled it off. It slid easily. She examined it carefully—thin and worn—and slid it slowly back onto her finger, her mind racing. She met his gaze. "Thank you."

"To do otherwise would be foolhardy, as your young Fireborn servant has already proven."

"You—you heard him? You spied on us?"

"With the welfare of my tribe at stake, how could I not?"

She took another bite of cheese, resentment bubbling, remembering how arbitrarily he had commanded that someone present her with a cloak. Of a sudden, the ring was more an irritant than a protection. "And who had to give up their ring so that I might wear it?" she snapped. "How many more resentments are you acquiring on my behalf, amongst these people who have already welcomed me so warmly?"

He leaned back against a log and stared at her, his eyes hooded and dark, his lips tight. "It was my mother's."

"Oh!" She couldn't stifle the gasp, for it was the last thing she'd expected to hear. "Thank you, again," she said softly.

"It's a fitting emblem between us," he said, his hair falling forward across his face, a long sheet of dark-shaded silver catching sunlight, obscuring his expression. "It was a sham."

It had hit her like a blow. A sham. "Of course."

"She bought it to pretend to be a widow and wore it until the day she died."

"But..." She stared at her finger, thought of everything that thin band of silver had represented. "What we did was not a sham." She raised her eyes to him and dared him to dispute her words.

"Surely you don't expect—"

Before she could lose her will and her nerve, she drew herself up and faced him with the question that had burned within her for hours. "How does this—" She motioned between the two of them then stared into his eyes, willing him to understand, desperate that she not have to go into embarrassing detail.

Unfortunately, it was clear from his arrogant cocked head and arched eyebrow that more detail was indeed necessary.

"I mean..." She felt her cheeks burning but refused to look away. "I know I have... have duties. And that you have... needs. But I don't quite understand how I'm to know, or if—" She broke off, but he was staring at her so silently it was clear she would have to come right out and ask him. "I don't know how this works. I don't know—well, I know you—I mean, a man—surely doesn't walk around all the time, stiff and... *alert*. And I know that when you are in that condition, you have certain needs and that this is what a wife is for." The words tumbled out faster than she could control. "But I don't understand how it all happens. Do you decide when you want to be—in that condition—and then inform me? Or does it catch you by surprise? Do we plan it ahead—or do we—"

"*Miss Fury!*" he exploded, his cheeks as red with flame as her own must be.

"I'm not Miss Fury," she corrected, "as you well know."

He opened his mouth to speak, then snapped it shut. Opened it again. Closed it again.

She was quite astonished. She'd never seen him without words. In fact, he strangely reminded her of Robin at that moment, a thought that alarmed her and made her feel almost smug. She regularly left Robin speechless. She'd never dreamed she'd be able to do so to this odious man.

"Perhaps you find it too delicate to discuss," she said, her tone purposely prim. "My mother said it was best to be clear about such things, but if you'd rather not—"

"*Perhaps,*" he snarled, "among those of your station you are allowed leisure time to do as you please, but that is not the case here. If you are quite refreshed, there are duties you can assist."

"Duties?" she asked, appalled. "Here? *Now?*"

"Not—not those—" Now he was gnashing his teeth. "There will be none of those kinds of duties. You may count yourself lucky on that behalf."

She tried not to show how relieved she was and bit into the apple again to hide her flaming cheeks. When she had recovered control, she swallowed and, examining the apple for fresh flesh, she asked, "The—the True Marriage you intend does not require physical intimacy?"

"I never intended—"

"But you said it, and that man was so angry."

"It was an insult to him and to any that have ever had a True Marriage. But by voicing the intent and by bonding in a place and way that would allow it, my point was made."

"Which is?"

"You are under my protection. As a True Wife, any who dared touch you would know to expect death. They understand. You should be safe."

"What is a True Wife?" she asked, exasperated. "He said I didn't even know what it is, and he's quite correct. I don't!"

"You saw the plaits at his temples?"

She nodded, starting the second apple.

"When he took his wife to bride, they exchanged locks. Each of them wore such plaits crafted from their blended hair with a magical blessing. It is a…" He scowled at the ground. "A rare ability to form such a marriage. A rare marriage."

"The flash of light when we touched?"

He nodded.

"How could that be? I harbour no romantic yearnings for you!" she exclaimed.

"At that moment, you seemed to make a pure commitment to it."

"Of course I did." She scowled back at him. "Did you think I would do it any other way? Perhaps some people enter into such relationships with false intentions, but I can assure you that a Fury—"

"Spare me your self-indulgent lectures on what it means to be a Fury. I can assure you I know more about that subject than you do."

She stiffened in outrage. "Do you imply that we—"

He shoved to his feet. "I do not imply. I know. But it has nothing to do with you, so we will end it there to spare your illusions. Now, if you don't mind, your duties."

"Duties," she repeated bitterly.

"The only duties you have are those owed to the community for taking you in, and as soon as you are fed, they will begin."

"I didn't think you wanted my help. I thought I was not to know of your preparations."

"You can help care for the children."

Children? She knew nothing of children, and the thought of being amongst them opened the wound of Otter's loss even more. "I really—I don't think I would be good with children. You must have other things—"

"There are few enough hands, with most of their mothers preparing for battle."

"Their mothers!"

He didn't repeat himself but gestured impatiently for her to stand.

When she did, holding the two apple cores in the palm of her hand, he curled his lip in a sneer. He took a core and flung it into the woods.

Of course. She felt foolish for not having done such already. She gritted her teeth, cocked her wrist and flung the other. It sailed half again as far as his. Without sparing him another glance, she savoured her warm, smug glow, tilted her nose into the air, and preceded him back into the heart of the grove.

"Miss—" He broke off, then corrected himself. "Persephone."

She turned one more time, bracing herself for whatever new attack he had prepared for her.

Instead, his glare was resentful but not hostile. "When the goddess told you not to do it… why didn't you listen to her?"

"I do not think the Earthborn gods could be so different from Fireborn," she said wearily. "And if there is one thing any bard can tell you, it is that where the gods are concerned, we are mere playthings. I do not put myself in the hands of those who would toy with me for their own idle pleasure."

She expected a flash of anger but was startled to see nothing but surprise on his harsh features, as if she'd voiced an idea he'd never pondered.

She was too weary to cherish the momentary pride at having done so.

❦❦

"What did you do with your virgin's blood?" The Crone watched her, squint-eyed and malevolent.

Persephone stared into the old woman's face, her mind racing. She had managed to stay out of the Crone's sight for most of the day. Why, now, did the old woman seek her out? Why did she want to know? Was she checking to see if she had really turned her back on Fireborn practices?

A chill rippled through her, one that left her feeling odd and vulnerable and aching.

Had Vespasian lied to her when he mocked her for attempting to save it?

If so, she would never admit it. She refused to give them reason to snicker that he had refused her bride's honour.

But if he was wrong, and if the Crone did think it useful, she didn't want his weakness exposed. If they didn't believe him to be making the right judgements and began to lose faith in him, if she couldn't trust these people to follow him, all her sacrifices were for naught.

The old woman still awaited her response.

"I believe," Persephone said with such deep respect, it would be difficult to discern the emotion beneath it, "that is an intimate matter between a husband and a wife." She lowered her gaze as if embarrassed for maidenly reasons.

"I'll ask him."

Persephone's chin raised a notch, and she met the Crone's inspection head on. "He will tell you the same thing." Even though she knew he wouldn't. Persephone asked, words that came from nowhere, but sprang to her lips to change the course of the subject, "His burdens are heavy and I am new to the roles I play. Please, if you would tell me, what might I do to ease his way? What might I do to see that he sleeps, or eats, or—" She ran out of words and felt her cheeks warm. She forced her voice to its usual crisp tones. "He is clearly strung tight and ready to snap, and I did not join myself with this band of rebels to see him fall short."

The old Crone snorted. "You've answered your own questions, then. See that he sleeps and eats. Not that you can do these things where he is sending you."

"But the children are here."

"Not for long. You'll be taking them to the crofter's hut."

With the adders.

Persephone fell to the log beside her. Her backside jarred with pain.

He was sending her to the place where the adders had almost killed her?

All thoughts of supporting him flew straight out of her mind, chased by a deep and urgent desire to put a dagger through his heart.

☙☙

He saw her coming before she saw him, saw her eyes blazing.

What in all the buggering caves of Hades did she dare find to enrage her now?

Pain pulsed at his temples, at his jaw, all the way down his spine. He pasted on the sneer that would be most likely to anger her and folded his arms and waited.

He noted the minute widening of her eyes, the moment of discomfort when she realised he was watching her approach, and then the visible effort as she straightened and crossed through battle preparations as if they were an annoyance put in her way solely to inconvenience her.

He deliberately dropped into an easy crouch, resting his elbows and body on the log behind him. If the men of her world would spring to their feet at her entrance, he would do nothing less than the opposite. He continued to sneer as he watched her approach. If she thought standing over him gave her any advantage, he quickly disabused her of that notion. "What offends your sensibilities this time?" He turned his voice to lazy boredom.

"You plan to send—" She broke off and swallowed. "Send the children to a place riddled with adders?"

"Ah." His sneer turned to a malevolent smile. "You are concerned for the children. The children you don't want to care for."

The tinge of pink in her cheeks confirmed what he already knew. It was her own terror that brought her raging to him.

"I have no experience with children. I can't think of any person less fit for such a job, and now you tell me I'm to keep them safe in the midst of an adder nest?"

"Not fit?" He sprang to his feet, despite his pain. "There is no one better fit to protect them. No one with your power! No one else who—if nightmares come true—can sway the Fireborn devils and their hired soldiers from doing to those children what they did to our Otter, and yet you complain of the responsibility—complain because the safest place for them might have snakes? Complain that it is more difficult to protect them from snakes than from a magical battle raging around them?" He almost—almost—restrained himself, but gave in to temptation and hurled a pulse of energy at the log beside her and watched it explode into smoke and dust as she leapt aside with a shriek.

"You aren't stupid. You know these things. And still you complain."

She grew rigid and pale. "You—you have made your point quite clearly."

To his astonishment, she walked away from him, her spine stiff and hands at her sides, trembling. His little show of pique and power had struck her so deeply? What new weakness was this? If he couldn't depend on her strength, what next?

Of course he'd had the adders cleared. How could she imagine otherwise?

He stormed away in the opposite direction, needing to put distance between himself and the fear and panic that they weren't ready.

When Night stepped into his path, he stopped short and dipped his head in the slightest of honours. "What is it?" he snapped, his voice showing no honour at all.

"Did you complete the marriage vows? Did you make the girl your wife?"

"Which do you doubt, my word or my ability to act as a man?"

"What did she do with her virgin's blood?"

"Don't tell me you have decided to dabble in Fireborn superstition."

"I want to know how seriously she takes her vow to leave it behind herself, you fool."

"That is not your business."

This time his nod was even less a nod, the respect so minimal he might rightly be accused of showing none at all. A sudden headache hit him, pain shot into his eyes, and he plunged deeper into the grove for respite.

☙☞

She still saw his black eyes, narrowed and glittering.

You aren't stupid.

His lip curled in disgust.

You know these things.

But she hadn't thought beyond her own terror.

You aren't stupid.

His voice hissed in her mind, curling down her spine.

Despite everything, despite what the others believed of her, he respected her ability to keep the children safe, whether through magic or through her ability to influence the duke's men, should the worst happen.

She should feel a sense of pride, but he robbed her of even that. Why couldn't he tell her what he needed of her? Why must everything he said to her be hurled as insult, leaving her too stung to see the underlying meaning?

Her fingernails bit into the tender palms of her hands, and she forced them to soften, forced her fists to open so that her fingers were rigid and splayed in the night air.

Stop acting like a child, she told herself fiercely. She was not a child, not a girl. She was a woman by the calendar and by her choice to wed.

The campfires flared high again, though no music broke the night. Great cauldrons of stew filled the air with the scent of herbs and meat, and again, families gathered with trenchers of bread, and again, Persephone watched Lark push food into Vespasian's hands and him begin to eat while barking orders.

Well that was one concern she need not have. He had those who were willing and able to fulfil his need for sustenance.

Her own stomach growled so that if she'd been in London, she would have had to excuse herself in humiliation and retreat from the room. Here there was no need. Here there was no one to notice or care, much less be offended. She reached deep into her pocket and found the last crumbles of cheese and wound her way back to the notched boulder that had become her place to sleep, to retreat from preparations that did not include her.

With her back against the cold rock, she put bits of cheese in her mouth and allowed the flavour to flood her mouth with moisture, a promise of food that would not be fulfilled until Bertrand found his way to her again.

She felt her lips twist in a bitter smile, that she was reduced to this. But better this than to show any how successful their shunning was at bringing her to her knees with hunger.

The savoury aroma followed her. She squeezed her eyes shut until the slight crunch of boot on ground brought them wide open again.

Again, the long-fingered hand offered her food.

A half loaf filled with stew. "Take it," he said. "You're little enough help strong. If you don't eat, you'll be none at all."

It was a fresh trencher, untouched. "Where did it come from?"

"You find it suspect?"

Belatedly, and yet blessedly before she'd reached to take it, she realised perhaps she should. "Why should I trust it?" She curled a strand of hair around her finger and watched the fires behind him, as if the need to snatch the food wasn't more than she could bear.

She felt his glare but did not meet it.

He shoved the bread at her. "They do not dare offend me in such a way." His voice was oddly strained.

She took it, tore a piece of bread and soaked it with broth until it dripped, and then plunged it into her mouth. The rich flavours of salt and wild thyme and chicken and onion exploded in her mouth, and she fought tears of relief.

"You will be fed as you should be fed."

Her mouth was too full to probe for answers to the questions this remark raised.

His other hand presented a cup of ale, and it took every ounce of her being not to burst into tears, but she did not. She accepted it carefully, with a gracious nod, and sipped when she longed to gulp, sipped daintily, relishing the moisture and the yeasty flavour upon her tongue. Only when it was swallowed, the last drop savoured, did she force herself to ask politely, "Have you supped already?"

He gave a curt nod.

"Enough?"

"What?"

"You don't eat enough or sleep enough. This isn't good for battle."

"And what do you know of battle?" he snapped.

"Enough to know that warriors should be nourished and rested."

"Pffth."

She drew back in offence. "Forgive me for enquiring." She turned herself back to her food and wished he'd leave her so that she could assault it more directly and desperately, without forcing herself to go slowly, to hide the extremity of her need.

"You will assist Grebe, who will take the children to the crofter's hut in the morn."

She examined his face and found nothing, no emotion, no more tension than usual.

"You expect the attack to come so soon?" She let out a gust of air. "I forgot. I am not to know."

"We will leave the grove and return to the village."

She nodded, remembering her first afternoon in the sacred grove and Tern's words. "You will not fight on sacred ground."

"We will defend it from without. We fled here for safety because they could not follow, but next time, there will be no fleeing. There will be a victory or a defeat, but no fleeing."

She felt the coil of tension in her own stomach.

"You do not bake bread."

Startled at his change of subject, she gave a half-shrug and finally swallowed. "I was never expected to know such skills."

"That has changed," he said, his lip curling in disdain. "You will have to learn, but not now. We will be fed."

"I am not accustomed to feeling so inadequate," she blurted, then immediately regretted it.

This time it was he who half-shrugged. "I'm sure you will experience it many more times."

He left her to devour the food without witness to her lack of manners and propriety.

⤖ CHAPTER FORTY-EIGHT ⥸

He paced restlessly through the encampment, the throbbing at his temples increasing with every step. They had to be drawing near, this hired army of hardened soldiers sent against them. None of his scouts had seen any sign of them, beyond the small party who had tracked the girl.

The quiet was deceptive. He saw family groups nestled together in desperate comfort, their last night with their children amongst them. Tension that rose, even from their sleep.

He saw Rue, alone, her grief shutting out everyone, even Lysander, who would bleed his last drop of blood for her.

Lysander, who kept watch over the rolling valley on this night, waiting for approaching troops.

It was too soon by at least a day, and yet…

Vespasian felt the danger like an unseen shimmer down the back of his neck. He'd done everything he could to prepare them, to instil in them a belief in their ability to defend and defeat, because to do anything other was to condemn them all. He kept his doubts and demons to himself.

He didn't realise where his restless wandering had taken him until he arrived at the pile of boulders, at the niche that sheltered the girl pressed tightly, almost desperately, against it.

How could she crackle with such energy when awake, so stiff and tall and reeking of arrogance, demanding attention with every movement, and then be so small and fragile in the night hours, wrapped tightly in the folds of the crimson cloak.

Well, then. She was safe. She could certainly take care of herself. At least she would be rested in the morn, even if few others were.

But the cloak trembled. He drew back, determined to leave her to her silent distress and found himself leaning over instead, reaching for the cloak.

A low growl sounded, a gust of hot air hit his knuckles, and he jerked them back.

The cursed dog growled at him as if he threatened her—he who was keeping her alive. The urge to blast the beast rose in him, and as always, he shoved it down. It had saved his miserable life by leading his men to him when he was adder-struck and then had made his life further misery. He waved it away impatiently. If he hadn't a right to raise the cloak that covered his own—

He could not form the word, even in his mind, the word that made her his.

He raised the edge. She shivered in her sleep. Pressing herself against a mass of cold rock, what could she expect? The beast that dared growl at him didn't bother to keep her warm. He dropped the cloak, determined to leave her to her sleep and instead, cast a warming spell with a wave of his hand and sank to the ground, his back pressed against the same cold boulder to rest but not to sleep.

There would be no sleep for him in these hours leading up to battle.

But a few moments' rest, yes, a few moments with the boulder supporting his head, the cold seeping into him to—please the gods—chill away the throbbing pain…

A few moments.

❦

A snarl awakened her.

Two snarls.

Every hair crackling with tension, she lay beneath the cloak, its unexpected warmth a comfort, and listened to the snarl, her fingertips tensing with magic, preparing for defence.

The soft, low growl.

Followed by the snarl near her head that she—after a moment of terror—recognised as the dog that hounded Vespasian's steps.

Silence.

Again, the soft, strange growl followed by the snarl.

She inched the cloak down until the cold hit the top of her head, her forehead, and finally her eyes.

The dog crouched beside her, its attention fixed on something beyond her line of sight.

Again, the growl.

And the dog's low snarling response.

Flinging the cloak aside, she rose, her arm cocked back to hurl magic—and she saw the silent figure, sitting an arm's length away, braced against the outcropping of rock.

The profile distinctive and unmistakable, right down to the hawk-like nose.

That emitted a soft growl of a snore.

The dog snarled again.

Vespasian was—he was here? With her?

Sleeping.

He, who did not sleep.

And snoring.

Of course with that nose he would snore.

And the stupid dog snarling as if preparing for attack.

And—and—laughter bubbled up within her, hysterical and wild, but she couldn't laugh—couldn't wake him, when he needed that sleep so urgently.

She slapped the beast's muzzle, and it lowered itself to the ground, though she could feel its baleful glare. She sat up, newly alert, and scanned the area for movement. If he was sleeping, she could not.

She braced herself against the cold stone and kept watch.

❧❦

He woke at dawn with a start and found himself the target of the girl's disdainful glare.

"You snore," she announced.

"I do not, and did not, for I was not asleep," he snapped.

"Of course you weren't," she said with a smirk.

Insolent brat.

She rose stiffly and headed into the wood to relieve herself.

He'd slept? Of all nights, to sleep when there was so much remaining to be done. Unsettled, he determined to be gone before she returned.

The encampment was already stirring, and his appearance drew a thousand questions, decisions, as if he hadn't made them all before. It was a reassuring repetition on this day of all days.

Bram stopped speaking in mid-word as Lark joined them, her lips soft and tender as she smiled up at Vespasian and offered him bread, heavily slathered with butter, folded over a thick slice of cheese. He reached to take it, and then stopped.

"You must be hungry," she said.

"Take it to Persephone," he said. "She is in need of sustenance."

Tern asked, astounded, "You would send Lark to feed that treacherous bitch?"

The pounding in his head that had been almost dormant exploded with a surge of cold rage. "You are speaking of my bonded mate."

Lark lowered her head as if slapped. "I'll find food for her, of course, but you must—"

He snatched the food from her hand. "I must make sure that she who literally holds our future in her undeserving hands has the strength to do so."

"Our future?" Bram demanded.

"Gather the children," he told Lark. "Take them out of earshot." He pretended not to see the tears in her eyes as she nodded and hastened away. He turned his attention to Bram. "Gather everyone under the goddess oak."

"Does the enemy approach?" he asked, tense.

"Do as I say!"

🕊🕊

Vespasian stood under the goddess oak at Night's left side, while Grebe stood at her right. The people restlessly awaited the words that would change all their lives and—gods help them all—end some. Yet they stood, proud and fierce. Vespasian felt a swelling of frustration and rage that it was happening too soon and too fast. He also felt the closest thing to belonging he'd ever known, and all for these people who had believed in him in his madness and thrown their lot in with him despite it.

They believed him as he believed the prophecy. He had convinced them that if they acted in faith, the True King would come. They had acted—would act—and the True King was still absent.

They stood there, proud and fierce, still.

She stood amongst the trees, hiding from their anger and resentment, just when he needed from her the arrogance that made his stomach churn in such familiar ways, it was almost a comfort. Of course she would not be what he needed her to be. Arrogance when he needed submission. Submission when he needed resistance. And now, meekness when he—when *they* needed her fire.

Yes, his stomach churned, and his anger found a very comfortable place to rest.

She met his eyes and flinched.

The old woman's hands rose, and she was old woman no more. "We stand before you, spirit and law and magic." Her voice rang with authority, and he was reminded that without her belief, none would have followed him. "In this moment as we are approached by those who would destroy us, let there be no doubt that we are united in one quest, our voices joined in one destiny."

What respect shone on those faces as they gazed upon her in all her magnificence.

"What is the law?" she asked, in ritual.

Grebe's voice was quiet when compared to hers, the voice of the law rather than the spirit, and yet it was no less powerful. "First, always, are the children, for they are the future, and they are life."

Nods met his gentle pronouncement, and if some eyes shone with moisture, none betrayed such by any move to wipe them. All remained fixed on their Wise Man of the law, whose life had been an example of all that was True of heart and mind and spirit.

Only one choked, angry sob broke the silence. Rue stood off to herself, her arms wrapped tightly around her body, swaying, alone in her grief, alone in her agony.

"In time of battle there can be but one leader, and that is the wielder of power," the old man continued.

Vespasian stared straight ahead, not meeting any of the gazes that he felt flickering towards him, seething at the thin figure huddled at the edge of the wood, huddled as if she could hide in her glowing red cloak.

"That is the voice of cunning thunder, of spirit lightning, of war. This is the moment for that voice."

Night spoke her final words. "It is the time for that voice."

She sank onto the gnarled roots that formed a throne with Grebe beside her, and Vespasian was the only one standing.

🌾🌾

It had come to this.

The man she loved stood for the wrong.

The man she loathed stood for the right.

She stood apart from love and joined with loathing.

This was her choice and her destiny.

Seeing him standing there, his ill-suppressed anger radiating from him in waves, she knew with a pang of grief in her heart that she had chosen well, had made the only choice she could. His was the absolute will and desire to defeat evil. He was her only hope. His eyes burned black with power, and she clung to that hope, that belief that in that tall, whip-thin body and harsh, forbidding visage was carried the weight of history and prophecy.

Oh, how she loathed him.

Oh, how she believed in him.

For not to believe was to surrender to the evil of children killed for power, of young girls' bodies strewn across a floor like so much offal, of the illusion of good stretched tight over the duke's core of wickedness.

In this man, this man of Dark character and quick, vile temper—

Lived their hope.

Her destiny was woven with his.

And she was sore afraid.

"Our plans have been made and rehearsed, and we know them as we know our own names." His voice was steel, without the weight and beauty of ancient tradition. No webs spun of gossamer as would have been in the Basilica. No dignity and grace as had come from Night and Grebe.

Only the heavy burden of reality. "First, we protect the children. When we part here, there will be time for goodbyes but not for tears. Do not frighten them with weakness, but empower them with strength."

How easily those orders sprang from his tongue, ordering mothers and fathers to bid adieu to their children, perhaps their last sight of them—without the emotion that was due them?

"The crofter's hut awaits them, and it has been made sound and safe by means both physical and magical. They will be protected by wisdom and power and cunning, and they will be kept safe."

The total lack of rage told her what she had suspected. They did not yet know. She braced herself.

"They will be led by Grebe."

A general acceptance met that announcement.

"And they will be protected by the power of a Fury."

She saw Rue tense, her body turn as she anticipated her husband's presence near the path to the standing stones.

But his eyes—*his* eyes, black and condemning—sought Persephone out in her place in the shadows, and she felt the disbelieving dawning of awareness around her, felt the bodies turning towards her, and heard Rue's harsh gasp.

"You do not trust her to protect them, she who killed my baby?" she cried.

Her voice pierced Persephone with a sharp dart of pain.

"Did my *wife*—" and how his voice, so silken when he wanted, caressed that word with sensuous grace that chilled her to the bone "—trust the wrong man?" His words seemed weighted with meaning. "Did she stupidly, foolishly, choose the wrong path?"

Persephone stiffened. He spoke the truth, but it stung, and with it, rose her own temper.

"It is the way of young girls," he sneered, "or so I've observed."

Rue fell silent, her body rigid with rage.

"It's the way of Furys to fling themselves into the fire and atone for such sins, is it not?" he demanded. "And it's in their power to ward and protect, and that is what she will do, this wife of mine with sins so heavy upon her heart." He raised one pale, elegant hand and, with an impatient gesture, beckoned her forward.

She could do nothing but walk through their midst. They stepped back as though the stench of betrayal clung to her. How dare he hold her up to such ridicule, even as he burdened her with a responsibility she neither asked for nor wanted.

His eyes glittered as she approached him, and she wanted to spit in his face. One long finger twirled, and she recognised the silent order and, gritting her teeth, spun to face these people who despised her.

"You do not trust her to fight for you," he said, "and none can blame you for that. But she is the power promised us in prophecy, the power that surpasses any you might put forth—"

"She is not one of us! She doesn't fight to defend her own blood," a buxom woman with curling ginger hair said.

Persephone recognised her. She was one of the laundresses who had mocked her, who had taken the evidence of her skill with bow and arrow and put it to shame. But she also recognised the pain in the woman's eyes and could only imagine the fear that lived there. She was about to put her child's life into the hands of one whose skills she deemed inferior, whose powers she didn't trust.

"I will protect them with my life," she said, and never had she spoken truer words, and yet, even they were not enough. She reached deep and found the vow that meant more to her than any other. Fist over her heart, she whispered, "Word of a Fury."

The woman stiffened, and her eyes drew down to narrow slits as she pulled her child closer to her. "But you are no longer a Fury."

Persephone felt the worlds like a blow, the truth in them a pain twisting in her heart as she fought for breath.

The ginger-haired woman cast an accusing glare. "Do the Fireborn not respect their binding vows?"

If this were a test, what a cruel test it was proving to be. Would they strip even this from her, the very blood from her veins, the source of her honour?

She thought of the man at her back, of the name she now bore, of the vows she'd made, and felt dizzy with the loss of all that was love, to be replaced by all that was disdain.

This was her path. She had chosen it quickly, and she would not change it even if she could. She found it within her power to say, "By the elements born of the earth," and bent to scoop a handful of cool dirt into the palm of her hand, its scent rich and loamy. "By earth."

She rose until, once again, she stood before her challenger. Without breaking her gaze, she spat into the soil. "By water."

With an arrogance of her own, she flicked a spark of flame at it, releasing the pungent scent of burning earth into the air. "By fire."

With a second flick of her fingers, she stirred a whirlwind in her palm that whisked its contents into the air. "And by air."

The woman's expression shifted to astonishment and then fear.

"I give you my vow, *my word as a Wyllt.*" She raised her face and included them all. "I will protect your children with all the power I have, in any way I can."

She was met by silence.

As if none other were present, the woman stared long at her and then stepped forward and gave the slightest of nods. "That is enough. May Elen guide you and protect them. Our hearts and our future go with you."

Persephone's nod was deeper, and she had no words to respond to such grace in the face of peril.

May Elen guide and protect…

The silent goddess who had said, *No, don't,* and who had not spoken since.

She felt that loss but also felt a heat on the back of her neck and whirled to find the man who she had accepted as her bound husband staring at her through narrowed eyes, unreadable and shut off from her.

"She will need a boy's clothes," he announced, flicking his glance away from hers. "Trousers and shirt and boots and cap, and a dark jacket or cloak. Who can provide them?"

Before Persephone could express her own surprise and questions, chaos broke out in raised women's voices. A sharp movement at the edge of her vision revealed that even Night reacted and seemed barely to keep her silence as her hands became fists in her lap.

"The strength of a woman does not need a man's ways!" a stout woman in the middle of the crowd shouted.

"If she has so much power, what need she to hide in a man's trousers?" another demanded.

"You insult us all!"

"Enough!" Vespasian's lips curled in his habitual sneer.

More than one woman's attention became focussed on the Crone in confusion, waiting for her to speak on their behalf.

The Crone remained silent.

"Know you not that she will be a target, that they will be seeking to 'rescue' her, or to kill her?"

Kill her? She felt the blood drain from her face but refused to show weakness.

"My *wife*—" and again, the word was caressed with silk "—is no stranger to boy's clothing."

The long ago night when this all had begun.

"She will be wearing a disguise and thus will be more fully able to do what she must to fulfil her duty and her responsibility."

No further protests were offered. Persephone's head spun with contrasts. Fireborn women would find the idea of her wearing a man's trousers obscene and indelicate. These Earthborn women deemed it an insult to their power. In the middle of all such thoughts spun the reminder that the duke might want her dead.

"We will see the children safely off, and then we will return to the village and prepare for war."

If those had been the last words spoken, they would have been ominous enough. But at that moment, a new voice, a beloved voice, spoke from the head of the path to the standing stones. His face etched with weariness but his body tall and strong, Lysander appeared from the emerald depths of the path. His eyes sought and found Rue, who turned away from him, her hair a wild nest of dirty tangles, her agony tangible in the air around her.

"They have come by water," he said.

He was met by stunned silence.

"Their ship is in the cove. They can be here in hours."

Pandemonium threatened—

But was halted by a sharp clap of magic that sprang from Vespasian Wyllt's raised hands. All froze and turned back, their fear and urgency palpable in the air.

"We will see the children safely off," he repeated, daring any to dispute him. He repeated his earlier command, "Then we'll return to the village and prepare for war."

If there had ever been doubt in her heart, it was gone.

His was the voice of authority and of hope, and now she had but to fulfil her own role that had been prophesied a thousand years.

His black eyes met hers, and if this had been a world where women curtsied, she would have done so willingly. Instead, she nodded and followed a woman who beckoned to her and said she would find her men's clothing. Minutes later, her cloak, gown, and chemise with its spot of blood on the skirt were all folded neatly into her pack. She emerged from behind the boulders that had provided her shelter for two nights and made her way once more through the milling families as they pressed pouches of food and clothes upon their children.

She made her way through their midst, her limbs clad in the softest deerskin and her feet in thick socks and well-made boots. She felt so vulnerable. She tugged the heavy jacket closer around her and the cap more firmly down over her eyes, her hair an uncomfortable knot beneath it.

She wondered how she would piss, and thought of her gown with its easily lifted skirt with regret. Heaven help her if her courses began before she was able to return to skirts. She laughed bitterly at the idea that bloody trousers were even on her list of worries.

But any thoughts—any thoughts at all—were better than watching the tender scenes played out before her, scenes that triggered fear and empathy for those bidding their children goodbye, so bravely participating in pretence of a day's outing and frolic. In her own selfishness, they triggered memories of her own family, of longing for the arms she longed to feel around her in comfort and strength, brothers and sister and parents so free with their affection. If any were here on this day, to receive her desperate embrace or wrap their arms around her in comfort—would she be as brave as these people, or would she succumb to the tears that threatened even now?

Oh, how carefully and with what great determination she shoved aside thoughts of the brother whose condemnation hung heavy between them, whose arms would offer both strength and comfort, had she not been the cause of his greatest pain.

Suddenly, she glimpsed wild hair and hollowed eyes and Rue, tragic Rue, huddled at the edge of the bustle, arms always clutching, always wrapped around herself, as she swayed.

Her brother's *wife*.

The dart of recognition hit straight and into the heart. Rue was a

Fury, too. Loved and cherished by a Fury son, Lysander, his heart in his eyes as he watched her. Rue who allowed none to comfort her, whose eyes glowed with madness.

Rue, a Fury.

On the other side of the great chasm that separated her world, Furys still lived and loved, and here—here where they surely had all that was just on their side, Furys had been brought to their knees by one of their own.

By her.

A small child darted in front of her, laughing and squealing, leading her mother on a merry chase. The mother with ginger hair lunged forward and swept the small girl with fine hair of strawberry blonde up into her arms. "I should let you run and not have your sweetie," she scolded sternly, even as her arms held the child tight against her full breasts. "My little Kit, such a scamp you are."

Persephone moved to the path that would lead them out of the grove and up the steep and difficult track leading to the crofter's hut. She stood there stiffly, her pack on her back, watching as Grebe gathered the children as easily as a shepherd gathering playful lambs.

She turned her back to them all, then, turning her back to the beginnings of loss.

It was only after her eyes rested on the tall form of the man tossing orders about with such arrogance and command that he could very easily be a king himself, that she realised she'd been looking for him, as a tongue relentlessly seeks out a sore tooth.

She needed that bracing reminder, the flash of cold astringent to remind her that foolish thoughts of the past were dangerous on this vital day. *He* needed no arms of comfort, nor would he offer them, nor would she want any such from him. A shiver swept down her spine.

Then children surrounded her, their large eyes frightened, despite Grebe's reassurances. Oh, merciful goddess, weeping children and mothers whose stoicism was rent by fear, these things could not weaken them on this day.

Without thought to how she knew what to do or say, she dropped to her knees in the midst of them. First reluctantly, then with great curiosity, they drew nearer, until their bodies squirmed about her. She gave a stern look to Grebe who, eyebrows raised, backed away with more than a little suspicion evident.

"None can know, for this is my most secret shame…" Widening her eyes large for effect, she bent even lower until they were all bent with her.

She whispered her secret, and yes, it was her shame, one that prior to this moment, only her family had known.

"I cannot sing."

It was met with giggles, and with scorn, because they were brats and scamps, the lot of them. But it had successfully distracted them.

"I need you to do this most important thing," she said.

She stood, slipped her silver flute from her sleeve, and raised it to her lips. When the first notes sounded, she began strolling up the path, surrounded by children whose clear voices rose in light, lilting song.

Llwyn Onn.

It's Mr Wyllt's favourite, Otter's sweet voice said in her memory.

She cast a glance back and found those black, glittering eyes resting on her… and felt a jolt.

She was a Wyllt. The one who should have been her comfort and strength would have been this man, this man she had despised for most of her life and who had held her in disdain for just as long. She turned away, her heart bleeding, refusing to look to him for any sign of approval.

She continued up the path that led the children away from death.

❦❦

Something was wrong. Everything was going as he'd planned, and yet—it was the children's voices raised in song, as if this weren't possibly the end of their world. How had she managed that?

Long after they had disappeared, swallowed up by dense green wood spattered with golden rays of morning sun, their voices drifted back like laughter on the breeze, interweaving with the music—the blasted Fury magic—of the lone flute. Around him, movement was urgent but not frantic. Was determined, not frightened, the anguish eased.

Somehow, *she'd* done that.

And yet instead of reassured, he felt unsettled. He thought of the last glimpse, before she'd taken their future away with her. Her bearing, as always, as regal as a queen, even when dressed in castoff men's clothing. The cock of her head, the angle of her elbows as she'd lifted the flute to her lips.

Her eyes.

For one fragmented moment they had captured him, and he had not been able to take in air. Those eyes had held something he'd never seen there before, something so unsettling he'd pushed it away, refused to consider it.

She had dared—dared!—look at him with eyes large and black and liquid and haunted, as if she *needed* something from him.

From *him*. He who was pulled in every direction, who carried the weight of their lives on his soul, and who had to be alert to every possible danger, to every possible permutation of events, who had to take blind flying leaps of logic in order to save them all, and she dared look to him as if she needed him to—

To what? He didn't know. He shook himself loose from the memory, and yet—he couldn't stop himself. He scanned the activity around him, saw how efficiently plans were becoming reality. Reassured, he plunged up the wooded path.

Long years on these very paths had given him their measure, and on this day he ran without thinking after the memory of the music.

What mistake had he made?

Only when he broke from the wood and, chest heaving, saw the small figures on a distant ridge—children gambolling like so many lambs, with a young, lithe piper leading them and ancient Grebe following behind—did it strike him, the magnitude of his error.

He had been given the power that dovetailed with his own, the prophesied power that would put the True King on the throne.

Yet to ease the concerns of his people who had every reason to hate her, to protect the children who were their hope and their future, to assuage his own bitter spirit that resented her for everything she stood for and everything she was, he had sent her—and her power—away.

✃ CHAPTER FORTY-NINE ✄

Robin stood at the ship's rail, his fingers white-knuckled as he awaited the command that would finally take him ashore. The fever raged in his veins, this need—this knowledge. She was near now, so very near.

He was afraid to examine what 'too late' might mean on this battle day. He turned away from thoughts of death and focused instead on life, her life, brimming and brilliant with promise.

The small, rocky cove was perfect for their purpose, deep enough to anchor, with beach enough to land, and no Ordinary presence discernible. Cliffs rose high above the rocks and sand, but that would prove no problem for men without horses, and if paths existed, even the horses could be put ashore and held ready for use.

He would demand her hand from those who had so wrongly hesitated, had so wrongly pushed her to wild action and to this moment.

Certainty burned within him. His future was clear, and she was at the heart of it.

She was as tightly twined into his destiny as his blood-filled veins twined into his heart.

The simple golden ring on his small finger heated with its magic, and he steeled himself for what was to come.

❦

As she crested the first hilltop beyond the ancient wood, her heels had wings. The music lilting from her flute danced in the air about their heads and around their feet, and long after they should have been weary, children laughed as a pheasant was flushed out of its brushy lair or a rabbit hopped through the bracken. As long as she had breath to play, there would be joy, not fear. How different this journey was, with the sun shining, hills blooming with purple heather and the salt of St George's Channel in the air. Yet with great urgency, she kept the pace brisk.

"Look!" A sturdy boy pointed at the sky.

High above, a raptor soared, its tail full and wide and long and notched, its body and upper tail and wing coverts a rich, warm reddish brown that caught the sun flashed fire. Smaller than an eagle and more slender than a buzzard, it soared against the blue sky.

"A red kite," Grebe said, and his voice was heavy with significance. "*Barcud,*" he added, the word fluid and music on his tongue.

"So rare," Persephone breathed, her skin prickling.

"Rare enough to carry portent on its wings," Grebe said.

"What does it foretell?"

"Attack. Bloodshed."

"That hardly requires a harbinger from the gods," she replied, suppressing a shudder.

"But perhaps a sign of the True King."

"May the goddess have mercy on us, and may you be right, because if ever we needed such…" Persephone let her voice trail away, thinking of the red-hued wings, the duke with his hair of flame.

Suddenly the kite swooped to the earth, and with an elegant flap of wings, back up again, a small, struggling mouse in its grip. It flew away to rip into its flesh, not caring that it was innocent, for innocence held no meaning in the kite's world.

The True King.

Hair of flame.

No. No. No, *never.*

A great anxious beast stirred within her. Battle was coming, and the future would be decided, and she would not be there.

Why should she want to be, she who was but a girl and less skilled than any? She had great power, but why should she want to use it in such a way? She had no desire to fight, but the anxiety sprang from knowing that she should. That it was important. That leaving it to others was dangerous and wrong.

Despite knowing there would be no answer, she dropped to her knees and offered a desperate prayer. *Oh, goddess, sweet goddess, show me the way.*

She remained kneeling until the rocks digging through the fine leather and into her knees drove her back to her feet again. She could not wait.

She hoisted her pack onto her back and raised her flute, leaving Grebe to herd the children behind her.

❧❦

The children were tired and easier to guide. They trudged forward, lured by the promise of food and a cool place to rest over the next ridge. It was in this momentary lull that Persephone finally spoke, not to children, but to Grebe. Though he had not indicated being open to conversation, she had to ask him the question that ate away at her. Scooping the youngest child with the strawberry blonde curls into her arms, she caught up with Grebe, who now led the way, his stride unexpectedly steady for his advanced age.

"What is it you've been wanting to ask ever since we set out?" he asked, his voice gruff with impatience.

So he would allow no subtlety? She stiffened her weary spine. "Is Vespasian Wyllt the True King?"

The old man's head snapped towards her, the thin braids swinging. "Is that it? You desire a crown?"

She stared into his watery eyes, confused.

"That's why you agreed to this mockery of marriage—"

"It is real enough," she snapped. "Real enough to keep me alive to protect your children!"

"Is it a *queen* you're wanting to be?"

"No!" Before the word queen had even crossed his lips, she'd felt the shackles, heavy as lead, weighing her down. No, no, a thousand times, no!

Seeming satisfied, though still suspicious, he watched the path. "You should know the answer to your own question, then."

"Just because I don't desire it doesn't mean anything. I did not ask for *any* of this, and yet here I am. Perhaps it is Vespasian—"

He let out a snort of disgust. "Do you not know of the Separation? Is your Fireborn knowledge so deficient that—"

"Of course I know. When Bardán Fury helped establish the line of Pendragon, he also established the Separation of Crown, Religion, and Magic."

"Bardán Fury," he spat. "You give him credit for such, when it was the ancients who first separated the three. Your esteemed ancestor cast aside the power and authority of women as nothing. He devised a system in which men held all. He corrupted a system as old as these mountains to his own ends."

She had no time to indulge in frustration over the inequities of power, as great as they might be. But the triune system of authority? He was right. It hadn't been inspired by the ancient Greeks. She frowned and considered what she'd seen in the grove. The Earthborn Crone as Spirit mirrored the Fireborn Priests as Religion. Grebe as the voice of Law might mirror the Crown. And Vespasian Wyllt as, she presumed, Magic? Had Bardán Fury's plan been based on a magical system other than the one he espoused? A system in his native Ireland? Something to consider, but for now, relief coursed through her. Vespasian would never be accepted as king, for his powers were too strong. And yet...

"He has the arrogance of one who sees himself as superior to all around him. He speaks with the authority of one who deems himself superior to all around him. You cannot deny that," she finally said.

"I cannot deny his passion and zeal—"

"His *obsession*," she spat.

"—have driven us forward and brought us to this point, nor can I deny how many of our problems begin when his judgment is poor, and that when he is most desperate, I have most to fear."

"As he is desperate now."

"He was desperate before he brought you back to us. That day, he was reckless."

That day. She tried to shut her mind against it, the memories of that day, of a startling and painful joining, of—

She stopped abruptly, causing the sleeping child on her shoulder to stir and murmur in distress. Mindlessly stroking the soft curls, she met the old man's rheumy blue gaze. "The flash of light. When our hands touched. Does it always happen in Earthborn rites?"

The old man turned his face resolutely away from hers and began walking again, and at first she thought he would not answer. But then he said, slowly, resentfully, "It is the first mark of a True Marriage."

"Impossible. We have no affection for one another."

He studied her closely. "What fuelled your decision, girl?"

"I'll do anything to stop the Duke Regent of Glastonbury."

But he seemed troubled. "You harbour no affection for him, and yet you in that moment made a binding so pure, it was blessed with the goddess's light."

"Pah," she spat without thinking. "The goddess didn't bless our binding. She tried to stop me."

He paled visibly, his breath growing short. "She tried to stop you— and you did not listen to her?"

She flung her free hand in the air as if dismissing a pesky servant. "I do not understand your goddess and your Shadows that suck me in deeper and deeper, that pull me away from the light. But they offer me the only chance I have of stopping a great evil."

"Girl." He grabbed her shoulder and spun her to face him. "You are mistaken about many things, but none more than this. You have been fed poison about what you call Shadow magic. It is not called that because it is Dark, but because when your people invaded these islands and brought your gods, you drove our gods and our magic into the shadows. Not because it is evil, but because it threatened the religion of the conquerors!"

"But I feel it—" she began.

"You have Dark within you, yes, but it is not Shadow magic."

"I don't understand."

"Night saw it in you at your birth as I saw it in Vespasian when he first came to us, after he had shamed himself and his goddess with his arrogance. Dark lives within the two of you, as well as powerful Shadow magic. The Dark is a curse, but how it binds you and how it devours you, I can't explain. I have no answers. Only that along with your curse, you bring us our only hope."

A curse. Old terror returned and swept through her. They were bound by a curse, and she had allowed him to deepen their bond, had willingly bound herself to him? No. Not this, not this now! "I told him it was a curse!"

"Your magic is not the curse. It is a gift that goes beyond our understanding, that you would receive such a thing."

"You confuse me!"

His voice grew hard and cold. "You were blessed and cursed at your birth. And now you bring both to us, and we must trust our lives and our future to someone who scorns us and demeans us and even betrays us. Someone who bears both a blessing that should have been ours and a curse that may destroy us. That is what we must endure."

❦❦

A streak of grey flashed low across the earth through the bracken.

A helmet rose over the rocks by the path, then a face with a menacing scowl, grizzled with beard, and with a ragged scar slashing from temple to bulbous nose.

Persephone grabbed a child with one hand and flung him behind her, her right hand rising to protect—

The grey streak became snarling dog, its sharp teeth piercing the jugular. Blood spurted. Eyes bulged. Arms thrashed and then hands closed on the beast's throat.

But the dog kept his grip, and before her and the children's horrified eyes the man's life pulsed away in shortening spurts of red, coating the dog and the ground around them.

Two more heads appeared, men rising to attack—

She flung her hands forward—and death—*death*, for it would not happen again, children would not be killed by the duke's men again—*death* flew from her fingertips in a burning, shrieking torrent—

They fell.

A wall of fire sprang from the ground before her.

Her fingers aching with pain, she prepared to try again, when Grebe grabbed her arm. "The fire won't hold long," he gasped. "Protect us while I take the children to safety!"

He had made the fire?

Grebe had the children running as she spun to attack their attackers, clenching and unclenching her hands in an attempt to shake off the pain, fearful that she wouldn't be able to muster a second defence.

The fire thinned before her, and she stifled a moan. The two figures were on the ground—had her attack hit them, after all?—but there were several more standing. A glance over her shoulder showed that the path up the mountain was empty. How much farther to the crofter's hut? Dare she run?

Warmth and dampness touched the fingers of her right hand, and she smelled the stench of burning blood and of vile, nasty dog.

Strength eased into her with the heavy weight of his body pressed against her legs as he stood with her, rigid as steel, fur bristling. He licked her fingers so thoroughly, they might have been drenched with grease.

With her other hand, she sent another flash of fire, fuelled by all the rage within her, all the fear and determination that they would dare hurt innocent babes, and watched it dance high. Screams erupted.

Her fire was not a barrier like that of Grebe but had found its marks. This time she did not wait, but took off up the path.

She rounded an outcropping and fell back against it, chest heaving, and this time it was her left hand that received the unexpected but welcome ministrations of the dog's tongue, the left hand that was eased of pain.

Sick rose in her throat, even as her legs grew numb.

Had she killed those men? She had to stop them, but Grebe had stopped them without killing, hadn't he? She didn't want this, this sickening guilt gnawing at her. But she wanted them dead, and she knew that she would do it again, and yet again, if it kept the path behind her safe and the children safe and—

A crunch of boots on gravel, slow and cautious, creeping...

The dog, the blessed, vile dog, grew rigid beside her and curled its lips back, showing sharp teeth and bloody muzzle and yet gave no warning growl, nothing to reveal their presence.

The steps grew nearer. She braced herself and sprang into the path as the dog launched forward at the throat of the duke's hired blackguard who had dared to survive her fire and her rage.

He rolled in on himself in defence, and she barely managed to stop and grab the dog by the dirty scruff of his neck as she fell on top of him and looked into the desperate, bloody, and beautiful face of Robin Fitzwilliam.

"Persephone!" His voice was ravaged, and his expression one of horror.

Belatedly, she saw herself and the splatters of blood from the dog's kill, beautiful, beautiful beastly dog.

Her heart—oh, her traitorous heart—wept at the sight of Robin, even as she scrambled back from his reaching arms. The dog stood between them, braced for attack.

She did not stop him, nor did she reassure or settle him, because she needed the dog to do what she might not—keep Robin Fitzwilliam at arm's length before she flew into those arms and lost herself there.

"Persephone?" he repeated softly, this time in question.

"Stand back." She raised her chin and clenched trembling hands at her sides. Before he could step closer and test the dog—the dog whose teeth had ripped the throat from one of the duke's soldiers, one of *Robin's* soldiers, she now understood—she forced her voice to coldness. "How many more hired murderers did you bring?" This time, the dog's low growl filled the air as she added her own snarl. "How many more innocent children will the duke kill while you hide your eyes?"

She read it his face, his disbelief, his pain. "Oh, my sweet, sweet girl."

"You still do not believe me. What, you think me mad? Or—" The next thought tumbled out with all its sharp-edged venom. "Or you find his decisions acceptable in a time of war? Killing innocent children to eliminate a source of danger is a regrettable but necessary command, Sir Robert?"

He dragged his fingers through his hair and shifted his weight uneasily. "What have they done to you?" he asked. "You reek of Shadows, of Dark—"

"I'm beginning to question what is Dark and what is not."

He held out a hand in supplication. "Come," he begged. "Come with me. Let me help you."

She backed away from him carefully, ever aware of stones and ruts in the path, of the disaster of stumbling and appearing weak, of appearing vulnerable.

For she was so vulnerable.

So damnably vulnerable to those green eyes, this man who would never know Shadows for he was too good, too kind. His virtue shone from him, and he was right, she reeked of Shadows.

But what benefit was his goodness and his virtue when she needed him? What use was it when it made him unable to see the truth that doomed them all?

He reached again, despite the dog, despite her own resistance. "Persephone, please—come to me. Let me hold you. Dear gods, let me hold you." He thought her mad, and he loved her anyway. For one sweet moment, she felt herself leaning forward in yearning, knowing how his arms would make the rest of the world fall away and the world right again.

A sharp blade of sorrow lodged in her throat, and she found it impossible to swallow around it, as her eyes burned with unshed tears.

She heard the sounds of children behind her, muffled sobs, Grebe's patient voice soothing, and knew her place, and knew in this she could not fail. In that moment she knew a truth more painful than any she'd yet had to accept.

Fierce knowledge rose in her. "You were supposed to be true," she said hoarsely. "You were supposed to help me, to believe me, and you didn't. I have never failed you, Robin Fitzwilliam. You failed me."

He staggered, stricken. "Then give me another chance!"

The glint of the cheap wedding band on her left hand mocked her. "It's too late." A child cried behind her—the children, the poor children—what they had seen, the blood the death! They were her duty. She would protect them as Otter had not been protected.

But the battle…

If a heart could truly tear in two and still beat, it would hold twice the pain, would it not? Beat twice as fiercely in one's breast? Spill its lifeblood in an outpouring of agony and still beat on? It was happening within her.

Before her, so pure and filled with virtue, stood her Robin. "You were not sent to attack the children," she whispered. "Those men—" Those men she had killed. "Were not here to kill us?"

He did not answer, but the truth was in his eyes. He did not believe those men were sent to kill her or the children.

And yet, hadn't it been in their scowls and radiating from them, their menace? Could they have orders that went beyond his knowledge? "Are there still others with you, or coming behind you?" she demanded.

He cast a stricken glance back at where the bodies lay scorched on the earth. "No more."

"I must see to the children." She turned away from him, praying he wouldn't follow her.

Praying he would.

Not thinking to fear—until she faced Grebe's suspicious eyes— what Grebe would see when he saw her with Robin Fitzwilliam.

℣℣

She turned her back on him and walked away, the dog at her side, leaving Robin standing, staggered, disbelieving.

She should have flown into his arms and instead had stood there in those disgraceful boy's clothes, with eyes haunted and hollowed, body trembling and fragile and delicate, so obviously filled with a yearning that matched his own... Yet she dismissed him. Refused him. Told him it was too late.

The children. How had she been given such a responsibility, to care for so many children, she who was little more than a child herself?

He scrambled after her. Of course, if there were children, they must be protected. She was choosing the valiant course and forcing him to see it, as well.

A flute, soothing and swirling with Fury enchantments drew him in. He approached the hut with its stone walls and thatched roof carefully, so as not to alarm them, but upon peering into the dark interior realised he need not have bothered. Sprawled on woven wraps, heads cushioned on arms, some of them curled together like puppies in a litter, the children slumbered. Fury enchantment, indeed.

Only one was not on the dirt floor. One small child with light curls nestled into Persephone's body as she leaned against the wall and played them into deep slumber.

A child with red-glinting hair and plump, pale limbs, one dirty thumb stuck in her perfect rosebud mouth. It stole his breath away, the sight of her holding a child. Would that be his child someday? Dared he even think such things, with their world in disarray? Yet dare he not? Was there any better reason to save a world?

Her eyes flashed up at him in warning, and his heart twisted with sweet pain. How could she possibly turn him away when to be in the same place with her, to receive her sharp rebuke or gaze upon her annoyed scowl filled him with such splendid joy, and he felt the anchor of his soul slip into place? How could she not feel it, as well? Could she turn away from this?

He knew as surely as he breathed, she could not.

He did not realise he was smiling at her until she darted a vicious glance between him and the old man and then hissed, "Stop smirking, Robin Fitzwilliam, and if you wake these children—"

He put a finger to his own lips, and she closed her mouth in frustration.

She slid the child into the old man's arms as he watched them both suspiciously.

"This is Sir Robert Fitzwilliam," she whispered, "as lazy and annoying a waste of skin stretched over man's frame as you'll ever see, but as true and noble as the sky is vast." She leaned closer to the old man, her tone quite urgent. "Do you trust me in this?"

The old man stared into her eyes for what felt like a very long time, and finally, he nodded.

"Good."

She rose to her feet and gestured to Robin to back his way out into the open again. Once outside, he found she had not followed him, but instead was still inside, bent over the pack she'd worn. When she joined him, she was wearing a reticule—a ridiculous bit of daintiness he recognised from her time in London, complete with embroidered birds with wings that trembled as if ready to take flight—secured to the waist of her trousers.

"I hope you're not planning to bring this new fashion to Town when you return?" he asked, straining for a light tone. "I can imagine no one who would be able to wear it as charmingly as you."

She did not even pretend to match his mood. "What of my family?"

He felt his smile falter and did not try to maintain it. "Your mother still awaits word from your father."

She nodded, tense and pale. "Electra?"

"Blooms."

This, at least, brought a small smile to her face. "And Dardanus?"

"Has found great favour in his king's eyes," he said without thinking.

Her eyes flashed black—blacker than he'd ever seen them. "The king?" she demanded. "What service could he possibly provide for King Pellinore?"

"It's over," he said gently. "The king is dead." He reached for her hand, but it was cold as ice in his, her own numbness, the blank horror in her eyes chilling him through. "Sebastian is king, and he has an heir in Electra's womb. This is what I'm trying to tell you. Even if the prophecy the rebels believed were true, this is not the time of prophecy. It's over. You can come home. To us all. To me." His relief surged through him.

"The king is dead. Long live the king."

❧ CHAPTER FIFTY ❧

The king is dead. Long live the king.

No. It couldn't be true. Her blood turned to ice. They were too late. Worse, they were wrong. Wrong.

But they couldn't be. She shoved aside Cosmo's prophecy—that the king would have hair of flame, that Electra would be queen—and groped—groped for something just out of reach. "How—how did the king die?"

"You know he has been unwell," Robin said carefully.

So carefully. Always so careful, always so afraid of upsetting her, distressing her, causing her to lose control.

"The day I left he was stronger than I'd ever seen him."

"He collapsed two days ago. His death was quick and merciful." He circled his wrist against his forehead. "And Sebastian... He wept tears of grief, true tears, walking amongst the people, and they kissed his hands and wept with him and loved him. If ever there was a man meant to be king—"

"Stop." She jerked away from the doorway, and the Dark, gods, the Dark that enveloped her... Cold fear took root. "And Cosmo?" This time, her voice quavered. "Is he here to fight?"

"Cosmo... is unwell."

"What has happened?" she demanded, the words sharp in her throat.

Robin avoided looking at her. "His prophecies have become more taxing."

"They never were before." This was wrong, all wrong.

"But your return will ease much of his distress," Robin said firmly.

He believed that. He believed she could return and that their world could shift back into what had been and what had been meant to be.

She wanted to beat her fists against him.

She wanted him to hold her.

She did nothing and allowed nothing, for nothing would ever be as it had been, or as they had wanted it to be. The very earth beneath her feet felt unsteady. "And the duke?"

"The king is not leaving the fighting to others this time. He is here."

Here to destroy them, to wipe them from the land, so that his reign would go unchallenged, so that none would know the truth. She curled her left hand into a fist, knowing that the duke—the king—would never, ever let her live. She would die accidentally. Lysander would not survive the battle, nor would anyone who might know the truth about him.

The king would weep at their loss and comfort his queen. The people would adore him. Robin would believe him, believe it all. And she could do nothing, because she was pinned to this spot, to a vow she had made to protect the children when it was thought she might actually be able to do so. When foolish, frustrating, arrogant Vespasian Wyllt thought he could control her by sending her away. She stared at Robin, her valiant Robin.

A vow.

"You must help me," she whispered. "Please, if you ever loved me—" She broke off, and guilt ate at her for those words, but she couldn't let herself care that she would use that very love against him, would trick a man who did not deserve trickery.

"Anything," he said, "you only need tell me what you desire."

How easily he said words like 'Anything', and 'Of course I'll believe you'. Because he did believe them when he spoke them, believed them to his very soul, that she would never ask more of him than he could give. Yet, when she did, how easily he had slipped away from such words, so sure she couldn't really mean them, so certain she could not possibly be right.

"I must ask you to promise me, to make the most solemn of vows, that you will let nothing harm these children."

"I will stand with you," he said. "None will dare harm them with me here."

"Vow it. Kneel and vow it," she said fiercely.

He stared at her in disbelief. "You know me. You know—"

"—that you failed me once before, and I would have your vow."

If she had struck him, he would not look more stunned, more hurt.

Yet how many ways had he failed her by not being her champion more stridently, by not protecting her more ardently from the world and from her family, until she'd chosen the Dark and the Shadows in an effort to find relief.

The pain in his eyes said that he knew it, as well. Her barb had struck home.

"Only if I might have your hand," he whispered. He reached for it, and the dog snarled.

With a wave, she settled the dog down to its haunches, though it still quivered with tension. She held out her hand, her left hand, and he dropped to a knee and took it in his and pressed his lips to her knuckles, and she caught her breath at the touch.

"I vow," he said, "by all the pantheon of Olympus that I will protect the children, that no harm shall come to them while I am their champion, that I will not fail you or them in this."

His image wavered before her eyes, distorted by tears that filled her eyes but would not spill—she would not allow them to spill.

She waited for him to see, to see… and waited longer. He did not release her hand, nor did he notice the cheap ring Vespasian Wyllt had placed on her finger, that even now mocked as much as it bound, and somehow she could not find the strength to point it out to him.

He who seemed particularly adept at not seeing things he should notice and mark.

She snatched her hand away, that restless beast stirring within her again. She must move, and quickly. But first—she had to know.

"How did they find me? How did you?" she demanded. "How could you know so certainly where I was?"

He raised his right hand, and on his smallest finger she saw a ring that was neither cheap nor mocking. It was heavy and golden and inscribed with runes. The small pearl on her right hand throbbed in recognition.

"The queen gave it to me," he said. "She sent me to find you."

The queen's gift to her, the ring, had been a tether? A way to keep her under royal surveillance?

Unsmiling, she slipped the queen's ring from her finger and pressed it into his palm. "Give this to your treacherous queen when next you meet."

"Treacherous? When she has such fondness for you?"

"You must leave Court, Robin," she said as she dragged her fingers through the tangles of her hair. "Leave it while you can, for you will never survive its intrigues."

"We will leave it together, and if you'd like, I'll make that vow, as well," he said earnestly.

"No! Not that one!" She fought to calm herself, to do what she had to do.

He tried to return the ring. "Wear it for now," he said, "for it might keep you safe. It might make it easier for me to protect you should anything go wrong." His brow creased in confusion when she backed away from him. "If you truly resent it, return it yourself when we return to London."

But she shoved his hand away, and the nasty dog beside her growled. "I will not see her again, not in this lifetime."

She jerked away from him. The dog blocked him from following her into the hut. She knelt before Grebe, the man of the law. "I vowed to protect them."

But his eyes were not on her. They were on Robin, standing uncertainly in the doorway, silhouetted against the bright light of day, representing all she had loved and held dear, and now forever removed from her. The old man's gaze went from Robin to her. "You have fulfilled your vow."

Did he mean what she thought, what she needed him to mean?

"Your horse is at the first turn-off, warded by Lysander with the other stock."

Hades.

"Go," the old man said. "Go now."

She stumbled to her feet, stepping over the sleeping form of a child using his small pack as a pillow.

The battle would not wage without her. She would be there. She must be there.

But first—she steeled herself to meet those eyes of green. "You promised to stay here. You vowed. You vowed."

"Of course. I'll stay with you as I promised."

"You are staying. I am not," she said.

"Persephone!"

She touched her fingers to her lips—wet lips, wet with tears—and kissed them, as she would never kiss him again. "I loved you, Robin. Oh, how I loved you."

Before her heart could stop her, she took off running for the passage through the rocks, down the narrow footpath between yellow gorse and late heather, flying not with joy but with fear, with sobs that wracked her even as she ran, with an image of his face etched with betrayal that would follow her to her grave.

Pain knifed into her side as she took the turn-off, scrambling to keep her footing as she careened around the bend. She sensed the wards and with a fierce burst of desperation, released them to see the small paddock that held the village's few horses and cows for safekeeping.

Hades, sturdy and elegant, tossed his mane and struck his hooves against the dirt as she approached. She flung herself over the wall, ran through the midst of alarmed animals, not caring that they scrambled wildly as she flew to the corner where Hades kept the other beasts at bay. She buried her face in his sleekly brushed neck, for Lysander had groomed him, of course he had, and his coat shone and his mane was thick and smooth, and for a moment all she could do was breathe in the familiar scents of her childhood, her girlhood, her life.

But she could wait no longer. She topped the low wall and then climbed onto his wide, strong back. Grabbing his mane, she leaned low over his neck, and together, they leapt the wall, flying through the air and landing on the other side with a jolt, and yet she didn't budge from his back, so carefully he carried her. She stilled him beneath her and recast the wards and watched the other livestock, now frantic, disappear. There was no time to calm them.

No time.

No time.

She bent low over Hades' neck, and he burst forward, a force of wind and muscle feeding on her own frantic need. All she could do was trust his footing, trust him to find his way as they flew down the slope, and within her heart grew a surge of hope. Hadn't he always kept her from harm? Hadn't her beloved Hades always taken her through Shadows and Dark and brought her safely home?

The rhythm of his hooves striking ground repeated the horror relentlessly.

The king is dead.

Long live the King.

❦❦

When they approached the last rise, with the standing stones looming ahead, high on the hilltop, and the path to the village just beyond, she slowed him to a walk, her heart pounding. She must find a safe place to leave him and go the rest of the way on foot.

She had guided him off the footpath and towards the first copse of trees when she saw it—the flash of flame on the path ahead of her.

Sunlight striking hair of flame on the figure of her greatest enemy.

She forced Hades sharply away, urging him into a gallop towards the trees—

But she saw the arm and saw it point towards her, the long flash of gold—a wand of gold. With a whip and a slash, he hurled a curse at her. Hades—her beloved Hades—reared with a squeal of rage, caught it full in his chest, and collapsed to the ground.

She screamed in anger and in agony as she fell free and hit the ground beside him. She sprang to her feet, over his heaving, valiant body, quivering beside her, and whirled.

With both hands, she hurled death.

From the depths of her Dark soul, she felt it flow, felt it rich and bitter and bile-filled and powerful streaming from her fingertips—

And the king—his handsome face serene with arrogance—waved one hand, and all her magic—her gift, her supposedly powerful magic—

Did nothing.

Nothing.

Nothing.

Pain screamed through her, the pain of attack, the pain of delivering death, and it meant nothing.

She throbbed with agony.

Sebastian—now the king—strolled towards her with his twisted smile, and the wreaths of Darkness circled him like vultures. Before she could react, his wand was pointed at her temple, its diamond tip glittering.

She waited for the hex that did not come.

The wretched, malevolent king touched her face with tenderness as he knelt over her. "You cannot hurt me, sweet sister," he purred. "Look at all that power you wasted, thinking you could hurt me. Don't you know the king is protected by even greater powers than yours?"

"Pendragon powers," she gasped. "Pendragon protections—but you are not a Pendragon!"

His lips curled into a smile as he stroked her cheek. "Do you need more proof that I am the True King than this?"

The wand dug into her temple, and she braced herself—

Footsteps approached and the wand quickly disappeared.

"Your Majesty!"

"I've found her," he cried. "Rejoice this day, for the queen's sister has been rescued!" Leaning close he whispered into her ear, "We are not finished."

She tried to strike again, but no magic sprang to her fingertips.

No power.

Only pain that left her shivering with weakness as she was swept into the midst of royal soldiers intent upon protecting her from her only means of salvation.

❦❦

Vespasian heard the shift in the air and dived.

An arrow struck the tree behind him, its flint tip buried, its shaft quivering with magic.

"Don't track it!" he barked, knowing the only reason a message would have been sent in such a way was with intent that he should do just that.

He stalked towards the arrow and with an urgent wave of his hand, detected no foul trickery and found the message affixed to the arrow's fletching. He felt the tension, the eyes of everyone upon him as the tight scroll of expensive parchment unrolled at the touch of his fingertips. With a sickening twist of his gut, he recognised the expectant blank surface and watched the elegant script, the swirl and grace of the ink's flowing pattern, the unforgettable voice in his mind as the words formed before him, for his eyes only, a spell he'd created himself whilst thinking himself clever and capable of earning his way into the charmed circle of friends around Sebastian Balmain.

He was swept back in time, and his face burned with humiliation until he managed to stifle it under an impatient need to read this unexpected missive.

In so reading, he felt the blood drain from his face and his veins turn to ice.

Impossible. He couldn't have her. Rage boiled up in him, up in an inferno that erupted in a roar. "Prepare for a siege!"

Night stood nearby, her wrinkled face drawn in dismay. "Who is doing the besieging?"

"There will be a long wait for the new king, if he thinks I have come this far to be so stupid."

He withheld the news from them all, that she who was supposed to be the salvation of their children was captive, with a single fine strand of her hair as proof. A few threads of black and silver, twisted into a knot at the heart of the scroll.

Vespasian took it and tucked it into his shirt, against his bare skin.

❧ CHAPTER FIFTY-ONE ❧

She stood stiffly, refusing to meet the new king's eyes as he circled her, his disdain for her male apparel clear in the subtle curl of his lip. His campaign tent was clearly something he'd had created before the old king's death, long before it was appropriate to display the royal Glastonbury seal on the front door-flap. The canvas was woven of darkest midnight blue and shimmering bronze stripes, making the interior need lamplight even in the bright of day. A thick Persian carpet covered the floor, and the narrow bed was crafted of gleaming ebony, decorated with bronzed details from Grecian urns and artefacts in the cathedral, with a small desk and chair to match.

Two foreign soldiers stood at attention just outside the tent, bronze helmets spilling blue plumes past their shoulders and onto their backs. She wondered if they spoke English or were chosen because they would not be able to repeat anything they might overhear.

When he finally spoke, his voice was unexpectedly gentle. "If I'd only thought to bring a trunk of your gowns. This alarming state…" He waved a languid hand that swept from her boots to her hair, tangled and loose now that her cap had been pulled from her head.

She stared through the open flap at the milling soldiers, many casting unsettling and lascivious glances towards the campaign tent. He was in here with her alone. What of her reputation now? she thought bitterly.

"Well," he said, "there's nothing can be done about it." Another languid wave of his hand, and the flap closed. "Untie your belt and lower your trousers."

There was no stifling her gasp, no looking anywhere except at his placid countenance. "I beg your pardon?"

"It grieves me to ask such a thing of you, my dear sister—"

"You are not my brother!"

"—but it is imperative that I see that you remain untouched."

"How—how dare you!"

533

"If you do not cooperate, I'll have to call for assistance."

She wanted to protest her innocence, but—but she wasn't untouched. If there was any knowledge she wanted to keep from him, it was her bonding with Vespasian Wyllt.

"My dear," he continued, and had she not known too much to trust him, his concern would have been compelling. "If it weren't that you've been with such a blackguard I would not put you through this." He let out a theatrical sigh. "Alas, I must."

When he raised a finger towards the flap-door, she realised he was about to make good his threat. He would not wrestle her to the ground; such would be unseemly. But he most assuredly would see to it that someone else did.

Hands trembling, legs threatening to give out from beneath her, she fumbled with the tie at her waist, and finally loosened it. Her reticule hung heavy against her thigh, and she considered its weight, its use as a weapon, but with him watching her every move, it was useless.

Slowly, painfully, she unbuttoned each flat button, holding the fabric together as best she could.

"I'm losing patience," he snapped. "Get on with it. Let me see."

"You can tell just by—by looking?" she asked, horrified, hands trembling, legs threatening to give out beneath her. "Surely there is a woman somewhere who—"

His laughter cut her off. "Don't be absurd. Did you think I intended to confirm your maidenhead? Dear child, I have no doubt it is intact."

She felt heat climbing her throat, her cheeks.

"It is your abdomen I wish to see."

She felt her skin chill with relief. He would not be looking at her private places. She held back a sob. She wasn't sure which was more threatening—that he would look, or that he would discover the truth. But when she felt his eyes studying her face too closely, she opened her mouth to protest again. "I have told you, he performed no rite on my—"

"Now."

She let the trousers gape wide to expose her hipbones and her humiliating lack of undergarments. Even this exposure was enough to make her eyes sting with tears.

He stared and frowned, and she clenched her fingers, willing even the slightest tingle to reveal some force at her disposal, but she felt nothing but numbness as his eyes crawled over her skin.

"You have none of your sister's softness to cushion a man. Such a pity." He turned away with a sniff. "You may cover yourself."

So relieved was she, her fingers fumbled more with the buttoning than they had the unbuttoning.

"I don't understand him. He's had all your reputed power at his fingertips and yet has made no move to steal it." The lines between his perfectly formed eyebrows grew deep. "If, that is, you have as much power as they all claim. I certainly have never seen it."

Thank the gods they had drugged her. Thank the gods he had never known.

The flickering light played across his face, gilding its planes and contours with such delicacy, he was as beautiful as an icon in the cathedral. But he swam in Darkness, heavy and choking as oily smoke. "Give me your hand."

She hid them behind her back, as if such action could do more than slow him.

He grabbed her upper arm, jerked her forward, twisted until her hand was in his, and—

He stroked his fingertips across hers.

With a scream, she wrenched her hand away, clutched it, gasping. Never—never—had anyone taken such liberties! "I'll kill you!"

His smiled. "How? You have no powers at all."

"What did you do to them?" she shrieked. "I had them before I attacked you, and now—" She broke off, unable to continue.

He looked genuinely surprised. "You think I took them without rite or ritual? Would that I had the ability to do such, my dear." Now his study of her grew even more intent.

He held out his hand to take hers again, but she snatched it away, backed up until the low bed pressed against her calves. "Don't touch me."

"I'm finding it difficult to imagine that you could possibly hold the key to anything, much less have possessed such powers as your family claim, since Vespasian has not exploited them. You are certain that he has not stolen them from you?"

She couldn't answer. She was certain, of course, but now, now another certainty had taken precedence. He spoke the truth—the horror and the truth.

No magic thrummed in her, ready for her calling. She was empty, a shell of what she had been before.

"Other than a weak attempt to assassinate me—"

Weak? It had shaken her to her core, and he called it weak?

"—you have proven incapable of putting up even the mildest magical defence. Also, Vespasian has known I have you for hours and hasn't bothered to respond to my message. One would think he would feel a bit more urgency over my possession of such a 'power', if such power actually exists."

This surprised him? She fought back bitter laughter. "I am hardly a person Vespasian Wyllt likes or admires."

"But he took you. Twice. He thought he could use you, and yet here you are, unused. It does make a soul wonder."

She wanted him to leave her. She needed silence. She needed to curl up in her pain without questions, without examinations, without being choked by oily black Dark curling around her. Yet she needed to know. "What message did you send him?"

"I made him an offer that any man of honour would accept. He has lost. There is no time of prophecy, no empty throne, no dead dynasty. He has lost whatever he thought he had in you—and of course, I wrote that you left him the moment you had an opportunity, of your own free will."

"Liar."

"I gave him an opportunity to avoid battle and bloodshed, to save the lives of the poor unfortunates who fell under his spell. All he has to do is give himself up."

"But you're prepared for an attack. Surely you don't think he will believe you." She tossed her head. "I don't believe you. You will destroy them, anyway."

The duke—nay, the king—slipped his gold wand from his sleeve and toyed with it, spinning it betwixt his fingers, watching its diamond tip collect and reflect sparks of light and magic. He raised his eyes to her, and they were heavy with the weight of sadness.

"Alas, history will show that the massacre could have been avoided, if the traitor Vespasian Wyllt had cared more for his people than his own skin."

His lips softened into a triumphant smile. He reached for a flowing cloak made of cloth of bronze. He swept it around him then raised its hood to cover his head. "I must inspect my troops. I would advise you not to get into any mischief whilst I am away, but it makes no difference. Everything is spelled for protection. You couldn't hurt anything even if you tried."

He tipped his fingers to his eyebrows in a mocking salute. "Nor can you escape. Rest well, sweet sister. The night will be long."

❦❦❦

Alone in the dark, she drew herself into a small ball on her side, clutching her knees tightly, for to let go would be to have the world spin out of control around her. Her head tangled with thoughts and memories of Dark, the feel of it on her skin, the scent of it in her nostrils.

The perfumed taste of Dark when she slept in her old chapel bedroom whilst the air was still heavy with moisture from Electra's rose-scented bath.

The swirls and tugs and tantalising temptations of the Dark that called out to her whenever she was near Vespasian Wyllt.

The sick-making, churning, oily black Dark that clung to the new king, the husband of her beloved sister.

The coiling of Dark in her own belly, restless, yearning to break free.

The old man's voice as he told her that it—the Dark—was *in* her, that she could not escape it, that it was at war with her own nature and yet part of her, as well.

Prayer tried to spring from her lips, to cry out for help as she had so often, but when she opened her mouth, no words formed, no sweet entreaties or fierce demands.

Gone was the day when she'd fling her will aside and beg a goddess to save her.

Gone was that innocent belief that the goddess loved her.

Instead, she had been abandoned for making the only choice before her, and she refused to beg, to abase herself for choosing strength over weakness.

She was alone, helpless, in the dark. The liquid voice so gentle in her ear found her an unreceptive listener.

Foolish child.

She did not answer.

Yes, my child, you chose dangerously and wrongly, and now you suffer.

"What choice would you have me make, then?" she demanded, any effort to ignore cast aside. "To die and give my family further cause to follow an evil man who stole a throne? Or have you forgotten that I had no choice? That at birth I was handed over to a destiny not of my choosing, and yet again, at my majority I was committed again, both times to a man both vile and wicked, and none of this was my choice. You gave me this destiny, and you dare rebuke me for the choice *I* made, when I had no choice at all but life or death? "

And if you had the choice again, the choice between honour and love?

"But I do not! What's done is done, and I have chosen, and I cannot regret my choice?"

You defied me and have chosen a man who can bring you only misery.

"I have chosen a path that can rid my people of evil!"

And so, by your choice, you claim your destiny.

Persephone stood, chest heaving, circling, looking for the source of this taunting voice for if she could see this goddess who dared speak to her of choices, she would surely slay her.

Suddenly the voice was no longer liquid, but was hard as granite, each word chipped and sharp and cold.

I lay this destiny upon you, child, that by your own choice, you will never know love.

A blade to the heart could not have pierced her more deeply, and yet she did not stagger or recoil, for hadn't she known this already?

I lay this destiny upon you, daughter, that the True King will come, and he who had most reason to welcome him will revile him, and you will choose again whom you must follow.

He would come. That was all her heart could take in, the hope—

however loaded with threat. The True King would come. She found herself clutching the high back of the chair to hold herself steady as relief coursed through her.

Yet, of course, there was more, for wouldn't such a destiny come as three?

I lay this destiny upon you, woman, that by choosing honour over love, you will find one and not the other, and you shall know misery, and it will be of your own choosing.

She wanted to cry out, but her throat was frozen.

And if you are true, it will be enough.

"What—what about the Dark?" she asked suddenly. "Do I—"

She broke off. The presence was gone, leaving emptiness and Darkness.

Once more, she felt a snarl of rage growing within her as she dropped to the floor and curled on her side and would not, would not, would not weep. Why did this mocking goddess taunt her with words of honour and love and choices, when it was the Dark that scared her? The Dark that claimed her, and she with no choice at all?

Why did the Dark in Vespasian Wyllt call to her, and the Dark clinging to the king repel her? She thought desperately of the vile Vespasian Wyllt, of all the horrible things he had done, and yet he would do anything—anything—to defeat the king. This alone should reassure her.

She worried at it like a sore tooth. The things he'd done, like sweeping Dardanus away into the Ordinary world for coins, using Dardanus's only Fury gift—his music—to such a dastardly purpose. But what was the purpose? *Always the money,* Lysander had said.

But Vespasian Wyllt didn't live in grand fashion. His clothes were good but had no flash and were of no better quality than that of his followers—who were all well-fed, healthy, well-clothed. Their community seemed self-sufficient, and yet had it always been? Or had the coins earned on a dirty, stinking London Street established them?

He had kidnapped her from her own ball.

No. Lysander had done so and admitted it was at his own urging that it had been allowed.

He had used a wand to hurt her.

By deflecting her own hex back at her, a hex she had aimed at him.

He had accused her of being a danger to his people.

And she had been, oh she had. Her magic erupting in a flash of flames that brought a hut down upon her, and yet he had helped Lysander save her, at his own peril.

He had set arrows upon her, faster and faster until she was sure the next moment would be her death.

To prove to her what her powers could actually do.

He had performed a rite so Dark, it involved blood sacrifice—and more—from the woman, Lark, and those were images she would never forget.

But he had been in a rage that he had been forced to do so.

That *she* had forced it, however unwittingly.

He had treated her worse than the lowest mongrel.

He had saved her from adders.

Only because he needed her power.

For his people. For this purpose. This battle.

He had assaulted her, had kicked mud in her face, had threatened her with death.

He had saved her life.

He'd taken her as wife and performed the deed that disgusted him so much, he swore it would never happen again.

He had sacrificed again and again. He would do *anything*. Anything for his people. Anything for the prophecy. Anything to rid the throne of Sebastian Balmain, who dared to make himself king.

Even to hold it empty—and what an act of lunacy and faith that was—for a True King who might never come.

Except… the goddess had spoken to them both. As little trust as Persephone had in such a goddess, the prophecy as promise seemed too real to disbelieve.

He would do anything.

Had done everything.

Had spent a lifetime preparing for this moment.

Curled and trembling on the thick Persian rug in this luxurious tent, she recognised what she'd never recognised before. She and Vespasian Wyllt had a prophecy in common. They had a curse in common. They had a Dark connection that bound them more surely than any hastily conceived marriage with its hastily performed consummation. But they had something else in common, as well.

She also would do anything to stop the evil that was spreading, the Dark that filled this luxurious campaign tent with its stench.

She would do anything. She already had.

Now, she was called on to do the last thing. She alone, of all the rebels, was close enough to touch the king. He had magical protections she could not breach.

But she was here, and she would find a way to kill him, even if it meant her own death.

Perhaps that was what the prophecy was about. If giving up her love, her family, and her joy was a price worth paying, so, too, would the sacrifice of her life be worth it.

She would kill the king if it cost her own life, secure in the knowledge that as long as Vespasian Wyllt lived, such a sacrifice would not be in vain.

⮞ CHAPTER FIFTY-TWO ⮜

Vespasian kept his fist clenched to hide the trembling, for if there were anything that would be disastrous on this day, it would be for his people to see his fear.

Sebastian had her. Had the children been captured? No. Sebastian would have said so.

He clenched his fists tighter. He had to be alone to think. "I'm going to check the lookout," he said harshly. "Tern, if anything here changes—"

"I'll handle it." Tern pointed at two deep buckets of sludge-tipped arrows. "These will be ready to protect the side path."

Vespasian nodded, pretended it mattered, when all he needed was to escape. Once on the path, however, he found himself less interested in solitude and filled with urgency to seek Lysander. Where were they, that Sebastian had been able to release an arrow—even a magical tracking arrow—and have it find him and yet not have been spotted?

He wove through the wood, finding no peace within. The closer he got to Lysander, the stronger his disquiet. He reached the standing stones, and at the far end of the hilltop, overlooking the plain below, the stone table that had once marked the opening to a great tomb. In its shade, Lysander stood scanning the horizon.

His arrival did not stir Lysander from his watch. Vespasian joined him, and the open plain with no sign of occupation left him feeling uneasy.

"Where are they?" Lysander asked, his voice low. "Surely they must be nigh."

Vespasian fingered the message in his hand. By all rights he should share it. But could he trust Lysander to use it wisely, if he knew that his sister was in Sebastian's hands?

Even if he couldn't trust Lysander not to do something stupid and disastrous to gain his sister's freedom, Vespasian had other news.

He walked between the upright stones, beneath the capstone that formed the tabletop overhead, to the small fire burning there. "I have heard from Sebastian," he said evenly, "and the king is dead. Sebastian has claimed the crown."

Lysander spun. "He pretends to be king?"

Pretends. Vespasian felt the lead in his stomach and swallowed. Was it pretence? Could this all be a tragic ending to a revolution unformed, and if it was unformed and too late, whose fault was that? The lead turned to acid. There was only one answer to that question. Turning away from it, he forced himself to reveal more damning information. "You know your sister is with child. A king and an heir. In short, he has declared there is no time of prophecy, and thus, no True King on the horizon."

Lysander said nothing. Said nothing, and Vespasian for once could not read his expression or the tension in his body. Was it defeat and fear that made the man rigid?

Belatedly Lysander asked, "Heard from him—how?"

"A spelled arrow, which I destroyed." He pulled the condemning message and its unrevealed secrets from the folds of his cloak and tossed it into the flames, watching the expensive parchment burn just as effectively and thoroughly as cheap paper. Only when the message was truly gone did he allow himself to leave the fire and walk past Lysander to the open spit of rocky outcropping that hung over the ridge before it spilled down to the valley below.

"Vesp, don't stand in the open."

But he did stand in the open. Sebastian was near, he knew it, waiting for his response, waiting to know whether he would give up in the face of a twist of fate he'd never anticipated or whether he would lead his people forward, possibly to their deaths, not knowing whether their cause even existed.

There truly was no choice, was there?

A gust of wind caught his cloak and sent it billowing behind him. Below him, the plain shimmered.

Shimmered.

As the last rays of the sun slanted low across the terrain casting deep purple shadows in contrast to golden light, the shimmer shifted, and the truth was revealed. With the setting of the sun, the spell dissipated in one final sparkle of magic. An army of foreigners with their tents in methodical semicircles around a gloriously beautiful, striped campaign tent captured the last fire of the sun. More than he'd ever imagined in his wildest nightmares. He had no words to express what he saw.

But Lysander Fury, may the gods damn him, had words, and he spoke them, in awe.

"Men went to Gododdin, laughing warriors,
Assailants in a savage war-band
They slaughtered with swords in short order,
The war-column of kindhearted Rhaithfyw..."

"What inspiration," Vespasian spoke, his voice somehow despite it all, cool. "Predicting our slaughter. Whatever would I do without you?"

"Are we a mite touchy, today? Surely you don't think any would ever mistake you for kindhearted Rhaithfyw?"

Vespasian stared at him.

Lysander stared back, his smile fierce and wide. "We shall be the laughing warriors, my friend. This will be no tragedy. This time the heroes shall prevail against the mighty."

And in that moment, even knowing that the sentiment was forced—had to be forced—he loved Lysander Fury as much as he could love any brother, which—while perhaps not a lot of what was, after all, a weak emotion—was all he had.

❦

A thought tantalised her in the darkness, drifting around the corners of her mind, just out of reach.

Dardanus.

The brother of her flesh and blood, the brother with the shared womb and pulse and... her guilt. Always, the guilt.

Dardanus.

Her thoughts swam in uneasy waves. Dardanus, always Dardanus and his only Fury gift. Even without magic, he possessed it. She wasn't certain whether it was real or imagination, but the silver flute against her right forearm seemed to warm in reminder.

She forced her fists to loosen, forced her aching body to stretch, and as she reached, the flute slid into her palm.

At first, she merely lifted it to her trembling lips and let air blow across it. The soft, fluid note thrummed through her body. It soothed her. It carried a blessing, almost as if her own dear Dardanus were here beside her.

Slowly, she pulled herself into a seated position, crossed her legs, and pressed her lips to the flute in a kiss, tears flowing down her cheeks. This was life without magic. A jagged hole deep within her bled at the agony. In her hands she cupped something beyond magic.

Not because it was magic, but because it was not. It was other. Different. Shared. In a life without magic, she would always and forever feel loss. She did not delude herself that she wouldn't. But she would not be empty. She blew—her breath, her air, her soul—into the flute. It came out as music, only music, and yet could ever such a thing exist as *only* music?

There is no Ordinary music or gold.

Music was the magic they shared, the Ordinary and the Magi. Music was her soul. So she played. Played with the aching of her heart and body, making music that trembled as her tears trembled on her cheek before falling. Music that quivered as her body quivered with grief and pain. Music that haunted and ached, followed by more, always more. For as long as Persephone Fury breathed, she would breathe music.

With the music came feather strokes across her cheeks, twining and stroking around her throat and neck and face. Strange caresses of something both silken and coarse, a twining of loss and comfort, and she opened her eyes to see silver hair floating and writhing in the air, a tickle of the scalp as it lifted and fell, and caressed her, caressed her, caressed her....

This was no magic, or not a magic of her making. Yet it came from somewhere. Somewhere, magic still knew her. Magic remembered her. She closed her eyes and let the music course through her in aching waves, and it was enough.

🦅🦅

The campfires covered the plain below them. Vespasian stood cloaked by darkness and magic and observed the movements of his enemy. A vast encampment lay below. The stone table atop the rocky outcropping had led Lysander Fury to them and now was a beacon to their enemy.

He had expected bloody attack, not silken lies and offerings of safety for those "so foolish as to follow the lunatic ravings of a cursed fool."

Lysander suddenly stiffened, his head angled, his face gently lit by starlight to reveal a tense frown. "Do you hear that?" he asked, his voice low. "The music?"

"I hear nothing." Leave it to the man to be distracted by music around a campfire rather than watching for movement.

"Vespasian…"

Lark's voice, soft and clear, caused his fists to clench and teeth to grind. "What is it," he snarled, wanting to take off her head for interrupting him.

"Your hair…"

He felt it then, the soft lifting and twining, as if toyed with by curling breezes. He reached up a hand to pull it into place, and it curled around him with a strength that seemed almost desperate.

He shook his hand, trying to free it, but the hair clung, coarse and silken against his skin.

"It's—it's only your silver hair," she whispered and said no more.

He heard the faint sound of a flute, drifting on the midnight breeze.

He felt the twisting pain, the fear, the loss.

He tugged his cloak more tightly around him, trying to shut it out.

The hair rose on the back of his neck, on his arms. Inside him, something visceral thrummed with need.

The need to act.

Now.

"Leave defenders in the village," he snapped. "Bring all others here. And—" He groped for words, for a plan, and none formed. "Defend." It was all he could say, all he could choke out.

"Where do you want the archers?"

"I don't care." But he did. He cared more than breathing, and yet at this moment, he didn't know. There wasn't room in him to think, to plot, to decide—

When all he knew was that he had to act.

Now.

Now.

He was moving—swiftly—and suddenly the dog was beside him, the blasted dog that had left with the children and now was with him as he took off for the treacherous trail through the adder-ridden boulders, down the steep slope to the plain below.

From behind him, Lysander demanded, "You great lummox— where are you going?"

"I'm going to free your sister," he snarled back.

"He has Persephone?" Lysander stopped asking questions and only called one last harsh warning. "Don't forget to shield yourself!"

"Go rut yourself, Fury," he snarled. And with that, he was in the crevice between the rocks, loose pebbles flying beneath his skidding, booted feet, rage and frustration boiling in him. His mind raced with anger at himself for succumbing to this daft urge, for scrambling wildly down the trail, bouncing off sharp crags and flat-sided wedges of stone. He knew what the others would say, that she'd betrayed them again, that she'd waltzed into their midst, and he'd been taken in because he was so fraught with obsession over the prophecy he would grasp at any straw, believe any lie, commit any folly, in the name of fulfilling it.

They would be right.

From nowhere, her defiant words came back to him. *Where the gods are concerned, we are mere playthings. I do not put myself in the hands of those who would toy with me for their own idle pleasure.*

How dare she toss away half his life—the only half that counted— with such nonchalance! How dare she introduce doubt in the one sure thing he could believe in, that he had a place in history, he, bastard son of nobody!

Blindly he ran, and blindly he slammed into a jut of rock. He fell back gasping in pain, blood streaming down his face. He forced himself to stop and re-gather, to breathe deeply and steady himself before he ended up crashing at the bottom, a mass of broken bone and flesh

She dared scoff at gods and goddesses, and this was the woman he had tied himself to. An unforgiving goddess who refused him and a spoiled woman-child who flaunted the gods and—

He held his cloak to his face, pressing to stop the flow of blood.

She might have betrayed them. But logic told him she had not.

Oh, how he lied to himself.

Desperation told him she had not. A need to believe himself incapable of making wild errors—he who had made so many—told him she had not. Worst of all, something deep in his gut told him that it didn't matter. Whether she had betrayed them or in her blasted stubborn arrogance had allowed herself to be captured, it mattered not.

If Sebastian had her and knew what he had, his uses for her power would be unmerciful and that in itself was reason to get her back.

But in his gut, as sure as the knowledge that he had a destiny to fulfil, was the knowledge that when he'd taken her to wife—however unwillingly and however much he might despise himself for doing it and despise her for allowing it—he had taken on this burden.

He had known her for a capricious, spoiled Fireborn bratling and had tied himself to her, and now he had no choice. He would find her, and if that meant he had to kill Sebastian to get to her… A curl of heat warmed him at that thought. He would consider his life blessed, indeed.

The night hung heavy and still with only the music breaking its silence. He couldn't roar or shout, but his silent demands carried the weight of his rage. *By all the drops of water in the sea, if ever you intended me to do this thing, if ever you believed this woman worthy, this is the time, damn you! Speak to me! Show me the way!*

Despite the tight passage, a streak of silver-grey flew by him, and then was ahead of him.

The dog, its grey almost white now, almost glowing.

He took off after it, heart pounding in his chest. The cursed, wild dog his only ally, and there were no more thoughts, just the final descent with only the glimmer of white fur sometimes visible ahead of him.

At the last tumble of rock at the foot of the cliffs, the expanse of land spread before him with the encampment in the near distance, the campaign tent lit from without by torches, a target.

From the tent came the unrelenting wash of music on the wind. Did she never run out of breath, run out of pain? If he could choke off the flow, he would, for surely if he hadn't heard the music, he wouldn't be on this fool's errand.

Had Sebastian no soul, that he could hear this and not go mad?

Like the rawest of neophytes, the arrogant swine had put his headquarters front and centre, open to attack.

Or like a king so confident, he toyed with his enemies by appearing as bait.

Or like someone who scouted the terrain, saw it open all the way to the rocks and knew only a fool would cross it in the light of the half moon and sky full of stars without an army at his back.

Gasping in the shelter of the last tumble of rock, Vespasian studied the ground ahead. The dog stood stiffly beside him, poised to leap forward, its coarse ruff bristling with impatience. It turned its long snout towards him and nipped his hand, and he had it drawn back to strike, but the dog took off a few steps and then looked back.

If a dog could glare, if a dog could snarl silently, this dog was doing both. Vespasian stepped forward. When he caught up with the dog, it moved again. The moon, only a quarter of the way up the sky, cast black shadows around the low rocks and bracken. Tense with the feeling that he was quite insane, he realised that he and the dog had no shadows.

He turned his head quickly, as if expecting them, perhaps, to be on the wrong side, playing games. No shadows at all. He stopped. The dog kept going, and in a few moments Vespasian's shadow formed—

He rushed forward as silently as his boots would allow and catching up with the dog, was back within whatever shield kept the moon from striking them, kept them in the dark, for all intents and purposes unseen and unseeable as they angled away from the encampment.

To a dark shape that whickered and stomped its hoof restlessly, a horse with empty saddle, and no rider near. Waiting.

Vespasian approached slowly, cautiously, but the horse did not shy from dog or man. He mounted it, confused, not certain that making himself an even larger target was at all wise.

Then he stopped thinking at all. He charged forward, the white dog as escort, and as he drew closer he found men, soldiers of fortune in uniforms he'd never seen. None on alert. None watching.

All stared in various forms of wistful despair at the tent, under her spell and responding to her pain, and suddenly, it had to stop, must stop, he must stop it before the entire world melted under her agony.

He pounded through their midst, flying on horseback, and—

Don't forget to shield, don't forget to shield.

—threw up the shields in hopes that they would protect him from whatever forces of magic these foreign soldiers had mastered, forces unknown on this isle, unknown because they'd been unneeded.

He dismounted from the horse and ran, his wand at the ready, cursing himself as the biggest fool that had ever lived as he saw the guards standing stiffly at attention by the tent and braced himself for battle.

Tears streamed down their faces, blinded their eyes. To his astonishment, he slipped inside undeterred.

He'd free the wretched girl, but more important, his prey was cornered, and Sebastian Balmain, Duke of Glastonbury, would die.

❧ CHAPTER FIFTY-THREE ❧

She felt him. He was there, *there*, on the other side of the tent wall. On an indrawn breath, pregnant with a note as yet unplayed, she stared at the tent flap. The very life breath of her music filled her in that sumptuous pause between inhaling night air and exhaling her soul through the flute, to become tears quivering in the air.

For if she could not release the agony in one way, it would demand a release in another.

The flap opened, and a silhouette appeared, tall and overbearing, with hair rising on the wind around him, catching torchlight and gleaming silver.

He'd come into the clutch of their enemy to rescue her?

Something deep inside her gave a feeble pulse in reaction to his presence and died. There was no Dark arousal, no surge of Shadow or Dark or—or any kind of magic at all, stirring to twine with his.

This was what she had wanted, to be free of their damnable connection.

Where there had been a pulse, there was now nothing but a faint ache.

"You stupid man! Are you mad?" She flew at him, fingers outstretched like claws. "They'll have us both!"

He caught her blow effortlessly on his raised forearm. "Clearly, I must be." Even in the near dark, she could see the curl of his lip in her mind's eye.

"Go quickly—before he discovers you!" Then it hit her. He didn't know. He'd come to free her because he didn't know. Humiliation overwhelmed her and she backed away, her flute clutched in her hand, silent and powerless. "I cannot help you. My magic—" She swallowed hard, tried to force the words around the lump in her throat. "It's gone."

"That's absurd." The flap fell closed behind him as he stepped forward. She backed away from his touch, but he was quicker than she.

His hand snatched hers, and she winced—squeezed her eyes closed—braced herself for the liberty he was taking.

To her shame, she whimpered despite her effort to be strong, an effort that failed because of that small sound.

But he didn't touch her fingertips. He raised them to his lips and drew in a breath across them, a healer's trick, to inhale the scent and texture of it, the taste of it, to test its strength and health. But this was different, this inhalation that drew air across her fingertips—air, nothing but air, no tingle, no spark, no power.

His grip on her wrist slackened. She felt his shock. But when she tried to pull free, his hand closed about her wrist more gently, and he reached to touch her face, and her shame was complete, for he felt her tears. His hand dropped away. "How—" he began.

With her free hand, she found herself cupping her abdomen protectively, wondering if he, too, would demand to see evidence that was not there.

"How—" he asked again, his voice strangled. "How many men have you killed?"

❧❦

Even before she spoke, he knew it mattered not. *Ysbryd y Myrrdin. Gods, buggering gods.* Obviously, enough. Too many.

"I don't know," she whispered. "The one who tracked me—"

"You used a wand. Who else?"

"There were so many, and I thought they were going to attack the children, and I—I don't know, I thought—I thought—" She pulled her hand free with a fierce jerk. "Why? What does it mean?"

The truth lodged on his tongue. The truth, that it was his fault, he hadn't taught her *enough.* That he'd believed that in the midst of all the Fireborn teaching against wands, they would have taught her *why.*

Or she would have learned why on her own.

What good was her intellect if she didn't bother to learn the important things?

The things he hadn't taught her.

There, together in the near-dark, he felt her trembling as she held her flute hand cupped protectively in the other. Sheltered the hand as if it were injured.

Suddenly, he knew.

The way she had cringed and had even let out a mewling whimper when he had taken her hand.

A cold fist closed on his gut. Her eyes were large, even in this dim light, and this most ridiculously strong and powerful of creatures trembled at his touch.

"He *touched* you."

He closed his hand over hers and, seeking power, found none, but he did not let go of her as rage washed over him. That—that blackguard had touched her in a way that no decent man would? Heat flamed deep within him, a heat of possession, of honour assaulted. No man should ever have made so free.

"I will kill him," she whispered fiercely into the night.

"I will help you."

After a long moment, she gave a jerky nod.

Then he felt the onslaught of filth.

As did she, for she jerked her hand free and placed it ridiculously on the frippery pouch that dangled from the sash at her waist.

He placed a finger on her lips, but the wretched girl jerked her head away, and it was all he could do refrain from snarling at her.

And—too late—he heard the stirring outside the camp, the movement. Confusion. Scurrying. Orders being barked.

With the cessation of music, the trance had melted away.

"You have to leave," she said. "You have to escape. They need you!"

"You're coming with me."

"No! I can do more here," she hissed.

She thought she could accomplish anything alone in her state?

"Nothing that happens to me matters. It's you they need."

"Buggering hell, what nonsense are you spouting?" He reached for her but she dodged backwards.

"There is a king and an heir. There is no time of prophecy. We lost. There is no time of prophecy, and we have no True King."

"Then shall it be a time of revolution, for as long as there is breath in my body, I will not submit to Sebastian as king."

"Revolution," she breathed, "without a True King? Without

prophecy?" She stared up at him in shock. "Yes," she said. And again, as if once was less than adequate, *"Yes."*

They both stilled, both turned their heads towards the tent door. On a wave of stench and death, his enemy—*their* enemy—approached. A shuffle of footsteps, and then, the spill of torchlight as the flap was pulled aside and an impossibly tall figure was poised there—impossibly tall because of the peak of the hooded cloak rising high above his head.

The king.

Yes, it was Sebastian Balmain, and yes, Vespasian had known him when he was but a mere Lord Aubyn, but this man had an aura of majesty. That profile would be perfection on gold coins, as if he'd been born to adorn them.

Vespasian felt the acid burn of a knife twisting in him at such recognition, but he would not be so foolish as to discount what his eyes and senses told him of his foe.

Which didn't mean he had to respect him.

Vespasian turned slowly, his wand dangling negligently from his fingertips, a slow smirk forming, and let instinct lead him. If the new king was caught unaware by his unexpected 'guest', such was not revealed by his countenance. One quick step brought Sebastian inside, and a motion of his hand brought the oil lamps and candles alight.

Beside Vespasian, the girl was rigid with a new tension. Her eyes were trained on the blond courtier following the king into the tent—

Whose eyes were equally riveted to her.

Persephone. A Fireborn name filled with arrogance, as delicate as a whisper, taunting and tormenting.

Who even now was standing white as a puffin's breast, her flute clutched in bloodless hands, her chin raised and lips pressed tightly together in obvious horror and shame.

For the blond man's eyes were taking in her attire, dusty and soiled and male, his expression unreadable. "Miss Fury, my pleasure," he said blandly, with a small bow. "To say that I am astonished by your presence here would be quite the understatement." He shot a questioning look at Sebastian.

"Greylund," Sebastian said, "you will await us outside and will not reveal the presence nor the state of Miss Fury to anyone."

The man bowed again to Persephone, cast an assessing glance at Vespasian, made a deeper bow to the king, and withdrew.

Persephone exhaled. Vespasian noted it. What was this man to her?

Sebastian tugged his gloves from his hands and tossed them onto the gilt-edged desk, and then adjusted a sleeve.

Persephone hissed a warning. "He has a wand!"

"Of course I do." Sebastian's patronising tone was either intended to anger her, or revealed a very unwise condescension. "Who do you think taught this lowborn bastard how to use one?"

She stiffened.

He turned his attention to Vespasian, his lips twisting into a semblance of a smile. "You are here to make your obeisance? To surrender? To betray the unfortunate souls who were swayed by your lies? Yes?" The king leaned back against the desk and folded his arms, a cat toying with mice.

"Sebastian." His one presumptuous word a direct challenge.

"Because I am feeling particularly benevolent, I will not have you put to death for daring to use my given name, a liberty which was not granted you when you were my grovelling servant and certainly not now that you are my subject." His cultivated ennui was even more condescending than his words, as if Vespasian were so far beneath his notice, even deliberate insult could not touch him. He gestured vaguely as he crossed to the table. "I would advise you to remember your place. Put your wand away, Wyllt. It's useless against the royal personage."

"It's useless against Pendragon protections."

"The same thing."

"I think not. I detect a certain—" Again, he felt his lips twitch into a smirk. "—inelegant scent that tells me so."

The king froze.

Vespasian immediately regretted his words. So. The man had no idea that his dabblings left him marked to those who could scent him? Of course, he wondered whether anyone other than he and Persephone would know. Still, it was knowledge he should not have revealed, and he felt by the rigid chill beside him that she had the same opinion.

"You will address me as 'Your Majesty', if you wish to live."

"But for how long?"

Sebastian arched a flame-hued brow on his perfect, porcelain brow.

"I cannot believe you intend us to live long," Vespasian continued. "Debasing myself to gain only a few more minutes of life isn't worth the taste on my tongue."

The cool demeanour cracked. "Perhaps I will enjoy this even more than I anticipated, and believe me, I have anticipated deriving great pleasure from your bloody demise." He stepped closer, his eyes glittering. His golden, diamond-tipped wand slid gracefully from his sleeve into his palm. He flicked it, and Persephone fell clumsily forward, collapsing at his feet.

With all the control that he possessed, Vespasian forced himself to remain unaffected.

Sebastian grabbed Persephone and held her to him, his wand at her throat. "I have yet to divine her worth, and yet you are here in a futile attempt to retrieve her, and I must ponder why."

The girl bristled with intent, and had she had magic at her disposal, Vespasian would have been poised to react with her, for he had seen her this way before, right before she exploded with rage, with power. Even without magic, she was unpredictable and stupid and brave and magnificent, and if she didn't get herself killed he would throttle her.

But she had no magic, and Sebastian had wrapped himself in Dark and dangerous protections.

I can do more here, she'd said.

The stupid, stupid—

He had to distract him. Vespasian turned his voice to silk. "I know how you kept the king alive. Clearly, you've found ways to manufacture that with which you were not Gifted."

Sebastian glowered.

"How did you kill him?" Vespasian asked. "It could not have been easy, if he was brimming with stolen life you'd put in him." He went in for the kill. "Although, even I must admit, the crown you filched becomes you."

"Bastard!" Sebastian spat. His wand swung away from the girl and aimed at Vespasian, and Vespasian blessed Lysander Fury for his reminder, for his shield was invisible but strong, though he felt a pang of panic that she was outside it—

A flick of Sebastian's wand, and ice flowed into Vespasian's veins, ice that left him frozen in place, unable to move, unable to breathe.

His shields… his shields were *nothing*.

Spots of black and red flashed before his eyes. If he'd been able, his pants would be wet with piss and worse. His heart was immobile, his lungs screaming.

Like this? It would end like this? A scream rose deep within him, a scream of pain and rage and humiliation—that he had walked into it, and like this—it was over.

The girl he'd bound himself to and despised and resented and had thought to free despite it all—pulled something from her ridiculous pouch.

He fought to breathe, to see—

She took an ugly, jagged-edged blade, curved like a sickle and encrusted with rust, and swung in a wide arc—slashing into Sebastian's wand arm.

Blood sprayed.

The vice released, and Vespasian collapsed to the floor, gasping.

The king roared his rage.

The blade swung again, the girl's movement a graceful dance as it sliced into his face, snagged deep in his cheek.

With a fierce shriek, she tugged hard, and the blade—

Gods, gods, gods…

The blade ripped loose and skin—jagged tears of skin—hung loose, exposing a nightmare image of bone and teeth and gore—The truth hit Vespasian—the king was protected against *magic*, but not this.

Sebastian reached up and found a flap of skin hanging and would have screamed—

But she stuffed a handkerchief in his mouth and brought the butt of her knife down onto his temple.

Already, outside there were men running. Vespasian acted without thought. He held out his open palm, and Sebastian's cloak flew into it. Then the wand. Finally he summoned the girl and she flew, colliding into his embrace.

A twitch of fabric and he was covered head to boots, his shoulders squared, his bearing erect, and he held her, twisting and screaming, tightly by the throat. "Don't make me strangle you!"

He stepped from the tent into a near collision with guards and the nobleman who had entered before. "My horse," he said, his tone bored.

"Your Majesty, he's not saddled—"

"Now!"

The horse appeared, and he tossed her up and then leapt behind her. "I will return, once I have taught my sister her place," he said, and with a kick of his heels, burst forward, taking the glorious beast in a leap straight over the campfire, leaving soldiers scattering in his wake.

It was a magnificent escape, even though in mere seconds, a half a minute, the hue and cry was raised.

"Physicians!"

"Send the physicians!"

"Stop him! That is not the king!"

The girl twisted and kicked. "He's still alive! I could have killed him!"

"Don't despair, you may have done," he said, "but in the meantime, we live. Forgive me if I don't share your desire to sacrifice yourself for the cause, as I'd rather accomplish what we must and live to enjoy the benefits."

Any response she might have made was cut off by whizzing of arrows over their heads streaming coils of fire in their wake.

"Rutting hell!" he snarled, bending low over her to protect her with his shields, as one after another, they appeared to freeze in mid-air and then explode.

"Bloody, rutting, buggering hell!" He struggled to control the stallion that didn't recognise the shield's protection and reared, fighting to flee the magical assault exploding over their heads.

The assault Vespasian recognised most clearly, for it was of his own planning.

The Earthborn—outnumbered by ungodly ratio—were attacking.

Lysander Fury had taken leave of his senses.

"Goddess save me from you and your kin," he hissed, "for you are clearly all mad!"

❧ CHAPTER FIFTY-FOUR ❦

The sky erupted over her head and rained down death.

First a milky glowing streak exploding and raining down over the soldiers around her, glistening droplets on their skin and hair and uniforms. A few, startled, reached to touch what clearly did not burn them or hurt them until another streak across the sky, this one a streak of fire, burst into a ball of flame above them, then into a shower of sparks that rained down destruction and ignited every bit of the milky glow. Screams filled the night.

The horse beneath them bucked; the world spun around her, a swirl of spell-lit night, teeming masses of soldiers shouting in foreign tongues.

"Forward!" Vespasian roared behind her, and again, "Forward!" He was driving the remaining soldiers forward, closer to the looming cliff ahead of them. He—in the guise of the king—was leading the charge against his own people!

Another volley of milky glow followed by fire shrieking across the sky, and again fire rained down around her, igniting everything it touched.

No, not everything.

Men screamed in agony. Yet the glow that fell into bushes, to the ground, onto the few horses she saw melted away. No sparks ignited them.

This magic—this horrific magic—burned men, but not beasts and bracken and heather and thorn.

She stared, repelled and awed at the carnage, as her nose lost the scent of filth and rot that clung to the king's cloak that Vespasian still wore and filled instead with the scent of burning flesh.

Again, the horse bucked beneath them, and she reached out, grabbed fists of its mane, her eyes burning, her heart filled with pity for this poor frightened beast. She leaned over his neck and crooned, just as she would her own beloved Hades.

Fighting tears, she crooned her grief and her love, and yes, her comfort to this beast who through no fault of his own was now in the midst of war. What brought her comfort seemed to bring him strength, as he burst forward to gallop at the wall of rock in the distance.

Beneath the source of the fire.

Vespasian's arms circled her with strength as he clutched the reins—too tight, no wonder the poor horse protested. She took them from his hands, determined to at least do this thing that required no magic, only experience.

He allowed it without question and continued to drive the men forward to their deaths.

For she saw it now, what he did. By driving them forward in a futile charge, he was driving them closer to the fiery assault, driving them straight into it. She should care, she should feel soiled to participate in such dishonourable trickery. Yet these soldiers killed for money and not honour, spilling the blood of people she had vowed to protect. Lust for gold had brought them to a foreign clime to die.

On the cliffs high above, she saw the standing figures, archers, shooting fire into the sky. Some arrows streaked white, some silver, some gold, and all the colours of flame. What magic had they wrought? What power, what amazing power these Earthborn had, and magics of which she'd never dreamed.

Women.

They were mere laundresses, mere women—and they owned the sky and all beneath it. She exulted in their power and their glory. Her own arms ached with the desire to wreak such havoc, to join the battle.

Her anger at Vespasian still simmered, for stopping her before she could attempt to land a killing blow. Yet here they were, in the midst of battle with hope of victory in the air.

But the desperation and rage roiling off the man at her back told a different tale. He closed his hand over her shoulder and squeezed tight. "To the east. We must get there as quickly as possible!" She felt the cloak slide from his shoulders and disappear into the darkness as they left it behind, his visible royal disguise having served its purpose. Now they were merely two figures on horseback amidst the mass of others.

She followed his pointing wand and wondered what he'd done with the king's. On, she urged the valiant horse, on into the night, across the uneven terrain, grateful for his bespelled hooves that flew across the surface despite holes and rocks. They plunged against the grain of a charging army, angling to the east when the army was charging south, and she braced herself against the collisions and the knowledge that if they didn't scatter in time to avoid the horse's fierce hooves, men would be trampled beneath them.

A soldier grabbed at her leg—pulled hard—but arms like iron bands closed around her and shifted her back onto the saddle. The soldier fell away, split open by a hex.

Out of the darkness, the boulders suddenly rose before them, and she slowed the horse with a sense of relief and confusion. What now?

Her back was suddenly cold where Vespasian had been pressed against it, as he dismounted and stood, waiting for her to do the same.

She slid her aching leg out of the stirrup, braced herself when the horse shifted, but clung to the saddle until her good leg found purchase. Finally she was on her feet, her dignity intact as he led the horse to where the boulders broke apart and created a shallow chasm.

She followed him, wincing. Her hip ached but was still strong.

She refused to be a physical hindrance, even though she was one in every other way.

She smelled and heard the gurgle of flowing water moments before she saw it before her, a small spring at the base of the rocks where Vespasian was letting the horse drink. Her eyes adjusting to the darkness, she dropped to her knees and scooped water into her hands, letting it splash wet and cold over her and then took more handfuls to quench her thirst.

Behind her, Vespasian slapped the horse on the rump and with a fierce command, sent it galloping into the night towards the bay and open expanse of sea, all that separated them from Ireland, and beyond. The horse, at least, would be safe.

"Come," he said, his voice gruff. He hadn't paused to drink but was already driving deeper into the shadows. She lurched to her feet to follow, doing her best to keep up with his long strides as he began to climb a hidden path that followed the fissure of rock up to, she presumed, the hilltop.

The way grew steeper, and her hip less and less functional, but she grabbed onto the rocks to help pull herself up. But she couldn't stop the gasps the effort brought from her, and suddenly he was looming over her, demanding, "Are you injured?"

"Not very."

"What does that mean?"

"My hip aches. Continue. I can keep up."

He let out an exasperated gust of air. "If it's not one thing, it's more," he muttered, and she saw the movement of his hands, the gesture of him sweeping his hair back from his face. "Do you need me to carry you?"

"No!"

"If you can't keep up—"

"I can! I will! Just go on, you—you—"

"Bastard, yes, I know." He turned away from her to continue.

"I did not say that, and would not!" At his pause and turning, and heavy silence, she added, "Not since you told me. I will not say such a thing again." She dispelled the awkwardness by adding, "But you are a beast and a blackguard."

"Indeed, I am." Still, he did not move.

"Go on," she spat. "I won't have you blaming it on me that we're slow. I may be useless and weak, but I can still move."

"You call yourself weak? Are you quite mad?"

"I have no magic. I'll be worthless in battle and will only slow everyone down, as I tried to tell you—"

"Fool!" he said almost viciously. "Even without your magic, you are the strongest person I've ever known."

She stared at his darkened face, wishing she could see his features, and relieved he could not see her state of dumbfounded shock.

"You attacked him like a virago. You were every inch *y Deraon* and—it was a wonder to behold. I was ready to kill you myself for making the attempt, and yet you were magnificent."

Again, the bitterness rose in her. "My aim was wild. I wanted his throat and only got his face and then—then, you! I could have finished it, ripped his throat open, but you grabbed me and stopped me before I could and—"

"We lived to fight another minute, another hour, and maybe that will be enough and maybe it won't, but we have it before us," he snapped then added, "Your vengeance is not without its sting. You destroyed his perfect visage."

"His visage? Had you left me, he would be *dead!*"

"So would *you.*"

"I was ready," she said and knew from the cold that seeped into her heart she spoke truth.

"We still would have a war to fight."

But if the new king was gone, the Fireborn surely would want someone worthy on the throne.

"Even without your magic, you have value. I don't know how and why, but this I know."

She shrugged and rubbed her aching hip. "I hope so, for you have saved me and now have me as burden."

"Persephone." She had never heard his silken voice go awkward and uncertain. "I would ask you to allow me to attempt something, something perhaps you'll find unforgivable, and I would not hold you weak or less than noble if you refuse."

The chill in her heart spread. "What?" she whispered.

She felt him take her wrist, raise her hand until their palms were pressed together, and only their fingers did not touch.

No. Not this, anything but this.

It took every bit of the strength he claimed she had not to recoil, not to strike him, not to run.

"Go ahead," she said, her voice stiff, unable to even ask why, only to submit.

"If you're certain."

"Do it!"

His hand curled and only the heels touched, and cold air rushed across her palm and then—

The light of his wand, glowing between them, casting his face in planes and hollows of silver and black, and she stared into his eyes because she could not bring herself to see his hands—his fingertips— touch hers.

The air left her lungs in a rush, and she would have fallen had she not been braced against the rock wall, but the assault—the assault—the rush of golden joy into her through that gentle touch of rough fingertips against her own.

It poured into her, this strength, this joy, this—

Magic.

She inhaled sharply, deeply, tasted it, stronger than lifeblood, a flow that pulsed through her, and she sobbed—she sobbed with the sheer joy of it.

Then the dog, the cursed dog flew at them and with a flash of bared incisors knocked them apart.

Her head hit the rock, but she hardly felt it, and she dropped to her knees, and crawled across the ground to him where he sprawled, gasping, and reached for his hand, clutched it, brought her own hand back for more, for *more*—

This time the dog did not just snarl and fly between them. This time it closed its teeth on her hand, broke skin, brought blood. She fell back, the need slowly seeping from her.

The lust.

She closed her eyes and reached and found it. Magic. Deep within her. Steady and pulsing, and *there.*

Overhead, the sky was still filled with streaks of light, and in the distance, the night still rang with screams. But where they were, wedged safely between walls of rock, neither fighting nor being attacked. The air glowed with the softest and gentlest of magics, both their bodies glowing, though the wand was no longer lit.

The dog stood between them, teeth bared.

She felt her cheeks flame, that she had climbed Vespasian Wyllt's body in an effort to get more. Yes, her magic was only a fraction of what it had been, but it was living in her. To crawl and beg more of that unspeakable touch was a source of shame.

For long moments, they could only lie there, waiting for the strength to resume their climb. Finally, he heaved himself to his feet and offered her his hand. She took it, and he pulled her to her feet then released her. "Are you ready?"

"Yes," she said, and the magic pulsed deep within her. "Yes."

She followed him the rest of the way, and not even her hip hurt her, nothing did, for she had magic, not with the fullness that had been hers before, but magic all the same. If she had this, couldn't more come? There must be a way to regain the power she'd had before.

There must.

When they neared the top, when the sound of arrows whizzing through the air on a stream of fire struck hard on her ears, she knew what she was feeling.

She wanted it back. The Dark that she thought she had hated. The loss was too hard, too deep, and she wanted it back.

Maybe she was succumbing to the Darkest urges and embracing them. It mattered not. She would not feel complete or whole again without them. They had been part of her from her moment of birth, whatever harsh price she'd paid for them.

But that wasn't all. The magnitude of what he'd done for her hit her like a blow.

She grabbed his arm, spun him to face her. "You gave me magic, how?"

"It's something that happens in a True bonding. One of the things. The Sharing of life and of magic. In... rare circumstances."

She could tell by his voice that this information was not easily given to her, nor did he find it comforting. But— "That's not what I'm asking. How did you give me magic? Whence did it come?" she demanded.

"From me."

Two words. Two words that brought her horror and rage. She flew at him. He grabbed her forearms, held them in his fierce grip, but could not stop her words. "You weakened yourself? You gave up our one advantage—your power?"

His refusal to answer was answer enough.

"Fool!" she cried.

"Evidently." He dropped her arms and continued until they broke out into the open, and she followed, to finally join the battle.

❧ CHAPTER FIFTY-FIVE ❧

She had never seen anything so beautiful.

They ringed the tops of the rocky cliffs, each like the figurehead of a proud ship, hair and skirts billowing in the wind, bearing proud and fierce and strong. Their blouse sleeves had been ripped away to reveal arms twined with muscle in a way that would horrify her mother and sister and any ladies of the Ton. Their hair was unbound and wind-whipped. Their cheeks and brows bore smears of soot, and their savage faces reflected fire-flashes as they released their arrows into the night and then whipped the next into place, ready to release on command.

These women protecting their world were more beautiful than any she had ever seen. Never had she felt so unworthy. Never had she felt so humbled. She stood alone in the midst of many, catching quick glimpses of Lark and Night at the fire under the rock table, of Rue crumpled against one if its supporting stones, her face wild with madness.

Persephone stood there alone, unwanted, and in her renewed but weak magical state, without even the power to offer that she had once borne.

Vespasian snarled into her ear, "*Ysbryd y Myrddin*, woman! This is not the time to stand in awe!"

She ran with him across the hilltop, seeing what she had not seen before. The women at the fire, the women archers, and others. Where were the men?

But before she could ask, they had reached Lysander on the foremost outcropping of rock overlooking the plain. But then she saw what they saw, and all other thoughts dropped away.

From this vantage point, the plain below danced with fires, new ones spreading like dancing sparks, as beautiful as they were distant. No twisted faces of death here, and screams so distant they seemed not screams at all but just the howling of the wind. Yet she was sorely aware that each spark and blaze of fire was accompanied by burning, horrific death. She, unlike these women warriors, had seen what their arrows wreaked.

But now she understood. They had seen what she had not, and it had filled their faces with grim resolve.

Even though Vespasian had driven the army forward into the teeth of the assault, it spread farther than their arrows could reach. Spread vaster than they had the arrows to destroy.

This army would be their doom.

"Might I ask," Vespasian said, his voice silken, his stance the very image of relaxed, yet radiating threat, "what lunacy seized you, that you split our people, attacked a force ten times our size, and dove straight into the teeth of the enemy?"

Lysander flashed him a grin, but she who knew every quirk of his brow, his lips, his face, knew the excruciating grief in his eyes, the ferocity in that smile. "In my life I have done things I believed to be just and right, and now they are ash in my mouth," Lysander said, and he did not have to look in Rue's direction for Persephone to know the source of his hollowness and his rage. "But on this night, if I am to die, it will be this way, my brother. I will attack, I will destroy. As we are all to die, it will be as heroes, not martyrs, and on that you have my word as a Fury."

Her heart swelled with recognition of a deep passion that matched her own, swelled with grief that he, too, felt their deaths coming, and swelled with pride that he refused to back down.

"Brother?" Vespasian asked, and had she not known this man to be the fiercest and strongest of any she had known, she would have thought there to be note of vulnerability in his voice, a softness in his black eyes as he stared sidelong at his lieutenant.

"What else should you be, you poor blackguard, if you wed the brat?" His voice held a note of affection—not just for Vespasian Wyllt, for whom he certainly must hold some amount of affection, but—but, for her. For the sister whose betrayal had turned his world to ash, with a dead son and a mad wife.

His hand touched her hair and then fell away.

And the thought that—at this moment—he might be going to forgive, to show affection, to be her beloved brother again, terrified her. She needed his strength, even his resentment. His forgiveness would unravel her.

He gave her hair a sharp tug, like he'd done when she's been just a girl, and the slight smirk of his lips frustrated her.

"You think you're too old for hair-tugging, imp? We will both be ancient with generations around us, and I will still tug your hair because you will still be just a brat to me."

"So it's living you're planning on doing now, is it?" Vespasian snapped. "I'm glad to know it. I've no need for Furys determined to throw themselves on swords of honour in their embrace of defeat."

She clung to his acid voice like a lifeline. Yet she could not stop herself from saying, as she looked across the field of battle below them, "There are no Furys out there to die." *To kill.* "I know it shouldn't make a difference…" She hated the way her voice broke, the weakness it implied.

"But it does," Lysander finished softly.

"It does *not*." Vespasian's voice cracked the air between them. "If fighting Furys will stop you, Lys, tell me now, because I have misjudged you as my ally if—"

"I did not say it would *stop* me."

Relief coursed through her. She needed them to be strong, to have no doubts, to be more than mere mortal men. Without that, there was no hope at all.

A streak of red shot into the sky from a place behind them—not from the battle, but from their flank, and she knew fear.

"They're attacking from the village!" she cried.

But around her, the flashes brought only the briefest of glances.

"We've cut off the other paths," Vespasian said. "No one can attack us from that side."

"Cut off?"

"Boulder-slides. Come back, I can't be worrying about you every minute!"

Tumbles of boulders, crashing down, erasing paths that had existed for centuries, if not millennia. They could not be assaulted from behind. They could not escape. The reality and weight of her charge came down upon her.

They had sent their children away so bravely, not as she'd thought, with the knowledge that some of them might never see their children again, but knowing that if this battle went badly, as surely it must—*none* of them would see their children again.

She would have had them all, their lives and futures, on her shoulders. All children of traitors, with only her to protect them against the Fireborn and foreign-born. If the weight of their lives didn't horrify her before, it now most certainly did.

Robin.

She wanted to see him once more, to tell him what she knew in her heart but had not said and now would never say—that his strength and his nobility might not be the stuff of warriors, but that it was the stuff of heroes. Because she knew that, in turning her burden over to him, she had given them the safest harbour possible.

Robin, my Robin.

She could never tell him how much his strength and his loyalty meant to her, even now that she had left him forever. Would he ever see beyond her trickery and betrayal? Would he ever understand the evil she saw, or would he only think she'd rejected him, *him*, not the malignant king. Would he ever know the power his honour gave her, the relief of knowing that those sweet children, unlike her Otter, might be protected, because he, her Robin, was so trustworthy?

The ache in her grew and would swallow her whole, but she could not let it. She had left him and now must do her part, however diminished it might be.

And then, she felt them… tendrils.

Tendrils of oily, heavy magic of the Darkest sort.

Rising from the plain below them.

What was the king doing?

What had he done?

❦❦

The foetor of decay. Blood—thick and rancid—assaulted him.

Stronger, more virulent, than when he'd been in the same tent with Sebastian. He had worried about what violence Sebastian might have imported from the Continent, weapon-spells and assault-hexes that they had never seen, and would have no quick defence against.

He scanned the terrain below them, looking for the source of this foetid power, and each time, his gaze was drawn back to the glowing tent.

But he'd been in the tent, and had seen nothing there, had not felt this then.

A throbbing, thudding pain exploded in his head. Images flew—

Mind magic.

Turned inside out, turned in on him, *on him*. Impossible! He staggered. Fell. He heard voices, distant and alarmed, and he wanted to shout, to warn them. Whatever invasion he suffered, surely, was to distract them at the moment of attack.

But he could not form words.

Images of the past, of his own self in a cheap tailcoat, waistcoat and breeches, his attempt to match in style what he could never match in quality, his unalluring features, the spark of pride and vanity in his eyes as he spoke—

This couldn't be happening.

These weren't memories from his own mind, but as he'd looked to others. To Sebastian.

He remembered in that flash of a moment how he'd dangled a forbidden knowledge, how Sebastian had responded with sly interest and attention, where before had only been disdain.

But Vespasian had not taught him mind magic. Mind magic had been born in him. It couldn't be taught.

A stab of pain as he saw himself in Ordinary London, finding that first girl, ripe with new life, luring her.

Sebastian's amusement—fascination, even—with the blood, the screams.

His own horror as he clumsily healed her, held the strong, sour posset to her lips and forced her to drink, to swallow. Desperate attempts to save her life when things had gone so horribly wrong, and finally, when it finally seemed that she would survive—taking her memories away from her and turning her back into the street near Covent Garden, a coin in her pocket. Not enough, not ever enough, but all he had to spare.

How pathetic he looked through Sebastian's eyes. He tried to block these images, this invasion. Then there were no thoughts, just images one atop another, faster and faster, as Sebastian flaunted the outrages he'd committed after Vespasian had left.

More girls.

More blood.

Life ripped from their bodies without grace, without ritual, without mercy.

No attempts at healing, for he wasn't there, *he* wasn't there.

Sebastian had found a way to distort and use what had been a Gift received from the hands of the goddess.

He'd known Sebastian was stealing life for the old king. The girl had told him. He'd known. But now… *seeing*. Knowing she'd seen…

What kind of power did Sebastian possess, to use Vespasian's own birth gift against him?

Blood collected for what purpose? They had never needed blood, had never used the blood, only the ovum.

Bodies discarded like carcasses, tossed into pits with offal from the Ordinary slaughterhouses.

Faces, girls both beautiful and plain, eyes glassy in death and horror, mouths twisted in the screams that were their last breaths, expelled in agony.

Pain—stabbing and pulsing pain.

This wasn't taunting. Nor was this to distract him while they attacked. This was his death. Not satisfied to merely destroy him, Aubyn was delivering death accompanied by every iniquity and trespass Vespasian had brought down upon the face of the earth in his youthful arrogance. Aubyn had proven himself superior.

The guilt, the pain, the self-loathing were more than his soul could bear, weakened and polluted as it already was.

Yet in this moment of truth, he was still Vespasian Wyllt. One question still echoed, still trumped them all.

How? His pride reared up in a roar of rage. How could this happen? How was Sebastian doing this to him? A new image flashed.

Immediate, fresh, *now*.

The interior of the campaign tent. A woman's distended belly, round and tight with an unborn child. New life. *No. No. No.* A golden dagger, raised, ready to stab—

The roar ripped from him, a canker splitting open and spilling what his body could not contain.

No. No. No.

His ears filled with it, his head, his pounding head, filled with it, the roar of his guilt, the accompaniment of his death, the music of the damned, delivered not by Sebastian Balmain but of Vespasian Wyllt's own creation.

Over the roar came the triumphant laughter he knew so well, the laughter of the golden boy turned golden man turned king.

ᔆ CHAPTER FIFTY-SIX ᔆ

Persephone spun, shocked, as Vespasian's body hit the ground beside her—rigid and quaking. She hurled herself to his side, frantic, afraid to touch him, afraid not to. "Lysander!" she cried. "Help me!"

But he had his focus aimed at the others, most of whom had frozen, prepared to run to their fallen leader. "Resume!" Lysander barked. *"Resume!"*

Only when they had did he drop to his knees beside her, joining her where she knelt. "It looks like—" he began, distressed, confused. "But that makes no sense."

"What? What makes no sense?"

"This is what happened when he fed us knowledge," Lysander said.

"He had fits?" she asked in horror.

"No. We did."

New rage filled her, that he would do this to her brothers, that they allowed it!

She met Lysander's eyes in instant realisation.

"Someone is doing this to him?"

"Impossible," Lysander said.

Not impossible. Nothing was impossible any more. She raised Vespasian's head, and it was heavy—so much heavier than she would have dreamed, and it shook—his teeth chattered, he jerked with apoplexy.

Panic rose in her. She had to stop this. Whatever it was, it had to end. She needed privacy. Her stomach was heavy with cold dread. She looked up and saw the Crone staring fiercely in their direction and knew she only had moments before the woman took over. "Your cloak," she demanded of Lysander, and a moment later his heavy wool cloak was in her hands. "Don't let anyone interfere."

Only moments to do what should be unthinkable, and now felt inevitable.

577

"Anyone," she repeated hoarsely. "Don't let anyone near."

She bent over Vespasian's body and with a whisk of her arm had them both covered with the cape that held her brother's scent, his skin, the earthy fragrance of the soap his wife had made for him when she was still sound.

When she still had a son, a life, a soul as yet unstruck by madness.

Persephone pushed such thoughts aside. She couldn't change what had been, but she could change what was to come. She flung herself across his body, even though his tremors sent cold repugnance through her. She found his hand—the same hand with which he had shared his magic—and with every fibre of her being screaming *No*—placed her palm against his, slid up its length, skin sliding against skin, until she found his fingertips, rough and cold, and forced—

Forced her fingertips against his.

A jolt of oily Dark shot through her, and with a screech, she flew through the air and landed at his feet, the cloak a crumpled mass of folds between them.

Vespasian had not repelled her.

Something else had.

It was the king. She tasted the oiliness on her tongue, smelt it in her tissues, the Dark, dank of the king's power.

She scrambled back up Vespasian's body, too desperate to care who saw. Had his face been so white before, his eyelids so waxen? A gnarled hand reached, but she batted it away, grabbed the hand that had been limp and now was rigid and slammed hers against it, forced her fingertips against his—and recognised the desperation beneath the Dark. The Dark had repelled her, but he—Vespasian—cried out for her. She felt it in her blood, in the pulse pumping through her as she pressed harder against him, pushed her fingertips against his and refused to release the pressure.

The Dark entered her body, suffusing her with its temptation to join in a sinuous dance. But this time, it was not a seductive power that held her there; it was a seductive power that she fought, that she denied, determined that the king would not prevail, no matter the cost, no matter the pain. Those small areas of flesh—mere fingertips—brought piercing torment when touching, where before the touching had brought sumptuous comfort. She couldn't back away, not now, not when she owed this man everything. She felt his awareness, his horror that it was she who helped him.

Let him rage. Let him hurl epithets and hexes at her, and she would hurl them back.

Please, she begged silently to the goddess who had been too silent too often. *Please, let him.* She no longer knew what she asked, let him rage? Live? It made no difference.

Let him.

The music took over.

❧❧

First, he only heard her breathing—a soft expulsion of air that he knew to be hers, so soft, and yet he heard it, even above the roar. Then he heard the crooning, like the whoosh of blood in his veins, something more than song, something pure incantation.

Finally he felt her fingertips, their excruciating pressure, and he would clutch them to him if he could, never let them go, for somehow—somehow her presence was lessening that of his enemy.

She had not asked.

She had simply inflicted herself on him and now was party to his past, the things he'd never shared with a soul, and she knew, she *knew*, and he had not allowed this, had not allowed her—

Could she see? Could she see his shame, his sin, his wrong-doing? The visions and images Sebastian had poured into him?

Her pulse became his. Her breath became his. Her calm became his. All else was gone.

All else was gone.

A warm weight was on him, stretched down his body, and he knew without having ever borne it before, without having felt the softness and the sharp angles upon him before, that it was she, her fingertips still touching his.

He sat up and flung her away, gasping.

❧❧

She landed face-first, her mouth filled with dirt, a pain that said her lip was split.

The gnarled hand grabbed hers, and the Crone would have examined her hand had she allowed it, but she did not. She jerked it away, rolled sideways on the ground to face away from them all, all who had seen the *touching*, and had seen her flung away like a nasty thing.

She didn't care. She had no time to care. She only had the time to reach deep, to find that place in her that should have thrummed with her magic, her coiling, restless magic, and felt only a whisper of its former power. She did not care whether she had enough. She only knew she was going to stop this king, must stop him *now*.

She dragged herself to her feet, stumbled to the edge of the cliff and looked down at the army that stretched forever, that would outlast the rebels, no matter how valiantly they fought.

Down there, was the king, the usurper, cloaked in Dark protections and willing to condemn as many to death as it took and not caring.

Of course he didn't care. He'd brought men he didn't know, men whose blood mattered nothing to him, whilst she was surrounded by people whose very fabric was torn by the loss of even one.

She thought of the wands that surrounded her, that protected their holders from the pain of imposing death. If she caused the death of one or a dozen, let her feel it, let her die with them, but let right prevail and the king and his plot fail. She felt the comfort against her skin, the silver flute held against her forearm so snug and safe, and she knew.

She let it slip down until it was in the palm that had been pressed against another in an act profane and taboo and yet redemptive.

She raised her beloved flute not to her lips, but to the sky.

If a wand harnessed magic and brought it to focus like a ray of sun bouncing off a mirror and turning leaves to fire, so did her music harness magic and spin it into power.

But this was something music could not accomplish.

This was something her sacred flute should never be called to do.

She held it as a wand, and aimed it, and dug deep for all that was in her, and called upon the coil of Dark, demanded its obedience, and shot a bolt of fire at that distant tent, not an arrow, but sheer magic, with all her rage and vengeance at its core.

Even from this distance, she heard the cries and saw movement like creeping creatures on a dark and distant floor as the flash hit, and soldiers scrambled, and her eyes stung and her vision went dark after such a flash....

But when it cleared, when she blinked through stinging tears, the tent still stood.

She reached again, this time with a scream of fury, and again, sent a bolt of fire, and again stared until the flash blinded her, and again, heard the screams, and this time her hand ached and her arm throbbed and her shoulder felt the impact as if it had been torn from her body, and she staggered back, stumbled, fell to her knees.

Knowing there were soldiers on that plain who would never breathe again, knowing from the ache—

But still, the tent and its foul king stood.

One more time, the last time. She knew it to be the last, for she had nothing left to draw on. She staggered to her feet and thrust her arm out—

And felt him join her.

Him.

The only him who existed.

The one who shared her power, her curse, and her desire.

His body braced her, at that moment he became as her backbone, her spine, the very bones and tendons of her body in its weakness. His arms surrounded her with strength and power, with a Dark pulse that entered her, joined with her, made her whole—

Made her dangerous.

Fierce.

Proud.

His hand covered hers over the flute, with only her fingertips exposed to the night.

They were one, he the strength and she nothing more than the power that built in her, deep in her, as it had longed to do for her entire life. Power that had been suppressed, reviled, a source of shame.

As well it should be.

For wasn't it a power that was so Dark, a power shared with a man whose own Shadows and Darkness were so deep, she feared him even as she depended on him?

In this heart-pounding, blood-singing moment everything she had been before seemed nothing.

This.

This moment.

This thing within her erupted with a roar of triumphant rage.

And from the flute, the beautiful flute never meant for such a charge, erupted a blast of power so Dark, it blocked out the stars and the moon and cast the plain before them in darkness so deep, even the fires did not pierce it.

Dark swallowed everything in its path.

Glorious and angry and vital, it swallowed the sky and the earth beneath it.

When it seemed so complete that there might never be another day, another sun—

Lysander screamed beside them, "Fire!"

Arrows screamed into the dark, trailing flames.

From the other side of the vast plain came their like, more arrows arcing towards them with such velocity that suddenly, they met in a blazing explosion that swept the sky and fell upon all below them and then—

Was gone.

No Dark.

No fiery furnace of a sky, and no ground blazing with inferno.

But across the plain, dozens and dozens and dozens of small, writhing fires—burning, burning, burning—

Lysander's face grew tight as he stared through the spyglass. He lowered it, averted his gaze.

Still she stood in the embrace of the man whose power matched and completed her own, their hands extended, the flute now cold. She felt its shame tremble through her, that it had been used in such a way.

She wanted to cradle it against her breast and comfort it.

She wanted to be cradled and comforted.

What had she done?

Oh, goddess, what had they done?

How many men have you killed?

Would she ever have magic again? Would she deserve to? She

trembled with fear, with need, and had nowhere to turn, nowhere to turn for comfort…

The ancient stones. She broke away. She stumbled past everyone, unseeing, unhearing.

When she found the stones with the heavy weight of slab balanced ever so precariously on their tips, she knew them in her heart, knew their desperation to hold it high and never waver, and she sank against one and pressed her back to it, cold and rough and hard against her, but solid, unyielding magnificent. She closed her eyes and felt the cold at her back, the heat of sacred fire before her.

No matter how precarious their load, they had not faltered. They would not falter. She was alone.

And safe.

❧❧

"The king," Vespasian asked, his voice hoarse.

But it seemed unnecessary to ask. In the midst of smouldering carnage, a lone tent still stood, glowing from within, a soft bronze glow. Lysander raised the spyglass again, and there was no surprise when he said, "They're leaving. He survived, he and two others survived. They're on horseback." Lysander's voice lowered to a growl. "We won't let them escape. I'm going after him. I'll take Tern and—"

"No." Vespasian fought to appear calm, to appear controlled, when he was nothing approaching controlled or calm. "His protections are too strong. We won't send any to be killed by him with no chance of returning the favour."

"What happened?" Night demanded, but he did not answer.

He had watched the girl walk away from him, stumbling over rocks in her path and yet going relentlessly forward—away—and he had felt awe.

What she had done.

Goddess, what she had done.

He didn't fool himself. He hadn't done this. She had done it. She had used him, but whatever had happened, whatever source of power had been harnessed, had been her doing.

Her *control.*

She who'd had none, suddenly had *all.* The battle was over, and they had sustained not a single loss. He didn't know what he had joined, what he had witnessed. She had gone stumbling towards the fire, and he suddenly knew a new fear, ridiculous and yet so very real, that, the way she trembled, she might fall straight into it. He sprang forward with legs that didn't want to move, ran after her, rounded the base of the stone to find her—

Curled at its base, staring blindly ahead, tremors rocking through her.

The flute lay crumpled in her hand. Crumpled, as if twisted by a vise or crushed by a vicious animal. A twist of silver that had once given wing to her music and now never would again. He reached—for what? What would he do? Could he do?

She looked up at him, and he waited for the accusations, the disgust at all she had seen. He braced himself, folded his arms, and met her gaze, leaning his shoulder against the stone as if it were merely convenient, not the only thing that kept him standing.

"What was he doing?" she asked, her voice barely above a whisper. "He was attacking you, but how?"

He looked away and didn't answer, his mind a turmoil of wondering. Could she really not know what had happened? Had she not seen? How could he answer when the only response was to admit he knew nothing, not what Sebastian had done, nor how to defend themselves.

"We can't tell them," she said. "They can't know how powerful he is."

"Night and Grebe have to know."

She leapt to her feet, power crackling so wildly, he felt it with her every movement. "Do you realise how close we all came to dying in this very place?"

"Of course I bloody realise!"

"Do you really think they should know this, before we understand, before we have—have an idea how to stop him, a plan?" she demanded, her voice low.

As always, she was so full of herself, it took everything in him to remain still and not throttle her.

"They saw what he did to you."

"What *he* did? What about what *we* did—what you did to me—right in front of their eyes?"

She paled, avoided his eyes. "You were dying!"

"You bloody near killed me yourself," he lied and was poised to attack again, until he saw the way her eyes glittered in the moonlight, shimmering like glass.

She was two breaths away from falling apart.

By all the gods and goddesses, he was barely three.

"We're not telling anyone anything tonight. Surely there will be sufficient opportunity enough for your incessant nagging tomorrow."

She gave her head a jerky nod, looked away and sniffed loudly, and he knew what fear and responsibility she bore on her shoulders. They had done something, but they knew not what. They had found a power, but they knew not what.

They were up against something even stronger than they were, when all was said and done.

They knew not what.

They knew nothing.

Rutting hell, he owed her his life. His life, and the salvation of his people, and everything he'd spent half a lifetime working for, atoning for.

Her. With all her youth and impetuous spirit as his burden.

Her.

What did she think of the burden she'd taken on, being shackled to him?

"You are a singularly horrid tutor," she said suddenly, irritably.

"You are an abysmal excuse for a pupil," he snapped back in confusion. "But why such an accusation now? I'll hardly dispute it, but I also cannot find it in me to care."

"Because we are bound by something—a True Marriage, it would seem. Yet I know little of them, because you have left me ignorant."

"Believe me, I never thought to need knowledge of such things myself. As for your training…" He allowed his tone to grow silken and sly, and felt stronger, settling into such a familiar role. "I taught you enough so that you did not destroy yourself, but not so much that you did not need to come back to me for more. Say what you will, but for my purposes, I taught you well."

He braced himself for the acid of her response, welcomed it, even.

"This time—" Her voice, soft and unexpectedly small in the darkness, spoke once more. "—this time we stopped him. This time he did not hurt the children."

He did not disabuse her of that notion, even though her words brought back a sharp, vivid image of a belly swollen with life, and a dagger's downward plunge, because from this knowledge, this vision, if nothing else, he could protect her.

Something eased in him with a relief as icy as a fresh stream of melted snow. She hadn't seen the visions Sebastian had forced into him when under assault. She couldn't have, or she would have attacked him for it. The same strange inability to use his mind magic on her must have kept her from sharing his visions, despite this bond of connection they shared.

She hadn't seen.

The earth swayed beneath him. Without the stone at his side, he surely would fall. He rolled his body until his back was fully braced against it, then slid to the ground, his hands resting on his knees, his eyes squeezed shut.

She was beside him in her dirty man's clothing, stinking of all they had seen and done on this night, and when he glanced at her, he saw her eyes shut, her hands on her knees in mimicry of his, and somehow, it was easier to rest, and his eyes drifted closed again.

❧ CHAPTER FIFTY-SEVEN ❧

The voices that broke her sleep were harsh, anxious, excited. She jerked her head up, and it struck the rock behind her with a sharp blow that left her breathless for long moments, even as she tried to make out what had stirred everyone so.

Children's voices… The children, singing *Llyn Onn*, their voices lifted on the breeze, with much laughter and exuberance.

Her spirit lifted at the sound, the knowledge that her vow had been kept. *Robin? What of Robin?*

Even with all these things, she sensed there was something different stirring the voices, a different urgency.

She leapt to her feet. Despite the throb in her head, she took off running, barely aware that Vespasian Wyllt was behind her, keeping pace with her.

At the sight of the morning sky, still painted in the hues of sunrise with the sun only now making its appearance on the eastern horizon, she stopped, dumbstruck.

As if spawned from that very sun, a smaller blaze of fire danced in the sky, trailing a streak of gold.

"*Pendraeg*," someone cried.

She saw the comet appearing as the head of a dragon, trailing a tail of fire.

"What does it mean?" someone else demanded.

And people were clearly torn between staring at the comet in the sky, and at their seer, desperate for Lark's reaction.

"Quiet," Night commanded. "Leave her be."

Lark, her golden hair lit by the sunrise until she glowed as brightly as the celestial being in the sky, stood stiffly, entranced.

Restless voices began to speak, but one harsh glance from Night kept all silent.

Across the land, all would see this and understand it to be a portent of a new age, a blessing upon their new king.

The new Pendragon.

Her misery rose in her, filled her with despair and disbelief. No, not this, not now!

The time of prophecy is over. There is no prophecy.

No!

The children's voices drew nearer, their innocent joy obscene against the stark terror that had swept the hilltop as all remained silent and waiting, confused and afraid.

Who would dare go against the gods, if this be their declaration?

Then Grebe stepped from between the rocks, the climb clearly having taken his strength, the braids in his hair hanging limp, each step a labour.

But then, children poured out from behind him, running to their parents, oblivious to the tension around them, and for those who greeted them, perhaps the fear did ebb as they swept their children into their arms with the emotion that they had not been able to show when sending them away. Tears flowed, sobs, and quiet voices and giggles and laughter, and yet, even amidst such homecoming, she saw Vixen's eyes dart over her child's strawberry blond curls to the sky.

When the last of the children had been pulled into familial embrace, she stopped breathing.

Robin.

He emerged from the pathway between the boulders, his hair ablaze with the first rays of sun, and Persephone stood taller, saw all around her stiffen in defensive reaction when they recognised the presence of a Fireborn enemy.

He wore shackles on his wrists. He was followed by Tern, whose eyes never left the prisoner.

She spun to Grebe. "Did you not tell them that he was helping you, that he was sworn to protect the children if—" She broke off at Grebe's stern expression, at the affronted gasp that swept the Earthborn.

"You entrusted their safety to a Fireborn?" Night demanded, her rage barely contained.

"Who, despite his ill birth and his misfortunate connections," Vespasian spat, his own disdain clear in every dripping syllable, "was the fulfilment of her vow. You did not question her presence last night, for only if her vow was fulfilled and her charges safe would she have been able to return to us. If you asked no questions then, it is too late to challenge her now."

Robin's eyes met hers in resignation and without accusation, even though he surely must blame her and her trickery and the vow she had drawn from him for his current fate.

She would have stepped forward and would have fought them tooth and nail to remove the shameful shackles, but when she looked up at him, when he stepped forward from the shadows of the rocks—

The fiery comet formed a halo around his head.

Lark's voice rose, as clear and pure as the bird for which she'd been named, *"An army will be moving to and fro, Blood will rule the land, He will be met with rejoicing and will bring the time of golden peace to all."*

The words of the blood-writ prophecy, the exact words.

Persephone snapped her gaze to that of Vespasian. "You told her."

His face was pale in the dawn, stunned. "Never."

Lark spread her arms, and tears spilled down her cheeks as she dropped to her knees and cried out, "Behold the day of rejoicing. Behold the True King!"

Perhaps there should have been protests and disbelief.

But there he stood with his hair of flame, the head of the dragon gracing him with its benediction, and around them, all around, these people dropped to their knees, these people who knelt to no man.

They dropped to their knees in joy and relief.

Their constancy had been rewarded.

They had been faithful, and finally, they had their king.

Persephone, and the man she had loved, and the man she had loathed, remained unbent, standing amongst the many.

Why did hope have the stench of death upon it, the thick scent of blood, of charred flesh, of destruction?

Yet hope it was, a thread of hope, because beneath the scent of death was the pulse of life, and when noble men lived, hope remained.

Noble men and women, none of them nobility, but of the earth. Her world turned upside down.

And beside her, the least noble of them all.

I lay this destiny upon you, woman, that by choosing honour over love, you will find one and not the other, and you shall know misery, and it will be of your own choosing...

Robin's eyes met hers, and now she saw in them things she'd never seen before, things she had never expected to see in their warm depths—the pain, the accusation, the confusion.

But she couldn't tell him, couldn't say the things he so desperately needed to hear.

I lay this destiny upon you, daughter, that the True King will come, and he who had most reason to welcome him will revile him, and you will choose again whom you must follow.

She could only take a step closer to the Dark man looming rigidly at her side and turn her gaze upon him.

I lay this destiny upon you, child, that by your own choice, you will never know love.

The Dark man whose anger bristled and harsh profile was etched, so stark and forbidding, against the dawn.

❧ End of Book One ❧

A Note to My Esteemed Readers...

... or, thoughts on the cherry-picking nature of my research.

You might say I've been Cherry-picking all my life.

My sister's name is Cherry, and I have spent a lifetime picking at her, partly because it's my nature and partly because it's in the Younger Sister's Code of Conduct. But that's a different type of Cherry-picking.

I have friends with bookcases full of research materials that they have absorbed, itemized, formed their own opinions about, and used to build the fictional worlds in which their characters live and their readers indulge. I love the books that are written by such writers and love seeing how real history and the writer's imagination mesh with such delicacy and precision.

I will never be one of those writers.

Don't get me wrong. I have bookcases full of research materials for *The Fury Triad*. Some are translations of ancient writings; some are the thoughts and beliefs of the occult during the era of my world; some are the most current academic thinking on Regency times. I have used the indexes to find specific information, have skimmed looking for inspiration, have gotten sucked into books just because. The one thing I have not done—and will not ever do—is become even the lightest-weight authority on the times. Instead, I look for the bits and bobs of real history that I can assemble to create my own world.

I never met a fascinating fact that couldn't send me off on a flight of fancy that led me into a wondrous new subplot or significant detail.

So, there you are.

I hope you enjoy Persephone Fury's world, and if you have questions about specifics, feel free to email and ask me about them. I may address your questions in my blog, and who knows—it may even be that the significant detail you question is documented and a part of real history, rather than my muse's imagination.

Happy reading—

Pooks

❧ ACKNOWLEDGEMENTS ❧

I was once asked, "How do you stay so motivated and enthusiastic about writing when it's such a grueling business, filled with so much rejection?" My answer is two-fold. First, my Dallas friends and my family keep me grounded. When I am with them, we talk about things 'not writing,' have an entire world and life beyond the business, and besides that, they are amazing people I dearly love. Second, my students are the true source of my energy. Every semester they walk into my classroom full of dreams, not yet beaten down by 'the business,' still fueled by 'the creation.' Seeing such faces semester after semester, keeps me infused with joy. If you have ever been in my classroom, I owe you a debt of gratitude. I hope you are still writing with joy, and if you aren't, get after it!

In the beginning, Mara Stein was cheerleader and midwife, reading every single word of *This Crumbling Pageant's* first draft as it was written—and then again, when it was complete. As I type, she is reading the final. It has been a long haul, and I sincerely couldn't have done it without her.

So much of this was written in the war room, I must thank those who share their frustrations, their goals, their enthusiasm, their thesauri—and all to a 30-minute timer: C.E. Murphy, Laura Anne Gilman, Diana Pharaoh Francis, Chrysoula Tzavelas, David J Fortier, Robin D Owens, Mikaela Lind, and more than I can list.

Incredibly, Yvonne Hewitt, Linda Furlet, Cindy Sloan and my sister, Cherry Werner also read the unabridged 230,000-word version. Ladies, I owe all of you chocolate chip cookies for life! And then there was the next draft, 80 pages shorter but still a massive effort, and yet once again beta readers were willing. Jodi Allmond Davis and Valier Smith Barricklow, you rock.

David D Levine and Nolan Isaacs, thank you for being 'the guys' who helped me determine whether this book might appeal to a male readership.

I also thank a wonderful friend and writer, Candace Williams, for writing and playing bridge while I wrote and especially for handing me one of the best character names ever.

Finally, Sherwood Smith stepped in with her brilliant insights and helped me refine Persephone's story and finally make it work.

I have a bad habit of choosing to write about things of which I know nothing. First choice, the entire fantasy genre was largely unplumbed by me when Persephone grabbed my heart. Thank you, Iain Brown, for giving me the thumbs up and a few directional pointers in the beginning. Sorry—I used wands, anyway! Judith Tarr helped me find my horse, Hades, a Kladruber, and also helped with certain technicalities of writing about horses. Her book, *Writing Horses, The Fine Art of Getting It Right*, was published after my book was finished. I am relieved to have it at my side as I continue writing my tale! Needless to say, all errors in horsemanship and horse culture are my own.

When I began Persephone's journey, I was part of an amazing community of writers, and can't begin to express how much I drew from their enthusiasm and generosity as we shared our love of the written word. Leigh Anne, Erica, Tricie, Karen, Kristy, Stephanie, Annie in Oz, the Barrister in London, and the amazing and much-loved Theresa in Portland have my thanks.

To single out names of those members of Book View Café who have helped me in recent years would be impossible. Their assistance was not on this project, but everything I learned from them about the business of publishing in this new and glorious age has been invaluable, and I'm proud to be a part of this professional group of writers.

I fling thanks with abandon at the Story Spring Publishing team—Melissa Smith, Chris Hagberg, Barbara Tarbuck, and the editors they brought in to make this happen: Deanna Noga and Michelle Montgomery.

Special thanks must go to Jessica Aldis, whose tender, loving red pen slashed and burned through the manuscript in ways that went beyond the call of duty, and for which I am ever grateful.

Finally, Diane Tarbuck, without whom this would not have happened. Her passion for Persephone's story and her meticulous eye for detail—along with her friendship—are vital components of the product that is now in your hands.

And now, I move onto the next book in the series, *The Dead Shall Live*. As always, my family will bear the biggest burden of dealing with a writer in the throes of creation. Sam, Douglas, James, Scott, Valier, Amanda, Amy Nohealani, Hatlyn, and Isis, you are my heart and my support. May all your endings be happily ever after.

Pooks
March 31, 2014

❧ ABOUT THE AUTHOR ❧

Award-winning screenwriter and bestselling novelist Patricia Burroughs—Pooks—began her writing career in romance with five published novels, one of which was a Finalist for RWA's RITA Award. For a time, Pooks was lured away from her novels to pursue a career in screenwriting, where she again won recognition in the form of a Nicholl Fellowship in Screenwriting from the Academy of Motion Picture Arts and Sciences.

With The Fury Triad, Pooks turns her pen to fantasy in a dark epic that combines swashbuckling adventure, heart-pounding romance, and plot-twisting suspense.

www.ingramcontent.com/pod-product-compliance
Lightning Source LLC
Chambersburg PA
CBHW050838030726
47503CB00007BA/2219